OF

LOVE

AND

LIFE

O F
LOVE
AND
LIFE

Three novels selected and condensed
by Reader's Digest

CONDENSED BOOKS DIVISION

The Reader's Digest Association Limited, London

With the exception of actual personages identified as such, the
characters and incidents in the fictional selections in this volume
are entirely the product of the authors' imaginations and have no
relation to any person or event in real life.

The Reader's Digest Association Limited
11 Westferry Circus, Canary Wharf, London E14 4HE

www.readersdigest.co.uk

ISBN 0-276-42585-5

CONTENTS

THIRTY NOTHING

Lisa Jewell

Dig and Nadine have been best friends
ever since they first met at school. Their
relationship is the most important thing in
both their lives—but they are adamant
that they could never, ever, be a couple.
But when Dig's first love, the beautiful
Delilah, reappears in Dig's life, he becomes
an adolescent schoolboy all over again.
Suddenly his oldest friendship is under
threat and he has to decide who it is he
really wants to be with.

Chapter One

Dig woke with a start.

The first thing he was conscious of was the taste in his mouth, a rancid coating of . . . what was it? Onions? Garlic? He slowly brought a hand from beneath his duvet and cupped it around his mouth. He let out a small puff of breath and sniffed it back in. Grim beyond belief. He clamped his mouth shut again.

The second thing he was conscious of was his head, which appeared to have had a large shipment of ball-bearings dumped in it overnight.

The third thing Dig became aware of was that there was a girl in his bed. A girl with messy blonde hair and bare bony shoulders and a tattoo of a sea horse on her left arm.

Dig slowly manoeuvred himself up on his elbow and surveyed the girl as if she were some kind of strange sea creature which had been washed up on his bed by the tide. She looked young. Surprise surprise. About twenty, probably. He wondered what she was called.

'Do you have any Nurofen?' Her voice was recognisably Irish. Northern Irish, to be precise.

'Uh-huh.' Dig's hand found the little tablets on his bedside table, and the glass of water he'd put there last night, a sign that at some point between getting home and going to bed he'd obviously been mentally and physically functioning. Which also indicated to him that relations had more than likely been had with this small, bony girl in his bed.

The level of traffic noise wafting through the half-opened window from Camden Road outside led Dig to believe that it was probably some considerable time after the six in the morning his head was telling him it was. He turned painfully to look at his radio alarm: 11.48am. It was also hot, stiflingly hot. Strange for the middle of November.

He passed the glass and pills to the bony girl.

'Thanks.' She gulped them down in one. 'What time is it?'

'Ten to twelve.'

'What!' She sprang out of bed, like a little pink whippet, and began jumping into her clothes: a tiny black vest top, no bra, G-string, combat trousers, pierced bellybutton, trainers. She heaved the curtains apart, sending Dig recoiling across the bed with one elbow over his face.

'Where am I? Is this Tooting Broadway?'

'What? No—no—Kentish Town—Camden Road.'

'Oh no! Oh no. I have to be in Clapham in ten minutes. Can I get a bus from here? Where's the Tube? D'you have a car?'

'No. Five minutes that way. Yes, but it's in for repairs.'

'I'll have to get a cab. I only have a fiver. D'you have any cash?'

Dig peeled the last tenner from his wallet and handed it to her.

She kissed it. 'I'll pay you back.'

'Where are you going?'

'Work. I'm a waitress—shit—it's going to be busy today—look at that sunshine—but it's only temporary, y'know, part time.'

'You're a student?' Something had come back to him from last night.

'Yeah, that's right.' She was scraping her hair back into some kind of knot. The sun was playing on her and she looked quite pretty.

'Where d'you study?' Dig was suddenly feeling vaguely sociable, as if he might quite like to see her again.

'God, you can't remember a thing we talked about last night, can you?' She smiled. She pulled a pair of yellow sunglasses from her rucksack and sat them on top of her head. 'Well'—she looked pleased with herself, a little embarrassed—'I'm at sixth-form college right now, but my tutors reckon I'll get a place at Oxford next year—*if* I get my grades.'

'What—er, what grades?' Dig rubbed at the stubble on his chin.

'A Levels, of course.'

'So—you're—how old?'

'Seventeen.'

Oh dear God! Seventeen!

She was standing at the door now, her rucksack on her back, looking all of a sudden like a child, like a small girl wearing big girls' clothes.

'Hey, look,' she was saying, waving his ten-pound note at him, 'I'll get this back to you—I promise. I have your number, I'll ring you.'

I'll ring you. *I'll ring you!* There was a child standing in his bedroom doorway, with a pierced bellybutton, waving his money at him and telling him she'd ring him. Hell, what was the world coming to?

'Oh, and by the way—Happy Birthday.' Then she was gone.

Happy Birthday. Oh yes, Happy Birthday indeed. Thirty years old. He was thirty years old. A thirty-year-old pervert. A dirty thirty old man.

He'd slept with a seventeen-year-old.

OK, so it was the stuff of dreams, the stuff men of his age made lascivious, lustful jokes about over pints in pubs. But to have really done it, to be confronted with the reality of a seventeen-year-old in his bed. It just didn't feel right. Dig suddenly felt a little too old to be chasing after much younger women.

The previous evening was starting to come back to him in dribs and drabs. Tequila slammers at Nadine's. Opening presents. Pints at the Lady Somerset with the rest of the crowd. All piling into a cab at midnight. Some club somewhere in town. (A club? They never went to clubs any more.) More tequila. And then dancing—dancing for hours. And that girl, that child . . . Katie! That was it, that was her name— Katie. Dancing with her and telling her, over and over again, 'It's my birthday! It's my birthday!' And then—a curry? Shit, it must have been nearly morning by then.

And that girl, Katie, had been there. And . . . yes, that's right, Nadine had started on Maxwell in the restaurant and she'd tipped her raitha into his korma for some reason or, more probably, for no reason whatsoever. Poor Maxwell. It looked like his days were numbered. And then? Well, they must have got a cab or something. He couldn't remember anything after that.

Dig wrapped himself up in his dressing gown and made his way to the kitchen where he got himself some coffee. He switched on his ioniser, lit a cigarette and let his hangover wash over him for a while.

The coffee and cigarette had pushed his breath to crisis point. He absolutely *had* to brush his teeth.

He stared at his reflection in the mirror as he brushed. There's the crunch, he thought, there it is. A couple of years ago I could have had a heavy night and woken up the next morning looking like something that vaguely resembled a human being, instead of this monstrous, dark-shadowed, grey-skinned sack of old bones that's staring back at me from my bathroom mirror. But now I'm thirty, and although I still have youth ahead of me, I have left the greatest part of it behind me, and my body will no longer collude in my systematic abuse of it.

Still, he thought, he didn't have much to complain about as he entered his fourth decade. He had a great social life and friends he'd known for years. He could pull pretty girls; he owned his own flat—OK, so it was small and noisy and it was up three flights of stairs, but it was his; he had the job of his dreams working as an A&R manager for a small record label in Camden—all right, so it was poor pay for long hours and very little success, but he loved it. His family lived just round the corner so he got to see his precious mum at least once or twice a week. And now he was thirty.

Thirty wasn't so bad.

Yeah. Thirty was fine.

Actually, it wasn't that different to twenty-nine.

Nadine rolled sideways towards Maxwell and let his big, bear-like arms wrap her up in a sleepy embrace. His neck smelt sweetly musty, and traces of last night's aftershave lingered on his skin.

'Cup of tea?' he offered.

'Ooh, yes please.'

Maxwell pulled his huge frame from the bed, squeezed himself into Nadine's much-too-small red-silk robe and padded off towards the kitchen. Nadine stretched herself out in the bed and smiled as she heard Maxwell performing his usual clattering pillage of the kitchen drawers and cupboards, unable even after three months to lay his hands on mugs and tea bags without first exploring every possible location.

She clicked on the radio and listened to the babble of Radio 5 Live presenters for a while, and suddenly realised that despite the traces of a headache lingering around her temples and the embarrassing memory of yet another scene with Maxwell in the restaurant last night, she was feeling quite inexplicably, deliriously happy. It was a Saturday morning, the sun was shining, there was a man in the kitchen making her tea, and she had no plans whatsoever for the rest of the day. Maxwell wasn't usually here at the weekend. She'd only seen him last night because it was Dig's birthday and Dig liked Maxwell and had insisted that she invite him. She wasn't used to waking up with a man on a Saturday morning.

This, she decided, was one of those moments, one of those utterly perfect moments in life, which you absolutely had to draw into your lungs and hold there and absorb every drop of, because that was what life was all about.

'There you go,' said Maxwell, gently placing steaming mugs of tea on the bedside table—mugs, Nadine noticed, that she never used, decorated with insipid roses and kept at the back of the cupboard. She felt a burst of irritation and her happiness bubble exploded over her head.

'For God's sake, Maxwell,' she bristled, waspishly, 'why do you always have to choose the ugliest mugs in the kitchen?'

'Eh?' Maxwell looked stumped, and Nadine felt flooded with disdain, at the precise moment she should have felt guilt.

'Haven't you noticed,' she continued, 'that when *I* make the tea I always use those Deco mugs or the *Simpsons* mugs or the *South Park* mugs. You know—the nice mugs? Haven't you noticed that I never, ever use these mugs?' She pointed at them in disgust.

'What's wrong with them?' Maxwell asked sadly.

'Huh! Exactly! That's exactly it! If you don't know what's wrong with these mugs then there is no point in having this conversation.' Nadine knew she was being unreasonable but she couldn't help it.

'Do you want me to change them?' he offered.

Nadine jumped out of the bed in exasperation and gesticulated angrily. 'No, Maxwell. I don't want you to change them, I just want you *not* to have chosen them in the first place. I want you to be as *repulsed* by these mugs as I am. That's what I want, Maxwell.'

Maxwell's kind face crumpled up with the strain of comprehension, and Nadine could see that he was trying, he really was trying to understand what she was saying to him and this annoyed her even more. The badly chosen mugs, taken in isolation, were not, evidently, a big deal, but set in the context of their three-month-old relationship they were yet another sign that Maxwell was the Wrong Boyfriend. She'd been trying to convince herself for three months that it could work, that despite the differences between them, despite his penchant for brightly coloured designer menswear, his infatuation with Celine Dion, his unfeasibly good manners, and the fact that he was a courier and she was a photographer who earned five times as much as him, she could make it work. Because Maxwell was as nice a bloke as you could ever hope to meet and Nadine felt that she deserved a nice bloke. But nice blokes aren't necessarily perfect blokes and Nadine was sorry for her pettiness and intolerance, but she couldn't, just couldn't, abide the differences between herself and Maxwell for another moment.

'Nadine,' Maxwell was saying, softly, 'I'm not really sure . . . could you explain to me why you're getting so wound up about a pair of mugs?'

'Oh God, Maxwell. It's not just the mugs. It's not the mugs. It's everything. It's us. It's me . . . this just isn't working . . .' Nadine listened to the words echoing in her head and thought how hollow they sounded. She wondered how many times in her life she'd used the same words before. 'It's me,' she always said, 'it's not you, it's me.'

And it was true. It *was* always her. She hadn't been dumped since she was twenty-one. It had been fine when she was younger, going out with unsuitable men, because all her friends were going out with unsuitable men, too. That's what you do when you're in your twenties. But then, gradually, one by one, all her friends had found decent men, good men, and splintered off. And now, in her thirtieth year, the game was over, the rest of the pack was in pairs, but she was still playing. And until a few weeks ago, she'd still been enjoying it.

But then she'd turned thirty and had begun to evaluate her situation and it had hit her then, the real reason why she went out with so many losers: she only went out with men who didn't threaten her friendship with Dig. The moment a boyfriend began to show any signs of resentment about the amount of time she spent with Dig, it was over. There existed between Dig and Nadine this sort of unwritten law that said that they weren't allowed to spend quality time with anyone but each other. Weekdays were for boyfriends and girlfriends; weekends were for Dig and Nadine.

Dig was Nadine's best friend, her favourite person in the entire world, and as long as they were friends she didn't actually *need* to be in love with anyone else. It would just complicate everything if either of them ever fell in love with another person.

The only problem was that they just didn't fancy each other; each one epitomised the antithesis of the other's 'type'. Dig liked tiny, girl-child-type women (which Nadine most certainly *wasn't*) who made him feel manly, and Nadine liked enormous hairy men (which Dig most certainly *wasn't*) who made her feel delicate. If they'd fancied each other, they would have been married by now. Probably.

Nadine looked at Maxwell, staring blankly at her, and she suddenly realised that he was going to be the last Wrong Boyfriend. Definitely. Without a doubt. Only Right Boyfriends from here on in.

She took a deep breath. 'Maxwell,' she said, sitting down beside him on the bed and gently removing the mug of tea from between his enormous fingers. 'I think we should talk.'

'So,' said Dig, regarding Nadine disbelievingly over a large plate of greasy meat and chips, 'let me get this straight. You dumped Maxwell because he chose the wrong mugs?'

'Well, yes. Among other things. I mean—we both know he wasn't right for me, don't we?'

'I really liked him . . . well, compared to some of the other men you've been out with this decade.'

'Yes. Of course. So did I. Who wouldn't? But he was so annoying, you know? The way he dressed, and the way he was always going on about his mum, and Celine Dion, and the fact that he was allergic to *garlic* of all things—I mean, how can you go through life being allergic to *garlic?*—and he was so pathetic, sometimes, so . . . so . . . so . . .'

'Nice?'

'Very nice. But just so . . .'

'Kind, pleasant, generous?'

'Yes. But, so . . . so . . .'

'In love with you?'

'Look'—Nadine pointed a speared chip at Dig—'he held his knife and fork like he was going to knit a sweater with them, OK?'

'You are unreal, Nadine Kite,' said Dig, slowly shaking his head from side to side in wonderment, 'you really are. What planet are you from?'

Nadine looked at him sniffily, sensing that her defence was shaky, to say the least. 'OK,' she conceded, 'I admit it. I am a fussy cow but, the bottom line is this: Maxwell wasn't right for me and I didn't want to go out with him any more. But, I know, *I know* that when I meet someone who *is* right for me, then I won't care how they hold their cutlery.'

Dig snorted sceptically.

'Yeah, right. Take the piss. But I know it. OK?'

Dig cut a swathe through the juices on his plate with a chunk of toast and smiled wryly at Nadine. 'Deen,' he said, popping the toast into his mouth, 'you know I love you dearly, but you are a complete and utter nightmare . . . Since you were twenty-two years old, since the day you left university and realised that you were never going to see Phil again, you have been out with every bloke who was stupid enough to ask you. As if three years with that weirdo wasn't enough. You have never once stopped and asked yourself if you actually *wanted* to go out with them, whether they were suitable, whether you fancied them, or if it stood a chance in hell of working out. You just use men to flatter your ego. You spend a couple of weeks doing everything within your power to ensure that they fall in love with you, and then the minute they do, you spend another two months building up a big enough list of faults and grievances to justify dumping the poor bastard.'

'I do not go out with every guy who asks me.'

'OK then. Name me one guy you've turned down—one guy.'

Nadine thought for a moment and then smiled wickedly. 'Well. Let me think. Oh yes, that's right. There was one bloke—you!' She smiled smugly. 'Got you! I turned *you* down.'

Dig shook his head. 'No no no. That doesn't count. We were kids then. I'm talking about *after* university, after the thing with Phil.'

Nadine went silent for a while as she flicked rapidly through her memory files. 'Well,' she said, 'it's not as if I get asked out every day or anything. You have to take these opportunities when they're offered.'

'Oh, come on! You haven't been single for more than a week in the last ten years and you haven't been out with anyone for longer than a few months. Work it out for yourself.'

'Oh yes,' leered Nadine, triumphantly, 'oh yes, of course! I forgot I was talking to the world's leading relationship expert. I forgot you were the man who had his heart broken when he was eighteen and hasn't let one single woman near it since. I forgot I was talking to the man who *woke up in bed this morning with a seventeen-year-old girl!*'

Dig blushed. 'Yeah, right,' he said, 'but at least I don't lead them on, at least they know what they're getting into. And besides, girls that young, they don't actually *want* anything serious, anyway. Not like you thirty-something women.'

Nadine raised her eyebrows ceilingwards. 'Oh,' she growled, 'don't start all that business again. I'm far too hungover for that argument. And anyway, I'm not thirty-something, I'm thirty-nothing.'

'What's the difference?'

'Well, thirty is more like a full stop on your twenties, really. I don't think you're actually *in your thirties* until you're thirty-one. Anyway, all I'm saying is, you're in no position to preach to me about how I should be conducting my love life.'

'OK, OK,' sighed Dig, smiling, 'so we're both as bad as each other. You dump decent men because they choose the wrong mugs, and I'm the Jerry Lee Lewis of Kentish Town . . . Let's face it—we're both crap.'

'Oh God, Dig. Look at us. We're both thirty now—we're *too old* to be crap. What have we been doing for the last ten years? I mean, I'm under no illusions about everlasting love, but we haven't even come close. We haven't had one long-term relationship between the two of us. We're pathetic. We're thirty years old, we're healthy, we've got flats, cars, jobs and security, we're both unbelievably nice people and we're going to wake up one morning and find ourselves all alone. All our friends will have big messy houses full of teenagers and grandchildren and noise and activity and we'll be alone, you in your anally tidy flat, me with fifty years' worth of glossy magazines arranged in piles, with nothing but memories of how it was to be young. That's not right. I don't want that. And the only way we're going to be able to avoid that is by doing something about it *now.*'

Dig had been nodding throughout this and now stuck one hand out towards Nadine. 'I agree,' he said, 'and I think we should make a pact here and now. I'll start looking for a more mature woman and you start looking for a bloke who measures up to your standards.'

'And the first person to start seeing a decent man or woman gets . . . gets . . .' Nadine quickly calculated the chances of Dig recognising a 'real' woman if she slapped him around the chops with her handbag, smiled and stuck out her hand, 'a hundred quid.'

Dig's eyebrow shot up into his hairline but he grabbed Nadine's hand and shook it hard. 'Yeah,' he said, 'OK. A hundred quid for the first person to start dating a decent person.'

'So that means a woman over the age of twenty-six, for you, and a man who I actually *like*, for me. OK?'

'OK!'

They shook hands across the table, each one as certain as the other that this was one bet that would never be called in.

Starfish and Kites

Dig thought Nadine was a bit of a drip when he was allocated the seat next to hers on his first day at the Holy Trinity Convent School for Boys and Girls in Kentish Town.

She had unruly red hair and squidgy white hands with dimples where she should have had knuckles. She was very small and very round, and her grey school skirt stood out starchily from her legs in an 'A' shape.

Nadine thought Dig was a bit of a nerd when he approached the desk next to hers. He was very skinny and very pale, with an overdeveloped head of thick black hair that looked, to her, like a bad wig.

Not surprisingly, none of the other children rushed over to get to know Dig and Nadine when the bell for their first break rang at ten thirty, and consequently they had to make do with each other for company while they sat in the playground.

'Dig,' stated Nadine, swinging her plump little legs back and forth, 'that's a really stupid name. Why are you called Dig?'

'It is not a stupid name. It's short for Digby.'

'Well, that's a stupid name, too.'

'No it's not—it's French.'

'Yes it is. "Dig". It's not a name. It's a *verb*.'

'What about you? You can talk. Nadine *Kite*. That's not a name, that's a thing that you fly in the sky.'

'Yes. I *do* know what a kite is, thank you very much.'

'Oh yes—I bet you've never flown one, though, have you? I have. My dad bought it for me. We take it out on Primrose Hill.'

Nadine fell silent for a second and took an extra big slurp of her

Banana Nesquik before shrugging. 'Who cares?' she said. 'Kites are for kids. Anyway,' she continued, changing the subject, 'how come you've only got one eyebrow?'

'It's not *one* eyebrow—it's two eyebrows that meet up in the middle.'

'Looks stupid.'

'Oh,' said Dig, 'thanks a lot.'

'Don't mention it.'

They both stopped talking and began sucking aggressively on their cartons of drink. Dig turned to Nadine and pointed at her hands. 'How come you've got no knuckles, then? How come they're *inside out*?'

'What do you mean?'

'Look,' he said, taking one of her little hands in his own and rubbing his thumb over the dimples in her joints, 'the skin there goes *in*, instead of *out*. They're not normal.'

'Yes they are!' She spread them out like starfish and gazed at them.

'No, they're not. Look at my hands.' He splayed his long white hand open, placed it over her starfish hand and pointed out his sharp knuckles. 'That's what knuckles are supposed to look like.'

'Hmph,' said Nadine.

There was a short silence.

'You can come with us—if you like,' said Dig.

'Where?'

'Kite-flying. Me and my dad.'

'Oh,' said Nadine. 'OK, then.'

They both sat then and stared at their touching hands, and let the warmth seep between their fingers while the playground echoed around them with the sounds of a thousand other children.

Nadine looked up at him then, into his kind, brown eyes, and decided at that moment that whatever happened in her life, she was going to marry Digby Ryan.

By the time Dig and Nadine had finished breakfast it was early afternoon, and a fairly strong wind had picked up around Primrose Hill, tugging clouds across the sun and throwing dead leaves into the air.

'Should have brought the kites,' said Dig, kicking up a drift of leaves.

'Should have worn trousers,' said Nadine, clinging on to the fly-away hem of her black chiffon skirt. 'Can we find somewhere to sit? This skirt's pissing me off.'

They sat beneath an oak tree, hands in pockets, legs crossed at the ankles, and stared across the park for a while, in silence.

Nadine turned to Dig. He looked so sweet. He wasn't bad looking, she supposed, smiling to herself. Quite cute, really. He was also wearing a somewhat serious, un-Dig-like expression on his face, and a couple of small creases had appeared in the area that should have been the gap between his eyebrows but was in fact just a bridge between the two. Nadine reached out to touch the little furrows with her fingertip.

'Oooh, yes,' she said, 'I can see the signs of ageing already.'

'What?' laughed Dig, touching the offending wrinkles.

'Worry lines,' said Nadine, resting her head on his shoulder, 'the care-free days of your youth are over, my friend.'

'You jest,' he said, leaning his head against hers and contemplating the brilliant blue and white sky above, 'but I think it might be true.'

Nadine didn't know what to say. 'Hey,' she changed the subject, 'what time were you born?'

'Erm, I'm not sure,' replied Dig, 'but it must have been in the evening, because my folks were in the pub when my mum's waters broke.'

'Well. There you go then. You're not thirty yet. Not officially. You've got another four or five hours in your twenties. So . . .'

'What?'

Nadine leaped to her feet, leaned down and scooped up a large armful of russet, auburn and mustard leaves. 'So,' she said, 'you're not too old to have a leaf fight,' and with that she threw the leaves all over Dig's head like oversized confetti, turned on her heel and ran away laughing.

She ran away, as she would recollect, in an anticlockwise direction, and she would later wonder what uncontrollable forces had led her to that decision. Because what Nadine didn't know when she made that seemingly trivial choice was just *how important* it actually was. Fate had snuck up on her unawares that day on Primrose Hill and as she ran screaming with laughter across the springy grass, Dig in pursuit with an enormous pile of leaves in his hands, little did she know that fate was about to leap into her path and change the course of her life for ever.

Because, had Nadine *not* taken the anticlockwise route that day, had she set off in the other direction, then they would never have bumped into Delilah.

He wasn't sure it was her at first. The hair threw him off a bit. It was a warm golden-brown instead of the peroxide white he remembered. And the clothes were different: classic, well cut and definitely expensive. But the moment he saw her face he knew.

It was Delilah. Delilah Lillie! He ignored the scratchiness of the leaves trapped inside his clothing and made his way to the iron railings that separated the park from the pavement. She was walking towards him on

Regent's Park Road, her hands full of carrier bags, a pair of sunglasses perched on top of her head. She was staring straight ahead and looked a bit stressed out. His pace quickened as she got closer.

'Di-ig. Where are you going?'

Dig ignored Nadine and carried on walking as if being irresistibly drawn towards a beam of light from an alien spaceship.

'Delilah?' he called. She didn't hear, carried on walking.

'Delilah!' He'd reached the iron railings now and grasped them with both hands as Delilah approached, a quizzical, slightly unsure expression on her face. 'It is, isn't it?' he began. 'Delilah. It is you, isn't it?'

Close up, she looked fantastically pretty, fresh-faced, glossy. She'd worn a lot of make-up at school and looked much younger now, barefaced. She was looking at Dig with a combination of confusion, anticipation, concern and embarrassment. She nodded.

'Dig,' he said, placing a hand on his chest, 'Dig Ryan.'

Her face softened with recognition. 'Oh my God!' she exclaimed. 'Dig Ryan! I don't believe it!'

'How are you? How've you been? It's so good to see you.'

'Yeah . . . yeah. I'm great, just great. How're you?' She was smiling widely, looking genuinely pleased to see him.

'Great. I'm great, too. Shit—this is amazing! God, I mean, what've you been up to, what're you doing now, where are you living?'

Delilah indicated the iron railings that divided them.

'Wait,' said Dig, 'wait right there. I'm coming round.'

He skipped back across the grass to where Nadine was waiting for him. 'Quick,' he gestured at her, grinning like an idiot, 'quick! It's Delilah. Come on!'

'Delilah?' muttered Nadine, a shadow falling across her face. 'Delilah Lillie?'

She let the handful of leaves she'd gathered for a counter-offensive fall dolefully to the ground and grudgingly followed the bounding figure of Dig across the park and towards the gates.

Delilah Lillie

Every school had a Delilah Lillie. They were usually blonde, they were always pretty and they were invariably the coolest girl in the school. Delilah Lillie was Debbie Harry, Leslie Ash and Kim Wilde all rolled into one. She had breasts before anyone else and a mop of thick bleached-blonde hair which hung over her eyes like flaxen curtains. She was moody and chewed gum and made her school uniform look sexy. All the boys wanted to go out with her and all the girls wanted to be her.

Nadine could remember Delilah's first day at school as if it were yesterday. The corridors and classrooms of the Holy Trinity Convent School for Boys and Girls had been rumbling with the rumours all day. There was a new girl in 4H and she was *really cool*. Her name was Delilah. She'd been expelled from her last school for, among many suggested misdemeanours, getting pregnant, sniffing glue, having sex in the showers, setting fire to the stationery cupboard and stealing the caretaker's car. She lived on the Gospel Oak Estate, the roughest estate in Kentish Town, and her dad was a burglar. She used to go out with Suggs from Madness and she'd slept with everyone in the sixth form of her last school. She was a junky, a criminal, a slag and a hard-nut. And she was sexy as hell.

Dig and Nadine sat on the grass outside the science block on their first afternoon back at school. They were fourteen years old. At Dig's feet was his constant companion, a folded and battered copy of the *NME*, and he had a big spot on his chin.

Nadine was wearing a baggy red school jumper, her thumbs emerging from tatty holes in the sleeves, and her tie was slung slovenly around her neck. Her frizzy copper hair was held back from her face with a green chiffon scarf and there were traces of mascara clinging to her pale eyelashes, mascara, Dig noticed, which hadn't been there last term.

Dig 'n' Deen, that's what everyone at school called them, because they were inseparable. You never saw one without the other. They occupied a quiet and comfortable position within the school hierarchy—too studious to be cool but too cool to be drips. No one gave them any hassle, but then no one particularly made an effort to befriend them either. Which was fine with them. They lived in a cosy world of study, John Peel, backcombed hair and kite-flying.

Nadine hadn't forgotten the pledge she'd made to herself at eleven years old, and if you were to feel around under her mattress you would find her most secret diary, the one she fills with her deepest and darkest thoughts and desires. It is an old school exercise book and it is decorated on the front and the back with doodles—practice signatures, in fact. All of them say the same thing: *Nadine Ryan*. Because even though they're not boyfriend and girlfriend, even though they've never even kissed each other, she is going to marry him.

Dig 'n' Deen are going to live on Gloucester Crescent in Camden Town in a big house with shutters and marble floors. Their bed will be a huge pine one with a fluffy white duvet and the sun will shine on to it every morning. They will have parties every Saturday night, and on

Sundays they'll pick up Dig's dad in their powder-blue E-type Jag and take him kite-flying on Primrose Hill. They will have four children— Sam, Ben, Emily and Alicia—and they will be incredibly happy.

It's not that Nadine has a crush on Dig or anything, it's just that she can't imagine anyone else marrying him and not being allowed to see him any more. One day they will be man and wife, but for now she is happy just to be his best friend.

'What have you got on Thursday mornings?' Nadine asked Dig.

'Erm . . . erm . . . erm . . .' He trailed off.

'Di-ig.' Nadine tutted and glanced up at Dig from her timetable, following his strange, glassy gaze with her eyes. He was staring across the grass to the netball courts, where a huddle of boys from the fifth form were vying for the attention of a tall girl with white-blonde hair, an awful lot of earrings and a very tight skirt.

'Aaaah,' said Nadine, '*that* must be Delilah Lillie.'

Dig remained rigid and speechless, staring at the glamorous figure across the grass, his jaw hanging ever so slightly open.

'She doesn't look like a junky to me,' said Nadine casually, surveying her through her eyelashes, 'she's incredibly pretty.'

Dig nodded. He opened his mouth to say something but his still-breaking voice cracked and he cleared his throat. 'She . . . she . . . she looks like Leslie Ash in *Quadrophenia*,' he finally managed to squeak.

Quadrophenia was Dig's favourite film of all time. And now there was a girl in the playground, a girl just over there who looked just like Leslie Ash, Dig's dream woman.

Nadine glanced across at her friend and saw the passion glimmering in his eyes, the longing oozing from his pores and the pain already piercing his soul as he looked at something he wanted so much but had already decided he could never have.

And that was when Nadine knew. That was the moment that Nadine knew that things were never going to be the same again.

All the legends that had accompanied Delilah to the Holy Trinity were proven unfounded within the first six weeks of term. She wasn't a drug addict, she wasn't a dealer, her father wasn't a burglar and she hadn't been expelled from her last school. She had simply moved from south to north London and been put into a new school. She *did*, though, live on the Gospel Oak Estate, and she *had* apparently been out with Suggs's little brother, although only for two weeks. However, this lack of sociopathic behaviour did nothing to dent her reputation as the coolest girl in school.

Nadine had been right. Things weren't the same between her and Dig after that first day of term. All Dig's priorities changed. Now everything was a constant reference to Delilah. He and Nadine would walk around the school grounds together, apparently aimlessly, but Nadine knew that they were Delilah-hunting, she knew that the moment Dig heard the sound of Delilah's gravelly voice echoing around a corner they would suddenly slow down and Dig would start walking differently and talking to Nadine in a really loud voice about something they hadn't been discussing before, usually something to do with music. He would walk past Delilah and stare resolutely ahead, avoiding her gaze.

Dig and Nadine's friendship ended one rainy Tuesday afternoon, just before the end of the first term. They were sitting together on the stairs outside the language lab when Delilah appeared from nowhere, clutching a pile of books to her chest and apparently in a hurry. But she stopped dead when she rounded the corner and saw Dig on the steps, stopped and stood squarely in front of him. For a second the air tingled with electricity, and silence reverberated around the three of them. Nadine stopped breathing and waited for one of them to say something.

'Hi,' Delilah said, finally.

'Hi,' said Dig, his voice not letting him down by cracking, but emanating resoundingly from beneath his ribcage.

Nadine sat with her hands on her lap and stared at the floor.

'You're Dig, aren't you?' said Delilah.

'Yeah,' he said, still in that deep voice, 'that's right. And you are . . .?'

Nadine whistled silently under her breath. You had to hand it to him, she thought to herself, that was pretty cool.

'I'm Delilah,' she said, 'Delilah Lillie. I'm in 4H.'

'Oh,' said Dig, 'yeah. Right. You're the new girl, aren't you?'

'Yeah,' she said, 'pretty new.' There was a second's silence then, and Delilah bit her lip and threw Nadine a sideways glance, a look which told Nadine everything she needed to know. I'm taking over now, that's what that look said, off you go, you ginger-haired nobody.

It was time to go, it was time to let Dig get on with this, without her. She pushed her papers together into a pile, swung her bag over her shoulder and got to her feet.

'Right,' she said unnecessarily, as neither of them was paying any attention to her, 'I'm off. See ya.' And then she walked, as fast as she'd ever walked, along corridor after corridor, until there was nowhere left to walk. And then she stopped, stopped in her tracks and turned to face the wall as the tears she'd been trying so hard to control spilled over her eyes and cascaded in sheets down her cheeks.

23

At around quarter past four on July 17, 1985 a loud bell from within the school walls pierced the silence, and the playground erupted.

It was the last day of school.

Folders and textbooks and feint-ruled pads with margins flew into the air, red-and-grey-striped nylon ties were unknotted from worn shirt-collars and spun like lassos around heads and 120 red-blazered sixteen-year-olds moved as one out of the school gates for the last time.

Nadine found her friends and they joined the crowds rushing towards Caledonian Park for an afternoon of drinking and pelting kids from other schools with flour and eggs. They drank flat cider from big plastic bottles. They talked about their plans for the summer and their plans for the rest of their lives. It was all ahead of them, but Nadine couldn't shake the feeling that the most important part was already behind her.

It was all over. Not just school, but what remained of her friendship with Dig. It wasn't going to survive this, she knew that. He was going to do his A Levels at a college in Holloway; she was doing hers at a grammar school in Archway.

He was still firmly ensconced in his partnership with Delilah, to the exclusion of everyone else, particularly Nadine. Delilah had him wrapped up like a fly in a web and he was happy to be there. There was nothing left over for Nadine.

A cloud moved across the sun, a small chill breeze wafted over her, and Nadine looked up just in time to see Dig and Delilah exchanging a kiss. The sun was just starting to set across the tops of the council blocks that lined the horizon, they'd run out of cider and two of her friends had fallen asleep on the grass. Nadine decided it was time to go home. She gathered her belongings together, got up and began walking.

Dig caught up with her at the park gates. He was breathless from running. 'Deen,' he squeaked incredulously, 'where are you going?'

Nadine could see Delilah across the park, sitting up stiffly, her back poker-straight, watching the exchange closely.

'Home,' said Nadine. 'It's getting late.'

Dig's face wrinkled in confusion. 'Oh,' he said, 'right.'

'So,' she said, 'goodbye and good luck, yeah?'

'What? I mean . . . yeah. But we'll still be meeting up, won't we? You know—the kites and everything?' He looked anxious.

Nadine shrugged. 'Oh,' she said, 'I think we'll probably be too busy, what with schoolwork and being at different colleges, you know?'

Dig's eyes clouded over with sadness. 'Yeah. I suppose you're right.'

Nadine squeezed a small smile through tight lips. 'So have a nice life . . .'

'Oh. Right. I see. You too. Yeah,' he said, looking like he had now given the matter some thought and was beginning to get used to the idea. 'Yeah. You have a good life, too, Nadine.'

And then they ran out of things to say. Nadine shot him one last smile and then turned to leave the park.

Outside the park, Nadine walked blindly towards York Way, her feet leading her homewards while her heart urged her to turn around, tear through the park towards Dig, her best friend, her soulmate, to make amends and reseal their bond, before it was too late. But she didn't—her pride wouldn't let her.

Chapter Two

ANTICLOCKWISE! ANTICLOCKWISE! Why had she gone anticlockwise? It was a fifty-fifty thing. She could have gone clockwise. She could have been back at Dig's by now, safe and cosy, instead of sitting in some hoity-toity tea-shop in Primrose Hill drinking overpriced cappuccino and watching her best friend regress within seconds to the fourteen-year-old schoolboy he'd always been.

And oh my God, look at her. Just look at her, will you? It's sickening. How can she look younger now than she did then? How can she be more beautiful, more poised, more *everything*? She has acquired polish and gloss. Her accent is now neutral. She has a dazzling smile and even a certain amount of charm. That's definitely something with a designer label in it that she's wearing so *effortlessly*. And look at the size of that rock on her ring finger—Gibraltar has nothing on it.

She has expensive hair—what is it that hairdressers in expensive salons actually *do* to hair to make it look expensive like that? She's wearing the sort of make-up that looks like you're wearing none at all, and she has that smell about her, not quite perfume, but something more intrinsic, like cleanliness, like morning dew.

Nadine looks at Dig. She hasn't seen him this excited for years. Every angle of his body is directed towards Delilah, his elbows, his knees, his head. Nadine may as well not be here, may as well not exist. She's a big ginger gooseberry again.

They're talking about Delilah's marriage, about the life she's been living for the past twelve years. She's not called Delilah Lillie any more, she's called, much to Nadine's delight, Delilah *Biggins*. Her husband is called Alex. He owns a small chain of brasserie-style restaurants in the north-west and they live together in neo-Georgian splendour in Chester. When he's not overseeing his empire, he's to be found on the golf course, squash court and cricket pitch. They have three horses and a swimming pool. Every couple of months Alex pays for Delilah to fly to New York first class and she shops till she drops.

It all sounds pretty dull to Nadine, but Dig's riveted by every word. But then, just as Nadine is about to nod off, the conversation suddenly changes direction. All is not as it seems. Delilah admits, her eyes glazing over with tears, that she's left Alex. She's taken off and left him in bed, with just a note to wake up to, which Nadine thinks is pretty cruel. But then, any man stupid enough to marry a heart-hazard like Delilah gets what he deserves, quite frankly. I mean, you can tell just by *looking* at her that she's going to leave you one day.

She doesn't expand on the subject and Dig doesn't ask her any of the *right* questions, about why she's left her husband and come back to London, but then he's a boy. She'd ask them herself but she's in too much of a mood to give her voice that inquisitive, interested edge it needs to form questions.

And that's another thing. You'd have thought, wouldn't you, that Dig would be demanding some sort of explanation right now, demanding to know why exactly Delilah disappeared and left him all those years ago, why she broke his heart into so many pieces that he'd never found them all to glue back together again? You'd have thought he'd be a bit *frosty* with her about the way she behaved back then, but he's not. He's acting like none of that ever happened, like everything is all right.

'So,' Dig is asking Delilah, 'how long have you been back?'

'I just arrived this morning, believe it or not. Got the first train down.'

'Really?' smiles Dig, the look of a man blessed with fantastic serendipity spreading across his face. 'And are you staying at your mum's?'

Delilah takes a slurp of her filter coffee—black, no sugar—and puts the cup down, shaking her head. 'Oh God no,' she says. 'I haven't spoken to her since I was eighteen. I moved out and went to stay with my cousin. Remember? Marina. That's where I'm staying now.'

Why? Nadine wants to scream. Why did you move in with your cousin when you were eighteen? Why didn't you tell Dig you were going? And why isn't Dig asking you these questions?

'And what are your plans?' says Dig. 'What are you going to do with yourself here?'

Delilah shrugs and looks anxious. This is obviously a tricky question for her to answer. Please, thinks Nadine, please say you're just here for a couple of days, you're very busy, people to see, places to go. Please say that you probably won't be seeing us again.

But Nadine already has this very strange, uncomfortable feeling that this isn't to be the last time they see Delilah, that Delilah is, in fact, going to be around one hell of a lot, a portent that is borne out seconds later when Delilah smiles and says, 'Well, I was just going to hang out, really, you know, catch up with old friends, that sort of thing.'

Dig's face performs a theatre of ecstatic emotions. 'Excellent,' he smiles, 'that's fantastic.' The two of them stop for a second then and beam, positively *beam*, at each other. Nadine smiles grimly and traces a happy face into the froth on top of her coffee.

'You two,' Delilah is saying, 'you two have changed so much. I would never have recognised you. Especially you, Deen. You're absolutely gorgeous. I love all these little clips in your hair. And I love your fingernails'—she takes Nadine's turquoise talons in her hands and examines them—'how do you get them to grow so long? Mine always split down here.' She indicates the pink of her perfect nails.

'Jelly cubes,' says Nadine, 'I eat jelly cubes every day. Rowntrees, lemon and lime flavour.' And she's thinking, Oh no, don't do this, Delilah. Don't do this whole trying-to-make-me-like-you thing. I don't want to like you. I am never going to like you because no matter how much you might have changed, I will never be able to forget the way you treated me at school, the way you disregarded me and belittled me and broke my heart. It has taken me a decade and a half to emerge from your shadow, to become desirable in my own right. Call me selfish, thinks Nadine, call me insecure and call me paranoid, I don't care. I just want you out of London, out of my life and out of Dig's life.

'So, you're a photographer, are you?'

'Uh-huh,' replies Nadine, 'that's me. I take pictures.' She tells Delilah briefly about the exotic locations and the financial rewards.

'Wow,' says Delilah, genuinely impressed, 'that must be amazing. I'm so jealous of you, I really am.'

Nadine forces a saccharine smile. 'Oh, don't be silly,' she says, wishing she could rise above all the small-minded, mean-spirited jealousy she's feeling. She looks across the table at Dig—he always brings out the best in her—but he's lost in Delilahland.

'Well'—Delilah is knocking back the dregs of her coffee and making moves towards her handbag—'I'd better get back. I've left my dog alone with a hundred starving cats. They've probably eaten *him* by now.' She smiles and drops a pile of coins on to the bill. 'I hope I'll see you both again soon. It would *so nice* if we could get together some time.'

'Yeah—definitely,' oozes Dig, 'definitely,' and Nadine can tell he's mentally reorganising his entire diary to make sure there's no question that they'll be able to 'get together some time'.

'Actually,' he says, reaching into the pocket of his black leather coat and pulling out a scrappy piece of paper and a Biro, 'let me take your number at your cousin's. I'm not up to much this week. Maybe we could go out one night. You know. Catch up on old times.'

No, thinks Nadine. No. Not again. This can't be happening again.

'That would be great, Dig. Thanks.'

Nadine's heart sinks.

On Monday morning, Dig gets to work at half past ten.

Late, by anybody else's standards, but perfectly acceptable by his, especially considering that he had to pick his car up from those thieving shysters in Tufnell Park on his way in.

Johnny-Boy Records is housed in a dinky little pink, stucco-fronted cottage in a Camden Town mews; it used to be Toby's home, when he started the label back in 1989, but now Toby lives in a five-bedroom house in Primrose Hill with his ex-model wife, their three strangely named children and a nanny, and the cottage is used as an office.

The inside hasn't changed much since Toby lived here; it's very cosy and homely. The floors are all distressed reclaim boards, there are table lamps and pictures and plants and flowers all over the place. In reception there is a widescreen Nicam TV and a big sofa where they watch *Neighbours* every day with their feet up on the Balinese coffee table. A wrought-iron spiral staircase leads to a galleried area overhead and from there another leads on to a tiny roof terrace where everyone eats their lunch in summer.

Dig loves the fact that his workplace is nicer than his flat. It's one of many reasons why he's stayed here so long. Seven years, in fact. He started off as an A&R assistant and was promoted to A&R manager the following year when his boss left to form a band of his own. Not that he actually manages anyone, he's a one-man department and he likes it that way.

Dig didn't use to be this slack. He used to be a workaholic. He'd be in at nine, work through lunch, stay till seven and then hit the trail, going to two or three gigs every night, because in those days Dig was on a mission to find the 'next big thing'. And in 1995 he found it: Fruit. The biggest sensation of the year. Their first single went to number one, as did the first album and stayed in the Top Fifty for nearly a year. They were on the front cover of all the music papers and appeared on every pop show on the telly.

It had been a mad year for Dig. He was head-hunted by every A&R department in London and consequently given a payrise by a somewhat scared Toby, big enough for him to finally leave home and buy a flat at the ripe old age of twenty-seven. His reputation was made. Everyone knew who he was and what he'd achieved. So he sat back and relaxed for a while, safe in the knowledge that no one could touch him because he was the guy who discovered Fruit.

'You're looking a bit pleased with yourself this morning,' says Charlie, their pneumatically blonde but strangely droll receptionist, shoving bits of paper into internal envelopes.

Dig considers his expression and realises that he does indeed have a smug smile hovering around his lips. He decides this is highly inappropriate for a Monday morning and removes it.

'You recovered from Friday night yet?' inquires Charlie, in a tone of voice laden with the suggestion that he'd been drunker than he thought.

'Just about,' he says, picking his mail out of the pile on her desk.

'You know that girl was only seventeen, don't you?'

Dig blushes and climbs the spiral staircase and ignores Charlie's calls of 'Lock up your daughters—paed on the loose!'

Dig pulls off his leather coat and hangs it up. He reaches into the inside pocket and feels around a bit until he locates what he's looking for. A small, manky shred of paper. He gently smooths it out and places it on his desk, next to his phone. He looks at it for a while and feels that smile forming on his lips again.

He won't call her now. He'll call her later. He'll have a cup of coffee first, open his mail, check his emails.

And then he'll phone Delilah Lillie.

Nadine always feels a little shiver of excitement going to work. First of all there's the unadulterated *thrill* of driving around in her white Alfa Spider, which is beautiful and which she paid for herself.

And then there's the sign outside her studio, nailed to the wall: NADINE KITE PHOTOGRAPHY. It gets her every time.

Her very own studio. She worked long and hard for it. Five years of underpaid and overworked assisting, first of all for a temperamental interiors photographer and then for a wonderful, old page-three photographer called Sandy, who'd been her inspiration.

Nadine never expected to make a living from photographing half-naked women. She aspired, as most photography graduates do, to a much higher plane. Fashion, maybe, or portraiture. But she started doing freelance photography at around the same time that 'lads' magazines became big business and over the years she had become *Him* magazine's most popular photographer, doing their main features and their cover shots. She'd found a niche for herself, a place where the rewards were high and the work enjoyable, a place she loved being.

Nadine is in a particularly good mood for a Monday morning. She's already been to the gym for one of her thrice-weekly workouts and it's left her feeling uncharacteristically energised and chirpy. The sun is shining and she's wearing a beautiful pink sequinned cardigan she picked up from a car-boot sale yesterday for a mere pound.

And she's single again! She loves being single, she really does. And this time she's going to stay single for as long as it takes to find a decent bloke. This time she's going to do it properly, and this time she has a rather attractive financial carrot to make sure she does.

Nadine flicks on the kettle in the tiny kitchen and stretches out on her pink leather sofa to read her mail. It's going to be a quiet day today. For once. A meeting at the *Him* office in Shaftesbury Avenue to pick the shot for the February cover and lunch afterwards with the commissioning editor. She'll use the rest of the day to catch up on paperwork and have a bit of a tidy-up. And maybe start phoning around her girlfriends to see if anyone has a male friend she could borrow to win this bet with Dig.

She smiles to herself. She *is* going to win, there's no doubt about that. Nadine has a fierce competitive streak, especially when it comes to Dig. Maybe it has something to do with working in a man's world. Maybe it's the way her parents always compared her unfavourably to her little brother. Who knows? But it's there, and it's got her where she is today. It's got her her flat and her car and a healthy bank balance. It's got her respect and status and a constant stream of high-quality commissions from some of the top magazines in the country.

And although she doesn't know it yet, it's just about to get her the prestigious Ruckham's Motor Oil calendar, a commission that will send her earning potential on a trajectory straight to the stars.

Mitchell Tuft, Ruckham's Brand Manager, asked her to bike over her portfolio last week. It was returned the same day with a blank compliment slip, and Nadine had assumed that was that.

But the phone has just rung and Mitchell Tuft is talking to her now about how much he loves her work and how he would like to offer her a month in the Polynesian Islands with some of the most beautiful women in the world and a pay-cheque big enough to mean that she could take the rest of the year off. If she was interested, of course.

'Well, yes, Mitchell. Yes. I'd be honoured. Of course. Yes. I look forward to it very much. Thank you.' Nadine puts down the phone and takes a deep breath to calm her racing heart. '£40,000,' she whispers to herself, '£40,000. For four weeks' work.' She gets to her feet and starts screaming. 'Oh my God! Oh my God—I'm going to be *rich!*'

She has to tell Dig. She picks up the phone.

'Dig! Dig! Guess what? I've got the Ruckham's calendar commission.'

'*Ruckham's!* You're joking!'

'No. I'm serious. I'm going to be rich!'

'Sod rich,' says Dig, 'who cares about money? You're going to be sent off to some exotic paradise with twelve fantastic, incredible, stunning women. Oh man—can I come? I'll be the bikini valet. I'll be the baby-oil applicator. I'll do anything. Please, please, *please*, can I come?'

'Sounds like you already have.'

'When are you going?'

'Middle of January. Isn't that perfect? Could there be a better time to get out of England and go to Bora-Bora?'

'Shit, Deen. You're going to paradise. And they're bound to put you up somewhere really swank. I am so jealous.'

'I'll bring you back a stick of rock.'

'Thanks. A lot. Anyway. Look. We'll celebrate at the weekend, yeah? I'm just on my way out so I can't chat. I need your advice.'

'Fire ahead.'

'Restaurants. I need you to recommend me a restaurant.'

'What for?' Nadine wrinkles her nose in confusion. Dig doesn't go to restaurants.

Dig's voice is almost trembling with excitement. 'I asked her out.'

'Who?'

'Delilah, of course. I just phoned her and I asked her out.'

'What do you mean, asked her out?' Nadine's mouth has gone dry.

'I mean, I said, would you like to come out for dinner with me? And she said yes.'

'You're joking, right?' Nadine can feel bile rising unpleasantly at the back of her throat.

Dig appears not to have picked up on the sudden change of tone in Nadine's voice.

' . . . It's all just coming together, Deen, y'know? That girl on my birthday night, Katie, she was like my wake-up call. If I hadn't woken up in bed with her, I wouldn't have felt so shit. If I hadn't felt so shit, I wouldn't have suggested going for a walk in the park with you. And if I hadn't gone for a walk in the park with you, I'd never have bumped into Delilah and I wouldn't have asked her out and I wouldn't be feeling as . . . *good* as I'm feeling right now. I mean, God—she's just *gorgeous*. Isn't she? Don't you think that she's actually *more* beautiful than she was when we were at school? . . . And nicer, too?'

Nadine feels her heart shrivel and is glad they're talking on the phone, otherwise Dig would be able to see the look in her eyes.

'Dig,' she hisses, petulantly, 'what are you expecting to actually *happen* with Delilah? She *is* still married, y'know.'

'Yes. I do realise that,' sniffs Dig, having finally picked up on Nadine's attitude. 'And I'm not expecting anything to *happen*. Well, not immediately. I just want to see her, that's all, just spend the evening with her.'

'OK. Fine. But I think you'll find that it's a disappointment. Being with Delilah. After all these years. She's not the same girl you knew at school, she's not the same cool chick. I'll bet she listens to Phil Collins, these days. And did you notice, the other day, she was wearing *pearl* earrings. I mean . . . that's positively middle-aged . . .'

'My God! What's the matter with you? You're basing your entire opinion of her on a pair of *earrings*? How shallow is that, Deen? Delilah's got class. She dresses beautifully—that classic look really suits her. And by the way—I did not ask her out to win our bet, but I have to say that I think it counts.'

'Forget it,' snaps Nadine. 'No way. Married women don't count.'

'Who said married women don't count? That wasn't in the rules.'

'Oh Jesus, Dig. Whatever. I really don't care. You go out on your stupid date with stupid Delilah and you have fun.'

'OK,' Dig says tersely, 'but where shall I take her?'

'What's wrong with the Bengal Lancer?'

'I can't take her there.'

'Why not?'

'Because—because she's Delilah, that's why. I want to take her somewhere special.'

'I'm sorry, Dig, I can't think of anywhere.'

'Fine,' Dig says angrily, 'just fine. I'll sort it out myself.' And then he hangs up, suddenly, leaving Nadine standing there in her studio, the receiver hanging limply from her hand and a film of tears forming rapidly over her eyes.

People come to London from all over the world to dip into its enormous wealth of diverse cuisines. There are Korean, Vietnamese, Turkish, Brazilian, Burmese and Havanese restaurants wherever you look. So why was the only restaurant that Dig could think of in the whole culinary melting-pot of London the Bengal Lancer on Kentish Town Road?

The Bengal Lancer was his favourite restaurant, without a doubt. The proprietor, Archad, was friendly and welcoming, the naan bread was the fluffiest in all of London and, most importantly, they served until midnight. But he couldn't take *Delilah Lillie* there for dinner, could he.

He'd finally called her at midday. Her phone number had sat next to his phone, burning a hole into his consciousness all morning, and he had hardly been able to contain himself. They'd had a nice little chat and he'd suggested Tuesday night, for dinner, and she'd said yes.

And then something surreal had happened. He'd been halfway through a sentence when Delilah had suddenly interjected with, 'Oh my God, I have to go—the cats are holding Digby hostage in the corner.'

Eh? 'Digby?'

'Yeah, my dog, Digby. I named him after you. Ha. Look. Phone me tomorrow. Let me know where to meet you, or whatever. OK?'

'Er, yeah,' Dig had said, losing his composure, 'OK.'

And then she'd gone. Hung up. Left him feeling . . . all . . . all . . . Digby? *Digby?* She'd named her dog *Digby?* In one way, he supposed, it was flattering. She'd obviously thought about him over the years. But a dog? He felt emasculated. God, he hoped it was a big dog, a Rotty or a Ridgeback. He'd die, just die, if it was something small and yappy.

And then Nadine had phoned with her incredible news about the Ruckham's calendar—jammy cow, she *always* landed on her feet—and he'd tried asking her for a recommendation for a good restaurant. And now he really wished he hadn't. She'd been *awful*. Really bitchy and unpleasant, not like her usual self, at all. God knows what was the matter with her. She'd just been given the best news of her career— £40,000! What Dig could do with £40,000—and she seemed just miserable. It seemed like she had something against Delilah, for some strange reason. It made no sense to Dig, no sense at all.

Just as he was wracking his brains over where to take Delilah, Nick Jeffries, PR Superstar, wandered into Dig's office. Not that you could really call it 'his office', as such—it was more of an alcove, really.

'Where can I take a girl, tomorrow night, dinner, not too expensive, not too spicy, not too far away?' Dig asked Nick.

'What sort of girl?'

'Sort of girl I've been in love with since I was fourteen who looks like a goddess.' Nick had a low boredom threshold so any attempts at conversation had to be succinct and to the point.

'Hmmmm'—Nick perched his skinny, combats-clad butt on the edge of Dig's table—'she in love with you?'

'She was. Not any more. Least, I don't think she is.'

'You still in love with her?'

'Don't know. Might be.'

'Hmmmm. Got it.' Nick clicked his fingers, reached across Dig, grabbed his phone and began punching in numbers.

PR people always did this, Dig had noticed, brought third parties into conversations via the phone.

'Freddie,' Nick was saying to him, 'mate of mine. Just opened a place in . . . oh, yeah, hi, Freddie. Nick. Listen. You got a table free tomorrow night? Two people? Great. Dig. Thanks, mate. Take care. You too. Tomorrow. All sorted.' Dig started as he realised that Nick had put the phone down and was now talking to him again. 'Eight o'clock. Exmouth Market. It's called *ex*. He'll give you a good table. He'll give you a good night. Don't worry. She'll *love* it,' he said with a wink and a grin.

'Yeah, but what sort of food is it?' asked Dig nervously.

'God, I dunno. Meat. Or something. It's a meat place.'

And then he was gone. Leaving Dig with a hundred unanswered questions, like, where in Exmouth Market? What sort of meat? How much? What sort of atmosphere? *ex* sounded a bit poncey, not much like his kind of place. But . . . oh well . . . it was bound to be trendy, and at least Delilah would be able to tell people that she'd been to some new place in Clerkenwell, before anyone else, while it was still hot. Yeah. He'd go. He'd take Delilah to *ex*.

It couldn't be that bad, could it?

It is.

That bad.

A pale Spanish girl with red lipstick has just led them to their table. It's an incredibly big table, stretching almost the entire length and width of the small concrete room. It is laid with immense white china plates and chunky tumblers. It is also the only table in the room. There is a large chandelier overhanging the table constructed from what look like—sun-bleached bones? The shades covering the high-voltage bulbs appear to be pterodactyl eggshells. Very *Jurassic Park*. Very bright.

They are seated next to each other (thankfully—Dig had imagined for one worrying moment that they were going to be seated at opposite ends of this huge table, smiling regretfully at each other all night) somewhere near the middle of the table.

Dig turns towards Delilah who is examining her cutlery with fascination. The fork is designed to look like a bird's leg, all gnarled and knobbly with talons for tines. The knife looks like some kind of feather thing, with vicious serrations, and the spoon is an egg, on the end of a twig. Delilah grimaces at Dig and puts them back down on the table. 'Weird,' she mouths, silently. Dig couldn't agree more.

There is no atmosphere in the place. Not one drop of it. Dig is suddenly blinded by the extent of his own stupidity to ever have taken a recommendation from Nick. He should have known Nick wouldn't have been thinking about what was best for Dig, he'd just have been thinking how cool it was that he had one mate who needed customers for his new restaurant and another mate who needed somewhere to eat and how cool it was that he'd managed to put the two of them together.

Still, thinks Dig, may as well make the most of it, the most of being alone in a room with Delilah Lillie—there's so much to talk about, so many questions to ask—but he can't because this place has an echo, and that Spanish girl is just standing there staring into space.

Dig wishes they had a menu or a wine list or something that he could look at, something to do. He smiles hopefully at the waitress, who immediately snaps out of her reverie and almost runs towards them. 'Yes?' she demands.

'Er—I wondered if we could maybe have a look at a wine list, maybe? And a menu? If possible. Thank you.' He grins, apprehensively, hoping she won't take his request the wrong way.

She positively *beams* at them then. Her mouth splits open from ear to ear, revealing a large set of intensely white teeth. And then she shakes her head. Still smiling, she says, 'No.'

Dig decides he must have misheard her. 'Sorry,' he says.

'No menus. You are *at home* tonight. You understand?'

Dig and Delilah shake their heads slowly.

'*ex* is *our home*. You,' she points at them, 'are *our guests*. Chef is *your host*. This . . .'—she indicates the table—'is *our dinner table*. This is like dinner party. You see?'

Dig and Delilah nod slowly.

'So. Chef has prepared one meal, four courses, for *his guests* and our *sommelier* will give you wine which will complement the food of the chef. And you will eat and you will drink and then, you will pay!' She has brightened considerably by this point. 'It is *brilliant* new concept!' she trills. 'So. You are comfortable?'

They nod again. '*Sommelier* will be with you soon,' she says, before walking to the counter and going back into a trance.

Dig and Delilah exchange looks. Dig is imagining how pissed off she must be about him bringing her here and is just about to embark upon a nervous apology when he suddenly realises that she's smiling.

35

'Damn,' she says, theatrically, 'I feel so rude. I should have brought our *host* a box of Black Magic.' Delilah begins giggling like a kid.

Dig sniggers and joins in. 'Here,' says Dig, leaning in to Delilah's ear, 'I hope we're getting Viennetta for pudding.'

They both dissolve into helpless laughter then, and the ice, it seems, is well and truly broken. Delilah Lillie, *circa* 1999, has a sense of humour! The Spanish girl finally has the sense to put some music on, lifting the atmosphere an iota above 'morgue', and Dig turns to Delilah, breathes in a lungful of her beauty and holds it inside, next to his heart, which is close to bursting with joy.

Nadine slouches on her cracked-brown-leather Deco sofa in her marabou-trimmed fifties-starlet negligee and her Bart Simpson slippers, sipping Cadbury's Highlights from one of her *South Park* mugs and trying desperately *not* to think about what might be happening with Dig and Delilah tonight. She's failing miserably.

She looks at the time display on her video: 9.45pm. They're probably eating pudding by now. Nadine's mind fills up with images of Dig spoon-feeding strawberries into Delilah's soft, red welcoming mouth and laughing as a pink trickle of juice dribbles seductively down her chin. She imagines him in his new Jigsaw Menswear jumper, the camel cashmere one which she helped him choose and which he looks so cuddly in, and his big leather coat which makes him look chunkier than he is. It's his best outfit of the moment, his special-occasion outfit, and he's bound to be wearing it tonight. She knows what he's like.

Nadine feels awful. She still can't get over the way she behaved yesterday on the phone to Dig. She still can't believe that she's fallen out with him, that he hung up on her, that they argued. It's all so out of character. Nadine wishes that life were like a word processor, complete with Undo and Delete buttons. She wishes that the entire phone call could be erased from both their memories.

As it is, the whole scenario is now festering away in her sub-and-not-so-subconscious like a sweaty sardine. The more she thinks about it, the more her general sense of gloom and despair deepens and the more she hates herself.

She is also hurt by what she, neurotically maybe, sees as the implicit assertion in Dig's comments that he doesn't like the way she dresses. 'Delilah's got class,' he'd said. 'She dresses beautifully.' What is that supposed to mean? Is that what Dig really wants? A classy woman? Someone who wears tailored suits and gold jewellery? Who has expensive highlights and pearl earrings? Nadine has always seen him with someone more interesting than that, someone with a bit more character, a bit more *style*. Someone a bit more like herself, quite frankly.

Nadine realises that her own sense of style is maybe a bit . . . challenging, for some people's tastes. She's used to comments from cabbies and bus drivers and even from boyfriends, some of whom have been embarrassed by her appearance. They don't understand why anyone who earns as much as she does would want to wear second-hand clothes or sew things herself.

Nadine has always assumed that Dig approves of her dress sense, maybe even *admires* it. She's always assumed that he isn't like other men—that he *understands* the language of her dress. But now it seems that he finds it as alien as every other man.

And then there's her flat. It's the flat of a mad woman. Look at it. Miffy the Rabbit wallpaper and princess telephone. Flashing-neon Elvis mirror and flamenco-dancing lampstand. Leopardskin and zebra-print fake-fur cushions. Cocktail cabinet. Cactus fairy lights. Stuffed toys. Tack, memorabilia and other people's junk. It's mayhem in here, but somehow it works. It's a great flat—everyone who sees it loves it—but if she lives alone for much longer it will go *too far* and she will probably start collecting newspapers and carrier bags full of old men's shoes. They will have to break down her door when someone finally notices that she hasn't been seen for a few months. 'Poor old thing,' they'll say, 'she had a lonely life. But at least she had her junk to keep her company.'

Oh God. Nadine is about to have a crisis. She wants to sit here all night, wallowing in her own misery and imagining Delilah in her 'classy' clothes and her huge solitaire diamond engagement ring, looking elegant and refined in some posh restaurant with lovely Dig, *her* Dig, wearing all his best clothes and being on his best behaviour, and making him fall in love with her all over again.

He can't. He *can't* fall in love with someone else. He just can't.

Where would that leave her?

Hot tears begin cascading down Nadine's cheeks. She's spiralling into a frenzied hysteria. A few days ago she was sane and normal. A few days ago she had a handsome boyfriend and a great life. A few days ago she was a free-living, happy girl with a brilliant job and a wonderful flat and a best mate who meant the world to her. Now she is a miserable, bitter and twisted old spinster with poison in her bloodstream and bad taste in clothes. She has fallen out with her best friend and fallen out with herself and she is once again the awkward, shy and frizzy-haired girl of her dim and distant youth.

And all because of Delilah-bloody-Lillie.

Chapter Three

HALF AN HOUR after their arrival at the painful *ex* Dig and Delilah have relocated to an Indian restaurant a few doors down the road. The mausoleum atmosphere they could just about handle, the lack of choice they could have lived with, the empty table was not too much of a problem and the strange waitress was almost endearing.

But when she'd approached them bearing two steaming bowls of slightly grey soup, all afloat with what looked like bits of brain tissue, and told them that it was *menudo*, a very famous Spanish soup made with tripe, and then hastened to assure them that chef was the most renowned offal chef currently working in London—they'd decided to cut their losses and run.

In the Indian they chatted away over a pile of poppadoms and a particularly good selection of chutneys.

'God . . . you know, Alex would have loved that place,' Delilah was saying. 'He loves offal—all those horrid bits—kidneys and livers and brains and things. Thank God he can get all that sort of stuff cooked for him at his restaurants, otherwise I'd be expected to do it.'

It was strange for Dig to hear Delilah talking like this, using words like 'horrid'. Delilah had customised her Kentish Town accent with new bits and pieces of pronunciation and intonation, accent and inflection picked up from her time mixing in another society, far removed from her own. She sounded unbelievably sexy.

'Thanks for tonight,' she said. 'I really appreciate it.'

'Oh—God—it's nothing. Sorry it's all been such a disaster.'

'Not at all—it's been great. And so good to see you. It's hard to know what to expect when you haven't seen people for so long—whether you'll still have anything in common or not. I've thought about you so often over the years, wondered what you were up to, where you were.'

'Oh yeah?' began Dig in trepidation. 'I wondered about you, too.'

'Really!' smiled Delilah. 'And what exactly did you wonder?'

'Well,' he said, seriously, 'I suppose, really, I worried, more than wondered. I was worried about you.'

The smile fell from Delilah's face. She fiddled with her napkin and deftly changed the subject. 'You know,' she said, 'I could probably have guessed that this is what your life would be like now. Music biz. Still living in the area, not too far from your mum, eh?' She smiled wickedly. 'And I think I could have guessed that you wouldn't have settled down yet. You always used to say that you didn't want kids till you were forty, till you owned your own record label—d'you remember?'

Dig smiled wryly. 'Yeah, I did say that, didn't I? I was going to be a millionaire and we were going to go off and live on a tropical island somewhere. I was going to be the next Richard Branson.'

'Oh yes,' she laughed, 'you were, weren't you? I was going to sit on the beach all day drinking cocktails and waiting for you to return from your yachting trip. How hysterical!' Her laughter turned into a nostalgic smile and she looked into Dig's eyes, suddenly serious. 'God, we were great together, weren't we? Invincible. Dig and Delilah! We thought we'd change the world one day. It's funny, when I first started at the Holy T, I used to see you and Nadine wandering about together, always looking so serious and *so cool*. I was so jealous of you two. I wanted to be like you. I worshipped the ground you walked on . . .'

Dig choked on a fragment of poppadom. How had his life changed so dramatically? How come when he was a spotty fourteen-year-old geek he'd had women like Delilah 'worshipping the ground he walked on', and now he was reduced to chasing around after teenage girls.

'I remember our first date. I was so nervous, but you were so nice. You listened to me. I wasn't used to that in those days. You gave me so much confidence in myself . . . you shaped my life in a way. I wouldn't be the person I am today if it wasn't for you. Isn't that weird?'

Dig nodded. It *was* weird. He'd never really thought about it before, but it was true. Parents expended so much energy worrying about the effect that their own actions would have on their offspring when it seemed that your character was determined, on the whole, by your peers. It was friends who formed you: your first mate, your first girlfriend, your first day at school, your experiences away from home.

Delilah, Dig suddenly realised, was an enormous part of him.

Getting the most beautiful girl in the school, the girl everyone wanted, and feeling the jealousy and respect of every boy around him had filled him with an unshakeable confidence in his ability to attract women, despite not being conventionally attractive. If it hadn't been for Delilah, he would have probably ended up marrying the first girl who'd let him sleep with her just in case no one else ever let him again. He still had that confidence all these years later, and he owed it to Delilah.

'So,' he said, nervously, 'tell me about Alex.'

Delilah looked slightly surprised. 'What do you mean?'

'Well, I don't know. What's he like? How did you meet him? What went wrong? That kind of thing. Unless . . . you don't want to . . .'

Delilah shook her head affirmatively. 'No,' she said, 'it's OK. It's fine.' She took a deep breath, and a warm smile spread across her face. 'I met him on Primrose Hill. He was a business studies student. I was . . . I fell over. He picked me up and took me to Casualty.'

'Were you hurt?'

'No—well, not really—just a cut, some stitches. It was nothing.'

'When was this?'

'Not long after you and I split up. I was eighteen. He was twenty-two. And so handsome. Here—look.' She grinned and began poking around in her handbag. She pulled out a photo. 'This is Alex.'

Dig took the photo from her fingers and studied it. A black-haired man wearing a DJ and bow-tie. He looked like Pierce Brosnan. God. Dig gulped and handed it back.

Delilah slid it back into her purse and continued. 'Even though we came from completely different backgrounds, we connected immediately. He was so strong and so together. Exactly what I needed.'

Dig felt the expression of interest freeze on to his features.

'Things were really tough for me around that time, and he became my best friend. There was no romance. But then he graduated and his father offered to set him up in business back in Cheshire, gave him the premises for his first restaurant.'

'So you went to live with him?'

'Not immediately. I had things to sort out here. But we kept in touch and when his restaurant opened he offered me a job and a room above.'

'And what was that like?'

Delilah shrugged. 'Weird,' she said, 'I'd never been out of London before that, and I'd never really worked. I was incredibly lonely and it was really hard work. I nearly came home, but there was nothing to come back to and I couldn't let Alex down. So I stuck it out. And besides, I think I'd already fallen in love with him by then.'

'So, what er . . . what was the *arrangement* then, with you and Alex?'

'What? You mean sleeping-wise?'

Dig nodded. A rude question, he knew, but he just couldn't help it.

'Well, there wasn't one. We were just friends and colleagues. He was my boss. Until my twentieth birthday, that is.' She smiled warmly at the memory. 'Alex had arranged a big dinner for me at the restaurant, all my favourite foods, candles, music, presents. He made a real fuss. And then he started saying things like how much he loved having me around, that he couldn't imagine his life without me. And then he got down on one knee and pulled out a little box with this'—she pointed at the rock on her finger—'in it. And he asked me to marry him!'

'And you said yes?'

'On the spot. There and then.'

'So. When did you, er . . . you know? You and Alex. When did you first . . .?'

'Sleep together? Not until our wedding night, believe it or not!'

Dig tried to look unfazed. 'And . . . how was that?'

'What—you mean—?'

'No . . . no. I mean. Not in detail. Just generally. Waiting until your wedding night. Was it a mistake? Was it OK?'

Delilah smiled tightly and screwed up her napkin between her hands. 'Well, you know,' she said, 'the first time's never anything to write letters home about, is it? And I, well, let's put it this way, sex isn't really a priority for me these days.' She laughed. Dig felt slightly shocked. 'You look shocked,' she smiled. 'Don't be. I'm just not a very sexual person any more. And Alex doesn't mind. He'd rather be working, or playing golf.'

Dig didn't know what to say. What a waste. What an absolutely shocking waste of a beautiful woman in the prime of her sexuality. How could any man possibly share a bed with Delilah Lillie and not want to shag her senseless every night?

'And you left him?'

'Hmm,' Delilah said, her face falling, 'I suppose I did.'

Dig composed himself to ask her the burning question. 'Why?'

For the first time in the conversation Delilah's body language closed in on itself and she became awkward. 'I'd rather not say,' she squirmed. 'It's er . . . it's rather personal.'

'OK. OK. No problem. But can I ask you just one more question?'

Delilah nodded cautiously.

'Are you back for good? This thing with Alex, is it over? Or what?' He looked straight into Delilah's eyes, hoping his gaze didn't betray the urgency inside, and then looked away again. 'I mean, are you staying?' Oh God, Delilah, he thought, *please say you're staying*.

Delilah stiffened slightly and cleared her throat. 'Haven't quite decided about that yet,' she said, 'not quite sure.'

'Oh,' sighed Dig, 'right.'

'I've, er . . . I've got some stuff to deal with in London, stuff I need to do to sort my head out. Emotional stuff. It all depends, really, on how that all works out, you know.'

She was being very cagey and Dig didn't know how to handle the conversation. It was obviously making her feel very uncomfortable. He would let it go—for now, anyway.

'So,' she said brightly, unselfconsciously changing the subject, 'what about you? How's *your* love life?'

'Well,' he smiled, 'existent. Active. But far from perfect.'

'Girlfriend?'

'Oh no,' he interjected briskly, 'I haven't got one of *those*,' as if she'd just said 'Mouldy toothbrush?' or 'Incontinent guinea-pig?'

'Anyone special since . . . since . . . well, since we split up?'

'No,' he answered. 'No. No one.' And then he laughed ironically as the sadness of this fact hit him.

'You're joking! No one special in twelve years? How come?'

He shrugged, blew out a lungful of breath. 'I dunno,' he said, 'I just really haven't wanted anything like that from anyone, haven't needed it.'

'I find that surprising,' she said, 'I always thought you were the one-woman-man type.'

'Well, I guess I used to be'—he smiled, 'when there was . . . just the one woman, if you see what I mean. But these days—I dunno—there just doesn't seem to be anyone else special out there.'

'D'you mind if I ask you something personal?' said Delilah.

Dig bristled pleasantly and nodded. 'Please,' he said, 'be my guest.'

'What's the deal with you and Nadine? Are you sleeping together?'

Dig choked. 'I'm sorry,' he spluttered, 'me and Nadine? What on earth made you suggest that?'

'Oh,' she replied, picking bits of coriander-flecked tomato out of the relish and chewing on them, 'just a vibe I picked up on, that's all.'

'What do you mean?'

'Well. When I bumped into you. In the park. At first I just . . . assumed that you were together, you know, a couple. You looked like a couple. And then when we were in the coffee-shop and you and I were chatting. I'd worked out by then that you weren't together, that you were just mates, but Nadine seemed . . . she was very *prickly*, almost like she was sulking. And I got the feeling that I was treading on her toes—that she saw me as some kind of *threat*. For whatever reason. I mean, tell me if you think I'm being ridiculous or nosy or anything.'

'Well. No. Nothing. Nothing's ever happened between me and Deen. Well, not really.' Dig was rubbing his chin and beginning to feel very uncomfortable. 'It's always been just a friendship, pretty much.'

'Look. I'm sorry. It's none of my business.'

'No. But you're right. Sort of. Nadine *has* been behaving very strangely lately.' He told Delilah how aggressive Nadine had been on the phone.

'And she's never behaved like this before now?'

'Never. That's the great thing about Nadine. I've always known what makes her tick, I've always *understood* her.'

'Anything happened in her private life? Man troubles?'

'Well, she's just finished with *yet another* unsuitable underdog boyfriend. But I don't think it's that. I think she's happy about that. And she's just been offered the most fantastic job imaginable—loads of money and a month in paradise. She should be really happy.'

'Well,' said Delilah, moving out of the way to make room for their waiter to unload his trolley of steaming food, 'she doesn't seem happy. She doesn't seem *at all* happy. And she's got a real problem with me.' She dipped her spoon into a dish of emerald-green spinach, flecked with creamy cubes of paneer cheese, and then flashed Dig an intense gaze.

'Have you ever considered the possibility that she might be in love with you?'

Dig snorted derisively. 'Nadine? Don't be daft! She wouldn't be in love with me if I was the last bloke on earth! She's my mate, that's all.'

'I wouldn't be quite so sure about that.'

'You don't know Nadine. There's no way, just no way, that she would *ever* feel that way about me. It's *unthinkable*. It's ridiculous! It's—it's—'

'True?' offered Delilah, raising an eyebrow at him.

'No! No! You've got it all wrong. You don't know Nadine the way I do. Nadine doesn't *do* love. All Nadine wants is a huge man with a small ego who she can boss around and then dump when she gets bored with him. She's the most independent person I've ever known. I don't think Nadine's *capable* of being in love, with anyone. Let alone with me.'

'Right. Well. Whatever, Dig. But I've been right about these things before. And *I* think that girl is in love with you. I can see it in her eyes.' She laughed wryly. 'And I can see in her eyes that she wishes I'd never come back on the scene. She sees me as competition.'

Dig had to bite his lip to stop himself blurting out that in his opinion Nadine *did* see Delilah as competition but only in terms of losing this stupid bet. Nadine just couldn't bear to lose. At anything.

'And tell me this,' Delilah continued, 'can you put your hand on your heart and swear to me that you've never, in all the years you've known Nadine, in all the years you've been friends, never felt more than just friendship? Never been tempted to take things a step further?'

'No! God! No. Never. I mean, there might have been a time, you know, *years* ago, when we were younger, just before university, just after you and I . . . But then she met some photographer guy at college and I sort of grew up and—no. No. Nothing ever happened. And now—it's been so long and we're such good mates. It just wouldn't happen.'

'Really? I can't think why not. She's very sexy, very attractive.'

'Oh I know. Of course she is. But she's . . . well, she's just Nadine, to me. Always has been. Always will be. And besides, she wouldn't want me even if I *did* fancy her.'

Dig was hating every second of this conversation. This was all nonsense. Him? And Nadine? The concept was making his brain hurt. He didn't want to think about it. And he certainly didn't want to talk about it with Delilah.

' . . . Well,' she was saying, 'I think you'd make a great couple. You've always had this bond. You've always been so similar.'

Similar? He and Nadine? Well, of course they were. That's why they were such good friends. But that didn't mean to say that they should *fancy* each other, did it? That didn't mean they should be a couple? And anyway, why was Delilah saying all this? What did all this have to do with tonight—with *them*?

'But, anyway. It's none of my business so I'll shut up now.'

Thank God, thought Dig, thank God.

Nadine was feeling more insane by the second. More and more unhinged, churned up, inside out, upside-down and all over the place.

She hadn't known what else to do with herself, so she'd phoned Dig. She'd known he was going to be out, of course she had. But there was always a slight chance, wasn't there, that he might have come home early? So she'd phoned him, listened to his answerphone message, the one with the James Bond theme playing in the background. And then she'd called him again. Five minutes later. Just in case, you know, he'd just that second walked into the flat. And then again, five minutes later. And again. And again. And again. Twenty-six times in all.

Pathetic. Absolutely pathetic. She didn't even have anything she particularly wanted to say to him. She just wanted to hear him say 'hello' so that she'd know he was home, that his night with Delilah was over, that *he wasn't with her any more*. That's all.

She could have called him on his mobile, but the bastard always had it switched off. Which was just as well, really. What would she have said? 'Are you having a good time with your dream-girl?' He'd have said, 'Yes, great, brilliant, you owe me a hundred quid.'

It was now eleven thirty and possibly the sort of time they'd be leaving the restaurant. They could be back in about half an hour, depending on where they were coming from and how quickly they could get a cab. But it was also the sort of time when they would be deciding whether they wanted the evening to end or not. If they decided to go on somewhere, then there was no knowing what time Dig would be home. Nadine didn't think she could stand it. She'd worked herself into such a frenzy by now that there was no way she'd be able to sleep.

Suddenly she knew what to do. She stood up, marched towards the coat stand, pulled down her ankle-length fake fur, threw it on, picked up her car keys and headed for her Spider, the front door slamming heavily behind her and her Bart Simpson slippers making barely a sound as she ran along the cold pavement.

After their meal Delilah seemed exhilarated, grinning widely and looping her arm through Dig's. Dig felt himself grow five inches taller. She asked him if he would take her to a gig—it had been so many years since she'd been to see a band. She didn't care who they saw—anyone, anyone at all, she said. Well, it was Dig's job to know exactly who was playing where, and he was on the guest list for at least a dozen different gigs around town every night of the week.

So he took her to see a band called Paranoid who'd just been signed by Johnny-Boy Records' Camden Town rivals and were playing at a new venue in King's Cross. They'd been hyped up to a colossal extent and this was their first live outing since they'd signed their contract.

'Oh my God! I just saw Robbie Williams!!' screamed Delilah, as they made their way down the steep basement steps leading to the main club area. 'Did you see? Robbie Williams!'

Dig smiled happily. This evening was going so well.

'I always liked him best, you know, when he was in Take That. I was *far* too old, of course, to be into Take That—it was a bit of a secret, really. Alex would have been horrified. But it's all right to like him now, isn't it? It's quite cool to like Robbie these days. Oh my God, Dig, being here with you, after all these years, being in London, going to gigs—it's like going back in time. I feel like a teenage girl again!'

Dig glanced quizzically at Delilah. Take That? Was this really the same girl who'd body-surfed through the crowds at a New Model Army gig at the Town & Country back in '84, wearing a shredded black T-shirt and stiletto-heeled pixie boots?

She grinned at him and he decided to forgive her—it was probably some kind of post-modern, ironic thing.

Downstairs was dark and dingy. The ceiling was low and the decor was all grubby red velveteen, scuffed mahogany and muted candlelight. They headed towards the bar at the back and Dig said 'All right' to a few people he recognised.

'Are you sure you don't want a proper drink?' he said, when Delilah asked if she could have an orange juice and lemonade.

'No. Really,' she said, 'I won't.'

'It's all right, you know. I'm not trying to get you drunk. I'm not going to try and take advantage of you, or anything,' he said, smiling, feeling quite giddy at the thought.

'Don't be silly,' she said, disconcertingly quickly, 'I know you're not. It's not that.'

He smiled, ordering himself a double scotch.

They took a table very close to the stage and spent half an hour celebrity-spotting. Delilah's face was tinted pink from candle-light glowing through a red glass dome on the table, and her glossy hair swung backwards and forwards as she talked and laughed and looked around her. As the support band left the stage, and the lights dimmed, the excitement mounted and Delilah turned towards him, smiled the most beautiful smile he'd ever seen and squeezed his hand on top of the table. She turned back to watch the stage, but Dig's eyes remained glued to her. She was perfect. Perfect.

The heater in Nadine's Spider had packed up, and she was freezing, even in her furry coat and slippers. She'd been parked opposite Dig's flat for more than two hours now, and there was still no sign of him. Where the hell was he? It was nearly two in the morning. She'd counted twelve cabs pull up in the vicinity since she'd arrived and twelve complete strangers disembarking. She'd crouched down in her seat every time she'd heard the familiar sound of a black cab applying its brakes and then sat up straight again when it wasn't Dig.

Her breath was leaving her lips in big icy clouds and she slipped her hands under her bottom to keep them warm. She knew she was being ridiculous. She knew that if anyone else had been doing what she was doing she would have felt terribly sorry for them, imagined them to be emotionally and psychologically deficient. But she wasn't someone else, she was herself, and it was *her* sitting in a freezing-cold car in a starlet negligee, fake-fur coat and Bart Simpson slippers at two in the morning, waiting for her best friend to get home from a date so that she could stand even the slightest chance of getting any sleep tonight at all. She knew she wasn't emotionally or psychologically deficient—she was just concerned for Dig's welfare. And besides, if she let herself admit that she was here because she was rancidly jealous, then she would never be able to look herself in the eye again.

Another rumble broke the silence of the traffic-free road. Nadine slunk down in her seat as the cab passed her and took a deep breath when she heard the engine slowing down. It pulled up a few metres ahead and Nadine craned her neck to catch sight of the two silhouetted heads in the back seat.

'Are you sure you'll be all right?' Dig asked, as the cab pulled up outside his flat, 'I really don't mind walking back from yours.'

'Don't be silly, Dig. Of course I'll be all right.'

'Here.' He forced a ten-pound note into her hand. 'I want to get this.'

'Why? Honestly, Dig. After everything you've done tonight, organised for me, I'm not going to let you pay for the cab, too.' She pushed his hand away from hers. 'Keep it. I don't want it.'

Dig finally gave up and tucked the note back into his pocket.

'So,' he said, pulling his leather coat around him and getting ready to get out of the cab, 'erm. Maybe see you at the weekend, or something?'

'Yeah,' smiled Delilah, 'maybe.'

Dig nodded happily. 'Cool,' he said, 'that's great.' He leaned towards the door handle, took hold of it and then turned abruptly to Delilah. 'I've had a really, really good time tonight, you know. Really. Best night, in a long time. Thank you.'

'Me too,' she said warmly. 'Thank you for the restaurants! And for the gig and for reintroducing me to London. I haven't had so much fun in years. It's been a real pleasure getting to know you again, Digby Ryan!' She laughed then and leaned in towards him.

When Dig looked back on this moment afterwards, it took on a stretched-out quality, as if it had happened over a period of a few minutes rather than the second and a half it had actually lasted. He could remember every last detail, the orange streetlight shining through Delilah's golden hair as she moved towards him, the little creases that formed in her lips as they puckered together, the shiver that ran down his spine as her hair whipped gently across his cheek and the spasm that rocked his body as he felt his lips being dampened by hers.

She pulled away slowly but left her arms where they were, loosely draped around his neck. She was staring deeply into his eyes and smiling. 'Mmm,' she drawled, touching her lips with the tip of her tongue, 'that was nice.'

Dig nodded and smiled and leaned in towards her again, his lips softening up for a repeat, but his descent towards her lips was impeded by her hands on his shoulders, gently pushing him away. 'That was nice,' she said, using a more measured intonation and raising her eyebrows, 'thank you.' She smiled. 'Thank you,' she said again.

Dig took his cue. He knew what she was saying. She was a married woman. She'd come to London to sort out her problems, not to get involved in any more. There'd be time. He lifted her hand and kissed the back of it. 'It's good to have you back,' he said as he stepped out of the cab and on to the freezing pavement, 'really good.'

Delilah leaned through the open window. She grabbed his hand. 'Sleep tight, lovely Digby Ryan,' she said. And then the cab pulled off, executed a perfect turning circle and bore Delilah away towards Primrose Hill.

Dig stood where he'd been dropped, on the side of Camden Road, and watched the receding cab, his hands in his pockets, his heart in his mouth and a smile on his face.

As the cab pulled away from the next junction and disappeared from view, Dig slowly pulled his hands from his pockets, bunched them up into triumphant fists and brought them down from the air above his head towards his chest. '*Yes!*' he said under his breath, '*YES!*'

Oh my God, thought Nadine, watching him from the shadows across the road, her face in her hands, her jaw slack, oh my God.

It's happening again.

Dig's in love.

Lime-Green Teeth

One morning, when Nadine was eighteen years old, an invitation dropped on to the doormat of her family home. Little did she know when she opened it that it was going to lead to one of the most unexpected nights of her life.

It was an invitation to a Holy T reunion. It had been organised by Anna O'Riordan, one of the perky, popular, button-nosed girls in their year, and was to be held at a wine bar in Camden Town. According to the invite it was meant as an 'opportunity to catch up with old friends and renew contact before we spread our wings to all four corners of the globe in the pursuit of a Higher Education'.

Anna O'Riordan always had been a pretentious cow.

The party was taking place on September 12, Nadine's last weekend in London. She was all packed up, had passed her driving test, chucked in her summer job and cleared out her bedroom, which now stood empty and sad, nothing left of her eighteen years but her Enid Blyton books and her etiolated kite.

It had been a scorching-hot summer and Nadine's usually chalky-white complexion had been toasted to a shimmery golden-brown festooned with freckles, and her auburn hair had picked up strands of honey-coloured highlights. She didn't know it at the time—what eighteen-year-old girl does?—but she was at her peak.

Nadine was, of course, blissfully unaware of her all-round gorgeousness and as she got ready for the party she felt incredibly nervous. Who was going to be there? What would they think of her? Would they even remember her? Would she have anything to say to anyone?

But, most importantly, would Dig and Delilah be there? The thought unleashed a mob of epileptic butterflies in her stomach. How was she going to handle that possibility? She envisaged herself walking into the wine bar and clapping eyes on them for the first time in two years. What should she be expecting? Delilah possibly full-term pregnant with a fag hanging out of her mouth? Dig looking like a man whose dreams have withered and died? Or maybe they just wouldn't turn up at all . . . Nadine began hoping nervously for this last option.

But as she walked from Bartholomew Road towards Camden that evening, the air still warm, the sun just starting to sink and a gentle breeze ruffling the crinkle cotton of her Indian skirt, she began to feel brave and strong. Why was she still bothered about Dig and Delilah after all this time? Who cared if they were there or not? She'd just spent two of the best years of her life at St Julian's, one of only twelve girls in a sixth form of ninety boys. Her confidence had grown beyond belief while she was there. She was a different person now and she had more important things to worry about than Dig and bloody Delilah.

She walked into the wine bar with her shoulders back and her head held high. She would show them, she would show everyone just how far mousy little Nadine Kite had come.

Dig was the first person she saw when she walked in. He was standing on his own, wearing ripped jeans, moccasins and an old check flannel shirt. His thick hair had grown untidily long, flopping on to his forehead and covering his ears. He was holding a bottle of Sol and examining the slice of lime in the neck, unsure what he was supposed to do with it. Nadine watched him with gentle amusement as he attempted to push the segment down the neck and into the bottle and, when this didn't work, pull it out again and try daintily to squeeze its juice into the beer. The slice released one drop of liquid and refused to yield any more, so Dig transferred it from his fingers to his mouth and began sucking on it.

And so it was that when Dig looked up and noticed Nadine staring at him, when their eyes locked for the first time in two years and their faces broke open into wide smiles of recognition, Dig Ryan was wearing a dazzling set of lime-green teeth.

'It's just meant to be for decoration, you daft bugger!'

'Deen!' he exclaimed, the lime segment falling from his lips and on to the floor. 'Didn't recognise you for a moment there. You look really . . . totally . . . shit. I didn't think you were going to come.'

'Of course I was going to come!' she laughed, hugging him to her. 'Why on earth wouldn't I?'

'I dunno,' he shrugged, smiling, 'I thought a St Julian's girl like you would be too posh for a do like this, it might be a bit beneath you.'

Nadine rolled her eyes at him. 'You shouldn't believe everything you hear.' Her gaze wandered up and down his face and she realised that Dig looked different. Not just older, but intrinsically *different*. Her eyes traversed his face and then she saw it.

'Dig Ryan,' she laughed, staring at him intently and making him squirm, 'what happened to your eyebrow?!'

'What?' he demanded, affronted, putting a finger up to it.

'It's . . . it's *separated*!'

'What are you talking about?'

'Your eyebrow. It's two eyebrows. What have you done to the middle bit?!'

Dig blushed, looked away. 'Phphphphphph,' he mumbled.

'What?'

'*I shaved it off, all right!—I shaved it off.*' He brought his beer bottle to his lips and took a large mouthful.

Nadine was doubled over with mirth. 'Oh Dig,' she cried, 'that's *hysterical*! You look so *weird* with two eyebrows. I just can't take it in! Oh come on,' she laughed, nudging him in the ribs, 'loosen up.'

A smile began to twitch at the corners of Dig's lips, and before long they were both laughing. 'It was Delilah's idea,' he wheezed through his laughter, 'she thought . . . she thought . . .' He fought to control himself. 'She thought it would make me look . . . *more intelligent*.' He dissolved again, and Nadine slapped her thighs and screamed with laughter.

'Oh don't,' she breathed, 'don't. I'm going to wet myself! You look so funny! Oh grow it back, Dig. You don't look like *you* any more!'

'Maybe,' laughed Dig, slowly regaining his composure, 'maybe. Anyway,' he said, indicating her empty hands, 'what about a drink? Do you want to go to the bar?'

Nadine shrugged, wiping a tear from under her eyes. 'Yeah,' she said, 'I guess so.'

They turned to survey the rest of the party then, and Nadine felt her spirits drop as she looked around her. 'Oh God,' she complained.

'I know. I know. I was going to leave after this drink, but I got trapped in the corner with Anna O'Riordan for quarter of an hour, telling me all about her summer in the States and her American boyfriend.'

Nadine sneered in sympathy. 'So,' she said, looking around her, trying to appear unbothered, 'Delilah not here?'

Dig shook his head, took another slurp of beer. 'Nah.'

'Couldn't face it, eh?' she smiled. 'Don't really blame her.'

Dig shrugged. 'Don't even know if she was invited. I haven't seen her since March.'

Nadine quelled the wave of excitement in her belly and tried to look unfazed. 'Oh,' she said, 'why not?'

'You tell me,' he said bluntly. 'One minute everything was fine between us. Then she started behaving really oddly.'

'Oddly?'

'Yeah. After her eighteenth birthday. She just . . . Here'—he stopped suddenly—'look. How d'you fancy making an escape. I'll tell you all about it over a decent pint. No one's noticed you're here yet. We could just go somewhere?'

Nadine nodded. There was nothing she would like more.

In a canalside pub, they bought pints at the bar and took them outside to a table overlooking the water. Nadine started ferreting around inside her duffel bag and brought out a packet of Silk Cut and a box of matches. Dig pretended to collapse. 'No!' he exclaimed, 'surely not. Not you! Not Nadine Kite! You can't *smoke*. It's not natural!'

She offered the packet to him, and lit them both up.

'Shit, Deen. You are the last person in the whole world I would ever have expected to smoke. When did all this start?'

'About a week after I started at St Julian's,' she said, exhaling. 'You were treated like a freak there if you *didn't* smoke. It was actively encouraged, in fact.'

'But I thought that St Julian's was supposed to be really old-fashioned and tough?'

'Myth,' she said, 'complete myth. That's what they *want* people to think, otherwise they'd only get people applying who wanted to doss around for two years.'

'So it was good?'

'It was the best. I've just had the best two years of my life.' She told him all about the smoky common-room and the flexible timetables, the 'Call-me-Tony' teachers and the non-existent dress codes.

They discussed Holloway Tech, where Dig had taken his A Levels. He'd got fairly good grades but he'd already decided that he didn't want to go to university. He'd spent the summer doing unpaid work experience for a record company in Soho and now they'd offered him a permanent job as office assistant, starting on Monday.

They talked about their families—his parents were fine and so was his little sister, who'd just started at primary school; her parents were fine, too, and her little brother had just got ten 'A' grades in his O Levels and was currently held on a par with Jesus Christ in the Kite household.

'So,' said Nadine, finally, 'you were going to tell me about Delilah? About what happened with you and Delilah?'

'Yeah. Right.' Dig dropped the end of his cigarette on to the ground and crushed it with the heel of his moccasin. 'I dunno, it was really weird. It all got a bit routine after we left school. She started doing this secretarial course, but she dropped out after the first couple of weeks because she didn't like the teacher, or something, then she started on some YOP scheme, working in a florist's and she hated that, too. So in the end she just got some shitty weekend job in a chemist, cash in hand, and that created a bit of friction because I had all this college work to worry about and I was making all these new friends, and she was just stuck at home all day with her old hag of a mother but I thought once I'd finished my A Levels I'd get a job, work hard, get promoted and then I'd be able to afford a flat, somewhere for us to live together. You know, I really thought we were going to be together for ever. I didn't think there was anything we couldn't work out.

'But the night after her eighteenth birthday I came home from college and Delilah didn't turn up. I phoned her at her mum's and one of her brothers answered the phone and said she wasn't there, he hadn't seen her since that morning, but that she'd left with a big bag and there'd been a lot of shouting and his mum was really angry with her.

'So all night, and the next and the next, I waited for her and I phoned her and nobody knew where she was and nobody seemed to give a shit. I nearly went to the police. But then I thought of something. Wherever she was, she'd need money. And she was eighteen now, she could sign on, and I knew she would so I bunked off college for a week and I hid behind a tree outside the DHSS, every day. She turned up on the Friday morning. She looked awful. I almost didn't recognise her. I ran up to her and I grabbed her, and d'you know what? She couldn't even look me in the eye. It was like she was ashamed or something.

'Anyway. In the end, she came back to my house. She stayed for a couple of weeks but she was so miserable—she didn't want to go out, she didn't want to watch telly, she didn't want to have sex. I tried getting her to talk but she just kept saying that nothing was wrong.

'Then one day I got back from college and she wasn't there. I asked my mum where she'd gone and she told me she'd popped out to get a paper. I knew instantly that something was wrong—Delilah would *never* pop out to get a paper. So I ran up to my room and all her stuff had gone. She'd left a note.'

'What did it say?' asked Nadine.

'Oh, exactly what I'd been expecting really. Sorry to hurt you but I can't be with you any more. It's not that I don't love you, I will always love you. But I have to go. It's over.

'I went round to her mum's place, demanded to know where Delilah was. But she just said, "I don't know no one called Delilah. I ain't got no daughter." And then she slammed the door in my face. Scary bitch.'

'Then what?'

Dig shrugged. 'Then just sort of trying to get over her, I suppose. Concentrating on my college work, revising, going to gigs.'

'You haven't seen her since?'

Dig shook his head glumly.

'Oh Dig,' said Nadine, putting on her best sympathetic voice, while thinking *Good, I'm glad, I hated that girl*. 'You poor thing. How are you?'

'Oh,' he said, brightening, 'I'm fine. I really am. It was bad for a while—but this work experience, it's turned my life around. I know what I want now. I've got a direction in my life and that really helps.'

'So . . . have you started seeing anyone else, you know . . . since?'

Dig shook his head. 'Nah,' he said, 'I've been too busy, what with my A Levels and work experience and everything. Nah.' He breathed in, looked up at Nadine. 'What about you? You . . . seeing anyone?'

'Uh-uh.' She shook her head. 'No.'

A smile tickled Dig's lips.

'What?' smirked Nadine.

'Oh. Nothing,' he grinned.

'What!'

'Nothing!' he repeated, light-heartedly. 'Just wondering if you'd—you know—have you . . . lost it, yet?'

'It?'

'Yes. It. You know!'

Nadine blushed crimson. She'd never talked about sex with Dig before. 'Oh,' she muttered, 'right. That. No. Not yet.'

Dig nodded knowingly and took a swig of his beer, a smile still lingering on his face.

'I'm only eighteen you know,' she smarted.

'Good,' smiled Dig infuriatingly, 'fine. That's just great.'

'I'm waiting,' she said, getting more indignant by the minute. 'It's just not something I want to rush into, that's all. I want to wait until *I'm* ready, and if I have to wait another ten years, then I will.'

'Deen. Calm down, will you! I think you're absolutely right.'

'Good,' said Nadine firmly, squirming slightly.

They fell silent for a second and sipped from their pints. Nadine looked up and found Dig staring at her intently.

'You seem so . . . different. You look so . . . so . . .' A blush spread across Dig's face as he searched for a word. 'You look so . . .'

'Ye-es?' joked Nadine, tapping her fingernails against the table-top.

'Jesus Christ, Deen, you look . . . *so fucking gorgeous.*' Dig's eyes seemed to bulge slightly as he said this and his blush went up a few gears from pale pink to throbbing purple.

Nadine snorted and burst into giggles, holding her cheeks in her hands. 'Oh,' she said finally, 'thank you!' Her blush matched his now, and the two of them sat side by side like a pair of matchsticks, giggling awkwardly. They stopped laughing every now and then and looked up at each other's crimson faces and started giggling afresh.

'Oh God—I am so embarrassed,' said Dig. 'I can't believe I just said that to you! To you! Nadine. My old mate, Deen!'

'Neither can I!' laughed Nadine. 'In fact, I'm so embarrassed that I'm going to have to go to the toilet!'

Nadine was still smiling by the time she'd walked from the beer garden, through the bar and to the toilets. This was so weird. Seeing Dig again after so long, sitting in a pub with him like a grown-up, drinking and smoking and chatting like adults. And that, just now, that compliment. That was *bizarre*. Dig thought she was gorgeous. And the way he'd said it—it reminded her of that day years ago at the Holy T, a summer's day when Dig had first set eyes on Delilah Lillie and he'd said that she looked just like Leslie Ash in *Quadrophenia*. And then he'd said, 'She is absolutely beautiful,' and she'd known then that she'd lost him. He'd used exactly the same tone of voice just then, when he told her that *she* was gorgeous—definitely—exactly the same.

A shudder ran down her spine.

They stayed in the pub until closing time, until a chill breeze had started blowing across their table and Dig had put one arm around Nadine's shoulders to stop her shivering.

His arm stayed there, on her shoulder, as they walked home, and Nadine wondered whether or not she liked it being there. What did it mean? Was it just a casual gesture, an act of affection? Or was it a prelude to something altogether unthinkable? After all those years of indifference and disregard, was Dig Ryan suddenly and unexpectedly going to do what she'd wanted for so long? Was he going to *want* her?

But what if something *were* to happen? What then? It would be the worst timing imaginable. Tomorrow was her last day in London. On Monday she was going to Manchester, to start a new life, to become a new person. Did she really want to start something here that would tie her to the past, tie her to London? Instead of spending her weekends getting to know Manchester, making friends, concentrating on her photography, she would be on trains, constantly whizzing up and down between Manchester Piccadilly and Euston, living out of a holdall, missing someone, wanting to be somewhere else.

That wasn't what she wanted.

But then, wasn't *this*—Dig, her, together, no Delilah, just the two of them—wasn't *this* what she had always, always wanted?

She looked up towards Dig. He was animated, chatting away about his plans for world domination in the music business, how he was going to give himself a year to eighteen months, tops, as an office assistant at Electrogram Records before he would start pushing his way forwards into the A&R department. A year or two there and then he would move sideways to a smaller label where he could be a big fish in a small pond, make an impact. It would be another year or so before he would discover the greatest guitar band in the world, make his name, make a packet and then—his master plan: Dig-It Records, his own label, a millionaire by the time he was twenty-five. Sorted. In the bag. No problem.

He was, Nadine realised, as full of ambition and plans for the future as she was. He had no room in his life for a long-distance love affair, that much was obvious.

They turned off Kentish Town Road and began the walk down Bartholomew Road towards her parents' house. She'd already decided she wouldn't invite him in. Her parents would make a fuss and say things like 'Well, howdy, stranger' and 'Long time no see' and he'd have to make small talk with them for ages about what he'd been up to for the past two years and how his parents were, and it was too late in the night for all that, so when they arrived outside her house she stopped at the bottom of the steps to the front door and turned towards him.

'Well,' she said, shyly, 'thank you for rescuing me from the horrors of the Holy T reunion. I've had a really nice night. It's been . . . er . . .' She searched for the right words to bring the night to a close without spoiling it but Dig wasn't really listening. He was anxiously staring into her eyes, his lips open and poised to say something, his body stiff.

'I have to see you again,' he stated firmly, his eyes nervous.

Nadine shot him a look. 'Well,' she began, 'of course . . . I mean . . . of course we will . . . it's . . . er . . .'

'No,' he growled, 'I mean *I have to see you again*. Soon. Tomorrow. What are you doing tomorrow?' His voice was desperate, he was holding her hands in his, tightly, too tightly.

Nadine was confused. She didn't know what to say. She squeezed his hands back and decided. She wanted to see him tomorrow, romance or no romance. She *wanted* to spend her last day in London with Dig.

'Nothing,' she said, finally, shrugging and smiling goofily, 'I'm not doing anything tomorrow.'

Dig smiled. 'Let's do something. You and me. Yeah?'

'Yeah,' smiled Nadine, relief at deferring the tearful farewells lighting up her face and widening her smile.

And then, before she knew what was happening, before she had a chance to decide whether it was what she wanted or not, Dig had wrapped his arms tightly around her shoulders, brought his face down towards hers and kissed her squarely on the lips.

Nadine was unresponsive for a second or two, her lips firmly glued together, her body tensed. But then the smell of Dig's flesh under her nose joined forces with the quite spectacular effect his lips were having on her groin and suddenly she relaxed completely into the kiss. Dig's mouth was soft and gentle, his breath tasted like hers, of beer and cigarettes. It was happening—it was finally happening—Dig Ryan was kissing her! She was being kissed by Dig Ryan! She and Dig Ryan were kissing!

Dig and Nadine slowly pulled apart, staring with wonder into each other's eyes.

'Well,' said Nadine, eventually, 'I'd better get in.'

'Yeah,' said Dig, 'right. OK. Give us a ring when you wake up, yeah? If it's a nice day we could go for a picnic or something.'

'Yeah,' Nadine nodded enthusiastically. 'That would be lovely.'

They exchanged another kiss and another look of wonderment and then Dig turned to leave. Nadine watched him for a while as he sauntered down Bartholomew Road. A warm feeling flooded Nadine's heart, a feeling of familiarity and cosiness seasoned with excitement and freshness. That's Dig Ryan, she thought to herself happily, that's Dig Ryan walking down my road, having just kissed me so firmly and passionately on the lips and turned all my insides to semolina, that's him, my soul mate, my dream man, the person I want to wake up with on Saturday mornings on a big pine bed. There he goes . . .

She smiled warmly to herself and was just about to turn and go indoors when she saw Dig, at the head of her road and thinking no one was watching him, suddenly break into a hop, skip and a jump, leap on to a garden wall, punch the air with his fist and whoop at the top of his voice before turning the corner and disappearing from view.

It was a golden late-summer morning when Nadine awoke at ten o'clock. Her mother was at church—and her father and brother had gone fishing together. At eleven o'clock she phoned Dig and arranged to meet him on Primrose Hill at half past twelve.

'Bring your kite,' he said. 'The wind's going to pick up later.'

Dig had two carrier bags with him when they met on the brow of the hill. He was draped all over a bench and smoking a cigarette. He had on the same jeans as the night before and a Happy Mondays T-shirt. He sat up straight when he saw Nadine approaching and his face broke open into a lecherous grin.

'You know that dress is see-through, don't you?' he commented lasciviously when she sat down next to him.

Nadine pretended to be embarrassed, but she knew full well the diaphanous qualities of her ankle-length Indian voile dress. She was wearing black-leather monkey-boots with pink laces and her hair was tied on top of her head into a cascading ponytail.

Dig peeled the carrier bags apart to reveal warm baguettes and tubs of taramasalata, bags of Kettle Chips and twelve bottles of beer. Nadine had brought a blanket, and they wandered around together until they found a spot that would afford them a little privacy.

And then, for the rest of the day, from lunch-time, through the afternoon and as evening approached, they lay on Nadine's blanket and kissed. They kissed for five hours. They kissed so much and so hard that Nadine's lips felt like blisters, and a stubble rash broke out on her chin. Every now and then they would break apart to eat a little something or to take a swig of beer, quickly finding each other's mouths again seconds later. They barely talked all day; when they weren't kissing they would stare dreamily into the distance, smiling at the overexcited children dashing around in circles. They watched the sun beginning to set in silence, silly smiles glued to their faces and their hands entwined.

And then, just as they were about to leave, their litter disposed of in a plastic bin, their blanket folded and their beer drunk, a breeze blew Dig's fringe off his forehead.

'Did you see that?' he said.

'What?'

Another breeze picked up the hem of Nadine's skirt.

'That,' he said, pointing at her skirt, '*that*,' he said, pointing at the furrows in the grass. 'Come on. *Quick*. Get your kite out!'

He grabbed her hand and they ran as fast as they could up towards the peak of Primrose Hill.

It didn't take long for Dig and Nadine's kites to become animated in the powerful wind that seemed to come from nowhere that evening. It was a warm wind, gentle but alive, tangling up their hair and clothes. The sun sank down slowly in the sky, and their kites danced in front of a golden backdrop. Finally the sun dropped beneath the horizon and the wind died away as suddenly as it had arrived and it was still and dark. Dig and Nadine looked around the hill. They were all alone, the last people there. They collected their kites from where they lay, spent, on the summer-dry grass, and arm-in-arm they began the walk back to Kentish Town.

'I've worked it out,' said Dig, as they walked down Prince of Wales Road. 'Even if I give my mum £20 a week rent *and* start payments on a car, say £20 a week, plus a Travelcard at £5 a week, I'll *still* be able to afford to come up and see you once a fortnight—I mean, it's not going to be much more than fifteen quid, is it, with a Young Person's Railcard?'

He turned to Nadine and smiled, squeezing her shoulders with his arm. She smiled tightly.

'And then, of course,' he continued, 'there'll be holidays as well, won't there? You'll come home for holidays, won't you?'

Nadine smiled nervously.

'Yeah, anyway. So what with holidays and weekends we should get to see quite a bit of each other. The three years should go in a flash and you'll be back in London before you know it and . . .'

Oh God, thought Nadine, this is exactly what I *didn't* want to happen.

'Dig,' she said, coming to a halt and turning to face him, 'actually, I don't think this is a very good idea . . .'

'What?' Dig's face clouded over in confusion.

'This,' she said. 'You and me. I don't think it's going to work out.'

'What do you mean?'

Nadine sighed. 'Maybe we should just take things a bit slower, you know.' She explained her feelings to him, about her new life at Manchester, wanting a clean break from London, needing to be unfettered by the past. Dig blinked a lot and nodded stiffly.

'D'you understand, Dig?' she asked. 'It's just not the right time. It wouldn't be fair on either of us.'

Dig nodded again and attempted a smile.

'So you understand?'

Once again, Dig nodded, but the nod slowly became a shake.

'No!' he shouted, backing away from her. 'No, actually, I don't understand. I don't understand *at all*. Jesus, Deen. Since the minute I set eyes on you last night I have been . . . I have been . . . oh God, I don't even know *what* I've been, but it's been great and I want to carry on feeling like this. I want to look forward to the weekends. I want to queue up at Euston station on a Friday evening with a change of clothing in a bag and ask for a return ticket to Manchester Piccadilly. I want a chance to get to know you properly, not just as Nadine Kite, my old mate, but as this new wonderful person I only met last night.'

'You've known me for years, Dig.'

'No! No I haven't! You were different before. You're a new person now and I can't just let you go without getting to know you properly, without giving us a chance. Jesus, Deen—I can't believe this is happening!'

Nadine stared at the ground. She couldn't believe this was happening either. She couldn't look into Dig's eyes. She was too scared of what she might find there. 'Sorry,' she mumbled, 'I'm sorry. But that's just the way things are. It's called bad timing and it's been the story of you and me, all through the years.'

'What do you mean?'

Nadine took a deep breath, opened her mouth and then closed it again. There was no point, no point whatsoever, in raking up the past. She shook her head. 'Nothing,' she sighed, 'nothing.'

'Look. Deen. Can't we even give it a try? Can't we at least see if things would work out, you know, instead of just writing it off from the outset? I know what you're saying, I really do, about new lives and fresh starts and all that, but, Deen, I have never felt like this before and I don't think I could cope if we didn't at least try.'

'Oh Dig! You don't understand, do you! Of course it will work! That's the whole point. You and I would be perfect together and that's exactly why I don't want to get involved with you. Not now. Not the day before I leave London. It's not what I want!'

'But you *do* want me?' asked Dig, his hand on his chest.

Nadine shrugged. Of course she wanted him. More than anything. But she'd made up her mind. If she said yes now, then she would lose control once again. 'No'—she shook her head firmly—'no, Dig. I don't want you. I know you might find that hard to believe, but I don't want you. OK? That's just the way it is.' She spun around and began walking brusquely down Kentish Town Road. There were tears tickling at the back of her throat and she refused to let Dig see her crying.

Dig chased after her. 'So that's it, is it? You're happy just to walk away and get on with your life without ever finding out what it could have been like?'

She nodded. Dig sucked in his breath and eyed her with scepticism. 'I don't believe you, Nadine Kite'—he shook his head slowly from side to side—'I really don't believe you.'

'That's your prerogative,' she replied sniffily, avoiding his gaze.

'Yeah,' he said, 'yeah. I suppose it is. And it's my prerogative to let you know that this isn't finished yet. I've never felt like this about anyone, ever. You are so beautiful and so special and so *amazing*, Nadine, and this'—he indicated the two of them—'*us*, this isn't finished yet. Just remember I said that, OK? You're wrong, tonight, you're in the wrong. You're making a mistake, Nadine.'

'I'm sorry,' she said, as they turned to face each other outside her parents' house. 'I should have been more honest with you—I just didn't think things were going to work out like this. I'm really sorry.'

'Look—Deen.' Dig took her hands and looked deep into her eyes. 'I hear everything you're saying about not wanting to get involved but can't we at least be friends? I have to know that you'll still be in my life. Can I write to you? Maybe just see you to hang out with when you're home for the holidays? Please?'

Nadine nodded. 'Sure,' she said, desperate now to finish what she'd started, to get indoors and away from Dig. 'Sure. Why not?' And then she turned away abruptly as tears started rising again and her eyes began shimmering. 'See ya,' she managed to squeak before sliding her key in the lock and stumbling through the door, letting it slam loudly behind her.

'*Is that you, love?*' She heard her mother's concerned voice from the living room, where her family were watching television.

'Yeah,' she said, holding back a choke. 'I'll be in in a minute.' She ran then, two steps at a time, towards her bedroom and collapsed sobbing on to her bed. As she lay there she heard a strange scuffling noise coming from outside. She peered between her curtains and saw Dig slowly backing away from the front door with his hands in his pockets and then she watched him walking down Bartholomew Road, dragging his feet awkwardly and heavily along the pavement.

'*Nadine. Nadine, what is this on the carpet?*' Her mother was hollering up the stairs. '*I really do wish you'd learn to pick up after yourself—you won't have me to do it for you after tomorrow, you know.*'

Nadine waited until she heard her mother's slippers shuffling back into the living room before slipping down the stairs.

She sat down heavily on the bottom stair and gently picked up Dig's grubby old kite. She brought it to her nose and sniffed it. It smelt of fresh air and plastic. It smelt of today, her day with Dig. It smelt of sunshine and hope and happiness.

She turned it over in her hands and noticed something written on the other side, in black Biro.

Dig 'n' Deen
September 13, 1987
For ever ♥

Chapter Four

NADINE HAD BEEN expecting the inevitable gushing phone call from Dig all morning, the phone call that would crushingly confirm what she already knew: that he'd had a fantastic time with Delilah last night, that he'd never been happier, that Delilah was the most amazing woman he'd ever met, *that he was in love*.

She was working on an advertorial feature for *Him* magazine and had been casting models all day with the magazine's art director and some tedious little marketing person from the Korean car company whose brief it was. She hated advertorial work. Horrid businessmen. Had no idea about art, no idea about creativity. Thought that *Him* magazine was just a more credible version of *Penthouse* or *Playboy*. Thought it was just a load of tits and arses. Which it was, to a certain extent. But there was more to it than that—articles on how to be a better boyfriend, how to be a better cook, dozens of pages of beautiful fashion photography, travel articles, sports, hobbies, health, music and film.

It was a quality magazine written by quality journalists and this was how Nadine justified her dependence on the magazine for her living.

They'd left her after lunch amid a sea of leftover Pret sandwiches and empty sushi containers and she'd finally been able to give in to her feelings of total and utter abject misery by throwing herself on to her pink couch and having a tantrum.

'Men!' she shouted at Pia, her assistant. 'Bloody men. All they want is perfection, all they want is tits like this and arses like that and legs this long and thighs that firm and youth and sex and lots of it.'

Pia, twenty-two, with tits like this and an arse like that, nodded wholeheartedly in agreement.

'They don't want reality, they don't want longevity, they don't want character or personality or anything even vaguely three-dimensional. Even Dig! Even lovely, sane, together Dig. I thought he was different, but he's not. He's just the same. Show him a pair of long legs and a pair of 34Cs, show him perfect bone structure and long blonde hair and he's away—whoosh—just watch him go.'

Pia nodded sympathetically.

'So shallow'—Nadine shook her head slowly in disappointment—'so very shallow. And he thinks he can win the bet—ha! Thinks that this counts! Well, it doesn't. Delilah *does not count*.'

Pia shook her head sagely.

'That girl,' continued Nadine, 'that girl made me miserable at school, miserable. And I know I'm a grown woman and I should have got over it by now, but I haven't. From the second I set eyes on her on Saturday it all came flooding back. I hate her. I really, really hate her—aaargh!'

'Fuckin' hell, Deen,' said Pia, 'd'you fancy Dig, or something?'

'Oh, don't be ridiculous.'

'Then why are you getting so worked up about this Delilah bird?'

'I'm not getting worked up,' she said. 'I just . . . it's just. Oh God— I dunno. I just don't want Dig to go out with Delilah, because I know what she's like, and Dig's my best mate and I don't want anything bad to happen to him. Because I love him. That's all.'

'But how come you've never been bothered in the past? About Dig's girlfriends?'

'Because they weren't real. Because they were pretend girlfriends.'

'Because they didn't threaten your friendship with Dig?'

'*Exactly!* That's exactly it!'

'You have really got to sort yourself out,' said Pia.

'I know,' sniffed Nadine, 'I know. Oh God—d'you know what I did last night?' She groaned and told Pia about the humiliating stalking episode outside Dig's flat.

'Hell, Deen you are losing it—totally. There's only one thing for it, you've got to win the bet. Take your mind off this Delilah tart. What was your part of the deal?'

'Oh, I had to go out with someone I genuinely liked instead of someone I *wanted* to like.'

'OK. So, who do you like?'

'No one. That's the whole problem. I don't like anyone.'

'Oh, come on. You must like someone. Everyone likes someone. What about that stylist from *Him*. The blond guy? He's cute.'

'David? No way. Too trendy, too vain, too pretty.'

'All right. How about Danny, that courier bloke who's always flirting with you? He's quite sexy.'

'Uh-uh. No more couriers, thank you. And besides, he has that spit-build-up thing in the corners of his mouth—yuck.'

'Jesus, Deen. You're a fussy cow, aren't you?'

'Well, apparently not. Apparently that's the problem—not fussy enough. I can't just go on looks or the fact that they fancy me. It has to be someone I can honestly imagine having a proper relationship with.'

'And have you ever managed that before? Have you ever been in love with someone who was right for you?'

Good question. Nadine thought back, through rows and rows of unsuitable men, wimps and weirdos and she didn't stop until she got to her first and only serious boyfriend, the man who broke her heart.

'Phil,' she said, finally. 'Phil was right for me.'

Philip Rich had been everything that Dig wasn't. He was ten years older for a start, at twenty-eight, which had seemed enormously old at the time, and had been the most handsome man at Manchester Polytechnic, with intense indigo eyes and a perfect Roman nose.

He drove a black MG Midget, he wore black-leather trousers and he had black shiny hair which was cut into a dramatic jaw-length bob. He was divorced. He arrived at college every morning carrying an aluminium briefcase and another metal-clad box full of state-of-the-art photography equipment. He was unfeasibly cool and from the minute Nadine set eyes on him she knew she wanted him.

She'd lived with him for three years. He failed his degree and then broke off their relationship two weeks before the end of university, took the last £50 out of their supposed 'summer travel' piggy bank and just disappeared one Tuesday afternoon. She'd been devastated.

'So, what went wrong?' asked Pia.

Nadine shrugged. 'I've got absolutely no idea,' she said, 'it's a mystery. He just took off.'

'Why don't you ring him?'

'What!'

'Ring him. Arrange to see him.'

'Don't be ridiculous! I haven't seen him for ten years! He's probably married by now.'

'Yes, but he might not be. He might be single and lonely.' Pia was an eternal optimist and a hopeless romantic.

'No,' said Nadine firmly, 'I can't phone him. He'll think I'm weird.'

'Of course he won't. He'll be made up. Have you still got his number?'

'Well, I've got his parents' number—somewhere—I think.'

'OK then—no excuses. Find it and phone them. Get his number. Meet up with him. You'll feel *so* much better about this Dig and Delilah thing.'

'D'you think?'

'I don't think,' said Pia sternly, '*I know*.'

'**Y**ou did *what*?!' Dig exclaimed loudly down the phone a few minutes later. 'You phoned *Phil*? What the fuck did you phone Phil for?'

'Well,' Nadine replied sniffily, 'why not?'

'Why not! How can you say "why not?" Because he was the most self-centred, arrogant, pretentious twat I have ever met, because he belittled you and controlled you and put you down. It took you months to get over what that bastard did to you. You were like a little mouse when you got back from Manchester.'

'I was not!'

'Yes you were! Don't you remember how you stopped wearing make-up, and the way you dressed, in all that baggy black stuff, and how you had no confidence whatsoever.'

'God, Dig! You're talking about nine years ago! People change, you know? Phil had a bad time at Manchester. He sounded completely different when I spoke to him on the phone.'

'Nadine. Why are you doing this? Why, after nine years of getting on with your life, are you suddenly phoning up someone you used to go out with when you were nineteen?'

'*Exactly!* That's exactly it. I am *not* getting on with my life perfectly well. That's the whole problem. As you yourself have pointed out, I'm getting on with my life perfectly *unwell*.'

'I don't understand.'

Nadine sighed. 'Phil is the only bloke I've ever loved, ever cared about, and I want to see him. That's all there is to understand.'

'Oh! *I* get it! This is for the bet, isn't it?'

'Oh, don't be ridiculous!'

'Of course it is! Why else would you suddenly decide that you just have to see some bloke you went out with ten years ago?'

'Oh,' exclaimed Nadine, sarcastically, 'oh, I see! It's perfectly all right for you to go off with Delilah Lillie after what she did to you. It's perfectly all right for you, but when *I* want to see someone who I used to be in love with, someone who hurt *me*, then there's something wrong with it! You hypocrite!!'

'I haven't *gone off* with Delilah! What are you talking about? We had dinner, that's all. We had dinner and we went to see a band!'

'And that is all I intend to do when I see Phil tonight. We're going to have a drink together and see how it goes.'

'Well, that's fine. You go and you have a good time. But don't expect to come crying to me when he starts pulling you apart again and you're handing out cash left, right and centre and your self-esteem is in tatters.'

'I can assure you, I won't!'

'Good!'

'Fine!' And with that she forcefully and noisily dropped the receiver back on to its cradle, threw herself down on to her studio sofa and started crying again.

Dig forcefully and noisily dropped the receiver back on to its cradle, lit a cigarette and sighed deeply. He'd phoned Nadine to make things up with her, to patch over their argument of Monday, and instead things had ended up a hundred times worse.

Philip Rich. How could it be possible that this awful character was re-entering his life after so many years.

Dig hadn't liked many of Nadine's boyfriends over the years but there'd been none he'd disliked as heartily as Philip Rich. Philip Rich with all his supposed good taste and maturity and sophistication. Philip Rich who'd morphed into Philip Poor so suspiciously quickly.

Philip Rich who'd picked up his tender, teenage heart with hairless, careless hands and snapped it clean in two.

The Worst Weekend . . . Ever

Nadine had been in Manchester nearly two months and Dig was in a bad way, still reeling from the emotional punch in the stomach she'd dealt him after their day in the park.

He sent her letters and comical postcards; he sent her promo copies of new singles, all freebies from his new job. He tried to keep things light-hearted, pretend that he was only interested in the so-called friendship he'd conjured up so desperately on Nadine's doorstep that night, pretend that he was too busy being successful and indispensable in his exciting job to have time to think about what had happened between the two of them on that September weekend.

Which was, of course, completely and utterly not true.

The truth was, that Dig Ryan had fallen madly, passionately and devotedly in love with Nadine Kite.

Nadine wrote back occasionally, not as often as he, and after seven weeks, three days and fourteen hours of this façade, Dig felt that strong enough foundations had been laid for him to suggest a weekend visit to

Manchester, without scaring her away. She put him off at first, but eventually they organised a date, and it was all he could think about for the week before he went.

So, here he was, clutching his weekend bag, striding purposefully up the concourse at Euston station towards the train that was to bear him Nadine-wards. She'd moved out of digs and into a flat now, and he presumed that he'd be bunged on to some kind of sofa and treated like a kid brother, but he didn't care. Just to be there would be enough.

It seemed she had a flatmate of some sort, who she referred to in her letters as 'Phil'—he was probably gay—but hopefully he'd be out a lot and he and Nadine could hang out together, listening to all the records he'd brought up with him from Electrogram.

He'd made an arrangement to meet Nadine outside, by the taxi rank, and as he emerged from the train station he looked around him for a fountain of auburn hair and a shimmer of translucent cotton.

He was therefore more than a little surprised when he turned around to see Nadine, her beautiful hair chopped off into a severe bob at her chin, dressed entirely in black and wearing a vicious slash of red lipstick across her mouth. She looked very pale and very thin and very trendy.

She was nervous with him as they sat in the back of the taxi on the way to her flat. She kept talking about this Phil character and how much she hoped Dig would like him and Dig was thinking, all right, all right, what's the big deal, it's you I've come to see, not your bender flatmate. But instead he smiled reassuringly and said that he was looking forward to meeting him, too, and he was sure they'd get on fine, and Nadine had looked disproportionately relieved to hear him say so.

Dig should have twigged when she started saying things like 'I don't know how much we'll be able to do this weekend, *we* haven't got much money at the moment' and 'there's a vegetarian café around the corner from *us* where *we* go for breakfast sometimes' but he didn't. He certainly should have twigged when she referred to '*our* bedroom', but he didn't. When he looked back on the whole episode the following day, he would wonder at his own stupidity and never again would he snort sceptically at those 'cross wires' comedy sketches on the telly.

Dig's first sense that something was afoot came as he crossed the threshold into Nadine's flat. It was absolutely horrible. It was on the second floor of a thirties block, built above a parade of shops, with paint peeling off the walls in enormous flaps. The flat itself had no central heating and was wretchedly furnished with the sort of furniture more usually associated with skips outside house-clearance sales.

'We're going to decorate it next term, when we've both got a bit more money,' said Nadine, hanging her black jacket from a hook in the hallway and leading Dig towards a door at the bottom of the corridor.

The door creaked open somewhat dramatically and there, sitting cross-legged on the floor, smoking a stinking Gauloise and reading the *Guardian* was the most enormous arsehole Dig had ever set eyes on.

He was barefoot and wearing pristine white jeans with a big black linen shirt. His hair was ludicrous, a wedge of over-polished black, tied back from his face into a stumpy ponytail. He was in possession of a proud and well-constructed nose of which, Dig could tell, he was inordinately enamoured and when he looked up slowly, calcu*late*dly slowly, from his paper to acknowledge Dig's presence in the room, his expression arranged itself into a strange and unnatural contortion of his facial features which didn't suit him in the slightest. Dig suspected he was trying to smile.

'All right,' he said, regarding Dig through squinted eyes before going back to his newspaper and his smouldering Gauloise.

It was antipathy at first sight. Dig had never before in his life felt so much dislike towards another person within such a short space of time.

As Dig stood awkwardly at the edge of the room, absorbing this unexpected surge of negative feelings and the fact that the lovely and ravishing Nadine was living in near-squalor with the Antichrist, the most terrible thing happened.

Nadine suddenly dropped her bag on to the sofa, kicked off her DM shoes, walked up to Phil, crouched down behind him and wrapped her lovely arms around his shoulders, squeezed him gently and planted a great big kiss on the back of his neck.

Dig's jaw dropped and his eyelids sprung apart. All of a sudden, everything fell into place; all of a sudden, everything made blindingly obvious, disgusting, foul sense. This ridiculous *person* was sharing his bed with Nadine Kite—the same Nadine Kite who had by her own admission been a lush and lovely virgin as little as eight short weeks ago, waiting sensibly for the right time with the right person, prepared to hold out till her thirtieth year if necessary. And now here she was giving it out, every night and with bountiful generosity, he presumed, to the foulest man he'd ever met.

Dig couldn't really remember much about the rest of the weekend. He didn't let his surprise show and he didn't ask Nadine about her relationship with Phil. He acted like he'd been expecting to find her in this cohabitation. He played it cool, he played the role of the scruffy, innocuous schoolfriend from years gone by, up to see his old pal for the weekend, exchanging nostalgic tales from the past and talking with overblown enthusiasm about his new job and his new car.

By the time Dig had decided that the whole weekend had sunk as low as it possibly could, and that all he had to do now was get through the night and then he could go home, things got even worse.

Dig was installed, as he'd predicted, on the sofa in the living room. And then, just as he was starting to drift off, to forget where he was, something woke him up. A squeak. Followed by another squeak. Followed by yet another. Rhythmic squeaks, one after the other. And then a soft banging, in time with the squeaks.

Dig's heart fell into his toes as it dawned on him what he was listening to—the sounds of Nadine, *his* Nadine, being soundly and roundly porked by Philip Rich. He felt instantly nauseous and pulled a cushion over his head, stuck his fingers in both ears and started humming to himself in an attempt to drown out the noise. By the time he pulled his fingers from his ears and emerged from under the quilt, all was quiet again.

He really, really, hadn't wanted to hear that. That was, in fact, the last thing in the entire world he had ever wanted to hear. He felt sick. He felt dirty. He felt disgusting. He felt contaminated.

He felt as jealous as fucking hell.

He left early the following morning, turning down Phil's offer of a lift in his MG Midget and refusing Nadine's offer to accompany him to the station also, as he really couldn't think of one thing that he would have to say to her if she did. So he shook hands with Phil and thanked him for his hospitality, and Nadine saw him off from outside the flat.

'God, Dig,' she said, 'thanks so much for coming—it's been really, really nice having you here. I wasn't sure how things were going to work out, you know, with Phil being around but—he really liked you!'

Oh God—she was so thrilled and he was quite obviously expected to be thrilled, too. He smiled grimly and said something inconsequential before a well-timed taxi appeared at the head of the road and he stuck his arm out for it. There was just enough time for a quick peck on the cheek before the cab took him away and deposited him, like a half-demented hostage being thrown from a moving car after twenty-four hours of interrogation, at Manchester Piccadilly.

As the day drew to a close, and Dig's frustration had matured nicely into a full-blown bad mood, he became overcome by a desperate desire to get steaming drunk. Anything to take his mind off Nadine and her ridiculous 'date'.

Nobody in the office had been interested in the suggestion of a post-work drink so Dig had attempted to track down Delilah to suggest that maybe they do something together. But there'd been no answer at the Primrose Hill number all day, and by the time he got home at eight o'clock he'd given up on the idea.

As ever, there were any number of gigs and general music-biz schmoozathons he could have attended but, glancing out of his window at a wet and chilly Wednesday evening, he decided on reflection that his fridgeful of big Buds, two packets of Marlboro Lights and something on video that he'd taped earlier on in the week would make for a mighty pleasant night in, so he plumped up his cushions, stretched out his legs and settled down for a night of vegetating.

At about nine o'clock his stomach started growling and he leafed through his ever-expanding library of take-away menus, deciding on a meat vindaloo and a prawn dopiaza from the Indian down the road.

Half an hour later his doorbell rang and he padded down his hall towards the entry phone clutching a twenty-pound note. 'Top floor,' he said into the mouthpiece, without waiting to be addressed. He opened his front door and listened to the sound of footsteps against the cold linoleum, resentful footsteps that grew slower as they neared the dizzying heights of the top floor. Restaurant-delivery drivers hated him for making them take the stairs and always arrived at his door in very poor spirits indeed. Consequently Dig had prearranged his features into his usual disarming toothy smile, ready to be charming and placatory.

The smile fell off his face like a badly hung painting from a wall, however, when a dishevelled, small and extremely ugly Yorkshire Terrier suddenly bounded up the top flight of stairs and came careering round the corner and straight into his flat, leaving a trail of tiny grubby footprints all over his oatmeal seagrass.

'Digby!' echoed a female voice around the stairwell. 'You bad boy! Come back here this instant!' The female voice was followed a couple of seconds later by the form of Delilah, equally as dishevelled as the damp Digby and shaking out a half-furled umbrella. 'Hi,' she said, stopping in her tracks when she saw Dig's shocked expression.

'Hi,' replied Dig. 'I was . . . er . . . expecting a curry,' said Dig, eventually, in the absence of anything more relevant to say.

'Oh,' said Delilah, 'and you got me instead!'

'Yeah,' laughed Dig.

'So,' said Delilah, running her fingers through her damp hair and peering around the doorway, 'are you going to invite me in?'

Dig started and moved out of the way. 'Oh God,' he said, 'of course. Yeah. Come in. Come in.'

He held open the door for her and caught his breath as her sheepskin coat flapped open briefly to reveal a thoroughly waterlogged cotton blouse sticking like clingfilm to her breasts. He had no idea what she was doing here, but she was a lot more welcome than a dopiaza.

That same evening, a quarter of a mile away to the east, Nadine finds herself sitting in a low-level seventies red-brick monstrosity going under the name of the Brecknock Arms. She's only been here a few minutes but she's already sensing, very strongly, that she's made a mistake. This is all Dig's fault, she thinks to herself. *He* drove me to it.

She is sitting on a torn red vinyl bar stool, wearing—inappropriately, she now feels—an emerald-green angora cardigan over a fuchsia crocheted dress, a silk poppy in her hair, drinking a watered-down pint of Theakstones and wondering what has happened to the mysterious and debonair Phil of her memories.

The man now sitting in front of her is *so old*. His face has the crumpled-newspaper look of an over-the-hill rock star. His once glossy black hair now hangs limply and finely over his ears and forehead in a style better suited to a man half his age, and his beautiful nose has acquired sharp lines and large open pores, overpowering his hollow face.

All Nadine's foolish, pathetic little fantasies about some over-the-top romantic reunion with her first love crumpled and died within seconds of walking into the Brecknock Arms. Phil was supposed to look the same as she remembered, with maybe just a touch of distinguished grey at the temples. He wasn't supposed to look like this.

Phil, on the other hand, had been speechless with joy to see Nadine walk in.

'Nadine Kite,' he'd drawled, grasping her hands, 'Nadine Kite. You're here! Look at you. You look great. I love your outfit, it's wild!' And then he looked like he was about to hug her, so Nadine deftly extricated herself from his grip and balanced herself on her bar stool.

Phil insisted on paying for the first round, despite Nadine's best efforts to swing the balance of the evening towards a *Dutch* sort of thing by paying for them herself, and he then, worse still, insisted on carrying her drink to their table, thereby potentially setting the tone for a night of false expectations and crossed wires.

'So,' she says, keeping her body language neutral and taking a measured sip from her Theakstones, 'Phil. How've you been?'

'Oh, you know. Not bad.' He takes a slurp of his beer and wipes his mouth with the back of one hand. 'You?'

'Fine,' she smiles, 'great, in fact.'

'So,' he says, 'what *inspired* you to get in touch again, after all this time?

Do I owe you money?' He laughs, extra loud to ensure that Nadine knows he's only joking, but it occurs to her that this is what he's really thinking.

'Well,' she replies, 'there was that fifty quid you took out of the piggy-bank! But seriously—I just wanted to find out how you were. What you've been up to. I just felt . . . I dunno . . . you spend so many years with someone, and then suddenly, overnight, they're not in your life any more. They just get on a train and disappear for nine years. I wanted to hear your story, I suppose, the "Story of Philip Rich"!'

Phil exhales through tight lips and eyes her sceptically. 'You got all night?' he asks.

Nadine nods, enthusiastically. She senses a story here, something behind that look, and suddenly decides that the only way she is going to be able to get through this evening is by pretending that Phil isn't really a part of her history, isn't a bloke she lived with and loved ten years ago, but is in fact someone she's interviewing for a magazine or researching for a novel. 'Start at the beginning,' she says. 'Start at the end of us . . .'

Nadine was disappointed to learn that Phil had gone back to London when they split up, gone back home and not to the remote Yorkshire village she'd been fondly imagining for some strange reason. He had come back, moved in with his parents, sold all his camera equipment, extended his bank loan and, with a shocking lack of business judgment, at the height of an international recession bought back the photographic lighting company he'd sold to fund his degree. He was made bankrupt six months later and had a nervous breakdown.

His life then, it seemed, took a series of very unexpected and out-of-character turns, and Phil spent most of the nineties trying to 'find himself' through one alternative route after another—crystals, meditation, Chinese herbs, Buddhism and Taoism. He moved from town to town and from woman to woman in search of happiness and fulfilment until his failure to find either led him to a drink problem and yet another broken relationship on a travellers' site in Warwickshire.

On the day he left the site, he walked three miles to Nuneaton in the rain clutching a bottle of Taunton Dry, walked into a launderette, swore at an old man and nicked the money he'd left out for his next wash. He stole £1.50 and for that he got a three-month prison sentence.

'Best thing that ever happened to me,' Phil said.

'What do you mean?' said Nadine, who was gripped by his story.

'It took a stretch inside to make me understand that some people aren't here for any big reason—they're just here. And I realised then that I'm one of those people and that it's all right just to be a normal bloke, do a normal job and have normal friends. It was like a huge weight off my shoulders working that one out. And the pressure just sort of disappeared.' Phil shrugged and lit a Rothman.

Nadine breathed out deeply. 'I can't believe how much has happened to you,' she said. 'It makes me feel so boring and . . . predictable. God— I haven't done *anything* with my life.'

'What about the photography? Still taking pictures?'

She nodded.

'Making a living from it?'

'Yeah,' she said, 'a very good living, actually.'

'Oh yeah?' His body language suddenly became very focused on Nadine. 'Got a nice flat and all that?'

'Yes,' nodded Nadine, proudly.

'That's great. I'm really pleased for you.'

'So,' she said, changing the subject back to him, 'when did you move back to London again?'

'Straight from the nick. March 1997.'

'Back to your parents?'

'Yeah.'

'And you're still there?'

Phil shook his head. 'Nah,' he said, 'nah. I've got a place in Finsbury Park now. A Peabody flat. My . . . er . . . grandparents sublet it to me.'

Nadine was confused. 'But you were at your parents' when I phoned their number?'

Phil shook his head, again. 'Nah. I was at mine, in Finsbury Park. I took the number with me when I went.'

'But . . . but . . . didn't your parents want to keep their number?'

Phil put down his pint and took a deep breath. 'No. They don't need their number any more. They're dead.'

The bluntness of his response took Nadine somewhat by surprise. 'I see,' she said. 'How long? How long have they been dead?'

Phil took a slug of his beer. 'A year,' he said, 'a year and a bit.'

'What? Both of them?'

'Uh-huh.'

'They died together?'

'Yeah. In an accident.'

'Oh, Phil'—Nadine instinctively grabbed his hand across the table— 'you poor, poor thing.'

'Yeah,' he muttered, 'well.'

'So. You couldn't bear to live in the house any more after they went?'

'Eh?'

'You know. Your parents' house . . .?'

'Oh. Right. No. It . . . er . . . I did live there for a while after they died. It was mine, legally. They left it to me.'

'And you sold it?'

'Erm . . . no. Not exactly. I . . . I . . . Oh God. This is another bad thing, you know. The house. Another bad thing.'

'Go on,' soothed Nadine.

'I haven't really talked about all this before, properly, you know.'

'Well, maybe you should.'

Phil sighed and took a deep breath. 'Yeah,' he said, 'you're right. I might as well tell you everything then, eh? Since you're listening.' He stopped and stared at her then, intently. 'You know something,' he said, 'you're still as beautiful as you ever were.'

Nadine blushed and looked away, embarrassed by the unexpected compliment and Phil's piercing gaze.

'Sorry,' he smiled, 'sorry. I shouldn't have said that. Anyway. The house. There was a fire.'

'Oh my God,' cried Nadine. 'How? What happened?'

'Huh.' He shrugged. 'It was my fault. I left a fag burning and went out. Can you believe it? One fag, one measly little fag.' He took one out of the packet in front of him and held it under Nadine's gaze. 'Something that small, that *puny*, it's hard to believe. If you'd seen what it did to my house—to three storeys and four bedrooms. It's frightening,' he said.

'What did you do?'

'Well, that's the thing, right. I don't know what happened after that. Not really. Only what other people have told me. I think I must have gone into some sort of shock. I went to the hospital, and they treated the shock, and then got in touch with my grandparents, who came and picked me up and took me back with them to Bournemouth. I don't really remember any of this. I reckon I had some kind of breakdown because I became quite unmanageable apparently and eventually my grandparents couldn't take it any more, so they sent me to a hospital.

'I was there for three months and they gave me pills and they gave me psychotherapy and they gave me counselling, and then they sent me home. My grandparents kicked another tenant out of their old Peabody flat and got it ready for me. I've been there for a couple of months, you know, trying to live a normal life, getting to know people.'

'So, you're all alone?' asked Nadine.

'Well,' he said, 'I met this girl called Jo a couple of weeks ago, down the pub with all her mates, and we got talking. Turns out she was a student, and her and all her student mates ended up coming back to my place.

They come round most nights now—all of them, just for a drink and a smoke and somewhere to hang out. It's nice for them to have somewhere to come and I like having them around. It makes me feel I'm not all alone.'

Phil fell into a silence then and Nadine fished her purse out of her bag. 'Let me get you a drink,' she said, her heart close to bursting with sympathy and pity. Poor, poor Phil.

Nadine took the drinks back to their table and Phil looked up at her gratefully. 'Thanks,' he said, 'thank you, Nadine Kite.'

And Nadine smiled back at him nervously and thought to herself that she was not just walking but positively *sprinting* up a path in her life that she was never, ever supposed to take, and then she thought to herself how even if she tried to turn around now, this very minute, and get off the path, it was already too late, far too late to ever find her way back.

Delilah hadn't arrived at Dig's empty-handed. As well as her tiny and unattractive dog, she had produced from somewhere, God knows where, a pair of enormous and ominously bulging suitcases.

'You going somewhere?' Dig asked, eyeing the cases with suspicion.

Delilah smiled. 'Well,' she said, 'that's the thing. It's not working out for us at Marina's. I've . . . er . . . I've just had a huge row with her.'

'With Marina? What about?'

'Oh God. Nothing. Nothing, really. She's just such a pious, sanctimonious old cow. I don't know why I ever thought it would be a good idea to stay with her. I'd have stayed in a hotel, you know, but I can't because of the dog. And *then* she threatened to tell my mum I was back in town, so I just packed a bag and walked.'

There was a brief silence as Dig absorbed this information, waiting tensely for the inevitable.

'So, anyway, I—er—was sort of hoping that me and Digby could maybe crash here for a while. We won't be any trouble, I promise you, and we'll be gone as soon as we can find somewhere else to go. And Digby's fully house-trained and very quiet.' The tiny creature suddenly threw himself on to Dig's corduroy sofa and began yapping incredibly loudly. ' . . . Well, usually he's quiet. He's just excited to be somewhere new. I'll cook for you and keep the place tidy. Not,' she said, peering around the door-way into Dig's spotless flat, 'that it actually needs it. So. What do you think?' She beamed at him.

Dig was speechless for a second, his head telling him that there wasn't enough room in his flat for a girl and a dog and two suitcases full of their belongings, while his heart told him that there was a devastatingly beautiful woman on his doorstep begging for a place to stay and of course he should invite her in. As he grappled with his dilemma, the awkward silence was broken by the buzz of the doorbell.

'*Take-away*,' said a muffled Indian voice.

'Top floor,' said Dig, suddenly flustered by the preponderance of issues bearing down on him all at once and the thought of so many people, animals and large objects jostling for space on his tiny landing. Something would have to give.

'Right,' he said, turning back to Delilah, 'I'd better give you a hand with these cases.'

'Oh,' squeaked Delilah, 'really? I can stay? Oh thank you!' And then she threw her arms around Dig's neck and hugged him hard.

Dig's arms crept slowly around her waist and through the dampness of her coat he could feel the shape of her backbone, the softness of the flesh that covered her hips, the squashiness of her breasts against his chest and as her lips found his cheek, Dig decided that this arrangement could actually work out after all.

Nadine is on *at least* her fifth large tumbler of vodka. And they've been *extremely* large. Equivalent to two or three pub measures. She started off drinking them with some lime cordial she found in the kitchen but gave up on the mixer after the first couple. Since then, she's been drinking them neat—without ice. She can't actually taste the vodka any more.

She'd said no, at first, when Phil had invited her back to his flat after the pub closed. Despite the fact that they'd ended up having a fairly pleasant evening together, helped along considerably by the four pints of Theakstones she'd consumed, the weight of the dreadful unfolding of events in Phil's life had started to make itself felt around her temples and she wanted to get away before things got any heavier.

But he'd looked so deflated by her refusal, almost like he was going to cry, and before she knew what was happening she was agreeing.

Phil's flat was in the Peabody estate off the Holloway Road, up three flights of echoing concrete stairs, and there were about half a dozen people already in his draughty living room when they walked in, listening to Gomez and sitting under a thick fleece of smoke. None of them looked up when Phil walked in, except for one tall, skinny girl with waist-length hair and enormous breasts straining beneath a child's T-shirt who unfolded herself from a cushion on the floor to greet him.

'Nadine, this is Jo. Jo, this is Nadine. Me and Nadine used to live together at university.'

'Oh yeah,' said Jo, handing Phil the bum end of a spliff and lowering herself back on to her cushion, 'didn't know you went to university.'

Nadine looked around her. Everyone in this room was so young and so distant, she felt as if she didn't exist in their eyes, as if she was of no consequence—which was ridiculous considering the fact that they were a bunch of students and she was a successful photographer with a sports car, a flat and a £40,000 commission. But if she was going to stand even the slightest chance of enjoying herself with these people, then she was going to have to get a lot more drunk than she was right now.

An hour and five large vodkas later and Nadine is suddenly feeling very self-confident, and that, combined with the incredibly strong spliff she's smoked, has given her surroundings a slightly surreal edge. She feels like she's in some kind of lovely floaty dream, and now Phil feels like one of those strange characters who wander in and out of dreams.

She's been using Phil as a sounding-board for the last half an hour, chewing his ear off about Dig and Delilah and what a mistake Dig's making and how he won't pay any attention to what Nadine has been trying to tell him *for his own good*, and how he's going to end up getting his heart broken all over again, and Phil, despite having so many problems of his own, has turned out to be a great, great listener, agreeing wholeheartedly with everything Nadine says and endearing himself to her more than he could possibly imagine in the process.

And now he's smiling at her and ferreting around his jeans pockets looking for something. He reaches into his pocket and brings out a tiny Indian pillbox. 'You sound like you could do with a little something to *lift* your spirits,' he says, pulling the lid off the tiny box.

'What's that?' Nadine asks.

'Little miracles,' he smiles. 'One of these, and the whole world will seem like a better place.'

Nadine's eyes open wide. 'Eeeeeeeeee?' she asks.

Phil nods and hands her a pill. 'You might just want half,' he says, 'if it's your first.'

'Oh no,' she says 'let me have a whole one.' Despite having lived what she considers to be a fairly colourful life, Nadine's never done an E before and she swallows it, quickly, and waits for it to take effect.

Half an hour later and she doesn't really feel any different. She's much more stoned, that's for certain, and much more pissed, and maybe that's why she's suddenly feeling so strangely drawn to Phil, suddenly feeling like she'd like to touch him, hug him, maybe even kiss him.

'Are you sure you're not really a *drug-dealer*?' she asks, jokingly, even though she's secretly started to think that maybe he is. It would explain all these students in his flat and the abundance of strong weed and the pill she's just swallowed.

'Nah,' he smiles. And then, suddenly and most unexpectedly, he turns and stares into her eyes and says, 'God, Nadine, you're so beautiful.'

Nadine chokes on her vodka. 'Oh,' she says, 'don't be daft.'

Phil shakes his head very slowly and stares at her. 'I'm not being daft,' he says. 'You're fucking gorgeous.' He leans in towards her as he says this, so that his face is only a couple of millimetres from hers. He locks his eyes on to hers, and she starts to feel vaguely uncomfortable but strangely excited. Inside Nadine's drug-and-alcohol-addled head, Phil is now larger than life—he is a legend. Phil has lived a big life, full of change and adversity. He has battled with depression. He has reinvented himself and pulled himself out of the quagmire time after time. He is strong and resilient. He is brave and unpredictable. He is everything that Nadine is not. He is better than Nadine.

And all of a sudden, through the blur of her thoughts, Nadine realises that this is what's been wrong with every man she's been out with since she and Phil split up. None of them have been better than her. They've all been weak and inferior—at least in her mind—and she has been unable to respect them.

She's had enough of weak men. She wants a strong man, a man like Phil. Phil isn't perfect—he is far from perfect—he is as flawed as it is possible for a man to be. But he is strong. He is special. He's different.

If Nadine were sober and happier, if Nadine hadn't just taken an E, she would be thinking exactly the opposite; she would probably call it a night now, start making her excuses, get her coat, order a cab, go home, because it is becoming increasingly obvious what sort of turn this evening is about to take, and there is a sensible, wise part of Nadine which knows that she shouldn't be following this path, knows that Phil has always managed to manipulate her and control her and that if she stays now she is more or less bound to let him do it again.

But she is not sober and she is not happy, so she smiles at Phil instead and thinks how much she's enjoying herself and how she still loves him in a funny kind of way, and how, if he was to try to kiss her, she probably wouldn't fight him off. As if reading her thoughts, Phil puts one hand on her shoulder and the other over her hand, and his fingers are moving over her flesh.

'I think,' says Phil, 'we should—go somewhere else—a bit quieter, y'know?' Phil strokes her hair and then brings the back of his hand down softly against her cheek. It is such a tender gesture that Nadine immediately turns to blancmange inside and knows that she has to do this, and that it's not wrong, it's all right, because Phil is good and Phil is beautiful and it will be beautiful and it's the right thing to do, the most perfect thing to do.

'I want to get to know you all over again, Nadine Kite. I want to be alone with you. Come with me.' He holds out his hand for her.

There is something so surreal about all this, about Phil, this flat, this evening, that Nadine is starting to feel like she's in a film or something, that none of this is really happening to her.

She takes his hand and follows him.

Dig was trying to be chilled out but was finding it very hard. Delilah had just committed the greatest domestic crime known to man. There were many domestic crimes—not replacing the toilet roll when it was finished, not rinsing things before putting them in the dishwasher, not putting lids back on things, not rewinding videos and not plumping up cushions—but that one, just now—leaving CDs out of their boxes—was the worst, by far. He'd tried so hard not to say anything. It had been his suggestion, after all, that she choose some music to put on. But he'd just meant for her to select one CD and put it on. Instead, she'd been completely overwhelmed by his shelves of alphabetically organised CDs and was now playing DJ, excitedly pulling one plastic case after another off the shelves. Dig lost the battle to control his neurosis.

'Erm—you couldn't put those back in their boxes, could you?'

'Sure,' replied Delilah, distractedly, pulling some shit by Vengaboys off the shelf and sticking it in the machine. She slid the Shania Twain album she'd just listened to back into its case and seemed satisfied that this act constituted a reasonable response to Dig's request.

Dig sat back and sighed. His CD shelves were full of music that he didn't like. He got it all free. Every day he came home with a handful of new CDs that he was never going to listen to. He used to consider these free CDs to be a perk of the job, but was now starting to feel that these freebies were more of an encumbrance.

He winced as he heard the opening bars to 'Boom Boom Boom Boom' and then stared in horror at Delilah, who was jauntily bouncing up and down and humming under her breath. She couldn't really like this sort of thing, could she?

'This is great,' she beamed at him.

Dig dropped his head into his hands. Nadine had been right. Delilah *wasn't* the same girl he remembered from years ago. Phil Collins would have been a *relief* right now. The old Delilah had thrown empty beer cans at Bucks Fizz on the telly and used a selection of well-chosen swearwords to express her disgust at such blandness and unoriginality.

The new Delilah had the musical taste of a twelve-year-old girl.

The passage of time could do cruel things to people.

Digby was sitting at his feet staring up at him with watery eyes. He vibrated briefly and then emitted a strange little high-pitched whimper.

'Delilah. I think there's something wrong with your dog. He keeps shivering and moaning.'

'Oh no,' said Delilah, 'he just needs to go to the toilet, that's all. D'you mind taking him?'

'Taking him? Where?'

'The nearest tree would be good,' she replied, sarcastically, Dig thought.

'Oh. Right. OK.' He glanced from his window and noticed that it was still raining. Great. He pulled on his leather coat and picked up an umbrella, attached Digby to his lead and then dragged him down the stairs to the chestnut tree outside his house.

Digby cocked his leg and then released the smallest squirt of urine that Dig had ever seen in his life.

'Is that it?' he barked at the dog. 'That . . . that dribble? Jesus.' He sighed and began dragging the dog back towards the house, but the dog seemed to have decided that he wanted to explore the neighbourhood.

'No,' shouted Dig, 'we're going in. You've had your lot.'

The dog stood his ground, looking pleadingly into Dig's eyes.

'That's it,' sighed Dig, 'if you can't behave like a grown-up, then I'm going to have to treat you like a puppy. Come here.' He leaned down to pick Digby up and the dog scampered backwards. He bent down again and the dog moved back even further. This continued until they were nearly in the road, and just as Dig managed to get his hands on the animal and pick him up, a large lorry drove past and threw the entire contents of an enormous puddle all over him.

Dig stood for a second, in shock, water rolling down his face from his hair, and his trousers sticking heavily to his legs.

'Oh,' he muttered, 'for fuck's sake.'

When he returned to the flat Delilah had moved away from the CD player, having left every single CD out of its case and strewn around the place, and was now busily unpacking, chucking items of clothing and undergarments randomly around the room.

'Oh,' she said, 'you're back. Did he go all right?'

'Yes,' murmured Dig, dripping on to the floor and waiting for a sympathetic comment from her about his dramatic state of wetness.

Instead, Delilah turned her attention immediately to Digby and began petting him furiously. 'Good boy,' she squeaked in some kind of strange, other-worldly voice, ''oos a good boy then? Did 'oo do a wee-wee for your uncle Dig, did you? Good boy!' And then she went back to her haphazard unpacking.

'I wouldn't mind turning in now, Dig, if that's all right with you? It's been kind of a long day,' she said with a sigh.

Dig looked at his watch. It was ten past ten. He didn't usually go to bed until at least midnight. He didn't have a television in his room. He hadn't even *begun* to digest his curry yet. He wasn't quite sure what he was going to do. 'Er—yeah—sure. I'll get the sofa-bed up for you.'

Shit, he thought as he made up the bed for her—without even a glimmer of an offer of help—I'm going to have to read a book. What a nightmare. He'd been reading *The Beach* for the last six months and was still only on page 85. He used it as a coaster for his morning cup of coffee, mainly. Dig wasn't one of life's great readers.

'Right,' he said, scratching his head, 'I'll see you in the morning. You know where everything is, don't you? Do you need me to wake you up tomorrow morning or anything?'

'No,' said Delilah, smiling, 'no. I'll just get up when you get up.' She walked towards him and placed her hands on his arms. 'Thank you, Dig. Thank you so much. This is so kind of you.'

She grabbed him then, and squeezed him to her in a bear-hug, and Dig thought, *excellent*, and lifted himself on to his tiptoes to match her height. He squeezed her back and buried his face into her cool, silky hair and breathed in that smell, that morning-dew fragrance. Oh Delilah, he thought. You have *no idea* what you do to me. You are so beautiful and so sexy and I just want to drag you into my bedroom right now and lick every inch of you.

Dig could feel Delilah caressing his back through his wet clothes and—*boing*—right on cue, there he was, Mr Happy, in his trousers.

'Oh Delilah,' he murmured into her hair, bringing his nose up towards her face, 'oh Delilah.' He closed his eyes and puckered up, almost exploding with the intensity of the desire he was experiencing, and then, suddenly, she was gone. Slithered from his embrace like a Vaselined cat.

She was halfway to the hallway. 'Sleep tight,' she said, and threw him a little wave before disappearing into the bathroom.

Dig shook his head in confusion.

What happened? One minute she was . . . and the next she was . . . And now he had a huge hard-on . . . He sighed, turned off the central light, looked briefly around his messy living room and went to bed.

Nadine awoke and sat bolt upright, covering her naked breasts with her hands. Phil sat up, too. They looked at each other. Phil grinned and pulled her firmly towards him. 'You are incredible,' he whispered into her ear. 'I could fuck you for ever.'

Oooh, she thought to herself, I wish you hadn't said that. I feel all *weird* now. In fact, Nadine was starting to feel all weird about this whole situation. What the hell was she doing here? What was she doing having sex with a deeply damaged man, on a cocktail of drugs and alcohol. It might have been rock 'n' roll but it certainly wasn't her style.

She knew that he'd tugged her heart-strings nearly to oblivion in the pub earlier on, and then he'd been a really good listener, he'd been sympathetic and attentive and kind, and then she knew that he'd hit her with some pretty powerful compliments and remembered how much she'd enjoyed the sex but now . . . well, what the hell was she doing?

Despite her lingering feelings of love and affection for him, Phil *really* wasn't her type, at all. Too thin, too pale and all that *very black* body hair that stood out in such stark contrast to his lime-washed flesh that you could see each individual follicle. And those long, shapely legs that looked like women's legs. She'd forgotten about those. But worst of all were his *underpants*—Nadine had never slept with a man who wore *underpants* before, particularly not bright-lemon underpants.

'Give me another half an hour and I'll see if I can make it *even better* this time.'

Oh what! Oh no. No no no no no. Nadine dragged her knickers up her legs and over her hips as quickly as she could, using them as some kind of symbolic chastity belt.

She stood up and pulled on her crocheted dress. 'Sorry, Phil,' she said, 'but I've got to go home now. Really.' She looked at her watch. 'Shit! It's nearly two! We've been ages.'

'Yeah,' smiled Phil proudly, 'I know.'

Nadine shuddered. She wanted to go home.

Chapter Five

BY THE TIME Dig's alarm went off at quarter past eight, he'd had a couple of gorgeous dreams and was ready to start the day.

The rain had stopped and the sun was positively bursting through his curtains. Delilah was wearing a pair of faded jeans, black crocodile-skin boots with high heels and a black polo neck when he walked into the living room. She was one of the few women who Dig considered suited to wearing jeans. She was crouching on the floor and leafing frantically through some paperwork, spreading the piles ever further and slurping on a mug of coffee as she went. She turned around when she sensed Dig behind her.

'Hi!' she beamed happily, rocking on her heels, 'sleep well?'

'I think so,' he said, scratching his head and balancing himself on the arm of the sofa-bed, which had not, he noted, been put away.

'So, Dig,' she asked, 'I meant to ask you last night. Heard anything from Nadine yet?'

Dig jumped a little—Delilah had a disarming ability to ask awkward questions at very unexpected junctures. 'Yeah,' he said, tersely, 'I spoke to her yesterday afternoon, actually. We had another row.'

'About me?'

Dig shook his head. 'Nah. About her. She's getting back in touch with this idiot she went out with at university. She saw him last night. I don't understand her.'

'Well,' said Delilah, decisively, 'I do. She's trying to get back at you.'

'What are you talking about?'

'It's obvious. She's pissed off with you for spending time with me, so she's phoned up her ex to try and make you jealous.'

'Oh, don't be ridiculous.'

'I'm not. I'm right. I know I am. She wants you to know what she feels like. Why else would she choose now, of all times, to get back in touch with this bloke?'

Dig shrugged petulantly.

'You gonna call her?'

'No.' Dig was aware that he sounded like a brat but he didn't care.

'Jesus,' sighed Delilah, 'you two are behaving like a pair of kids.'

'She started it,' said Dig, continuing his brat theme.

'So. Why can't you finish it? Just pick up the phone and say, "All right, Deen, fancy a drink?" You'll go out, you'll chat, within an hour everything will be back to normal—I guarantee you. Honestly. You two should be married to each other and instead you're not even *talking* to each other—it's infuriating!'

Dig winced at this new reference to him and Nadine.

'D'you want another coffee?' he asked, gesturing at her mug.

'Er . . . no thanks,' she said, 'I'm actually really late for something.'

'Oh yeah? What's that then?'

'Oh—nothing really. I've just got be somewhere in twenty minutes.'

She suddenly became deeply distracted, busily rearranging things in her handbag and clutching the spare set of door keys he'd given her the night before. 'Erm,' she began, biting at her lower lip, 'Dig. I . . . er . . . need to ask you a favour.'

Oh God, thought Dig, what now?

'Sure!' he smiled. 'No problem!'

'I was sort of hoping, if it wasn't too much trouble, that you could maybe have Digby today?' She smiled at him apprehensively.

'Eh?' said Dig.

'Well, I wouldn't normally ask, but I'll be on trains and God knows what today, and I don't know when I'll be home, and it would just make everything so much easier if he wasn't with me . . .'

'But I've . . . um . . . I've got to go to work, Delilah. I can't look after him. Can't you just leave him here?'

Delilah shook her head sadly. 'He's awful when he's left alone—he makes this terrible noise, like goats being tortured or something—painful. And he deliberately pees on beds. It's a spite thing. Can't you take him with you? Please Dig—please. I'll make it up to you tonight—I'll cook you my famous lamb casserole—it's Alex's favourite! Please!'

Dig stared into Delilah's huge blue eyes and felt his resolve diminish rapidly to nothing. Toby wouldn't mind about the dog and poor old Delilah really, *really* needed him to help her—she would be so grateful, and grateful women were, generally speaking, a *very good thing*.

So he nodded and he smiled and he said, 'Yeah, sure, why not?', and Delilah hugged him yet again, and Dig thought to himself that he really was building up a good, big stock of brownie-points here and that at some stage all this Good Samaritan stuff was going to start paying dividends, surely, and he hugged her back.

Delilah didn't get back to Dig's flat until half past ten that night. She didn't tell him where she'd been all day and Dig didn't ask, and there was certainly no mention whatsoever of the promised lamb casserole.

Nadine was experiencing what could fairly be described as the worst hangover of her life. Without a doubt. Her head was throbbing, her heart was racing, her blood was fizzing, her stomach was churning and she was feeling as miserable as sin. She was having rather severe difficulty piecing together the fragmented bits of last night's events. She could just about remember having sex with Phil (bleugh), but she had absolutely no idea how such a terrible thing could have happened.

She'd managed to crawl out of bed forty-five minutes ago and had been dragging her pained body around the flat ever since, trying to make it do the things it normally did in the mornings, like wash its hair and make its toast and brush its teeth. It had been extremely difficult and extremely unpleasant, but she'd managed it somehow, and had been about to leave for work when she'd heard the phone ringing.

'Hello,' she sighed, painfully, perching on the arm of the sofa.

'Is that the sexiest woman in Kentish Town?' said a strange male voice.

'I'm sorry?'

'Hello, darlin'. It's me, Phil.'

Nadine experienced a sudden knot of tension in her stomach.

'Hello . . . hello . . . are you there?'

'Oh . . . yeah . . . sorry.' Nadine let her weary body flop sideways on to the sofa. 'So . . . how are you?'

'Yeah. Great. Great. You?'

'Not so great, actually.'

'Feeling bad?'

'Yeah—you could say that.'

'Can't say I'm surprised, really. All that vodka you were drinking and then—you know—that pill.'

'What pill?'

'You know—I gave you a pill—when you were getting upset about things.'

Oh yes. That E! Oh my God—she had, hadn't she? She'd taken an E. Jesus—she was thirty years old and she'd just taken her first E. That would explain *a lot* of things about last night.

'You might feel a bit low, today, a bit blue. Just drink a lot of coffee.'

God—she was so stupid. She could have killed herself.

'Yeah. Right. I will . . . Thanks.' She buried her face into the cushions on the sofa and closed her eyes. She was aware that the line had gone silent but was feeling too dreadful to be able to think of anything to say.

'Hey, Nadine'—Phil's voice broke the silence—'you know something? I haven't slept since you left. I've been up all night. Just thinking about you, about *us* . . . about how great we still are together.'

Oh no, thought Nadine, oh God.

'I've been wanting to phone you since you left. And I just wanted to say thanks, for getting in touch, for listening, for being you.'

Nadine wanted to say something nice—she felt *so sorry* for him—but all she could manage was a weak laugh.

'So I . . . er . . . just wondered. What are you up to later? Thought we could, like, meet up. Or something. Yeah?'

Nadine sat up straight. This was all a bit much, all a bit full-on for eight thirty on a Thursday morning with a raging hangover. 'Oh well,' she stalled, 'later? Erm, well—the thing is, I'm off to Barcelona so . . .'

'Oh right, yeah. Fair enough. You'll want an early night, I suppose.'

'Yeah. That sort of thing.'

'Well, when are you back? Maybe we could get together then?'

'Back on Tuesday evening, actually.'

'So—maybe late next week?'

'Yeah. Maybe.'

'Great. Cool,' he said, and the line went quiet again. 'Erm, Nadine?' he said, eventually.

'Yeah.'

'I just wanted to say to you, I'm so glad you're back in my life. I should never, ever have let you go, before. I should never have let my ego come between us the way it did. I'm older now and I've learned so much in life, and one thing I've learned is that true love is what life is all about and nothing should ever, *ever* get in its way. And you were my true love, Nadine. I knew it then and I sure as hell know it now.'

Nadine's cheeks pinkened with horror.

'I can't believe I'm lucky enough to be given a second chance with you. I wanna make it work this time, I wanna make it perfect. Yeah? So I'll give you a ring on Tuesday, OK? And we'll meet up?'

'Yeah,' said Nadine, not knowing what else to say and wondering, not for the first time in her life, why it was so hard to use the word 'no'.

The next morning Dig waited until he heard the door slam behind Delilah and her footsteps bouncing down the front steps before crawling out of bed and into the living room.

Bloody hell—it was a nightmare in here. She hadn't even opened the curtains. There was half a bowl of porridge encrusting on the coffee table, half her wardrobe strewn across her bed, and Digby was shivering furiously under the radiator.

'Great,' Dig muttered under his breath.

He couldn't stand this, he really, really couldn't bear it. He knew he was being anal, he knew other people would be able to ignore all this . . . this *shit*, all this stuff everywhere, clothes and mess and paper and dogs. Other people would just think, Well, it's not perfect, but she's a friend and it's only a bit of mess. But Dig just couldn't. He couldn't concentrate. He couldn't relax. He couldn't *breathe*, for God's sake.

He moved towards his stereo and traced his finger across the 'B' section of his CD collection. There was only one thing for it, only one person who could help him now. He reverently laid the disc in its tray, slid shut the door and pressed play. When it came to a mess of this magnitude, there was only one man for the job.

The One and Only.

James. Brown. Get down.

Dig swivelled the volume as loud as it would go without bouncing ornaments off his shelves and set to it.

Dig loved to tidy, he really did. It was one of his favourite occupations. But this was a bit trickier than usual because it wasn't his stuff. It was bits and pieces from somebody else's life, stuff that belonged on the shelves and in the cupboards of a house he'd never visited, in a part of the country he'd never been to. And a lot of it was underwear.

Digby still sat quaking under the radiator and watched Dig as he feigned disinterest in her bits of white-jersey underwear, lumping them together nonchalantly, like old rugby socks, almost as if someone might be watching him for signs of sad-old-gitness. He collected her mugs and bowls and glasses of water and put them in the kitchen sink. He rolled up the duvet and shoved it in the hall cupboard, along with the pillows. He heaved the sofabed back into its cavity, retrieved his cushions from where they lay scattered around the room, plumped them up and arranged them into a nice overlapping pattern across the sofa back.

He stepped back to appraise his cushions, screwing up his face as he joined James to hit a high note. Now—where to put all these beautifully folded bits of designer clothing? He spotted one of her vast suitcases in the corner, dragged it into the middle of the room and threw it open. And then he stopped in his tracks. Paper. Loads of it. Loose-leaf papers in clear plastic folders. Notebooks. Folders. Letters. Clues.

He shuffled the papers around a bit to make room in the case for her clothes, and let his eyes wander across the official-looking letter that lay on the top as he put her clothing, piece by piece, into the case.

Dig scanned it quickly.

November 10, 1999

Dear Delilah,

I have been trying to phone you since you walked out of our session yesterday afternoon but your housekeeper was unable to tell me where you were.

I am very concerned about you, Delilah, and can only hope that you haven't carried out your threat to return to London. I understand your need to uncover the past, especially in the light of what you told me yesterday, but I really feel that this trip will not be in your best interests and could in fact be detrimental to your progress at this stage in our work together.

However, if you do insist on going ahead with your plans, then I beseech you to talk to Alex about it. He has supported you in everything over the years and shutting him out now would be unfair on both of you.

I don't think there is anything else I can say, except to urge you once more to postpone this visit until you're stronger.

Warm wishes,

Dr Rosemary Bentall

Clinical Psychologist

Dig closed his mouth, cleared his throat and quickly piled the rest of the clothes on top of the paperwork. His heart raced in rhythm to the music as he tried to go about his business, but he found it impossible to feel normal. 'Uncover the past'? What did that mean? And what the hell was Delilah doing seeing a shrink? Delilah wasn't mad.

This threw a new complexion on everything. When Delilah had told Dig that she was in London to 'sort her head out', he'd thought she was here to contemplate her marriage, which was why he'd kept out of her face. But it was nothing to do with her marriage. It was to do with the past. Of which he was a part. It was his business, now. He had a right to know.

Far from putting Dig off Delilah, finding out that she was a fruitloop had intensified his feelings for her. It made her more real, more attainable in a way, like finding out that she was more than just the coolest girl in school, finding the soft spots that she'd let only him see, was what had made him fall in love with her all those years ago. People with weaknesses made Dig feel strong in the same way that small women made him feel big.

Since reading the letter, Dig had been consumed by an overwhelming desire for intimacy. He missed the way he'd been in his youth, he missed the time in his life when he'd been carefree and careless with his heart, when he'd been capable of falling helplessly and hopelessly in love. He'd been such a soft-hearted romantic when he was young, his heart on his sleeve and his emotions on a plate. And since he'd first set eyes on Delilah, last Saturday, he had begun to experience similar sensations again. It was incredibly exciting to discover that he was still capable of feeling this way.

For the first time since he was a teenager, since that hideous weekend in Manchester, Dig could imagine, without a hint of panic, a future life which involved somebody else. He could imagine seeing the same face on the pillow next to him every single morning, and he could imagine saying 'we' a lot instead of 'I'. He could envisage the golden world that Nadine had conjured up in the café the other day, the world full of teenage children and mess and noise and joyful rites of passage.

Dig was ready to open up again. He was ready for anything, including getting hurt.

Nadine stopped off at her local corner shop on the way home that Friday evening and bought a fresh loaf of bread and a packet of bacon. She deserved a big fat bacon sandwich after her hugely strenuous work-out at the gym this morning.

She'd spent most of that day thinking about what had happened between her and Phil on Wednesday night, and shuddering a lot—how could she? how could she? *how could she?*—but she hadn't heard from him since Thursday morning, so maybe, just maybe, *please God*, he was just going to disappear down whatever dark, dank hole he'd emerged from, and she'd never have to see him again.

She dropped a thick stack of paperwork on the table in her hallway, hung up her coat and kicked off her shoes. As she passed the telephone she noticed the answerphone flashing and did a double take. It was telling her that she had eighteen new messages!

The display must have malfunctioned. Either that or something bad had happened. Oh God. Maybe her mother. Or . . . or . . . maybe it was Dig, trying to make things up with her, maybe he wanted to see her that night. Nadine's heart began racing as she pressed the Play button.

'Er—hi,' began the first message, 'Nadine. It's me. Phil.' Nadine's burgeoning excitement deflated like a punctured tyre. 'It's . . . erm . . . it's eight fifteen. On Friday morning. Just phoning to say hi and that I hope you have a great time in Barcelona, and I can't wait till you get back.'

So much for her theory that he'd forgotten about her, thought Nadine. She tapped her fingers impatiently while she waited for the next message, hoping for the sound of Dig's voice.

'Hi. It's me again. It's . . . eight thirty now. I know you're not there, but I was just thinking about you. So . . . I'll call back. Bye.'

Oh for God's sake. Nadine didn't have time to listen to this crap. She had bacon sandwiches to eat, packing to do, Channel Four comedy shows to watch. A beep heralded the next message.

'Me again. It's nine thirty now. I was thinking—maybe I could see you off at the airport tomorrow. Maybe. If you like. I just really, really need to see you, Deen. Soon. So give me a call. OK?'

Oh God. Oh God. Nadine fast-forwarded to the next message.

'Nadine Kite. It's me again. 'It's ten fifty. I've got to go out now. I'll . . . er . . . I'll call you later.'

'Nadine Kite. I'm back. It's amazing, everything feels so different.

You've changed everything. I feel like I'm alive again.'

Oh Jesus. Oh no. Oh no. Nadine heavy-heartedly wound the tape on to the last message.

'You'll be home any minute. How many messages have I left? Yeah. Too many, probably. Look, I have to see you. Tonight. OK? I'll call you again. Please, Nadine Kite. I have to see you. Bye.'

Beep, said the machine, *you have no more messages*.

A chill went up and down Nadine's spine. Oh God.

She felt herself beginning to panic. The flat felt suddenly oppressive and horribly, horribly empty. The phone sat ominously in its cradle, frighteningly silent but pregnant with the prospect of the next ringing tone and the sound of Phil's voice invading her home and her freedom.

She sat like that for a few minutes, listening to the sound of her own heartbeat in her ears, trying to assimilate the fact that what she'd done on Wednesday night wasn't over, and was in fact just beginning.

Oh God, she thought, I can't handle this. I've got to get out of here.

She picked up her handbag, threw on her coat and left her flat, the door slamming loudly behind her.

She was going to the place in the world where she felt safest. She was going to Dig's and she was going to apologise for her hideous behaviour, and by the time she left, everything was going to be back to normal.

Dig had planned a candle-light dinner for Delilah, over which he would talk to her, *really* talk to her, about her trip to London, about that letter from her shrink, and her mission to 'uncover the past'. After all, he couldn't help her if he didn't know what her secret was.

He'd been to the fishmonger in his lunch hour and bought a pound of absolutely enormous prawns—complete bruisers—plus a great thick wedge of Loch Fyne smoked salmon and a small pot of caviar. He'd bought a packet of blinis and a large pot of smetana from the organic supermarket on Parkway, and had boiled some dinky miniature new potatoes and served them crushed with melted butter and rock salt. Nice and simple.

But sitting now opposite Delilah, Dig's prawns tasted like unwashed towelling socks. His smoked salmon tasted like damp kitchen roll, and the blinis had all the flavour and consistency of old cardboard.

'Mmmmmm,' he murmured, through a mouthful of mush, 'these prawns are excellent, aren't they?'

Delilah nodded sadly, and sighed.

She had slipped into a pair of pyjamas, and her hair was hanging limply around her face. Dig had seen her looking better. She hadn't said a word since they'd sat down to eat a quarter of an hour ago, just nodded and sighed in response to his questions.

This evening was not turning out how he'd planned.

Delilah had claimed to be feeling unwell when she'd finally returned from wherever it was she'd been all day at eight thirty that evening.

Dig had been trying so hard to get her to open up, but it seemed he'd chosen the wrong night. All his questions hit a dead end and were ricocheted back at him. Delilah was quite patently *not* in the mood for talking. Dig's heartfelt concern from earlier in the day had dissipated, and now he was just plain irritated.

Delilah was pushing a tiny, ant-like ball of caviar around her plate with the tine of her fork. This latest silence had lasted about two minutes, so far. The longest yet. What was it, thought Dig, what was it that was so painfully unbearable about silences between people? It was like a failure. A silence in the midst of a lively conversation could negate in a second everything that had come before.

'So,' began Dig, admitting defeat, breaking the silence, 'what are you up to tomorrow?' He felt like an emotionally withdrawn father trying to make conversation with a recalcitrant teenage daughter.

Delilah gently rested her fork on her plate and sighed again.

'I've . . . er . . . I've got a lot to do tomorrow . . .' She trailed off.

Dig sensed an opening. 'Anything I can help with?'

Delilah shrugged. 'No,' she said, eventually, 'no—I'll be fine. But thanks.' She looked up briefly through heavy eyes and then down again.

Dig sighed with frustration.

'What are *you* doing?'

'What?' replied Dig, slightly shocked by Delilah's first opening gambit of the evening.

'Tomorrow. What are you doing tomorrow?'

'Oh. Right. I don't know.' That was a point, thought Dig. It was Saturday tomorrow, and for as long as he could remember, Saturday had been Nadine day. A fry-up either round the corner from her, or round the corner from him, and then, depending on the weather, a walk in the park, flying the kites, or just sitting in and watching some sport on the telly before getting ready to go out. That was what he did on Saturdays. Well, that was what he *used* to do on Saturdays, before he and Nadine had fallen out with each other. He wasn't quite sure what he would do now that they weren't talking to each other.

The thought made him feel single. Which struck him as odd, because he'd been single, pretty much, for the last ten years. But, with Nadine in his life, he'd never actually *felt* single. He'd never had to contemplate huge, empty weekends with no one to share the minutiae.

Dig felt his stomach swill with unexpected anxiety. What would life be like, without Nadine? It was impossible to imagine. Horrible, probably, absolutely horrible. That settled it. He would definitely, definitely make things up with her, tomorrow. He would phone her first thing and they would go out for breakfast and everything would be back to normal.

He smiled and looked up. Delilah was still pushing the bead of caviar around her plate and appeared to be having trouble controlling her breathing. As he watched her, he saw a slick of sweat appear on her upper lip and the colour drain entirely from her face.

'Are you OK? Delilah?'

She dropped her fork noisily on to her plate, scraped back her chair, cupped her hands to her mouth and ran towards the bathroom.

A moment later Dig heard his prawns, his caviar, his blinis and his smoked salmon hitting the toilet bowl in a dramatic stampede from Delilah's stomach.

He sighed and began clearing away the food. He heard the shower being operated and the lock going on the bathroom door. Well, that was that, then. It looked as if Delilah's problems and her secret mission to uncover the past were to remain a mystery for at least another night.

Dig was just about to blow out the candles, when he heard the door-bell ring.

Dig's disembodied voice on the entry phone sounded surprised to hear her—'Oh, Nadine. Hi'—almost like he'd been expecting someone else.

She took the linoleum-clad steps two at a time, oblivious to her already tender, post-gym leg muscles screaming at her to stop. She hadn't yet thought about how she was going to tell Dig that she'd had E'd-up sex with Philip Rich within hours of meeting up with him again and how he was now turning out to be a bit of a psycho, plaguing her with phone calls. She hadn't thought about any of that. None of that mattered any more. All she wanted to do was make up and be friends again.

She rounded the corner at the top of the last flight of stairs and stood nervously outside Dig's front door. He was standing in his hallway, look-ing tired and uncomfortable, wearing his best shirt and his new jeans.

'Hi,' she said, squeezing out a smile. She felt inexplicably tearful.

'Er—hi.' Dig looked distinctly unthrilled to see her.

'Sorry to—er—turn up like this.'

'That's OK.'

'Are you going to invite me in then, or what?' She grinned, attempting to bring a little levity to the tense atmosphere.

Dig didn't smile, didn't say anything, just scratched his head and moved out of her way.

'So—how've you been?' she asked.

'Oh—fine. Fine. You?'

'Yeah. Fine.'

There was a silence. It was awkward.

She dropped her bag and coat where she always left them and made her way into the living room—which was when she became slowly aware of the seductive surroundings, of the veritable *come-on* spread out all over the table, and candles, and the music—it sounded like— sounded like—*Robbie Williams*? Couldn't be, couldn't possibly be. Dig wouldn't be listening to Robbie Williams. And the lights were very low, and what was that *thing*, that furry little thing on the sofa? It looked like one of those Russian hats, except smaller and hairier. Nadine screamed when it jumped off the sofa and started walking towards her.

'Oh God!' she exclaimed, clutching at her heart. 'What is that?'

'It's a dog,' said Dig, helpfully.

'Yes. I can see it's a dog. But what's it doing here?'

'It's—er—he's Digby.'

It took a second for Nadine to twig. She thought it was a feeble joke at first, and then it dawned on her. Digby. Delilah's dog. This was Delilah's dog. What the hell was Delilah's dog doing in Dig's flat? Nadine was starting to think that she'd stumbled into some parallel universe; empty prawn shells, jars of caviar, Robbie Williams, small dogs—she fully expected a wife and kids to appear from nowhere at any second.

And then her thought processes began to clarify.

Sexy food—low lighting—Delilah's dog. Oh God.

At the very second that Nadine worked out what was going on she heard a click and there was a sudden blast of light and steam from the bathroom door. And there she stood, emerging from the steam like a rock star coming on stage through a cloud of dry ice, her hair tied up in a towelling turban and her body wrapped in a minute towel that barely covered the tops of her thighs. She smiled widely when she saw Nadine.

'Deen,' she said, 'what are you doing here? We weren't expecting you.'

Oh God. Oh God. Nadine's chest constricted and her breath came fast and furious.

She looked at Delilah, towelled and scrubbed and steaming.

She looked at Dig, shirted and combed and blushing.

She looked at the table, laden and clothed and sparkling.

She saw Dig and Delilah exchange a look. There was a moment of dreadful silence.

Then Nadine picked up her coat and bag and pushed Dig out of the way. She slammed the door closed behind her and ran down the stairs. Behind her she heard Dig's door opening and his voice echoing down the stairs: 'Deen, where are you going?' She heard his footsteps, faster than hers, catching up with her, and she increased her pace.

She spun herself around the twists and turns of the narrow stairwell, her hand gripping the rail, her feet moving faster than Michael Flatley's.

Dig caught up with her on the street.

'Nadine! What's going on?'

'Nothing—I'm going home.'

'But what's the matter with you?'

'I don't want to talk about it. Just go back inside. Go and look after your precious, *beautiful* Delilah! Poor helpless innocent little Delilah. Go and wrap yourself back around her little finger. Go on!'

'Nadine!' Dig grabbed her arm. She shook his hand off her.

'*Leave me alone!*'

Dig stood back and eyed Nadine with surprise. 'All right then,' he sniffed, 'all right. Fuck off then, go on—fuck off.'

For a moment they stood and stared at one another, both breathing heavily and both wearing expressions of disbelief that something this horrible could be happening to their perfect friendship.

Nadine opened her mouth to say something, then turned and ran away. A gap in the four lanes of traffic on Camden Road prevented her from killing herself as she sped across the road towards her car, flinging open the door and grinding her gears before screeching away.

The last thing she saw before she took off was Dig, standing in his socked feet in the middle of Camden Road, rain pouring down his face, staring after her with his jaw hanging open and his hands outstretched in front of him in a gesture of pure bewilderment.

Nadine started talking to herself as she threw her little white car around corners, across roundabouts and over traffic lights, muttering, under her breath, like a mad woman.

What had she done? What was happening to her? What had happened to all those years she'd spent being cool and together and happy and well adjusted? Had she actually been but a whisker's width away from this insanity all along, without ever realising.

In the space of less than a week Nadine had dumped a perfectly lovely man because she didn't like his choice of mugs, had spent an entire evening phoning Dig when she knew he was going to be out, had actually driven round to his flat in the middle of the night in her Bart Simpson

slippers, to spy on him, had impulsively telephoned her horribly beautiful ex-boyfriend of ten years ago only to find that he was just horribly
horrible now, had ignored this, and slept with him anyway, on a cocktail
of drugs and alcohol, and now she'd done that. That thing just now, in
Dig's flat. That hideously embarrassing, Scarlett O'Hara-style exit, all
flouncing and tripping and hands-held-to-throat drama-queen.

Tears sprang to her eyes. Dig had told her to fuck off. Her stomach
lurched and wriggled and rucked. She felt nauseous. She scratched at
her tears distractedly and tried to ignore the little voice inside her head
telling her something that she'd known all along, really, ever since
Delilah had first reappeared six days ago, the little voice that was telling
her that the reason she was so jealous was that she wanted Dig for
herself, that she loved Dig—that she was *still in love with Dig*.

'*Ridiculous!*' she exclaimed, slamming the heels of her hands against
the steering-wheel, '*completely, totally and utterly ridiculous!*'

How could she possibly still be in love with Dig? She'd always loved
him, of course she had, but this was a completely different story. She'd
never felt jealous of him before. She'd sat next to him at parties and
nightclubs while he was chewing young, flat-stomached girls' faces off.
She'd listened with relish to every last detail of every last encounter he'd
ever had with nubile, perky-breasted little imps. All without even the
smallest sign of the green-eyed monster.

'He's *my* Dig, Delilah Lillie,' she moaned, as she drove past her house
for the fourth time, frantically looking out for a parking space, '*he's my
Dig, not your Dig. Go and get your own Dig, you bitch. Leave mine alone.
He's my Dig, my Dig, my Dig, my Dig . . .*'

But it was too late, she knew that now, too late for her and Dig. She
was never going to see Dig again, ever. It was over . . .

At this thought, yet more tears erupted like a geyser all over her face.
Rain cascaded down her windscreen and tears ran down her cheeks,
and she couldn't see a bloody thing.

She indicated left to make one final attempt at parking somewhere
within walking distance of her home and swung her car violently
around the corner. And then she saw it—there it was, definitely—a car,
about to pull out of a space, literally twenty feet from her own front
door. She slammed her indicator to the right and brought her car to a
screeching halt parallel to the car behind it, so full of determination and
defensive territorialism, her eyes so clouded with tears and her vision so
obstructed by the sheets of rain bouncing frantically off her windscreen
that she didn't see the thin, bowed-over figure in front of her, she didn't
notice that he'd stepped out into the street, without warning, from

between two parked cars, and the first she knew of his existence was the sound of his knees crunching against her bumper.

'Oh Jesus!' screamed Nadine, her hands jumping off the steering-wheel to cover her mouth. 'Oh no, oh *Jesus*!' She pulled on her hand-brake till it almost came off in her hand and threw the car door open. A passing car swerved out of the way and let loose a loud and frightening blast of its horn. Nadine ran to the front of her car. 'Oh God, oh God!'

There was a small, raggedy bunch of bones lying at the foot of her bonnet, not moving, its limbs arranged at strange angles.

'Oh no oh no oh no,' she thought to herself, whimpering slightly, 'I've killed someone, I've only gone and killed someone.'

She crouched down next to the crumpled figure and leaned in towards his face.

'Hello,' she ventured tentatively, gently prodding his shoulder, 'hello. Can you hear me? Are you all right?' The figure remained still. Nadine started thinking *ER*, thinking recovery position, thinking mouth-to-mouth resuscitation, thinking 'oh my God will someone please call an ambulance?' She was paralysed with fear and indecision.

And then the man moved, moved just a few inches, and groaned. Nadine stared at him. He groaned again.

'Oh God—you're alive! Oh thank God!' Tears of relief began to flow down Nadine's face.

The thin, wet figure turned slightly from where he lay on his stomach, on to his side, and began moaning under his breath, 'Oh my leg, my fucking leg.' He was beginning to sit up now, his back to her, clutching his knee and rocking back and forth.

Nadine stopped in her tracks—she recognised that voice. And, now she came to think of it, that hair was pretty familiar, too. And those jeans. And that raggedy old jumper.

'What the fuck were you playing at?' The man turned to face Nadine with this last question, and his jaw dropped when he looked at her.

'Nadine!'

Oh God, thought Nadine, her eyebrows dancing in disbelief, this can't be happening, this just *can't be happening*.

'Phil!' she reciprocated painfully, staring in horror at her worst night-mare. 'Are you OK?'

Nadine peeled down Phil's sodden and grimy jeans while he perched on the edge of her bath, wincing and clenching his teeth. He was, she noticed, wearing lemon underpants. She hoped they weren't the same pair he'd had on on Wednesday night.

As his jeans unfurled she sucked in her breath. His lower thigh was blooming into huge, misshapen roses of black and purple and grey. There was a small trickle of blood seeping from a deep graze where her number plate had embedded itself into his skin. His knee was swollen up to twice its normal size. 'I'm taking you to the hospital,' she said.

'No,' stated Phil, too firmly.

'Yes,' retaliated Nadine, disbelievingly, 'come on.'

'No. No hospitals. It's only a bruise. I just need to rest it.'

'Phil—you're bleeding. And look at the size of your knee. Will you please let me take you to the hospital—you should have this X-rayed.'

'No,' he stated again, 'I'm not going to the hospital. If it hasn't gone down by tomorrow, then I'll go.'

Nadine took a deep breath. 'OK,' she said, 'so let me take you home.'

Phil winced again and doubled over in agony. 'Aaaah,' he moaned under his breath, 'aaah. Have you got any painkillers?'

Nadine passed him a couple of Advils from her bathroom cabinet and headed towards the kitchen to get him a glass of water. As she stood over the sink, she started feeling a little uncomfortable. She still hadn't asked Phil what exactly he'd been doing hanging around in the rain outside her house at half past nine on a Friday evening and she wasn't sure that she wanted to.

She turned off the tap and headed back to the bathroom. Phil wasn't there. Her heart missed a beat. Maybe he'd gone. Gone away. Stumbled back out into the darkness. A selfish and worried voice deep inside her said, 'I hope so.'

She stuck her head around the living-room door—no sign of him. Neither was he in the toilet nor in the entrance hall. She pulled back the 1950s *Homemaker* print curtains in her living room and surveyed the street outside. It was empty.

And then she wandered into her bedroom, not expecting at all to find him sprawled all over the Bollywood duvet cover on her bed in nothing but his lemon briefs and a pair of black ribbed socks, smoking a cigarette and with the remote control for her TV in his hand.

'Had to lie down,' he said, sucking on his Rothman and wincing a bit theatrically. 'Don't suppose you've got a TV guide, have you?' He blew out a stream of smoke and regarded Nadine defiantly through faded-denim-blue eyes. He was challenging her, daring her to make him leave.

Nadine flinched a little in the face of his audacity. She didn't want him on her bed. She didn't want him in her flat. But what could she do? She'd nearly run him over out there. That was her fault. Bad driving, lack of concentration. And just look at the state of his leg—there was no way he'd be able to walk on that unaided, and she couldn't *force* him into her car, she couldn't force him to do anything.

She approached her bedside table stealthily and placed the glass of water on a mother-of-pearl coaster embedded with tiny little mirrors.

'There you go,' she said, in her best jolly voice. 'I'll—er—just get you a TV guide, then. Won't be a sec.'

'Cheers.' He was staring ahead at the TV, not even looking at her.

She glanced at him as she left the room, at the rock-star pallor, the twelve-year-old-girl legs, the white skin sprouting incongruous black hairs in places, the thin arms and the yellow briefs. An involuntary shudder worked its way up her body.

But the minute she walked into her living room she started feeling bad. Oh God, she thought. Poor Phil. Poor poor Phil. He's all alone in this world. His parents are dead. His house is burned down. And now I've run him over. None of this is *his* fault. None of it.

And it was me—*me*—who invited him back into my life. It was me who phoned him out of the blue and me who sat in a pub with him, ghoulishly pushing him for more and more details about the tragedy that was his life. He didn't ask to get involved with me again. He didn't force me to take an E. He didn't force me to have sex with him.

She sighed and began pulling animal-print cushions from her sofa as she searched for last week's Culture section from the *Sunday Times*. It was only one night, she told herself. Just one night. She would let him stay in her bed—she would sleep on the sofa—and then she'd drop him home tomorrow on her way to the airport.

It was the least she could do.

Chapter Six

THE FRONT DOOR SLAMMED, staccato heels clattered down the front steps and Digby bounced joyfully on to Dig's bed.

'OK,' thought Dig, chucking him under the chin, 'I'm awake now.' It was eight forty-five. Dig couldn't remember the last time he'd been awake before eleven on a Saturday morning. And not just awake, but unhungover and somewhat refreshed. He'd been in bed by ten thirty the previous night—because Delilah had wanted to turn in early—and pretty much stone-cold sober.

He stepped out of bed into a little rectangle of sunshine that was warming up his seagrass and strolled towards the window. As he pulled his curtains apart he saw Delilah on the street below. She was standing on the corner of Hilldrop Crescent and Camden Road looking around distractedly for a cab. She was wearing her sheepskin over a very smart suit and high heels, and her hair was held back from her face with sunglasses. In one hand she held her incredibly expensive-looking little Hermès doeskin attaché case and in the other a huge Hamleys carrier bag, poking from one corner of which was the tip of what looked like a large rabbit's ear. Dig scratched his head and wondered where the Hamleys bag had come from, what the rabbit was doing in it and how come he hadn't noticed it when he'd cleared the living room for dinner last night. Delilah must have hidden it somewhere. Why?

He watched as Delilah impatiently paced back and forth, swivelling her head constantly as she listened for the rumble of a cab. Dig untwisted the security lock on his sash window and lifted it up a couple of inches, letting in a blast of fresh autumn air and the roar of early-morning traffic.

A cab appeared on the horizon and Delilah lifted the attaché-attached hand to hail it. Dig pushed his head further through the gap in the window, straining to hear Delilah's voice above four lanes of traffic.

He was sick of this. Sick of tiptoeing around Delilah and avoiding the truth. Sick of doing everything in his power to make her life comfortable while she rewarded his efforts with nothing more than evasion, bad moods and the dubious honour of looking after her dog.

It was clear to Dig that the only way he stood a chance of getting close to Delilah now was to know all her secrets, to know everything that Dr Rosemary Bentall knew. And if she thought that he was too immature to deal with them, then he was going to uncover them for himself.

He poked his head a little further through the window and, as if by magic, just as Delilah grabbed hold of the cab door-handle and twisted her head towards the driver to tell him where she wanted to go, a hush fell across Camden Road. The traffic stopped and the wind died and Delilah's words were carried from her lips on a puff of fresh air and deposited on Dig's window-sill. 'Waterloo Station, please.'

Within two minutes Dig had dressed, knocked back half a mug of cold coffee left by Delilah in the kitchen, thrown on his leather coat, scooped Digby up in his arms and was pacing up and down Camden Road looking for a cab.

He briefly wondered at this strange, alien world, this early-morning

Saturday world peopled by the kind of men and women who didn't spend every Friday night down the pub, who didn't go to bed at two in the morning and who didn't have to spend their entire Saturdays stumbling from one attempt at curing their hangovers to another. There was something appealing about that, something refreshing. A whole new array of possibilities. His thoughts returned once more to the golden world of Nadine's imagination—the one with the kids and everything. It was becoming more alluring by the minute.

Dig flapped his free hand up and down like an overexcited schoolboy who knows the right answer when he saw a little amber lozenge glowing mutely in the distance. The cab pulled up next to him.

'Waterloo station, please—and I'm in a real hurry.'

'No problem,' said the driver, pleased at the prospect of a breakneck drive around the near-empty streets of London. 'No problem at all.'

It was 5.30 in the morning and Nadine was doing one of her five-minute, condensed, early-morning preparations. It was possible, if in a big enough rush, to do everything one normally squeezed into forty-five minutes in only five. She'd packed the night before, laid out her travelling outfit, put coffee, milk and sugar in a mug, and had a good long bath just before she had gone to bed so she wouldn't have to shower.

The only thing she had to do this morning that she didn't normally have to fit into her five-minute regime was to make sure that Phil was up and ready to go. She'd spent the night on her sofa, and when her alarm went off, the first thing she'd done was throw open the bedroom door and switch on the overhead light. It was cruel, but she didn't care—this was a military-style operation.

'How's your leg?' she'd said, when she popped her head around the door thirty seconds later.

'Uuuuuppphhhh,' Phil had said, throwing his arm over his face.

'Come on,' she'd said, all brisk efficiency, 'all you have to do is put your clothes on—here.' She lobbed them on the bed. 'You've got'—she looked at her watch—'two and a half minutes. Chop-chop.'

Thirty seconds later and Phil did not appear to have moved a muscle, let alone a limb.

'Phil! Will you please move it!'

'Fucking hell, Deen,' he mumbled, squinting at her from beneath his own elbow, 'you've turned into a right little sergeant-major.'

'Yes—well—lots of things about me have changed,' she said. 'Let me have a look at your leg.' She strode around to his side of the bed and flung the duvet back mercilessly.

Phil watched her carnivorously, a smug smile twitching the corners of his mouth. 'Ooh yes,' he drawled, 'I like you much more like this. All stern and Miss Whiplashy. Are you going to spank me?' He said this last in a flesh-crawlingly horrible little-boy voice.

Nadine blanched. Jesus. Who was this repulsive person?

She tutted and turned her attention to his leg, which resembled an overcooked chipolata sausage, all gnarled and blackened and knobbly. 'Jesus,' she said, 'you really are going to have to do something about that leg, you know. Do you want me to drop you at the hospital now, or can you make your own way there from home?'

Phil looked at Nadine with bemusement. 'I don't think I'm going anywhere, to be honest.'

Nadine let the duvet drop back over Phil's legs and regarded him with growing horror. 'What do you mean?'

'I mean—this leg ain't going to get me anywhere beyond the bedroom door, not for a while, anyway.'

'What? But it was fine yesterday—you walked all the way from the road to here and then you made it on your own from the bathroom to the bedroom and . . .'

Phil nodded. 'Yeah—that was *yesterday*. It's sort of seized up overnight.' He wiggled his leg and winced. 'It's gone all stiff. I can hardly move it. I reckon I'm gonna need a wheelchair to get me out of here.'

Nadine gulped. Her five-minute plan was unravelling—this was a nightmare. Part of her thought Phil was lying about his leg—he was in mighty high spirits for someone who was supposed to be a cripple. But what could she do? She could hardly accuse him of lying, could she? She couldn't yank him out of bed and into her car. The only thing she could do was believe him. And if she was going to believe him, then she was going to have to get the situation sorted. She couldn't leave him in her flat—alone—without her. It was unthinkable. She looked at her watch again. She had a bit more time now that she didn't have to drop Phil off at Finsbury Park, time to organise things.

Think—think—think . . . But the only thing that Nadine could think was that it was five thirty in the morning and there was no one—not even her father—who she would feel comfortable phoning at this time of day to help her remove an immobile ex-boyfriend from her flat.

She reached for the phone book.

'What are you doing?' asked Phil, suddenly alarmed.

'I'm going to call the hospital, see if they'll send someone round for you with a wheelchair.'

'No!' snarled Phil, grabbing her wrist, 'I told you—no hospitals.'

Nadine loosened his grip on her arm and eyed him uncomfortably. 'OK.' She placed the phone book carefully on the floor. 'Why not?'

'Because,' he said, 'because it's . . . er . . . I've got some stuff in my bloodstream that shouldn't be there—*comprende*? And the last thing I need right now is hassle off a junior doctor—all right?'

'OK—OK. I won't call the hospital. But I've got to call someone. Is there anyone I can call?' she asked hopefully. 'A friend or something—maybe that Jo girl—who could come and collect you, or sort out a wheelchair for you?'

Phil winced again and shook his head. 'Not at this time of the morning,' he breathed, 'no way. Jo's probably still out clubbing and, as you know'—he eyed her poignantly—'there's no one else . . .' He lowered his eyes and let his shoulders slump forwards.

Nadine was harpooned, once again, by guilt. Oh God. She kept forgetting. Every time she started feeling antipathetic towards Phil, he would say something to remind her how mean-hearted she was, she who had everything, a family, friends, a beautiful home—legs that worked.

She sighed and gave in to the guilt. It couldn't hurt, could it? To leave Phil here in her flat. I mean—what could he *actually* do, when you thought about it. Make a mess? Big deal. Eat all her food? It was only going to go off otherwise. Invite his young student friends over? Where was the harm in that. Still be here when she got back? She shuddered. No—that wasn't going to happen. No way.

'OK,' she said, firmly, 'you can stay. But promise you'll get some help. Promise you'll call Jo a bit later. Yes?'

Phil did that awful little-boy thing again, pouting ever so slightly. 'I pwomise,' he said, and Nadine had to fight back a burst of nausea.

'Right,' she said, backing uncertainly out of the room, 'I'm just going to load up the car. I'll be back in a second.'

She felt vaguely sick as she lugged boxes and boxes of aluminium-clad photographic equipment down her front steps and out to her Spider. It was still dark outside, and invisible birds chattered happily from shrouded tree tops. Jesus, she thought, am I mad? I'm leaving my beautiful flat, my refuge from the world, in the hands of Philip Rich, a man I was hoping just yesterday that I would never, ever see again as long as I lived. He's lying in my bed, in his foul underpants, on my lovely Indian-cotton sheets, under my Bollywood duvet cover *that I made with my own hands*, and I don't want him to be there, but there's nothing I can do because my flight to Barcelona leaves in two and a half hours and there's a team of models, hairdressers and stylists expecting to meet me in an hour, and if I'm not there I'll get sacked.

She threw her coat over the boxes in the boot to stop them being bounced about, slammed down the door and locked it, taking a deep breath to try to calm her nerves.

Back indoors, she opened the door to her bedroom, warily and heavily.

'Right,' she said, over-brightly, a spare set of keys clutched in one hand, and her bag slung over her shoulder, 'I'm off.' She walked briskly towards the bedside table and dropped the keys. 'Spare set of keys for you,' she said. 'Just drop them back through the letter box when you go. Make any phone calls you need and—um hope everything works out with the leg. And, Phil . . . I'm so sorry for what happened last night. I hope you can forgive me.' She forced a smile and Phil picked her hand up from where it hung at her side. Very slowly he brought her hand to his mouth and kissed the back of it, deeply, passionately and intensely.

'Nadine Kite,' he drawled, letting her hand drop from his lips but not letting go of it, 'you're the best. The best girl ever. I could so easily fall in love with you all over again, you know. In fact'—he smiled and squeezed her hand—'I think I might already have done.'

Nadine managed to extricate her hand from his without seeming rude and began backing away from him. Her face was flaming red, which was annoying, because Phil was arrogant enough to presume that she was blushing with desire and pleasure rather than the all-consuming revulsion and horror she was feeling.

'I really have got to go now, Phil,' she said, looking at her watch, 'I'll try calling later, from the airport, or something. Good luck.'

Phil stuck one hand in the air and smiled again. 'Farewell, lovely lady,' he said, in a pretend Shakespearean tone, and then performed a ridiculous little twiddle of his hand and the mock-bow of a courtesan.

Nadine smiled stiffly, found the door handle and left the room.

She felt horribly sad as she closed the door on her lovely little flat, like a mother forced to leave her beautiful daughter alone with a lecherous baby sitter. 'Sorry,' she mouthed as she made her way towards the car.

Dig slunk down in the back seat as he recognised the shape of Delilah's head in the cab in front, leaving just his eyebrow visible above the partition. His driver had certainly made up time, flying through the streets of north London, and now Dig's cab was sitting directly behind Delilah's at the traffic lights on the Strand, about to turn left on to Waterloo Bridge.

Dig glanced at his watch. It was twenty past nine. The lights changed and Dig grabbed the armrest as the cab took the corner a little too fast.

'*Which entrance do you want?*' came the tinny, disembodied voice of the driver as they approached the Imax cinema on Waterloo roundabout.

'*Eurostar? Mainline? The Underground? Which one, mate?*'

Oh God. He was going to have to say it, wasn't he? Ten years ago he'd have been excited at the prospect, but now—well, it was a bit embarrassing, really.

'Can you just, um'—he cleared his throat—'would you mind just following that cab?' He cringed a little as he heard the words leave his lips and saw the driver's eyebrows arch sceptically.

'*Bet you've wanted to say that all your life*,' he chuckled happily.

Delilah's cab pulled up in front of the creamy stone steps leading towards the main concourse of the station and Dig watched her extricating herself from the vehicle.

His cab squeaked to a halt behind hers and the driver eyed Dig as he attempted to pay the fare from an almost entirely prone position in the back seat, sliding a ten-pound note through the crack in the window and crouching down to open the door only once he was sure that Delilah had fully disembarked and was halfway up the steps.

As Dig picked his way carefully up the magnificent stairway, Digby started quivering with excitement in his arms. He could smell her—Delilah. He let out an excited, high-pitched groan and tried to wriggle his way out of Dig's arms, towards his mistress. 'Shhhh,' said Dig, clamping his hand over the dog's tiny, damp snout. 'Shhhh.'

On the concourse Dig hid behind a row of phone booths to watch Delilah's movements. She was striding towards the ticket office, her heels clicking against the marble flooring.

Dig waited until Delilah was firmly ensconced in a queue and then dashed furtively to a leaflet stand offering colourful information about day trips to Hampton Court and Loseley Park. He dropped his head and pretended to study the leaflets as Delilah picked up her change and turned to leave the ticket office.

Delilah was walking slowly now, heading back towards the far end of the station, past platform nine, eight, seven, six—stopping at the Accessorize shop, feeling up some fur wraps, leather gloves, fake pashminas, beaded handbags, before wandering past platform five, four, three, popping into Knickerbox, fingering bits of silk and satin, gingham bras and tiny jersey vest tops printed with rosebuds.

As she emerged she glanced up at the board above platform one. Dig followed her gaze from where he stood in the doorway of a closed pub, on the other side of the concourse. He squinted to make out the words: 9.52 to GUILDFORD via CLAPHAM JUNCTION.

OK, he thought, Guildford here I come.

Dig moved stealthily down the platform, following Delilah's swaying hips, and when Delilah stopped midway down the platform and mounted the train, Dig increased his pace. He got into the carriage one down from her, so that he could keep an eye on her through the adjoining windows. There she was, sitting with her back to his carriage, thankfully, and flipping through a sheaf of paper.

Between stations, Dig cupped his chin in his hand and stared through the window, watching as the tiny, rust-filled, overgrown gardens of Battersea, Clapham and Streatham gave way to the conservatories and aluminium-framed windows of Wimbledon, Kingston and New Malden. As the train slunk through Surbiton, Dig threw a furtive glance towards the next carriage. Delilah had stopped flicking through papers now and was staring out of the window, nervously nibbling at the skin around her fingernails. God, thought Dig, as inappropriately as ever, she really is so shockingly beautiful.

Anonymous station after anonymous station zipped by in little flashes of red, white and blue Network Southeast insignia, and within twenty minutes Dig found himself being deposited somewhere called Walton-on-Thames.

Delilah dismounted and turned left, leaving Dig in a perfect position to follow her unseen. His heart, which had slowed down while sitting on the train, resumed its frenetic tattoo as he pulled his sunglasses from his coat pocket and slipped them on.

Delilah disappeared into the ticket hall up ahead, and Dig quickened his pace, narrowing the gap between them. He rounded the corner into the ticket hall and saw Delilah crossing the road outside the station, striding purposefully away from him.

He headed briskly through the chilly hall and nearly jumped out of his skin when a man with a big scar on his cheek suddenly bellowed into his face, 'Can I see your ticket please, sir?'

Dig glanced at the man and then at the road opposite, where he could see Delilah shrinking to doll-sized proportions. Oh bloody hell. He could stay here and waste five minutes trying to sweet-talk this fellow into letting him off with a fine or he could just make a run for it.

'Sir, I need to see your ticket.'

Oh sod it. He clutched Digby tightly to him, threw the man a deeply apologetic look and legged it. It was a risk—but the risk paid off. The ticket collector sighed deeply and returned to his newspaper.

Dig stood impatiently at the edge of the road, waiting for a bus to complete its U-turn before dashing across towards the now empty street he'd last seen Delilah disappearing up.

Dig breathed in sharply and slowed down when he heard Delilah's heels echoing around the next corner—thank God, he'd been worried that she might have disappeared into one of the overgrown Wendy houses that lined this meandering avenue and that he would be left stranded in Walton-on-Thames for the rest of his life.

Finally, the interminable road gave way to a fork, and signs of civilisation and human life began to appear: a school, a church, a low-level office block, people. Within a few seconds a busy high street emerged, and Dig found himself jostling for space on the pavement with large, meaty-armed families, with nervously shuffling pensioners and pushchairs, prams and double buggies. Delilah kept striding.

Dig ducked into a doorway when Delilah stopped in her tracks ahead of him. What must he look like, he wondered, all sweaty and unkempt, with a weird dog, dashing around furtively and hiding in doorways?

Delilah was consulting one of her bits of paper, turning it round and viewing it from all angles in a manner that suggested she was looking at a map. Dig looked at his watch: 10.51am. They'd been walking for bloody ages. He hoped they were nearly there—wherever the hell 'there' was. He didn't think he could stand the suspense for much longer.

Delilah slid the piece of paper back into her doeskin attaché case and continued on her way, her heels beginning to echo again as the pedestrian population thinned out once more.

Outside a pink pub, she turned right, and Dig followed her down a steep footpath, his heartbeat increasing with every loose pebble his trainered feet dislodged. At the bottom of the footpath Dig stopped and caught his breath and had his first reality check of the day. What the *fuck* was he doing? Where was he? Why was he here? He didn't do things like this, people in films did things like this, not him.

The river lay beyond the fringe of trees in which Dig was hiding. Despite the name of the town, Dig was slightly surprised to find it there, wide and curved and sparkling, small flotillas of rented boats peopled by families in overcoats skimming the surface, a large lock to the left, a small reservoir to the right.

Finally, Delilah came off the path and disappeared up a small turning, and Dig breathed a sigh of relief as he realised that they were probably there. They had to be. He didn't want to walk any further.

At the top of the turning were three houses, set well back from the road and all backing directly on to the river. Delilah was walking towards the middle of the three houses, her pace diminishing, the Hamleys bag no longer swinging. Even from fifty feet away, Dig could hear her nervously clearing her throat.

He stationed himself behind a small skiff that was being decorated and had been left upturned, painted half white and half green. It was called 'Sun King' and had been pulled on to the verge, where it provided Dig with more than sufficient cover.

Delilah slowed down even more as she approached the large, handsome house. And then she did something really annoying. After all this, after a ten quid cab ride at the crack of dawn, after nearly being done for fare evasion, after walking through some godforsaken bit of Surrey for nearly half an hour, after everything that Dig had been through this peculiar morning to discover what Delilah was up to, she rewarded him by placing both of her bags on a bench and sitting on it.

Dig grimaced and ground his teeth. What the *hell* was she doing? Sitting down. In Walton-on-Thames. Sitting down—on a bench—for no discernible reason—just sitting there. In Walton-on-Thames. *Why?*

Dig took the weight off his toes and sat back on his bottom. The ground underneath was cold and damp, but he didn't care—he was knackered and hot, and now he was also deeply frustrated.

Delilah had crossed her legs on the bench and draped one elbow across the back of it. Dig watched her knock her sunglasses from the top of her head to her nose and then do something vaguely peculiar with her hair, arranging it over her face, almost as if she were drawing curtains, and then she turned up the collar of her sheepskin jacket. She was, Dig realised with a sense of mounting excitement, attempting to disguise herself. This was more like it, he thought gleefully, this was more like it. He was about to witness some kind of illicit rendezvous, some kind of espionage, something a bit . . . *exciting*.

Nearly an hour later Dig was starting to run out of enthusiasm.

His body had lost every degree of the heat it had built up on the walk here. His hands and nose were freezing and his arse had gone numb. He was starving hungry and bored stiff.

Nothing had happened for nearly an hour—Delilah was still sitting on the bench, still wearing her sunglasses and still hiding behind her hair.

Five more minutes, Dig told himself, and then I'm going home.

And then he heard something—a click, followed by another click, followed by laughter. Someone was finally coming out of one of the houses. He tucked Digby into his coat and rearranged himself to give himself a better view of the proceedings.

The front door of the middle house was wide open now and Dig could see the silhouetted form of a family as they jostled to leave the house, bickering and squawking and shouting. Delilah, he noticed, had swivelled slightly on the bench and was regarding the open door with interest, her fingertips touching the arm of her sunglasses.

'Maddie, stop it!' he heard a woman's voice shouting, in perfect Surrey tones. 'Leave the dog alone!'

A large Newfoundland bounded through the door and across the gravel, bearing a small child on his back, who was gently whipping the dog's bottom with a plastic ruler. 'Gee up, Monty! Gee up!' squeaked the pretty, dark-haired little girl.

'Get off the dog, Maddie!' A tall woman emerged from the house, carrying a large duvet and a pressure cooker. She was too thin and had obviously been extremely beautiful in her youth. Her hair was jet black and cut into a big tousled wedge which suited her. She was wearing an enormous ex-army greatcoat with a fur collar and green wellingtons.

She was followed by a young boy of about ten, who had his nose stuck in a Harry Potter book while simultaneously dribbling a football across the crackling gravel.

The mother pulled a clunking set of keys from her battered old handbag, selected one with her teeth and thrust it into the keyhole at the back of her silver Mercedes estate. The door sprung open, and the dog, the duvet and the pressure cooker landed in the boot.

'Maddie. Get into the car!'

The dark-haired boy kicked his football towards the garage and slid into the back seat, his eyes still glued to his Harry Potter book, and Maddie hopped into the back seat next to her brother.

Well, thought Dig, this is all very sweet—cute dog, cute girl, wonderful domestic vignette and all that—but what the hell has this got to do with anything?

The woman sounded her car horn and Dig jumped a mile. She wound down her car window and stuck her head through it.

'*Sophie!*' she roared, banging the car horn with the heel of her hand again in exasperation. '*Will you get down here immediately!*'

The front door squeaked open a few seconds later and Dig saw Delilah stiffening on the bench, cupping the side of her face with one hand in a further attempt, he presumed, to disguise herself, as a very tall and slim young girl emerged into the sunshine.

'*Honestly, mother,*' the young girl shouted, turning to look at her while she locked the front door behind her, '*the neighbours must think you're a bloody child-abuser.*' She tutted and tucked her door keys into the pocket of her rucksack. She looked about twelve years old, and was wearing black pedal-pushers, chunky fluorescent trainers and an outsized grey fleece. Her hair was long and parted in the centre and was a warm, shining golden-brown, in stark contrast to that of the other members of her dark-haired family. She was the sort of fresh-faced, lanky and even-featured young girl who Dig could imagine being approached in shopping centres by scouts from modelling agencies. She might have been only twelve, thirteen years old, but she was gorgeous.

As she walked around the car and approached the passenger door, Dig got a better look at her. Full, plump lips, wide blue eyes with dark lashes, creamy skin and a sulky, resentful attitude. Her mother said something to her as she slid into the passenger seat, and she smiled— a reluctant smile, he noticed—and as she smiled she turned towards Dig and, like a brick lobbed through a window, a thought splintered his mind.

Oh my God, she looks just like Leslie Ash in *Quadrophenia*.

He turned to look at Delilah, who hadn't moved a muscle since the young girl emerged from the house, and then he turned back to the girl, who was strapping herself into her seatbelt. Uncanny, he thought, uncanny the resemblance between the two, the same height, attitude, lips and smile, the same rangy figure, swaying hips and peaches-and-cream complexion. The same . . . exactly the same. Realisation coursed through him and he began to experience difficulty breathing. He was back in the playground at the Holy T, cross-legged on the grass, perusing his new timetable and experiencing the character-forming shock of seeing Delilah for the very first time. Jesus, he thought, this is eerie. That girl, he thought, that girl is the spitting bloody image of Delilah.

He turned to look at Delilah again, who was clutching the back of the bench with two white-knuckled hands and staring helplessly at the Mercedes as it reversed out of the driveway and away from her. Her hair had fallen away from her face and her jaw was slack with shock and dismay. As the car straightened itself out on the street, Delilah mindlessly pushed her sunglasses from her nose to her hair, and Dig could see tears shimmering on her cheeks. He felt bad. He felt elated. He felt cheated. He felt horrified. He felt scared. He felt excited.

He looked back at the car and at the girl in the passenger seat, who was now arguing with her brother in the back. Is it possible, he thought to himself, that that beautiful, sullen, wonderful girl, is my daughter?

Nadine hadn't had time today to think about Dig and Delilah, about Phil in her flat, about anything very much apart from exposure levels, light readings and F-stops. Which was a good thing. But then, after four hours of lugging all her equipment around the streets of Barcelona, sweet-talking policemen and bribing shopkeepers into letting her use locations, not to mention holding back the drooling crowds of men trying to get a look at Fabienne, the eighteen-year-old star of the new

Renault advertising campaign, in a gold-sequinned bikini, it had started raining. And Nadine had had to abandon the shoot for the day.

She was sitting in her hotel room now, listening to the rain ricocheting off the tiled roof overhead, and trying desperately to resist the temptation to phone home. It would do her no good at all to hear the sound of Phil's voice echoing down the line from hundreds of miles away. It would only upset her. Better not to know. But the second she managed to tear her thoughts away from Philip Rich, lying in all his underpanted splendour on her bed, in her flat, her mind filled instead with the equally alarming image of Delilah in Dig's flat, all scrubbed and shining and ready to have sex with Dig. Urgh. She shuddered at the thought.

Jesus, thought Nadine, last night was just *horrible*.

She looked at her watch. It was only three o'clock, but the dark, low cloud that hung over Barcelona made it feel more like early evening. She threw open the door of the mini-bar and eyed it furiously, challenging it to offer her *a real drink*, something that could even *begin* to take the edge off her wretchedness and misery, and sheer, belly-rotting jealousy. Come on, you pathetic excuse for a fridge.

She eyed a quarter-bottle of Louis Roederer and a dinky little bottle of Jose Cuervo. There was something horribly sad about the idea of doing tequila slammers alone, in the middle of the afternoon but, in her current frame of mind, it appealed to her.

She pulled a tooth mug off her bedside table, poured in the little bottle of tequila, filled it to the top with lovely, cold, frothing champagne, covered it with her hand, slammed it down hard on the table-top and necked it in one.

The bubbles and the taste made her shudder. Disgusting. She burped loudly and licked the champagne off the palm of her hand.

The alcohol reacted immediately, lending a lovely soft focus to the room, the view from her window and her mood. Now she wanted a cigarette. Not just wanted but *craved* a cigarette. Her room was non-smoking. Her window was fixed closed.

She poured the remainder of the champagne into the mug, gulped it down, put on her shoes and a cardigan, picked up her door key and made her way downstairs to the hotel bar.

Nadine was hidden in a cosy little corner of the bar, nestled on to a tiny, squishy sofa but within easy eye-contactable distance of the barman. It was five thirty and it was still raining outside. Nadine was drunk.

'God—there you are! Thank God!' A small pixie-faced girl with cropped black hair collapsed next to Nadine on the sofa. 'We've been looking everywhere for you.' It was Pia. 'Fabienne's doing all the shops in the lobby and Sarah's doing a corridor-by-corridor trawl for your butchered body. We've been phoning your room all afternoon. I was about to call the police.'

'God, I'm sorry,' said Nadine, suddenly very conscious of her lips not working in harmony with her tongue, of the fact that if she didn't watch out she could very easily start slurring. 'I didn't think. I'm sorry.'

Pia grimaced. 'You're *pissed* aren't you? Breathe on me,' Pia ordered, pointing her minute nostrils towards Nadine's mouth. Nadine let out a small puff of air. 'You are! You're drunk! Blimey, Deen. It's not even six o'clock yet, and you're off your trolley! Well,' she said, getting to her platformed feet, 'there's only one thing for it. I'm going to find Sarah and Fab and get them down here. I expect a full round of whatever that is you're drinking, on the table by the time I get back. OK?'

'OK.'

Pia was back within minutes with Sarah, the Sloaney, blonde, pencil-thin make-up artist, and Fabienne, the voluptuous and ripe-fleshed Renault-ad girl. Nadine supposed that in company like this she was probably the dumpy redhead with the stupid clothes on. Nadine smiled to herself. She didn't care. She *loved* drinking with beautiful women. You got loads of attention and everyone talked to you. Nadine settled down to enjoy what was obviously going to be a top girly night.

By eight o'clock the previously sedate bar had exploded into Saturday-night mayhem, due to the quartet of English girls drinking champagne cocktails in the corner. Pia had been entertaining them, as ever, with hilarious accounts of the men in her life, peppering her stories with well-chosen swear-words and physical demonstrations of various events using her tiny little stick-drawing body to great comic effect. Nadine was so drunk by now that she was hugely appreciative of Pia's diverting behaviour, meaning as it did that she could just sit there grinning like a fool and not have to make any kind of intelligent conversation, when she suddenly realised that Sarah was asking her a question.

'Sorry,' she muttered, pulling herself back into the proceedings.

'I said, are you still going out with that really cute-looking bloke I met last time I saw you?' said Sarah.

Nadine racked her mind. The last time she'd seen Sarah socially was about six months ago when she was going out with? . . . with? . . . Jimmy, of course, the thirty-nine-year-old chiropodist who was—well, not *bad*-looking as such, but certainly not what you would describe as a 'really cute-looking bloke'. Sarah couldn't possibly mean Jimmy.

'You know,' said Sarah, noticing Nadine's confusion, 'the guy with the big eyebrows—he had some kind of weird name. The A&R guy.'

Nadine choked on her cocktail. 'What!' she exclaimed, wiping her chin with the back of her hand. 'You mean Dig?'

'That's it,' cried Sarah, 'Dig! I knew he had a silly name. Yeah, Dig. What happened to him—are you still seeing him?'

Nadine laughed over-loudly and shook her head. 'Dig and I are just friends,' she said, 'we're not going out together.'

'God, you're joking,' said Sarah, 'could have sworn the two of you were as together as Posh and Becks. There was a real chemistry there. I remember it really well—he had his arm around your shoulders.'

'Yeah, well,' said Nadine, 'we've known each other for a long time. We're very affectionate with each other.'

Sarah was shaking her head. 'No,' she said, 'no. There's more to it than that. I told Neil about you two when I got home that night. I said to him that I'd never been able to understand why you never went out with decent men, but that it looked like you'd finally found one.'

Nadine laughed again. This wasn't the first time someone had told her what a lovely couple she and Dig made—many other people had made that mistake over the years—but tonight, with her heart broken and her head full of Delilah and all the stuff that had happened over the last week, it was hugely reassuring to hear. Her stomach did a strange floppy thing that made her feel all weak. She wanted to hear more about what a great couple they made. She needed to hear it.

'So why haven't you two ever got it together?' asked Sarah. 'Is he gay?'

Nadine snorted and slapped her thighs. 'Dig? God, you're joking. He's deeply heterosexual. *Too* heterosexual, if anything.'

'So why not? Oh—don't tell me. He's trapped in some long-term relationship with the wrong woman?'

'No! He's a serial monogamist, like me—except his relationships are even shorter than mine.'

'So, the two of you are unattached, you're affectionate with each other, you're best friends and you've known each other half your lives?'

Nadine nodded.

'Why the hell aren't you going out together? That's more than most supposed couples have going for them, y'know?'

Nadine nodded again and felt a little hysteria building in her stomach.

'Don't you fancy him, even a little bit?' asked Pia, nudging her playfully in the ribs.

Nadine was about to give her usual knee-jerk response to this question, asked of her in the past, many times. 'Oh no,' she was about to sneer, 'he's too small for me.' That's what she always said. And then she'd make some joke about his skinny legs and his big eyebrow and his sticky-uppy hair, and everyone would laugh and the subject would get dropped immediately. But tonight—tonight she was going to be honest. She needed to get it off her chest, off-load on to someone else the frightening realisation that she was in love with her best friend.

Nadine looked at Pia and grinned mischievously. 'We-ell,' she grinned, and all three girls began screeching with pleasure, 'he is kind of cute.' Blood rushed to Nadine's head as the words left her lips. She felt strangely excited and unburdened. Her mind started sending her picture postcards from the past. There was one postmarked September 12, 1987, a shot of Dig wandering down Bartholomew Road in the dark, jumping up on that wall when he didn't know she was looking and punching the air. There were the doodles she'd drawn all over her old diary when she was a teenager. *Nadine Ryan Nadine Ryan Nadine Ryan.* And there was Dig's old kite, the one he'd given her the day they went to Primrose Hill. *Dig 'n' Deen, September 13, 1987, For ever.*

More pictures flashed through her mind. Flying kites on Southend beach with Dig and his dad. Waiting for buses on Saturday mornings with Dig to go down to the Notting Hill Record and Tape Exchange.

She pictured Dig's flat, his spotless little kitchen, his plumped-up cushions and fluffed-out duvet. She imagined the two of them, sitting side by side on his blue-cord sofa drinking big bottles of Bud, watching the telly, smoking and snuggling up to each other, the warmth where their thighs pressed together, the weight of his head on her shoulder, the smell of his sweet, beery breath when he turned to share a joke with her. All that stuff she'd taken for granted for ten years, all that lovely, warm, easy, intimate Diggy stuff. All that lovely stuff that Delilah was currently getting her perfectly manicured mitts all over.

As these thoughts surged through her mind, Nadine became filled with a sense of resolve and strength. She couldn't let Delilah win, not again, not this time.

Nadine squinted to focus and glanced at her watch. Quarter past eight. Quarter past seven in London. She felt her pocket for her door key, got up from her seat without a word and strode purposefully towards the lifts. A smile twitched at the corners of her mouth while she waited for the smoothly humming lift to slink its way down to the foyer and collect her.

In her room, Nadine threw off her shoes and landed with a bounce on her freshly made bed. She found the bit of laminated plastic that gave instructions on how to make an international call and began dialling.

She was going to tell Dig that she was in love with him.

Her heart raced as she waited for the call to connect. 'Come on,' she muttered to herself, 'come on, pick it up.' The phone rang, five times, six times, seven times, and Nadine was about to hang up when there was a click, a second's silence and the muffled sound of someone's skin rubbing against the mouthpiece. Nadine caught her breath.

'*Hello?*' came a woman's breathless voice.

Nadine dropped the receiver and it landed with a crash on to the cradle. Delilah. Delilah Lillie. Answering Dig's phone. In Dig's flat on a Saturday night. The slightly insane smile that had been etched on to Nadine's face for the last quarter of an hour disappeared. Stinging, salty tears sprung to her eyes, taking its place.

Nadine pulled a handful of Kleenex from the box on her bedside table and rubbed her damp face into them. Her hysterical happiness turned to hysterical misery, and the more she wiped away her tears, the more she produced. She'd lost again—lost to Delilah Lillie. She'd had ten years to love Dig, to have Dig, to be Dig's—*ten years*. And she'd left it a week too late.

Chapter Seven

DIG HAD SAT NUMBLY for a moment after the family disappeared in their Mercedes estate, unable to absorb what had just taken place. He looked over at Delilah, who had turned to face the water and was staring pensively across the river, and, for a moment, he desperately wanted to rush over to her and take her in his arms and share her trauma.

Instead he waited for a while and watched her. After a few minutes she stood up, picked up her two bags and strode towards the middle house. She stopped at the front door, pulled the gigantic bunny from inside the Hamleys bag and perched it on the doorstep.

It was a grey and white rabbit, with a large bow round its neck, and was carrying in its paws a red-felt heart with the words 'Birthday Girl' printed on it.

Jesus Christ, Dig thought, this is so heavy. And then he started doing some pretty basic maths. Today was November 21. He counted nine months backwards on his fingers: February 21. Delilah's eighteenth birthday. The last time they'd had sex. The last time they'd been happy together. Just before everything had gone sour and Delilah had disappeared. Oh God. Dig dropped his forehead on to his fist with frustration and confusion. This was so heavy, so unbelievably heavy.

Delilah was crouched down on the front doorstep of the middle house. She was fussing with the rabbit, arranging it, trying to balance it. She leaned in towards it, and Dig was rooted to the spot with sadness and tenderness when he saw her suddenly grab it in her arms and squeeze it tightly, her face buried against its cheek and tears rolling down her face.

Enough, he thought to himself, I've seen enough.

He got to his feet and very quickly, before she turned around, scampered down towards the towpath and ran, through the crowds, along the river, down the high street and back to the station.

His thought processes were dizzying as he went from train to Tube, from Tube to bus and from bus to front door. Absolutely breathtaking. He was frightened, exhilarated and nauseated, all at the same time.

Most days the most important thing Dig had to think about was his car breaking down or having a row with Nadine or forgetting to send his mum a Mother's Day card. Today he was being forced to reconsider his entire existence, his history, his identity.

He felt bigger, physically larger, as he paced his flat back and forth that afternoon, waiting for Delilah to get back. He felt older, too, like all those people he'd seen out and about at quarter to nine this morning.

His initial instinct was to say nothing to Delilah when she returned. He might have been reeling from the shock of it all, but Delilah would be feeling worse. He'd spied on one of the most intensely private moments of her life. He'd been somewhere he had no place to be. He felt guilty. The last thing Delilah would need on her return from such a traumatic event was Dig sticking his nose in, asking questions, turning the whole shocking situation into his own drama.

But as afternoon turned to evening and the sky darkened and his head became so inflated with questions it felt like it would explode, his mood changed. He became angry. Delilah was in the wrong. No matter whether that beautiful girl was her daughter or not and whether he was the father or not, no matter what the truth of the situation, Delilah should have involved him. She should have told him why she was in London. She'd treated him like a child with no capacity for dealing with adult realities. Which was, he supposed, true on many levels. But still, she'd found other uses for him, hadn't she? He was grown-up enough to own the flat she was staying in, to have paid cash for the sofa-bed she was sleeping on, and he was responsible enough, apparently, to look after her precious dog every day.

As his frustration and impatience had grown during the course of the afternoon he'd tried phoning Nadine. Over and over. He'd never before needed to speak to Nadine so badly, never needed to hear her voice, the voice of normality and routine, of lightheartedness and easiness, the voice of his best friend in the world. He didn't care about all that awfulness the previous evening. He just wanted to see her. But where was Nadine when he needed her? Not at home, that was for sure. Nadine's absence in his hour of need had served only to compound his sheer, throbbing panic, and by the time he heard the key in the lock and lifted himself from the sofa to confront Delilah at the front door, he'd lost all sense of reason. He no longer cared whether or not Delilah was emotionally ready to discuss the girl in Surrey, and he was no longer ashamed of his act of deception and craftiness in following her there this morning. All Dig cared about now was getting answers to questions.

'So,' began Dig, 'what happened to the rabbit?'

Delilah jumped and clutched her heart. 'Oh God, Dig,' she said, 'you nearly gave me a heart attack.' She hooked her sheepskin on to the coat-stand and clicked the front door shut behind her. Digby bounced off the sofa and went hurtling towards her. Dig leaned against the living-room doorpost and folded his arms.

'What did you do with the rabbit?'

Delilah glanced at him curiously and then with concern. 'What rabbit?' she asked, slipping her sunglasses off her head and dropping them on to a table before heading off to the kitchen.

'Oh, you know, the big one with the floppy ears. You had him when you left the house this morning.'

Delilah stopped in her tracks for a moment and then spun round towards Dig. 'Ah!' she said, brightly, '*that* rabbit.'

'Yes,' said Dig, '*that* rabbit.'

'Oh he was a—er—gift. For a little girl I know. In Surrey. It was her—um—birthday.' She pulled open the fridge and removed a large jar of pickled onions, twisted off the lid nervously and forced an onion the size of a satsuma into her mouth. 'Mmmm,' she mumbled through the sphere, 'yummy.'

Dig looked at her with disbelief.

'Did she like it?'

'Hmm?'

'The little girl. In Surrey. Did she like the rabbit?'

Delilah shrugged and crunched. 'Yes. I think so.' She popped another onion in her mouth, picked up the jar and walked out of the kitchen.

Dig leaned back against the work surface and put his face in his hands. Great, he thought, bloody great. I really am a *smooth* operator, aren't I? I really handled that so well.

It was time to start this all over again.

'Delilah,' he said, striding into the living room, 'I know about Sophie.'

His heart bounced into his throat as the words left his mouth. It was the most dramatic thing he'd ever said in his life. He suddenly felt like an actor playing a part in a silly soap opera.

Delilah looked up at him. She'd been unzipping her black-suede boots. She kicked one off mindlessly and continued to stare at Dig.

'What?'

'Sophie. I know about Sophie.'

'Sophie who?'

Dig walked over to the sofa and sat down next to Delilah. He turned towards her, looked into her red eyes and felt himself relax. He stopped feeling like a soap actor.

'I followed you today, Delilah. I followed you to Surrey and to the river. I watched you. I saw everything.'

Delilah froze momentarily, one boot suspended from her hand.

'I saw the girl. I saw Sophie. She's beautiful . . .'

Delilah placed the boot carefully on the floor and rested her hands on her kneecaps. She stared into space for a moment and then turned towards Dig. 'Why did you do that, Dig?' she sighed, and Dig suddenly felt ten years old again.

'I don't know,' he shrugged. 'I didn't give it too much thought really. Just saw you outside, waiting for a cab this morning, and something snapped. I didn't plan it, or anything . . .' He tailed off.

There was a moment's silence, leaving Dig more than enough time to ponder his lack of emotional finesse. There were a million questions he could ask her right now, but only one truly definitive one. He took a deep breath and opened his mouth.

'Is she—Sophie—is she mine?'

Delilah spun round and stared at him. Dig held his breath. This was it. This was, potentially, the biggest moment of his life.

Delilah's eyebrows knitted together and she frowned. And then she grimaced. 'No,' she stated, 'of course not.'

Dig exhaled, felt his heart start beating again, a little too fast. He licked his dry lips and nodded distractedly. 'Ah,' he murmured, feeling curiously deflated, 'of course not.'

Dig took a deep breath and forced himself to keep pushing. He hadn't come this far to let it all slip away again.

'But she is yours—right?'

Delilah was silent again. She let out a huge sigh and turned towards Dig. 'I can't believe you followed me, Dig. I really can't.' There was a trace of disappointment in the tone of her voice which cut right through him like a switchblade.

He looked at her then and felt suddenly and icily detached from her. Who was she? Who the hell was this girl, who he thought had left him twelve years ago because she was scared of commitment but who'd actually gone off and had someone else's baby, who lived some fairy-princess existence in the countryside that he couldn't even come close to relating to, who had a horrible dog and terrible taste in music, who was incapable of hanging up a wet towel or cleaning a cup?

The Delilah of his dreams and memories was a girl; this person eyeing him with disappointment and disdain was a woman, a woman who'd given birth and had to give her child away, a woman who had moved on in her life and had left her past behind her. Including him.

He'd been a fool to imagine that there was a future for him and Delilah. He felt faintly ridiculous to have ever considered such a notion.

Dig suddenly felt a burst of intense anger.

'Jesus, Delilah,' he shouted, 'what the hell was I supposed to do? You turn up here at my flat without warning, you—you kiss me in the back of a cab, you dump your dog on me, you make—you make—you make a . . . a . . . *mess*, you tell me *nothing* about what you're doing here. You treat me like a mug. You haven't made me a casserole. I clean up after you all the time. And then I ask you a perfectly *normal* question and you don't even give me the decency of a straight answer. I'm sorry, Delilah, if I stuck a toe into your private areas, but I didn't know what else to do.'

Dig gulped when he realised he'd just said 'stuck a toe into your private areas'. What a ludicrous thing to say . . .

'I just want some answers, Delilah,' he sighed, before getting up off the sofa and walking meaningfully towards the kitchen.

He pulled open the fridge door and enjoyed the blast of cold air against his flushed skin. He picked up the last of his big Buds and made a pig's ear of trying to get the lid off on the corner of the work surface before giving up and taking it off with a bottle-opener. Had he ever, he wondered, been less cool?

He stomped back into the living room and sat next to Delilah again.

She turned towards him and placed a cool hand over his hot one. Her face had softened. 'Dig. I'm sorry. You're right. I've been unfair. I hadn't really thought about any of this from your point of view. I've been so preoccupied, trying to track the family down, trying to avoid . . . trying not to see other people, and you've been so patient and so sweet. You've kept out of my way and I don't know what I'd have done without you.'

Dig pulled his hand away. 'There you go again,' he said, 'you're doing it again, treating me like a pet, or something, treating me like Digby here.' He pointed at the dog. 'Well, you might have named him after me but I am *not* a Yorkshire terrier, Delilah, I am not your pet,' he finished indignantly, his features set with pride, his thoughts in shock at the sheer idiocy of some of the things he was coming out with this evening.

Quote of the Night: 'I am not a Yorkshire terrier', closely followed by 'you haven't made me a casserole'. It wasn't like this on the television.

'Look, Delilah. I'm not very good at this sort of thing, as you've probably noticed. But I'm confused. I appreciate what you must have gone through for the last week—well, the last twelve years, I imagine. I appreciate how hard this must all have been for you, how emotional and tough. And I understand why you kept it all from me, I really do. But I haven't had a moment's peace since you kissed me in the back of the cab on Tuesday. You sent me down the wrong turning when you did that. Made me think you were here because of me. You being here has made me re-evaluate my entire life. I was *happy* before you turned up. And then you kissed me. And then you moved into my flat. And then I thought we'd had a bloody kid. I've fallen out with my best mate over you. And now—and now, I'm just in a right old two and eight.'

Nice finish, he thought, really stylish closing line.

'Please include me in your life, Delilah,' he said, 'please tell me everything. What happened twelve years ago?'

Delilah pinched the bridge of her nose between two fingers. 'God, I've made a real mess of this, haven't I?' she sighed. 'It wasn't supposed to be like this. I was just supposed to come to London, find Isab- find Sophie, have a look at her, make sure she was all right and then decide what to do about . . .' She cast her gaze downwards, cryptically, towards her crotch. Dig eyed her with confusion but she ignored him and carried on. 'I had no idea I was going to bump into you and Nadine and how that was going to make me feel.'

'How d'you mean?'

'Look—I saw you first, on Saturday, in the park. I saw you before you saw me and I actually sped up, you know, to avoid you.'

'Why?'

'It just wasn't part of the plan. But then you saw me and you caught up with me and I found myself feeling nostalgic. And I thought, why not? Why not have a bit of fun while I'm in London. You know, I'm the same age as you and Nadine, but the life I live and the life I've *lived*, I feel like a middle-aged woman most of the time. Which is fine. But when I sat there in that coffee-shop with you and Nadine I suddenly felt so old and you seemed so young, with your wacky clothes and your free-and-easy lifestyles, and I was so envious of you both.

'So I went back to Marina's and started thinking about the old days, about going to gigs with you and wearing outrageous clothes and behaving like a rebel, and I suddenly really missed that person. I missed that person who didn't give a toss what anyone thought, who was streetwise and rude and true to herself. So I met up with you. I wanted a holiday from being Delilah Biggins, Chester Wife, I wanted a night out as Delilah Lillie, Kentish Town Rebel, and there was no one I enjoyed being Delilah Lillie with more than you, Dig.

'It was only going to be the one night. That's why I kissed you, I suppose. I didn't think I'd ever see you again, and I was so full of adrenalin and so excited to be out with you, away from Alex, away from the country and back, very briefly, in my youth, that I just got carried away. And I kissed you. I shouldn't have. I know you, Dig. I know how sensitive you are. I should have realised how seriously you would have taken that kiss. It was stupid and self-indulgent of me. Please forgive me . . . I didn't mean to lead you on.'

Dig nodded sagely, wondering at the irony of a beautiful woman asking his forgiveness for kissing him on the lips.

'I didn't think twice about turning up here and asking you for a bed. You've always been one of the kindest-hearted men I knew, Dig. It didn't occur to me that you still had any feelings towards me—I felt like a charity case, not a woman, when I turned up on your doorstep. I was so desperate, I didn't think about your feelings. I'm sorry. And I'm sorry about the mess. I'm terrible, I know that. I always mean to be tidier—I always intend to put things away—but then I get distracted and I completely forget. And as for the casserole,' she smiled, 'let me take you out for one. Tonight. Please! I'll take you anywhere you like, for any kind of casserole you like.'

'How about a curry-flavoured one?' teased Dig.

'Absolutely,' smiled Delilah, 'a curry-flavoured casserole it is.'

'God, Delilah. I'm sorry to have lost my temper with you like that. It was out of order and it was selfish. It's just been so frustrating, and then I've spent all day thinking I was a dad.' He laughed wryly. 'I shouldn't have got on your case—not after the day you've had. You must be feeling shitty.'

Delilah shook her head and smiled again. 'D'you know what?' she said. 'I'm really not. I thought I would be, but I'm not. Because she's fine, isn't she? Sophie's just fine. The woman who adopted her—her mother—seems a bit of a panicker, but then, maybe if my mother had been a bit more like her . . . She's just fine. Lovely house, brother and sister, she's got everything. The thing I was most scared of was that she'd look like her father—that I'd see him in her. But he's not there—not at all. She's all me. She's fine.'

'Delilah,' said Dig, seriously, 'promise me, over dinner, promise me you'll tell me everything. About Alex and Sophie and who her father is and what happened? Yes?'

'Yes,' nodded Delilah, 'I promise.'

'Bengal Lancer?'

'Bengal Lancer sounds great.'

Dig grabbed his coat and passed Delilah her sheepskin, and just as they were about to leave the house, the phone rang.

'Leave it,' he shouted out to Delilah, 'let the answerphone pick it up.'

'No,' she said, 'I'll get it.'

She was frowning when she wandered back into the hall a few seconds later.

'Who was it?' asked Dig.

She shrugged. 'God knows,' she said, 'they hung up when I answered. I did 1471 but it was *"from a network which doesn't transmit numbers"*.'

Dig shrugged, too, and held the front door open for Delilah.

At the Bengal Lancer, Archad greeted Dig warmly and with surprise.

'You are very early this evening,' he joked, looking at his watch, and Dig thought, Yes, I am—I have never, in fact been here before eleven o'clock, I have never been here sober and I've never said a word to you that wasn't pliant with alcohol.

Archad seated them in a booth at the back of the restaurant and handed them a pair of menus, smiling with excitement at Delilah as he backed away. As Dig looked at Delilah across the table he had a sudden *déjà vu*—the two of them, in Exmouth Market, on Tuesday night—when he'd been so entranced by her, so thrilled to be sitting in a restaurant with *Delilah Lillie*, the Love of his Life, praying that she'd stay in London, hoping that . . . hoping that—What had he been hoping? Hoping that something would happen, he supposed, that someone would let him fall in love with them, *hoping that something would change.*

And there was no denying that things had changed, although not in any of the ways he might have imagined. It had been a week of firsts.

He'd woken up before nine on a Saturday and arrived at the Lancer before eleven. He'd taken a woman out to dinner, he'd been seen in public with a Yorkshire terrier, and he'd been to Walton-on-Thames. But most importantly, he felt unblocked. He felt free and alive. Delilah had changed everything. He was ready for love.

'Are you ready to order?'

'Yeah,' he said, closing his menu. He didn't have to look at the menu to know what he was going to order. 'So, what are you going to do now?'

'What do you mean?'

'Well—now that you've found Sophie. What are your plans?'

He tensed his body as he waited for her to answer. Please say you're going home, he thought, please say you'll be packing those enormous suitcases and going back to Chester with your weird dog. Please.

'Are you trying to get rid of me?' teased Delilah, grinning at Dig.

'No!' he almost shouted. 'No! Of course not. I just wondered . . .'

'Well. I guess I'll be going back home. To Alex.'

'Is that what you want?'

She nodded. 'More than anything. I've missed him so much.'

'I don't get it,' said Dig, 'if Alex means so much to you, why didn't you tell him you were coming to London? Why did you leave him? You must have really hurt him.'

Delilah nodded again, stiffly, and Dig was alarmed to notice her eyes glaze over with tears. Oh shit—now he'd made her cry.

'I'm sorry,' he said, grasping her hand, 'I didn't mean to . . .'

She shook her head. 'It's all right,' she said, 'it's fine. It's just that—you're right. I should have told him what I was doing but I was in such a state, it was all so unexpected, I couldn't think about anything else for two weeks and then I just took off. I just never thought it would happen to us, it didn't seem possible, and I never wanted it, I really never wanted it and . . .'

'Delilah!' barked Dig. 'Slow down, for God's sake. I've got no idea what you're talking about.'

'Oh God—I'm pregnant, Dig! I'm pregnant. Can you believe it? We had sex three times this year *and* we used a diaphragm and I still managed to get pregnant!'

Dig clicked his hanging jaw closed. 'A-ha,' he said.

'And I never wanted a baby. Never. What would I know about being a mother? Look at the example I had.' She raised her eyebrows indignantly. 'I've already given one away and I don't want to do that again. But I can't have a baby, Dig, I just can't! I don't want one and Alex would be so angry. He complained enough when I got the dog.'

Dig was panicking. More heavy stuff. Oh God. 'Can't you—you know,' he stammered, 'can't you?'

'Get rid of it? Oh God—I've thought about it. That was one of the reasons why I came down to London. I couldn't have an—an—a termination at home. It would have been round Chester in seconds, and it's no one's business, is it?' She eyed him angrily. 'And ever since I found out I was pregnant I haven't been able to stop thinking about Isab— about Sophie. She's been haunting me. I suddenly felt like I couldn't make any decisions about this'—she looked at her groin again and Dig realised what she'd been trying to say earlier on when she'd eyed her crotch so cryptically—'until I'd put a full-stop on the Sophie chapter. The agency told me she'd gone to a good family, a nice family, but at the time I didn't care. I just wanted her away from me—gone. I couldn't bear to look at her or touch her. I didn't care where she went to live just so long as I never had to see her again. Because, you see, she looks like me now, but when she was born she looked just like him—she really did.'

'The father?'

She nodded, and her face hardened, and Dig sensed that they were approaching the crux of the matter. He leaned back into the red velvet of the banquette and waited for Delilah to start talking.

Silver Toenails

The sun was shining the day after Delilah's eighteenth birthday. She'd spent the previous night at Dig's, as she did nearly every night. He'd taken her out for a birthday treat to a wine bar off Oxford Street and they'd shared a bottle of Mateus Rosé and felt like grown-ups. Her mother's house was empty when Delilah let herself in at nine thirty. She'd left a birthday card outside Delilah's bedroom door. It was the first time her mother had remembered her birthday in ten years, and Delilah felt a curious surge of warmth rising in her chest.

In her bedroom, Delilah ripped open the envelope and pulled out an embossed card with a picture of a girl riding a pony on the front.

Daughter Dearest, said the printed message inside the card,
Once you were a tiny thing, with toes and thumbs so small
And now you are a woman, strong and proud and tall
I've fed you and I've loved you, I've nurtured you through strife
But now it's time to let you go and learn to live your life
I'm so proud of you, daughter dearest
Happy 18th Birthday

She'd signed it 'All love, Mum' and she'd even scribbled a couple of kisses underneath her name. Delilah felt choked with strange emotions. Despite the fact that a stranger had worded the message inside the card, it was her mother who had chosen it. It was the kindest, least selfish thing her mother had ever done. Delilah felt a wondrous sense of her life opening up: she and Dig were going to get engaged, he was going to get them a place to live, she could sign on at last and stop working at that shitty chemist, and now this—an unprecedented gesture of maternal love. The future looked brighter than it had ever done before.

She had a bath, washed her hair, slipped into her dressing gown and enjoyed the rare peace and quiet in her usually chaotic home. On her bed, she stretched out a long, white leg, picked up a bottle of silver nail polish and began to paint her toenails.

Downstairs, the front door slammed shut, loudly enough to make Delilah jump. She got to her feet and peered down the stairwell, towards the front door ahead.

It was Michael, her stepfather. He was leaning heavily against the door, his clothing awry, his face caked in dirt and bloody scabs.

'What happened to you?' she said, climbing down the stairs. Michael looked at her sheepishly. 'Jesus Christ, look at your face.'

Delilah had known Michael since she was five years old. He was a quiet, repressed, almost terminally shy man who rarely spoke. Delilah suspected he had learning difficulties. He'd been teetotal when he'd met Delilah's mother, just after her father died of cirrhosis, but thirteen years and five children later was a consummate drinker, his life punctuated by pub opening times and visits to the off-licence.

Michael let Delilah manoeuvre him into the front room and on to the threadbare sofa. He stank. She peeled his leather jacket from his obese frame and threw it over the arm of the sofa.

'Where've you been, Michael? What's happened?' Delilah often found herself talking to Michael as though he were a child.

Michael shook his head distractedly.

'Did someone hit you?'

He opened his mouth to speak and Delilah was almost knocked sideways by his vaporous breath. 'Oh Jesus, Michael, you're pissed. It's bloody ten o'clock in the morning and you're pissed.'

'Your mother,' he said, shaking his head slowly, 'your mother.'

'What did she do?'

'She kicked me out, didn't she? Kicked me out last night. Your mother. Hadn't even finished eating my tea. And it was sausages and all.'

'Why did she kick you out, Michael?'

He shrugged. 'Hadn't even finished my tea . . .'

Delilah raised her eyebrows. She wasn't going to get any sense out of him, that much was obvious. 'Here,' she said, 'I'll go and put the kettle on, make us both a coffee, eh?'

'Yes please, D'lilah—that would be nice.'

Delilah had always felt sorry for Michael. He'd gone straight from the home of his overbearing and abusive mother into the home of another overbearing and abusive woman, taken on her four children and given her another five. Despite the indubitable quality of his sperm, there was no respect in this household for Michael, and now that Delilah was escaping, could see a future beyond these four oppressive walls, she almost wanted to help him. He was more a victim of the Lillie curse than her, in a lot of ways. He was never going to escape.

She walked back into the front room holding the two mugs of coffee. Michael looked pathetic—fat, unkempt, drunk and pointless.

'There you go,' she said, guiding the mug into his dirty fingers, making sure he'd got a firm grip on it.

She stood over him while he took a first tentative sip. As he put the mug down, Delilah could see he was smiling.

'Thank you, D'lilah,' he said, 'thank you.'

And for a moment Delilah felt warm and good.

'Delightful . . . de-lovely . . . delicious . . . Delilah,' said Michael. He laughed to himself under his breath. 'Delightful . . . de-lovely . . . delicious . . . Delilah . . . delightful . . . de-lovely . . . delicious . . . Delilah.' He was laughing loudly now and rocking back and forth as he repeated his strange mantra. Delilah began to back away—he was weirding her out—but suddenly the smile fell from his face and he began to cry. He stretched his vast arms upwards and grasped Delilah by the waist. He buried his face into her stomach and began muttering into the cotton of her dressing gown. 'Thank you, D'lilah, thank you, D'lilah.'

Delilah didn't know what to do. His hair was greasy and smelt bad. His breath was hot against her flesh, his arms suffocating around her waist. She tried to peel his fingers apart and extricate herself from the foul embrace, but the more she tried to get away from him, the harder he held her. Beautiful Delilah, he kept saying, such a beautiful girl, such a nice girl . . . such a nice girl.

She could feel a damp patch on her stomach where his snot and tears were seeping through the cotton. Her heart began to race as a feeling of being trapped overcame her. And then suddenly she was on her back. Suddenly Michael had her by the wrists and was pinning her to the sofa. But you're not a girl, he was saying, you're not a girl, not any more, you're a woman now, aren't you, you're eighteen, and you're a woman, and you can do whatever you like, and I can do whatever I like because we're both adults, isn't that right, isn't it, and his breath, his breath smelt like raw meat, and his tongue, when it forced its way through her clenched lips, tasted of stale vomit. Delilah heard a song in her head while it was happening. It was a song she'd heard on the radio at Dig's that morning. It played over and over in her head in rhythm with Michael's laboured thrusting. As she listened to the song in her head, she stared at her feet, her eyes focusing on the smudge of silver nail polish left on her toe, a reminder of the last thing she'd done while she was still happy. Because, even as it was happening, Delilah knew for sure that she was never going to be happy again. And then the front door went. Delilah heard her brothers shouting and careering around, and her mother's harsh Golden Virginia voice telling them to shut up. Thank God, she thought, thank God, Mum's home, she'll look after me.

'Mum,' she wheezed, trying to lever Michael off her, 'Mum. In here.'

She should have known better. All those years of disinterest and she'd let herself be sucked in by one flimsy birthday card, let herself believe that her mother cared.

'You filthy little fucking slapper!' Delilah felt herself being dragged from the sofa by her elbow and thrown to the floor. 'You whore!' She felt the toe of her mother's shoe connecting with her stomach.

'Can't you get your own man, is that it?' she said. 'What's wrong with that eyebrow-on-legs you're always hanging around with? Isn't he giving you enough?'

She didn't give Delilah a chance to wash herself, or pack more than a few essentials. 'Get out of my house and never come back! As far as I am concerned, I don't have a daughter any more.'

She'd slammed the door behind her, opening it again two seconds later to throw Delilah's jacket out after her, on to the pathway.

Delilah picked it up, dusted it off and began to walk. As she walked, she turned briefly to look behind her at a house where she'd known no joy, and she knew for a fact that she would never see it again.

Dig gulped. 'Why didn't you come to me, Delilah? That day. Why didn't you come to me?'

Delilah had been looking at the ceiling, but now she dropped her head, and the tears that had been suspended in her eyes tumbled down her cheeks. She rubbed her face with her pink napkin and looked into Dig's eyes for the first time since she'd started talking.

'I didn't want to be with *anyone*, Dig. I was ruined. Michael ruined me that day. You have to understand that. I couldn't even think about being anywhere near you and your lovely mum and your neat little house and your clean, clean lives. And when you found me that day, at the DSS, I just wanted to disappear. I was standing there with you in the rain and you were so concerned about where I'd been, there was so much love in your eyes—and all I wanted was for the rain to turn to acid and dissolve me, there and then, dissolve me and wash me away down a drain.

'I tried to make it work with you, for your sake, not for mine. But every time I touched something in your house, every time I got into bed with you I felt like I was contaminating things, dirtying your sheets. Every time you touched me I wanted to tell you not to. I was totally fucked up, Dig, the most fucked up I've ever been, and when my period was late I just lost it. Packed up my stuff and went back to Marina's.

'Of course, it was the last place I should have gone. Once it was confirmed that I was pregnant there was never any question of an abortion, it didn't even come into the equation. Marina's such a devout Catholic. It was unthinkable. And I was too much of a vegetable to do anything about it. I just sat in my room, staring at the walls, feeling this thing growing inside me day by day, totally resigned to my fate, totally resigned to bringing this thing into the world, to giving it life. I felt like a vessel, not a human being. I wasn't Delilah Lillie any more. I didn't wear make-up any more, stopped dying my hair, didn't watch telly, listen to music, anything.

'But that was when I met Alex—he was studying on Primrose Hill. I was nine months pregnant and I tripped and fell. He took me to the hospital and they had to induce the baby because I was bleeding internally and there was a chance that it might have gone into trauma from the fall. So Alex was there when Sophie was born. I told him everything, about Michael. He was so acceptant—he didn't even flinch. He made me feel so calm. Clean, almost. I don't suppose there are many twenty-two-year-old men who would have had the maturity to deal with a situation like that, are there? I knew he was special.

'He kept in touch after that day, took me out every now and then. And then—well—you already know the rest, don't you? Alex always understood, about the sex thing, about me not wanting it. He didn't have a problem with it. I've been seeing someone about it—a shrink—trying to get better, trying to be a sexual person again. It's a very slow process. Every now and then I burst over with love for Alex and I want to give him something. He never asks me for it. I offer it, when I feel strong, when I feel clean. And, if I'm really honest, when I get scared that he's going to find it somewhere else. And I offered it to him six weeks ago and now I'm pregnant, and I thought that coming back to London, finding Sophie, would help me decide what to do. And it just hasn't, Dig. It hasn't at all.'

She started crying then, not loud sobbing, but silent tears. Jesus, thought Dig. We might be the same age, but Delilah Lillie is centuries older than I'll ever be. Thirty, to me, just means being a slightly-older-than-I'd-like-to-be teenager. Thirty to Delilah means a lifetime of growing and surviving and really living.

'So,' Delilah was saying, 'that's the story. That's Sophie's heritage. She'd be *so* proud, I'm sure, to know where she came from.'

'Fuck, Delilah,' sighed Dig, eloquently, 'what a nightmare.' He shook his head slowly and exhaled loudly and hated himself for being so ill-equipped to deal with this sort of situation, especially as it was him who'd been so desperate for Delilah to open up and talk about things in the first place. He felt his brain scrambling with the effort of finding something, *anything* substantial or helpful to say.

And then, through the fug of thoughts, it came to him, the one thing he could say that he knew was true, that he meant whole-heartedly and that might actually help Delilah.

He took hold of her hands and looked her in the eye. 'You'll be a wonderful mother,' he said. 'You shouldn't worry about that.'

Her face softened and she sniffed loudly. 'Do you think so?' she said, and Dig thought to himself that tonight was the first time in a week that he'd seen the old Delilah, the tender, vulnerable, scared girl he'd fallen in love with all those years ago, the Delilah who'd leaned on him so heavily and needed him so much, and made him feel like a man even though he'd been only eighteen years old.

He felt strong suddenly and gripped Delilah's hands even harder. 'You want this baby, don't you?' he said. 'You really want it?'

She nodded, snottily.

'And you're scared, aren't you, scared that you won't be able to love it, like you couldn't love Sophie?'

She nodded again.

'And like your mother couldn't love you?'

'Mmm.' She blew her nose into her napkin.

'Delilah—you're not your mother. I sometimes find it hard to believe that you're from the same gene pool as your mother. You are so full of love. You loved me, I know you did, and look how much you love Alex. You love your horses. You love your dog. And I think that deep down somewhere, you did love Sophie. I saw your tears today on her doorstep, I saw the way you looked at her. You love, Delilah, and you will be a great, great mother. Really.'

Delilah looked at Dig with watery eyes and he was moved to see the warmth inside them. 'Thank you, Dig,' she sniffed, 'thank you. That means a lot. It really does. It means—it means—you know—Alex—he'd be such a wonderful dad.' She started to brighten. 'He doesn't think he would. But he would be, I know it. And we've got ponies and dogs and ducks and trees to climb and secret gardens to explore. Any child would be happy there, don't you think? Even with an old bag like me for a mother!' And then she laughed and Dig laughed, and he noticed that she'd picked up her cutlery and was spooning cubes of chicken tikka on to her plate, and he supposed that must mean that the crisis was over. But there was still something he wanted to ask her.

'Don't you ever want revenge? Don't you ever want to kill Michael?'

Delilah stopped, her spoon suspended over her plate.

'No,' she said, thoughtfully, 'no. He's going to spend the rest of his life with my mother. In that house. That's punishment enough. That's a life sentence.' She deposited some rice on to her plate.

'I would have,' said Dig, decisively, 'I would have killed him. If you'd come to see me that night and told me what he'd done I would have gone straight round there and killed him. Honestly.' Dig stopped when he realised that Delilah was smiling at him. 'What?'

'Oh, Dig. You're so lovely, aren't you? So good.' She patted his hand, which he'd unconsciously furled into a fist, and Dig blushed. 'Why the hell haven't you got a girlfriend? What are you doing wasting your time with all these young things when you could be making someone so happy? Someone real?'

Dig averted his gaze from hers and busied himself piling curry on to his plate, barely aware of what he was doing. His face was burning crimson. He wasn't used to people telling him how lovely he was.

'I mean,' continued Delilah, 'you're hardly the archetypal playboy, are you? It's not you. It doesn't suit you. Don't you ever want—more?'

Dig laid down his cutlery and rested his head in his hands, as much an attempt to cover his blazing face as to compose himself.

'Never even thought about it till you turned up,' he said, frankly. He told her about the girl he'd slept with on his thirtieth birthday and the conversation he and Nadine had had over breakfast, which neither of them had taken at all seriously. He told her about his reaction to bumping into her in the park, how excited he'd been about their dinner date, how spellbound he'd been by her that night and blown away by their unexpected kiss in the back of the cab. He described the feelings of growth and change that her presence instilled in him, his sudden need to extend himself and expect more from life—more money, more success, more respect, more ambition and, most importantly, more love.

'This morning, when I left the flat to follow you, I was looking at all those people out and about, doing their thing, with their kids and their jobs and their responsibilities, and for the first time ever I found myself thinking, Yeah, I could do that, I could be like those people. You know, a nice woman, a kid, a dog—a nice, *big* dog—a proper flat instead of a shoebox, holidays twice a year, in-laws, anniversaries, early nights, all that. But then I realised something. It's too late, isn't it? I've left it too late. Basically, the foundation for all that stuff is the right woman— yeah? None of that is going to happen without the woman, that's where it all starts. But there aren't any decent single women around.'

'What are you looking for, Dig? Who's your ideal woman? Describe her to me.'

'Well—she'd be beautiful, of course, and slim, definitely. Blonde would be good and nice perky tits. Sorry'—he shrugged—'I'm shallow about that sort of thing—I can't help it. And—well—she'd be the same sort of age as me—or she could be a very mature twenty-two, I suppose.

'She'd have to be intelligent, but not intellectual. Intellectual people scare the life out of me. She'd have to have a healthy appetite, you know, really enjoy her food. Especially curry. And it would be great if she could cook.

'She'd like pubs, have similar taste in music to me, be sociable, but sensible, too, if we're going to have babies. She couldn't be too much of a party animal. I'd want her to be someone who I could rely on, who'd be where she said she was going to be, not too flighty.

'And . . . and'—he tapped his fingernails off his teeth as he considered—'money would be good.' He nodded. 'I wouldn't object to a woman with a nice healthy bank balance. A family girl would suit me, too—someone who's as close to her parents as I am, who understands the little apron-strings I can't quite cut off.. And'—he clicked his fingers at the arrival of a new thought—'*tidy*. She would absolutely have to be reasonably tidy. I mean, I wouldn't expect her to be quite as over-the-top as me, obviously. But reasonably tidy would be good.'

'So, you're not too fussy, then?' smiled Delilah, teasingly.

Dig smiled and leaned back in the banquette. 'I guess,' he said, 'the most important thing is a girl who I can look at in bed when I wake up on a Saturday morning and just think—great, it's the weekend and I'm with my girl, and whatever we do today it's going to be great because she's my best friend and I love being with her.'

Delilah was nodding and smiling. 'Well, congratulations,' she said, offering him her hand to shake, 'that was the correct answer. You are, officially, mature enough to handle a grown-up relationship. But hmm . . . let me think . . . there's only one problem, isn't there?' She was camping it up, rubbing her chin with her fingertips and feigning confusion. Dig wondered what the hell she was doing.

'What's that?' he said.

'Well, where *on earth* are you going to find a woman to fit those criteria. I mean, they don't exist, do they?'

'Exactly!' said Dig. 'Exactly.'

'There's just no such thing as a beautiful, intelligent, single woman who likes curry and pubs, who's tidy and sensible and family-minded and who you could consider to be your best friend, is there?' She slapped her forehead with the palm of her hand in mock-exasperation. Dig was thoroughly confused by her strange carrying-on.

'Not in my experience, no,' he said, conclusively.

'Oh, but wait! Silly me! I know just the girl. I can't believe I didn't think of her before. She's perfect for you. You'll love her.' She leaned down to pick up her handbag and started ferreting around in it. 'I'll give you her number.'

Dig was suddenly all ears. 'Oh yeah,' he said, 'who is she? What's she like?'

'She's like your perfect woman, Dig. She's thirty, she's beautiful, she's successful, she's sweet and she's kind, and you'll absolutely love her.'

'Yeah but—will she like me?'

'She'll think you're perfect,' said Delilah, scribbling on a piece of Filofax paper. 'You're just her type, I promise you.' She clicked the lid back on to her pen and slid the piece of paper across the table towards Dig. 'Ring her,' she said, sternly, 'ring her right now.'

Dig picked up the sliver of paper and held it in front of his nose. His face creased in confusion. 'But—but—I don't get it. This is *Nadine's* number.'

Delilah smiled at him.

'Why have you given me Nadine's number?'

Delilah frowned. 'Blimey, Dig,' she said, 'no wonder intellectuals scare you. You're not exactly bright spark of the month, are you?'

'Oh,' said Dig, smiling grimly, 'oh, *I see*. You're back on one of these matchmaking crusades. *I* get it.' He shook his head and handed the piece of paper back to Delilah. 'You just don't get it, do you? This isn't going to happen. Nadine and I are never going to be like that. If it was going to happen, it would have happened by now.'

'*Why?*' exclaimed Delilah. 'I don't understand. What the hell is the matter with you two? Why hasn't it happened?'

Dig rubbed his face with the palms of his hands. 'I dunno,' he sighed, 'it just wasn't meant to be, I guess. I tried and she wasn't interested.'

Delilah slapped her hand down on the table-top and made Dig jump. 'So you have! I knew it! I knew that there must be something more than just this supposed platonic friendship bullshit. Tell me what happened.'

Dig was starting to regret his candour—it was taking him places he had no interest in being. He took a breath and composed himself to tell Delilah the story of September 1987.

'So,' he said, afterwards, 'Nadine didn't want me, OK? She told me: "I don't want you." You don't get the truth much plainer than that. She wanted more than me. And it took me a while to get used to the idea, you know. For months I found it hard to be around her without wanting to—you know—but it's good now. She's my mate. She's a huge part of my life and I'm grateful for that. Life without Nadine would be empty and meaningless. But, Delilah—I know you mean well and everything, but forget it, OK. Because it just isn't going to happen.'

Delilah was shaking her head. 'God, Dig. I wish you could sit where I'm sitting just for a few moments, see what I see, what *anyone* can see when they look at you and Nadine. I wish you could see it, get over some stupid, childish shit that happened twelve years ago and see it objectively.' She sighed deeply and passed the piece of paper back to Dig. 'Keep this,' she said, folding it into his palm, 'keep this bit of paper. Maybe one day you'll find it in your wallet and you'll remember this conversation and you'll do the right thing. Yes?' she said, beetling her eyebrows and squeezing his clamped hand.

'Yeah,' sighed Dig, 'whatever.'

He slid the piece of paper into his coat pocket and set about trying to consume some of the food that was congealing on his plate.

What a day, he thought to himself as he masticated on a flavourless piece of lamb—why did food always taste so awful when he was with Delilah?—what an unbelievable day. He suddenly felt exhausted beyond words. He wasn't hungry, he wasn't thirsty, and there was no way he could revert to smalltalk with Delilah now.

But the funniest thing of all was that in spite of the painful conversation they'd just had and everything that had happened in the past week, as he sat there contemplating his cold curry and absorbing the strange atmosphere, Dig suddenly realised that all he wanted in the whole world was to see Nadine.

Chapter Eight

BANG BANG BANG

'Uuurgghh.'

Bang Bang Bang '*Nadine!*'

'Oh. Jesus.' Nadine peeled open one eye and then the other. The blurred images of textiles, bits of furniture and the watercolours on the wall that were forming on her retinas meant nothing to her.

'*Nadine!* Are you in there? Let me in.' *Bang Bang Bang*.

It was Pia. It was . . . she was . . . oh, God. Nadine's head was like a . . . like a . . . a horrible thing, just a horrible, horrible, *horrible* thing. Where was she? Where the hell was she? What was this place? Barcelona, she suddenly remembered—she was in Barcelona. But what day was it?

She finally managed to extricate herself from the bedclothes and crawled across the carpet towards the door. 'Coming,' she managed to croak, as she dragged herself along on hands and knees, 'I'm coming.'

She hauled the door open and blinked into the bright light. Looming above her was Pia.

'Christ, Deen,' squeaked Pia, crouching down and putting her skinny little arm around her shoulders, 'are you OK?'

'Mmmm,' grunted Nadine, shielding her eyes from the light, 'my head. My head. What day is it? How long have I been asleep?'

'It's still Saturday night, Deen,' said Pia, stroking some hair out of Nadine's face. 'It's nearly half ten. You've been gone two hours.' She clicked the door closed and lay down on the floor next to Nadine's prone figure. They lay and contemplated the ceiling for a moment.

'You know your phone's off the hook, don't you?' said Pia, turning towards Nadine, who had covered her face with her elbow and was groaning under her breath.

'When you didn't come back, we tried to phone you, and when it was engaged we just assumed you must have run up here to phone Dig. After two hours we started thinking that even *you* couldn't spend that long on the phone. So, did you? Did you call Dig? Were we right?'

Nadine nodded. 'Mmmm,' she mumbled.

'Yes!' exclaimed Pia triumphantly. 'I knew it. Jesus—that Sarah really opened a can of worms, didn't she, coming out with all that stuff about you and Dig? You should have seen your face, Deen—it was priceless! So—what did you say to him? What happened? Did you declare undying love, or what?!'

Nadine pulled herself to a sitting position. It was all coming back to her now. Oh yes—it most certainly was. Oh bloody hell. Oh bloody bloody hell. 'Oh no,' she muttered, 'oh Pia. I can't believe what I did. It's too awful. I can't tell you.'

Pia's face blossomed with excitement. 'What?' she screeched. 'What happened—will you just tell me—please. I can't bear it!'

'I left a message on his answerphone.'

'Oh no!' Pia clasped her hands over her mouth. 'What did you say?'

Nadine shuddered and caught the cigarette that Pia had just thrown her. 'Well—first time I phoned him, *Delilah* answered.'

'Who's Delilah?' Pia lit her cigarette and threw the lighter to Nadine.

Nadine sighed. 'Delilah,' she said, 'remember? I told you about her last week. The Love of Dig's Life. They were teenage sweethearts.'

'Oh, yes,' nodded Pia.

'So when I heard Delilah's voice just now on the phone, in Dig's flat, like she *owned* the place, I went a bit mad. I burst into tears first—snot and everything—and then afterwards I calmed down a bit. And then— oh God—I managed to convince myself that I needed to be a grown-up about all of this. I decided that the best thing to do would be to confront Delilah, talk to her, find out what her intentions were, kind of thing. So I called back—but this time there was no answer. I hung up. I was *furious*, convinced that they were both there, deliberately not picking up the phone. I got myself really wound up and before I knew it I'd picked up the phone again and—and—when the answerphone clicked on I let rip.'

'Oh God—what? What did you say?' Pia asked.

'I said something along the lines of'—she cleared her throat—'"I give up. He's yours. Have him."'

Pia winced.

'Oh but it gets worse,' warned Nadine, ruefully, reddening as her words echoed in her ears, 'it gets much worse.'

She'd thought she was being so calm, so mature, so *wise*.

'Have him,' she'd said, trembling, a hastily lit and illicit cigarette shaking between her fingers. 'He's yours. I've had ten years to do something about it and I didn't, so I guess it's fair enough. I'm not going to let you get to me any more—oh no—I'm moving on, Delilah, and you're welcome to him. Have him, wind him round your finger for a while and then dump him again. See if I care. Break his little heart again. It's not my problem any more. I'm done. I'm through. Goodbye.'

She'd put the phone down then, her heart thumping loudly and before she'd even had a chance to think about what she'd just done, she'd had another thought and was picking up the phone and dialling.

She'd stubbed her cigarette out viciously as she waited for Dig's stupid James Bond message to finish. She was on a roll now and couldn't stomach delays and time-wasting.

'And,' she'd said, hysterically, after the beep, 'another thing. This is a message for you, Dig. *I lied!*' she'd cried, adrenalin almost leaking from her ears, 'I lied when I said I didn't want you. OK? L-I-E-D. Because I did. I did want you, actually. And I always have and I still do. And—and—I'm drunk. I'm very, very, *very* drunk. I'm plastered. And I've been thinking about things and thinking about *your* things, you know, your flat and your sofa and I miss you and I lied. Just so long as you know that I lied. Have a good life. Bye. I'll always love you. Bye.'

And then she'd hung up, feeling quite pleased with the way it had gone. 'That's that sorted, then,' she'd thought to herself, her mouth set hard and her hands still shaking. She'd lit another cigarette, opened her mini-bar, made some kind of hellish cocktail from brandy, gin and San Miguel, knocked it back, been to the bathroom, thrown it up and then collapsed on the bed into a stuporous and immediate sleep.

'Oh hell, Deen,' tutted Pia. 'You've really done it now, haven't you?'

Nadine nodded heavily and collapsed backwards on to the bed. 'This is—awful. This is the most awful, awful thing. Just awful . . .'

'You know something, Deen. If all that was true, then it's good that you said it. Life's too short and you're not getting any younger and at least this way you'll know. You'll know one way or the other. And I'll bet you that by the time we get back to London, Delilah will be gone. I mean—*Delilah*—honestly. There is *no way* Dig could end up with someone called Delilah. It just wouldn't happen. It's not real life.'

Nadine wanted Pia to go now. The conversation was getting unbelievably silly, and her head hurt, and she just wanted to lie there for a while on her own, torturing herself with word-perfect recollections of the messages she'd left on Dig's answerphone.

Oh God.

It was all over now. Things were never going to be the same again.

A sense of madness descended upon Dig as he drove towards Nadine's.

That message. It can't have been real. It just can't have. Must have been some kind of joke. There was just no way—no way.

'Did you put her up to this?' he'd asked Delilah after the stunned silence that had followed the end of the second message. Delilah had just shaken her head, numbly.

'Do you promise?' he'd asked desperately.

'Of course I didn't,' she'd snapped. 'Don't be so ridiculous. I've had slightly more important things to worry about the last few days than constructing some kind of elaborate practical joke. I told you. It's what I've been telling you all along. That's all. It's the truth and now you're actually going to have to do something about it. I'll put the kettle on,' she'd sighed, stroking his arm, 'you'd better give her a ring.' She'd looked horribly tired and Dig had felt guilty, inadvertently dragging her through yet another emotional quagmire after the day she'd had.

He'd phoned Nadine after he'd recovered from the initial shock and had been more than a little surprised to find that she was having a party. He couldn't believe that she hadn't invited him. Some girl whose voice he didn't recognise had answered the phone, and there'd been loud music in the background. He'd said, 'Is Nadine there?', and she'd said, 'I dunno, I dunno. Hold on.' She'd sounded very drunk, and when he was still holding on nearly three minutes later he'd hung up and attempted to watch the telly, instead, intending to deal with it in the morning. No point discussing it with her now, he'd thought, she'll be too pissed. Better to wait until tomorrow, until we've both had a chance to think about this. But waiting had, of course, been impossible. This had to be talked about now. It was too weird and too scary. It was *madness*.

It was a clear night for once as Dig drove in a daze towards Gordon House Road. A Saturday night, he reminded himself, the night when he and Nadine would usually be in a pub somewhere, either locally or in town, either with friends or just the two of them, either single or with current partners. They would be getting their last round in about now, a curry would be imminent. The world would be a simple place, full of warm friendship and deep affection and unspoken feelings of love and togetherness all wrapped up in a lovely, lagery blur. Nadine would be wearing some outrageous dress or other that she'd picked up earlier in the week from a second-hand shop, and wherever they were, her loud laughter and loud clothes, her vociferousness and her humour would light the place up, even the dingiest corner of the dingiest pub.

Could that incredible, bright, flamboyant and utterly unattainable woman, that self-assured and infuriatingly independent woman really be the same one who'd left that hysterical message on his answerphone? Nadine? Maybe she was on drugs. Maybe someone at this party of hers had slipped her a little something. Yes, he decided, turning left into her road, that was the only explanation. Nadine was on drugs.

He could hear the music pounding from her flat even before he'd got out of his car—which was another worrying thing. Nadine had never had a party at her flat before. She'd had parties, but she'd always hired rooms and studios and restaurants because she couldn't bear the thought of her lovely, mad, overstuffed, piled-up, spilling-over, bright and colourful flat being trashed by a load of drunken friends who she'd feel too guilty to shout at. Dig felt concern rising in his chest.

It took a few minutes for someone to come to the door. Dig watched the smudged blur of a human form making its way to the internal front door through the thick opaque glass. Looked like a bloke. Dig cleared his throat and breathed in deeply, trying to quieten his thumping heart. He felt suddenly and overwhelmingly awkward. What was he going to say once he was face to face with Nadine?

'Yeah—who is it?' rumbled a hoarse male voice on the entry phone.

'It's Dig,' he shouted back, 'who's that?'

'Dig! Little Dig! Cool. Excellent!' He could hear various locks and chains being undone and then the door slowly opened. A very thin, gaunt man with a mop of dirty hair and a threadbare lambswool sweater on shuffled out into the hallway. He was barefoot against the mosaic terracotta tiling in the communal hall and was holding in one hand a can of Kestrel and half a mangy-looking spliff. And he was limping.

As he opened the front door he placed his hands on Dig's shoulders and grinned at him even more. 'Looking good, Dig, looking really good. Man, it's great to see you.'

He enveloped Dig in a minor hug then, and Dig was almost knocked out by the smell of fags and booze. Who was this person? It was only as the man released him from the hug and pulled back to appraise him that Dig realised who it was. He hadn't recognised him because he'd been smiling, and he'd never seen him smiling so genuinely before.

'Phil?' he said, uncertainly.

'Come in, man, come in. I tell you—it's blinding in there.' He began limping across the tiled flooring again, towards the door.

Dig followed him, suspiciously. Phil? What was Phil doing here? And what the hell had happened to him in the last ten years? He looked terrible. There was nothing left to remind Dig of that shiny, pretentious, leather-trousered tosser he'd first encountered all those years ago.

As they entered Nadine's pink-foil-wrapped hallway Dig stopped in his tracks. This wasn't right. These weren't Nadine's friends. They were all far too young. There was a girl sitting on Nadine's Art Deco cabinet, the one she'd picked up off a skip in Highgate one night after a party and had made Dig help her carry all the way home. And now there was a girl he didn't know sitting on it, sitting on a pile of Nadine's precious magazines, swinging her fat-trainered feet back and forth and hitting the shiny walnut of the cabinet clunk clunk clunk. There was a bloke sitting at her feet on the floor, tapping his feet manically, to the beat of some kind of unidentifiable dance music emanating very loudly from Nadine's living room.

Dig followed Phil's skinny, limping figure towards the living room, stepping over the man on the floor, and began scanning the flat for any sign of Nadine. He saw a nugget of ash drop from the end of Phil's spliff, and rubbed it into the dark-green carpet with the sole of his foot as he passed over it, tutting under his breath at Phil's lack of respect for other people's carpets. He was starting to make a little sense of the situation now. These were obviously *Phil's* friends. Nadine had thrown a party and invited Phil and he'd invited some of his mates, and it explained entirely why Nadine hadn't invited him—quite apart from the fact that they weren't on speaking terms: because she knew he didn't like Phil.

Poor Nadine he thought to himself. She must be hating this. I bet she's wishing she'd never even suggested the idea now. And I bet she's wishing she'd never got in touch with Phil again, out of the blue—he's not exactly heart-throb material any more. And all this weirdness here might go some way to explaining her bizarre telephone messages.

He scanned the room for Nadine, his brain throbbing in time with the flashing lights. All her furniture had been cleared out of the room—her leather Deco sofa, her mirrored cocktail cabinet, her bookshelves and bucket chairs, her fluffy leopardskin cushions and purple suede pouffe. Every picture and mirror on the wall had been knocked to a dishevelled angle and—oh no—her favourite mirror of all, the oval bevelled one with the chrome frame, had been smashed cleanly in half.

Unable to spy Nadine anywhere, Dig began walking towards Phil, who had gone to sit on the window-ledge with his bad leg resting on an upturned plastic crate in front of him. The tip of his tongue was just protruding from his lips as he licked the corner of a Rizla, and his face broke open into another gummy smile when he saw Dig approach.

'Dig. Mate. Sit down.' He slid along the window-seat and patted the space.

Dig didn't want to sit next to Phil. 'Erm—actually—I wouldn't mind just going to say hello to Nadine first. I haven't seen her yet. D'you know where she is? Is she in here?'

Phil burst into uproarious laughter. 'Come on,' he said, 'sit down. *Sit down.*' He patted the seat next to him again. 'Nadine told me you two had fallen out. Over a girl, yeah?' He was pinching pale-green grass from the most enormous bag of grass that Dig had ever seen.

'Yeah,' Dig said, 'sort of. It's all really complicated.'

'Isn't it always, mate, isn't it always?'

'Look—I really need to speak to her. Where is she?'

Phil exploded into another peal of blood-curdling laughter. 'I couldn't say, precisely, Digby. No—not precisely. You'd have a long search on your hands, let's put it that way.' He guffawed happily to himself and then looked up at a young man with a mop of peroxide hair who'd just whispered something in his ear. He whispered something back to him and patted his arm. "Scuse me a minute, Dig. I'll be back in a tick.' He heaved his bad leg off the crate and hobbled towards the corner of the room with the young man.

Dig frowned. What was that supposed to mean, 'I couldn't say, precisely'? That sounded . . . ominous. Deeply, deeply ominous. Dig began to feel the slightly nauseous sensation of butterflies in his stomach.

What had Phil done to her? He stood up and strode towards Phil, who was just tucking a banknote of some description into his jeans pocket.

'Where is she? Where the fuck is Nadine?'

'I told you, man. I don't know for sure . . .'

'What do you mean, you don't know? This is her flat. Where is she?'

'I dunno,' Phil shrugged, 'Spain, somewhere.'

'Eh?' Dig grimaced. Spain? That was the last thing he'd been expecting.

'Yeah. Spain. She's on a business trip, taking pictures of tits and arses.' He laughed again and lowered himself back on to the window-seat.

Dig's head began to swim. Spain? Actually, that did sound kind of familiar now he came to think about it. She might have mentioned something about a Spanish trip a while back. But that explained nothing. It didn't explain her desperate visit to his flat last night. It didn't explain the messages on his answerphone and it certainly didn't even *begin* to explain this nightmare of a party currently taking place in her lovely flat. Dig rubbed his face with the palms of his hands and sat down heavily next to Phil on the window-seat.

'When did she go?' he sighed.

'Early this morning. Woke me up and all,' he laughed, 'expected me to get up, cheeky bint!'

'You were here this morning?'

Phil nodded.

Dig digested this unsavoury little fact with a dry gulp. Phil was here, this morning. Which meant, of course, that Phil had been here last night. Dig shuddered.

'So,' he managed to squeak, 'what's the story, then?' He attempted to imbue his voice with a blokish camaraderie but couldn't quite veil the creeping nausea rising in his gut. Surely not. *Surely not.*

'The story, man? What story?'

'You. And Nadine. What's happening?'

He could hardly bear to hear Phil's answer.

'Not too sure myself, mate,' he grinned. 'Nadine just phoned me, out of the blue. We went out for a drink, went back to mine, and suddenly she was all over me, like nothing had ever changed, you know. That girl is something else, isn't she? That girl is—*hot.*' He nudged Dig and Dig had to stop himself punching him in the face.

'So, it's all on again. Me and Nadine. I've got the front-door key, mate.' He winked and Dig felt sick.

'So,' he said, taking a deep breath, 'where are you living now, Phil?'

Phil shrugged and indicated the room with his eyes. 'Wherever I lay my hat, Digby, wherever I lay my hat.'

'And have you—have you laid your hat here?'

'It certainly looks that way. I could do much worse than Nadine, couldn't I? She's an angel, that girl, a true angel. She's got a lovely little place here and a nice bit of money coming in. You seen her motor?' He made an 'O' of his mouth.

'So Nadine's asked you to move in?' Dig's eyes were starting to bulge with the improbability of it all.

'That's right, mate. That's right. Bit of a result, *non?*'

'But—but—but—'

'That's taken you a bit by surprise, hasn't it?'

Dig nodded.

'Look,' said Phil, draping one arm around Dig's shoulders, 'you've got to understand a woman like Nadine. She's got everything, right. She's got the looks and the job and the flat and the car. But she hasn't got a man. Not a real man. And then she turns thirty—the old biological clock clicks in and it gets her thinking—about the old days—about what we had together. She phones me—her lost love. Who can blame her? I was a bit surprised, to be honest, by how fast everything happened, especially the sex—you know—on the first night. But it was blinding, Digby, blinding. Some of the best sex I've ever had.'

Dig felt bile rising in the back of his throat. He swallowed it.

'So I give her a load of what I know she wants—sweet talk, messages on the answerphone, declarations of undying love—and the next night, I'm in. Foot in the door, hat on the old metaphorical bed. In—like—Flynn.' He nodded smugly and inhaled deeply on a spliff. 'It's a shame

LISA JEWELL

she had to go away. She would have loved this.' He indicated the party.

'Does she know you're having a party?' muttered Dig.

'Nah. Nah. But she won't mind. You know what she's like. Sweet. Laid back. Make yourself at home, she said, help yourself to anything, this is your flat now, treat it like your own.'

Two small girls with spiky ponytails wandered towards Phil. 'Yes, sweethearts,' he smiled. One of them leaned down to his ear. He nodded and then the three of them disappeared into the corner of the room.

Dig's eyes were wide open and his mouth was shut tight. This was all surreal. He must be dreaming all of this. Nadine was in Spain. Phil was in Nadine's flat. Nadine had had sex with this mop-haired skeleton. She'd invited him to live with her. All this at the same time as phoning *him* and leaving bizarre messages on *his* answerphone. No no no. The entire universe had gone stark staring raving mad.

He felt suddenly and horribly claustrophobic. There were too many people in here, not enough air, too much noise. He had to get out of here, absolutely had to get out, fresh air, clear his head . . .

As he left the room he saw the two girls walking away from Phil and examining something in their hands. Phil tucked yet another banknote into his jeans pocket.

Right, thought Dig, OK. Phil's a dealer. Phil's a dealer.

He put the realisation into a mental To-Do list for digesting later, when he was out of here, away from here, gone.

He found the front door handle and forced it open, stumbling into the relative tranquillity of the tiled hallway. He stood statue-still for a split second. His head was spinning. He pushed open the main door and felt a sense of release when he heard it slam loudly behind him.

His feet sounded like a giant's feet as he clambered clumsily down the front steps. Where had he parked his car? Where? Shit. Yes. Over there. That's right. He ran down the pavement, unlocked the front door, slipped into the driver's seat, leaned into the beige upholstery, breathed out—big, long, deep, out. Pulled on his seatbelt, switched on his ignition, reverse, forward, reverse, out of here, gone.

The world seemed to get brighter as Dig left Gordon House Road. Brighter and lighter. Slowly, yard by yard, Dig's head cleared. He turned left into Highgate Road and tried to focus his thoughts. He should be doing something, that was what he was aware of above all—he should definitely be doing something. What? What should he be doing? Nadine had invited that man into her flat. She'd slept with him. She'd given him a key. She had no one to blame but herself. But parties—drugs, students, trashed carpets—she hadn't asked for any of that.

140

Dig pulled up at the traffic lights at the top of Highgate Road and rested his head on his steering wheel. This had been the weirdest twenty-four hours of his life.

As he lifted his head to check the lights, another light caught his eye. A light on Kentish Town Road to his right. A deep-blue, trapezium-shaped light. It said 'Police'. Of course, he thought, of course. Absolve himself. Let someone else deal with it. Clean it up. Sort it out. That's what they were there for, after all. That's what we paid them for.

The car behind him hooted as he dithered in front of the now-green light. He slipped into first, flicked his indicator to the right and pulled up in front of the police station.

Dig returned to Nadine's flat, with DCs Farley, Stringer, Short and McFaddyen. He rang on the doorbell, asked for Phil, waited until both doors were opened and then stood back and allowed the officers to go about their business.

He'd never seen anything like it. Within seconds, hordes of people began spilling from the house like insects, hurriedly pulling on jackets and shoes and hats as they went. A second later the music died, leaving the entire street with a strange, dead, ringing sound. And then a couple of minutes later Dig watched with a morbid fascination from his hiding-place across the street as Phil himself was marched firmly towards the waiting police car and lowered into it.

He was still smiling.

Dig remembered what Phil had said at the party: 'Wherever I lay my hat, Digby, wherever I lay my hat.' Of course. It made perfect sense to Dig. He probably thought of prison as just another place to lay his hat and, no doubt, when he got out, he'd find somewhere new to 'lay his hat', some other poor woman's lovely flat.

He didn't believe a word Phil had said earlier on. There was no way, *just no way*, that a wrinkly old git like Philip Rich with his dead eyes and his dirty hair could possibly have got Nadine to drop her drawers, to invite him to move into her flat. It made him feel sick just thinking about it. There must have been some other explanation for it. There must be more to Philip Rich than met the eye. Dig had always had his suspicions about him, never trusted him. He would get to the bottom of this peculiar state of affairs. But first he needed to speak to Nadine.

For the first time ever Dig felt protective and tender towards Nadine, Nadine who needed no one, least of all Dig Ryan. He'd protected her property. He'd looked after her. The thought left him feeling curiously warm inside.

He watched the blue-and-white car pull away from Gordon House Road and then walked sadly towards Nadine's house. The front door was open. He moved into the hallway and towards Nadine's flat.

Inside he wandered around desolately. The mass stampede from the flat had created even more damage. Nadine's pink-foil wallpaper had been shredded by people all rushing to the front door at the same time. The pile of magazines on the Deco cabinet had been thrown to the floor and mashed underfoot. Wine bottles and lager cans littered the carpet.

Dig's head filled up with images of happier times, thoughts of all the evenings he'd spent here with Nadine in her eccentric little castle, listening to music, getting stoned, getting ready to go out, discussing their disastrous love lives. He'd been with her when she'd first been to see the flat. She'd fallen madly in love with it and he'd tried to persuade her it wasn't right for her. It's characterless, he'd told her, it's got no soul and it's overpriced. But she hadn't listened to him. She'd bought it for the asking price and had, of course, proved him entirely wrong, compensating for the beige Anaglypta, dark-stained-oak and magnolia walls of her childhood with flights of fancy and bright colours, turning the dull, echoing flat she'd bought into a mad, welcoming, warm and cosy refuge from the world. Dig loved it in Nadine's flat.

Imagine, he thought with a sudden sense of dread, if something happened and I was never allowed to come back here again. Imagine if something happened to Nadine and I never saw *her* again. What would be the point, he wondered, of going on? Would he have any desire to get up in the mornings or to go out at the weekends if there was no Nadine?

Imagine if she died. Imagine if she got run over by a bus and someone phoned him and said, 'It's Nadine, something's happened.' He couldn't, he just couldn't countenance it—he'd never smile again . . .

Dig was surprised and just a little horrified to find that his eyes were filling up with tears as he explored this morbid train of thought. He gulped to force them back and wiped away an escapee as it slid down the side of his nose. How ridiculous. He must be over-tired. That was the only explanation.

. . . and imagine, his mind forced him to keep thinking, imagine if something happened to Nadine and you never got a chance to apologise for not phoning her last night when she was so upset, never got the chance to explain to her about Delilah, to ask her about that message on the answerphone, to find out why she lied to you all those years ago about how she felt about you.

There was so much that needed talking about, and where was Nadine? In Spain, that's where, in bloody Spain, while his head pounded and his heart ached and his life twisted itself in and out.

Dig sighed heavily and lowered himself on to his haunches. He picked up one of Nadine's poor, destroyed magazines and held it to his chest.

Please come home, Nadine, he said to himself, please come home.

Chapter Nine

NADINE PILED ALL HER CASES and aluminium-clad boxes on to the pavement and eyed her front door with suspicion.

She felt for her key in her pocket and breathed in deeply as she brought it towards the keyhole. She'd managed to work herself up into a complete paranoid frenzy over the course of the weekend about what might have happened to her flat while she was gone. She had images in her mind of spilt wine, broken glass, wild parties and police raids. Ridiculous, of course, she knew she was being ridiculous. Pia and Sarah had spent most of the past three days persuading her how silly she was being. 'Don't be daft,' they kept saying, 'don't be so over-dramatic. The flat's going to be just fine. Phil will be home by now, back in Finsbury Park,' they soothed.

Instead they encouraged her to discuss the whole 'Phoning Dig' fiasco. That was *much* more interesting as far as they were concerned—a real-life soap opera for Pia, unfolding in front of her very eyes. They were all convinced she'd done the right thing, especially Sarah, of course, who'd started the whole bloody thing in the first place and was already planning what she going to wear to the wedding. They'd been on her case all weekend to phone him again.

'No way,' she'd insisted, 'don't even waste your time thinking about it. I am never phoning Dig again. Ever, OK?' She had a plan anyway. A plan to work her way out of the awful nightmare she'd landed herself in. If Dig *did* ever phone her again, for whatever bizarre reason, then she'd just tell him that she'd been playing Truth or Dare with the girls and that phoning him was the punishment they'd concocted for her.

OK. So it was a crap excuse. But at least it was an excuse. And actually, she supposed, men were generally so bemused by the carryings-on of drunken women *en masse* that he'd probably just accept it as gospel. Of course, he'd think, 'Women—they're weird, we all know that.'

She stabbed the front-door key into its hole.

It was going to be fine, she told herself. Everything was going to be just fine. Her flat would be fine. Her life would be fine. It was all going to be perfectly—fine. She took a few deep breaths to psych herself into believing that everything really was going to be fine before slowly twisting the key in the lock and pushing the door open.

She flicked the hall light on and clamped her hand over her mouth.

A strange, strangulated little yelp slipped through her fingers.

A million thoughts landed in her mind at once as she absorbed the physical reality of her trashed hall, the most insistent of which was that this was some kind of dream precipitated by the preceding three days of irrational concern. Like a mirage. Yes—that's right—a mirage.

This comforting thought lasted less than a microsecond before reality hit with a vengeance. Her flat was destroyed. She'd been burgled. Her hand still clamped to her mouth, she slumped her shoulders and fell to her knees, bags and cases slipping from her shoulders and hands, her keys clanging to the ground. Oh God. Look at this place. Look at it. Look at her walnut cabinet. Look at all her magazines everywhere. Look at the pink-foil wallpaper, all scuffed and ripped.

She hobbled on her knees down the hallway. Spilt wine, fag-ends, ripped pages from magazines, huge, dirty footprints—everywhere. There was a lump the size of an egg in her throat. She breathed deeply to prevent useless tears escaping and got to her feet using the bathroom doorframe to pull herself up. She pushed open the bathroom door and waited helplessly while it creaked open.

'Oh God,' she moaned, when she saw what was within, 'oh no. Oh no.' Tears began spilling, despite her attempts to control them.

She began moving more quickly then, from room to room, from kitchen to living room, and everything she saw increased the knot in her stomach and the sadness in her heart. Her flat. Her lovely, lovely flat. The flat she'd created with her bare hands, from skips and second-hand shops, from clearance sales and her parents' generosity, month by month, year after year, piece by piece. All ruined. All dirty. All broken.

Anger started to erupt inside her as she stepped over empty wine bottles, and she felt a primal scream building in her chest. Her fists clenched themselves tightly and then she let it go. She opened her mouth, closed her eyes and screamed, not a scream of fear but a deep, sonorous scream of pure rage.

'*Fucking Bastards!*'

She began half-heartedly to collect bits and pieces together—empty beer cans, half-full beer cans afloat with stinking, swollen fag-butts and spliff-ends. There were articles of discarded clothing lying around the place—*other people's* discarded clothing. She hadn't been burgled—that was obvious now. There was nothing actually missing. Just lots of grim stuff added, things moved around and other things broken. She hadn't been burgled—she'd been partied.

Phil. Fucking Phil.

She'd known this was going to happen, from the minute she'd closed her front door behind her on Saturday morning to the minute she'd opened it again just now. Her instincts had been spot on. She felt sick. She found it impossible now to rustle up even the smallest shred of sympathy for Philip Rich. She was *glad* in fact, glad his parents had died, glad his house had burned down. He deserved it. All of it. He deserved worse. He deserved much more.

She kicked the doorframe, collapsed to her knees and began to howl. She wailed and thrashed and sobbed and shouted. And then had rapidly to pull herself together when she heard the doorbell ring.

'Oh Jesus,' she muttered to herself, pushing tear-sodden tendrils of hair from her cheeks and wiping her eyes. She got heavily to her feet and stumbled towards the front door. As she crossed the hallway towards the main door she saw a sight she knew would stay with her for ever, a vision that brought goosebumps to her flesh and a lump to her throat, that turned her stomach to liquid and her knees to jelly, the sweetest, most beautiful thing she'd ever seen in her life. Everything that had occurred in the past week and a half, from sleeping with Phil to running him over, from having her flat trashed to leaving appalling messages on answerphones, every bad moment of every bad day, every feeling of insanity and misery and unhappiness just dissolved when she pulled open her front door and saw Dig standing there.

He was wearing a frilly apron, a cap and a daft smile.

In one hand was his precious purple Dyson, in the other a dustpan and brush and at his feet sat a tiny, quivering Yorkshire terrier.

'I've come about the cleaning position,' he grinned. 'I've got excellent credentials and references. I've been voted the cleanest person in NW5.'

Nadine melted then and dissolved into fresh tears. 'Oh Dig,' she snuffled into his shoulder, 'oh Dig. Thank God you're here. Thank God.'

Dig squeezed her back, hard as anything, tighter than he'd ever hugged her before.

'God, I've missed you,' he said, smiling at her.

Nadine smiled back at him and looked into his soft, dark eyes, pain just falling away from her as she did so. 'It feels like ages,' she sniffed.

She looked down at the trembling dog. 'Is that the feather duster?'

Dig laughed and leaned down to pick him up. 'No,' he said, 'this is the world's smallest and most unappealing dog and this small and unappealing dog is getting the early train back to Chester tomorrow morning. Aren't you, mate?' The dog looked at him fearfully, as if he'd just suggested the knacker's yard.

'What?' said Nadine. 'On his own?'

Dig threw her a pitying look.

'Oh,' she said, breathlessly, 'you mean Delilah's going home?'

'Yes,' smiled Dig, 'Delilah's going home. Back to her husband. Back to have a baby.' He smiled.

'But—but—but . . .'

'Nothing ever happened between me and Delilah, you know. Nothing. We had one kiss. I've done a lot of thinking since you went away and there's a lot of stuff you need to know, Nadine. About Delilah. You need to hear about Delilah. You've got her so wrong. She's a good person. She's a very good person who's had a very hard time. And we need to talk about Phil. About why he let this happen to your flat. He *isn't* a good person. But,' he said, seriously, 'most importantly, we really, *really* need to talk about us.'

'What do you mean—about us?' Her stomach fizzed at the very concept, at the fact that Dig had even mentioned it.

'Look,' he said, ushering her into the hallway, 'get your rubber gloves on and get into the kitchen. We'll talk as we clean.'

There was a lot of talking that rainy Tuesday afternoon and a lot of explaining. Dig had spent twenty minutes on the phone the previous day to a DI Wittering, who had been more than expansive on the subject of Philip Rich, a character who the Metropolitan Police had been familiar with since his ex-wife had first reported him twelve years earlier for the theft of her black MG and the contents of her savings account.

They'd come into contact with him again seven years later when his suicide was reported to them by a distraught woman called Mandy Taylor, claiming to be his fiancée. She'd watched in horror as he threw himself off Putney Bridge two weeks before they were due to be married. He had, apparently, taken the precaution of emptying their joint bank account before taking his life and when Mandy Taylor bumped into him coming out of a pub off Tottenham Court Road six months later she'd been too shocked to press charges.

His parents—who were alive and well and had attended his funeral—refused to have anything to do with him and these days he was a squatter dabbling in a bit of small-time drug-dealing.

'You mean, he made all that up? All that stuff about his parents and his girlfriend and everything?'

'He's a con artist, Nadine. He's been a con artist from the day you met him.'

After a tip-off from Phil's elderly father, Haringey council had evicted him and eight students from a flat in Finsbury Park on Friday morning, and it seemed he'd decided that Nadine and her flat would make a much better alternative to finding a new building to squat.

'Of course,' sighed Nadine, 'of course. That flat. It didn't seem right. All those students and that strange furniture. And . . . and'—she was growing quite animated as so many of the events of the last few days began to make sense—'and—that's why he left me all those messages. That's why he was hanging around outside my flat. That's why he wouldn't leave. He had nowhere else to go. I thought he was desperate to see me, but he was just desperate for a roof over his head. Oh my God. To think . . . I just . . . oh God, Dig, I'm such an *idiot*. I can't believe I fell for all that . . .'

Her face fell even further after Dig had related the story of Delilah's visit to London, of Sophie and Michael and her unplanned pregnancy.

'Oh Jesus,' she said, 'I feel so bad. All that time I spent bitching about her and hating her and she was going through so much. And I had no idea. None at all. I just thought she was here to make trouble, to take you away from me. Oh God, Dig, I feel like such a bitch . . .'

It was getting dark by the time they'd finished cleaning the kitchen and discussing the events of the past week and they still hadn't even brushed on the subject of the answerphone messages.

Both of them were aware that it was next on the agenda but both of them industriously spun out the other subjects until finally, at five o'clock, they ran out of things to say. The atmosphere in the kitchen was plump with the prospect of their next conversation.

'Well,' said Dig, getting off his knees and looking around the kitchen, 'I think we've done in here. Pretty much spotless, I'd say.'

'Mmm,' murmured Nadine, looking around her and feeling awkward with Dig for the first time in years. 'Do you want to get started on the other rooms now? Or we could have a cup of tea? Or you can go if you like? You don't have to stay. I'll be all right. I'll make you dinner, though, obviously, if you do stay. So . . .' She trailed off and turned abruptly towards the sink, stowing a jumbo-sized bottle of Domestos into a cupboard and feeling her cheeks flush to a warm pink.

Dig smiled at her back. Of course he was going to stay. This was the only place in the world he could think of that he wanted to be right now. It was where he'd wanted to be since Saturday night. Here, in Nadine's kitchen, with Nadine looking fantastically cute in threadbare old grey jogging bottoms, a crappy old Paul Weller T-shirt that he'd given her years ago and a lime-green pinny with Miffy the Rabbit patch pockets. Her thick copper hair was all over the place, her toenails were bubblegum pink and she had a smudge of something grey across her upper lip that made her look like she had a 'tache. She looked like a madwoman. She *was* a madwoman. A gorgeous, lovable, sexy, red-haired, successful, together, strong-minded and about-to-be fabulously wealthy madwoman. He smiled again. What a combination.

Nadine spun around. 'I just thought of something,' she said, 'we should do it now—in case we don't get round to it later—all that furniture on my bed—I'm going to need a hand getting it off. Do you mind?'

Digby had made a nest for himself on the corner of Nadine's duvet that was still showing, and Dig gently scooped the creature off the bed with the palm of one hand and laid him on his jacket in the hallway.

'Aw,' smiled Nadine, watching him tenderly, 'cute. You're quite fond of him, aren't you?'

'No,' he said. Then more softly, 'Well, he's all right, I suppose. He's sort of grown on me the last few days. But he's just not my kind of dog. Well, he's not *any* kind of dog, really, is he? I mean, look at him.'

They both cast their eyes downwards at the slumbering little ball of greasy whiskers and bulging eyes. He sighed deeply in his sleep and emitted a little whistle.

'He's knackered,' said Nadine.

'Well,' said Dig, 'it's not surprising, really. He's had a tough few days.'

'Haven't we all,' said Nadine, moving back towards the bedroom.

'It's been a very strange week,' agreed Dig.

'Mmm,' murmured Nadine, turning pink again, 'to put it mildly.'

'But good, I think—a good week.'

'In spite of everything?'

They were on either side of Nadine's bed now, each holding an arm of her leather sofa.

Dig nodded.

'Why?'

Not just yet, thought Dig. In a minute.

'Here,' he said, 'let's get this sofa into the living room.'

Nadine nodded stiffly, and on the count of three they heaved the ancient sofa off the bed and lumbered around with it for a while until they'd manoeuvred it through the bedroom door and into the living room. Exhausted, they both collapsed on it and gasped in unison.

'D'you remember getting this thing in here, when you moved in?' asked Dig, turning to smile at Nadine.

'Yeah. Of course I do. This was the first thing I bought for the flat. From that old house-clearance place that used to be up on Agar Grove. £38.50. I always wondered what the 50p was for.'

'I thought you were mad. Why would anyone want to buy some rancid, stinky sofa with horsehair falling out of the bottom and cracks all over the place? I kept trying to get you to go to Habitat but you just weren't interested in anything new—or clean—or'—he cast Nadine a cheeky look—'*nice*. "Oh no, I don't want something that hasn't been used by at least twelve people before me—oh no, that's *far too clean*— you mean, it came in a box? How common."'

Dig flinched and laughed as Nadine picked up a cushion and hit him over the head with it. 'You bastard! You're just jealous because you've got no imagination. "Ooh, I *just* don't know—shall I go for the mid-beige or the light beige? Or maybe I'll be *really* daring and go for the deep beige. Or do you think that'll clash with the navy blue . . .?".'

Dig picked up a cushion now and boffed Nadine with it, harder than he'd intended, accidentally clipping her on the temple with his knuckle.

'Ow!' she yelled, rubbing the side of her face. 'That really hurt!'

'Oh God,' said Dig, immediately dropping the cushion and sliding along the cracked leather towards Nadine, 'oh God. I'm sorry.' He cupped the side of Nadine's face with his hand and stroked his thumb across her temple. 'I'm really sorry, Deen.' Her skin was smooth and flushed under his and her eyes were still slightly red around the rims. She looked so young and vulnerable. He brought his thumb down to her upper lip and wiped away the grey smudge.

As he touched her and looked into her green eyes Dig could feel something stirring deep down inside him, something almost magnetic forcing his body and his face closer and closer to hers. She eyed him with a mixture of fear and excitement.

Dig could tell she'd stopped breathing.

So had he.

'Oh, Deen,' he said finally, pushing a messy copper curl away from her face, tucking it behind her ear, 'we're such a pair of idiots, aren't we?'

Nadine nodded, and Dig knew then that they were on the same wavelength, knew that he wouldn't have to do too much explaining.

And for once Dig wasn't stuck for words. For once he was going to open his mouth and all the right words were going to come out of it. Because, for once, Dig had it all planned.

He took a deep breath and started talking.

'We've been a couple for the last ten years, do you realise that? We go shopping together. We go on holiday together. We spend our weekends together. We even spend alternate Christmases with our parents. We bicker. We hug. You know all my colleagues, I know all yours. The only thing we *don't* do is sleep together and wake up together. And I used to think that that was because you'd rather die than even contemplate the idea of being—*intimate* with me.'

Nadine opened her mouth to say something and Dig put a finger up to hush her. 'Shhh,' he said, 'listen to me. 'Remember that weekend—in Manchester, when I came to stay?'

Nadine nodded again.

'I didn't show it at the time because I didn't want to make you feel bad, but I didn't know that you were living with Phil until I got there— I still thought I was in with a chance. And that weekend—it was the worst weekend of my life, Deen. Pretending I didn't care was the hardest bit of acting I've ever done. I had to listen to you and him—having sex—and I thought my heart was going to break, I really did.

'It wasn't Delilah who broke my heart, Nadine, it was you. And I never got over it. I really didn't. And now I know what I've been doing for the last ten years. With all these young girls. Now I know why I haven't had a decent, proper girlfriend in all this time. It's because I didn't *need* one. *You've* been my girlfriend, Nadine, and I've subconsciously chosen women who were no threat whatsoever to what I have with you. And all this time I've thought that I could be happy living this compromise for the rest of my life, happy loving you and having sex with other women because I thought that friendship was all I'd ever get from you. But then you left that message on my answerphone and now everything's changed. Did you mean it? Did you mean what you said? About lying— about wanting me?' He stared into her unblinking eyes.

Nadine stared back into his in wonder. She felt almost faint with excitement. 'Yes,' she said, 'I meant it.'

'So why?' said Dig. 'Why did you tell me you didn't want me? Why did you reject me? Why did you go off to Manchester and fall in love with someone else?'

Nadine sighed. 'Because of Delilah,' she said.

'Delilah? What did Delilah have to do with it?'

'You were my best friend—my world. Delilah broke my heart when she took you away from me. It wasn't just *you* that she wanted at the Holy T, it was what you and I had—that intimacy, that exclusivity, that complicity. She wanted to take my place. Dig 'n' Deen. Dig and Delilah.

I knew it, and I hated her. I didn't know who I was without you. My last two years at school were miserable and lonely.

'And then I went to St Julian's and I felt strong again. I became someone in my own right, and when we met up and spent that weekend together and you started making all these plans for the future, I just got scared. I couldn't bear to lose you all over again, not when I'd only just found myself. So I rejected you. It made me feel strong. I wasn't expecting to meet Phil, to fall in love so quickly, and I really thought, that weekend when you came up, that you'd got to grips with the idea that we were never going to be together. And, you know, I've done it too, what you've done. The reason I've been out with so many unsuitable people is because I had the most suitable person right here, all along. I haven't been looking for love because I haven't needed to. Because I love you and I don't want to love anyone else and I really don't think I *can* love anyone else . . .'

'No! That's exactly it. Neither can I. I thought I could love Delilah, because I'd loved her before. I thought it would be different. But it wasn't. I tried to love her, but I couldn't . . .'

'And I thought I could love Phil again! But . . . bleughhh.' She grimaced and she laughed, and Dig laughed, and for the first time in ten years Nadine could feel herself getting a grip on one of those happiness seeds. She could feel her hand tightening over the little seed, she could feel it nestling against the palm of her hand, and this time she was not going to let go of it.

'It's always been you, Nadine. You and me. Dig 'n' Deen. Nobody else stood a chance, did they?'

Nadine shook her head and smiled widely. 'I used to think that you and I would get married when we left school. I used to think . . . here— wait.' She ran from the room, into her bedroom, ferreted around inside her wardrobe for a minute and then came back clutching something in her hands. 'Look,' she said, handing it to Dig, 'look at this.'

It was a diary. It was old and musty. Dig turned it over. And there it was, written over and over again in self-conscious adolescent handwriting.

Nadine Ryan. Nadine Ryan. Nadine Ryan.

'And look,' said Nadine, turning the pages, 'look at this.' She pointed at a section entitled 'Mrs Nadine Ryan'. 'Read that bit,' she said.

Dig threw her an amused look and started reading. He chuckled as he read. 'Oh yes, I like this bit—powder-blue E-type,' he smirked.

'*Four children!*' he cried at one point.

'Gloucester Crescent. Yes. I could live in Gloucester Crescent. So,' he said, closing the book and turning to face Nadine, 'when shall we start?'

'Start what?'

'House-hunting, of course.'

Nadine searched for the sarcasm in his voice, but it wasn't there.

'Jesus, Nadine. We've wasted so much time, haven't we? Ten years. Let's not waste any more. Eh?'

And then he put the book down, took Nadine's hands in his, and he kissed her. On the lips. And even though he'd thought it might feel strange, kissing Nadine, it didn't. It felt the opposite of strange. It felt so unbelievably right.

And Nadine gripped Dig's hands in hers and felt his lips moving against hers, and she couldn't believe they'd waited so long to do this because this was what her lips were designed for. For kissing Dig Ryan.

They fell backwards together into the leather of Nadine's Deco sofa and smiled at each other, and then they kissed again.

It grew dark while they kissed and soon the only light in the room came from the cactus fairy lights over the fireplace, and in that cool, green glow, in the debris of her flat, on a rainy November evening, Dig and Nadine finally got it together.

Epilogue

DIG LOOKED OUT through the tangles of ice-blue clematis and snowflake jasmine that framed his study window. The sky outside was turquoise and smudged with white. The air was warm and full of pollen. It had taken its time but, finally, in the second week of July, summer had come to London.

Dig's study was a minimal refuge in the chaos of their new home. He'd acceded to Nadine's taste in interior decor and let her run amok with her strange wallpapers and bits of bohemian junk in the rest of the flat. It was funny how easy he found it to live with Nadine's mess—it was so much a part of her that he almost loved it. He could *breathe* amongst her clutter. But in here was all white walls and modern furniture, anglepoise lamps and linen filing boxes from Muji. His old corduroy sofa sat against the wall.

This tiny, neat, well-organised room was now home to Dig-It Records, the smallest independent label in the world. Only two weeks old and only one band to its name but—they were *the* greatest guitar band since Oasis. Absolutely. Dig could feel it in his gut, his heart and his soul. He just had to persuade the rest of the world now.

This new life still felt a little like playing at grown-ups. He and Nadine kept expecting someone to come to the front door in a uniform and ask them what the hell they thought they were doing living in this adult's house in this adult's road, to march them out, throw them into the back of a van and deposit them in a bedsit in Tufnell Park.

Dig gulped back the dregs of his tea and looked at the clock. Six thirty. Nadine should be back any minute. He smiled at the thought. It was her turn to cook tonight. His stomach growled in anticipation.

The doorbell rang and Dig made his way wearily down the hallway but he snapped out of his long-day-in-the-office reverie when he opened the door and saw a stunningly beautiful woman with golden hair and skin standing on the doorstep.

'Delilah!'

Delilah's face burst open into an enormous smile and she threw her arms around Dig and squeezed him hard.

'Oh Dig,' she said, 'it's so great to see you!'

'What are you doing here?'

'God. I'm *so sorry*. I was determined not to turn up unannounced again, not after last time. I kept trying to call you and there was no answer so I wrote to you. Two weeks ago. We've been shopping all day and then we turned up at your flat this afternoon and there was no one there, so we drove to your mum's and she told me you'd moved up in the world and she wasn't wrong—I mean, *look at this place!*'

She poked her head into the hallway and began looking around. She was wearing a pure white crepe viscose dress, short and flirty with shoe-string straps. On her feet were pale-blue strappy sandals. Her hair was twisted up and clipped back with some kind of plastic claw affair. Dig could see her knickers through the semi-opaque viscose. She was wearing a G-string. He gulped.

The sound of a car door slamming drew Dig's attention away from Delilah's underwear and towards the road. There was a large four-wheel-drive Jeep parked opposite, and a tall man was unloading stuff from it—funny bags made from quilted fabric, and plastic boxes. He was about six foot four with coal-black hair and an imposing physique. He was wearing jeans in the same effortless way that Delilah wore hers, with a grey V-neck T-shirt. He was very brown and, when he turned around, quite guttingly handsome. He threw Dig a smile and Dig worked it out. Alex.

Alex reached further into the Jeep and brought out something very carefully with both arms—a Ming vase, maybe, thought Dig, or a particularly large Fabergé egg. No—it was another plastic contraption with a large handle, and nestled within it was a small pink thing wearing a stripy all-in-one.

Alex picked up all his quilted things and plastic things and headed towards them. Delilah beamed. 'Dig,' she said, 'let me introduce you to the two most gorgeous men in the world. Dig—this is Alex—Alex, *this is Dig.*' Dig was touched to notice a trace of pride in Delilah's voice when she said his name. He went to shake Alex's hand and laughed because his hands were all being used up for other things. Alex laughed, too, and Dig was shaken again by the resemblance to Pierce Brosnan.

'And,' continued Delilah, taking the contraption with the pink thing in it from Alex and thrusting it towards Dig, 'this is the fantastic Oliver—isn't he *beautiful*?'

Dig looked down into the contraption, at the funny little sausage of pinky-white flesh and into the cloudy blue of the sausage's eyes and tried to think of something to say. 'Lovely,' he managed, eventually.

They went indoors then, and Dig felt inordinately proud as he showed this perfect family his elegant and classy new home, with its high ceilings and original features, this airy two-bedroom flat that spoke of hitherto alien concepts such as *being settled* and having *made it.*

He made tea and sat his guests down in the garden, on dark-green wrought-iron furniture. The garden looked spectacular—tiny but mature, all brambly rose bowers and ivy-clad walls. The air was heavy with heat and fragrant with jasmine. The sound of a violin being played somewhere further down the street wafted into the garden.

Delilah fiddled with a plastic bottle and slipped it into the sausage's mouth. 'Dig,' she said, looking around her, 'this is incredible. Gloucester Crescent. Did you win the lottery or something?'

Dig laughed. 'No,' he said, 'I wish. No. This is a childhood dream of Nadine's. A *very expensive* childhood dream. I have never been poorer in my entire life. I had more money when I was eighteen, earning £6,000 a year. But we sat down together and worked out that we could afford it, even with me giving up my job. Just. We both made quite a lot on our old flats and Deen's doing so fucking well and—oops.' He covered his mouth and glanced apologetically at the sausage.

Delilah laughed. 'His language skills aren't quite up to picking up swearwords just yet. He's only four weeks old. Don't worry.'

'Anyway, Nadine's career has really taken off, since the Ruckham's calendar—she's earning a mint. The mortgage repayments are crippling, we can't afford to go out or buy clothes or go on holiday or anything but'—he looked around him—'it's worth it, you know. I could die here, do you know what I mean?'

They both murmured affirmatively and for a second or two it was silent. Delilah and Alex glanced at each other and exchanged a look.

'Shall I tell him?' said Delilah.

Alex nodded happily.

Delilah turned to face Dig, anticipation in her face. 'Dig,' she said, 'we've got something we'd like to ask you. Well—two things, actually.'

Dig felt his face muscles tense up. Delilah asking him favours was, in his experience, a very worrying thing.

'Ye-es,' he said, smiling stiffly, trying to sound excited.

'The first thing is—and I know, you're not religious or anything, but neither are we so it doesn't matter—but I'd—*we'd*—be so honoured if you would be Oliver's godfather.' She beamed at him and Dig was surprised to notice a little flush of pleasure in his stomach area. He looked down at the sausage and felt a burst of warmth. He looked at Alex and Delilah, who were both staring desperately at him as if they'd just proposed marriage, and he smiled. 'Shit,' he said, 'yeah. Definitely. I mean—yeah!' And everyone just sat there and beamed for a while.

'That's fantastic,' said Delilah grabbing the back of Dig's neck and kissing him on the cheek. Alex gave him a large hand to shake, and Dig couldn't believe how happy he was to be asked to stand in a church and tell lies with a stupid suit on, all for the sake of a dimply sausage who couldn't have cared less either way.

'So,' he said, happily, 'what was the other favour?' He was on a favour roll now—he could handle favours like this.

'Well,' said Delilah, her face becoming serious, 'it's—er—actually, hold on, just a sec. Alex—can I have the car keys?'

She plopped the sausage down into Dig's arms, took the keys from Alex and disappeared back into the house.

Dig sat for a while, holding the sausage as if it were an unpinned hand-grenade.

'Here,' said Alex, smiling, 'let me take him. You don't look very comfortable there. It takes a bit of getting used to, this baby lark.' He grinned warmly at Dig and gently scooped the pink thing from his arms.

Dig felt awkward for a second, now that Delilah was gone, not sure what he and Alex were going to have to talk about, but Alex saved him from himself.

'Dig,' he said, and Dig nearly jumped out of his skin because his voice was so deep—he sounded like he should be doing trailers for Hollywood movies. 'Dig. I wanted to thank you.'

Dig threw him a not-sure look.

'For what you did for Delilah last year.' He was *very* posh.

'What do you mean?' said Dig, thinking about his complete lack of doing anything for Delilah last year, except for following her around.

Alex put the sausage back in its contraption and tucked a blanket round its legs. 'For looking out for her. For having her to stay. For talking her out of not having this little chap. She told me what you said to her, about being a great mother, about her ability to love. You were very wise and you were right. I dread to think what would have happened if you hadn't talked her round.'

They both turned to survey the pink thing and Dig felt himself blushing. 'Well,' he said, 'God. You know. It was nothing. It was . . .' And then, just in the nick of time, just before Alex would have reached the conclusion that he was an illiterate buffoon, the proper grown-up bit of Dig came to the rescue and he realised there was something important he wanted to say. 'It was the least I could do,' he said, breathing easy, 'after all, Delilah did the same for me.'

'Oh yes?' said Alex, crossing his legs and looking at Dig with interest.

'Yes. She set me on the path to true happiness.'

'Really. How?'

Dig looked at Alex and tried to gauge how honest he could be. His eyes were brown and gentle. He looked like he could take a bit of romance. 'She stopped me being blind. I'd been in love with someone for twelve years and was too much of a coward to risk rejection so I just made do with being her friend. Delilah showed me that I could have more. That this girl loved me, too. I thought she was interfering at the time. But she was right. And now I've got the girl of my dreams.'

Alex smiled. 'And you're happy?'

'I have never been happier in my life. This is it'—he indicated their surroundings—'this is my castle and Nadine's my queen.'

And Alex and he exchanged a long, deep look, and Dig knew that Alex knew exactly how he felt and that they were both lucky, lucky men. Dig decided he liked Alex.

'What are you boys talking about?' said Delilah, striding back into the garden. Dig was about to make a joke of some description when he noticed what Delilah was holding in her arms.

'No way,' said Dig immediately, crossing his hands in front of his chest.

'You don't know what I'm going to ask you yet.'

'I don't need to. I don't care. There's just no way . . .'

In Delilah's arms, shivering even in this balmy heat, was Digby. He wagged his tail when he saw Dig and tried to escape from Delilah's arms.

'See,' whined Delilah, 'see how much he loves you. He's never forgotten you, you know. He's had this empty look about him since I took him home last year.'

'What do you want? Do you want me to look after him? OK. One night only, though. One night and that's it.'

Delilah shook her head slowly from side to side and deposited the dog on Dig's lap. 'It's a bit more than that,' she said, nervously, 'you see, you wouldn't think it to look at him but he can be quite aggressive, and the thing is, is that—and there's no way we could have known this— but he hates babies. Hates them. And he hates Oliver. Snarls at him. It's awful. And I couldn't bear to give him away to a stranger. And I just keep remembering how well the two of you got on together. And . . .'

'He hates babies?' asked Dig.

'Mmm,' Delilah nodded, sadly.

'All babies?'

'Well. Yes. At first we thought it was just Oliver, but now we've noticed it's all babies.'

A large, smug smile spread across Dig's face, and he shook his head. 'Sorry,' he said.

'Can't you just give it a go? You could have a trial run?'

Dig shook his head and looked up when he saw someone walk into the garden. A stunning redhead in a blue crushed-silk dress wearing red 1950s plastic sunglasses and butterflies in her hair.

She stopped in her tracks when she saw the group in the garden and looked quizzically at Dig. And then she smiled widely when she recognised Delilah and stooped to hug her. Delilah introduced her to Alex and Oliver.

'Nadine,' said Dig, tucking his arm around her waist and drawing her hips towards his shoulders, 'Delilah's just asked us a favour. She needs a new home for Digby and she thought maybe we'd like to have him.'

Nadine smiled at Digby. 'Oh,' she said, 'well . . . we *could*, I suppose.'

'There's only one thing, though. He hates babies.'

'Hates babies?'

'Uh-huh.'

'Oh dear.'

'Oh dear indeed.'

Delilah looked at them questioningly and they smiled at each other and then at her, and Dig spun Nadine round so that she was sideways on. Nadine pulled at her dress so that it clung tightly to her body and there, silhouetted by the white-gold sun and barely perceptible, was a tiny, hard, perfect little bump.

Delilah screamed, and leaped to her feet, asking a million questions all at once about due dates and scans.

Alex smiled warmly and shook their hands.

Digby ran around barking in an attempt to draw attention to himself.

And Dig and Nadine just beamed at each other because although it was scary as hell, although it was entirely unplanned, although they felt far too young and far too immature to bring another life into the world, and although they had no idea how they were going to afford it, none of that mattered because that little bump was the best thing that had ever happened to them.

LISA JEWELL

The story of how Lisa Jewell became a best-selling author sounds a little like a fairy tale. She had just been made redundant from her job as a PA in a shirt-making company. The week afterwards she went on holiday with her boyfriend Jascha and a large group of friends. 'I wasn't sure what I was going to do next and thought I might try temping. One evening my friend Yasmin sat me down and asked me what I really wanted to do and I said that I'd like to write a female version of Nick Hornby's book *High Fidelity*. She promised to take me to my favourite Thai restaurant if I managed it but, if I failed, I would have to take her.'

Lisa Jewell quickly wrote three chapters and sent them off to ten agents. Back came nine rejections but the tenth asked to see more of the novel. She was thrilled but was worried that she wouldn't be able to finish it while also working full-time. Jascha, who she describes as 'the most amazing man on the planet', asked her to move in with him so she could afford to work part-time and finish her novel. The book, *Ralph's Party*, was published to critical acclaim and quickly became a best seller.

She says she loves being a writer but admits she doesn't always like writing. 'Writing is very hard. I don't understand how anyone can say they actually enjoy it,' she says. 'The days when you write really well and

you get lots done are just brilliant. But the days when you don't write well are just hideous.'

Since publishing *Ralph's Party*, Lisa Jewell has become friends with a group of women writers whose books have been dubbed 'Chick Lit' in the media. 'We email each other all the time, procrastinating. Sometimes we go drinking together as well. There is no competitiveness or bitchiness, we're very supportive.'

In *Thirtynothing* the central characters have to get to grips with growing up. After living a sort of extended adolescence throughout their twenties, by the end of the book both Dig and Nadine feel ready to change and to take on adult responsibilities. This is a subject that fascinates Lisa Jewell. She is thirty-two herself and found turning thirty very traumatic. 'I loved being young and I couldn't really see what it was about middle age that I had to look forward to. But even though I have now turned thirty myself, my life hasn't changed that much. I'm having too much fun at the moment to settle down and have babies, which I'm told will bring a whole new dimension to my life—when/if it happens.'

In a truly romantic style, Lisa Jewell married her amazing boyfriend, Jascha, in a town hall on the Italian Riviera, and they now live happily in North London.

Sally Cummings

Kiss and Tell

Donna Hay

Jo may have had big dreams of being a serious actress, but when her husband leaves her with their two children and a nanny to support, she has to find work wherever she can. So when she is given the part of Stacey in one of TV's top soap operas, *Westfield*, Jo is delighted—even if it does mean she has to compromise her artistic integrity and kiss the detestable leading man. As long as the soap is a success, Jo can pay the bills, but as the show's ratings plummet so do Jo's hopes for the future.

CHAPTER ONE

'YOU MAY KISS THE BRIDE.'

Jo smiled up at her new husband as he lifted her veil and lowered his head to kiss her. As their lips touched, a hush fell over the congregation, broken only by the sound of her mother's sobbing.

Then, suddenly, the doors at the back of the church creaked open and a woman stood there, silhouetted against a shaft of light. All heads turned to follow the elegant blonde as she stalked up the aisle towards them, her face hidden by her sweeping Philip Treacey brim.

'What the — Who is she?' Jo glanced at the man at her side. 'Steve?'

'Well, Steve? Aren't you going to tell her who I am?' The woman turned to Jo, her smile mocking. 'Perhaps I'd better introduce myself? I'm—'

'Cut. Sorry everyone, the boom was in shot. Can we go again?'

A groan went up from the congregation. All eyes turned accusingly to the man holding the furry boom mike, who looked sheepish.

'Shit,' the blonde muttered. 'That's the first time I remembered my lines.' She turned and stalked back up the aisle.

'Right, if we could just go back to the kiss?' The first assistant director was silent for a moment, listening to the director's instructions on his headphones. 'And . . . action.'

This time it went without a hitch. As the first assistant called cut, there was a collective sigh of relief and everyone started talking at once. The vicar disappeared behind the choir stalls for a cigarette, a make-up girl arrived to touch up the mystery woman's lipstick, and the actress playing Jo's mother retrieved her copy of the *Guardian* from under the pew. As the grips moved the heavy grey camera into position for the next shot, Jo turned to her husband of just three minutes.

'If you ever try to stick your tongue down my throat again I'll knee you so hard in the balls you'll be singing soprano. Is that clear?'

Brett Michaels leered. 'Go on, you loved it really. I know you single mums are desperate for it.'

'The day I get that desperate I'll shoot myself.'

'You don't know what you're missing, love. I've never had any complaints before.' Brett's muscles bulged inside his morning suit. As macho Steve Stagg, he was *Westfield*'s resident sex symbol. He was square-jawed, brutishly handsome and the most obnoxious man on TV.

Bastard, Jo thought, as she walked away, picking her way over the snaking electrical cables. She wandered outside. It was a muggy July day and she could feel her gravity-defying hairdo wilting under her veil in the heat. The crew swarmed amid the gravestones of the churchyard, clutching scripts, checking light levels and discussing camera angles.

The real vicar was watching in bewilderment from the steps of the vicarage. Jo greeted him with a wave. 'Nice day,' she called.

'Is it?' He raised his eyes gloomily. 'I don't know what the PCC are going to say about all this. I only agreed to do it because I thought it might help our organ restoration fund. I didn't realise you were going to take the place over.'

'Sorry.' Jo hurried away guiltily. What else could she say? It was always the same with TV crews. When the *Westfield* circus rolled into town, everyone was expected to make way for it.

She pulled at her frilly neckline to cool herself down. She'd been sweltering inside her wedding dress for nearly six hours and her feet had swollen inside her white stilettos. It had been a long day, and not a very easy one. Jo disliked location filming at the best of times, and this certainly wasn't one of the best. They'd arrived at seven that morning to find the unit manager arguing with a man from the council about parking arrangements. A lorry full of lighting equipment was stuck in traffic somewhere on the York outer ring road, and, worst of all, the catering van hadn't turned up. Everything had got hopelessly delayed, which meant hours of sitting around interspersed with bursts of frantic activity.

Tempers might have been fraying on set, but at least the fans were enjoying it. 'Coo-ee! Stacey love! You look gorgeous!' A small crowd of onlookers waved and cheered from the other side of the wall. Jo raised her hand in greeting. After four years in *Westfield*, she'd got used to people calling her by her character's name.

The public's devotion never ceased to amaze her. *Westfield* would never be as big as *EastEnders* or *Coronation Street*, but the twice-weekly soap set in a York housing estate was still cult viewing. It basically told the story of two women—the formidable Ma Stagg and her extended family of thugs and delinquents, and tart-with-a-heart Maggie Evans. Maggie's countless failed relationships had left her with two daughters. Jo played the eldest, Stacey, a kind-hearted but not too bright girl, who ran the local hairdressing salon with her younger sister Winona.

Today was a huge day for her character and for *Westfield*. It was the day when Stacey married Ma Stagg's eldest, macho minicab-driver Steve. No wonder the public had turned up to watch. For the past year they'd followed the on-screen courtship, with all its ups and downs. Now they huddled under the watchful eyes of the Talbot TV security guards, clutching banners with STACEY 4 STEVE on them.

Gravel crunched under Jo's shoes as she picked her way down the path towards the catering van, which had finally turned up. Some of the wedding guests gathered round the hatch in their morning coats and elaborate hats, clutching styrofoam cups of coffee. Jo joined the queue and ordered a coffee and doughnut before walking back to her trailer. On the way, she passed another, bigger caravan with blacked-out windows. This belonged to Eva Lawrence, *Westfield*'s oldest and biggest star. She'd been playing bossy matriarch Ma Stagg ever since the show started, and she never let anyone forget it. Her outrageous demands and tantrums had earned her the nickname Eva the Diva.

She never mixed with the rest of the cast, emerging from her trailer only when she was summoned for a take. The only one who was allowed anywhere near was her simpering personal assistant Desmond, a middle-aged man with all the backbone of a jellyfish.

As with everything else at *Westfield*, there was a pecking order in the accommodation. Eva and Brett had trailers to themselves, closest to the set. Jo's was furthest away, and shared with the rest of her screen family. They were already there as she wrestled her crinoline through the narrow doorway. Lara Lamont, who played her younger sister Winona, was slumped in the only comfortable chair. She acknowledged Jo's arrival with a brief glance while yapping into her mobile phone.

'What do you mean, they won't let me choose my own stylist? Don't they know I'm doing them a big favour, posing for their crappy fashion shoot?' She shifted her long legs fractionally to let Jo struggle past.

At the far end of the trailer, Viola Washington, who played their mother Maggie, took off her blonde wig and shook her hennaed curls free. 'That's better. I thought my scalp was going to melt with that thing on.' She fanned herself with her wig. 'God, it's like an oven in here.'

Away from the cameras, Viola abandoned Maggie's broad Yorkshire accent for her usual RADA drawl. She was a cultured, intelligent woman in her fifties, and about as far away from brash man-eater Maggie as it was possible to get. 'So how did it go with Steve the Stud?'

Jo shuddered. 'Being kissed by Brett Michaels is like snogging a bicycle inner tube, only not quite so arousing.'

'Tell me about it, darling. I had an unfortunate little love scene with him last Christmas, remember?' Viola pulled a face at the memory. 'By the way, the press office dropped off a note for you. I stuck it in your mirror.'

Jo plucked out the envelope. Meanwhile, in the background, Lara was rapidly reaching diva pitch.

'No, you listen to me, Bernie. You tell them if I don't pick the stylist the deal's off. Understand? Off!' She flung the phone down on the counter top. 'Who the hell do they think they are?' she hissed. 'It's not as if I even need the stupid bloody publicity.' She swept her trademark long black hair off her shoulders and frowned. 'What's that you've got?'

'Just an interview request.' Jo stuffed the note into her bag. 'I'll give them a ring when we finish filming.'

'You're not going to do it, are you?' Lara stared at her in horror. 'Why don't you get the press office to give them some quotes? Next you'll be telling me you answer all your fan mail!' Lara sneered. Jo blushed. Before she could answer, Lara's phone trilled again and she snatched it up.

Jo and Viola exchanged glances. Lara Lamont was twenty years old and exotically beautiful. Until three years ago her biggest claim to fame had been a walk-on part in a Burger King ad. Then a *Westfield* casting scout had plucked her from the obscurity of a Leeds youth theatre and catapulted her into the limelight. She now spent her nights out in trendy clubs, dated boy bands and—if the press rumours were to be believed—had an expensive cocaine habit. Most dangerously of all, she had started to confuse fame with talent.

Jo finished her doughnut and brushed the crumbs off her frock. She took a quick look at herself in the mirror and winced. It was very Stacey—shiny white satin with a ruched-up skirt, puffy sleeves and a low-cut bodice scattered with handfuls of rhinestones. Her dark blonde hair was caught up in a mass of ringlets under a sparkly tiara. Dolly Parton meets Bo Peep, she decided.

'My mother would love me in this,' she said wistfully.

Viola looked sympathetic. 'Still putting pressure on you to get married, is she?'

'Pressure? My mother would make the Moonies look laid back.'

What her mother failed to understand was that finding the right man wasn't easy. She was thirty-three years old, with two children and a job that put her in the public eye. She'd had more than her fair share of men who wanted to date her because she was famous and experience had made her cautious. Besides, she already had one failed marriage behind her. She was in no hurry to rush into another one.

'Maybe you should give up on men?' Viola suggested. 'Stick to women. I could fix you up, if you like?'

Jo smiled. Viola played a nymphomaniac on screen, but away from the cameras she ran an animal sanctuary in the Yorkshire Dales with her lifelong partner Marion. The newspapers had tried to do a few shock-horror lesbian exposés on her, but had given up when they realised her life was neither shocking nor horrific, but actually rather dull.

'Thanks, but I don't think my mother would ever forgive me,' Jo said. 'It's bad enough having an actress for a daughter. If I turned out to be gay as well she'd never be able to hold up her head at the Nether Yeadon Ladies' Bridge Club again.'

Lara switched off her phone. 'You'll never guess what!' She looked around at them. 'Trevor Malone's been sacked.'

'You must have got it wrong,' Viola said. 'Trevor Malone's fireproof.'

'Apparently not.' Lara waggled the phone at them. 'Not from what I've just heard, anyway.'

The stunned silence was broken by a rap at the door and the production assistant calling out, 'They're ready for your next scene.'

As usual, they were filming the scenes out of order, starting with the wedding ceremony inside the church. For the rest of the afternoon they were doing outside shots of Jo arriving with her mother and sister, who were still trying to talk her out of going through with the wedding.

It was slow going. Jo lost count of the number of times she ran up and down the church steps. She could feel herself getting a headache, which wasn't helped by the scratchiness of her veil or the thrum of the generator in the background. Added to which the muttering between takes seemed to get louder as the afternoon wore on.

Poor Trevor, Jo thought. As far as everyone was concerned, Executive Producer Trevor Malone was *Westfield*. He'd come up with the original idea fifteen years before. He'd created the York housing estate and all the characters who lived there. He decided who was to be born, and who was to die. It was like telling God that he wasn't up to the job any more.

By the time filming finished for the day, the press office had given up trying to deny the rumours.

'Why did they get rid of him, do you think?' Jo wondered as she and Viola took off their make-up in their trailer.

'I don't know. Falling ratings, I expect. *Westfield* hasn't been doing too well lately. I suppose they think they should get someone new in.'

'Yes, but to sack Trevor. I feel so sorry for him.'

'It's us I feel sorry for. You don't know what it's like when a new executive producer takes over. They want new blood. Sexier characters. You wait and see. It's not just Trevor's head that will roll.'

'Oh God.' Jo slumped in her chair, her wedding veil in her hand. *Westfield* was her security. And with two children to bring up, the last thing she needed now was to be on the dole and looking for acting jobs.

'You'll be all right.' Viola noticed her dismayed expression. 'You're young and pretty, and the viewers like you. It's the oldies like me they'll want to get rid of.' She leaned forward, examining her neck. 'I wonder if I should have my face lifted?' she mused.

But Jo wasn't listening. In spite of what Viola had said, she wasn't reassured. And if they could get rid of Trevor, surely no one was safe?

She was looking forward to a peaceful hour or two to reflect on the problem when she got home, as it was Duncan's turn to look after the children. But, as soon as she put her key in the door and heard squabbling from upstairs, she knew it wasn't to be.

Ignoring the thuds from overhead, she went into the sitting room, where Roxanne the resident but very part-time nanny was curled up on the sofa, getting stuck into some juicy phone gossip. She frowned as Jo entered the room. 'Look, I've got to go,' she said. 'Yeah, that's right. She's come home.' She put the phone down with a martyred sigh.

'What are the girls doing here?' Jo asked.

'*He* dropped them off half an hour ago. Said he had some work to do.'

'Again? But that's the second time this week.'

'Yeah, I know. I'd say something about it if I were you.' Roxanne picked at her split ends. She was a lanky twenty-year-old with an unfortunate complexion and all the infectious enthusiasm of a slow worm.

Jo's heart sank as her fragile domestic arrangements crumbled around her. Why was her ex-husband always doing this to her?

She dumped her bag and fleece jacket on the hall stand and went into the kitchen. As she flicked the switch on the kettle there was a crash from upstairs. Jo leaned against the worktop and braced herself. Sure enough, a moment later she heard feet thundering down the stairs.

'Mummy, tell her!'

'You tell her to keep her hands off my things.'

'I wasn't touching your things. I wouldn't want your stupid things.'

Jo switched the kettle off and reached into the fridge for a bottle of wine instead. So much for slowly unwinding from the day.

'What's for tea?' Chloe asked. She was six years old and alarmingly like her father, with her fair curls, blue eyes and absolute certainty that she was always right.

'Give me a chance, I haven't thought about it yet.'

'Daddy's got a new car,' Chloe said, changing the subject abruptly.

'Has he indeed?'

'It's a Land Rover Discovery,' Grace added. Grace was eleven going on nineteen. She bristled with cool, from her braided hair to her oversized trainers. But underneath she was as shy as her sister was outgoing. 'You should see it, it's really cool. Why can't we have a car like that?'

'Because we can't afford it.' And neither could Duncan. At least, that's what he always told her whenever she asked for some money for the children. She topped up her glass and decided she owed Duncan a furious phone call. 'Right, that's it. I'm going to phone your father.'

'I hope you're not going to start swearing?' Grace said reprovingly.

'I don't swear.'

'Yes, you do!' Chloe pointed out. 'We heard you. The last time you had a row, you called Daddy a—'

'Well, this time I'm going to stay perfectly calm,' Jo cut her off. 'But you'd better go upstairs just in case,' she added as an afterthought.

The phone was answered by a young, foreign-sounding girl. Jo was struggling to make herself understood when Duncan came on the line.

'So much for working,' she said tartly.

'As a matter of fact, Thea is helping me research my next chapter.'

'I bet she is.'

Duncan sighed. 'Is that why you called, to interrogate me about my love life? I thought all that finished when we split up?'

'I couldn't care less who you sleep with,' Jo snapped. 'Why did you send the girls home?'

'I thought I explained to your half-witted nanny, I have to work.'

'And what do you think I do? You know I have a script to learn—'

'Oh, come on, it's hardly the same thing is it? How long will it take you to learn a few lines? Especially when most of them are only one syllable.'

'We can't all produce works of art all day. Some of us have to earn money, real money, instead of contemplating our navels.'

To her annoyance, Duncan just laughed. 'Oh dear, here we go again. Why do I feel another lecture coming on? How poor hard-done-by Jo has had to sacrifice her promising theatre career to feed her children because bad old Duncan refuses to churn out commercial trash.'

'I'd be amazed if you churned out anything,' Jo retorted. 'One novel in three years is hardly prolific, is it? When are we going to see this next masterpiece of yours?'

'When it's finished. Which won't be very soon if you keep disturbing me.' He hung up.

Jo slammed down the phone, wondering how she'd ever married someone so self-centred. But she'd been just the same, once upon a time.

They'd met at university. She was studying English and drama, he was one of her lecturers. Despite the ten-year age gap, they'd shared the same dreams. He was going to write the definitive modern novel. She was going to take the acting world by storm. But then real life intervened. A year after leaving college Jo found herself pregnant. By the time she'd got over the shock, she and Duncan were married.

Grace's birth might have been an accident, but it changed her life. Suddenly playing all the major Shakespearean heroines by the time she was thirty didn't seem as important as taking care of her precious baby daughter. Duncan grudgingly agreed to stay in his college job to support them. The plan was that when Grace was older Jo would go back to work so he could concentrate on his writing.

Which she did, for two years. And then Chloe came along. Duncan wanted Jo to have an abortion, but she refused. Frustration and arguments followed, and within a year of Chloe's birth they'd split up.

Jo listened to Chloe's imperative tones ringing out from the sitting room. How ironic that the child Duncan hadn't wanted to be born should turn out so much like him.

Her script lay on the work surface. She put it guiltily to one side and started to prepare supper. Perhaps, if she could keep Roxanne off the phone long enough, she might be able to snatch half an hour to go through the next day's scenes.

But no such luck. She was draining pasta over the sink when Roxanne appeared in the doorway. 'Right, I'm off now,' she announced.

'Off? Where?'

'Out with my friend Wendy. You said I could go, remember?'

Jo racked her brains. No, she couldn't remember. She put on her best wheedling face. 'Look, I don't suppose—'

'No.' Roxanne shook her head. 'I can't cancel. Wendy's waiting for me. We're going down Micklegate. I can't let her down, can I?'

'No, I suppose not. Off you go, then. Have a nice time.'

'I will. Don't wait up.' Jo looked at the length of leg appearing from her bottom-skimming skirt and wondered if she should say anything. Would her parents in Thirsk approve of her going out like that? But by the time she'd opened her mouth, Roxanne had already gone.

'Yuk, what's this?' Grace made a face as Jo put her plate in front of her.

'Spag bol, what does it look like?'

'That's got meat in it, hasn't it? Vicky Carling says meat is murder.'

'Vicky Carling doesn't have to eat it, does she?'

Grace pushed her plate away. 'I'm a vegetarian.'

'What's a vegetarian?' Chloe piped up.

'Someone who doesn't eat meat.' Grace thrust her face towards her sister. 'You know what you've got on your plate, don't you?' she said ghoulishly. 'Little chopped up bits of baby calf and—'

'That's enough, Grace!' Thankfully the phone rang, saving them from more grisly details. Chloe raced to it first.

'Hello, Grandma.' Jo put down her fork. Just what she needed. 'Yes, I'm fine. Yes, Grace is fine too. Mummy?' She ignored Jo's frantic head shaking. 'Yes, she's here. Do you want to speak to her?' She handed the phone over. Jo took it reluctantly.

'I'll deal with you later,' she threatened. 'No, not you, Mum.'

Audrey only ever rang for two reasons. One, so she could berate her for being a working mother and the other—

'You'll never guess who I had coffee with this morning? Marjorie Redman. You remember Marjorie? You and her daughter Susan used to go to Brownies together?' She went on, 'She was telling me Susan's just got herself engaged. To a merchant banker.'

'Lucky old Susan.'

'I know. And she's such an unfortunate-looking girl, too. All that hair on her upper lip. And that squint. I don't know how she managed it.'

Jo could hear the naked envy in her voice. Competition for eligible men was fierce among the mothers of Nether Yeadon. After five years as a divorcee Jo sensed she was becoming a social embarrassment.

'Well, you know what they say, Mum. Love is blind.'

'Of course, Marjorie's delighted,' Audrey went on. 'She was beginning to give up hope. But it just goes to show, it's never too late.'

'Mum, Susan's only thirty-three. She's hardly on the shelf.'

'Yes, I know. But by the time a woman gets to your age most of the men are either divorced or . . . you know, the other way.'

'So, Susan's tracked down the last single, straight man in North Yorkshire. Good for her.'

'There's no need to take that tone, Joanne,' Audrey sniffed. 'I just thought you'd be interested. After all, Susan is a friend of yours.'

'Was there something else you wanted, Mum? Only I've got a lot of work to catch up on this evening.'

Oh God, why had she said it? Cue Audrey's second favourite subject.

'You work too hard, you know. If only you had someone to share the burden with—'

'I have a nanny.'

'You know what I mean.'

Jo sighed wearily. 'Yes, Mum, I know. But I don't have to wash the nanny's socks or worry about who she's sleeping with behind my back.'

'Well, if you're going to take that tone—' The phone went down with a crash, leaving her holding a buzzing receiver. She knew she would have to ring back and apologise. But not yet. First she was going to load up the dishwasher, run herself a long, hot bath and tackle that script.

Most of her scenes for the following day were with Viola. Jo sank under the bubbles and concentrated on the lines. She'd barely been in the bath five minutes when the door burst open and Chloe and Grace fell through it.

'Will you help me with my maths homework?' Grace demanded.

'It's hardly my strong point.'

'Doesn't matter. If I get it wrong I can just say it's your fault.'

As Grace dashed off to fetch her books, Chloe took off her clothes and climbed into the tub. Jo sighed and put down her script. It looked as if, yet again, Stacey and her emotional dramas would have to wait.

By nine o'clock, she'd finally talked the girls into bed and poured herself another glass of wine. Huddled in her towelling bathrobe, she sat at her dressing table. She picked up a brush and tried to pull it through her hair. Even after three washes it was still tangled with lacquer. She scowled at her reflection in the dressing-table mirror. She might not have Susan Redman's squint or hairy-lip problem, but she was no Kate Moss either. Her nose was too short, her mouth too wide. Her hair was just about blonde, thanks to a few fading summer highlights, and cut in a thick, layered bob. Her eyes were large and expressive, but the colour of dirty pond water with permanent shadows of exhaustion.

She was just picking up her script yet again when the phone rang. It was Viola. 'I just thought you ought to know, I've found out who our new executive producer is going to be,' she announced breathlessly.

Jo steeled herself. 'How bad is it?'

'The worst,' Viola said. 'It's the Grim Reaper.'

She sounded so grave Jo nearly laughed. 'Who?'

'Richard Black. The Grim Reaper. Don't tell me you've never heard of him?'

'Well, no—'

'Darling, the man's a monster! How do you think he got his nickname? His appearance means instant death,' Viola said. 'You remember

A Country Village? That sweet little afternoon soap? Who do you think sent the bulldozers in and turned it into a shopping centre?'

'No!'

'And you must have heard what happened to Eithne Pollock?'

'Wasn't she in *Coachman's Way*?'

'That's right. She lived for that programme. It was all that kept her going after her husband left her for a chiropodist. But Black sacked her.'

'What happened to her?'

'You might well ask,' Viola said darkly. 'The last I heard, she was demonstrating electric sanders on the Home Shopping Channel. I tell you, the man is death. The question is, which of us will be next?'

With that troubling thought on her mind, Jo fell into bed with her script. She'd just finished reading and turned out the light when she heard feet pattering across the landing. A moment later, Chloe's warm little body was snuggling up to hers.

'Mummy,' she whispered. 'Can we have a hamster?'

'I don't think so, darling.'

'Mummy, have we got millions of pounds in the bank?'

Jo pulled away and looked down at her. 'What makes you ask that?'

'Simon Beckett says we have. His mum reckons because you're on telly we must be filthy rich.'

'Simon's mum shouldn't believe everything she reads in the papers.'

'And she says that's why you never help out at school. She says you'd probably expect a few thousand to turn up at the summer fête. That's not true, is it?' Chloe frowned.

'Of course it isn't.' Jo cuddled her closer. It hurt when the girls got teased or picked on because of who she was.

'So we don't have millions in the bank?' Chloe interrupted her thoughts.

'I'm afraid not.'

'But have we got enough to buy a hamster?'

'We'll see.' A moment later Chloe was asleep. Jo lay awake, listening to her soft breathing.

If only they did have millions in the bank, she wouldn't be worrying . It hadn't occurred to her until now just how much she needed *Westfield*. The job might have its drawbacks, but it had given her financial security. After she'd split up with Duncan, Jo had found herself alone with two small children and no money. For months they'd struggled along in a dingy, damp flat, on virtually nothing, while she searched for work. She'd done all kinds of odd jobs, from waitressing to selling fitted kitchens, just to make ends meet. In the meantime, she'd tried to find acting work. But she'd lost count of the auditions she'd had to turn down because she couldn't find anyone to look after the children, or because the job would involve filming away from home.

And then, just as she was beginning to give up hope, along came *Westfield*. Trevor Malone's offer was like a dream come true. It might not be the challenging career she'd dreamed of, but at least it meant she could buy a house and build a life for herself and the girls.

And now she was in danger of losing it all. Jo stared into the darkness. 'It's not just Trevor's head that will roll.' Viola had said. Guilty and selfish as it made her feel, Jo just prayed it wouldn't be hers.

By the following day, news of the Grim Reaper's imminent arrival had spread around the *Westfield* studios. As Jo drove through the security gates, she spotted a removal van parked outside the main building, which housed all the production offices. Slowing down, she recognised Trevor's battered old desk being loaded onto the back of the van.

'The king is dead. Long live the king.' Rob Fletcher, who played her brother-in-law Tony Stagg, drew up alongside her on his bicycle. He might be a wife-beating womaniser on screen, but away from the cameras he was quiet, bespectacled and a member of Greenpeace. 'How long before the rest of us are being bundled out like that, I wonder?'

The *Westfield* set, with its outdoor lot, indoor studio sets and annexe of dressing rooms and wardrobe department, stood away from the main production building, separated by a tree-lined courtyard. Jo parked her yellow Cinquecento in its usual spot in the artists' car park, but instead of heading straight for her dressing room, she took a detour into the studio building. Rob's comment had unsettled her and she needed to be reassured that at least somewhere it was business as usual.

Ahead of her the set dressers were busy in the café set, laying the tables and filling the chiller cabinet with pre-packed sandwiches. These were the regular sets, which featured in every episode. From the far side of the building came the sound of hammering and a tinny radio as the other temporary sets were put up for the episode they were due to film the following day.

When Jo had first arrived at *Westfield* it had seemed strange to see the sets, looking much smaller and shabbier than on screen, arranged side by side amid camera equipment, lighting and props. Now it all seemed as familiar as her own home. But for how much longer? she wondered.

She wasn't the only one who was feeling apprehensive. Everywhere Jo went, there were pinched, anxious faces. People were snapping at each other. Every snippet of gossip was seized upon and dissected.

'I wonder when he's coming?' mused Viola, as they gathered in the greenroom later that morning. It reminded Jo of a student common room, with its fug of cigarette smoke and clutter of coats, bags and scripts on every armchair. Besides Jo and Viola, there were Rob Fletcher and another actress, Judy Pearce. Brett was in a corner, playing with his Gameboy in a great show of indifference.

'No idea. They're keeping it very hush-hush.'

'I just hope we get another payday before we all get the boot.'

'Well, I think it's outrageous,' declared Judy, who played Ma Stagg's downtrodden daughter-in-law Andrea. 'We should talk to the union about it. They can't treat us like this.'

'I think you'll find they can, darling,' Viola said. 'You can complain all you like, but if you've got any sense you'll just keep your head down and hope for the best like the rest of us.'

'Well, I think they've made the right choice.' Brett looked up from zapping aliens. 'I've always said we needed some changes on *Westfield*. It's about time we got rid of some dead wood.'

'I take it that doesn't include you?' Jo asked.

'Of course not.' Brett's lip curled. 'They wouldn't dare get rid of Steve. He's the only reason women watch this show.'

Jo fought the urge to slap the smirk off his face. The worst of it was, he was probably right.

'This is ridiculous. They can't just keep us all in the dark like this,' Jo declared. 'I think we should go up and find out what's going on.'

'You don't mean—the top floor?'

'Why not? What's to stop us going up there? We have a right to know.'

Everyone stared at her. The top floor was the Mount Olympus of *Westfield*, where all the heads of department lived. Artists were only ever summoned there when they were in trouble, or about to get a big new story line. No one, but no one, went up there of their own accord.

'Maybe you're right,' Viola agreed slowly. 'Maybe someone should go up and find out what's going on.'

Jo nodded. She was still nodding when she felt all eyes turn in her direction. 'What . . . me? Oh no, I couldn't.'

'It was your idea,' Judy pointed out.

'Yes, but I wasn't volunteering!'

She was still wondering how she'd been pushed into the job as she stepped through the doors of the executive lift onto the top floor.

Her footsteps were silenced by acres of cream carpet as she crept down to the end of the long corridor to what had once been Trevor Malone's office. She felt out of place in her combat trousers, T-shirt and battered old Reeboks. Fortunately there was no one around, although she could hear muffled voices behind closed doors as she passed them.

Jo found Trevor's door and gingerly pushed it open. A vast, empty space roughly the size of a football pitch greeted her. Ahead, through a wall of glass, the *Westfield* set lay like a toy town. From here she could see everything—the tiny streets, with their shops and house fronts propped up by huge timber struts, and the studios beyond.

She turned away, and nearly fell over a battered old cardboard box sitting in the middle of the floor, bearing the words: RUBBISH FOR DISPOSAL.

Then something caught her eye. A glint from under the flap of the box. Jo knelt down to look and her breath caught in her throat.

There, stuffed into the box with all Trevor's old papers and books was a small glass statuette. Jo lifted it out carefully. His National TV Award. She remembered the night he'd collected it, how they'd all crowded onto the stage, the applause ringing in their ears. Trevor had stood in the middle of it all, too choked with pride to speak, just gazing at it. His award.

She felt her eyes blurring. And now someone had just dumped it in a box to throw away. They'd got rid of the man, and now they wanted to get rid of his memories too.

'What do you think you're doing?'

The voice startled her so much she nearly dropped the award. Her eyes travelled from the Bruno Magli slingbacks, up the slim legs, past the sharply cut black suit to meet a pair of hostile grey eyes.

She stood up until she was level with them. 'I'm Jo Porter.' She stuck out her hand, but the woman ignored it.

'I suppose you've been sent by Maintenance?' she snapped.

'I—'

'You should have been here half an hour ago. I want this rubbish cleared before Mr Black's furniture arrives.'

Jo was about to point out her mistake, then thought better of it. At least if she took Trevor's box she could save it from the garbage chute.

The woman stalked out of the office, leaving Jo boiling with indignation. High-handed bitch!

As she staggered down the corridor, her legs buckling under the weight of the box, she met the woman by the lift doors. She was flicking through some post, ignoring Jo as she struggled, puffing and panting, to balance the box on one knee while trying to reach the lift buttons.

In the awkward silence that followed, she tried to make conversation. 'So—er—have you worked for Richard Black long, then?'

The woman looked her up and down. With her sleek dark hair, knuckle-duster cheekbones and a voice that could etch glass, she oozed superiority. 'I've been *Mr* Black's PA for nearly two years.'

'You must know him quite well, then?'

'Well enough.' Was that the faintest trace of a smirk?

'What's he like?'

Her well-bred nostrils flared. She looked as if she would rather be making small talk with the box. 'We get on extremely well.'

As if that's any recommendation, Jo thought, as the lift doors whispered open. She hauled the box inside then turned back to face the woman. 'So—um—any idea when he's arriving?' she panted.

'Oh, you'll meet him soon enough.' Her tight little smile was the last thing Jo saw before the lift doors closed on her.

Trevor Malone lived on the top floor of a converted Victorian house in a once sought-after but now seedy part of Harrogate. Jo still wasn't sure if she was doing the right thing as she parked her Cinquecento outside. After all, she'd only known Trevor through work.

She opened the boot and dragged the box out onto the kerb. Squaring her shoulders, she hauled the box up the stone steps towards the battered front door.

No one answered when she rang the bell. Jo was just about to give up when the door opened and a frail, elderly man stood there.

'Oh, I'm sorry,' she began to apologise. 'I was looking for—'

'Jo?'

She peered closer. 'Trevor?'

'What a wonderful surprise.' His smile lit up his lined, tired face. 'What are you doing here?'

'I—er—' She tried not to stare. Crikey, what had happened to him? He looked as if he'd aged thirty years overnight. 'I came to bring you this,' she pulled herself together. 'You left it at the office.'

'Ah.' He looked down at the box. 'So I did. I wondered if it would turn up.' He crouched down, lifted the flaps and took out the award. For a long time he just stared at it, not moving. Jo's heart sank.

Then Trevor looked up and she saw the shimmer of tears in his eyes. 'Thank you,' he said. 'You don't know how much these things mean to me.' He gazed reverently at the statuette. 'I wanted to collect them myself, but I couldn't bring myself to go back.'

He was so overcome she felt tears pricking herself. 'I'll help you carry them upstairs, if you like?'

'Thank you, my dear. You're very kind.' He placed the award back in the box and straightened up. 'Perhaps you'd like a cup of tea?'

'Well, I—' Jo was about to refuse, until she saw the desperate loneliness in his eyes. 'That would be very nice,' she agreed.

She followed him into the dark passageway and up several flights of narrow stairs.

'Go through to the living room,' he said, when she finally gasped her way to the top-floor landing. 'I'll put the kettle on.'

His flat was sparsely furnished and very eighties, with black ash and smoked glass everywhere. Jo sank into the deep embrace of a black leather sofa and looked around her. One wall was lined with photos of most of the *Westfield* cast. There were no family photos, she noticed. It was rumoured that Trevor was gay. Others reckoned he was just married to *Westfield*. Looking at the photos made her feel even more sad.

How could everyone have forgotten him so quickly? He'd only been gone three days, and already it was as if he'd never existed. It had become bad luck even to whisper his name.

'Looking at my rogues' gallery?' Trevor shuffled back in with a tray. 'Some people have certainly changed, haven't they?'

Especially you, Jo thought.

'It was so kind of you to come.' His hands shook slightly as he poured her tea. 'You're the first person who's spoken to me since—you know.'

'The others send their love. They keep meaning to call, but you know what filming schedules are like.' Jo couldn't meet his eyes.

'I really miss the place,' he sighed. 'Silly, isn't it? I still can't get used to getting up in the morning and not having anywhere to go.'

His forlorn face brought a lump to her throat. 'You'll be back, you'll see. They won't be able to run the place without you.'

'I doubt it, my dear. I wouldn't want to come back, anyway. Not once Richard Black gets his hands on it.'

Jo shivered. Why did people keep saying that? 'Do you know him?'

'As a matter of fact, I gave him his first job, nearly fifteen years ago, as a production assistant on *Westfield*. He just turned up at the studios one day, out of the blue, and demanded I take him on. Couldn't have been more than seventeen at the time. He was an arrogant sod even then.'

'So what's he like?'

'Totally ruthless. If Richard wants something, he won't let anyone or anything stand in his way.' His mouth thinned. 'I remember at that very first interview I asked him what kind of job he wanted. He looked me straight in the eye and said, "Yours." And he's been after it ever since. I handed him the knife, and now he's stabbed me in the back with it.'

'What do you mean?'

'Oh, you know how these things work in television. A whisper here, a few rumours there. He's been spreading dirt about me, telling everyone I'm not up to the job. He's got friends in high places. People listen to him.'

'But surely they listen to you, too? After all, you created *Westfield*!'

'Once upon a time, maybe. But things change.' Trevor looked wistful. 'TV companies don't want good drama. They want sensationalism, something to push up the ratings. And that's what he's promised them.'

'Things will work out. You'll find another job.'

'I doubt it, my dear. Who'd want an old fool like me? No, at least I've got enough sense to know when I've been put out to grass.'

They chatted for a while about the old days, until it was time for her to leave. As he saw her to the door, Trevor suddenly clutched her arm.

'Be careful, won't you?' he said. 'Don't trust him. I did once, and look where it got me.'

Jo smiled ruefully. 'I aim to stay out of his way if I can.'

'I'm serious!' As he thrust his face close to hers, she caught a whiff of whisky. 'Watch out for him. Because he'll certainly be watching you.'

'Thanks for the warning.' Jo planted a kiss on his thin, bristly cheek. 'Take care of yourself, Trevor,' she said. 'And don't forget to come and see us if you're passing.'

He shook his head. 'Thank you my dear, but somehow I don't think I'll be seeing *Westfield* again.'

CHAPTER TWO

THE SUN STOPPED SHINING on the day of the funeral three weeks later. The sky was steel grey and a damp mist clung to them as they lined the graveside. It could have been a scene from *Westfield*. Brett, Rob and Eva huddled together on one side of the grave. On the other was Viola, flanked by Jo and Lara, all dressed in sombre black.

Except this wasn't make believe. This was all too horribly real.

It had all happened so suddenly. A stroke, according to the coroner's report. Trevor died quickly and painlessly in his sleep. But Jo knew, and so did everyone else, that it was a broken heart that had killed him.

There were no relatives or friends at the funeral. The cast and crew of *Westfield* were his only family. Burly cameramen shouldered his coffin from the church in grim silence. As it was lowered, Lara stepped forward, a rose in her hand. She was wearing a new Dolce and Gabbana frock coat, and, as she paused dramatically beside the grave, Jo heard the click of a camera.

'I don't believe it,' Viola hissed through her tears. 'She's brought a bloody photographer!'

'Probably another exclusive deal.' Jo could just imagine the headline: SOAP TRAGEDY—LARA LAMONT INVITES US TO THE FUNERAL AND SHARES HER GRIEF.

Sickened, she turned away—and then she saw him. A tall, dark figure, standing under a yew tree on the other side of the churchyard, the collar of his raincoat turned up against the clinging mist.

As the mourners began to disperse, Jo picked her way across the grass to where he'd been standing. But he was gone. She reached the trees just in time to see a dark green Audi disappearing up the road.

'Come to make sure old Trev's dead and buried, I suppose.' Jo swung round and found herself facing the smiling, oleaginous features of Charlie Beasley, showbiz reporter and chief muckraker of the *Globe*. He was deceptively harmless looking in his spectacles and grey suit.

'Don't you vultures have any respect?' she snapped.

'You know who that was, don't you?' Charlie ignored the question. 'Richard Black. The Grim Reaper himself. Might have known he'd be hanging around in a graveyard with a name like that.'

Jo stared down the road. So that was him.

'This couldn't have worked out better for him if he'd planned it,' Charlie went on. 'Now he hasn't got Trevor looking over his shoulder, he can do as he likes. Of course, it's not such good news for you lot. Rumour is he's got some big changes planned. Must be a bit worrying, eh?'

Jo bit her lip. After four years on *Westfield*, she knew when a tabloid journalist was trying to trap her. She walked away, quickly.

Charlie panted to keep up with her. 'I've heard the Grim Reaper's already sharpening his scythe. But I suppose you know all about that.'

'I don't listen to gossip. That's your job.'

'Oh, this isn't gossip, love. It's fact. He's drawn up his hit list. And guess who's at the top of it?'

Jo gritted her teeth. 'I don't know and I don't care.'

'You haven't heard?' Charlie blinked in mock surprise. 'Viola's for the chop. And so are a few of the others. They say he's getting rid of anyone over fifty. Sad really, isn't it?'

It was more than sad. It was heartbreaking. If it was true, Viola would be utterly devastated. If it was true. 'No comment.'

Jo reached her car and fumbled in her bag for her key.

'Besides, it's got to be good news for you, hasn't it? With Viola and that lot out of the way, you could end up one of *Westfield's* biggest stars. I reckon you've got a lot to thank Richard Black for.'

'I've got nothing to thank him for. If it wasn't for him, Trevor Malone might still be alive!'

She could have bitten off her tongue. Charlie's brows shot up. 'Are you saying Trevor died because he was sacked from *Westfield?*'

'No.'

'You think he died of a broken heart, is that it?' Charlie's eyes gleamed. 'And as it was Black who got him sacked, he's the one who caused his death. He virtually murdered him, is that what you're saying?'

'I'm not saying anything.' Jo found her key, unlocked the car and dived in.

As she started the engine, Charlie bent down and grinned through the window. 'Thanks, Jo,' he said. 'Your comments have been most helpful.'

GRIM REAPER CLAIMS HIS FIRST VICTIM, declared the headline on the *Globe's* front page the following morning. Under it were the words: 'He killed Trevor, says soap star Stacey.'

Jo spotted the paper on a rack outside a newsagent's as she was driving the girls to school. She jammed her foot on the brake, nearly causing a multiple pile-up behind her.

'Mum!' Grace, who was trying to finish off her homework in the back, yelled in outrage. 'You've made me scrawl right through my map!'

'Sorry.' Jo moved off again. It was a mistake. It had to be.

But it wasn't. She bought a copy of the newspaper after dropping the girls off. She was still sitting behind the wheel of her car, staring in horror at the words on the page, when her mobile phone went off.

It was Louise, *Westfield's* press officer. 'Have you seen the *Globe?*'

'I'm looking at it now.'

'You didn't really say all that, did you? Please tell me you didn't.'

'Of course I didn't. Well, not all of it, anyway. I might have said something. Oh God, I don't remember!' She certainly didn't remember saying that Richard Black was a murderer, or that he had an innocent man's blood on his hands. But it was there, in black and white.

'Why on earth didn't you talk to me first?' Louise raged. 'You know what reporters are like. They're sharks, sniffing around for blood.'

'I only said what I felt,' Jo defended herself lamely.

'Yes, but it wasn't true, was it?'

'How do you know? I saw Trevor just before he died. He was heart-broken at being sacked.'

'But he wasn't.' There was a silence at the other end of the line.

Jo gripped the phone. 'What are you saying?'

'Nothing.'

'Louise!'

'Look, let's just say there's more to this story than meets the eye, OK? You should have checked your facts with me first.'

'I know. I'm sorry.' Jo bit her lip. 'Perhaps I could apologise—'

'No!' Louise bellowed. 'Don't say a word. You've already done enough damage. Not a single word. To anyone. Do you understand?'

'Yes,' Jo agreed meekly.

'Of course, it would have to happen today,' Louise said. 'You do realise it's Richard Black's first day? What do you suppose he's going to say when this lands on his desk?'

'Perhaps he won't see it?' Jo suggested optimistically.

It was hardly a realistic hope. As she slunk into the *Westfield* studios half an hour later, it felt as if the whole world had got hold of a copy.

Typically, the first person she met was Brett Michaels. As he swaggered past her in the corridor, he leered and drew a finger across his throat. Her empty stomach churned.

And there was worse to come. Someone had stuck the Situations Vacant page from *The Stage* on her dressing-room door.

'Very bloody funny!' she snarled, slamming the door.

'My God, I'm amazed you dared show your face this morning.' Viola was examining the bags under her eyes in the mirror.

Jo slumped down in her chair. 'I take it you've seen it too?'

'Darling, hasn't everyone? Someone's enlarged it on the photocopier and stuck it up in the greenroom. You are daring!'

Jo stared despairingly at her own reflection. 'So has anyone spotted our new boss yet?'

'Not so far. We've seen his poisonous PA though. Kate, I think her name is. She came stalking through here about an hour ago.'

Jo bit her lip. 'Oh, Vi, I should have kept my mouth shut, shouldn't I?'

'It might not have been the best career move you've ever made,' Viola agreed. 'But personally, I think you did the right thing.'

'You do?'

'Absolutely.' Viola nodded. 'Suicidal, but definitely the right thing. Someone needed to speak up. I'm just glad it wasn't me, that's all.'

The morning's filming went by with only the occasional snigger and sideways remark for her to contend with. By lunchtime Jo was beginning to breathe again. Perhaps she was worrying over nothing? She finished her scenes, changed back into her jeans and sweater and was on her way home when she met Kate coming towards her.

'There you are,' she said. 'I've been looking for you. Mr Black would like to see you in the top-floor conference room. Immediately.'

'Any idea why he wants to see me?'

'I should have thought that was obvious.' Kate gave her a withering look.

They made their way up to the top floor in silence. Jo passed the time plucking invisible fluff off her sweater.

'Haven't I seen you somewhere before?' Kate said.

'Er—I don't think so.' Jo squirmed as the PA studied her.

'No, I'm sure I've seen you on the top floor—'

'Here we are.' The lift doors opened and Jo rushed out.

Kate glanced at her watch. 'Five minutes late. Everyone will be waiting.'

'Who's everyone—?' Jo never finished the question, as Kate pushed open the door marked CONFERENCE ROOM. Suddenly she found herself confronted by a sea of faces. Everyone, from the cast, the crew and the production team, to the girls in admin and accounts, was there.

The room fell silent and all eyes swivelled in her direction as Jo made her humiliatingly public entrance. She tried to slink in at the back but Viola had saved her a seat so she was forced to shuffle her way to the front row. And then she was face to face with the Grim Reaper himself.

He was younger than Jo had imagined, no more than mid-thirties, although his severely tailored suit made him appear older. He stood at the front of the room, flanked by Kate and Louise the press officer, surveying the assembled company through narrowed eyes.

So this was the famous Richard Black. No wonder everyone was so in awe of him. He seemed to tower over them all, and not just because of his commanding height.

'Now we're all finally here, perhaps we could make a start?' He didn't raise his voice, but the room instantly fell silent. 'As you all know, my name is the Grim Reaper. But I prefer to be called Richard.' Everyone laughed politely. Jo was too terrified to crack a smile.

He wasn't smiling either. She studied him covertly, taking in the strong face, the short dark hair with just a hint of curl, the hard, cynical mouth. He wasn't exactly handsome, but there was an aura of power about him that was disturbing.

'I won't beat about the bush. *Westfield* is in trouble. Big trouble. I wouldn't be here if it wasn't. I've been brought in to put things right. Now I realise I might not be the most popular choice for the job. But, whether you like it or not, I'm the best chance you have of saving your jobs. If the ratings keep falling the way they are, in six months' time this whole show could be axed.'

There were murmurings among the audience. No one had realised the situation was this bad.

Or was it? Jo watched him closely. 'Don't trust him,' Trevor had said. 'I intend to do everything necessary to put *Westfield* back where it belongs,' Richard went on. 'And that includes changing story lines and getting rid of characters who have outlived their usefulness. Some of you will have to go.' Jo swallowed hard. Was he looking at her? 'I shall be looking at the situation closely over the next month or so before I make any long-term decisions. Now, having said all that, I hope we can all work together. But if anyone thinks they may have a problem with the way I do things, perhaps it would be best if they left now.'

There was silence. Jo shrank in her seat as all eyes turned to her.

'And one more thing,' he added. 'Some of you may have read certain reports in the gutter press this morning.' *Oh God, here it comes.* Jo stared at her shoes and willed herself to disappear. 'Now I realise emotions may be running high following the recent . . . tragic events.' He cleared his throat. 'Which is why I'm taking no action on this occasion. But I can't allow this constant bleating to the press to continue.' His gaze swept over them like an Arctic breeze. 'From now on, all comments must be directed through the press office. If anyone gives any unauthorised interviews, I won't hesitate to sack them. Is that understood?'

There was a general murmur of agreement. Jo forced herself to lift her eyes from the toes of her trainers and realised with a shock that he was looking straight at her, piercing and direct. Heat flooded into her face.

'Good,' he said quietly. 'In future, if you have any complaints, please bring them to me, not Charlie Beasley.'

'Well, I reckon you got off lightly there,' Viola said as they emerged from the lifts into the production-centre reception ten minutes later.

'You think so?' Jo could still feel her face burning.

'God yes,' agreed Lara, flicking back her long dark hair. 'I thought you were in for a right bollocking.'

She couldn't have been more mortified if he'd dragged her up to the front and flogged her in front of everyone. And he knew it too. 'I still think he's a bastard,' she muttered.

'Well, I wouldn't want to get on the wrong side of him,' Lara said. 'Although he's dead sexy, isn't he?'

'He put me in mind of Mr Darcy,' Viola nodded. 'You know, very aloof on the surface, but loads of simmering passion underneath.'

Jo stared at them both. 'I don't believe you two! Have you forgotten what he did to Trevor?'

'Not that again!' Viola raised her eyes heavenwards. 'My God, Jo, haven't you dropped yourself in it enough?'

'Besides, Trevor can't have been up to the job, or *Westfield* wouldn't be in so much trouble, would it?' Lara added.

'So that makes it all right, does it?' Jo turned on her. 'Don't you understand, it's not what they did, it's the way they did it? Just throwing him out like—an old Hoover bag. And we all know who was behind *that*—'

'Can I have a word?' She'd been so busy sounding off she hadn't noticed Louise, the press officer, approaching. 'In private,' she added, grabbing Jo's arm and steering her towards the press office.

Louise crossed the room to her desk and began sorting through the mountain of papers. 'About what you were saying,' she began.

'I know, I know,' Jo held up her hands. 'It's OK, I'm not going to start shouting to the press again. It was a stupid thing to do. But you can't stop me having an opinion.'

'Trevor Malone wasn't sacked,' Louise said. She was in her thirties, a plump, dark-haired girl with a permanently harassed expression. 'It was his decision to leave *Westfield*.'

'But I don't understand,' Jo faltered. 'Everyone knows they brought Richard Black in to replace him.' Then the truth dawned. 'Oh, I get it. You mean he was offered some kind of made-up job, like associate executive consultant in charge of paperclips—'

'He could have stayed in his old job, with his old salary. All he had to do was share some of the day-to-day responsibility with Richard.'

'Let him make all the decisions, you mean? Well, I'm not surprised he left. It doesn't sound as if he was given much choice, does it?'

'It wasn't like that.' Louise handed Jo a piece of paper. 'Look, I'm not supposed to be telling you any of this. But I thought you should know. This is the press release I prepared on the day Trevor Malone left *Westfield*. Go on, read it. It's all there.'

Jo skimmed through the document. It didn't add up. 'I don't understand. It says here—'

'It says the head of drama at Talbot TV planned to sack Trevor because he really wasn't up to the job any more. He *wasn't*,' she insisted, as Jo opened her mouth to protest. 'Anyway, Talbot wanted to bring in Richard Black. But he said he'd only come here on condition that he could work alongside Trevor. Apparently they go back a long way.'

'Trevor gave him his first job,' Jo murmured.

'Well, Trevor wasn't having any of it,' Louise went on. 'His pride couldn't take the idea of sharing *Westfield* with anyone. So he packed up his stuff and left. But he made sure everyone believed he'd been sacked.'

'That's the bit I don't get. Why would he want people to think that?'

'Aiming for the sympathy vote, I suppose,' Louise shrugged.

Jo looked down at the press release. Trevor had deliberately used her, and she'd fallen for it. 'So why didn't you send this out?'

'Richard wouldn't let me. He said he didn't want to get embroiled in a war of words. But, if you ask me, it was out of loyalty to Trevor. It's just a shame the old man didn't feel the same way, isn't it?' She took the paper out of Jo's hands. 'Promise me you won't breathe a word of this to anyone? My job would be on the line if Richard found out.'

Jo stood up, her brow furrowed. 'But you can't deny it did kill Trevor, leaving *Westfield*? I mean, Richard must have that on his conscience?'

Louise shook her head. 'It was Trevor's liver. He had a serious drink problem. Another little fact Richard made sure we hushed up.'

Jo thought back to the last time she'd seen him. The smell of stale alcohol on his breath.

She left the press office, still dazed. As she made her way back towards the studios, she spotted Richard Black striding towards her.

She froze. Oh God, what must he think of her? Maybe it wasn't too late to apologise? As he drew level, Jo gave him a big smile.

'I just wanted to say—'

But she never got a chance to say it. He whisked straight past her. He didn't spare her the briefest glance, but Jo knew he'd deliberately ignored her.

She watched him go, feeling crushed. So much for staying out of his way. She had the feeling she'd just put herself right in his firing line.

'**D**o we have to go?' Chloe and Grace sat side by side on the sofa, their expressions pained.

'Yes, we do. School starts next week.'

'But we hate shopping!'

'Especially for school uniform. Yuk!'

Jo gritted her teeth. 'Look, I'll tell you what. We'll get it done quickly and then treat ourselves, shall we?'

That got them. 'What kind of treat?' Grace wanted to know.

'Can I have a hamster?' Chloe piped up.

'Well, I was thinking more of tea in Betty's,' Jo admitted. 'But we'll see, shall we?'

By the time she'd spent three hours buying skirts, blouses and PE kits, and arguing with Grace about why kitten-heeled mules were not sensible school shoes, she felt exhausted enough to agree to anything.

Chloe bore her new pet exultantly into Betty's tea room, followed by a grumpy-looking Grace.

'It's not fair,' she grumbled. 'She's got that and I haven't got anything.'

'You can share the hamster.'

'No, she can't!' Chloe's eyes were wide with outrage.

'I don't want your stupid old hamster.' Grace snatched up the menu. 'Anyway, I'm going to save up and buy a python. They eat hamsters.'

'They don't!'

'Do!'

'Tell her, Mummy. Tell her she can't have a python.'

'You can't have a python. And stop playing with that thing, Chloe. I'm sure you're not supposed to bring animals in here.'

Fortunately they forgot their squabble and concentrated on choosing the biggest cake on the trolley. Jo poured herself a cup of tea from the silver pot and closed her eyes, wallowing in the momentary peace. Outside it had started to rain. Office workers and late shoppers were hurrying home, their coats turned up against the sudden downpour. Jo nibbled a ham sandwich and felt glad that she wasn't one of them.

But her happiness evaporated when she glanced round and spotted Richard Black standing at the PLEASE WAIT HERE TO BE SEATED sign. And he wasn't alone. Jo barely had time to digest this fact before her instincts slid into automatic.

'Mummy, why are you under the table?' Chloe's head appeared upside down.

'I'm hiding from my boss.'

'Where?' Jo grabbed her just as she was climbing onto her chair for a better look.

'Sit down! I don't want him to see me.'

'Why not?'

'Because he's mean and he hates me.'

If she was in any doubt about that when he first arrived, the past four weeks had confirmed the fact. It wasn't just that he ignored her. He seemed to ignore everyone. It was the way he ignored her. He had an unnerving habit of turning up in the middle of filming and hanging around behind the cameras, watching but not watching, managing to be hostile and unaware of her presence at the same time. It was quite a gift.

Jo peered out from under the table. 'Can you see where he's sitting?'

'Over in the corner, I think. Is he the cross-looking one?'

She edged her way back into her seat. 'That's him.'

'Who's that woman with him?'

'That's his PA, Kate. She's a sort of secretary.'

'Why does he need a secretary on a Saturday afternoon?' Grace asked.

Why indeed? Jo watched them as they sat in the corner, studying their menus, surrounded by designer carrier bags. They'd obviously been shopping together, which could only mean one thing: Kate and Richard Black were an item. It didn't surprise her.

'So what are you going to call that thing?' Grace asked Chloe.

'Pudding.'

'What kind of a stupid name is that? You should give him a cool name, like Fatboy Slim.'

'I'm not going to call him Fatboy, am I? That's a horrible name, isn't it, Mummy?'

'If you say so, darling. Now please close that box up before we get thrown out.' Jo couldn't take her eyes off Richard. He was wearing a suit, for heaven's sake. On his day off.

Thankfully the tea room was crowded so they managed to get through their tea without being spotted. Jo paid the bill, grateful to escape. She was just gathering up her shopping when Chloe let out a scream.

'Where's Pudding?'

They all stared at the empty box. 'He must have escaped.' Grace stated the blindingly obvious. 'I bet you didn't shut the box up properly.'

Chloe immediately started howling. 'Pudding! I want Pudding!'

Her voice rose above the muted clink of cups and cutlery. From a neighbouring table, Jo heard one middle-aged man hiss to his wife, 'Listen to that! If she was my grandchild, I'd give her bloody pudding!'

'Let's just look for him, shall we? He must be somewhere.'

Jo and Grace got onto the floor, while Chloe screeched above them.

'Can I help?'

She lifted her eyes from the carpet to the handmade brogues of Richard Black. Great. Just what she needed. 'We're fine, thank you,' she said with as much dignity as she could muster.

'I've lost Pudding!' Chloe shrieked. Richard looked unnerved. He'd obviously never been this close to an hysterical child before.

'Her hamster escaped,' Jo said. She wished she could do the same.

'I see. And what exactly were you doing with a hamster in here?'

'Well, you see, he gets so lonely in his cage, I just thought I'd bring him for a browse around Debenhams—' Jo gritted her teeth. 'What do you think I'm doing with it?'

'We've just bought him,' Grace explained.

'Ah.' He nodded wisely. 'In that case, may I make a small suggestion?'

'Yes?'

'I don't think you'll find him like that. If you keep flailing your arms around you'll just frighten him even further away.'

So now Richard Black was an expert on rodent psychology, was he?

'And what do you suggest?'

'You should offer it some encouragement.' He handed Jo's plate, with the remains of her sandwich, to Chloe. 'Here, break this up into crumbs. Perhaps we can lay a trail to entice him back.'

Chloe stopped howling and obediently got to work. She seemed reassured now that Richard was on the case. Jo fought down feelings of annoyance. She just wished he'd bugger off and leave her to deal with this crisis in her own haphazard way.

As if things weren't bad enough, suddenly Kate was standing over them too, her Jimmy Choo slingbacks tapping impatiently.

'Richard, what—? Oh, it's you.'

'Watch where you're putting your feet,' Jo warned. All she needed now was for Pudding to be impaled on those vicious spiked heels.

Kate ignored her. 'Are you coming, Richard?'

'In a minute.' He took the crumbs from Chloe's sticky hands and knelt down beside Jo. She watched him scatter them on the carpet under the table. 'Right,' he said. 'Now all we've got to do is wait.'

It felt as if they were kneeling there for hours. The whole room seemed to be holding its breath as everyone stopped to watch.

Jo cringed. This was a nightmare. 'Look, I don't think this is going to—' she began, but suddenly Chloe was pointing excitedly.

'It's Pudding! He's come back!' Sure enough, a sandy ball of fluff came snuffling out from the shadowy recesses of a corner table, blissfully hoovering up the crumbs in his expanding cheeks. Richard scooped him up gently as the whole tea room erupted in spontaneous applause.

'Safe and sound,' he said.

'Thanks.' Jo took the hamster from him.

'No problem.' He stroked the hamster with his finger. 'Pudding, eh? Perhaps you should call him Houdini?' For a brief moment she thought she saw the shadow of a smile. Then it was gone.

He stood up, brushing the crumbs off his knees. Chloe blinked up at him in awe. 'Are you the man Mummy was hiding from?'

'Don't be silly, darling. I wasn't hiding from him!' Jo covered her scalding embarrassment with a forced laugh.

'Yes you were. You said he was mean and he hated you!'

Kate snorted. Jo couldn't meet Richard's eyes. She couldn't imagine what he must be thinking. Or rather, she could. Only too well, in fact. 'Come on, I think we'd better get this little one home, don't you? Before he does another disappearing act.'

Just her luck, they all left at the same time. They made an awkward group, sheltering under the awning from the rain.

'Well—er—thanks again.'

'Where are you parked?'

Why did he have to ask that? 'We haven't—' Chloe piped up, but Jo clamped her hand over her mouth.

'It's just round the corner.' She pointed vaguely. 'So—um—we'll be going. Come on, girls.' She shepherded them out into the rain.

'Why did you say that?' Grace demanded, as they ran across the wet street. 'You know we left the car at home.'

'Yes, but I didn't want him to know that, did I?'

'Why not?'

'Because then he might offer us a lift home, that's why.'

'So? What's wrong with that? At least we wouldn't get soaked!'

What indeed? Jo couldn't answer. She just had the vague feeling that the less time she spent in Richard's company, the less chance he'd have to disapprove of her.

They took a detour down the narrow, cobbled street of Stonegate, and were just crossing Duncombe Place when Chloe suddenly cried out, 'Look, it's your boss again!'

There was no escape this time. Richard's Audi was already slowing down beside them. The window glided down and he leaned across.

'Where did you say your car was parked?'

'It isn't,' Chloe answered cheerfully. 'Mummy just said it was so you wouldn't give us a lift.'

Oh bugger. Jo closed her eyes, mortification washing over her.

'Really, there's no need,' she tried to laugh it off. 'We only live off Clifton Green. We can easily walk it in ten minutes—'

'And we have a dinner reservation in Leeds for eight,' Kate pointed out quickly. 'I'll never have time to shower and change.'

For a second it looked as though that was the end of it, until Chloe wailed, 'But Pudding's box is getting soggy. What if he escapes again?'

'And I've never been in an Audi convertible before.' Grace ran an admiring hand over the gleaming paintwork.

'Looks like you're outvoted, doesn't it?' Richard leaned across and opened the back door.

Outmanoeuvred, more like. The children had caused her some embarrassment in her time, but this was definitely the worst, Jo decided, as they squeezed into the back seat, dripping all over the flawless upholstery. In front of her Kate's shoulders were rigid.

Jo looked out of the window, trying not to listen to Richard and Kate's whispered conversation. It didn't take a genius to work out they were having a domestic. Or that she was the cause of it.

Then suddenly, the car stopped sharply, flinging them all forward.

Kate got out, slamming the passenger door. Without a backward glance, she strode off, her high heels clicking on the wet pavement.

'Have you two had a row?' As usual, Chloe's timing was impeccable.

'Leave Mr Black alone,' Jo said hastily. 'Let him concentrate on his driving.'

But Chloe hadn't finished with him. 'Is that your wife?' she asked.

'No.'

'So you're not married, then?'

'No.'

Jo slunk down in her seat. All Chloe needed was a twinset and she could have been Grandma Audrey. 'Darling, I don't think . . .'

'Mummy isn't married either,' Chloe said. 'She was, but she and Daddy split up.' Richard didn't answer. 'Daddy's got a new girlfriend. But Mummy hasn't had a boyfriend for ages, have you, Mummy?'

'I'm sure Mr Black isn't interested in hearing about my personal life.'

'Daddy says he's not surprised,' Chloe went on. 'He says Mummy's impossible to live with. He reckons a man would have to be a saint to—'

'Oh look! A cow!' Jo shouted, pointing out of the window.

'Where?' Chloe clamoured to have a look.

'Sorry, I could have sworn I saw one.'

'A cow, in the middle of York? How lame can you get?' Grace said scornfully.

Jo stared at the back of Richard's head. She had the horrible feeling he was secretly laughing at her. 'Turn right here,' she said in a clipped voice.

They pulled into their road of tall, grey-stone Edwardian terraced houses. She was out of the car before he'd put on the brake.

'Thanks for the lift,' she said.

'Not at all.' Richard glanced at the girls, who were fighting over the doorkey. 'It's been most . . . entertaining.'

CHAPTER THREE

STACEY TO FACE AXE—OFFICIAL, the headline in the *Globe* proclaimed. Underneath was a *Westfield* still of her looking suitably mournful, with the subhead, 'Charlie Beasley's Tips For The Chop'.

Jo tried to stop herself buying a copy of the paper on her way to work, but she couldn't. It was like probing an aching tooth.

'The stars of *Westfield* will have even less to smile about today, as they gather in the office of new Executive Producer Richard Black to learn their fate,' she read, as she waited at the traffic lights. 'Black, known in the business as the Grim Reaper, was brought in by Talbot TV bosses to halt the show's drop in the ratings. After six weeks in the job he's now ready to make drastic changes, including axing some familiar faces.'

Jo tossed the newspaper onto the passenger seat in disgust. All week, the tabloids had been speculating about the forthcoming changes at *Westfield*. And then on Friday they'd all received notes telling them Richard Black would meet them the following Monday 'to discuss their future'. Suddenly the rumours seemed harder to dismiss.

Jo's concentration was in tatters, but luckily she didn't have too many scenes that morning. In between takes, Richard Black had been summoning the cast one by one. Some emerged looking relieved, others in tears. The atmosphere was leaden with expectation.

'I've got a brain tumour,' was Viola's doleful pronouncement as she and Jo met on the café set. She was sitting at one of the tables while the cameras arranged themselves around her. Her gloomy face was reflected on monitors all around the set.

'No!' Jo sank into the seat opposite. 'How do you know that? You haven't been summoned, have you?'

'No, but it's got to be, hasn't it? You know all those headaches my character's been having lately? It's going to be something serious. You wait and see. Any day now they'll be tagging my toe and carting me off to the morgue!'

'You won't be the only one,' Jo sighed. 'I suppose you've read Charlie Beasley?'

'That reptile! Take no notice of him, darling. It's all speculation.'

'Yes, but Richard Black's got every reason to sack me, hasn't he? I'm already down as a troublemaker, remember?'

'I'm sure that's not true.' Viola grimaced as one of the set dressers slid a bacon sandwich in front of her. 'Oh God, do I have to? You know I'm a vegetarian.'

'You're supposed to be an actress, aren't you? Pretend it's a veggie burger,' Brett sneered from the sidelines. He was hanging around waiting for his cue. 'Heard the news?' he said. 'Judy Pearce has got the push.'

'You're kidding!' Viola's mouth fell open. 'I don't believe you.'

'Suit yourself. But when I left the greenroom she was on her third box of Kleenex.'

'Can we have some quiet on the set, please?' Aidan, the first assistant director, called out. 'Positions please.' Jo got up and took her place behind the café door, ready for her entrance.

'And . . . action.' As Jo opened the door, she deliberately emptied her mind of what was going on and tried to concentrate on her scene.

Ironically enough, Stacey and Viola's character, Maggie, were supposed to be discussing rumours that a property developer was going to send the bulldozers in and flatten the whole of Westfield to create an enormous park-and-ride site. It wasn't easy but they managed to get through the scene. Viola then went off to the greenroom to find out the latest news while Jo was left with the terminally awful Brett Michaels.

He oozed onto the set, looking tough in his trademark vest and stone-washed jeans. As he sat down beside her, Jo was nearly choked by the overpowering effect of his cologne. 'God, what are you wearing?'

'Like it?' he leered. 'One of my fans sent it to me. She said it summed up my character.'

'You mean it gets right up people's noses?' Jo shuffled her chair away.

'Very funny. I wonder if you'll still be laughing when the Grim Reaper's finished with you.'

'I could say the same thing. You haven't been summoned to the top floor yet, I notice.'

'No need.' Brett reached across and helped himself from a plate of sausage rolls that the set dresser had placed on the table. 'I know exactly what's going to happen to me.'

A slow, painful death, I hope. 'And what's that?'

'Nothing. My character is the most popular in this show, and Black knows it. He wouldn't dare get rid of me.' He grinned, revealing a mouthful of half-eaten sausage. 'And I bet Steve will be even more popular when he's a grieving widower. I wonder how they'll kill you off?'

'They won't need to,' Jo said. 'I'll probably kill myself at the thought of a lifetime with you!'

Just then the props girl rushed over. 'You weren't supposed to eat those!' She pointed at the crumbs Brett was hoovering off his plate.

'So?' Brett leaned back in his chair and gave her one of his sexiest smiles. 'You can run off and fetch some more, can't you, darling?'

'But you don't understand. They were old stock from the canteen. We cut the green bits off—'

Maybe there is a God after all, Jo thought as she watched Brett rush off set, looking sick.

They took a break for lunch, but no one really felt like eating. Instead Jo headed for the greenroom to join the others. Lara had just emerged unscathed from her interview with the Grim Reaper, and was all smiles.

Meanwhile, in the opposite corner of the room poor Judy Pearce was hunched beside the coffee machine, doing a phone interview with *Inside Soap*, explaining how glad she was her contract hadn't been extended.

'No, really, I'm relieved,' Judy insisted. 'This marks a new beginning.' Jo and Viola exchanged wry looks. 'There's so much to look forward to. No more typecasting. No more being creatively straitjacketed—'

'No more regular pay cheques.' Jo could understand what Judy was saying, but she would happily go on wearing a creative straitjacket if it meant she could pay the bills and feed her children.

Judy put the phone down and collapsed back in her chair. 'Thank God that's over,' she said. 'I need a gin. Lying always makes me thirsty.'

'So, have they said what's going to happen to you?'

'Apparently I'm going off to help run an orphanage in Romania.' She shook her head. 'Can you imagine? My character hasn't had a selfless thought in five years and suddenly she's turned into Mother Teresa.'

While she went off in search of alcohol, Jo stared at the clock. Richard Black had promised to see everyone by six o'clock. That could mean another four hours of waiting and wondering.

The greenroom phone rang, and everyone jumped. Jo and Viola looked at each other.

'That'll be him,' Viola whispered. 'I wonder who he wants next?'

God, I hope it's me, Jo thought. If she had to wait any longer they'd be scraping her off the walls by six o'clock.

But it wasn't. 'Oh well, here goes.' Viola gave her a brave smile as she headed for the door. 'Wish me luck.'

'You won't need it,' Jo smiled back. If anyone needed luck, it was her.

After a quick break she was called back on set. This time she was in the hairdresser's where Stacey worked with Lara's character Winona. The set, with its pink fittings and floral wallpaper, was as familiar as her own home. Yet somehow she couldn't seem to find her way around today. She bumped into the hair dryers and tripped over cables.

'What's got into you?' Lara said irritably. With her own future settled, it didn't occur to her that anyone else might still be feeling the strain.

Meanwhile, more people emerged from their ordeal, the gossip flew thick and fast around the set. Jo listened to it all, her stomach churning. Even when Viola appeared and gave her an excited thumbs-up, it did nothing to ease her flutterings of apprehension.

Then, just when she thought she couldn't stand it any longer, Brett appeared on set and said, 'It's your turn to see the Grim Reaper. His PA just called the greenroom. He's ready for you.'

Jo walked across the courtyard to the production building. She felt at a distinct disadvantage in her sprayed-on jeans and pink clingy Lycra top with lips and nails to match. Looking like this, however could Richard Black take her seriously? Nervously, she tried to smooth her hair down as the lift doors opened and she found herself on the top floor.

There was no one to meet her at the lift and the top floor was strangely silent. Jo teetered along on her white stilettos towards Richard Black's office at the end of the corridor.

Kate's desk in the outer office was empty. Jo hesitated. Should she go straight through and knock on Richard Black's door? But as she took a step towards it, a sound from inside stopped her in her tracks. There was a lot of whispering going on, followed by some husky laughter. Then she heard Richard say, in a slightly annoyed voice, 'Kate, I'm working.'

'You're always working. Come on, let me try and relax you.'

Jo edged closer. Surely they weren't—they couldn't be—

'God, that feels good.' They were! Shocked, Jo went into sharp reverse—and backed straight into a towering rubber plant.

The next few seconds seemed to pass in slow motion. In the silent office, the toppling plant sounded like a giant redwood crashing to the ground. Jo made a last frantic grab at it, but lost her balance and fell on top of it, taking a pile of files from Kate's desk with her.

As she struggled to release herself from the dense foliage, the door was flung open and there were Richard and Kate.

'What are you doing with those files? They're confidential.' Kate stormed over and began gathering them up.

'It was an accident.'

'And what are you doing up here anyway? No one sent for you.'

'Yes, you did.'

'I certainly didn't. And I think I would have remembered, don't you?'

'But I got a message—' Colour drained from her face as the truth dawned on her. Bloody Brett Michaels! This must be his idea of a joke.

'I—I'm sorry,' she stammered. 'I must have got my wires crossed—'

'It doesn't matter.' Richard came to her rescue. 'You're here now, so we might as well get on with our meeting. Come into my office, would you?' He stood aside to let her enter. Jo strutted past him with as much dignity as she could muster while still picking bits of leaf out of her top. 'Perhaps we could have some coffee, Kate?' he added.

'As soon as I've finished tidying up this mess.' Jo caught Kate's look of suppressed fury as Richard closed the door on her.

The office had changed a lot since Trevor's day. Gone was the cluttered chaos of spilling filing cabinets and overflowing desk. In its place was a vast, clean space with white walls, flawless cream carpet and gently curving pale wood furniture. A small laptop computer was the only thing that marred an otherwise empty desk.

'Please take a seat.' Richard directed her to one of the strange bendy-looking chairs. He sat down on the other side of the desk, picked up some papers and shuffled through them.

'As you know, I'm meeting everyone today to discuss their future at *Westfield*. I've spent the last few weeks exploring the dynamics of the show, and how everyone fits into it.'

He glanced up at her. Jo fixed him with an unblinking stare. 'I think you'll agree, we've taken quite a few wrong turnings with your character over the past few months. According to the demographic profiles, Stacey isn't popular. She's perceived as being too bland. Her marriage was a mistake, too,' he went on. 'The focus group reports all state that people would prefer—'

'Look, you don't have to go on with this,' she interrupted him. 'I'm being sacked, right?'

Surprise flickered in his dark eyes. 'What makes you say that?'

'I don't need a focus group to tell me you don't like me.' She lifted her chin. 'I don't blame you. We didn't exactly get off to a good start, did we?' She stood up. 'Let's face it, Mr Black, whatever your research had come up with you were never going to keep me on, were you?'

She had the brief satisfaction of seeing him lost for words. Making the most of it, she walked to the door, willing herself not to trip up and spoil her exit.

'Ms Porter? Jo?' She was halfway out when he spoke.

Jo hesitated. She wanted to finish off with a spot of huffy door-slamming, but her curiosity got the better of her. 'Yes?'

'How would you like to have an affair?'

She turned and stared at him. It was impossible to tell what was going on behind those eyes. 'Is this some kind of joke?'

'I'm not laughing.' He didn't look as if he ever did. 'I believe we could pull your character around. The way I see it, your main problem is that you've been allowed to become a cipher to Brett. It's time we tried you with your own story line. That's what made me think of an affair.'

It all seemed too good to be true. 'But Stacey's only just got married!'

'I know. That's what would make it so interesting. Everyone knows she's a devoted wife. No one would expect her to fall passionately in love with another man. Imagine the tension that would create.'

'So who would I have an affair with?'

'I haven't decided yet. I think we'll bring in someone new.'

Someone new. No more fighting off Brett's wandering hands.

'So? What do you think?'

She was too dazed to think anything, except that she would like to rush across the room and kiss him. 'I thought you didn't like me?'

'I never let my personal feelings interfere with my work. You're a very talented actress, but you've been underused. I mean to change that.'

She realised he hadn't answered her question. Or perhaps he had.

'So does Brett know about this yet?'

Richard shook his head. 'I'm seeing him tomorrow morning. Apparently he has his own ideas about how his character should develop.'

'I bet he has.'

He sent her a shrewd look. 'Do I take it there's a certain amount of tension between you and Brett?'

Jo bit her lip. She didn't want him to think she was difficult. 'I never let my personal feelings interfere with my work,' she parroted his own words back at him.

'I'm very glad to hear it.' Was that the shadow of a smile? He closed his file and stood up, dismissing her. As she headed for the door, he suddenly said, 'Wait a moment.'

She held her breath as he came around the desk to her. He reached out his hand and for one insane moment she thought he was going to pull her towards him for a kiss.

'I couldn't help noticing—there.' He plucked something from her hair and held it out to her. 'You had a bit of leaf in your hair.'

'Thanks,' she said. To distract from her withering embarrassment, she added, 'So what's going to happen to Brett, if I get a new love interest?'

There was a twinkle in Richard's eyes. 'Oh, I have something in mind for Mr Michaels. Something that will really challenge.'

'Gay? Fucking *gay*?'

Brett stormed around the sweetshop set, knocking props flying. He kicked the door so hard his foot went straight through the plywood.

'Temper, temper.' Jo and Viola exchanged wry looks over the counter.

'Does that man know what he's doing? Does he? How can my character be gay? It's impossible. The man drives a *cab*, for God's sake. He's got testosterone pouring out of him!'

'So did Rock Hudson, and look at him.'

'Well, I think it's a terrific idea,' Rob Fletcher said earnestly. 'It's such a brave thing to do, to take a character like Steve and fearlessly redefine the accepted gender parameters—'

'Why don't you let them redefine *your* parameters, if you're so keen?' Brett growled.

'Come on, Brett, it's only a soap,' Jo reasoned. 'No one's going to take it seriously.'

'*I* take it seriously. And so will my fans. Let's face it, ninety per cent of women only watch this crap show because of me. How will they feel when they find out my character's gay?'

'Maybe you'll start to appeal to the men instead?' Viola suggested.

His jaw muscles twitched. 'It's all right for you, you're a bloody lesbian. You don't care what anyone thinks of you. Well, I'm not going to stand by and watch that moron assassinate my character.' He stalked off the set, scattering technicians as he went.

'Where's he off to?' Aidan asked.

'Gone in search of his feminine side, I think,' Viola replied.

Jo smiled. Maybe Richard Black did have a sense of humour after all.

 # CHAPTER FOUR

'Ow! That hurts.'

'It wouldn't if you kept still—oh, I give up.' Jo dropped the hairbrush as Chloe wriggled away yet again.

'Why do you have to work today? It's Sunday. You never go to work on a Sunday.'

'I told you, we have some special filming to do in a hospital, and they'll only let us do it today.'

She was trying to put on her make-up and cram down her breakfast when Grace came clumping downstairs.

'I wish we didn't have to go to Grandma's,' Grace grumbled. 'She's always moaning at us. "Wash your hands, wipe your feet, you surely don't expect me to walk the streets with you looking like that—"'

Jo hid a smile. Given the choice, she wouldn't go either. But it was Roxanne's day off, Duncan claimed to be working again and so her mother had graciously agreed to step in and look after the kids.

A little too graciously, in fact. 'No trouble at all,' she'd chirped, when Jo plucked up the courage to call. 'Stay for supper when you pick them up. Your father and I hardly ever see you these days.'

No martyred sighs, no disapproving remarks. Jo felt wary. Either

Grandma Audrey had discovered Prozac, or she was Up To Something.

She was just making another assault on Chloe's untidy curls and trying to find her script when Roxanne swanned in wearing her dressing gown, the *Sunday Times* under her arm and a plastic bag on her head.

'Why are you wearing that?' Chloe was transfixed.

'I'm deep conditioning my hair. I've got a date tonight.'

Jo suppressed a surge of envy. 'Has anyone seen my script?'

'I forgot to tell you, I'm playing an angel in the infants' Nativity,' Chloe said.

'That's wonderful, darling.' Jo tipped her bag out onto the table, scattering keys, pens, ancient parking tickets—but no script.

'And you've got to make me a costume.'

'Me?' Jo looked up, as Grace snorted into her cornflakes. 'Don't they have teachers for that sort of thing?'

'All the other mummies are making them.'

All the other mummies stay at home having tennis lessons and Tupperware parties, Jo wanted to retort.

'Anyway, it's not for ages yet,' Chloe said reassuringly. 'Nearly three weeks. I know you can do it, Mummy.'

Jo looked apprehensive. 'I suppose I'll have to.'

'Is that what you're looking for?' Roxanne nodded at Pudding's cage.

'Oh my God!' Jo stared in horror. 'Right, who did it?' She whirled round to face them. 'Who used my script to line the hamster's cage?'

'Someone with excellent taste, I should imagine.'

'Daddy!' The girls scrambled from the table to greet Duncan as he stood in the doorway, looking irritatingly calm. She'd almost forgotten he'd promised to take the girls down to her mother's for her.

'You really should learn to calm down, darling. Why don't you try meditating?'

'Good idea.' Jo extracted her script and shook the crumbs off. 'And would that be before or after I've helped the girls with their homework, done the ironing, been to the supermarket—'

'OK, OK, no need to go on. You're not my wife now.' Duncan turned to the girls. 'Right, who's for a trip to sunny Nether Yeadon?'

'Me!' Chloe and Grace rushed to get their coats. Jo followed them.

'Now don't forget to say please and thank you, will you?' she warned. 'Grace, try not to bite your nails. And Chloe—'

She was still nagging when the front door closed on her. Jo felt a pang of jealousy as she peered through the glass. The girls were climbing into Duncan's Discovery without a backward glance. No wonder, their father was always laughing and joking and never behaved like a miserable trout. If only she wasn't so short-tempered all the time.

Roxanne paused on her way upstairs. 'You know, your ex is quite nice really,' she commented.

Jo watched the car drive away. 'He can afford to be,' she muttered.

They'd been given permission to film in an outpatients' section of the local hospital that wasn't open on a Sunday. The location team had obviously been hard at work, trying to make it look as much as possible like a busy casualty department.

According to the story line, Eva's character, Ma Stagg, had been beaten up by her new man friend, who, unknown to Ma, was a bigamist and part-time drug dealer. She'd been rushed to hospital and now her dutiful daughter-in-law, Stacey, was anxiously waiting for news. Her mother Maggie was with her, although why she'd bothered to come when she was Ma Stagg's sworn enemy no one could quite explain.

'Vi, when Jo asks you how you're feeling, I believe your line is "Fine". Not "Why, what have you heard?" ' Aidan pointed out for the fifth time.

'Sorry, darling, I wasn't thinking.'

'Yes, you were,' Jo accused her. 'You were thinking about that wretched brain tumour again, weren't you?'

'I can't help it. I know Richard said I had nothing to worry about, but that was two months ago. How do I know he hasn't changed his mind?'

'He won't.' Although Jo was beginning to wonder that herself. Eight weeks on and her new love interest still hadn't materialised. Meanwhile, she was still in Brett's clutches. Although, after visiting a couple of gay clubs with Viola and getting a rapturous response, he was getting used to the idea of becoming a gay icon.

The scene was wrapped up quickly, and Jo moved on to her next, which unfortunately was with Eva the Diva. She was proving to be a difficult patient, propped up on a trolley in a curtained-off cubicle, puffing away on a Silk Cut while a tearful make-up artist pleaded with her.

'But you've just been beaten up!' she was saying. 'Couldn't I just give you a teeny little black eye—'

'You're not touching this make-up and that's final.' Eva's tiny eyes narrowed under their sooty coating of mascara.

'It's no good,' Aidan sighed, after another twenty minutes of pointless wrangling. He listened to the voice coming over his headphones. 'The director says we've got to go for a take, make-up or no make-up.'

'Thank God.' Jo glanced at her watch. She'd promised her mother she'd be there at six, and it was nearly five already. And the cameras hadn't even started rolling yet.

Luckily, Eva seemed in a good mood since she'd won her battle over the make-up, and the scene moved quite fast. But it was nearly seven when Jo finally got on her way. The Sunday traffic was terrible. Jo tapped her fingers on the wheel and cursed expressively. This could well trigger another Cold War with her mother.

And if her lateness didn't do it, her appearance certainly would. Jo sneaked a cautious look in the rearview mirror, and winced. Her face still bore traces of Stacey's tarty screen make-up, and she had a large spot brewing on her chin. And she could only imagine what her mother would make of her scruffy jeans, sweater and trainers.

She pulled into the sweeping gravel drive of The Pines and felt the familiar urge to scream. Audrey was waiting on the steps for her. 'There you are, I— What have you done to yourself?' She looked horror-stricken. 'You could have changed!'

'Yes, Mum, I could.' Jo fumbled with the lock of her Cinquecento. 'If I'd had an afternoon to spare I daresay I could have had a manicure and a bikini wax too. But I've been working.'

Audrey tutted. 'That's the trouble with you working mothers, you never have time for anything, do you?'

Jo smiled sweetly and went past her into the house, her trainers squeaking on the polished parquet. 'Where are the girls?'

'Helping your father with the compost heap. Don't you want to go upstairs and freshen up?' She blocked Jo's way.

'Not really. I'll just collect the girls and go home, if you don't mind.'

'But you're staying for supper, aren't you?'

'I'd love to, but I can't. It's been a long day and I want to get the girls to bed—' Then she noticed her mother's expression. 'Oh no, Mum. Not another one!' she groaned. 'Who is it this time?'

'I don't know what you mean,' Audrey sniffed.

'You're trying to fix me up again, aren't you?'

'I may have invited Rosemary Warrender round for supper.' Her mother couldn't meet her eye.

'And she wouldn't by any chance have a son who's single?'

'Actually he's divorced. And don't look at me like that, I know you'll like him. He's a dentist,' she said in an awed whisper. 'I've told him all about you. Rosemary and I are sure you'll hit it off.'

'Really?'

'I know you think I'm interfering, but I'm only doing it for you.'

'I realise that, Mum, but I'm not interested.'

'How can you not be interested? For heaven's sake, Jo. I'm beginning to think no man will ever be good enough for you.'

Before she had a chance to respond, the door flew open and the girls tumbled through. Chloe was howling.

'Mummy, she smacked me!'

'No, I didn't.'

'You did! Tell her, Mummy.'

'Get your coats, girls. We're going home.'

Instantly the howling stopped. 'But I thought we were staying for supper?' Grace protested. 'Grandma's made chicken pie. A real one, not out of the freezer like we have.'

Jo couldn't bring herself to look at her mother. 'It sounds lovely, darling, but we'll have to come back another time.'

And she herded the children quickly into the car.

'But I don't understand,' Chloe protested as she swung the car out of the drive. 'Why couldn't we stay at Grandma's?'

'Because she and Mummy had an argument, stupid,' Grace cut in. 'Grandma wants Mummy to get married, and she doesn't want to. Isn't that right, Mummy?'

'Something like that.' She'd have to learn to keep her voice down.

'You're not going to get married, are you, Mummy?' Chloe's eyes were huge with concern in the rearview mirror.

'Of course she isn't,' Grace scoffed. 'She's far too old to get married. And she'd never choose anyone we didn't like, would you, Mummy?'

'No, darling.' Chance would be a fine thing.

'I wouldn't mind if you married Richard,' Chloe said. 'I liked him.'

'I'll bear that in mind,' Jo said, and laughed all the way home.

Her argument with her mother, plus rampaging premenstrual hormones, meant she slept badly and woke up the following morning with a pounding headache and a foul temper. By the time she'd packed the girls' lunch boxes, found various lost items of PE kit and listened to Roxanne waxing lyrical about her wonderful new boyfriend, she was just about ready to kill.

And just to make her happiness complete, when she reached the *Westfield* studios she found some idiot had parked a battered old pickup truck in her parking space.

Jo slammed her car door and stalked towards it. But as she approached, a huge grey shaggy head suddenly appeared at the window and a volley of deep-throated barking sent her into sharp retreat.

She finally found a parking space round the other side of the building and then trudged all the way back to the studio block.

'Sorry I'm late.' Jo stormed into Make-up and flung herself into the nearest chair, beside Viola. 'You won't believe it, but some selfish bastard has just dumped his van and his scruffy mongrel right in my space.'

'Do you mind? You can call my parentage into question if you like, but Murphy's is as pure as the driven snow,' said a voice behind her.

Jo looked up. There, reflected in the mirror, was the most beautiful man she had ever seen.

'Irish wolfhound,' he drawled. He had a voice like Hugh Grant.

'Sorry?'

'Murphy. My dog. He can trace his bloodline back to the last century.'

'Ah. Right.' She willed herself to say something intelligent, but her tongue was welded to the roof of her mouth.

'Sorry about your space.' He pushed his flopping blond hair out of his eyes. He was tall, narrow-hipped and totally gorgeous, in faded Levi's and an old leather jacket. 'I was late myself. I'm supposed to be here for a photo session. I wasn't thinking when I dumped the truck.'

'It doesn't matter.' She'd already forgotten about it, mesmerised by his intense turquoise eyes.

'We haven't been properly introduced, have we?' He held out his hand. 'I'm Marcus Finn.'

'Jo Porter.'

'So you're Jo?' A slow smile lit up his face. 'I understand we're going to be lovers?'

If he hadn't been holding on to her hand she would have slipped out of her chair in shock. As it was, she could only whimper.

'Marcus is your new love interest,' Viola said with a knowing smile.

'What? You mean you—? Since when?'

'I was cast last week.' He frowned. 'You look upset. Is there a problem?'

'N-no, not at all. It's just no one told me.' No one told her he would be so young, either. Or so incredibly sexy.

'I hope you're not disappointed?'

Jo's mind reeled. 'No,' she said. 'I'm not disappointed.'

'Good.' He looked her up and down with leisurely interest. 'Neither am I, as it happens.'

'You lucky bitch!' Lara hissed as they gathered outside on the set later that morning, waiting for the next camera angle to be set up.

'I don't know what you mean.' Jo huddled inside her *Westfield* anorak as the icy November wind whipped around her ears.

'Like hell you don't! Why didn't they cast him for me? He's far too young for you,' Lara pointed out with her usual tact. 'Imagine snogging him all day and getting paid for it.'

'I'm a professional. It makes no difference to me.' She pulled up her collar, hoping Lara wouldn't notice her blushing furiously.

203

'Yeah, right. So you don't mind if you kiss him or Brett Michaels?'

'I'd rather kiss a baboon's bum than— Oh, hi, Brett.' Jo beamed as her screen husband loomed into view. He scowled back.

'Have you met Marcus?' Lara asked.

Brett grunted. 'Can't see what all the fuss is about. Looks like a complete tosser to me.'

'Takes one to know one,' Jo grinned, as he stomped off to argue his lines with the director. 'He's not his usual cheery self this morning.'

'Are you surprised?' Viola had drifted up to join them. 'He's got some competition, hasn't he? He's frightened he won't be the Number One Hunk when our Mr Finn hits the screen.' Viola looked around, 'So where's the lovely Marcus now, then?'

'No idea. Louise from the press office whisked him off about half an hour ago. I think he had some publicity shots to do.'

'Lucky Louise,' Viola sighed. 'He really is gorgeous, isn't he? I tell you, if I wasn't a lesbian and twice his age I'd definitely be interested.'

Brett's evil mood lasted all morning, and he seemed determined to take out all his frustration on Jo. All they had to do was walk down the street having an argument. But every time she did the scene well, Brett would either corpse or fluff his lines so they had to do it again.

While he held up filming for what seemed like the fiftieth time, Jo flopped down onto the step outside the pub and looked around, hugging her knees to keep out the bitter wind.

As she flicked through her script, she felt someone watching her. She looked up. There was Marcus, loitering behind one of the cameras. As their eyes met, he winked and hit her with the most lethally sexy smile she had ever seen. Jo jerked her gaze back to her script, blushing like a schoolgirl. She didn't allow herself to look up again until the first assistant called a break in the filming. By then, Marcus had gone.

Complaining bitterly about the cold, they all made their way down to the canteen to thaw out. Louise, the press officer, met them in the doorway, looking frantic.

'Have you seen Marcus?'

'Have we?' Lara rolled her eyes. 'God, he's gorgeous!'

'He's also meant to be doing an interview. I've been plying the woman from *TV Times* with doughnuts for the past half-hour, but I think she's beginning to suspect something.' She turned to Jo. 'If the worst comes to the worst I may have to offer you as a substitute.'

'How nice to feel needed.' Jo picked up a tray and went to the counter, where Joyce the canteen assistant was waiting for her, arms folded across her massive bosom.

'Only cold stuff now,' she announced flatly. 'I've turned off the fryer.'

'You're kidding!' Jo's jaw dropped. 'But I've been looking forward to a fry-up for the past two hours. It's the only thing that's kept me going.'

'You should have come in earlier then, shouldn't you? The fryer goes off at half past one, you should know that by now.'

'But I'm starving!'

'There's sandwiches. And it's no good you looking at me like that,' she added. 'I don't run this place for your convenience, you know.'

Obviously not, Jo thought.

No sooner had she sat down with a limp-looking tuna and cucumber on brown than there was a commotion outside and a shaggy, slobbering monster hurtled through the door, followed by Marcus clinging on to a rope lead. Jo recognised the monster from Marcus's truck.

They skidded to a halt at the counter, and the dog reared up, putting his huge paws on top of the till. 'Take no notice of Murphy, he's just a bit peckish.' Marcus grinned apologetically. 'He'll be all right when he's had his bacon and sausage fix, won't you, boy?'

He'll be lucky. Jo glanced at Joyce's twitching face. 'You can't bring that . . . that thing in here!' She pointed a shaking finger at Murphy.

'Why not?'

'Because—it's against health and safety regulations!'

'But he gets so upset if I leave him on his own.' Marcus fixed her with a sorrowful look. 'Can't he stay, please? He won't be any trouble. And neither of us has had a decent meal in two days.'

Jo chewed her leathery sandwich crust and watched, fascinated, as Joyce's mouth disappeared into her pouchy face. Her cheeks grew redder and she looked as if she was about to combust, until—

'I'll put the fryer on,' she grunted. 'Sausage and bacon, did you say?'

'And eggs and fried bread, if it's not too much trouble?'

'Did you see that?' Viola whispered. 'She's never done that before.'

She's never met Marcus Finn before. Jo watched him stroll across the canteen to where Louise and the woman from *TV Times* were waiting, both looking hacked off. Within minutes they were all smiling, the journalist was feeding Murphy the remains of her doughnut and Louise was blushing like a schoolgirl. Wherever he went, he seemed to leave a trail of fizzing female hormones in his wake.

'He's totally gorgeous,' Lara sighed. 'I wonder if he's attached?'

'Only to his dog, by the look of it.' Jo pushed the remains of her sandwich away. It was too disgusting to persevere with.

She watched in envy as Joyce shuffled over with a sizzling plate of fry-up. As she pushed the plate in front of Marcus, he looked up and gave her a dazzling grin which sent her reversing into the chilled cabinet.

'Even she's got the hots for him,' Lara whispered.

Viola shook her head. 'He looks like trouble to me.'

'I know. That's what's so sexy about him.'

'So what attracted you to *Westfield*?' The journalist was asking.

'The money mostly.' Marcus fed a piece of bacon to Murphy.

'You mean you weren't a fan of the show before you started?'

'To be quite honest with you, I've never seen it before in my life.' Jo could see Louise's smile growing steelier by the second. 'But now I'm here and I've had a chance to meet my co-stars'—he looked directly at Jo, who choked on her coffee—'I must say I can't believe my luck.'

The interview was wrapped up soon afterwards. As the journalist put away her notebook and tape recorder, Marcus came over to their table.

'Thank God that's over!' He sat down beside Lara and picked up her cup. 'Can I have a swig of your coffee? I've got a monster hangover.'

'Would you like a paracetamol?' Jo offered.

'Thanks. I knew you were an angel the moment I set eyes on you. Although to tell the truth, I'd be better off with a hair of the dog.'

'I suppose you were out celebrating last night?' Viola said.

'So they tell me.' Marcus winced. 'Although I can't remember a thing about it, I woke up in someone's back garden this morning.'

'Sounds wild.' Lara tossed back her dark hair.

Sounds awful. Jo suddenly felt very old. As Lara and Marcus discussed their worst hangover experiences, she found herself pinned to her seat by Murphy. She distracted him with the remains of her sandwich.

Just then the others were called back for their next scene. Normally Jo would have headed straight for the greenroom, but with Murphy's head now firmly across her knees she was stuck to her chair.

'Well?' said Marcus. 'Did I do OK?'

She looked up, straight into those melting aqua eyes. 'Sorry?'

'The interview. You were watching me the whole time. I assumed you were making sure I didn't make an idiot of myself?'

Jo felt a warm tinge in her cheeks. 'Actually, I wasn't listening.'

'That's a pity,' he smiled. 'I need someone to keep an eye on me.'

Louise came over before she could reply. 'Well done, Marcus. I think you made a good impression there,' she beamed. 'Now, would you like me to show you round the studios?'

'Thanks, but Jo's already offered.'

'Oh. I see.' Louise looked crestfallen. 'Well, if there's anything you need, you know where to find me, don't you?'

'What was all that about?' Jo asked, the moment Louise had gone.

'I'd much rather you showed me round. You don't mind, do you? Only I think we should spend some time getting to know each other.' He tilted his head beguilingly. Viola was right, she thought. Marcus was definitely Trouble.

They walked from the main production building across the courtyard towards the studios. Jo pointed out the row of Portakabins that housed the greenroom, the dressing rooms and the make-up and costume departments, aware all the time that Marcus was watching her and not paying the slightest bit of attention to anything she was saying.

'And these are the studios.' She flicked on a switch, flooding the vast, barn-like building with light.

'So where is everybody?' Marcus looked around.

'They don't shoot in here on a Monday. That's when they do all the scenes on the outside lot. I noticed you were there this morning.'

'I just fancied a look around. I hope I didn't put you off?' He suddenly seemed very close. Jo tripped over a snaking electrical cable in her haste to get away.

She pointed out the interiors for the pub, the shops, café and various houses. 'We rehearse in here on a Tuesday and Wednesday, and film all three episodes on Thursday and Friday,' she explained, aware that her voice was going up and down.

'A five-day week?' Marcus stepped behind the pub bar and ran his hand over the beer pumps. 'I don't think I've ever done one of those.'

'It doesn't always work like that. If you're in the middle of a big story line you might be in every day, but otherwise it could be just two or three days a week. And you usually get a break afterwards. I think we might be busy over the next few weeks, though. Once we—er—'

'Start our affair?'

'I'm afraid there's no beer in those pumps.' Jo changed the subject abruptly. 'With the number of takes we do, we'd all be paralytic.'

'I'll remember that.' He came back round to her side of the bar. 'Oh well, I thought it was too good to be true. Alcohol *and* a beautiful woman to sleep with. It's just a shame they're both an illusion, isn't it?'

As he moved closer, Jo took a step backwards and was immediately goosed by Murphy's cold wet nose.

'I'll show you the dressing rooms,' she squeaked.

She led the way, Marcus and Murphy close behind her, and stopped in front of a door. 'Here we are. God, you're lucky. Looks like you've got your own dressing room.'

'Is that a good sign?'

'Put it this way, only Brett and Eva get their own rooms. I still have to share with Viola and Lara.'

'Lara—is she the pretty one with the long dark hair?'

Jo pressed her lips together. 'That's her.'

Like all the other dressing rooms—apart from Eva's, of course—it was simply furnished, with just a dressing table and mirror, a wardrobe and a couch. 'Well, here we are. It's pretty basic, but you can bring in your own stuff to make it more homely if you like.'

'It's brilliant.' Marcus flung himself down on the couch. 'This is a lot comfier than some of the floors we've been sleeping on lately, isn't it Murph?' The dog thumped his thick, shaggy tail in agreement.

'Don't you have your own place?' Jo asked.

'You could say I'm kind of between addresses.'

'Since when?'

'Since my last girlfriend kicked me out.' He yawned. 'I've been dossing down with friends until I get myself sorted out.'

'So you're—er—single at the moment?'

'Apart from Murphy. He's my minder.' He ruffled Murphy's head. 'And he's got great taste in women too. He soon sees off the unsuitable ones.'

Jo smiled nervously. 'Sounds ominous.'

'Oh no, he likes you, I can tell. Which is just as well, really.' Marcus pushed the fair hair off his face so she could see into the clear, ocean-green depths of his eyes. 'I think I should warn you, I have a terrible habit of falling in love with my co-stars.'

She was still struggling for a suitable reply as the door opened and Richard Black came in.

'Marcus, I— Oh, I see you two have already met?' He frowned at Jo.

'I've just been telling Jo how much I'm looking forward to working with her.' Marcus's eyes twinkled.

'I see.'

Unfortunately Murphy chose that moment to get off the couch and trot over to investigate her groin with his nose.

'Yes, well, if you'll excuse me, I'd better be getting back on set.' She pushed him off, deeply embarrassed. 'I'll—um—see you soon.'

'I hope so.' Marcus's grin sent her stomach plummeting down to her stilettos.

She'd barely reached the end of the corridor when Richard caught up with her.

'I'm sorry if it was a shock for you, finding out about Marcus like that,' he said. 'I wanted to tell you myself, but I've been in endless production meetings for the past few days.'

'It doesn't matter,' Jo said.

'So what do you think of your new love interest?'

'He looks perfect to me.'

CHAPTER FIVE

'YOU'RE VERY DRESSED UP. Going somewhere nice?'

'Only work.' Jo feigned great interest in the contents of the toaster.

'Oh yeah? And since when have you started wearing skirts for work?' Roxanne asked. 'And make-up. You never usually wear make-up—'

'Well, I'm wearing it today, aren't I?' Jo saw her blink of surprise, and felt contrite. 'More toast?' she offered.

'Anyone would think you had a fancy man.'

'And what's that supposed to mean?'

'It was a joke, no need to bite my head off. I mean, you wouldn't really have a fancy man, would you? Not at your—' She broke off.

'Not at my age?' Jo finished for her. Roxanne was right. She was behaving like a teenager, but she couldn't help it. After three weeks of working together, she had a fully fledged crush on Marcus Finn.

According to the story line, Stacey, and Marcus's character Vic, were supposed to fancy the pants off each other. They were desperately trying to keep their feelings under control. But all that pent-up passion was there, just waiting to explode. For once, Jo knew just how Stacey felt.

She also knew it was ridiculous and pointless. Marcus was too young for her. And yet . . . she was only thirty-three, just eight years older than him. And he did seem to spend a lot of time flirting with her. Perhaps he liked older women?

'Hello, Mummy. You look funny.' Chloe's nose wrinkled as she came into the kitchen. 'You smell funny too. Is that perfume?'

'Look, what is this?' Jo slammed down her mug. 'Can't I dress up once in a while without someone calling the fashion police? I just felt like looking nice for a change, OK? Is that such a crime?'

Roxanne slid diplomatically from the table. 'I think I'd better get you two ready for school. Mummy's obviously in one of her moods.'

'I am not in a mood.'

'Maybe she's having a period?' Grace suggested. 'We had a lesson about it at school.'

'Why does everyone keep talking about me as if I'm not here?'

'What's a period?' Chloe ignored her. 'Does it make you want to dress up and paint your face all funny?'

'Have you got your costume for the Nativity?' Jo changed the subject as the others giggled. 'It's the final rehearsal today, isn't it?'

Chloe nodded. 'But I don't want to go to school today. I don't feel well.'

'Nor would I, if I had to wear that stupid costume!' Grace sniggered.

'It isn't a stupid costume!' Jo shot her eldest daughter a warning look. 'What's wrong, darling?'

'My tummy hurts and I feel sick.'

Jo felt her forehead. She was a bit clammy. 'I'm sure this tummy ache isn't too serious. Maybe it's just first-night nerves? All actors get them.'

'Really?'

'Of course. I know some professional actors who are actually sick before they go on stage.'

It seemed to do the trick. Chloe went off to school with Roxanne, swinging her Nativity costume in a carrier bag.

When she got to work, the first person Jo ran into was Kate, looking sharply elegant as ever in a taupe Nicole Farhi suit.

'I've been asked to give you this,' she said.

Jo looked down at the thick, cream envelope. 'What is it?'

'It's called a letter.' Kate smiled. Clearly this was what passed for humour on her planet. 'It's an invitation. To Mr Black's drinks party next week. I need your reply by tomorrow at the latest.'

'Is anyone else going?'

'Well, we're hardly likely to have invited just you, are we? Oh, and by the way, Richard's having a breakfast meeting for the cast and crew tomorrow at eight thirty. He wants you to be there.'

'But I can't!'

'What do you mean—you can't?'

'I've made other arrangements for tomorrow morning.'

'Well, you'll just have to cancel them, won't you?'

'But it's my daughter's Nativity play. I can't miss that, can I? Couldn't you just have this meeting without me?' she pleaded.

'Richard is expecting you.'

Richard would just have to un-expect her, wouldn't he? There was no way she was missing Chloe's big moment.

She headed for the greenroom to find the others howling at an interview Brett Michaels had done with the *Radio Times*.

'Listen to this.' Viola gasped for breath. '"I reckon if Shakespeare were alive today, he'd be writing scripts for *EastEnders* and *Westfield*." What does he know, anyway? He'd find a *Carry On* film highbrow.'

Jo was hardly listening. She'd spotted Marcus in the corner with Lara, their heads close together as they practised their lines. Lara kept flicking back her long dark hair, a sure sign she was flirting.

Viola looked at Jo. 'You look nice. Got a job interview?'

'Not you as well?' Jo sighed. 'Blimey, it's only a skirt. I didn't know it would cause such a fuss.' She glanced over to catch Marcus's reaction. He was too captivated by Lara to notice. A disappointed lump rose in her throat. So Marcus had found someone new to flirt with.

They were interrupted by Ros, the organising stage manager, whose job it was to watch over the goings-on in the greenroom and make sure the artists were where they should be.

'I've just had a call from Wardrobe,' she said. 'They said to tell you they're sorry, but they're running late so could you go down and collect your clothes for your first scene?'

It was easy to see that Wardrobe were under pressure. Jo could hear the rumble of the washing machines halfway up the corridor. She opened the door and found herself enveloped in the warm, damp fug of drying laundry. Somewhere in the middle of it, Bernice the costume designer was hard at work ironing, while her sidekick Gaby consulted the bulky diary into which was scribbled the various scenes and what each character was supposed to be wearing.

'Well, look at you.' Bernice smiled. 'You're looking very   '

'Don't say it!' Jo held up her hand. 'Yes, I'm wearing a skirt. No, I don't have a job interview, or a fancy man. And I'm not having a period.'

'Ooh, get you!' Bernice and Gaby exchanged wide-eyed looks. 'Are you sure about that, dearie?' Gaby asked. 'Only you're crabby enough.'

Jo sat down. 'So what am I wearing today?' she asked. Then she saw Gaby's sly smile. 'Oh no. Please don't tell me it's the cerise angora?'

'Sorry. That's what it says in the book. You were wearing it in the last scene, so you've got to be wearing it in the next one.'

'I'm always wearing it.' Jo watched Gaby disappear through the doorway that led into the long, dark room beyond, where the characters' clothes were kept. 'Why does all my stuff have to be so awful? Why can't I have something a bit more chic? More designer?'

'On our budget?' Gaby returned with an armful of clothes. 'Tell you what, you talk the scriptwriters into letting you win the lottery and we'll see what we can do. In the meantime—'

'It's the cerise angora. Yes, I know.' Jo snatched it out of her hands. It was just horrible. Too short, too fluffy, too garish, with a disgusting sequinned motif on the front that looked as if she'd just been sick down it. Which was exactly what she felt like doing whenever she wore it.

But she could have been wearing a strategically placed copy of *Sporting Life* and Marcus still wouldn't have noticed. He barely acknowledged her as she stepped onto the hairdresser's set. He was too busy larking around behind the reception desk with Lara.

'So, Jo, you and Vic are lusting after each other, but you know you can't do anything about it because it wouldn't be fair on Steve,' Aidan reminded them. 'Now you've got to stand by and watch while he makes a play for your kid sister. And Marcus, you're redirecting all your pent-up passion to Winona because you can't have Stacey.'

That's a joke. Jo scowled at them. Any pent-up passion certainly wasn't heading in her direction.

The crew suddenly parted as Eva Lawrence stalked on set, followed by her ever-faithful assistant Desmond. She took her place at the basin with an air of wounded resignation, clutching a salon gown around her.

'Oops, looks like Eva's upset someone again!' Lara whispered. It was a standing joke that whenever Eva the Diva became too demanding, the script department got their own back by writing in a scene at the hairdresser's, knowing how terrified she was about losing her wig.

In this particular scene, Jo's character Stacey was supposed to be chatting with Ma Stagg over the washbasins when Vic came in and started flirting with Lara's character Winona. Jo found she could play Stacey's simmering jealousy without even trying.

'So how come a beautiful girl like you doesn't have a boyfriend?' Vic asked, when the cameras started rolling.

'Maybe I'm just choosy?' Winona teased back.

Vic leaned closer. 'What does a man have to do to get your attention?'

'Watch it!' Eva hissed as Jo squirted shampoo in her eye.

Winona smirked. 'What do you suggest?'

Jo watched, frozen with shock, as Marcus planted a kiss on Lara's mouth. The next second a piercing shriek echoed around the studio. It was coming from Eva the Diva.

Jo looked down at what appeared to be a drowned black cat in her hands. Without thinking, she screamed and flung it across the studio. It sailed up into the air and landed with a flop high up on the lighting gantry overhead. It was only when she heard Eva's strangled cry and saw her wispy grey head that she realised what she'd done.

'Oh God, I'm so sorry!' She didn't know whether to laugh or scream.

'You stupid cow!' Desmond leapt forward and flung a towel over Eva's

head. 'There, Miss Lawrence, we'll get you a Valium,' he soothed.
Shooting a final, furious look at Jo, he bundled Eva off the set. From
under the towel came the sound of incoherent whimpering.

There was a shocked silence, then the whole studio exploded.

'Christ, did you see that?'

'I thought I was going to die! I don't know how I kept a straight face.'

'We'll take a break, give her time to calm down.' Aidan's voice rose
over the babble. 'And for God's sake, get that wig off the ceiling.'

Mortified, Jo escaped to her dressing room. It wasn't long before Lara
followed, bringing Marcus with her.

'Ooh look, it's the *Westfield* wig-lobbing champion!' Lara giggled. Jo
retreated behind Viola's discarded *Guardian*. Why did she have to bring
him in here? Dressing rooms were supposed to be private. They could
have gone to the greenroom if they'd wanted to chat.

Lara was prattling on about some fabulous new members-only bar
that had just opened in Leeds. 'You mean you haven't been there yet?
You've got to go! How about tonight?'

'Sounds like fun,' Marcus drawled. 'How about you, Jo? Do you fancy
a night out clubbing?'

Jo crushed the pages of the newspaper, her knuckles white with fury.
As if ignoring her wasn't enough, now he was making fun of her too.

'Actually, I couldn't think of anything worse.'

She folded up her newspaper and stood up. Marcus watched her.
'Where are you going?'

'To the greenroom. I'm sure you two would prefer to be alone. I know
I would.'

She swept out of the dressing room. But she hadn't gone very far
when Marcus caught up with her.

'Was it something I said?' he asked.

'I don't know what you mean.'

'Oh, come on, I can tell you're in a mood.'

'I'm surprised you even noticed.'

She started to walk away but he grabbed her arm, swinging her round
to face him. 'Is this about me and Lara?'

Her eyes flashed. 'Why should I care what you two get up to?'

'It is, isn't it? You're jealous because you think I fancy her.'

'Don't flatter yourself!' She turned her face away. 'Anyway, it's obvious
how you feel about her. You've been chatting her up all day.'

'Only because I had to. It's in the script, remember?'

'And is it in the script that you have to ignore me?' The words were
out before she could stop them.

'Actually, it is.' He tilted her chin to look up at him. 'Look, we're supposed to be fighting our feelings. I chat her up and you get jealous.'

'Yes, but that doesn't mean you have to do it in real life!'

'Maybe not, but that's the way I work. I can't just switch my emotions on and off. I have to feel them here.' He took her hand and laid it over his heart. Jo felt the warm, hard muscles underneath his T-shirt and her knees turned to jelly.

'You mean to tell me,' she said slowly, 'that you've been ignoring me and deliberately flirting with Lara so it would look right in the *scene*?'

'And it worked, didn't it?' Marcus's aqua eyes sparkled. 'You really wanted to rip her hair out by the roots, didn't you?'

'Please don't mention hair.' Jo looked sheepish. Maybe she *was* a bit jealous. And Marcus was right, that afternoon's scenes had been some of the easiest she'd ever done. But even so . . .

'I wish you'd told me this before,' she grumbled.

'But it wouldn't have worked then, would it?' Marcus grinned. 'Although I have to say you made it pretty hard to ignore you this morning. You looked so sexy in that skirt—'

The sound of throat-clearing made her turn round. Richard Black was at the other end of the corridor. How long had he been there?

Long enough, judging by the look he was giving them.

'Can you tell me where I'd find Eva's dressing room?' he said. 'I understand there's been some difficulty on the set.'

As Marcus gave him directions, Jo shuffled her feet and stared at the floor. She felt like a guilty schoolgirl who'd been caught snogging behind the bike sheds. And she hadn't even done anything. Yet.

Jo spent the whole journey home wishing she'd never given in to such a mad impulse. Why had she agreed to go clubbing with Marcus? What was she trying to prove? That she could compete with the likes of Lara?

She didn't know what to wear, either. Not a lot, if Lara's photos in the newspapers were anything to go by. She seemed to get by with little more than some strategic body piercing.

As she drew up outside the house the front door flew open and Roxanne appeared on the step. 'Jo! Thank God you're home! It's Chloe. They sent her home from school—'

Jo didn't wait to hear any more. She pushed past Roxanne and headed for the sitting room.

Chloe was lying on the sofa, looking even whiter than the toy polar bear she clutched. 'Oh Mummy,' she wailed. 'I've got first-night nerves. I was sick on a shepherd.'

'Shh, darling. It's OK. Mummy's here.' Jo knelt down and touched her forehead. It was clammy with sweat.

'She's been sick three times.' Grace was curled up in the armchair. She looked both disgusted and impressed. 'She vomited on the rug. And that cushion. And she was nearly sick on the hamster too.'

'I wasn't sure whether to ring you at work.' Roxanne hovered, holding a plastic seaside bucket. 'She seemed OK an hour ago. Then she suddenly got worse—' As if to prove it, Chloe suddenly jacknifed upright and retched. Jo grabbed the bucket just in time.

'It's probably a tummy bug,' she said. 'These things take hold so quickly. The important thing is to keep her cool. Can you bring me a damp flannel?' As Roxanne rushed off, Jo turned back to Chloe. 'Mummy will make you more comfortable.'

'Do you think I'll be well enough to be in the Nativity tomorrow?'

'I jolly well hope so. I'm looking forward to seeing this show of yours. You'll be fine in the morning, you'll see.'

But there was the evening to get through first. And Jo knew she wouldn't be spending it clubbing. Leaving Roxanne to mop Chloe's sweaty brow, she went into the hall and called Lara's mobile.

Lara answered immediately. 'Really? Oh, that's bad news.' Lara tried—and failed—to sound disappointed as Jo explained the situation. 'Still, never mind. I'm sure Marcus and I will have fun without you.'

I bet you will, Jo thought, putting down the phone.

It turned out to be a long night. Chloe clung to her all evening, stopping only to throw up every hour or so. At first Grace was fascinated, but after a couple of hours she pronounced it all too gross to bear and stomped off to her room for an early night. Roxanne had already retreated upstairs with the portable TV and a copy of *Cosmo*.

Jo washed Chloe's face, changed her into fresh pyjamas and settled her down in her bed. She looked so small, snuggled up under the big double duvet.

'Do you think they'll let me be in the show tomorrow, Mummy?'

'Of course they will, sweetheart. Why shouldn't they?'

'I was sick on Jamie Dunsford. And Mrs Parkin was very cross. What if they make someone else an angel instead of me?'

'Then they'll have me to deal with,' Jo said firmly. 'How are you feeling now?'

'A bit better.' Just to prove it, Chloe was suddenly and comprehensively sick all over Jo's lap. She then fell into a deep and peaceful sleep, leaving Jo to stagger bow-legged to the bathroom.

The perfect end to a perfect day, she thought. And what were Lara and Marcus doing now? Dirty dancing in a darkened nightclub? Whatever it was, it was more fun than sponging sick off her jeans.

She pulled them off and tossed them into the washing basket and was just wiping down her shirt when the doorbell rang. Jo glanced at the clock. Who could be calling at half past eleven?

It was Marcus. He stood in the doorway, clutching a bottle of wine, looking devastatingly sexy in black jeans and his old leather jacket.

'I came to see what changed your mind,' he said.

'Didn't Lara tell you? Chloe was sick.' She yanked her shirt down, conscious of his gaze lingering on her thighs.

'I know that's what she said. But I wasn't sure if it was just an excuse?'

'You seriously think I'd lie about my daughter being ill?'

'I suppose not.' He looked sheepish. 'How is she now?'

'Sleeping, thank God.' Jo glanced over his shoulder into the street. His pick-up truck was parked under a street lamp. 'Where's Lara?'

'Snogging with the DJ, the last time I saw her.' He tilted his head. 'Well? Aren't you going to invite me in?'

Jo summed up the situation shrewdly. 'You mean Lara ditched you so you thought you'd come round here instead, is that it?'

'No!' He looked hurt. 'Actually, I'd decided to come round before Lara ditched me.' He smiled appealingly. In spite of herself, Jo couldn't help smiling back. 'So can I come in? Please? I've brought a bottle of wine.'

It was tempting. But after the evening she'd had she just couldn't face it. 'Sorry, I'm hardly in the mood for entertaining.'

'You're certainly dressed for it.' His eyes travelled up her bare legs again. Jo manoeuvred herself behind the front door.

'Some other time, maybe. I'm a bit tired.'

'Oh, go on. One drink won't hurt, surely?' He stopped and sniffed the air. 'What's that smell?'

There was a nasty sour aroma coming from somewhere. In panic, Jo realised it was her shirt. She had to get changed, and it seemed quicker just to give in than to stand and argue. 'OK, one drink,' she agreed. 'The kitchen's through there. I've got to get dressed.'

'Not on my account, surely?'

She ignored him and hurried upstairs. She crept round her bedroom, tracking down jeans and a sweater in the darkness trying to quell the excitement that bubbled inside her. He was a friend, that was all.

Marcus had already made himself at home in the living room when Jo got back downstairs. She found him lounging on the sofa, a glass in his hand. Murphy was stretched out on the floor beside him.

'I couldn't leave him in the truck. He yells his head off.' Marcus saw her dismay as he handed her a glass. 'I hope you don't mind?'

'I suppose not.' Jo picked her way over the thrashing tail. She sat down cross-legged on the floor and sipped her wine. The silence lengthened awkwardly. What should she say? Jo wondered. They had nothing in common, except work. 'How did you get into acting?'

'It seemed like a good idea at the time. I kept being kicked out of school, and it was pretty clear I wasn't going to end up at university. Drama school seemed like an easy option.'

'Which college did you go to?'

'Most of them,' he grinned. 'I'm afraid I'm not very good at sticking to things. Especially rules. I think it's genetic. My family isn't known for its staying power. We get bored too easily.' He held out the bottle to her. 'More wine? You've hardly touched yours.'

'No, thanks. I've got to be up early in the morning. I'm watching my daughter be an angel. And believe me, that doesn't happen very often.' She smiled at him. 'Tell me more about your family.'

'You wouldn't believe me if I did.' He slid onto the floor next to her. 'Most people seem to find my family set-up a bit weird, to say the least.'

'Sounds intriguing.'

'Let's just say we're not what you'd call a traditional nuclear family.'

As he painted a picture of his chaotic home life, Jo was shocked. His parents, various brothers and sisters and assorted friends and hangers-on lived in a kind of commune deep in the Gloucestershire countryside. But it didn't end there. From what Marcus said, it sounded as though his father had repopulated the local community single-handed.

He leaned over, topping up her glass. He'd moved closer so their shoulders were touching and his thigh was brushing against hers. If she just turned her face a fraction he would be close enough to kiss . . .

Then, as if he could read her mind, he said, 'Can I stay the night?'

'What?'

'Can I stay? I'm in no fit state to drive.' He held up the empty bottle. 'And frankly, I've got nowhere else to go. I've sort of run out of friends' floors.' He looked downcast, like a little boy.

Jo thought about it. 'Well, I suppose you could have the sofa—'

'I'd rather sleep with you.'

She nearly dropped her glass in shock. Talk about direct!

'I'm afraid my daughter's beaten you to it,' she said, trying to sound light-hearted. 'Besides, I hardly know you.'

'What's there to know? You know you want me. And I want you.'

Jo finished her wine with a gulp. 'You don't waste any time, do you?'

'What do you want me to do? Play games? Go through a big charade of asking you out, swopping phone numbers, going on a date?'

'Isn't that how relationships usually start?'

'Who said anything about a relationship?'

It was like a bucket of icy water over her head. 'I see. So we're talking about a one-night stand, are we?'

'A night, a week, a lifetime—who knows?' Marcus shrugged. 'Why can't we just enjoy the moment, and see what happens?'

He reached up and traced her jawline. 'I'm just trying to be honest with you. I like you. And I think you like me. Maybe we could have a relationship, I don't know. Like I said, I've never been very good at sticking to anything. But I know we could be very, very good together—'

He brushed her lips with his finger. The slightest touch, but it sent electric shockwaves through her. Mesmerised, she watched his mouth coming closer. Another second and he would be kissing her—

Suddenly there was a loud yelp as Murphy shot to his feet.

'What happened?'

'I think I knelt on his paw. It's OK. Murph, don't be such a wuss.' Marcus ruffled the shaggy head. 'Now, where were we?'

'I think I was just about to make some coffee.' Jo escaped to the kitchen and leaned against the door, her heart doing a frantic salsa against her ribs. Oh God. Marcus Finn, gorgeous blond love god that he was, actually wanted to sleep with her.

And she wanted to sleep with him. She absent-mindedly emptied half the coffee jar into the cafetière. But it was all wrong. She might be old-fashioned, but jumping into bed with someone, no matter how amazingly sexy, wasn't her style. If Marcus cared anything about her, he'd respect that. And if he didn't . . .

She carried the tray back into the living room. 'Look, Marcus, I hope you don't think I'm being—' she started to say, then stopped. He was stretched out on the sofa, snoring gently.

'Marcus?' She put down the tray and took the glass from his hand.

Jo smiled wryly. So much for white-hot passion. With a sigh, she went off to the airing cupboard in search of a spare duvet.

She had a highly erotic dream that night. She was covered in banana yoghurt and Marcus was licking it off. Her body became one huge quivering erogenous zone as his tongue delicately explored every inch of her. Her navel, her breasts, the hollows in her collarbone, her ears . . .

She stirred. Something *was* licking her ears. She opened her eyes.

'Bloody hell!' She tried to move, but she was pinned to the bed by twelve stone of hairy canine. '*Help!*'

Murphy sensed her panic and started barking, giving her a faceful of stale doggy breath. He leapt off the bed and bolted for the door just as Chloe, Grace and Roxanne came through it.

'Mummy, why is there a strange man on our sofa?'

'He's—um—a friend.' Jo clutched her chest, checking for broken ribs.

'What sort of friend? A boyfriend?' Grace was suspicious. 'He's not moving in with us, is he?'

'Of course he isn't moving in. What time is it?'

'Ten past eight.'

'Ten past eight?' She flung off the duvet. 'Why didn't anyone wake me?'

'We were too busy watching that man.' Chloe, thankfully, seemed none the worse for her night of throwing up.

Jo searched for her dressing gown. 'Go and get dressed, girls. I just need a quick shower.'

'But that man—'

'He won't bite you. Now hurry up!'

The girls shuffled off, but Roxanne lingered behind. 'So who is he?'

'His name's Marcus and he's just joined *Westfield*.' Jo delved under her bed. 'Have you seen my other slipper?'

'How old is he?'

'Twenty-five, I think.'

'So he's a lot younger than you, then?'

'Astounding, Einstein.' Jo threw on her dressing gown and headed for the door. But not before she'd caught the look Roxanne gave her. It was a look of envy mingled with disgust. *Toy boy*, it said.

After she'd washed, dressed and dried her hair, Jo found Marcus at the kitchen table, ploughing his way through a bowl of Rice Krispies. Chloe watched him like a scientist conducting a particularly fascinating lab experiment.

'Your dog doesn't look very friendly,' she said.

'Don't you believe it. He's a gentle giant.'

'What if he eats Pudding?' She glanced anxiously at the hamster.

'He won't. He never touches pudding, he's watching his figure.' He looked up at Jo and grinned. Her stomach did a backflip.

'So, who wants breakfast?' she said brightly. As Chloe reached for the Sugar Puffs, Jo noticed Grace hanging back in the doorway.

'I'm not hungry,' she muttered.

'You, not hungry? That's a first.' Jo flipped the switch on the kettle. 'Shall I make you some toast?'

'I told you, I don't want anything!' With a scowl at Marcus, Grace

219

slammed the door. Jo listened to her footsteps stomping up the stairs.

'I wonder what's wrong with her?'

'She doesn't like *him*.' Chloe, blunt as ever, nodded towards Marcus. 'She said he was horrible, and she said if you marry him she's going to run away from home and live with Daddy.'

Mortified, Jo forced herself to meet Marcus's eye's. He was smiling.

'I suppose this means we'll have to cancel the register office?' he said.

He left soon afterwards. There was an awkward moment as they stood on the step.

'Are you sure I can't offer you a lift?' he asked

Jo shook her head. 'It's Chloe's Nativity this morning.' She bit her lip. 'Look, Marcus, about last night—'

'Sorry I fell asleep just as things were beginning to get interesting.'

'That's just it, I don't think they were. It's not that I don't find you attractive,' she said quickly. 'It's just—I take sex very seriously.'

'So do I.' His eyes glinted.

'That's not what I mean—'

'I know exactly what you mean.' He took her face in his hands and his lips brushed hers. 'But don't worry, I haven't given up on you yet.'

With a wink, he was gone, Murphy at his heels. Jo closed the front door, turned round—and bumped straight into Chloe.

'He kissed you!' she crowed. 'He *is* your boyfriend, isn't he, Mummy?'

'No, he isn't.' Jo looked up. Grace was on the stairs, watching her with silent reproach. Before Jo could say anything, she ran back up to her room and slammed the door.

Later, with Grace cold-shouldering her, and Roxanne treating her as if she was a cradle-snatcher, it was a relief to get to work that afternoon, after watching a perfect performance from Chloe.

Lara and Viola were already in the dressing room, having been working all morning. Lara was on her mobile as usual, while Viola was engrossed in an article in *She* on non-invasive cosmetic surgery.

She looked up as Jo entered. 'Have you heard? Lara's getting married!'

'You're kidding? But she hasn't even got a boyfriend!'

'She has now. Some DJ she met in that club last night.'

'Blimey.' Jo gaped at Lara. 'So what's she doing now? Breaking the news to her parents?'

'You must be joking! She's calling her agent to try to fix up a magazine deal for the wedding.'

Jo shook her head. 'That girl doesn't buy a packet of Tampax without trying to sell the exclusive rights to someone.'

'Sorted!' Lara turned off her phone. 'Bernie reckons he can do a deal with *Goss* magazine for the wedding, if we get married on Valentine's Day. And they might even cover the cost of the honeymoon.'

'What? You mean you'd even have a photographer following you around the bridal suite?'

'Why not?' Lara shrugged. 'I can't wait to tell Leon.'

'Leon? This is your new boyfriend, is it?'

'Fiancé. Although we haven't got the ring sorted out yet. We'll probably have to get *Goss* involved with that, too. It'll make a great spread.'

'So what's he like, then?' Jo asked.

'Leon? He's really cool. He's a kind of entrepreneur. You know, night-club promoter, DJ, pop-video producer—all that kind of stuff.' She inspected her fingernails. 'He thinks I should make a record. To cash in on my famous name, sort of thing.'

Viola and Jo exchanged horrified looks. Leon might know a lot about the music business, but he'd obviously never heard Lara sing.

'So what happened to Marcus?' Viola asked.

'God knows. He disappeared after we got to the club. Said he had to see someone. His dealer, probably.'

Jo's smile faded. 'You don't think . . . he does drugs?'

'Jo, everyone does drugs.'

'I don't.'

'Everyone who's anyone,' Lara said crushingly.

They were interrupted by the dressing-room phone. Jo picked it up. 'Hello, Jo Porter speaking.'

'So you've finally turned up, have you?'

She recognised the voice on the other end of the line, and her blood ran like ice through her veins. 'Richard?'

Viola started dancing around in front of her, doing some kind of frantic flapping mime. Jo was still trying to figure it out when Richard said, 'So where were you this morning?'

Oh God. The breakfast meeting. 'Look, I can explain—'

'My office. Now.' He cut her off. 'And this explanation had better be bloody good!'

'Oh God, I'm really sorry,' Viola said. 'With all the excitement about Lara, I forgot to warn you. Richard was absolutely spitting when you didn't show up this morning. You're in massive trouble.'

'Thanks,' Jo said. 'I think I'd already worked that out for myself.'

By the time she reached the top floor she'd decided a grovelling apology would be in order. She was in the wrong, after all. She should have let him know personally that she couldn't make the meeting.

Kate couldn't hide her malicious smile as she showed her into Richard's office. He was standing at the window with his back to her, but from the rigid set of his shoulders she could tell that he hadn't calmed down at all.

'Well? What have you got to say for yourself?' His voice was low and full of leashed anger.

'Look, I'm really sorry about this morning. I realise I should have let you know personally, but—'

'But something came up, is that it?' He turned round slowly. 'It's too late for apologies. I expected you here at eight thirty this morning.'

'Yes, but—'

'I told you to be here. What went wrong? Couldn't you get out of bed?'

She gritted her teeth. He didn't want to hear her explanation, he just wanted to bully her. 'I'd made other arrangements.'

'But I wanted you here. And since I'm the one who pays your vastly inflated salary I expected you to do as I ask!' He rested his hands on the desk and leaned towards her. 'Everyone else managed to fit this meeting into their extremely busy lives, so why not you? Or does your love life take precedence over your other commitments?'

'Love life?' She stared at him. 'I don't know what you mean.'

'Then perhaps you're not aware of the latest gossip?' He picked up a copy of the *Evening Press* and flung it across the desk at her. 'Imagine my surprise and delight when I pick up the paper and find *that* little snippet staring at me. No wonder you couldn't drag yourself away!'

Jo read it over several times. It was just a tiny paragraph on the inside page, but it exploded in her brain like a Scud missile.

'*Westfield* Stars in Secret Love Tryst', it said. And underneath: 'They may have to fight their mutual attraction on screen, but in real life it seems actress Jo Porter has already succumbed to the charms of her gorgeous *Westfield* costar Marcus Finn. Marcus, soon to be seen on screen as her new love interest, was spotted leaving Ms Porter's Clifton home early this morning.'

'But . . . this is a load of rubbish!'

'Are you saying he didn't stay the night?'

'Well, yes, he did, but it wasn't like that!' she protested, as Richard's eyes narrowed. 'He's just a friend, that's all.'

'A very close friend, if that story's anything to go by.'

'I—' She started to explain, then stopped herself. 'I don't think my private life has anything to do with you.'

'You're absolutely right.' His icy response took her aback. 'Frankly, Ms Porter, I couldn't care less if you entertained half the male population of

North Yorkshire. But I do care when it starts to affect your work. I expect one hundred per cent commitment from you. And if you can't give that, then maybe it's time you started redefining your priorities.'

'Now just a minute! When have I ever missed a day's filming? When have I ever been late on set? Just because I miss one meeting—'

They were interrupted by the arrival of Kate. 'Sorry to butt in, but I've got an hysterical Roxanne on the phone for you.' She looked disapprovingly at Jo. 'Apparently it's a matter of life and death—'

Jo didn't wait to hear any more. She rushed to the phone on Richard's desk and snatched it up, hammering the buttons with trembling fingers until she picked up the right line. 'Roxanne, what it is? Is it the girls? Is it Chloe? Don't tell me she's been taken ill again—'

'No, she's fine. I just thought you ought to know—Pudding's gone.'

It took a moment for her pounding heart to slow down. 'What?'

'He wasn't in his cage when I came back from the shops at lunchtime. His door was open and he'd gone.'

As the adrenaline rush subsided, Jo didn't know whether to laugh or cry. 'So you phoned me to tell me the hamster's run away from home?' She glanced at Richard. He was standing at the window again, staring out. She could only imagine what he must be thinking.

'What do you think we should do?' Roxanne wailed. 'The girls will be so upset.'

Jo suppressed a sigh of irritation. 'Look, Roxanne, I really can't think about this now. You sort it out.' She put the phone down.

Richard turned round to face her. But before he could say anything Jo was ready for him. 'The hamster's left home. Yes, I know it's trivial as far as you're concerned, but it's important to the girls. Just like Chloe's Nativity was important to her. That's where I was this morning. I told Kate but you can check with the school if you don't believe me. The number's in the book.'

She saw his eyes flicker but her anger had taken over. 'And please don't try to lecture me about my priorities, Mr Black. Because as far as I'm concerned my children come before anyone and everyone else. Even you. You might like to think you're some kind of omnipotent power up here in your big office, but in my list of priorities you feature precisely nowhere!' And with that, she slammed out of his office before he had a chance to respond.

Richard Black lived on the top floor of a smart warehouse conversion on the banks of the River Ouse, overlooking King's Staith.

'I've always wondered what these places were like,' Viola said as she, her partner, Marion, and Jo squeezed into the lift. 'I hear they cost a fortune, especially for a river view.'

'I'm sure Richard can afford it.' Jo flattened herself against the wall to make room for Marion's bulk. In her mannish suit and stout shoes, her brown hair cut in a severe bob, she was a complete contrast to Viola, whose floaty multicoloured dress made her look like a bird of paradise.

Jo wasn't looking forward to this. She'd managed to steer clear of Richard up until now, but this would be like walking into the lion's den. She was terrified he would bawl her out again in front of all the other guests. And although deep down she knew that wasn't really his style, it didn't stop her palms growing clammier as the lift moved upwards.

The doors opened straight into an apartment roughly the size of a small football stadium. Most of the guests had already arrived and were huddled at one end of the cavernous space. A brace of waiters worked the room with trays of wine and canapés. As they entered, a woman in black appeared and helped them off with their coats.

Viola caught her breath. 'Oh my God, it's so—so—'

'Minimal?' Jo helped herself to a glass of wine from a passing tray.

The room was starkly bare apart from two enormous white sofas squaring up to each other across a huge expanse of polished pale wood floor. Two of the walls were comprised almost entirely of glass, offering a fabulous panoramic view of the river and over the rooftops of York. In one corner a spotlight illuminated a single twisting hazel branch in a sculpted glass vase. Other than that, there was nothing. It was like the nuclear winter of interior design.

Jo looked round for Richard and found him, on the other side of the room, talking to a couple of *Westfield*'s regular directors. He was dressed immaculately, wearing an expensive-looking suit that matched his dark colouring. As if sensing that he was being watched, he turned round. As his eyes met Jo's, the unexpected lurch of sensation in the pit of Jo's stomach nearly made her drop her glass. Then, before she'd managed to regain control, he slowly and deliberately turned his back again.

'What do you think, Jo?'

'Sorry, what did you say?' She dragged her attention back to Viola and Marion, who were helping themselves to handfuls of nibbles from another passing tray.

'I was just saying,' Viola said. 'They haven't got a single Christmas decoration up. Do you suppose they're Jehovah's Witnesses or something?'

'Just incredibly trendy, I think. Christmas is probably too naff for them. God knows what they'd make of her house. Every inch was covered with baubles and tinsel. It was like Santa's Grotto gone mad.

Jo glanced back at Richard. Even now, at a party, he seemed totally in control. His dark, hawklike gaze scanned the room, missing nothing. Although for some reason it never strayed her way. She was surprised how much that piqued her.

Viola frowned at the dinky little canapés Marion was holding. 'I don't know about you, but I need some serious food. Shall we go and investigate the kitchen?'

'You go ahead,' said Jo. 'I'll catch you up.'

Violet and Marion headed off to the kitchen, leaving her alone. Jo looked for Richard. The people he'd been talking to had drifted back to the group, leaving him on his own. She watched him apprehensively. She knew she couldn't leave it like this, with neither of them speaking. She had to rebuild some bridges, and it was now or never. She gulped down her wine, took a deep breath, and headed towards him.

She was halfway across the room when he looked up and saw her. Instantly he turned on his heel and headed in the opposite direction. For a second she stood, stranded in the middle of the room, not knowing what to do next. Richard's exit had been so abrupt, so downright bloody *rude*, she didn't know how to react. She glanced around, certain that the whole room must have witnessed her public snubbing. But no one seemed to be looking her way except Kate who was smirking into her glass of Semillon Blanc.

Embarrassment gave way to outrage. *Bastard*, she thought. Here she was, trying to offer an olive branch, and he'd thrown it back in her face. Well, sod him. If he wanted to be like that, so could she.

She walked into the kitchen, which was just as pristine as the rest of the apartment. It looked like an operating theatre, with millions of tiny bulbs reflecting pinpoints of brilliant light off the highly-polished aluminium work surfaces.

Viola and Marion were tucking into the buffet together with Brett Michaels and his latest girlfriend, a pretty young thing with the longest of legs and the shortest of wispy slip dresses.

'This place is incredible, isn't it?' Viola said. 'Can you really imagine anyone living here?'

'That depends what you mean by living, doesn't it?' Jo replied. After the way Richard had snubbed her she was in the mood to dish the dirt. 'People like Richard and Kate don't live like the rest of us. They have lifestyles. I mean, look at all this.' She swept her hand round the kitchen. 'I don't suppose either of them actually uses any of it. It's probably all for show, just like everything else in this arty-farty flat.'

'Jo . . .' Viola whispered her name but she was in no mood to stop.

'Take that bin,' she said. 'Have you ever seen anything so ridiculous? You couldn't get an After Eight wrapper in there without it overflowing. But I bet it cost more than my month's mortgage—'

She was suddenly aware of an ominous silence in the room. Turning slowly, she found herself looking up into the Arctic gaze of Richard Black, standing in the doorway.

'Sorry to interrupt. I only came in to get some food.'

They all watched in silence as he picked up a plate and began to help himself from the buffet. Jo felt as if she'd been turned to stone. All except her face, which flooded with hot, humiliated colour.

'Wonderful—er—party.' Viola struggled to break the tense silence.

'Is it?' Richard shot Jo an icy glance and then stalked back through the open doorway.

Jo and Viola stared at each other in silence, then Viola stifled a scream with her fist. 'My God, did you see his face? I just wanted to die!'

'I think I just have.' Jo downed her glass of wine and poured herself another with shaking hands. She'd really done it now. I don't care, she told herself. He deserved every word. So why did she feel so wretched?

'*Get that fucking dog off my sofa!*'

Kate's scream from the far end of the apartment, nearly made her drop the bottle. They all rushed to open the door.

Murphy was stretched out on one of the pristine white sofas, his tail thumping happily against the cushions while Marcus looked mildly on.

'He's not doing any harm,' he said.

'Not doing any harm?' Kate said. 'Do you know how much these sofas cost? Do something with him!'

'What do you suggest?'

'I don't know, do I? Put him out on the roof terrace.'

'But what if he gets lonely and tries to jump?'

'Then tell him to call the bloody Samaritans! Just get him out of here!'

Everyone started laughing, but Jo didn't join in. She was too busy staring at one of Marcus's hands, which was firmly fixed on the well-upholstered bottom of Louise, *Westfield's* press officer.

Jo hardly recognised her. She'd swopped her usual sober suit for a sprayed-on pair of leather jeans and a black T-shirt, neither of which did her any favours.

'I'll take him.' Louise stepped forward and grabbed Murphy's collar, hauling him off the sofa. 'Come on, boy. Let's go walkies.'

Jo watched her drag the shaggy hearthrug towards the glass doors. She was obviously on good terms with Murphy and his master.

'Hi, angel. Long time no see.' She jumped as Marcus flung his arm round her shoulder. He looked gorgeous, in a loose white shirt and faded jeans, his freshly washed hair flopping in his eyes. 'Missed me?'

'Not really.'

'I was going to phone you, but so much has been happening I never got round to it. You wouldn't believe what's been going on.'

'I'm sure I wouldn't.' Louise was coming back towards them, pushing her way through the crowd like a heat-seeking missile. Jo quickly disentangled herself from Marcus's embrace. 'Hi, Louise.'

'Hello, Jo.' She was wearing a lot more make-up than usual. Somehow it didn't look quite right on her plump, kind face.

'Isn't she fabulous?' Marcus put his arm round her waist. Louise turned an unfetching shade of pink under her thick foundation. 'Lou's saved my life. She found out that me and Murphy were sleeping in the truck and she's been letting us stay at her place. Isn't she an angel?'

'She must be.' Jo noticed the possessive way Louise slipped her hand into Marcus's, and felt a twinge of pity for her. She wondered if she knew Marcus was commitment-phobic. If not, she soon would.

That could have been me, she thought. If she'd let Marcus into her bed . . . She was surprised at how relieved she felt.

She left them to it and went off in search of the bathroom. Like everywhere else in the apartment, it was all very sleek, shiny and minimal, from the mirrored walls to the fluffy white towels and gleaming chrome and polished marble surfaces.

She checked her reflection and reapplied her lipstick. What am I doing here? she thought. She didn't want to be at this party, and Richard certainly didn't want her here. The best thing she could do was leave.

She emerged from the bathroom and started hunting for her coat. There must be a cloakroom somewhere. She pushed open the first door she came to and found herself in Richard and Kate's bedroom. Blue moonlight flooded in from the window wall, illuminating the vast white expanse of bed, the only furniture in the bare room.

She was about to retreat when she suddenly realised she wasn't alone. On the other side of the room, outlined in moonlight from the window, was Richard.

He had his back to her, and a slight breeze from the open window lifted his dark hair as he stared out at the river. Smoke coiled from a cigarette, apparently forgotten between his fingers. He'd taken off his jacket and his shirt gleamed blue-white in the moonlight. For a split second she forgot who he was and where she was, and watched him. She'd never noticed what an amazing athlete's body he had, his broad shoulders tapering to lean hips and long legs.

'Did you want something?' His voice startled her.

'I was—um—looking for my coat.'

'You're not leaving?'

'I think it's best, don't you?'

He turned slowly. His face in the moonlight, was unreadable. 'Why?'

'It's obvious, isn't it?'

'Don't tell me, my—what did you call it?—lifestyle offends you so much you can't bear to stay a moment longer. Is that it?'

Jo squirmed. 'No, but—'

'But you don't approve of the way Kate and I live?'

'I didn't say that.'

'I believe you did. You were quite voluble on the subject, in fact. Even our bin offended you, as I recall.' He stubbed out his cigarette in an equally designer-like ashtray.

'Look, I'm sorry. I had no right to say those things. I was just angry at you—for ignoring me.' There. She'd said it.

Richard frowned. 'When did I ignore you?'

'When we arrived. I was coming to talk to you and you walked away.'

'My mobile went off. I went outside to answer it. I tried to find you afterwards. That's why I came into the kitchen. But you were busy talking to your friends at the time.'

Shame washed over her. 'Like I said, I'm sorry,' she mumbled. 'But I really think it would be best if I went now.'

'Wait.' She was groping for the door handle when he spoke. His voice was so soft she barely heard it, yet it was enough to stop her in her tracks. 'Do you want a cigarette?'

She turned to face him. He'd moved from the window to sit on the bed, and was opening a packet of Marlboros. He clamped one between his lips and held out the rest. 'Well? Do you want one?'

Jo shook her head dazedly. 'No thanks.' She watched, fascinated, as the brief flare of his lighter illuminated his face.

He took a long drag, his eyes meeting hers through the haze of smoke. 'By the way, you were right. It is an absurd bin. I've been telling Kate that ever since she bought it. But it didn't cost a month's mortgage.'

'Oh?'

'More like a top of the range BMW. Joke,' he said, as Jo's face changed. 'Sit down if you like. I won't bite.'

She moved cautiously to perch on the end of the bed. 'Don't you want to go back to the party?'

'To be quite honest, I can't stand parties. And I'm sure everyone will have a much better time if I'm not there.'

'What makes you say that?'

'Let's face it, half the people in that room only came because they were afraid I'd sack them if they didn't.'

'That's not true.'

'Isn't it?' His eyes were cynical. 'They call me the Grim Reaper. No one can look at me without seeing their P45s.'

Jo couldn't help smiling. 'Maybe it's your image?'

'My image? I didn't even know I had one.'

'Of course you have. Everyone has. It's what the world sees.'

'And what exactly does the world see?'

Jo tried to think tactful. 'Someone aloof and unapproachable.'

'Maybe that's the way I like it?'

'Then maybe you shouldn't wonder why people are afraid of you?'

'Are you afraid of me, Ms Porter?'

She looked into his face. 'No,' she whispered. What she was afraid of was the strange sensation that suddenly hit the pit of her stomach.

'So how do you think I could make myself more . . . approachable?'

'Um . . . I'm not sure.' She tried to drag her mind back from the alarming track it had found itself on. 'Maybe you should lose the tie?'

'What's wrong with my tie?'

'Nothing. It's just you're always wearing one. It's hardly relaxed, is it? You make people feel as if they're here for a job interview.'

'So what should I wear? A cardigan? Would that be relaxed enough for you?'

Oh God, now she'd offended him again. She was about to make a flustered apology when she caught it. The faintest twitch at the corner of his mouth. Shocked, she realised he was teasing her.

'So, how's the prodigal hamster? Did he ever come home?'

She frowned. 'How did you know about . . .' Then it came back to her. She'd taken the call from Roxanne in his office. 'No, I'm afraid poor Pudding may have ended up being the cat next door's main course.'

'Your daughters must have been very upset?'

'Inconsolable is the word, I think. Poor Chloe still insists on leaving the cage door open at night, just in case he decides to come back—' She broke off, seeing him yawn. 'I'm sorry, I shouldn't be boring you with my domestic dramas.'

'I don't find you remotely boring.' Their eyes met, and Jo felt a sudden, unexpected jolt. She looked away, confused. 'Actually, I'm a bit jet-lagged. I flew in from New York this morning.'

'Really? Business or pleasure?'

'Definitely business. Some American network bosses are interested in buying *Westfield*.' He rubbed his eyes. 'I've been out of the office for the past two days, otherwise I would have seen you sooner.'

'Me? Why?'

'To apologise. I was wrong to fly off the handle about you and Marcus. You were right, your personal life is none of my business.'

'But there's nothing going on between me and Marcus. He just turned up on my doorstep late one night, that's all.'

'And now he's turned up on Louise's.' He searched her face. 'How do you feel about that?'

'Sorry for Louise, I think,' she shrugged. 'Marcus Finn isn't exactly ideal boyfriend material.'

'Don't you find him attractive?'

'Well, yes. But there's got to be more to it than that, hasn't there?'

'Like what?'

'I don't know . . . chemistry, I suppose.'

'Chemistry?'

'You know. When you look at someone and everything feels just totally right.' He turned to look at her and suddenly she found she couldn't say any more. The air between them seemed to be crackling.

Then from down the hall came a blast of Marvin Gaye, breaking the tension and releasing her from the spell.

'They'll be wondering where we are,' she said. 'Maybe we should go back and join the party?'

'Good idea.' Neither of them moved. It was Jo who reluctantly dragged herself to her feet first. After a moment, Richard stubbed out his cigarette and followed her.

Several couples were already slow dancing when they rejoined the party. Among them, she noticed with surprise, were Marcus and Kate. Although they were hardly smooching. Kate was holding him at arm's length like a smelly dishrag.

As soon as she spotted Richard she came over to join them, Marcus trailing after her. 'He's drunk,' she hissed. 'And his wretched dog's eaten all the canapés.'

'Only because no one else was touching them.' Marcus leaned over and planted a damp, wine-flavoured kiss on Jo's mouth.

'Where have you been, anyway?' Kate looked put out. 'I've had to entertain this lot all by myself.'

Jo glanced guiltily at Richard. Nothing remotely intimate had happened between them, so why did she feel as if it had?

'Come on, angel, let's dance.' Jo flinched as Marcus folded his arms round her waist. 'I've been longing to get you on the floor all night.'

'What happened to Louise?' she asked, as he pulled her into his arms.

'No idea. Gone home, I think. She got in a bit of a strop earlier, just because I was talking to Brett Michaels's girlfriend.'

'I can imagine. Maybe you should have gone after her?'

'Why? I'm having a good time. Besides, she doesn't own me.'

'Obviously not.' Marcus was a very sexy dancer. He held her so close their bodies seemed to be moulded together. Jo felt his hands snaking up and down the length of her spine without a tingle of interest. She was right. There was definitely no chemistry there.

Then, over his shoulder, she caught a glimpse of Richard and Kate. They were working the crowd, smiling, chatting and laughing together, the perfect couple. He wasn't even looking her way. If there had been any chemistry between them five minutes ago, it had soon been forgotten.

CHAPTER SIX

'NO WAY, DUNCAN. You're not doing it.'

'Can't we just talk about this like reasonable adults?'

'There's nothing to talk about. You're not having them and that's that.'

'They're my kids too. And you always have them at Christmas. I've never complained, have I?'

'Yes, but I don't take them to the other side of the world, do I?'

'It's only for a couple of weeks.'

A couple of weeks? Only the most magical weeks in a child's life. And Duncan wanted to take the girls to Florida.

'They'll have a fantastic time. You wouldn't want to deny them that, would you?'

'No, but couldn't you take them some other time?' she pleaded.

'I've already explained that. Some friends have rented a villa for Christmas and New Year and they've invited me and the girls along. Just think about it, Jo. They could be spending Christmas at Disney World.'

She felt herself wavering. He was right, the girls would have a terrific time. But Christmas was special. The thought of not seeing their excited faces on Christmas morning tore her apart.

'Tell you what,' Duncan suggested. 'Why don't we let the girls decide?

They're old enough to make up their own minds, don't you think?'

Jo agreed. But she should have known Duncan would get in first, wooing them with tales of spending Christmas Day with Mickey Mouse.

'Dad says there'll be films all the way,' Grace told her excitedly.

'Sounds wonderful.' Jo tried to hide her disappointment, but Grace noticed.

'We don't have to go, if you think you'll be lonely,' she said.

'Me, lonely? Heavens no! I'll have a lovely time.'

'But what will you do on Christmas Day?' Chloe picked up on her sister's concern. 'You'll have to eat a whole turkey by yourself!'

'I expect I'll go and share Grandma's,' Jo lied. 'Don't worry about me, I'll be fine. We'll have our Christmas together when you come home.'

'With cards and presents?' Chloe asked.

'Everything. I'll even keep the tree up.'

'It'll be bald by then,' Grace said, but she looked slightly more cheered. 'You're sure you don't mind?'

'I think it's a lovely idea. And it won't seem like a minute before we're together again.'

Jo had been right, it didn't seem like a minute. It seemed more like years. The house felt empty without the girls, especially as Roxanne had gone back to Thirsk to spend Christmas with her family. It was only when she found how oppressive silence could be that Jo realised how much she missed the blaring music and the squabbles.

Christmas morning was the worst. She woke up before dawn and lay, staring into the darkness, imagining the girls asleep in their beds on the other side of the Atlantic. Missing them was like an ache inside her.

It could have been worse. She could have gone to her mother's for Christmas. Audrey had invited her, although once she'd let it slip that she would also be inviting Rosemary Warrender and her still available son, Jo had decided against it.

She'd promised the girls she'd save their gifts until they got home, but there were a few others to open. Some Clarins stuff from Viola. An Ibiza club remix CD from Roxanne. A book on DIY from her father, who had long since given up any hope of her finding a man. And some expensive underwear from her mother, who obviously hadn't.

The girls rang just after lunch. They sounded so happy and excited Jo could have gone on listening to them gabbling for ever, but then she heard Duncan warning them not to stay on the line too long.

'We've got to go,' Grace said. There was a long pause, then she added quietly, 'I miss you, Mum.'

'Me too, darling.' A lump rose in her throat. Grace was always the cool one, never wanting to be cuddled or fussed over. Jo ached to cuddle her now.

By eight o'clock she'd had a bath, changed into her old dressing gown and eaten roughly her own body weight in Twiglets. She was curled up on the sofa watching the big movie when the doorbell rang. Jo rolled off the sofa to answer it.

'I hope you don't mind me calling?' Richard said.

She stared at him in the doorway, his overcoat turned up against the freezing wind, rain dripping off his dark hair. 'No, of course not. Would you, er, like to come in?'

He shook his head. 'I won't disturb you. I only came to give you this.' He pulled a small cardboard box from inside his coat. 'I just happened to be passing a shop yesterday, and I noticed it.'

Mystified, she took the box, wondering what on earth could have brought him across York on Christmas night, and in such filthy weather. She nearly dropped it as she felt something scuffle inside.

'Oh God, it's not . . .' Cautiously she undid the end of the box. The yellow street lamp illuminated a pair of shining black eyes. 'A hamster!'

'It's all right, isn't it? I mean, I haven't squashed the poor little bugger or anything? He's been living in my sock drawer since last night.'

'No, he's fine. He's gorgeous. The girls will love him.' Except the girls were several thousand miles away. She opened her mouth to speak, but no sound came out. Then, to her horror, she burst into tears.

He hesitated a fraction of a second. Then she felt his arms go round her, holding her stiffly. 'I take it this isn't to do with the hamster?' he said.

'I'm sorry.' His coat felt damp against her cheek. 'I'm really sorry.'

Then it all came out, in a long, incoherent babble. About Duncan and the girls being in the States, and her being alone.

'I know I'm being selfish and pathetic, but I miss them so much.' She sniffed back a sob.

'It's OK.' Richard patted her shoulder. She could feel his unease in every rigid muscle of his body.

'I'm sorry.' She pulled away and wiped her face on the back of her hand. 'You must think I'm a complete idiot.'

'Of course not.' He didn't sound too convinced. 'You're upset, that's all. Anyone would be.'

'Thanks for the hamster. It was really kind of you to think of the girls. And to bring it all this way on Christmas night. You and Kate must have a thousand better things to do.'

'Actually, Kate's gone to Sussex to spend Christmas with her family.'

She frowned up at him. 'And you didn't go with her?'

'I'm not really the type for big family get-togethers.'

'You mean you've been on your own all day?'

'So have you.'

'True.'

They both looked down at the hamster snuffling inside his box. Finally, Richard said, 'Well, I won't keep you.'

'Do you want to come in for a drink?' The words were out before she had time to think about them.

He hesitated. 'Are you sure? I don't want to impose.'

'You won't. I was just thinking about cracking open a bottle of wine. I won't feel so guilty if I share it with someone.'

She showed him into the sitting room, handed him the wine to open and left him depositing the new hamster in Pudding's cage while she ran upstairs, splashed her face with cold water and changed into a pair of jeans and a grey cashmere cardigan. By the time she got downstairs Richard had poured them each a glass of wine and was standing by the fire.

They sat down on opposite ends of the sofa. But despite the safe distance between them, Jo still felt wary. There was something different about him. She just couldn't put her finger on what it was . . .

Then it dawned on her. 'You're not wearing a tie.'

'Oh. I decided to take your advice.' He looked down at his chinos and blue chambray shirt. 'Although it takes a bit of getting used to.'

'It's a big improvement.'

'Thanks.' His grin was so unexpected, Jo nearly dropped her glass in shock. She'd never seen the Grim Reaper smile before. He should definitely do it more often, she decided. It transformed him. He looked less forbidding, younger, and infinitely more attractive.

As the evening wore on, she was surprised how easily the conversation flowed. Jo even found herself telling him all about the girls, and Duncan, and how their marriage finally broke up the day she came home and found him in bed with one of his students.

'I was hurt more than shocked,' she said. 'I'd always suspected Duncan had other women. I just never imagined he'd bring them home to our bed.' She sipped her wine. 'Neither of us was really happy. We probably would never have married if I hadn't got pregnant.'

'Then maybe it's a good thing you split up when you did. There's nothing worse than growing up in a house full of misery and hate.'

Jo looked sidelong at him. The firelight flickered on his sombre face, highlighting the high cheekbones and long, straight nose. 'You sound as though you speak from experience?'

'Maybe.' He changed the subject. 'And you've never thought about getting married again?'

'Well, you can't exactly pick one off the shelves at Men'R'Us, you know.' She finished her drink and reached for the bottle, topping up both their glasses. 'Most men my age are either married, or divorced, or so terrified of commitment they run a mile when they find out you're a single mum with two kids.'

'So I'm guessing there's no man on the scene at the moment?'

'Are you kidding? The last time I had a man in my bedroom was over a year ago. And that was only the BT engineer putting in an extension.' She stopped short. 'I mean, I've had offers,' she went on quickly. 'But I have to be careful. I don't think it's right for me to be trailing loads of boyfriends through the house. The girls need stability.'

'I wish my mother had felt the same.' Richard stared broodingly into the fire. 'After my father walked out on us she brought in a succession of uncles and stepfathers, each more disastrous than the last. She said my brother, Jez, and I needed a man about the house. But it was my mother who needed them, not us.'

He finished his drink. Jo silently refilled it, and waited for him to go on. 'She married twice. The first was a compulsive gambler who managed to lose our home and every penny we had, and the second . . . Well, it was all a long time ago.'

But not forgotten, judging from his expression. 'I'd like to hear about it.'

He hesitated, then he said, 'Edward Sheppard. He was a doctor—well respected, enough money to give my mother the life she wanted for us. He was supposed to be our salvation.'

'But he wasn't?'

'No, he wasn't.' Richard's voice was flat. 'My mother thought he was such a saint, taking on a woman with two kids, but my God, he made her pay. He never let her forget what he'd done for her . . . for all of us. She used to put a brave face on it, but I knew what was going on. I saw the bruises.'

'He beat her up?'

'Only behind closed doors. He had his good name to consider.' His face was bitter. 'My brother and I were at boarding school, so we didn't see the worst of it. And he knew my mother would never tell anyone. She was too ashamed that it was her fault, that she'd let us down.'

'But why didn't she leave him?'

'How could she? She'd run out of options. She had no money of her own. We depended on him for everything.'

'So she stayed with him?'

'Not exactly. When I was seventeen, she sent Jez and me back to boarding school. One morning she waited until Sheppard had gone to do his morning surgery, then she went into the garage, put a hosepipe on the exhaust and killed herself.' He recited the facts in a toneless voice. 'She knew if she walked out on him we'd be penniless. I suppose she thought if she was dead he'd have to look after us.'

As he lifted his glass to his lips, Jo had to clench her hands together to fight the sudden, overwhelming urge to put her arms round him. She couldn't even begin to imagine the pain he must have gone through.

'What happened then?'

'What do you think? It made me feel sick to watch him, playing the grieving widower, when it was he who killed her. He let them all believe she did it because she was depressed. But I knew the truth. And I made sure he knew it too.' He swallowed hard. 'I said I didn't want anything to do with him, or his money. I told him I'd look after myself, and Jez. The next day I left school and started looking for a job.'

'Which is how you met Trevor Malone?'

He frowned. 'How did you know that?'

'Trevor told me. He said you were an arrogant sod.'

'I was! To tell the truth, I was actually as scared as hell. I had no experience, no qualifications. I didn't even know the first thing about working in TV. As far as I was concerned, it was a job, and it paid well enough for me to find a place where Jez and I could live.

'I was lucky. And I was willing to work hard. I was only the gofer, but I put in more hours than anyone else, I volunteered for the jobs no one else wanted to do. In the end I made such a nuisance of myself they had to promote me. Trevor Malone was great, too. He taught me a lot. He was more of a father to me than either of the men my mother married.'

'But he tried to make it sound as if you'd put him out of a job?'

Richard shrugged. 'He was an old, sick man, just trying to salvage what was left of his pride. I can't blame him for that.'

'But it can't have been easy for you, taking over at *Westfield*. And I made things worse with that stupid story in the *Globe*. I'm sorry.'

'You weren't to know. Besides, I'm the Grim Reaper, remember? I can take it.' His smile didn't reach his eyes. 'I demand perfection and total commitment from everyone I work with. I'm ambitious, arrogant and probably impossible to live with.'

'And those are just your good points?'

He grinned again, and Jo felt her stomach do an absurd backflip. She reached for the wine bottle just as Richard did the same.

'I'm sorry.' He let go of the bottle as if it had been electrified.

236

'No, please, you have it.' She tucked her feet up under her. Was it her imagination, or were they sitting a lot closer than they had been?

She watched him refill her glass, then his own. The wine must be going to her head, because she was seriously starting to fancy him. If she wasn't very careful she might be tempted to do something about it. And that would be A Very Bad Idea.

'So why does Kate stay with you, if you're that impossible to live with?' Now why did she have to go and bring Kate's name into it?

'Kate understands me,' he said shortly. 'We're alike in a lot of ways. We both know what we want out of life—and what we don't.'

'And what don't you want?'

'Marriage. Kids. All the domestic stuff that goes with them.'

'You mean you don't want children? Not ever?'

He smiled wryly. 'Don't look so shocked. Not everyone's desperate for that kind of commitment.'

'I realise that, but—'

'It's not that I hate kids or anything,' Richard went on. 'It's just I don't think I'd be any good at all that messy, complicated family stuff. I'd rather concentrate on my career. And I know Kate feels the same.'

She stared at him, amazed. 'Well, I suppose it's your choice. But I just couldn't imagine my life without Grace and Chloe.'

'Really? Even if it means making more sacrifices?'

'I don't see that I've made any sacrifices—'

'There's your career, for a start. I've been going through your CV,' he said, as Jo's eyes widened. 'You're a talented actress. You're wasted at *Westfield*, and you know it.'

'Is this your way of telling me I'm sacked?' Jo joked feebly.

'Of course it isn't. I'd never want to lose you.' Their eyes met, and held.

'Well, I'm not going anywhere,' she said firmly. 'Perhaps you're right. Perhaps I would have achieved a meteoric career if I hadn't had my children to consider. But I wouldn't swop them for all the BAFTAs in the world. A career can't take the place of a family.'

'It can't let you down or screw you up, either.' Richard's eyes were hard. He finished his drink. 'I'd better be going. It's nearly midnight.'

'Is it?' Jo glanced at the clock. Had they really been talking for four hours? It didn't seem that long. She uncurled herself from the sofa.

'I'll leave my car and walk back. I've drunk too much to drive.'

'In this weather?' Jo watched him shrugging on his overcoat. 'You could—um—stay the night? I mean, you could sleep in Roxanne's room. She's away until tomorrow night—' She gabbled on, painfully conscious that every word sounded like a come-on.

'I don't think that's a very good idea, do you?' Richard smiled. 'I seem to remember your hospitality landed you in the *Globe* last time.'

'I doubt if even Charlie Beasley is so desperate for a story he'd hang around in the bushes on Christmas night. Especially not in filthy weather like this.' She followed him into the hall.

'All the same, I'd better be getting back.' He turned up the collar of his overcoat. 'Thanks. I've really enjoyed this evening.'

'Me too.'

She watched him go, his broad shoulders hunched against the rain. It wasn't until he was halfway down the street she realised how badly she'd wanted him to stay.

CHAPTER SEVEN

'WELL, THIS IS IT, DARLING. Our big moment of passion. I hope you're ready for it?' Marcus winked over the rim of his coffee cup.

'Don't get too excited. It's difficult to get passionate when you've got three cameras pointing at you.'

'Oh, I don't know. It sounds quite kinky to me. Besides, I'm practising for when it happens for real.'

'Don't hold your breath, will you.'

He grinned. 'Come on, you know you're just playing hard to get. You want me as much as I want you. And you might as well know, I've made a new year's resolution to get you into bed.'

Jo choked on her coffee. 'Marcus! How many more times do I have to tell you, I'm not interested?'

There was only one man on her mind at the moment, and unfortunately it wasn't Marcus. No matter how much she tried to forget about Richard, the memory of Christmas night wouldn't go away. She hadn't felt that close to a man for a very long time. And she was sure he felt the same. But how could he? He was still involved with Kate. And even if he wasn't, he'd made it clear Jo wasn't his type.

That was what she told herself in her gloomier moments. But then her wildly romantic, optimistic side took over and she'd start picturing them together. Just one big, happy family . . .

'So why don't you want me?' Marcus interrupted her fantasy.

'Sorry? Oh, I don't know. Where do I start? You're wild, irresponsible and you've already got a girlfriend, Louise, remember?'

'Oh, her.' Marcus shrugged, 'Actually, we've split up.'

'Since when?'

'Since I realised I couldn't get you out of my mind.' He gave her a look that would have melted the knicker elastic of half the women in Britain. 'So what do you think? Can I come round tonight?'

'No!' His persistence made her laugh. 'I told you, I'm not interested in a one-night stand.'

'God, you women are all the same! Why can't you just enjoy the moment, instead of analysing where things are going the whole time?'

'If you have to ask that, Marcus, then you and I aren't going anywhere.' He looked mournful, like a kicked puppy. 'Look, I'm really flattered. But it's just—well, the chemistry isn't there.'

Marcus's eyes gleamed with the light of challenge. 'You want chemistry? I'll give you chemistry.'

A few minutes later they took their places to rehearse the scene.

'Remember, this is the scene where all your pent-up feelings are about to blow,' Aidan instructed them. 'You know what you're doing is wrong, but you just can't help yourself. So really let rip with those emotions.'

Whether she was just fresh from her Christmas break or she had some pent-up feelings of her own she needed to unleash Jo wasn't sure, but as they did the scene she could feel real anger and frustration building up inside her head. Marcus picked up on her cue and soon they were yelling and screaming their lines at each other. But when Jo forgot herself and slapped his face, everyone was startled. Especially Marcus.

'I'm sure that's not in the script,' he muttered, rubbing his cheek.

'Sorry.' She bit her lip. 'I got a bit carried away.'

'No problem. As long as you don't mind me doing the same?'

'That was brilliant.' Aidan listened to the director's instructions on his headphones, then gave them the thumbs up. 'He says to keep that in.'

'Do we have to?' Marcus scowled.

But the next time she slapped Marcus, instead of flinching away he came right back at her, trapping her face between his hands and pulling her towards him for a passionate kiss that stopped her mouth and nearly her heart and entire nervous system too.

'How's that for chemistry?' he whispered. Then he stalked off, leaving her to listen dazedly to the applause and catcalls of the rest of the crew.

Stunned, Jo made her way back to her dressing room. But when she opened the door there was Marcus.

'OK, we'll do it your way,' he said. 'This—relationship thing. We can give it a go, if you want?'

'Not again!' Jo sighed. 'Look Marcus, I told you, it wouldn't work.'

'How do you know that, if you don't try? We could go out, if you like? A proper date. How about that?'

Jo looked at his eager face. 'You're very sweet and I'm terribly flattered, but really I'm not interested.'

He shook his head. 'You're a hard woman, Jo Porter. You're lucky I don't give up that easily.' As he left, he handed her a scrap of paper. 'Here's my mobile number. Call me when you change your mind.'

'Don't you mean "if?"'

Marcus grinned over his shoulder. 'I know what I mean.'

After a tiring day, she was looking forward to a long, hot soak in the bath, followed by a few mindless hours in front of the TV. But as she turned into her terrace of grey-stone Edwardian villas, she spotted her mother's beige Honda parked outside the house and remembered Audrey was paying one of her visits.

As she opened the front door she was greeted by a furious-looking Roxanne. 'If anyone wants me, I'm upstairs,' she snapped.

'What about the children's tea?'

'Ask *her*.' Roxanne shot a sullen glance towards the kitchen, whence came the sound of clattering pots and pans and Audrey's voice.

Jo gritted her teeth and followed the sound. In the kitchen she found the girls slumped at the table looking as if they'd lost the will to live, while Audrey stood at the cooker, stirring something in a pan. As Jo opened the door Grace and Chloe rushed to greet her like a couple of castaways who'd just spotted the rescue ship.

She hugged them and went over to greet her mother. 'Hi, Mum. Something smells nice.' She sniffed the air appreciatively.

'Yes, well, I thought my grandchildren could do with some proper, home-cooked food for a change, instead of all that convenience rubbish.' Audrey offered a powdered cheek. 'I really don't know why you keep that girl on, Joanne. She's neither use nor ornament.'

Here we go again. 'Roxanne's OK. And the girls adore her.'

'Yes, but she's not very experienced, is she? She obviously hasn't the first idea about nutrition. No wonder those girls always look so peaky—'

Jo left her ranting to herself and tiptoed back out of the kitchen. She had a bath and tried not to think about the hostilities that were brewing downstairs. Just as she stepped out of the tub and tucked a towel round herself, the doorbell rang.

'Can someone get that?' she called. There was no answer. A moment later, it rang again. 'Will someone please answer that bloody—'

As she came charging out of the bathroom, wearing a towel, her hair dripping, she was confronted by Richard in the hall below with her mother.

For a split second they stared at each other. Then Audrey cut in, 'It's all right, dear, you get dressed. I'll look after your guest.' With a meaningful flash of her eyes, she led Richard into the sitting room.

Oh shit. Jo ran round the bedroom, throwing open drawers and cupboards and pulling out their contents. The last thing she needed was to leave Richard at the mercy of her mother. She unearthed a pair of black trousers and a white Kookai top from the depths of her wardrobe. That would do. Casual but not too scruffy.

As she hurried downstairs Audrey came flying out of the sitting room. 'Why didn't you tell me you were expecting someone?' she hissed.

'But I wasn't expecting—'

'And look at you. You haven't made much effort, have you? Couldn't you have done something with your hair? Here, let me do it.'

'Mum! I'm not five years old.'

Jo snatched the comb back from her mother's hands and went into the sitting room. Richard was perched uncomfortably on the edge of the sofa while Chloe curled up beside him, messily eating a yoghurt. Grace was stretched out on the floor, watching *Neighbours* at full blast. Jo's heart sank. Welcome to family life, she thought.

'Are you sure I can't offer you a drink?' Audrey asked.

'I'm fine, thank you.' Richard was stiffly polite.

'I'll take the children into the kitchen so you two can be alone, shall I?' Jo listened to her manhandling the protesting girls down the hall.

'Sorry about my mother,' she said.

'Not at all. She's been taking very good care of me. So far I've been offered two cups of tea, three gin and tonics and a round of ham sandwiches.' His dark eyes twinkled.

Jo looked apologetic. 'I'm afraid she sees every man as a potential son-in-law.' Oh God, why had she said that? Now he'd think she was fishing. 'Not that there's any chance of that.'

'I know what you mean.' He smiled.

She sat down on the sofa. 'So what can I do for you?' she asked. 'This is getting to be quite a habit, isn't it? You dropping in.'

He nodded. 'Actually, I wanted to talk about the last time I came. I didn't know whether I should come round or not. I've been turning it over in my mind for days. But in the end I knew I had to see you again.'

241

Jo's heart did a mad tumble. So she hadn't imagined it. He fancied her, too. She forced herself to stay calm. 'Any particular reason?'

'We—er—both had a bit too much to drink that night.' He stood up and paced the room. 'I told you some things I've never told anyone before. Things even Kate doesn't know. About my family and so on.'

'I see.' This didn't sound like a declaration of love.

'The thing is, I don't want it to go any further. The press would have a field day if it was to get out. It's not just for my sake.' His words came out in a rush. 'There are other people to consider. My brother, for instance. I don't want anyone to get hurt.'

'Do you seriously think I'd go to the press with a story like that?' Jo shook her head in disbelief. 'What kind of person do you think I am?'

'I didn't mean it like that. I'm just asking you to be discreet, that's all. You talked to them before, didn't you?'

'That was different. I was tricked into giving that story.'

'Exactly. That's why I'm asking you to be extra careful this time.' He sat down beside her. 'I'm appealing to you as a friend,' he said softly.

A friend! She didn't know whether to laugh or cry. 'I think it's for the best if we forget that evening ever happened, don't you?' She glanced away so she wouldn't see the look of relief in his eyes. She was already hurting enough.

'You're probably right,' he agreed. There was a long pause. 'I hope I haven't offended you, coming round like this? I just thought it was important that we both knew where we stood.'

'Yes, well, I think we both know that now, don't we? So—was there anything else? Only I do have things to do this evening.'

'Of course. I'm sorry.' He stood up. 'Thanks again—for being so understanding.'

He opened the door and Audrey fell through it. 'Going already?' Her face was a picture of disappointment. 'Won't you stay for dinner?'

'No, thank you. I think I've already outstayed my welcome.'

'What did you say to him?' Audrey barely waited until the front door was closed before she launched into Jo.

'Why ask me? You probably heard it all through the door anyway.' Jo was too angry to care if she sent her mother off into a sulk. Angry with Richard, and with herself for ever thinking she had a chance with him.

'It's such a pity.' Audrey watched wistfully through the window as Richard's Audi drove away. 'He seemed such a nice man.'

'Yes, he is, isn't he?' Jo couldn't keep the edge out of her voice. 'Unfortunately, he doesn't feel the same about me.'

'Well, it's about time you found yourself someone who did.'

'You know something? You're absolutely right.' Jo reached for her bag and started to rifle through it.

'What are you doing?'

'For the first time in my life, Mother, I'm taking your advice.' She found the scrap of paper she was looking for, picked up the phone and punched in Marcus's mobile number.

Jo took another slug of her ice-cold designer beer and winced. God, it was horrible. Pretentious, overpriced and completely lacking in taste. Just like the rest of this place.

I'm having a great time, she told herself, but her conviction was beginning to wear thin. She felt overdressed in her cream linen shift dress, her feet hurt like hell, and her temples were throbbing in time to the thumping techno dance music. Whatever happened to going for a quiet drink? she wondered.

The evening had got off to a bad start when she'd called for Marcus at the address he'd given her and Louise had opened the door.

It took her a moment to recognise *Westfield's* press officer beneath the puffed, blotchy face. She looked as if she'd been crying for days. She wore a faded pink dressing gown, her dark hair falling into her eyes.

'Louise! I—er—didn't expect to see you here?'

'Why not? It's my flat.'

'But I thought—' She was still groping for the right words when Marcus appeared, wearing just jeans and drying his hair on a towel.

'You're early.' He grinned. 'Come in, I won't be long.'

He disappeared to get ready, abandoning her in a desperately awkward silence with Louise.

'Would you like a cup of tea?' Louise offered.

'Thanks.' Jo followed her into the kitchen. 'Look, Louise, I don't know what's going on here, but I would never have agreed to go out with Marcus if I'd known you two were still together.'

'We're not. He's just staying here until he gets a place of his own sorted out.' She wiped her nose with her sleeve and smiled. 'It's OK, we've talked and I'm fine about it. Honestly.'

'Ready?' Marcus appeared in the doorway, looking amazingly sexy in new black jeans and T-shirt. Louise, who had been rinsing mugs under the tap, suddenly dropped them and rushed out of the room.

Marcus watched her go. 'What's up with her, I wonder?'

'Isn't it obvious? God, Marcus, why didn't you tell me you were still living with her?'

'I didn't think it was important. I told you, we've split up.'

'Yes, but she's obviously not over you yet, is she?' Jo gnawed her lower lip. 'Maybe we'd better call it off tonight.'

'Why?'

'I think Louise needs more time to adjust to the—er—situation.'

'That's her problem, isn't it?' His green eyes were harder than she'd ever seen them.

Now, suffocated by a fug of cigarette smoke, sweat and cheap perfume, she was beginning to wish she'd walked out when she'd had the chance. She looked around for Marcus and spotted him over the crush of elongated, youthful bodies, caught up at the bar. As she watched, a group of girls pushed their way towards him. One of them, dressed in PVC hot pants and a bra top, tapped Marcus on the shoulder and handed him a pen. Then, to Jo's astonishment, she suddenly unzipped her shorts and wriggled out of them, exposing her pert, perfect bottom for him to sign. Grinning, Marcus obliged. But as he handed back the pen the girl suddenly wrapped her arms around his neck and practically sucked his face off, while her friends shrieked encouragement.

Jo waited for the jolt of jealousy. But to her surprise, she was more concerned that she would never again see the tenner she'd sent him to the bar with.

'Mineral water, as requested.' He appeared in front of her and pressed another ice-cold bottle into her hand. She couldn't even drown herself in alcohol as she was driving. This is it, she thought. I am officially on the Date From Hell. And the sooner she could get away, the better.

Then it came to her. 'I've been thinking . . . Maybe we should go back to my place?' she whispered. 'The girls would love to meet you.' She smiled at him. 'After all, now we're having a *relationship* you're going to be playing a big part in their lives, so they should get to know you.'

Even in the darkness she could see he'd turned pale. 'It's so wonderful that you like kids,' she went on. 'You don't know how hard it is to find a man willing to take on a woman with children. Especially not as lively as my two.'

'T-take on? Lively?'

'Of course, they don't mean any harm. But they really need a man around. You know, a father-figure? You wouldn't mind if they called you Uncle Marcus, would you? At least for now . . .'

'Er—no, of course not.' Marcus scrambled to his feet. 'But maybe we should make it another night? I'm—er—worried about Louise. We've—um—probably got things to discuss, don't you think?'

'Maybe you're right.' Jo hid her smile behind her hand. 'I'll drop you off, shall I?'

CHAPTER EIGHT

Jo LOOKED AT HERSELF in the mirror and nearly choked. Why Lara had ever asked her to be a bridesmaid she had no idea. Looking at the dress, she could only assume it was because of some long-held grudge.

It was like a tribute to bad taste. Everything about it was seriously abhorrent, from the eye-watering orange colour to the hacked-about neckline and ragged hem.

'Ooh, must have a shot of that, love—hold it. Perfect!' She flinched as a flashbulb exploded in her face. *Goss* magazine had been there to capture every excruciating moment of the Valentine's Day extravaganza. They'd gone with the happy couple to choose the rings, to meet each other's parents, and on the carefully orchestrated hen night, for which Jo had been forced to undergo a major make-over with a bossy stylist. They were now in the bridal suite, where, watched by assorted make-up artists, stylists and photographers, the bride was having a slanging match with her mother.

'I told you, you're not wearing it!' She and her frock filled the doorway to the en suite bathroom. It was a vast, billowing creation made, apparently, from chicken wire and parachute silk. Alexander McQueen meets the Montgolfier brothers, Jo decided.

Lara's mother looked fetchingly normal by comparison, in a lilac two-piece and matching hat. 'But I bought it specially—'

'I told you the stylist would bring your outfit, but you didn't listen, did you? Oh no, you had to go and buy something like *that!*'

'But what's wrong with it, dear?'

'What's wrong with it? This is supposed to be a stylish occasion, in case you hadn't noticed. You'll show me up.'

'I think she looks lovely.' Jo noticed Mrs Lamont's trembling lip and stepped in quickly.

'Who asked you?' Lara turned on her. 'And where's Marcus? He's supposed to be giving me away.'

'Oh, surely not, dear. I thought your father—' Mrs Lamont flinched as Lara swung round again. She was a terrifying sight, her jacked-up bosom heaving, her eyes flashing malevolently underneath false lashes.

'I hate you all!' she yelled. 'This is my big day and you're all going to spoil it!'

'Hold it there, love!' Somewhere behind Jo a flashbulb popped.

'Now, Dawn, dear, don't get yourself all upset—'

'Don't call me that! I told you never to call me that! My name's Lara, can't you get that into your thick head? Lara, Lara, LARA!' With a tortured sob, she flung herself across the kingsized bed.

'She's overwrought. It's excitement, I expect,' Mrs Lamont whispered to Jo. 'She was exactly the same when she was a little girl.'

It's a shame you didn't slap her legs while you had the chance, Jo thought. Even Chloe was beyond throwing tantrums like that.

'Maybe I should go downstairs and see what's happening?' Jo suggested, edging towards the door. She couldn't stand much more.

'If you see Marcus, tell him to get up here *this minute*!' were the last words she heard as she closed the door on the hysterical bride.

The Leeds hotel where the wedding was being held was so drop-dead stylish there was a six-month waiting list to book a room there.

Jo gazed around the teeming reception area with awe. It looked like an invasion from Planet Celeb. A gaggle of supermodels towered over the latest cool boy band. A black American rap singer exuded attitude in the corner, surrounded by a posse of leather-clad homeboys.

Viola joined her just as a couple of trendy breakfast TV presenters wandered past, followed by a Booker prize-winning novelist.

'Here, have one of these.' Viola slipped a glass into her hand. 'Freezer-chilled vodka. You may need several of them, if you're going to carry off that frock with any kind of conviction.'

'You don't exactly blend into the background yourself.' Jo smiled at her flowing tunic and trousers in swirly gold print.

'Well, you know, I thought I'd make the effort. Seeing as we're mixing with some real top-notch stars.'

'You can say that again. I don't know anyone, do you?'

'Neither does the bride.' Viola lowered her voice. 'Apparently it was in her contract that she had to have certain celebrities here or she wouldn't get her money. Can you believe it?'

'Knowing Lara, I'm afraid I can.' Jo craned her neck. 'So which one's the bridegroom?'

'I think it's that one over there. In the white biker's jacket. With the ponytail.'

'Not the one who looks as if he's been upholstered at World of Leather? He's old enough to be her father.'

'He's also rich and well-connected enough to launch her pop career.'

Viola looked around. 'Ooh, don't look now, but here comes Mr Darcy. Doesn't he look frighteningly sexy in that suit?'

Jo glanced over her shoulder, straight into the laser-beam eyes of Richard Black. She hadn't spoken to him since that night at her house, over six weeks ago. She'd managed to convince herself that her fleeting attraction was over. But seeing him again was like a punch in the solar plexus. Oh bugger, I really do fancy him, she thought weakly.

'That Kate isn't with him. Shall we go over and say hello?'

'No! I don't—' But it was too late. Viola already had hold of her elbow and was steering her across the room towards him.

'Richard! Thank God, another familiar face. We were beginning to think we were at the wrong party, weren't we darling?' Viola beamed at Jo, who was too tongue-tied by Richard's penetrating stare to reply. Why didn't he say something?

Then, finally, he did. 'What,' he said slowly, '*are* you wearing?'

Jo couldn't help laughing. 'You should see the bride.'

'That bad?'

'Worse. Stick a couple of gas burners up her skirt and she could take Richard Branson round the world.'

His slow smile lit up his smoky grey eyes. Jo felt her heart kindling in response.

Then Kate appeared. She was dressed in a brilliant scarlet Dolce and Gabbana suit and matching Philip Treacey hat that looked sensational with her dark colouring but did nothing for her boot-faced expression.

'Oh, it's you.' Her cold gaze dismissed Jo instantly and she turned to Richard. 'When is this circus going to start? I'm not sure I can stand much more.'

'Not enjoying yourself?' Viola looked sympathetic.

'Not particularly. I don't even know why we had to come.'

'We came because we were invited.' Richard's voice was low.

'So? I've lost count of the number of invitations we've turned down because *you* didn't feel like going.'

Jo and Viola exchanged glances. Sensing a row brewing, she decided it was time to beat a retreat. 'I don't suppose anyone's seen Marcus?'

Her question had an alarming effect. Kate and Richard forgot their bickering and both turned on her sharply.

'Why do you want him?' Richard demanded.

'He's supposed to be giving the bride away.'

Kate snorted. 'He's such an unreliable bastard he probably hasn't bothered to turn up.'

'Thanks. That's just what I wanted to hear.' As if Lara wasn't hysterical enough. 'Look, if you see him, tell him I'm looking for him, will you?' Gathering up her skirt she pushed her way through the crowd.

She finally found Marcus hunched on a low wall under a silvery eucalyptus tree in the courtyard, smoking a cigarette. From his crumpled clothes, three-day stubble and bloodshot eyes he looked as if he'd been burning the candle at both ends and in the middle too.

'You look awful,' she said. 'What have you been doing to yourself?'

'Sleeping in the back of the truck. Louise kicked me out of her flat.'

'About time too,' Jo said briskly. 'You deserve it, after the rotten way you've treated her. You've taken advantage of her for far too long.'

His fingers shook as he inhaled deeply on his cigarette. Jo frowned. She'd never seen him like this. She sat down on the wall. 'So what's up?'

'You really don't want to know.' He took another drag of his cigarette. 'Let's just say I failed to come up to someone's expectations.'

'And this someone—I imagine it's a woman?'

'Of course.'

It must be Louise. 'Let me see—she wanted commitment and loyalty and fidelity and you didn't?'

He smiled wearily. 'How did you guess?'

'Because it's always the same story with you.' Jo shook her head. 'Look, she's probably upset now. But I expect once she stops breaking her heart she'll realise what a lucky escape she's had.'

'I hope you're right. She could make my life hellish if she doesn't.'

He was right there. As press officer, Louise was in a prime position to drop juicy snippets of gossip to the wrong people.

'I know someone else who could make your life hellish. The bride will be wanting your head on a pole if you don't get a move on.'

Marcus grinned. 'I love dominant women. Are you this bossy in bed?'

'You'll never know, will you?' At least he was back to his old self again. Weeks after their disastrous date, Marcus had finally realised he was wasting his time with Jo and they'd settled into an easy, flirtatious friendship.

'Come on,' she said. 'We've got thirty seconds to get you upstairs and make you look presentable before the bride throws another tantrum.'

They were making their way back into the hotel when Marcus suddenly said, 'Thanks.'

'What for?'

'For talking to me. And for being the only woman in the world who isn't madly in love with me.'

Jo laughed. 'Bighead!'

'No, I mean it. You're a real friend.' Before she could react he stopped, pulled her into his arms and kissed her in a very unplatonic way.

'Excuse me.' They sprang apart at the sound of Richard's voice. He was standing in the doorway watching them, his face curiously blank. 'I just thought you ought to know, the bride's on her way downstairs.'

'Oh hell!' Jo grabbed Marcus's hand. 'Forget about making yourself presentable, we'll head them off in the lobby.'

They were all coming down the staircase when Jo and Marcus arrived, breathless. Lara swished in front, followed by a brace of stylists, a photographer and her manager, Bernie, gabbling into his mobile. Then came Jo and Marcus, and Lara's mother, now barely recognisable in a Vivienne Westwood bustier and black capri pants, teetering down the stairs on a pair of Prada mules. Lara's father trailed behind, his dapper morning suit standing out among the colourful circus.

'But you're my only daughter!' he was saying.

'I know, but *Goss* wants Marcus to give me away.'

'But, Dawn, love—'

'*I told you not to call me that!*' Lara screeched. 'Look, you're lucky I even let you come. I fought long and hard to get you and Mum an invitation, so don't you try and spoil it for me!' She flounced off, leaving him standing helplessly at the foot of the stairs.

Jo twirled a radicchio leaf idly between her fingers and decided she'd never been so bored in her entire life.

Beside her, Marcus had recovered from his earlier depression and was engaged in some serious flirtation with Toni Carlisle, the outrageous blonde ladette star of Talbot TV's youth show *All Talk*.

Meanwhile she was stuck with Brett Michaels and an overweight breakfast-show presenter. Brett was sullen and furious that Toni Carlisle was ignoring him, and the TV presenter, kept trying to practise his twinkling charm on her.

She gazed round the room and immediately caught the basilisk stare of Louise, Marcus's former girlfriend. She looked as if she wanted to rush across the room and staple Jo's head to the table.

Jo hastily glanced away—and found herself facing Richard's equally hostile gaze. This was getting ridiculous. Louise she could just about understand, but what could he possibly have against her?

By ten o'clock, when the music started and Leon got behind his massive mixing desk to treat everyone to his latest mega-hype-club remix, she decided she'd had enough. The pounding techno beat was so loud it made her fillings buzz. Every time she turned her head a *Goss* photographer was pointing a zoom lens up her nose. It was all very wearing.

She went upstairs to the bridal suite to change. She just hoped there wouldn't be a photographer waiting to capture that on film too.

But there wasn't. Instead she found something much worse.

Marcus was sprawled naked across the kingsized bed, his sculpted muscles golden against the crisp white linen. Toni Carlisle, also naked, was stretched out beside him.

As Jo froze in the doorway, Marcus rolled over onto his stomach and grinned at her. 'Angel! Want to join the party?'

'Go on. Live a little.' Toni giggled. 'You know what they say. Two's company, three's a blast.'

'No thanks.' Jo forced herself into the room, carefully averting her eyes from Toni's silicone breasts. 'Does Lara know you're in here?'

'Where do you think we got the key?'

They both fell about giggling. They were obviously on something but Jo didn't want to know what. She grabbed her clothes from the end of the bed and headed off to the bathroom, slamming the door behind her.

She was just buttoning her shirt when she heard a shout from outside, followed by a splintering crash. A second later, Toni screamed.

'What the hell—' Without thinking, she flung open the bathroom door . . . and found herself right in the middle of a nightmare.

The room was full of people. Half a dozen tough-looking men and women swarmed around, throwing open wardrobes, pulling out drawers and emptying their contents onto the floor.

As Jo stood frozen in the doorway, one of them barged past her into the bathroom and started searching in there.

'Will someone please tell me what's going on?'

'These people are police officers. They're searching the room.' Marcus looked as unconcerned as if they'd arrived to deliver room service.

'What?' She noticed the uniformed officer guarding the door. 'But why?'

'Apparently someone in the hotel tipped them off that we might have drugs in here.'

'But that's ridiculous, I don't know anything about—what are you doing with that?' She sprang forward as one of the police officers emptied her bag out on the bed. Immediately a hand closed on her shoulder.

'Would you mind sitting down, madam?'

'But he can't do that! That's my property he's mauling.' She took a step forward but she was grabbed from behind and forced into a chair.

'Better do as she says, angel.' For once Marcus wasn't smiling.

Jo sank into the chair. How could he be so calm? She'd done nothing, yet her heart was hammering a bongo beat of fear against her ribs. Keep your head down and your mouth shut, she warned herself. This is all a terrible mistake. They won't find anything. There's nothing to find . . .

'I've found something, Sarge.'

One of the policemen emerged from under the bed. Jo caught a glimpse of a battered old tin as he passed it to the man in uniform.

'Oh dear,' Marcus said. 'I wonder how that got there.'

'You tell me, sir.'

'I hope you're not saying it has anything to do with us?'

'I think we should discuss this down at the station, don't you?' The policeman's gaze swept the room. 'I am arresting all three of you for possessing an illegal substance. You do not have to say anything but it may harm your defence if you do not mention when questioned—'

'But you can't!' Jo shot to her feet. 'I"m innocent. I don't know anything about drugs.' She carried on protesting her innocence as she was hustled out of the back entrance to the waiting police cars.

'This is all wrong. You're making a big mistake,' she kept saying as she huddled in the back of the car with the others. This isn't happening, she kept telling herself. They can't lock you up for something you didn't do. Any second now they'll realise what they've done and let you go.

She was still telling herself that as the custody officer read out the charges against her and took away her shoes, earrings, bag and even the belt from her jeans.

'But I haven't done anything!' Her throat was sore with fear and panic.

'Of course you haven't. Neither have most of the others in here.' He gave her a quick smile. 'Put her in number five,' he instructed the accompanying officer.

It was only when the heavy steel door clanged shut and she heard the jingle of keys that her indignation turned to panic. She stared at the chipped dark blue paintwork, her stomach churning.

'No good you staring at the door, love. You could be in here hours.'

She turned, slowly. There were two other women there already. A thin girl with straggly dark hair and hunched shoulders stood in the corner, chewing her nails. A fierce-looking woman with badly bleached hair and dark roots sat on a bench. Jo didn't fancy her chances against either of them.

'First time, is it?' Roots eyed her sagely. 'Thought so. It's always the worst. Why don't you come and sit down?'

She patted the seat next to her. Jo perched on the edge, ready to flee if necessary. 'How long will they keep us here?'

'Well, I've been here since last Tuesday.' Roots grinned, as Jo's face crumpled. 'Only joking. They can only keep you twenty-four hours without charging you. But they usually like to get you sorted out within six hours, otherwise it means more paperwork and hassle.'

'*Six hours!*' It would be nearly morning by then. The girls would be wondering where she was. Roxanne would be panicking . . .

'Might be less, might be more. Depends how busy it is. I just call it an occupational hazard. Makes a change from freezing your backside off on the streets when there's not much trade about.'

All this time the dark-haired girl had been shuffling sideways along the wall towards her. Suddenly, she said, 'I know you!'

Jo edged away. 'I—I don't think so.'

'I'm sure I've seen you somewhere before.' Her voice was rasping. 'You don't work on that corner up near the Wakefield Road, do you?'

Jo shook her head, too terrified to be offended. With her tangled hair and her wild bloodshot eyes, she reminded her of the girl from *The Exorcist*. Any minute now she'd whip her head round 360 degrees and cover them all in green vomit. Jo could hardly wait.

An hour ticked by, slower than any she'd ever known. She was allowed to speak to the duty solicitor on the phone. In a sleepy voice he'd assured her that she'd be out in no time.

'No point in me coming down if they're going to let you go,' he'd yawned. 'Don't worry about it, I'm sure your friends will vouch for you.'

'Yes, but what if they—' she asked, as the receiver went down.

Jo stared at the phone. What if he was wrong? What if Marcus and Toni didn't vouch for her? What if they let her take the blame? People had been locked up for much less.

She spent another half an hour or so trying not to cry, aware that the dark girl was watching her with the peculiar intensity that only the very mad could achieve. She suddenly let out a bark of laughter.

'I know who you are! You're Stacey. Out of *Westfield*.'

She was just about to deny it when Roots chimed in. 'Oh my God, so you are! I never miss an episode. I always tape them if I'm working.'

'R-really?' Jo smiled weakly.

'I suppose you found out about that slag from the minicab office?' Dark Hair was looking frighteningly intense again. 'Bitch. I know where she lives, you know. I could go round there for you, if you like?'

Oh great. Trust her to get stuck with the Psycho Branch of the *Westfield* Fan Club.

Thank God, just then there was a rattling of keys outside the door. A police officer called her name and Jo practically threw herself into his arms. At that moment she would have admitted to anything, if only he'd get her out of there.

As it was, she didn't have to. Less than an hour later she was free. She walked dazed and shaking into the brightly lit reception area, clutching her belongings in a small plastic bag.

The first person she saw, alone on a line of hard plastic chairs on the other side of the counter, was Richard Black.

'Jo!' He shot to his feet as soon as he saw her. She tried to smile bravely, but somehow she couldn't manage it. Just seeing him there, the first familiar face she'd seen since the whole terrible nightmare began, was too much for her and she burst into tears.

'Oh God, Richard, it was so horrible!' She sobbed against his shirt as he pulled her into his arms. 'They wouldn't listen to me, they just locked me up in this awful place—'

'Shh, it's OK. You're safe now.' His breath was warm against her hair. 'Come on, let's get you out of here.'

It was raining as he led her out of the back door to where his Audi was parked in an alleyway. 'The front's swarming with press,' he explained shortly. 'They'll be round here too, in a minute.'

Sure enough, they'd barely reached the car before someone yelled her name. A moment later came the pounding of many feet. Jo stared, transfixed with shock and horror, as they rounded the corner. There were dozens of them, all shouting at her. Richard flung open the car door and shoved her inside. 'Hold tight and for God's sake keep your head down!'

Jo cowered on the back seat, flinching at the machine-gun whirr of cameras all around her. Then suddenly the engine roared into life, and the car shot forward, scattering the reporters like skittles.

She waited until she sensed they were safely away, then uncurled herself. She looked out at the dark night. It had started raining again.

'They're not going to go away, are they?' she murmured. 'We might have got rid of them this time, but they'll be back.' A thought struck her. 'Oh God, what if they go after the girls? Or my parents?'

'Calm down. Louise will do what she can to squash it and by tomorrow morning they'll be chasing after some other poor sod. You'll see, it'll all blow over.'

Jo caught his eye in the rearview mirror. He didn't look convinced and neither was she. The story was too juicy to disappear overnight.

They were both too preoccupied to talk as they drove back to York. Jo huddled in the back of the car, going over and over her ordeal in her mind. At last they turned off the A64 and headed towards the city's outer ring road. As they neared her home, Jo's heart started pounding faster. What would be waiting for her when she got there?

'I shouldn't think the story will have reached here yet,' Richard said. 'They'll probably still be looking for you in Leeds.'

'I hope so. Right now I just want to get home and make sure the girls are OK.' She watched the rain streaming down the window. 'What do you think happened to Marcus? Will they let him go?'

'I'm sure he can look after himself.' His curt reply surprised her. He was probably just exhausted, she thought.

'I haven't thanked you properly—for coming to rescue me,' she said humbly. 'I wouldn't have known what to do if you hadn't been there. I just want you to know I really appreciate it.'

She jerked back in her seat as Richard swung the car off the road and screeched to a halt. He swung round in his seat to face her. 'I don't want your appreciation,' he said. 'Just tell me one thing. Did you do it?'

Her head reeled with shock. 'How could you even ask me that?'

'Because I need to know.' He took a deep breath. 'Look, I know how you feel about Marcus. I caught you kissing him earlier on, remember? It's hardly beyond belief that you might have done something stupid if he asked you to—'

'Is that really what you think of me? You really believe I'd be capable of something like that—' She swallowed hard, fighting for control. 'I didn't do anything. The police believed me, so why can't you?'

'Jo—' Hot tears blurred her eyes. She jerked her face away and fumbled for the door handle. 'Where are you going?'

'Home.' She flung the door open and scrambled out. 'I can walk the rest of the way, thanks. I don't need your help. Not now you've made it clear what you really think of me!'

He sighed. 'Look, Jo, I didn't mean—'

She slammed the door on his protest and walked away. A moment later she heard the engine rev hard behind her and he roared past.

Jo kept walking, although she was so overwhelmed by misery it was an effort of will to put one foot in front of the other.

Richard thought she was guilty! Hurt, shock and betrayal gnawed away at her, leaving a hollowed-out feeling in the pit of her stomach. Of everything she'd been through that night, this was the worst.

She turned the corner and was confronted by a small crowd gathered around her gate. And they were all waiting for her.

Jo looked desperately up the street, but Richard's car had long since disappeared. There was nothing else for it. Squaring her shoulders, head down, she ran through the rain towards her house.

'Jo! What have you got to say about your arrest?' They closed in on her like jackals on a carcass. Jo pushed through them.

'Is it true you were having a threesome when the police came in?' Charlie Beasley's nasal whine rose above the rest.

'Just fuck off, will you?' She lifted her eyes for a fraction of a second. Just long enough for a flashbulb to explode in her face.

Charlie grinned. 'Thanks, darling. That'll look great in the late edition.'

Jo pushed her way through her gate and up to her front door. She fumbled in her bag for her key, but her vision was too blurred with tears to see anything. In the end she gave up and banged on the door.

'Roxanne? It's me, Jo. Let me in.'

'Jo?' The door opened cautiously and Roxanne's pale face peeped out through the narrow gap. 'Oh, thank God! Hang on, I'll take the chain off—' The door closed then opened again, just wide enough for Jo to squeeze through. They both threw themselves against it, slamming it on the reporters who instantly swarmed forward.

'I'm so glad you're back.' Roxanne's voice shook. 'It's been horrible. They've been shouting through the letterbox—' She burst into tears.

'Shh, it's OK. I'm here now.' Jo hugged her. 'Are the girls all right?'

'I—I think so. I put a video on for them and told them to stay upstairs. I think they're asleep. I didn't know what to tell them,' she sobbed.

'It was a misunderstanding.' Jo held her closer. 'But it's all sorted out now. It's over.' Then she noticed the suitcases side by side at the foot of the stairs. 'Roxanne, what are your bags doing there?'

'I'm sorry. I had to phone my mum and dad. I didn't know what else to do.' Her red-rimmed eyes pleaded for understanding. 'They told me to come home. They said they didn't want me staying in the house with you. My dad wanted to come and pick me up straight away, but I told him I had to wait until you got back. I couldn't leave the girls.'

'Thanks.' Jo shuddered to think what would have happened if she'd walked out on them. But she couldn't blame Roxanne's parents. They were trying to protect their child, just as she would Grace and Chloe.

Jo summoned up a smile. 'Do you want me to give you a lift? I'm sure if you waited until morning some of this lot would be gone.'

'I can't. Dad says I'm to get a cab and he'll pay at the other end.'

'No, I'll pay. It's the least I can do, after everything you've been through tonight.'

While Roxanne went off to call the taxi firm, Jo risked a glimpse through the crack in the living-room curtains. They were still out there, camped in her tiny front garden, trampling the shrubs and kicking over Chloe's lovingly arranged miniature rockery.

'Mummy?' Grace stood, pale-faced, in the doorway. 'What's going on? Why's Roxanne calling a taxi?'

'She's—um—going on a little holiday.'

'Is she coming back?'

Jo and Roxanne exchanged glances. 'I hope so, darling.'

'Why are all those people shouting?'

'There was a mistake and I had to go to the police station,' she said. 'But those reporters have got it all wrong and want to print a story about it in their newspapers. They'll be gone by tomorrow, you'll see.'

'And you're not going to prison?'

'I'm not going anywhere,' Jo assured her. 'But the next couple of days might be quite difficult and I need you to be brave for your sister's sake. You're old enough to understand, but Chloe isn't. She might get scared.'

'I'll look after her.' Grace looked so pathetically young in her Forever Friends pyjamas, Jo felt a choking lump in her throat.

The cab came and somehow Roxanne managed to manoeuvre herself and her suitcases through the clamouring reporters. Her departure set off another barrage of hammering and questions through the letterbox.

Meanwhile, upstairs, Jo huddled with the girls under her double duvet, her throat aching from trying not to cry.

She was staring into the darkness, listening to the rain and the voices outside and trying to work out her next move, when she heard a noise coming from downstairs. Below them, in the kitchen, came the slow creak of the back door opening.

Jo crept onto the landing and strained her ears to listen. Someone was definitely moving about down there.

The bastards had got in! For a second she stood there, paralysed with shock and fear. Then outrage, galvanised her into action. She crept downstairs, grabbed the first weapon she could find—an old flat iron they used as a doorstop—and crept towards the kitchen door.

'Hold it, you bastard!' With a yell of fury, she flung open the door and hurled herself at the darkened shape of the mystery intruder.

She hadn't banked on him fighting back. She felt her wrists pinned in a powerful grip. Panicking, she dropped the flat iron. There was a howl of pain and the intruder lost his hold on her. Jo grabbed her chance and lunged for the light switch.

'Christ, woman, what the hell do you think you're doing?' Richard clutched his foot and swore under his breath.

'What am I doing? What are you doing, prowling around my home in the middle of the night?'

'I came to help you.' His teeth clenched in pain. 'I think you've broken my bloody foot.'

Jo folded her arms across her chest. 'How did you get in?'

'You left your keys on the back seat.'

'And you decided to use them?'

'I told you, I came to help you.'

'What are you going to do, give me a lift to the Priory Clinic?'

He ignored her. 'We haven't got much time. I parked round the corner and sneaked in through the back to avoid the reporters. If we're quick we can get out before they realise what's going on. How long will it take you to pack a bag?'

'Now hang on a second—'

'Do you want to stay here and take your chances with that lot?'

Put like that, she didn't have much choice. 'I'll wake the girls up.'

Richard had told her to pack as little as possible and he groaned when Jo dragged the two suitcases into the kitchen. 'I thought I told you to travel light?'

'Believe me, this is light. You should see what I talked them out of packing.' She bit her lip. 'Grace is bringing the rest down in a minute.'

'The rest?' His words dripped with ice. 'What rest?'

'Chloe refused to leave without her Barbies. Sorry,' she shrugged. 'I'm afraid they have a rather extensive wardrobe.'

'So I see. Anything else?'

'Only the hamster,' Grace said. 'We've got to take Richard, haven't we Mum? He might not survive on his own.'

'Richard?'

'They insisted on naming him after you. Sorry.'

Richard's face didn't crack. 'You'd better bring him then, hadn't you? Only tell him he can carry his own flaming suitcase!' Grabbing a bag in each hand he headed for the back door, muttering darkly about 'wretched women'. Jo would have laughed if her stomach hadn't been in such a knot.

'You still haven't said where we're going,' she said as they turned off the outer ring road. It was the first time she'd been able to speak after the hair-raising start to their journey. A couple of reporters had spotted them piling their luggage into the car and rushed to give chase. Richard had had to put his foot down to lose them, which left Jo clinging by her fingernails to the dashboard and impressed Grace no end.

'To my cottage. It's in the Dales, just outside Richmond.'

'I didn't know you had a cottage.'

'No one does. That's why you'll be safe there.'

Jo glanced at the girls sleeping on the back seat. 'We would have been in a real mess if you hadn't turned up.'

'I couldn't just leave you to cope on your own.' He stared at the road. 'So what happened to your nanny? I thought she'd be with you.'

'She went home.' She told him about Roxanne being summoned back to Thirsk.

'But that's appalling!' Richard looked horrified.

'You can't blame her parents for jumping to the wrong conclusions. They don't know what happened in that hotel room. No one does.'

'Including me?' He glanced sideways at her.

'It seems to me you've already made your mind up, like everyone else.'

'Look, I'm sorry if I upset you earlier, but I had to know the truth. What were you doing in that hotel room anyway?'

She told him. It was a relief to be able to give her side of the story to someone at last.

'So there's nothing going on between you and Marcus?' he said.

'I told you, he's just a friend. Or he was. After tonight I don't care if I never see him again.'

'Me neither. I think his days on *Westfield* are numbered.'

'You do believe me, don't you? About what went on tonight?'

'I've always believed you. I just needed to hear it from you.' He shot her a look. 'I know you'd never do anything to hurt those kids.'

Jo stared straight ahead at the swishing windscreen wipers, unable to speak for the lump that filled her throat. 'Can we change the subject? I just want to forget the whole thing, if I can. Tell me about your cottage.'

'It's nothing special, I'm afraid. I bought it as an investment to let out to holidaymakers. It's about half a mile from the nearest village, so you won't be bothered with neighbours,' Richard went on. 'There's a woman comes in to clean once a week, but I'll call her in the morning and tell her not to bother. The fewer people who know you're there, the better.'

'Fine.' Jo could feel her eyelids drooping. Her whole body ached for sleep. But she did her best to stay awake as they left the lights of the motorway behind and followed the winding roads deep into the Dales.

Richard turned off the road and headed down what felt like a narrow, rutted track. Then he made a right turn and stopped.

'We're here,' he said.

She helped Richard haul the bags out of the car. She was just about to wake the girls when Richard stopped her. 'Don't disturb them,' he whispered. 'We'll carry them inside.'

Jo followed him into the cottage, Chloe in her arms. It gave her a guilty pang to see him carrying Grace, her head lolling on his shoulder. Poor Richard, he must be wondering what he'd let himself in for.

'Sorry it's a bit basic.' He dumped Grace on the sofa. 'We usually just get birdwatchers and hikers staying here, and they spend more time outside than in.' He reached over and flicked on the lamp. 'I keep meaning to do it up a bit, but I never get round to it—'

'It's fine.' Jo took in the bare furnishings, the freezing cold and the strong smell of damp. It was far from perfect, but at least it was safe.

She laid Chloe down next to Grace on the battered old sofa and for a moment they stood and watched them sleeping peacefully, their heads together. Then Richard said gruffly, 'I'll go up and make the beds.'

'Let me.' Jo moved towards the stairs but he stopped her.

'I'll take care of everything. You need to rest.'

'But what about you? You've had a long night too.' There was a five o'clock shadow on his chin and dark welts of weariness under his eyes.

'You're right.' His eyes met hers uncertainly. 'I was going to ask if you minded me staying the night? I don't know if I could face making the drive home. You can say no if you're not happy about it—'

'Of course you can stay. It's your cottage, after all. But won't Kate be worrying where you are?'

'Kate doesn't worry about me.' Was it her imagination, or was there a hint of bitterness in his voice? 'But you're right, I'll call her on the mobile later. After I've sorted out those beds.'

Jo settled herself on the sofa with the girls. She felt herself relax, listening to the thumps overhead. Richard was taking care of everything. After so many years on her own she'd forgotten how good that felt.

'Jo?' She woke up with a start. Richard was standing over her. Befuddled by sleep as she was, she imagined his expression looked almost tender in the lamplight. 'Shall we go upstairs?' he said softly.

She was instantly awake. 'What? Upstairs? You mean—'

'I've finished making the beds, if you can help me carry the girls?'

'The girls. Of course. Yes.' The sofa springs groaned as she struggled to her feet. Thank God Richard couldn't read her mind.

Together they hoisted the girls into their arms and carried them up the narrow staircase to the bedroom.

'I've put you in the room next door. I'll take the sofa.' Richard said.

'Are you sure? I wouldn't want to put you out at all.'

'Jo, it's four in the morning. It'll hardly matter where we sleep if we don't get to bed soon.'

She woke up to find bright sunshine streaming through the tiny dormer window. She looked around, taking in her surroundings. It didn't take long. The room was only slightly larger than the single bed she occupied. When she stretched out she could touch the faded roses on the opposite wall with her fingertips. Talk about small.

Her breath misted in the cold air. It was freezing.

She was trying to make herself get up when the girls came into the room, bundled up in several layers of jumpers.

'It's really cold.' Grace shivered. 'And there isn't a telly.'

'I don't suppose Richard needs one, if he never comes here.'

'Why are we here, anyway?' Chloe demanded. 'Grace said it's because we're on the run from the police.'

'Did she indeed?' Jo shot Grace a warning look. 'Well, we're not. We're having a sort of holiday, that's all. That sounds like fun, doesn't it?'

'I'd rather go to Disney World.' Chloe went over to the window. 'It's got a really big garden,' she reported. 'Can we go and explore?'

'Wait until I'm up.' Jo extended a cautious toe out from under the covers. 'What time is it?'

'Nearly half past ten.'

'What?' Jo swung her legs out of bed and winced as her feet touched the cold, bare boards. 'Why didn't anyone wake me? Where's Richard?'

'He's gone.'

'Gone? When?'

'Dunno,' Grace shrugged. 'His car wasn't there when we got up.'

'Didn't he leave a note or anything?'

'Don't think so. What are you shouting at me for?'

'Was I? Sorry.' Why was she so disappointed? Surely she hadn't expected Richard to hang around the cottage with them all day? 'Oh well.' She forced a note of cheerfulness into her voice. 'We can't lie around in bed all day, can we? Better see what we can find for breakfast.'

Not very much, was the answer. Luckily the last occupants of the cottage had left a few basic provisions, although the girls curled their lips at the idea of Ryvitas and raspberry jam.

'I'm afraid that's all we've got.' Jo stuck her head in another empty cupboard. 'We'll sneak into the village and buy something decent later.'

She was determined to approach their situation with a positive frame of mind. But her optimism faded as she struggled to get to grips with her new surroundings. It wasn't just a TV the cottage was lacking. There was also gas central heating, a basic plumbing system and any kind of kitchen appliance that didn't come out of the Ark.

Determined not to die of hypothermia, she bundled the girls into their coats and took them outside to collect wood for the fire. It was freezing cold and the wind whipped her hair round her face as she watched Chloe and Grace dart around the garden. At least they'd managed to forget about the previous night's trauma. And so had she, she realised, as she hauled an armful of wood into the cottage. This place was exactly what she needed. It would be perfect, if only Richard were here . . .

By the time they got back to the cottage they'd already missed lunch and the girls were complaining of starvation. Jo decided to abandon her plan to build a fire until later and trek off to find the village instead.

They followed the narrow winding lane, tramping between the fields with the cold wind whistling through their coats. It was a relief when they finally spotted the spire of the village church. Soon they were in a pretty little hamlet full of quaint cottages in mellow, honeyed grey stone. They found a village shop-cum-post office, and Jo stocked up on groceries. She also bought a bottle of wine, as a thank you gift for Richard.

'Can we have some sweets?' Chloe asked. Jo turned round to answer her—and then she saw it. Her own face, strained and blotchy with tears, on the front pages of the *Globe*, the *Sun*, the *Mirror* and the *Sport*.

Her heart shot into her mouth as she dropped her shopping, scattering loo rolls, cereal boxes and bags of oven chips all over the floor.

'Mummy! Can we have some sweets?'

'What? Oh—yes, I suppose so. But hurry up.' She gathered up her shopping, her hands shaking. She paid for her purchases, keeping her head down and her scarf pulled up over her face. On impulse, she grabbed a handful of newspapers and paid for them too.

'That'll keep you busy.' Miraculously the woman behind the counter didn't seem to recognise her. 'I love a bit of gossip, don't you? See what all those celebs are getting up to.'

She almost ran all the way back up the lane to the cottage, the girls struggling breathlessly to keep up. Once safely inside the front door, she drew the bolt across and pulled the curtains.

'Why are you doing that?' Chloe asked. 'It's not night time.'

'It's—er—more cosy, don't you think?' She hurried around the kitchen, making sandwiches, her hands shaking. All she could think about were the newspapers she'd stuffed in the back of the cupboard.

Once the girls were settled in the sitting room with their sandwiches, sweets and comics, Jo shut herself in the kitchen. She took out the newspapers and spread them over the table.

It was worse than she could ever have imagined.

WESTFIELD STARS IN THREE IN A BED SEX AND DRUGS ROMP, was the lurid headline on the *Globe*. The rest of the story was even less accurate. According to Charlie Beasley's version of events, she and her lover 'sexy stud' Marcus Finn had enticed 'outrageous blonde TV nymphet' Toni Carlisle into the bridal suite for an orgy. The *Sun* had them snorting coke, while the *Mirror* had them all as crack addicts.

Jo ripped up the papers and stuffed them into the bin. She wanted to scream with pain and fury, but she couldn't. She couldn't do anything. All she could do was sit helplessly by while the newspapers made up terrible, poisonous lies about her.

She sat on the kitchen floor beside the bin, her face buried in her hands, and sobbed. Once she started crying she couldn't stop. She heard the kitchen door creak open and Grace's voice whisper, 'Mum?'

'Go away.'

'But we—'

'Look, just go away and leave me alone, will you?'

The door banged shut. Jo tried to call them back, but all that emerged were more great, gulping sobs.

 # CHAPTER NINE

SOME TIME LATER the door opened again.

'Jo?' She knew Richard was standing over her but she couldn't look at him. 'Jo, what is it? What's going on?'

She couldn't answer him. She was crying so much she could hardly breathe.

He must have caught sight of the newspapers she'd stuffed in the bin. He sighed. 'You've seen them, then? I hoped you wouldn't.' He knelt beside her, and she felt his arm round her. 'Come on, it's not that bad.'

'N-not that bad?' She managed to gulp the words out. 'H-how much bloody worse could it be?' And she started sobbing again.

Richard's arm tightened round her shoulders. 'I told you, it'll all blow over by tomorrow. Besides, no one really believes all that rubbish.'

'So what? It doesn't m-matter if it's true or if they believe it. Mud sticks.' She wiped her face with her sleeve.

'But the people who care about you know the truth. Who gives a damn what anyone else thinks?'

'That's easy for you to say!' She turned on him viciously. 'Your children don't have to face their friends at the school gates. They have a hard enough time as it is, without the other kids calling their mother a whore and a—a junkie!'

'Well, you're not making it any easier for them, are you? Don't you realise they're out there terrified because they think you're having some kind of breakdown? They need you to be strong, not fall apart on them.'

'I can't help it, can I? You don't know what it's like—'

'I know what it's like to have a mother who's so wrapped up in her own problems she can't see what she's putting everyone else through.' His eyes blazed with anger. 'If you want to help those kids I suggest you stop feeling so sorry for yourself and start thinking about them!'

He released her and slammed out of the room. A moment later she heard his car roar off.

Jo crouched on the kitchen floor, hugging herself. Bastard. What did he know? He wasn't the one who had to go out and face the world every day. And as for being wrapped up in her own problems . . .

Well, maybe she was. She hadn't handled this very well, she knew that much. Poor Chloe and Grace, she must have terrified them, losing it like that. Richard was right about that, too. They needed her to be strong for them. She couldn't let them down.

She stood up and went outside to look for them. There was no sign of Grace and Chloe. Just a note propped up on the mantelpiece, hastily scribbled in Grace's writing—*Gone with Richard.*

She went up to the bathroom, splashed her face with cold water and pulled a brush through her hair. Her swollen face looked back at her from the chipped bathroom mirror.

She was doing her best to build the fire with the wood she'd collected when she heard Richard's car outside.

'We've been to the fish-and-chip shop.' Chloe raced into the room.

'And Richard let me drive the car up the lane to the road,' Grace added proudly. 'He says I'm a natural.'

'Really? That's nice.' At least they didn't seem any the worse for seeing their mother reduced to a howling mess.

Then Richard came into the room. Jo ducked her head and concentrated on building up the fire. She could feel him watching her.

'Go into the kitchen and lay the table, would you, girls?' Amazingly, they went like lambs. Jo heard them clattering about in the kitchen.

'That wood's too damp. It'll never light,' Richard said shortly.

'Look, I'm sorry.' She stared at the black, empty fireplace. 'I shouldn't have lost it like that. You're right, I *was* just feeling sorry for myself.'

There was a long silence. 'I'm sorry too,' he said at last. 'You had every right to be upset.' He crouched down beside her. 'I just got so angry when I found the girls cowering like that. It reminded me of my brother and me—' Jo risked a glance at him. His smoky eyes were full of sorrow. 'But then I realised, you're nothing like my mother was. You're strong.'

Jo smiled weakly. 'I don't feel very strong at the moment.'

'Maybe not. But you'll pull through this.' He reached up and pushed a stray lock of hair off her face. The gesture surprised them both and they froze, just as the door flew open and Chloe fell through it.

'Dinner's ready!' she yelled.

The moment was forgotten as they sat round the scrubbed kitchen table with the girls, tucking into their food. Richard showed Jo how to light the Aga and a pleasant warmth filled the room.

'Sorry it's not more imaginative,' Richard said. 'The village isn't exactly blessed with takeaways.'

'This is fine,' Jo assured him. 'Although somehow I never pictured you eating fish and chips.'

'Yes, well, it makes a change from the flesh of innocent virgins.'

'Is that really what you eat?' Chloe looked at him, wide-eyed.

'Only when I'm working.' He flashed a look at Jo. He seemed so different tonight.

She looked round the table. The girls were giggling about something and despite all her problems, for the first time in a long time she felt truly at peace. Why couldn't it always be like this, she wondered.

'Looks like you've made a couple of fans,' she said, when they got around to clearing the plates. The girls had gone to bed after a spirited game of Monopoly. To Jo's embarrassment, they'd insisted on Richard going upstairs to say good night. 'I'm sorry if they've been a nuisance.'

'They've been fine.'

'All the same, it can be a bit much if you're not used to them.'

'Jo, I have seen a child before. I was one myself once, remember?' His eyes twinkled. 'Just because I'm not keen on having kids myself doesn't mean I hate them. I just don't think I'd be a good father, that's all.'

'But you're brilliant with children! Anyway, just because you've had a bad upbringing yourself doesn't mean you're going to repeat it with your own family. If anything, it might even make you better at bringing them up, because you wouldn't want to make the same mistakes.'

'Maybe you're right,' he agreed. 'I must admit, sometimes I wonder what it would be like to have a family to come home to. A real home.'

'But you've got a home.'

Richard's smile faded. 'I've got a place to live. It's hardly the same thing.' He paused. 'Yours is a real home,' he said.

She laughed and slipped the plates into the water. 'Mine is a pigsty!'

'No, it isn't. It's warm, and it's full of laughter and love. Like you.'

Jo turned round, and suddenly they were facing each other, only inches apart. Her heart bounced like a turbo-charged yo-yo.

'Mum! Chloe's being a pain. Come up and tell her, will you?'

Grace's yell from upstairs was like a bucket of icy water. They moved apart. Jo didn't know whether to feel relieved or disappointed.

There must be something about country air, she decided, fumbling for her watch on the bedside table. It was almost ten o'clock again.

She lay in bed, listening to the voices from downstairs. She could hear Grace, and Chloe's high-pitched squeaks, and . . . Richard?

She hurried out of bed and into her clothes. As she threw open the curtains, she was amazed to find it had started snowing overnight. Soft flakes fell against her window and a deep blanket of white covered the ground. It was like a scene from a Christmas card.

Then she heard Richard's voice again. She wasn't quite sure how to face him after last night. She wondered what might have happened next, if Grace hadn't called out when she did.

She found them all in the kitchen. Richard and Chloe were at one end of the big scrubbed pine table, while Grace buttered her way through a heap of toast at the other.

'Mum!' She grinned. 'Have you seen outside? It's snowing! Real snow, not that grey slushy stuff we get in town.'

'I know, darling.' But Jo's eyes were fixed on Chloe, who had her entire Barbie collection spread in front of her. She was dressing them from their extensive shoebox wardrobe. Nothing unusual in that, except that Richard was helping her.

'No, you've got it wrong again!' Chloe snatched the doll out of his hands. 'This is Aqua Dazzle Barbie, she has to wear the sparkly swimsuit. That goes on Snow Queen Barbie. See?' She held it under his nose.

'I'm not very good at choosing women's clothes.' Richard sighed. He looked up at Jo and smiled. He was looking very dark and desirable in a black sweater and jeans. Her stomach lurched.

'Shouldn't you be at work?' she squeaked.

'I thought I'd work from here today.' He folded one of Barbie's minuscule cardigans. 'The roads will be a nightmare. It'll take me so long to get back to York I might as well not bother. If that's OK with you?'

'Of course. Why shouldn't it be?' Jo tried to suppress her leaping excitement. 'But won't they need you in the office?'

'I've got my laptop and my mobile if anyone wants to contact me. I've told Louise that you're off until further notice. And Kate's more than capable of running the office in my absence.'

I'm sure she is, Jo thought. She put the kettle on the hob, and then she noticed that morning's *Globe* lying on the worktop.

'I walked into the village to get it earlier,' Richard said. 'It's OK, you can read it.'

There were no splashy headlines this morning. Gingerly she flipped the page—and there it was, on page five. A photo of Marcus, looking furious, getting into a Bentley with Murphy under the headline DIS-GRACED SOAP STAR GOES HOME TO FACE THE MUSIC. According to Charlie Beasley, Marcus's father was Lord Finnimoore of Wyston, and the Hon. Marcus was heir to several thousand acres of Gloucestershire.

'That can't be true!' she whispered.

'Apparently it is. Bit of a dark horse, isn't he?'

'You can say that again. I thought his family were a bunch of hippies!'

'They are. Very rich and well-connected hippies, though. Which is probably how he manages to stay out of jail.' His voice was bitter.

Jo went on reading. There were a couple of paragraphs about Toni Carlisle being admitted into rehab, but nothing about her.

'It looks like they've forgotten all about you, doesn't it?' Richard said quietly. 'You could probably sue them if that's what you wanted, but I think it's probably better if we just let it die a natural death.'

Jo nodded. 'A court case could take months, and then it would all get dragged up again. I just want to forget it ever happened.'

After breakfast the girls started clamouring to go outside and play in the snow. Jo was caught up in the rush to find boots and coats.

'Aren't you coming outside with us?' Chloe looked disappointed as Richard opened up his briefcase and took out his laptop.

'I'm afraid I can't. I have to work.'

'Can't you just forget about work for one day?'

'I'm sure Richard's got far too much to do,' Jo cut in quickly. 'Come on, we'll go outside and build a snowman.'

She followed the girls out into the garden, her boots plunging into the deep, crunchy snow. She could see him sitting at the window, his dark head bent over his computer screen.

She tried to keep the girls quiet, but it was impossible. They weren't used to real snow, and they couldn't help whooping and shrieking as they fell about in it. Every so often Richard lifted his head to look out at them. Jo could feel his irritation at the constant interruptions.

Finally she got the girls organised into making a snowman, but after half an hour they'd made nothing more than a small, unsatisfactory pyramid with a misshapen head that kept rolling off.

'It looks stupid.' Grace drop-kicked the head into the trees.

'Oh, I don't know.' Jo did her best to be encouraging. 'I think it looks

like that snowman in the video. You know, "We're walking in the air—"'
She flapped her arms and floated round the garden.

'MUM!' Chloe and Grace chorused.

'Could I make a suggestion?'

Jo turned, mid-float. Richard was standing in the doorway, looking rugged in a thick cord jacket. She was so hot with mortification she could almost feel herself melting a hole in the snow.

'Yes?'

'Perhaps you're going about it the wrong way?' He crunched through the snow towards them. 'If you want to make a real snowman, the best way is to start like this.' He crouched down and began gathering up snow.

Jo watched him, her arms folded. 'So you're an expert, are you?'

'I've obviously had more experience than you.'

'Why don't you put the kettle on, Mummy?' Chloe said patronisingly.

Jo stomped into the kitchen. She knew where she wasn't wanted. Actually, it was quite a relief to be inside. The Aga spread a cosy warmth through the cottage. Jo peeled off her damp gloves and boots and pulled up a chair after she'd put the kettle on, propping her feet up on the oven door to watch the steam rise off her socks.

Outside, she could see the girls rushing around, gathering up armfuls of snow and bringing them back to Richard, who was constructing an extremely impressive snowman. He really had them under his spell, she thought. Unlike her other boyfriends in the past, who'd tried to bribe them with presents, he seemed to win them over just by being himself.

She nearly fell off her chair. *Unlike her other boyfriends* . . . what was she thinking of? Richard was very, very far from being a boyfriend.

She finished making the coffee, took the mugs outside and set them on the windowsill.

'I've made the—' She didn't even get the words out before a snowball hit her square in the face, filling her mouth with snow. 'Right, who did that?' she spluttered, as the girls screamed with laughter.

'He did!'

Grace and Chloe pointed at Richard. 'Only because they told me to,' he protested. He held up his hands. 'Jo? What are you doing with that? It was just a joke, there's no need to—ow!'

'I may not be able to make a snowman, but I'm a deadly aim,' she said calmly. She turned away to pick up the mugs, and a snowball bounced off the back of her head. She looked back, and another caught her on the chin. The girls were almost hysterical by now. Richard was leaning against a tree, looking smug. 'That does it,' she muttered. She advanced towards him slowly.

He watched her, his eyes narrowing. 'Truce?' he suggested.

'No chance,' she said sweetly. She reached up and shook the branch. There was a soft thump, and he was covered in snow.

It all happened very quickly after that. Jo saw the look of menace in his eyes and backed away. She turned to run, but Richard made a flying tackle, grabbing her legs and bringing her to the ground. As she screamed and wriggled and begged for mercy, he began stuffing handfuls of snow into her jacket and down her shirt.

'No! Please, don't, I'll do anything—'

She looked up into his laughing eyes, just inches away from hers, and suddenly attraction hit her like a blow in the solar plexus. She stopped squirming and lay there, his weight on top of her, pinning her down.

It seemed to hit him at the same time. His smile slipped and he froze, his eyes looking deep into hers.

Chloe's giggling broke the spell. Richard rolled off her and sat up. 'We'd better have that coffee before it gets cold,' he said.

They sat on a fallen log, watching the girls play. Jo could feel the sexual tension crackling in the air, and this time she knew she wasn't imagining it. The question was, what were they going to do about it?

Richard answered for her. He drained his cup and stood up. 'I'd better go and finish that work.'

They stayed a cautious distance from each other for the rest of the day. Richard spent the whole afternoon hunched over his computer, while Jo entertained the girls and pottered around the kitchen preparing supper. It felt as if they were circling each other, each waiting for the other to make the first move.

It was a weird evening. Jo had never been so heart-stoppingly, nerve-twangingly aware of anyone in her whole life.

She couldn't tell what he was thinking, but she had the feeling he was as nervous as she was. There was no laughter, no easy conversation flowing between them. Every look, every word, every movement was laced with meaning.

Somehow Grace had picked up on her nerves and realised Richard was the cause of them. She'd also decided to act as an unofficial matchmaker. As soon as supper was over and the plates were cleared away she declared in a loud voice that it was time for bed.

'But I thought we were going to play Monopoly?' Chloe whined.

'Not tonight,' Grace said firmly. 'We're tired and we want to go to bed. Now.' She manhandled her sister towards the stairs. 'Don't worry, Mummy, I'll put her to bed,' she insisted. 'Then you can stay here with Richard.' She added a few eye rolls and encouraging semaphore hand movements, just in case neither of them had got the message.

The bedroom door closed overhead, plunging them into awkward silence. 'Subtle as a sledgehammer,' Richard said wryly.

'I never thought I'd say it, but I think I preferred it when she was slamming doors and sulking every time a man came within ten miles.' She glanced sideways at him. 'At least it means she likes you.'

'I'm flattered.'

What happens now? Jo wondered. The air tingled with expectation. For want of something constructive to do, she went into the kitchen and fetched the bottle of wine she'd bought the day before, and two glasses. When she got back to the sitting room Richard was standing at the window, staring out into the night.

'I bought this in the village yesterday. I don't know if it's any good—'

'Not for me, thanks. I've been thinking—they've probably managed to clear the main roads by now. Maybe I should be heading back?'

Disappointment hit her like a punch in the stomach. 'Why?'

He turned slowly to face her. 'I think we both know the answer to that one, don't you?'

She looked down at the bottle in her hands. 'I suppose Kate will be wondering where you are.'

'Kate doesn't give a damn where I am!' His vehemence startled her.

'Then why are you going?'

'Because of what's happening with us. There is something happening, isn't there? And I guess I'm right in thinking that if I stayed here tonight we might do something we'd both regret.'

'Who says we'd regret it?'

'Oh come on!' Richard said. 'Surely you can see it wouldn't work?'

'Because of Kate?'

'Because of us. You don't need someone like me in your life.'

'What you mean is you don't need someone like me. That's what all this is about, isn't it?' Anger flared in her eyes. 'You're afraid that the girls and I might mess up your oh-so-perfect lifestyle.'

'There's nothing perfect about my lifestyle. And maybe I'm afraid I'll end up needing you too much.' His eyes were dark with pain. 'Jo, I know what loving someone can do, remember? I grew up watching my mother falling in love with men and having it all blow up in her face. I don't want the same thing to happen to me.'

'Who says it would?' She took a deep breath. 'Look, what happened to your family was terrible. But you mustn't let it stop you being happy.'

'I am happy.'

'No, just because you're not miserable doesn't mean you're happy.'

'Spare me the psychobabble! You don't know me well enough.'

'No, you're right. I don't.' She stalked into the kitchen and started on the washing up. She was staring at the water running into the sink when he came into the room.

'I'm going now.' She didn't turn round. 'Jo?'

'What? What do you want me to say? Bon voyage? Have a safe trip?'

'Don't do this, Jo—'

'Do what?' She swung round to face him, a frying pan in her hand. 'If you want to go, then go. I'm not stopping you.'

'You think I really want to go? You think I haven't dreamed about being alone with you like this? Christ, I've thought about nothing else for weeks.' His voice was husky. 'But it's not going to work, Jo. We can't start something we can't finish.'

'Then there's nothing more to say, is there?' She turned back to the sink and started scrubbing the pan as if her life depended on it. She was still scrubbing when she heard the front door close. Only then did she allow herself to break down. He was right. They both wanted and needed such different things in life, their relationship didn't stand a chance. But that didn't take away the terrible, searing pain.

'Jo?' The pan scourer fell from her hands. She turned round. Richard was standing in the doorway, his dark hair dusted with melting snow.

'Who am I kidding?' he groaned. 'This thing started the day I first set eyes on you. And there's not a damn thing I can do about it.'

He crossed the kitchen in a couple of strides. A moment later, she was in his arms and he was kissing her, passionate and fierce. Jo clung to him, kissing him back just as passionately.

Richard finally pulled away and looked down at her. 'You don't know how long I've been waiting to do that.'

They curled up together on the rug in front of the flickering fire. Jo couldn't remember when she'd felt this happy, snuggled up next to Richard. The weight of his arm round her shoulders felt so right somehow. They talked a little, laughed a lot, and listened to the whirr of the hamster's wheel as Richard the rodent did his nightly exercise routine.

'Doesn't that wretched animal ever shut up?' Richard muttered.

'Leave him alone, he's sweet. Besides, you bought him.'

'Only because I wanted an excuse to see you again.' He held her closer. 'And then, once I got to your place, I realised what a mistake I'd made.'

'Charming.'

'You know what I mean. Seeing you totally confused me. I knew you were everything I'd spent my whole life trying to avoid, and yet I couldn't get you out of my mind.'

'Thanks very much! I'm not that much of a disaster area, you know.'

'No, but I am. I didn't think I'd be that good for you, either. I'd just managed to convince myself I'd got you out of my mind when I turned up at that wedding and saw you with Marcus Finn. I didn't know whether to be furious with him or with myself for letting you go when I had the chance.'

'I told you, Marcus isn't my type.'

'Thank God for that. Otherwise I'd definitely have to fire him.'

Jo stared at him in disbelief. 'Of all the arrogant—' He leaned over and stopped her mouth with a kiss. Her pulses leapt in response but she pulled away, still uncertain.

'What about Kate? I don't want to think of anyone getting hurt because of me.'

'Kate won't get hurt. She's not the type.' He sat upright. 'I suppose that's what attracted me to her in the first place. We were never a couple. Just two independent, ambitious people in a mutually satisfying arrangement.' His jaw was hard with tension. 'Although, frankly, I don't think Kate's all that satisfied with it either. She's been acting strangely since before Christmas, taking herself off with friends every night and weekend. We're hardly what you'd call together any more.'

'And is that why you wanted me? As a replacement for Kate?'

Richard's eyes crinkled. 'Jo, if I'd been looking for a replacement for Kate, do you seriously think I would have chosen someone like you?'

'God, you're such a creep!' Jo picked up a cushion and took a swipe at his head. Richard ducked at the last minute and lost his balance. Jo seized her advantage and threw herself on top of him, straddling his long, lean body between her thighs. 'Say you're sorry,' she demanded.

'Make me.' Before she could make a move his hands flashed out, pinning her wrists and pulling her towards him so their faces were just inches apart. She breathed in the clean, male smell of him, heard his breathing grow ragged. She could feel his erection pressing warm against her belly. She looked into his eyes, burning dark with longing.

'Make me,' he whispered again.

They stumbled up the stairs and barely made it inside the door before Richard pushed her against it. They pulled at each other's clothes, kissing deeply, their hands exploring and caressing bare skin.

Jo heard herself crying out as he stroked her breasts, circling her nipples with his fingers, then his tongue before travelling down, down . . . She arched her body, a drumbeat of desire deep in her pelvis. She'd never experienced such passion or desperate physical longing.

They just made it to the bed.

'Sorry,' Richard groaned afterwards against her skin. 'That was a bit lacking in finesse, wasn't it?'

'I'm not complaining. Besides, we can do the finesse bit next time.'

'Next time?' He pulled away, his damp skin peeling from hers. 'You think I've got enough energy for a next time?'

Jo smiled. 'I'm counting on it.'

'You're an insatiable woman.' Richard bent his head and kissed her again. He folded her into his arms and collapsed backwards onto the bed, pulling her in a giggling heap on top of him.

They spent most of the night making love and talking. They talked about anything and everything, sharing their memories, their hopes, their dreams. Most of all they talked about their future.

'I'll talk to Kate as soon as I get back,' Richard promised.

'Will she be very upset?' Jo ventured.

'The only thing that would upset Kate is the thought of losing her lifestyle. But she can have the flat and anything else she wants.'

'But where will you live?'

He turned his face towards her. 'I was thinking, I might do this place up and move in here. And maybe I could stay over at your place sometimes? If you think the girls wouldn't mind—'

'Are you kidding? They'll be thrilled.' Jo grinned. 'Are you sure you're ready to take us on?'

His eyes gleamed in the silvery moonlight. 'I'm looking forward to it.'

She drifted into a contented sleep in Richard's arms and woke up to find pink dawn sunlight filling the room, birds twittering noisily outside, and the bed beside her empty. Smiling to herself, she lay back against the pillows, luxuriating in the warm hollow of the bed where Richard's body had been. She didn't deserve to be this happy. Surely something had to come along to spoil it?

Then she heard the voices drifting up from downstairs and she realised that 'something' had already arrived.

She pulled on her dressing gown and hurried downstairs. They were in the kitchen. Richard was at the Aga, watching the kettle with scowling intensity. Kate was sitting at the table, her head in her hands. She looked awful. Her eyes were pink and swollen, her smudged mascara blended with the deep circles under her eyes, and her hair was hastily pulled back off her face in a tatty rubber band.

Kate lifted her face from her hands and regarded Jo stonily. 'Oh, it's you.'

Richard pushed a mug in front of Kate. He also looked utterly miserable. His jaw was clenched, his dark eyes devoid of expression.

'Would you like a coffee?' he offered.

'Thanks.' Jo glanced at Kate, then back at Richard. He frowned and gave the slightest shake of his head. So he hadn't told her yet. In which case, why was she so upset? And why, come to that, was she even here?

'Here, have mine.' Kate pushed her mug across the table towards her. 'The way I'm feeling I can't face coffee at the moment.'

Jo pulled out a chair opposite Kate's and sank into it. 'I didn't expect to see you?'

'Didn't you? Well, life's full of surprises, isn't it?' Kate's voice was edged with ice. What the hell was going on?

Jo glanced at Richard. He was staring into space, oblivious to what was going on around him. He looked so unreachable it frightened her.

Suddenly he galvanised himself into action and emptied his untouched coffee down the sink. 'Let's just go, shall we?' he muttered.

Jo stared at him. 'Go where?'

'I'm taking Kate back to York. I'll send someone down to pick up her car later.' He turned to Kate. 'Ready?'

'I can't wait.' She stood up. 'The sooner we get home, the better.'

Home. Jo's head reeled. Whatever had happened, Kate still believed she and Richard were a couple.

Jo watched Richard unhook his overcoat from the peg behind the door. He didn't look at her. It was almost as if she'd ceased to exist for him.

'Richard?'

Finally he looked up at her, and she almost wished he hadn't. He didn't even look like the same man. She hardly recognised the dark, frowning face with the haunted eyes and rigidly set jaw.

'Are you coming?' Kate stood in the doorway, her arms folded.

'Wait in the car, Kate. I won't be a moment.' His eyes never left Jo's face. Kate sighed heavily and slammed the door.

'What the hell's going on? What's she doing here? Why didn't you tell her about us?'

'I couldn't tell her, not yet. She's—had some bad news.' Richard raked his hand through his hair. 'It's complicated. I owe you an explanation but I can't give you one, yet. Not until I've sorted things out.'

'Sorted what out? Richard?'

He started to speak, but Kate's voice interrupted them. 'Are you coming, or what? It's bloody freezing out here!'

'In a minute.' He glanced over his shoulder, then back at Jo. 'Look, I promise I'll talk to you later. When I know what's going on.' He picked up his case. 'It'll be all right, I promise,' he said. And then he was gone.

CHAPTER TEN

'THAT'S IT, JO. If you can just get a bit closer—go on, lean in together—lovely.' The photographer snapped a few more frames. 'Now, if we can have you a bit more cheek to cheek, that's it—'

'It's all right, angel, you can get a bit closer. I haven't got anything catching.' Marcus pulled her closer.

'How do I know that?' Jo's *What's On TV* cover smile was frozen in place. 'The amount of women you've slept with, you could have diseases medical science hasn't caught up with yet!'

He laughed. 'Are you mad at me or something?'

'Heavens no, why would I be mad at you? Just because you dragged my name through the mud and nearly got me jailed for life!'

'Don't be so melodramatic, darling, they wouldn't have put you in jail. Besides, how was I to know the police were going to turn up? Although I'd like to know who tipped them off. I wouldn't be surprised if it was the Grim Reaper.'

She pulled away from him. 'Why would he do that?'

'I wouldn't put anything past him. He's always hated me.'

'But he wouldn't risk *Westfield's* reputation just out of spite.'

'Oh, so you're on his side now, are you? What's brought this on? Don't tell me you've fallen for his warmth and charisma?'

She could feel her face flaming. 'Fuck off, Marcus.'

'Ooh, have I touched a nerve? I noticed he was quick to jump on his white charger and rescue you. He left me hanging out to dry.'

'Only because you'd admitted you were guilty. Besides, you didn't exactly need his help, did you? You had Daddy and an army of barristers, remember?'

Marcus's face clouded. The news that he was the Hon. Marcus Finnimoore, heir to half a county, had seriously dented his street cred.

'Anyway, it's all over now,' he said.

Is it? Jo thought bleakly. A week after she and the girls had come out of hiding, her life was slowly getting back to normal. Roxanne was back, having defied her parents and turned up on Jo's doorstep at midnight. And her own parents, thankfully, had been oblivious to the whole thing.

By the time they had returned from the Languedoc the scandal had blown over. Duncan had offered to act as a character witness—'You just send them to me, I'll tell them you're as sexually adventurous as an amoeba'—while the cast of *Westfield* had been sweetly supportive. Except Brett, of course, who found the whole thing a huge joke.

She could have put the entire miserable episode behind her, except for one thing. She still hadn't heard from Richard. She'd stayed at the cottage for two days after his hasty departure. Two days of watching through the window for his car to come up the drive. Finally she couldn't bear it any longer. She'd summoned a taxi, rounded up the girls and headed home. Fortunately, by then, the press had got bored of staking her out and moved on to pursue another scandal.

But still she didn't hear from Richard. According to the gossip, neither he nor Kate had been at work for days. What if they'd had a heart to heart and Richard had realised Kate was the one for him after all?

After another two days of waiting for news, Jo screwed up her courage to call him herself. His mobile was switched off and the answer machine was on at the flat. She didn't have the nerve to leave a message.

After the photo shoot, she and Marcus had an interview with a journalist from a TV listings magazine. Jo sipped coffee and struggled to keep a smile on her face as she answered the usual inane questions about her character, and ignored all the intrusive ones about her private life.

The interview overran by several minutes. Afterwards, Jo grabbed her bag and dashed off to the studio building. Her first scene that day was in the corner shop. According to the storyline, Ma Stagg had found out about Stacey's affair with Vic, and wanted to put a stop to it.

As she picked her way across the studio she heard uncontrollable screams coming from the brightly lit set. Her heart sank. She'd forgotten Ma Stagg's grandchildren, Keifer and Keanu, were supposed to be in this scene. Usually she could tolerate the kids' tantrums, but her patience was at breaking point this morning.

And here was someone who could push her beyond the limit. Jo braced herself as Brett swaggered over.

'You're late, junkie,' he greeted her. 'Been round the back tooting charlie, have you?'

'Of course, Brett. How else could I get through a day with you?'

His brow furrowed. Jo could see his lips moving as he puzzled over her remark.

Jo ignored him and tried to concentrate on her script, but the sound of screaming filled her head, making it impossible for her to think straight. Everywhere she looked there was chaos. Children howling, Eva teetering dangerously close to a tantrum, the production crew muttering tensely among themselves.

'Do you know what I've heard?' Brett was saying. 'Coke gives you an even bigger buzz if you stick it up your backside.'

Jo raised her eyes slowly to meet his. 'Do you know,' she said. 'You took those last five words right out of my mouth?'

She thrust her script into his hands and stalked off, ignoring the chorus of astonished noises that followed her. Anger propelled her out of the building and across the courtyard to the canteen. She sat down at a corner table and put her head in her hands.

She'd spent four years at *Westfield* and she'd never realised how much she hated it until now. Four years of playing the same dreary bimbo, doing interviews and photo shoots, living her life in a goldfish bowl. The whole business with her arrest had made her realise how public her life had become. The only thing the job had going for it was a regular income, but even that barely made up for what she had to go through day after day. And yet, she couldn't give it up. She needed that security, no matter what the price. She was tired, bored and trapped.

She felt a warm, wet rasping on her cheek. She looked up and found herself staring into Murphy's friendly brown eyes. Marcus stood over her, a cup in one hand and a doughnut in the other.

'I've brought the tea, and Murph's brought the sympathy,' he grinned.

'Thanks.'

'I mean it.' He sat down opposite her. 'So what's the problem?'

'I don't know. Just the job getting to me, I suppose.' She wished she could tell him what was really on her mind, but she didn't dare share that with anyone. 'Maybe I'm just coming down with something? I haven't felt too good the past few days.'

'If I were you, I'd go straight home before the Grim Reaper catches you. He's seriously pissed off.'

'You've seen Richard?'

'Unfortunately.' Marcus grimaced. 'All I did was say hello to him in the corridor and he practically took my head off. I'm telling you, that man doesn't forgive or forget—where are you going?'

'To see Richard.' She pushed back her chair with a clatter and rushed out of the canteen.

At least she didn't have to face Kate standing guard outside his office. A temp sat in her place, filing her nails and reading Jonathan Cainer. She looked up, mildly surprised, as Jo stormed past her.

'You can't go in there. He's in a meet—' By the time she was on her feet Jo had already flung open the door.

Five heads turned to look at her. Jo barely took in the faces of the script editor and the storyline writers. All her attention was focused on the man behind the desk.

'Jo.' He stood up. His appearance shocked all the anger out of her. His face was gaunt and there were dark hollows under his eyes. He turned said to the others. 'Perhaps we could continue this meeting later.'

They all filed out of the office, leaving Richard and Jo alone.

'What's happened to you?' Jo whispered.

'I'm sorry.' Richard sank back into his chair. 'I know I should have called you. I picked up the phone a few times, but I didn't know what to say.' He buried his face in his hands. 'It's all such a mess.'

'What is? Richard, what's happened? Are you ill? For God's sake, tell me. It can't be any worse than what I've been imagining.'

'Can't it?' His eyes were dark and haunted. 'Kate's pregnant.'

All the blood drained from her head, leaving her faint and weak. She sank down into a chair. 'No! It can't be true.'

'I wish it wasn't, but it is. I've seen the test results.'

'But how—when?'

'Some time around Christmas. She's known for a couple of weeks but she couldn't bring herself to tell me. She wasn't sure how I'd react.' He sighed heavily. 'I hardly understand it. We've always been so careful.'

'She certainly picked her time to give you the good news.'

'I'm sorry. I know you must have been wondering what the hell was going on. But the truth is, I didn't even know myself. Kate and I have spent the last few days and nights just talking, trying to make some sense of it. I've never seen her in such a state. She's gone to pieces over this.'

'How is she now?'

'Still pretty shell-shocked, but coming to terms with it.' He paused. 'She's keeping the baby.'

Jo's head went back in shock. 'But I would have thought—'

'She'd want an abortion? I assumed that too. But she's had some kind of medical problems since she was a teenager and apparently the doctors have warned her that a termination would be a risky surgical procedure for her. She's got no choice but to go ahead with the pregnancy.'

'And how do you feel—about her keeping the baby?'

'It's her decision, obviously. I have to go along with whatever she wants. And I wouldn't be happy about getting rid of a baby just because it's not convenient. Especially if it means putting her health in danger.' He leaned back in his chair. 'It does make things complicated, though.'

Complicated? From where she was standing, it made them totally impossible. 'Does she—know about me?'

'Of course, I told her. I said I was going to, didn't I?'

'Yes, but that was before—'

'Kate's pregnancy doesn't change anything as far as I'm concerned. It's you I want to be with, not her.'

'How can you say that? This baby changes everything.'

'Why?'

'Because that's what babies do, whether you want them to or not!' Jo stared at him, exasperated. 'It's going to need both of you for support.'

'Of course I'm going to support it.' Richard lifted his chin. 'I've already told Kate I'll pay for whatever she needs—'

'I'm not talking about money!' Anger flared in her eyes. 'Babies don't just need nappies and toys and private school fees. They need love and care. They need a loving home. And they need both their parents.'

'Your daughters don't have both their parents.'

'Yes, and it's bloody hard work, which is why I wouldn't want anyone else to go through it. I manage because I have to. But that doesn't mean I wouldn't prefer it if I had someone to share it with.'

'You've got someone. You've got me now.'

'And soon you'll have a child of your own to worry about. Do you really think I could let you abandon it while you play happy families with me and the girls?'

He narrowed his eyes. 'So what are you saying?'

'I'm saying'—she took a deep breath—'I'm saying you should try and make a go of it with Kate. You and Kate had a relationship once. You could do it again.'

'That was before I met you.'

His eyes met hers across the desk. Jo felt herself weaken and looked away. 'Like I said, this baby will change both your lives for ever.'

'You think it will bring us closer together? Quite a tall order for a baby, isn't it? Especially when I want to be with someone else.'

'You might feel differently once the baby's born. It's the most wonderful feeling in the world, watching your child grow up, seeing it take its first steps, hearing its first word. You couldn't miss all those things.'

He looked down at the desk in front of him. Jo sensed he must have been having the same thoughts himself. 'But I want you, too,' he said hoarsely. 'I love you. Is it such a crime for me to want us to be together?'

'We can't,' she whispered. 'I couldn't let you do it, and deep down you know you wouldn't want to. How long before you end up resenting me for keeping you away from your own flesh and blood?'

He stared at her in silence. 'So that's it, then?' he said finally. 'Even if I walked out on Kate tonight you still wouldn't have me?'

Of course I'd have you, she wanted to cry. Deep down her heart ached for him to do just that. But her head knew how wrong it would be.

She stood up. Her legs felt weak. 'I'd better go.'

'I'm sorry for letting you down so badly.'

'It's not me you should be worrying about now.'

She forced herself to keep walking down the softly carpeted corridor towards the lift. Her throat ached, and it was all she could do to stop herself crying and rushing back to him. But there was no point in going back. Their future had been resolved, and nothing could change it now.

CHAPTER ELEVEN

'AT LEAST THE ACCOMMODATION'S NICE,' Viola commented, as they pulled into the wide sweeping drive that led to the clifftop hotel.

Jo stopped the car and got out. It hadn't been an easy journey, with four of them and a travel-sick Irish wolfhound crammed into her car. Jo's head ached from trying to concentrate against a background of Marcus's tinny Discman and Lara screeching into her mobile phone.

'What do you mean, the record company isn't interested?' she snapped as they tumbled out of the car. 'You said they'd love my demo. You *promised*, Leon. Yeah, well, I'm fed up with listening to you, too.'

She shoved the phone in her pocket and stalked up the drive, leaving the others to struggle with her luggage.

Viola sent Jo a meaningful look. 'I think the honeymoon's over.'

'And her pop career, by the sound of it.' She turned to Marcus, who was trying to light a cigarette. 'Are you going to give me a hand with these cases?'

'Don't be too hard on him,' Viola said. 'I expect he has servants to do that at home, don't you, Trust Fund Boy?'

'Bog off, you old lezzie.'

'Charming! I suppose that's what they taught you at Eton?'

Jo listened to them trading insults, but she didn't have the energy to join in. She'd been very tired lately. And the idea of two days filming in sunny Robin Hood's Bay wasn't going to raise her spirits.

A month had passed since she'd had that heart-to-heart with Richard.

Since then they'd tried to avoid one another. It was harder to keep away from Kate, whose pregnancy was now the talk of the *Westfield* studios. Soon she would be strutting around, proudly displaying her bump. Jo didn't know how she'd cope.

Or maybe she wouldn't have to? The week before, she'd called Julia Gold, her agent, and told her she was thinking of leaving *Westfield*. After a lot of squawking and swearing, Julia had finally agreed to look around for other offers. 'But don't hold your breath,' she'd warned. 'You don't know what it's like out there these days.'

It can't be any worse than it is here, Jo thought miserably, as she trailed after the others towards the hotel. Just to make her feel even worse, the first person she saw when she walked into the hotel reception was Kate, signing in at the desk.

'Bloody hell, what's she doing here?' Marcus groaned.

'Hello, darling.' Viola said as Kate came towards them. 'I was just saying, pregnancy obviously suits you. You're positively blooming.'

'I don't feel blooming,' Kate snapped back. 'The sea air's making me feel sick.'

She stalked off to the lifts. 'Well, I never,' Viola declared.

Jo shrugged. 'It's probably her hormones.'

'Not her. Him.' Jo followed Viola's gaze towards the double doors. Richard had just walked in, carrying a bag. 'Arriving separately, eh? And he doesn't look very happy. I wonder if they've had a bust-up?'

Richard glanced up at them and nodded briefly. Jo forced herself to smile back, dismayed at the lines of tiredness etched round his eyes.

'It's none of our business,' Jo said.

'Spoilsport!' Viola made a face. 'Since when has that stopped you enjoying a bit of gossip?'

'Ooh, look! It's Stacey, isn't it?' Jo was saved from answering by the shriek behind her. She turned round as a middle-aged woman in a headscarf thrust her face right up to hers. 'It *is* you! I knew it. I never miss an episode.'

By the time Jo had finished signing autographs the others had drifted off to their rooms. She collected her keys and had her bags sent up to her room, and went outside to get some fresh air.

It was a cold, grey March day and the salty wind carried a spattering of rain as she followed the path over neat lawns to sit on a bench overlooking the sea. Jo hugged herself as she listened to the muted roar of the waves crashing against the rocks below her. This wasn't supposed to happen! How was she meant to cope with Richard here? She hadn't bargained for that, on top of everything else.

The trill of her mobile phone broke into her thoughts. Jo plunged her hand into her bag to retrieve it.

'Are you sitting down?' Julia Gold never bothered to introduce herself. She just assumed everyone was hanging on the end of the phone, waiting for her call. 'I've just found you the most fantastic job.'

Jo straightened her shoulders, instantly alert. 'You've found me a job?'

'Well, as good as. You'd have to audition, but unless you make a monumental fuck-up the part's yours. The producer's desperate for you.'

As she described the role, Jo felt herself go light-headed. It was the kind of thing she'd always dreamed of. *Heartland*, a sixties period drama series set in a rural Yorkshire village, were bringing in some important new characters and they wanted her to play the new headteacher at the village primary. It meant more money, more prestige, and a chance to escape from the daily grind of soap life.

Jo switched off the phone, still in a daze. This was brilliant news. But even though she felt like jumping up and down there was still a tiny, hard lump of dread in the pit of her stomach.

She would have to leave *Westfield*. That meant never seeing Richard again. But then, why was that such a bad thing? Surely seeing him every day and knowing they couldn't be together could only hurt her more?

Still troubled, she walked back to the hotel and up to her room. As she put her key in, the door next to hers flew open and Murphy trotted out, followed by Marcus. He grinned when he saw her.

'I've been knocking on your door for hours. Where have you been?'

'Just walking and thinking.' She didn't tell him about the job offer. She was still getting used to the idea herself.

'At the same time? Ooh, clever girl. I can't quite get the hang of that myself.' He swept his hair out of his eyes. 'I'm just taking Murphy for a stroll along the cliffs while I try to work out a way of avoiding dinner.'

'Why would you want to do that?'

'Haven't you heard? We've all been summoned to the restaurant by the Grim Reaper at eight.'

'Oh God,' Jo groaned.

She retreated to her room to unpack and absorb this latest piece of bad news. Great. This evening was just what she needed.

As she finished unpacking, she came across the unopened box of Tampax in the bottom of her suitcase and felt a fleeting moment of panic. She was late. She'd never been late in her life, except when—

Bile rose up, burning her throat. No, that would just be too monumentally unlucky. Besides, there could be lots of other reasons. Stress, for one. She'd certainly had more than her fair share of that recently.

And tonight would be even more stressful. Jo considered her options as she showered and washed her hair. She could just refuse to go. Or she could develop a tactical migraine. Or she could just go and get the damn thing over with. After all, she was leaving *Westfield*. In a few weeks they wouldn't be able to hurt her any more.

But in the meantime, she had the next few hours to get through. And it was no help when she walked into the bar at ten to eight and found to her horror that Richard was already there. On his own.

Panic assailed her. She started to creep away, but he turned and saw her. Stay calm, she told herself as she walked towards him.

'Drink?' he offered.

'Gin and tonic, please.' She sent him a sidelong look as he ordered their drinks. He was wearing a sharply tailored black suit that made him look so sexy it almost hurt. His face was still gaunt and shadowed, but if anything it just made him look even more darkly attractive.

Her drink arrived and she downed it in a single gulp. Richard looked surprised. 'Another?'

'Please.' He was drinking whisky, she noticed. Was he drinking to dull the pain, like she was?

'So—er—how are the girls?' he asked.

'Fine.' Jo took a steadying gulp of her drink. 'So—um—how's Kate?'

He slammed his glass down, making her jump. 'Look, I can't do this. I can't just behave like we're polite strangers. I miss you like hell. I spend every waking moment thinking about you. It's driving me out of my mind.' She flinched at the raw despair in his eyes. 'Why do you think I came down here? It was just a pathetic excuse to see you again.'

'But you brought Kate?'

'I didn't bring Kate. She came by herself, although God knows why. We might still be living under the same roof but we're not having any kind of relationship. Anything she and I had died the day I met you.' He slid his hand across the bar and covered hers, his long fingers curling round her wrist. 'God, I want you so much,' he groaned.

'I want you too.' There was no point in denying it.

'So what are we doing? Why can't we just be together?'

'You know why.'

'So we've just got to go through the hell of seeing each other every day, is that it?'

'Maybe not.' She took a deep breath. 'Richard, I've been offered another job.'

'What kind of job?' His fingers tightened round her wrist.

'A very good one, actually.' She told him about *Heartland*. 'It would be a great career move, and it would mean I could still be based at home—'

'And you wouldn't have to see me again?' Richard's eyes narrowed. 'That's why you're doing this, isn't it?'

'What if I am? What good is it doing either of us at the moment? And it'll only get worse when Kate has the baby—'

'Someone talking about me?' They sprang apart. Kate stood behind them, looking chic and superior in a narrow-fitting cream cashmere sheath that showed off her still enviably flat stomach. She sidled between them and waved to the barman. 'I'll have a vodka and tonic, no ice.'

'Is that wise?' Richard asked.

'Probably not, but who cares?' She smiled bitterly at Richard. 'Don't tell me you're worried about the baby, darling? Bit ironic, isn't it, considering you'd rather it wasn't born at all.'

'That's not true!' Jo gasped.

'Isn't it?' Kate's eyes glittered with malice. 'Let's face it, this pregnancy has been a bit of an inconvenience all round, hasn't it? But at least you two don't have the misery of carrying it for nine months.' Her drink arrived and she took a massive slug.

'Why are you having it, if you feel like that?' Richard muttered.

'Because I have to, don't I? I'm not going to risk killing myself just so you can rush off into the sunset with your girlfriend.'

Just at that moment Viola and Lara arrived with the rest of the crew. Jo was so relieved she nearly hugged them.

'Sorry we're late,' Viola greeted them cheerfully. 'Lara had a few calls to make. No sign of Marcus?' She looked round the bar.

'Last time I saw him he was taking Murphy for a walk along the cliff.' Richard glanced at his watch. 'We can't wait. He can join us later.'

By the time Marcus finally appeared, it was half past eight and they were already halfway through their starters. Jo eyed him with dismay as he weaved his way across the restaurant. He'd obviously been doing some serious damage to the mini bar.

'You're late,' Kate snapped. 'We've started without you.'

'Now how often has a woman said those words to me?' He flung himself into the empty seat next to Jo and reached for the wine bottle. Jo caught Richard's steely look and longed for the evening to end.

Unfortunately there was a long way to go before then. She pushed her fork around her plate, her stomach too taut with nerves and unhappiness to eat more than a couple of mouthfuls. Her wine glass sat untouched in front of her, while Marcus kept helping himself from the bottle, growing louder and more lively every minute. Meanwhile, everyone's smiles were growing more and more fixed.

Thankfully the meal finally ended and they all drifted into the lounge for coffee. Jo's heart sank when she saw Marcus weaving in behind her clutching a bottle of brandy.

'Thought we might need a chaser.' He collapsed in an armchair and beamed round the table. 'Well, this is nice, isn't it? Reminds me of my old prep school, with the headmaster keeping an eye on us all.' He topped up his glass and lifted it mockingly at Richard. 'Why are you here, by the way? Is this some kind of power kick for you, having us all bowing and scraping? Do you get off on it, or something?'

'Not as much as you get off on behaving like an arsehole, obviously,' Richard snapped. Even Marcus looked wary. Oh God, they're going to fight, Jo thought.

'What's all this? Looks like I arrived just in time.'

Never in a million years would Jo have imagined she would be pleased to see Charlie Beasley. But as he stood there, smiling like an insurance salesman, she could have kissed him. With him was a squat, bearded man, a camera slung around his neck.

'Don't let me stop you,' he beamed. 'But let me know if you're going to punch him, won't you? Tony would hate to miss the shot.'

Richard didn't take his eyes off Marcus. 'What do you want?'

'Just a couple of words with Marcus here. I wondered if you had any comment to make on this.' Charlie pulled a photo out of his pocket and handed it to Marcus. 'Recognise her?'

Marcus stared at it for a moment. Then, slowly, he tore it in two.

Charlie's smile didn't waver. 'I'm amazed you managed to keep it quiet for so long,' he said to Marcus. 'You covered your tracks well, I'll give you that.'

'Not well enough, obviously.' Marcus's smile didn't reach his eyes.

'Oh God, what's he done now?' Lara giggled. 'Robbed a bank?'

'He's married.'

'Bloody hell!' Viola gasped.

'B-but I don't understand,' Jo stammered. 'When—?'

'Seven years ago. It was seven years, wasn't it Marcus?' Charlie said.

'You tell me. I was stoned at the time.'

'She was the reason you were kicked out of your posh boarding school.' Charlie recited the facts gleefully. 'Little Samantha Frost. The caretaker's daughter. She was sweet sixteen.' He looked proudly round the table, like a conjuror who'd just produced a rabbit from a hat.

'Is this true?' Jo gasped.

'Probably.' Marcus stifled a yawn. 'Like I said, I was stoned at the time. I vaguely remember rushing off to the register office or something.'

'But why?'

'God knows. I think it had something to do with her not sleeping with me unless she had a ring on her finger.' He refilled his glass. 'Although as I recall it was all a bit of a wasted effort. She was fairly abysmal in the sack.'

'Or maybe you were just too stoned?' Richard muttered nastily.

'So why haven't you divorced her?' Kate wanted to know.

'Never got round to it. To be quite honest, I'd forgotten all about the silly little cow. We're not exactly on Christmas card-exchanging terms.'

'She could have divorced you, couldn't she? If you've been separated all these years—'

'That's just it, you see,' Charlie interrupted. 'They're not quite as separated as Marcus here likes to make out. Isn't that right, mate?'

'If you say so—*mate*.' Marcus's eyes narrowed dangerously.

'You see, Marcus likes to pay a visit to the marital home every so often. Just to claim his conjugals, so to speak.' Charlie beamed round at his audience. 'She lives somewhere on your dad's estate, doesn't she? Very handy, that. And of course Daddy picks up all the bills as usual.'

'That's enough.' Richard suddenly stepped in. 'You've got your story. I think you'd better go now.'

'But I just wanted—'

'Are you going to leave, or do I have to throw you out myself?' Richard rose from his seat. He looked so angry even Charlie wasn't going to take any chances.

'OK, OK, I'm going. Like you said, I got what I came for.'

There was a long, uncomfortable silence after he'd gone.

'Well, I don't know about you, but I could do with a drink.' Marcus reached for the bottle, but Richard stopped him.

'I think we've all had enough,' he said.

'But the party's just getting started—'

'Then I suggest you continue it in the privacy of your own room.'

They faced each other across the table. For a frightening moment Jo thought Marcus was going to argue, then he backed down.

'Fine.' He stood up. 'I don't much like the company here, anyway.' Grabbing the bottle, he stumbled towards the door.

The party broke up soon afterwards. Richard went up to his room and Kate announced she needed to go outside for some fresh air. Jo, Lara and Viola stayed in the bar to gossip about the evening's events.

'Can you imagine?' Viola said. 'I had no idea, did you?'

'I'm amazed no one found out sooner. I expect they've been trying to dig up some dirt on him ever since he started on *Westfield*.'

'They didn't have to dig very deep, did they?' Viola shook her head. 'Charlie Beasley must have thought all his birthdays had come at once.'

'Actually, when he first turned up I thought he'd come for me.'

They both turned to look at Lara. 'You? Why?'

'I'm getting a divorce.'

'Oh my God, how awful for you. What does Leon say about it?'

'He doesn't know yet. I've just been on the phone to my solicitor to sort it out. He says we've got irreconcilable differences.'

Jo turned to Lara. 'What kind of irreconcilable differences?'

'I dunno, do I?' she shrugged. 'That's just what my solicitor reckons. I think it's 'cos I want a record contract and he hasn't got me one.'

'Oh well, in that case I'm not surprised you want to get rid of the bastard.' Viola drained her glass. 'That's positively mental cruelty.'

Two gin and tonics later, Jo left them still mulling over Marcus's revelations and Lara's divorce plans, and went up to her room.

As she passed Marcus's door, she heard voices coming from inside the room that galvanised her and made her forget all thoughts of bed.

'You really are a bastard, aren't you? Why didn't you tell me you were married?' There was no mistaking that voice. Jo stopped to listen.

'I didn't think it was that important,' she heard Marcus drawl.

'Not important? Marcus, I'm carrying your child. Don't you think that gives me a right to know?'

Jo froze. Her blood turned to ice in her veins.

'My child? I thought it was Richard's?'

'Don't play games with me, Marcus. You know as well as I do that you're the father. I've checked my dates. It had to be Christmas.'

The Christmas Kate had supposedly been spending with her family. Jo felt sick.

'So maybe it *is* mine. So what? We've been through all this.' Marcus sounded bored. 'I told you to have an abortion. I've even offered to pay for it, for Christ's sake. What more do you want?'

'I want you to be with me. I want us to bring this baby up together. I love you.' Kate's voice was so pleading Jo might have felt sorry for her if she hadn't had the overwhelming urge to kill them both.

'And what about Richard?'

'I don't give a damn about Richard and you know it.'

'So why did you tell him he was the baby's father?' There was a long silence. 'Don't tell me, you were trying to make me jealous? Hoping I'd come forward and lay claim to my rightful heir?'

'It's not funny!' A sob caught in her throat. 'I thought you might at least do the decent thing.'

Jo pushed closer to the door. Next moment there was a *basso profundo* bark from inside and Murphy suddenly leapt from the bed and hurled himself at the door. Jo toppled backwards with a yelp of alarm as he began scratching at the woodwork from the other side.

'I think there's someone out there,' she heard Kate say.

Jo didn't wait to hear any more. She scrambled to her feet and searched in her bag for her key. Sod it, it wasn't there.

The door opened and Murphy flung himself at her, trapping her against the wall. Marcus stood in the doorway.

'Hi! I'm—er—just looking for my key,' she said feebly.

'Well, if you don't find it you can always sleep in my room.' He winked at her, whistled Murphy back inside and closed the door. Jo made a face at it. What a creep, flirting with one woman while he was breaking another's heart. Even if that woman was Kate, who frankly deserved everything she got.

'**B**limey, what have you been doing with yourself? I don't know if I'll have enough panstick to cover those shadows,' Madge the make-up artist greeted her cheerfully as she staggered into the caravan early the next morning. 'Hangover, is it?'

'Something like that.' Jo took her seat at the mirror. She had slept very badly, tortured by dreams of Marcus, Kate and Richard.

As Madge arranged a blue plastic cape round her shoulders and got to work backcombing and spraying her hair, Jo closed her eyes and tried to make sense of what she'd heard the previous night.

Kate and Marcus. It just didn't add up. They barely even liked each other, let alone anything else. Jo couldn't remember a time when they'd been in the same room without getting into a bitching session.

'Could you not screw your face up like that, lovey?'

'Sorry.' Jo tried to relax, but inside she was burning with anger. How could Kate be so selfish? She wasn't going to get away with it.

'Morning, everyone.' Marcus sauntered in, grinning all over his face as usual. 'Hi, angel.' He leaned over to kiss her, but she flinched away. 'Ooh, what's up with you?' He flopped into the chair next to hers. 'Thanks, darling.' He smiled appreciatively as one of the other make-up artists handed him a cup of coffee. 'God, I need this.'

'Tired, are you?' Jo looked sideways at him as Madge applied sweeps of pink blusher to her cheeks.

'Not especially. Why?'

'I just thought you might not have slept too well last night. Maybe your conscience was playing you up?'

His smile slipped a fraction. 'I slept like a log. I always do.'

'Well, I suppose you can, can't you? I mean, you've got no worries. Not like other people.'

'You *are* in a bad mood, aren't you?' Marcus did his best to sound light-hearted. 'What is this, Pick On Marcus Day or something?'

'Possibly. You see, unlike you I didn't sleep too well last night. I had a lot on my mind.'

'Anything in particular?' His eyes were wary.

'Just something I overheard.'

'There you are, lovey. All done.' Madge removed the plastic cape.

'Thanks.' As she slid out of the chair Jo's eyes met Marcus's in the mirror. His face, where the make-up artist hadn't sponged a thick layer of foundation, was satisfyingly pale. So he knew she knew. Now it was time for his lying bitch of a girlfriend to find out too.

She found Kate on a lounger beside the heated indoor pool.

'If you're looking for Richard, I think he's talking to the director.'

'It's you I wanted to see. Can I have a word?'

Kate stifled a yawn. 'So what is it you want, exactly?'

'The truth. Is this really Richard's baby you're carrying?'

'Of course it's Richard's. What a ridiculous question.'

'Then I must have got it wrong. You see, Marcus swore it was his.'

'He told you that? But I thought—' Then she saw Jo's face. 'Very clever,' she hissed. 'Well, so what? What difference does it make if it *is* Marcus's baby?'

'What difference does it make?' Jo stared at her, appalled. 'How could you do it? How could you lie to Richard like that?'

'Because who's going to support me if Richard doesn't?' Kate's voice was sharp. 'Marcus won't, he's made that very clear.'

'You could support yourself.'

'What, me and a kid on a glorified secretary's wages?' Kate uncurled herself from the lounger and stood up. 'It's all right for you. You're a celebrity. You don't have to live in the real world. Well, I do. I know what it's like to have to get by on sod all. It's humiliating and demeaning.' Jo watched in amazement as Kate transformed before her eyes. Her face took on a mean look, and her accent slipped into flat Yorkshire vowels that were more Hull than Home Counties. 'I'm not going back to that for anyone. And if it means telling a few lies, well, so what?'

'But you're ruining Richard's life.'

'Says who? He was happy with me before you came along.' She stopped. 'That's what all this is about, isn't it? You want him for yourself? You're in love with him!'

'Of course I'm not.' It hurt to deny it but she couldn't bear to admit her weakness to Kate. 'Richard and I were over before we'd even begun. I just don't want to see him hurt, that's all.'

'Oh yeah? And what can *you* do about it? Tell him?' Kate's eyes flashed with malice. 'That would be nice for him, wouldn't it? The whole world would know he'd been taken for a fool.'

'No one else need know.'

'Oh yes, they would. Because I'd tell them.' Kate's chin lifted in triumph. 'If you breathe a word of this to Richard I swear I'll go straight to every tabloid in town. I wouldn't need either of them then, would I? I'd be set up for life.'

'You wouldn't dare!'

'Try me. Now, if you don't mind, I need my rest. All this stress is very bad for baby.' She'd barely sat down before she was on her feet again. 'What was that? Did you hear someone moving about outside?'

Jo crossed over to the window and looked out. 'I can't see anyone.'

'What if there was someone out there?' Kate looked panic-stricken. 'They might have heard the whole thing.'

'Why should that bother you? Five minutes ago you were ready to sell your story to the highest bidder.'

'Exactly. And if it gets out I won't get a penny!'

Jo swung round, a red mist rising behind her eyes. Before she knew what she was doing, she had struck out at Kate. It wasn't a hard shove, but it caught her off balance. Jo watched in horrified fascination as, arms flailing, Kate toppled into the swimming pool.

'Bitch!' she screeched, when she finally surfaced, splashing and floundering. Jo could still hear her screams and curses halfway to the set.

CHAPTER TWELVE

'SO IT NOW GIVES ME great pleasure to declare Wisebuys of Wigginton officially open.' Jo cut the yellow ribbon that stretched across the doorway. A smattering of applause broke out, most enthusiastically from the manager at her side. He was a dapper little man in his fifties, with a boot-brush moustache and hair that was suspiciously black for his age.

Jo acknowledged the applause with a weak smile. After a tense two days filming in Robin Hood's Bay she was supposed to be taking some time off. She was so tired the last thing she'd wanted to do was drag herself out of bed on a Friday morning to open a supermarket. But she'd promised to do it weeks ago, and she didn't want to let anyone down.

'If you'd like to come this way, we're ready for the trolley dash.'

'I'm sorry?' Jo frowned at the manager.

'The trolley dash. The competition winners?' He tutted impatiently. 'We ran a promotional competition in the *Evening Press*. The winners get to keep whatever they can bung in their trolleys in two minutes.'

'Oh, I see. And you want me to start them off, do you?'

'No, I want you to take part. Your agent agreed it weeks ago,' he hurried on, sensing opposition. 'And I've got customers in there looking forward to it. I don't want to let them down.'

'OK,' she sighed.

'Oh, and there's just one more thing. We want you to wear this.' With a flourish, he produced something red, flaccid and rubbery from behind his back. Jo stared at it in dismay. It looked just like a—

'A Willy,' the manager explained. 'That's what we call them—Willies. After Wisebuys Willy, our mascot? He's a cock. It's a novelty hat, see. You put it on your head, like this.' He stretched it over his hands. It was like a swimming hat with a flabby cockscomb on top.

Oh God, what did it matter anyway? As long as it got her out of this hellhole. And the sooner the better.

The trolley-dash contestants, two women and a man in a Fair Isle cardigan, were already lined up, empty trolleys poised. They spared Jo the briefest glance as she took her place at the end of the row. Their eyes were already fixed on the shelves ahead, working out their strategy.

'Ready, everyone. On your marks, get set—GO!'

It was like the chariot race from *Ben Hur*. She was barely halfway up the canned goods aisle before the man in the cardigan veered across her path, sending her crashing into a display of tinned peaches. She struggled to her feet and, as she rounded the next corner, the two women closed in on her, smashing their trolleys into her ankles. Jo stopped, screaming with pain—and it was then that she spotted the newspaper stand.

'Watch it!' Cardie Man cannoned into the back of her as she stood, gripping her trolley handle to support herself, her eyes fixed on the front page of the *Globe*. *Exclusive! MY SECRET NIGHTS WITH MARCUS FINN—Woman at centre of* Westfield *love triangle speaks out.*

'Where do you think you're going?' The manager stepped into her path as Jo headed for the door. 'You can't go yet.'

'Watch me.' Jo ripped off the rubber hat and thrust it into his hands. 'You won't get your cheque.'

'I don't care.'

His voice followed her as she ran across the car park. 'I knew we should have paid the extra grand and got Dale Winton!'

It was a miracle she made it to the *Westfield* studio in one piece. She screeched into the car park, abandoned the Cinquecento at a careless angle, and made her way up to the top floor of the production centre.

A small crowd of script editors, directors and location managers had gathered round what had been Kate's desk. The temp was vainly trying to fight them off.

'I told you, I don't know anything,' she kept saying. 'Yes, I know you've got a meeting scheduled but I can't do anything about it if he's not here, can I?'

So Richard hadn't turned up to work. Jo didn't blame him. She took the lift back down to the ground floor. Louise might know where Richard was. It was the press officer's job to know everything, just so they could stop anyone else finding out.

'No, I don't know where he is, or when he's coming back.' Louise was hidden behind a toppling mound of newspapers, a phone clamped to each ear. 'No, there's no comment to make. Thank you.' She slammed both the phones down and looked up at Jo with murderous eyes. 'I suppose you're looking for Marcus too?'

'Well no, I—'

'I don't know where he is. I hope the lying bastard's burning in hell.' One telephone rang again. 'Oh fuck off!' She buried her face in her hands.

'Sounds like you need a break.' Jo came round to her side of the desk and slid her arm round Louise's plump, heaving shoulders. 'Come on, let's go to the canteen and see if we can bribe a coffee out of Joyce.'

They were lucky enough to get to the canteen during the ten-minute slot Joyce had decreed for serving beverages. Jo found them a quiet table in the corner and parked Louise there. 'So what's the problem? This isn't just pressure of work, is it?'

As Jo primed her with cappuccinos, Louise poured out her troubles. How she was still in love with Marcus, how deep down she'd always hoped he might come back to her. She was so naive Jo wondered how she'd managed to function on the same planet for so long.

'And all this time he and Kate were—together.' Louise blew her nose noisily on a scrappy tissue. 'I just can't believe it. I really thought it was you he liked. I was so jealous of you. That's why—' She broke off.

"That's why?' Jo prompted her gently.

She lifted large, swimming grey eyes to meet hers. 'That's why I—I tipped off the police that night at the hotel.'

'You did what?' Jo crashed her cup down. 'You mean it was you who told them we were taking drugs in that hotel room?'

'I didn't actually say it was you—'

'No, but I still got arrested! Do you know the trouble you caused? I spent a night in jail because of you!'

'I know, and I'm sorry. As soon as I'd done it I knew it was vindictive and stupid, but I just couldn't help myself. I'm so, so sorry,' she sobbed. 'I was so angry and upset—I just wasn't thinking.' She squared her shoulders. 'You'll be glad to know I've decided to resign.'

Jo looked at her puffy red face. Poor Louise. She was as much a victim as the rest of them. 'You don't have to do that.'

'But after what happened—'

'Look, Marcus Finn made us all look pretty stupid, one way or another. He's certainly not worth losing your job over. Let's just keep it our secret, shall we?'

'Are you sure? Oh, Jo!' Louise started sobbing again. 'I promise I'll never make you do another photo shoot as long as I live! I'll—'

'You could help me find Richard.'

'Richard? But why do you want—oh!' The truth dawned in her clear grey eyes. 'You don't mean you and he are—?'

'I don't know what we are.' Jo sipped her coffee. 'I just want to make sure he's OK, that's all.' She had another reason to see him, but she'd pushed that to the back of her mind.

Louise looked regretful. 'I wish I could help you but I don't know where he is. I went straight round to his flat this morning myself but there was no answer.'

'Maybe he just wasn't answering the door?'

'I thought that too, but then the concierge downstairs said he'd seen him putting some cases in his car two days ago. He hasn't seen Kate either. You don't think she and Marcus have run off together, do you?'

'I doubt it,' Jo said. 'Marcus was willing to leave her high and dry when he found out about the baby, so I doubt if he'd come rushing to her rescue on his white charger now—That's it!' She leapt to her feet.

'What is?'

'Something Marcus said once about Richard coming to rescue me on his white charger. God, I've been such an idiot. He's bound to be there.'

'Where? I don't follow you—'

'That's OK. Just make sure the press don't either.'

It was an effort of will and memory to work out where the cottage was. It took several wrong turns before Jo recognised the chocolate-box pretty village with its local store where she'd bought the newspapers that fateful day all those weeks ago.

She followed the twisting lane, straining her eyes for the half-hidden turning that led to the cottage. Then she spotted a flash of metallic dark green through the trees to her right. Richard's Audi.

As Jo manoeuvred in beside it, the adrenaline rush that had kept her going all the way over the Dales suddenly deserted her, and doubts began to set in. What if he didn't want to see her? What if—the horrible thought slowly dawned on her—he was more heartbroken and humiliated than she'd imagined, and had come down here to end it all?

'Richard!' Her trainers crunched across the gravel as she ran to the front door and hammered on it with both fists. 'Richard, it's me. Are you in there?' There was no answer. 'Richard, open this door!'

'Looking for me?' Jo nearly collapsed with relief as Richard emerged from around the side of the house, wearing an old workshirt, paint-spattered jeans and carrying a brush.

'Richard! Thank God you're all right.' She ran to hug him, but he backed away.

'I'm covered in paint,' he said. 'Any reason why I shouldn't be all right?'

'I was worried. I thought you might have done something stupid—'

'Bit late for that, isn't it? It seems to me I've already made an idiot of myself.' His eyes were hard and cynical. 'Well, as you can see, I'm all in one piece. So you can stop worrying about me, can't you?'

He turned and strode off. Bewildered, Jo followed him round to the back of the house. He was already halfway up a ladder, slapping paint on the wall in angry strokes. The smell of the emulsion made her feel sick.

'Richard, why are you so angry with me? What have I done?'

'It's what you didn't do.' He twisted round to face her. 'You knew, didn't you? About Kate and Marcus? Why didn't you tell me?'

Jo paled. 'How did you find out?'

'I heard you and Kate talking by the swimming pool. Very illuminating it was too. I learned a few things about both of you, I can tell you.' He snatched up his brush and started slapping on more paint.

'Richard,' Jo pleaded with his turned back. 'I wanted to tell you about Kate, but I couldn't. She threatened to go to the papers if I said anything. She said she'd make sure you were publicly humiliated—'

'And you really think I would have been that worried? Can you seriously imagine that I'd rather spend the rest of my life being duped than risk a day of people pointing and staring at me? Christ, I've lived through worse than that. I'm the Grim Reaper, remember? The man the tabloids love to hate?'

A lump rose in her throat. 'I—I'm sorry. I didn't think—'

'Or didn't care?'

'What's that supposed to mean?'

'Oh, come on, I heard what you said to Kate. You told her you didn't love me. Do you know how it felt, hearing you say that?'

'That's not true!' She strode across the garden towards the ladder, ignoring her stomach's heave of protest. 'Why do you think I came here today if I don't care about you?' Her eyes were level with his scuffed Timberland boots. 'I admit I should have told you about Kate. But you've got to believe me, I only did it to protect you. I thought you'd want your personal life kept quiet. Remember just after Christmas, when you were worried about the press getting hold of the story about your family?'

'That was different,' he said gruffly. 'I had to protect my brother. I don't give a damn about myself.'

'Yes, well, I didn't know that, did I? I made a mistake. I wish I *had* told you, then maybe we'd be facing all this together.' The smell of paint hit her stomach, which responded with a Mexican wave of nausea. 'Richard, do you think you could come down? I can't go on talking to your boot like this, and if I stay here much longer I think I'm going to be—'

Too late. Jo clamped her hand over her mouth and dashed off.

Thank God it was a false alarm this time. By the time Richard caught up with her she was on her hands and knees in the rose bushes.

'Sorry.' She sat back on her heels and disentangled her hair from the thorny branches. 'I seem to be making a bit of a habit of this lately.'

'Meaning?'

'What?' She squinted uncertainly at him.

'You said you've been making a habit of this. Maybe it's the fact that I've been living with someone who throws up on a regular basis, but is there something I should know?'

She looked up at him. There was no point in putting it off any longer. 'You'll probably find out eventually. I'm pregnant. And before you insult me by asking—yes, you're the father,' she went on, as Richard started to interrupt. 'I know, I'm an idiot, I should have told you I wasn't on the pill. But we were a bit too carried away at the time, if you remember?' She could feel herself blushing. This wasn't quite the way she'd envisaged breaking the news.

She wished he'd say something. 'Ironic, isn't it?' She forced some lightness into her voice. 'But don't worry, I'm not like Kate. I won't be slapping a paternity suit on you and demanding maintenance. It's my mistake and I'll take full responsibility.'

'A mistake? Is that how you see it?'

'Don't you?'

'No, I don't. But then I love you, and you obviously don't give a damn about me.'

'Of course I love you! Why else do you think I'm here?' Tears filled her eyes and spilled down her cheeks. 'I'm sorry, I can't help getting emotional. I seem to do that a lot lately too.'

'You're not the only one.' As he crouched down and folded her into his arms. 'Christ, you don't know how wretched I've been,' he muttered into her hair. 'When I heard you tell Kate you didn't love me—'

'I only said it because I didn't want her to feel she'd got the upper hand. I didn't know you were listening.'

'Thank God I was, or we'd still be in the same bloody mess now.' They held each other tightly. Jo felt as if she never wanted to let him go. 'What did Kate say when you confronted her?'

'Just what she'd threatened. I told her I was moving out and that if she wanted a man in her life she should talk to the baby's real father. At first she tried to say it could be mine, which we both knew wasn't really true. Then when she realised I wasn't buying her lies, she went ballistic. She said she wasn't leaving the flat and if I wanted to earn myself a few more juicy headlines by turning a pregnant woman out on the street, I was welcome to try.'

'What did you say?'

'Nothing. I told her I didn't care where she lived, as long as I didn't have to live under the same roof. Then I packed my bags and walked out. I presume she must have gone straight to Charlie Beasley, because the next thing I saw were the headlines in this morning's paper.'

'Ah, so you've seen those, have you?' They looked round. Charlie himself was fighting his way through the overgrown rosebushes towards them. 'Good, aren't they? Should shift a few copies.'

Jo felt Richard tense. 'What are you doing here?'

'More to the point, what are you?' Charlie's eyes gleamed behind his spectacles. 'I had no idea you and Jo had such a close—working relationship. I don't suppose I could have a piccie for the paper?'

Richard looked down at her, and she saw the unspoken question in his eyes. She smiled and nodded. At least their news might knock Kate off the front page.

'I think we can do better than that,' he grinned at Charlie Beasley. 'How would your paper like a *Westfield* exclusive?'

 EPILOGUE

'AND . . . CUT.'

Everyone on set relaxed. The chargehands moved in to gather up the cables as the cameramen moved into position for the next shot. Jo eased her bulk carefully out of her car seat. Pregnant women and Mini Travellers didn't go together. Neither did a thick 1960s angora coat and the hottest July day for thirty-odd years.

She smiled gratefully as a make-up girl descended with a cool sponge for her hot, perspiring face. At least they were working outside. Aberthwaite, the picture-book village where *Heartland* was filmed, was looking particularly glorious today, with rampant roses, clematis and honeysuckle spilling round every cottage doorway. Across the square, the rest of the cast were already gathering for lunch outside the Fox and Rabbit. Jo sighed longingly, wishing she could join them.

Working on *Heartland* couldn't have been more different to *Westfield*. She missed Viola, of course, but the cast and crew had made her feel really welcome. And best of all, as this was the last episode of the current series, she had a lovely long holiday to look forward to.

'Looks like you've got visitors.' The make-up girl nodded towards the other side of the square, where Chloe and Grace were running towards her. Richard was sauntering behind, looking relaxed and sexy in aviator sunglasses, black cords and a white T-shirt that showed off his newly acquired tan. He'd grown his hair slightly longer, which suited him.

'Not bunking off work again?' She squinted up at him teasingly.

'It seemed a shame to waste the day, especially with the girls being on school holidays. We thought we'd come and watch you work instead.' He lowered his shades so she could see the warm smoky grey of his eyes. 'We wondered if you fancied some lunch at the pub?'

'Please. You go over and order. I'll be with you when we've finished the next scene.'

Half an hour later they were sharing a plate of huge ham salad sandwiches under the overflowing hanging baskets. The air was fragrant with honeysuckle and old-fashioned roses. It was all sheer bliss.

'We've been shopping for the baby,' Grace announced excitedly.

'Again? It's not due for three months and it's already spoilt rotten.'

'But you should see what we've got him. Some tiny little jeans from Baby Gap. They've got fly buttons and everything.'

'Can we watch it being born?' Chloe asked. 'Matthew Watson in my class saw his little brother being born and he said it was better than a horror film.'

'We'll see.' Jo pushed the plate away, her appetite suddenly lost. 'Why don't you two go and play on the swings if you've finished eating?' As they rushed off, she said, 'They'll be selling tickets to their mates next.'

'Maybe we could organise a photo shoot with *Goss* magazine?'

Jo grinned. 'That reminds me. Did you see that piece in *Hello!*?'

'The four-page spread on Lara Lamont's life after divorce, you mean?' Richard shook his head wryly. 'You've got to hand it to the girl, she never misses an opportunity. Photo or otherwise.'

'So what else is new on *Westfield*? Is Ma Stagg still in her coma?'

''Fraid so. Doesn't look like she's coming out, either. Not unless Eva Lawrence agrees to her new contract.'

'I still can't believe you did that,' Jo giggled.

They sat in silence for a moment. Then Richard said, 'I saw Kate today.'

'Oh?' Jo's smile faded. 'How is she?'

'Hardly blooming. The baby's due in a few weeks and she's still chasing Marcus for money. No one's seen him since he walked out of *Westfield*. Kate seems to think he might be bumming round the States.'

Jo nibbled thoughtfully on a cucumber slice. 'That sounds like him. He's probably a rich woman's plaything over in Beverly Hills.'

'Leaving Kate to pick up the pieces,' Richard said. 'I know I shouldn't after what she did, but I can't help feeling sorry for her. That's why I agreed to let her stay on at the flat. I hope you don't mind?'

'Why should I?' Jo had no reason to resent Kate now. After all, she herself had everything she really wanted.

She gazed at Chloe, laughing and shrieking on the swings while Grace pushed her higher and higher, and smiled. She had Richard, and she had her family. Kate would never know that kind of happiness, because she didn't understand the value of it. 'I think she's been punished enough,' she said.

Charlie Beasley had seen to that. When Kate went to him with her story, she'd expected him to write about her as some kind of doomed romantic heroine. Instead, Charlie had done a bit of digging and come up with the story of Kathy Gilbert, the wannabe word-processor operator from Doncaster who'd shed her past, acquired a fake finishing-school accent and a designer wardrobe, and reinvented herself as the daughter of a wealthy Sussex family. To have her past exposed so cruelly was just about the worst fate Kate could have suffered.

'We're ready for your next scene, Miss Porter—sorry, Mrs Black.' The PA blushed at Richard. He had that effect on women, Jo realised. But strangely, he never seemed to notice.

She lumbered to her feet. Thank heavens they'd managed to shoot around her massive bulk with clever camera angles. 'Well, I suppose I'd better be going. Are you going back to work later?'

He shook his head. 'As it was such a nice day I thought they could manage without me.'

'They're having to do that quite a lot lately, aren't they?'

'And they'll have to do it a lot more in a few months' time. Didn't you know I was a New Man?'

'I sort of liked the old one.'

He grinned. Marriage hadn't changed the way that grin made her heart skip.

DONNA HAY

Donna Hay's lips are sealed when it comes to answering one of the most intriguing questions about *Kiss and Tell*—just who are the characters in her novel based on? And who exactly was the inspiration for her soap character, Brett Michaels, 'the sexiest man on TV', or for the wonderfully self-obsessed Lara Lamont? 'I can't answer that,' she says with a laugh. 'Let's just say I've taken bits and pieces from a lot of people. Journalists I know who work on television magazines keep asking, "Is so and so based on this character or that?" But I never comment,' she says discreetly.

As a freelance journalist who specialises in covering soap operas, Donna Hay is perfectly placed to write a behind-the-scenes novel about a soap opera. She is a regular feature writer for *What's On TV* magazine and since 1998 has had her own column in *TV Times*. Her first job in journalism was writing picture love stories for teenage magazines but she soon got sidetracked into feature writing. She became features editor of *Prima* magazine before eventually going freelance. But while she was working as a journalist she was also writing fiction in her spare time. She credits 'a bit of a midlife crisis' with giving her the push to finally achieve her dream of being a novelist. 'I'd been writing fiction for so long but not managing to find a publisher. I always comforted myself with the fact there was still time, after all, Catherine Cookson wasn't published until she was in her forties. And I

suddenly realised that I was edging towards that age myself. I decided that if I didn't get my first book published by the time I was forty I would give up. I joined the Romantic Novelists' Association's New Writers' Scheme, which gave me a deadline for finishing the book.' The scheme encourages new writers to submit a manuscript, which is then given a detailed critique by a professional writer or editor. Donna Hay sent in her first novel, *Waiting in the Wings*, and quickly found both an agent and a publisher. The novel went on to win the Romantic Novelists' Association's New Writers' Award in 1999.

She enjoys combining the two strands of her writing. 'I like the immediacy of feature writing, the fact that it's finished quite quickly. Whereas with a novel it can feel as if it is never going to end.' *Kiss and Tell* is her second novel but she has already completed her third, which is due out next year, and she is currently hard at work on her fourth.

Donna Hay lives in York with her husband and her daughter Harriet (pictured above with her mother), who was the inspiration for aspects of Grace and Chloe in *Kiss and Tell*. She was brought up in South London but moved north ten years ago. At first she missed London but now she thoroughly enjoys living in the North. 'It's a cliché but the pace of life up here really is much calmer.'

Sally Cummings

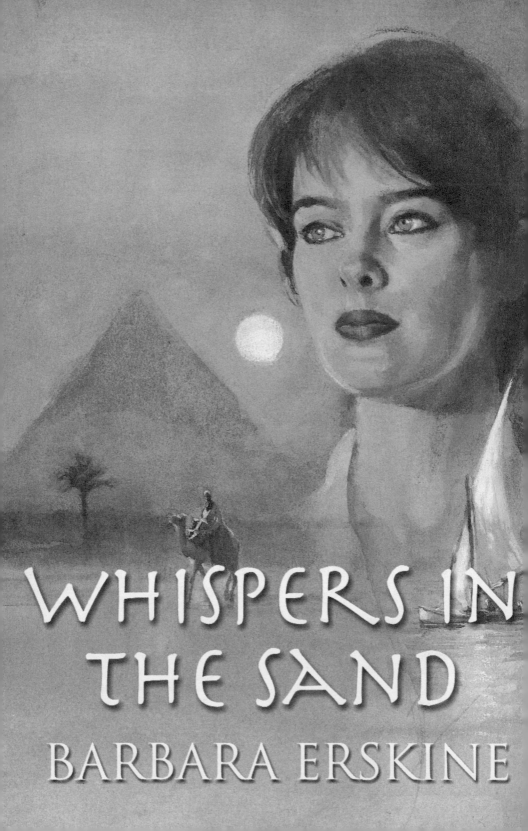

WHISPERS IN THE SAND

BARBARA ERSKINE

Over a hundred years ago, an intrepid woman

artist, Louisa Shelley, travelled down the Nile,

recording her journey in her paintings and her

diary. Now, her great-great-granddaughter, Anna,

retraces Louisa's cruise, reading the diary as she

travels, and is soon entranced by the passionate

Victorian love story that unfolds.

But as she reads on, Anna discovers a chilling

secret behind an ancient Egyptian scent bottle

that once belonged to Louisa. Anna has inherited

this bottle—has she also inherited its curse?

𓀀𓅱 ANCIENT EGYPT

IN THE COOL incense-filled heart of the temple the sun had not yet sent its lance across the marble of the floor. Anhotep, priest of Isis and of Amun, stood before the altar stone. He had lit the noon offering of myrrh in its dish and now watched as the wisps of scented smoke rose in the dimly lit chamber. Before him, in the golden cup, the sacred mixture of herbs and powdered gems and holy Nile water sat in the shadows waiting for the sun's ray to hit the jewelled goblet and fall across the potion. He smiled and raised his gaze to the narrow entrance of the holy of holies. A fine beam of sunlight struck the doorframe and seemed to hover in the hot shimmer of the air. It was almost time.

'So, my friend. It is ready at last.' The sacred light was blocked as a figure stood in the doorway behind him; the sun's ray bounced crooked across the floor, deflected by the polished blade of a drawn sword.

Anhotep drew breath sharply. Here in the temple he had no weapon. 'The sacrilege you plan will follow you through all eternity, Hatsek.' His voice echoed round the chamber. 'Desist now, while there is time.'

'Desist? When the moment of triumph is finally here?' Hatsek smiled coldly. 'You thought to waste the sacred source of all life on that sick boy pharaoh! Why, when Isis herself has called for it to be given to her?'

'No!' Anhotep's face had darkened. 'The goddess has no need of it!'

'The sacred potion distilled from the very tears of the goddess is hers, by right. She alone can renew the broken body of the pharaoh!'

'It is the pharaoh's!' Anhotep moved away from the altar. As his adversary stepped after him, the purifying ray of sunlight struck the crystal

303

surface of the potion, turning it to brazen gold. For a moment both men stared, distracted by the surge of power released from the goblet.

'So,' Anhotep breathed. 'The secret of life eternal is ours.'

'The secret of life eternal belongs to Isis.' Hatsek raised his sword. 'And it will remain with her, my friend!' With a lunge he plunged the blade into Anhotep's breast, withdrawing it with a grunt as the man fell to his knees. For a moment he paused as though regretting his hasty action, then he raised the bloody blade over the goblet, and in one great sweeping arc hurled it and the sacred potion it contained to the floor.

'For you, Isis, I do this deed.' Setting the sword down on the altar he raised his hands. 'None but you, oh great goddess, holds the secrets of life and those secrets shall be yours for ever!'

Behind him Anhotep, his bloodied hands clutching his chest, somehow straightened, still on his knees. He groped for the sword above him on the stone. Finding it, he dragged himself painfully to his feet and raised it with both hands. The point of the blade sliced between Hatsek's shoulder blades and penetrated down through his lung into his heart. He was dead before his crumpled form folded at the other man's feet.

Anhotep looked down in despair. At the base of the altar the sacred potion lay as a cool blue-green pool on the marble, stained by the curdling blood of two men. His breath coming in small painful gasps, he staggered across to a shelf in the shadow of a pillar. There stood the chrismatory, the small, ornate glass vial in which he had carried the potion to the holy of holies. He reached for it, his hands slippery with blood, and turned back to the altar. Falling painfully to his knees, he managed to scoop a little of the liquid back into the tiny bottle and pressed in the stopper as far as it would go. In one last stupendous effort he pulled himself up and set it back down on the shelf in the darkness.

By the time they found him lying across the entrance to the holy place, he had been dead for several hours.

It was the high priest's order that the two priests be embalmed and their mummies be laid inside the holy of holies, one on each side of the altar, and that it should then be sealed for ever. Then prayers were said for their souls, stipulating that they serve the Lady of Life in the next world as they had failed to serve her in this.

The two priests sleep in the darkness of the tomb. There is no sound. On the shelf between the pillar and the wall the small bottle sealed with blood lies hidden. Inside, the life-giving potion, dedicated to the gods, made sacred by the sun, thickens and grows black.

In the silence comes the sound of scraping, faint and far away. It is an intrusion, a sacrilege in the thick of the dark. The tomb robbers work without speaking, swiftly and with certainty that this at last is the place for which they have been searching for so long.

When the door cracks asunder and is levered from its place, there is no one there to protect the contents of the grave.

The mummies are carried out onto the sand. They are broken, desecrated, turned back to dust. In the corner, hidden, the tomb robbers find the bottle. They carry it outside into the desert, glance at it and toss it away. Glass by now is common. It has no value to the seeker after gold. When they leave the tomb lies open. The spirits of the dead feed on the sunlight and the silver blessing of the desert moon and grow stronger. But in the night the men who laid sacrilegious hands upon forbidden places encounter the servants of the gods. The gods will always protect the sacred vial of Isis's tears, and the robbers die, their bodies are eaten by jackal and crocodile as the judgment of the gods demands.

𓏤𓏤 ENGLAND, PRESENT DAY

'WHAT YOU NEED, my girl, is a holiday!'

Phyllis Shelley was a small, wiry woman with a strong, angular face, which was accentuated by her square red-framed glasses. Her hair cropped fashionably short, she looked twenty years younger than the eighty-eight to which she reluctantly admitted.

She headed for the kitchen door with the tea tray, leaving Anna to follow with the kettle and a plate of scones.

'You're right, of course.' Anna smiled fondly. Pausing in the hall, she stood for a few seconds looking at herself in the gilt-framed mirror. Her dark hair was knotted behind her head, bringing out the grey-green tones in her hazel eyes. She was slim, tall and classically good-looking, but her face was tired and thin and the crow's-feet round her eyes were deeper than they should have been for a woman in her mid-thirties. She sighed and pulled a face. She had been right to come. She needed a good strong dose of Phyllis!

Tea with her father's one remaining aunt was one of the great joys of life. The old lady was indefatigably young at heart—strong and clear thinking—and she had a wonderful sense of humour. In her present state, miserable, lonely and depressed, three months after the decree absolute, Anna needed a fix of all those qualities, and a few more besides. She turned to follow Phyllis out onto the terrace.

'You look well, Phyl.' Anna smiled across the small round table. It was a wonderful autumn day, leaves shimmering with pale gold and copper, the berries in the hedges a wild riot of scarlet and black.

Phyllis greeted Anna's remark with a snort. 'Considering I'm so old, you mean. Thank you, Anna! I am well, which is more than I can say for you, my dear. You look dreadful, if I may say so.'

Anna gave a rueful shrug. 'It's been a dreadful few months.'

'Of course it has. But there's no point in looking backwards.' Phyllis became brisk. 'Life, Anna, is to be experienced. Lived,' she said slowly, as she poured two cups of tea. 'It may not turn out the way we hoped. It may not be enjoyable all the time, but it should be always exciting.'

Anna laughed in spite of herself. 'The excitement seems to have gone out of my life at the moment.'

If it had ever been there at all. There was a long silence. She could feel Phyllis's eyes on her and she bit her lip, seeing herself through the other woman's critical gaze. Spoilt. Lazy. Useless. Depressed. A failure.

Phyllis narrowed her eyes. She was a mind-reader as well. 'I'm not impressed with self-pity, Anna. You've got to get yourself off the floor. I never liked that husband of yours. You married Felix too young. And I think you've had a lucky escape. You've still got time to make a new life. You're young and you've got your health and all your own teeth!'

Anna laughed again. 'You're good for me, Phyl. I need someone to tell me off. The trouble is I don't really know where to start.'

The divorce had been very civilised. There had been no unseemly squabbles; no bickering over money or possessions. Felix had given her the house in exchange for a clear conscience. He, after all, had done the lying and the leaving. And his eyes were already on another house in a smarter area, which would accommodate his new life and his new woman and their child.

For Anna, suddenly alone, life had become an empty shell overnight. Felix had been everything to her. Even her friends had been Felix's friends. After all, her job had been entertaining for Felix, running his social diary and keeping the wheels of his life oiled. She organised all the areas of his life that were not already organised by his secretary. And in order to maintain that organisation uninterrupted it was made clear, only after the fashionable wedding in Mayfair and the honeymoon in the Virgin Islands, that there would be no children. Ever.

They had married two weeks after she graduated from university with a good degree in modern languages. He was fifteen years older. That decision to stay on until she had finished her degree had been, she now suspected, the last major decision she had made about her own life.

She had two hobbies: photography and gardening. On both Felix allowed her to spend as much money as she liked and even encouraged her interest. Both were, after all, fashionable and relatively harmless, and she had allowed them to fill whatever gaps there were in her life.

Strangely, she had put up with his occasional indiscretions, surprised at how little they actually upset her, and suspecting but never admitting that this was because, perhaps, she did not love him quite as much as she ought to. Nevertheless, the news that his latest girlfriend was pregnant hit her like a sledgehammer. A torrent of rage and frustration broke over her head in a tidal wave, which terrified her as much as it shocked her husband. He had not planned this change in his life. He had expected to carry on as before, visiting Shirley, supporting her and the child, but not becoming too involved. His instant enchantment with the baby had shaken him as much as it had pleased Shirley and devastated Anna. Within days of the birth he had moved in with mother and child and Anna had consulted her solicitor.

'You must start with a holiday, Anna dear,' Phyllis was saying. 'Change of scene. You need to go somewhere exciting. Meet new people. In fact you need to go to Egypt.'

'Egypt? Why Egypt?'

'Because when you were a little girl you talked about Egypt all the time. You had books about it. You drew pyramids and camels and ibises and you pestered me, every time I saw you, to tell you about Louisa.'

'You're right. And I haven't thought about her for years.'

'Then it's time you did. I think you should go out there and see the places Louisa saw. When they published some of her sketchbooks ten years ago I was tempted to go myself.' She smiled. 'She was an amazing woman, your great-great-grandmother,' Phyllis went on. 'Amazing, brave and very talented.'

Frowning, Anna considered Phyllis's words, aware that the old lady's beady eyes were fixed unswervingly on her face.

'Well?' she said.

Anna smiled. 'You know, I think I might just take your advice. I haven't exactly got a lot of pressing plans.'

Phyllis sat back in her chair. Closing her eyes, she turned her face to the sun and a small smile played across her features. 'Good. That's settled then.' There was a pause, then she went on, 'This is heaven. There is no nicer time of the year than the autumn.' Her eyes opened again and she studied Anna's face. 'Have you spoken to your father yet?'

Anna shook her head. 'He hasn't rung me since the divorce. I don't think he'll ever forgive me for separating from Felix.'

'Silly man.' Phyllis sighed. 'He's got more and more impossible since your mother died and that's a good ten years ago now! Don't let it upset you too much, darling. He'll come round.'

Anna looked away. She was not going to cry. By now, she should have got used to her father's insensitivity and his blatant lack of interest in her, his only child. She sniffed hard, realising suddenly that Phyllis had disappeared back into the house.

Phyllis was only gone two minutes. 'I have something here that might interest you.' She did not look at Anna as she sat down once more. She had dropped a package onto the table in front of her. 'A few months ago I decided to have an old desk restored. The veneers had lifted badly.' She paused. 'The restorer found one of the drawers had a false bottom and inside he found that. It's Louisa's journal.'

'Really?' Anna took the packet and stared at it in sudden excitement. 'But that must be incredibly valuable!'

'I expect so. And interesting.'

'You've read it?'

Phyllis shrugged. 'I had a quick look at it, but the writing is very difficult and my eyes aren't so good these days. I think you should read it, Anna. It's all about her months in Egypt.'

The diary was on the back seat of the car when it was time to leave. The last crimson rays of the sunset were fading as Anna climbed in and, reaching for the ignition, looked up at her aunt. 'Thank you for being there. I don't know what I'd do without you.'

Phyllis shook her head in mock anger. 'You would cope very well indeed, as you know. Now, book that holiday. Promise?'

'I'll think about it. I'll promise that much.'

'Have you been to Egypt before?' the man in the seat beside her asked.

It was nearly four months since that glorious autumn day in Suffolk, but now, at last, she was on her way. Outside, the ground staff at Gatwick were completing the final checks on the loading of the plane.

Anna did not look up from her guidebook. 'No, I haven't.' She tried to sound unenthusiastic without being downright rude. She did not relish being trapped into conversation with whoever destiny had chosen to be her neighbour on the plane.

'Nor me.' She felt him glance at her sideways, but he said no more, groping in the bag by his feet for his own reading material.

Anna risked a quick look to her left. Forties; sandy hair, regular features, long eyelashes. She was suddenly sorry she had been so curt. But there was plenty of time to make up for it if she wanted to.

It was hot and stuffy on the plane and her head ached. She couldn't move in the closely packed seats and she could feel the arm of her neighbour wedged tightly against her own. She leaned forward and reached into the bag at her feet and brought out Louisa's diary. She had been saving it to read on the trip. Perhaps this was the moment to start.

The paper of the leatherbound notebook was thick, deckle-edged and in places foxed with pale brown spots. Carefully she turned to the first page of florid italic script and began to read.

February 15th, 1866: And so, the boat has reached Luxor and tomorrow I leave my companions to join the Forresters on the Ibis, *which I see already tied up nearby. It will be wonderful at last to have some privacy especially after the constant chatter of Isabella and Arabella with whom I have had to share a cabin all these weeks from Cairo. I am sending a packet of sketches and paintings back with them on the boat and hope to start a new series of drawings of the Valley of the Tombs as soon as possible. The British consul has promised me a dragoman, and the Forresters are said to be a kind, elderly couple who will allow me to travel with them willingly, without too much interference to my drawing. I long to be able to see more of the desert. The nervous excitement of my companions so far on this adventure has prevented us from venturing any distance from our boat and I cannot wait to begin my explorations further afield.*

Anna looked up thoughtfully. Imagine the frustration of not being able to explore because your companions were too nervous. Shifting a little in her seat to try to make herself more comfortable, she turned back to the diary.

'Louisa, dear. Sir John Forrester is waiting for you on the deck.' Arabella bounced into the small cabin in a froth of white lace and cambric. 'He has come to take you across to his dahabeeyah.'

Gripping her voluminous skirts tightly in one hand, Louisa climbed the companionway steps and emerged into the sunlight.

Sir John Forrester was a tall, skeletally thin man in his late sixties. Dressed in a heavy tweed jacket, plus fours and boots, he turned to greet her, his white pith helmet, the only concession to the climate, in his hand. 'Mrs Shelley? How very nice.' His bow was courteous, his eyes brilliant blue beneath bushy white eyebrows. He greeted her companion then instructed the two dark-skinned Nubians with him to remove her luggage to the felucca drawn up alongside the paddle steamer.

Now the moment had come, Louisa felt a small pang of nervousness. She had shaken hands one by one with the men and women who had been her companions over the last few weeks, nodded to the crew, tipped her cabin servants, and at last she was turning towards the small sailing boat which would ferry her across to the *Ibis*.

Sir John followed her down the ladder and within seconds the boat was heading across the turbid water towards the *Ibis*. Behind her, Arabella lingered on deck, her face shaded by her pink parasol, and waved at Louisa's departing back.

The *Ibis* was a graceful vessel propelled by two great lateen sails and steered from the back by a huge tiller. The elegant accommodation, Louisa had soon discovered, included cabins for herself, the Forresters and Lady Forrester's maid; a saloon filled with divans and a large writing table; and quarters for the crew.

This time she was to have a cabin to herself. Tearing off her hat she flung it on the bed and looked around approvingly. After the dark wood and brass fittings of the paddle steamer this cabin, tiny though it was, was beauty itself. Her narrow bed was spread with brightly coloured woven fabrics, there was a carpet on the floor, fine blue and green shawls were draped across the window, and the basin and ewer were made of beaten metal.

Of Lady Forrester there had been no sign. 'Indisposed, my dear. She'll join us for dinner,' Sir John had said vaguely as he showed Louisa to her cabin. 'We'll sail as soon as possible. Not far. We'll tie up on the other side of the river so you can set off for the valley tomorrow. Hassan will be your dragoman. He will act as your guide and interpreter. Good chap. Highly recommended.' He smiled knowingly. 'And you'll have to share Jane Treece, Lady Forrester's maid. I'll send her in to you directly.'

And here she was, a woman of about forty-five, with hair pulled severely off her face beneath her cap, dressed, like her, in black. 'Good evening, Mrs Shelley.' The woman's voice was deep and educated. 'Sir John has asked me to act as your maid and chaperone.'

Louisa hid her despair as best she could. She had hoped to be free of such formality. It would, though, be helpful to have someone unpack her dresses. Her sketchbooks and her precious watercolour box, her paintbrushes, she would allow no one to touch but herself.

Turning, she stared at the evening gown which Jane Treece laid out for her. Her vision of casting aside her corset and petticoats, and the formal black which her mourning demanded, and putting on the blessedly cool, softly flowing dresses made for her all those long months ago in London, were beginning to recede once more. 'I had assumed we would be more casual on so small a boat,' she said cautiously.

'Indeed.' The word conveyed shock, scorn and such superiority that Louisa was in no doubt that her assumptions had been dreadfully mis-judged. 'Sir John and Lady Forrester keep every formality on the *Ibis*, Mrs Shelley, I assure you,' Jane Treece said. 'Sir John's man, Jack, and I see to it that everything runs as well here as it does at home in Belgravia.'

Louisa bit her lip to hide a wry smile. Trying to look suitably chas-tened she allowed the woman to help her on with her gown and pin her hair up in loose ringlets beneath a black lace veil.

The main saloon of the boat was as exotic as her own cabin, but the silver and china laid on the table for dinner was English. The food itself, though, was Egyptian, and delicious. Louisa ate with enjoyment as she explained to the Forresters why she wanted to paint the Egyptian scenery. Augusta Forrester had emerged from her own quarters looking as elegant as if she were entertaining at home in London. A small, silver-haired woman in her early sixties, she had managed to retain a pretti-ness of feature and a charm which made her immediately attractive. Her attention span was, though, Louisa discovered quickly, very short.

'When Mr Shelley died,' Louisa explained as they ate, 'I found myself lost.' How could she ever tell them how lost without her beloved George? She had contracted the same fever that had killed her husband and, although she had recovered, it had left her too weak and too listless to care for her two sons. They had gone to stay with George's mother, and Louisa had been persuaded that a few months in a hot climate would restore her to health. She and George had planned to come to Egypt one day. It was George who had regaled her with stories of the temples and tombs that were being discovered in the desert.

Glancing from Sir John to his wife, Louisa saw that the latter was no longer listening to her, but the mention of Augusta's nephew, Edward, brought her back from her daydreams, and for a few minutes she sat attentively as her guest described how that young man, a friend of George's, had rescued her, arranged her passage, and persuaded his uncle and aunt to take her to see the excavations. Without his help, she would have been destroyed.

His uncle and aunt were, however, not quite as unconventional as their nephew, and her dreams of conversation and laughter, and the convivial travel that she and George had so often discussed, were far from what the Forresters had in mind.

Anna looked up. Her neighbour appeared to be asleep. Beyond the thick glass of the window, the distant ground had turned the colour of red and ochre and gold. The colours of Africa. With a tremor of excitement, she stared down for a long time before leaning back in her seat and opening the diary again. Skimming down the cramped, slanted writing in its faded brown ink, she flipped through the pages, glancing at the sketches that illustrated the narrative.

Hassan brought the mules at first light so that we could escape the worst of the heat. He loaded all my painting equipment into the panniers without a word, and we rode to the valley without speaking.

Anna rubbed her eyes wearily. She turned on a few pages.

I saw him again today—just a faint figure in the heat haze. A tall man, watching me, who one minute was near me and the next minute was not there. I called out to Hassan but he was asleep, and by the time he had reached my side the man had vanished into the strange shimmer thrown by the heat of the sand. I am beginning to feel afraid. Who is he and why does he not approach me?

That sounded exciting. Exciting and mysterious. With a small shiver, Anna looked up with a start to see that her neighbour was looking down at the diary on her knee with evident interest. Anna sighed. His glance was an invasion of her space, an intrusion. Closing the diary, she forced herself to look up and smile. 'Not long now.' She turned towards him. 'Are you going on a cruise too?'

He was an attractive man, she realised, but even as she thought it his face closed and she saw it harden and the warmth vanished.

'I am indeed, but I very much doubt it is the same one as you.' His accent was difficult to place, very faint—slightly Scots perhaps— because that was all he said. He turned away from her, and putting his head back against the seat closed his eyes once more.

She felt a surge of anger and resentment. Well, that had certainly put her in her place. Turning abruptly towards the window she stared out, astonished to find that far below them it was already dark. In the distance, she could see lights. They would soon be arriving at Luxor.

By the time she had been through passport control and retrieved her suitcase, Anna was exhausted. She hung onto her case, grimly waving away the offers of help from a surge of gesticulating, shouting, would-be porters, and joined the queue for the bus.

A hasty glance round the bus showed her that her neighbour from the plane was not there. She wasn't sure if she was relieved or sorry. She had not enjoyed his rudeness. On the other hand his would at least have been a familiar face among all these strangers. Was she the only person there on her own? It seemed like it as she sat down on a seat towards the back. She gazed out into the darkness feeling suddenly bleak and lonely, and then realised with an excited sense of shock, which put all thoughts of her loneliness out of her head, that beyond the reflections of the bus windows she could see palm trees, and a man in a white turban perched on the rump of a tiny donkey that was trotting along the road in the dark.

The *White Egret* was a small boat, a Victorian paddle steamer accommodating eighteen passengers. It was moored on the outskirts of the town. They were welcomed with hot towels for their hands and a drink of sweet fruit juice, then they were given their cabin keys.

Her cabin was small but adequate, her case already waiting for her in the middle of the floor. Her new domain provided her with a single bed, a bedside locker, a dressing table and a narrow wardrobe. It was scarcely luxury, but at least she did not have to share it with a stranger. Throwing her holdall, camera and shoulder bag down on the bed, she closed the door and quickly unpacked, laying out her few cosmetics on the dressing table. Among them she stood her little Egyptian perfume bottle—it had seemed only right to bring it to the land of its origins. About three inches high, the glass was a deep, opaque blue, decorated with a thick white-feathered design, the stopper sealed with shaped wax, pushed flush with the top. Phyllis had given it to her when as a child it had caught her fancy, and it had stayed with her ever since.

There was time for a quick shower before dinner. Throwing off her clothes, she turned and ducked into the little bathroom. She stood for five minutes beneath the tepid trickle of water, letting it wash away the weariness of the journey, before forcing herself out of her reverie and reaching for her towel.

Pulling it round her, she stepped back into her room. The temperature in the cabin had dropped. Shivering, she stared round, puzzled. There was no air-conditioning control that she could see. Pulling on her green cotton shift and slinging a lightweight sweater round her shoulders, she stopped in her tracks again, frowning. There was definitely something odd about the temperature in the room. Shrugging, she gave one more glance round the cabin and then she headed for the door.

This was the moment that she was dreading. She had to go out and meet the other passengers, her first sortie into life as a single woman once again. With a deep sigh she let herself out into the carpeted corridor outside and, noting with relief how warm it was, began to make her way to the dining room.

She found herself seated at one of three round tables, each of which accommodated six people. Beyond the windows she could see nothing of the land or the river she had come so far to visit. The only sign of Egypt was the appearance of a solemn procession of waiters, dark-skinned, dressed in white—two or three per table at least.

Her companions were, to her relief, immediately friendly. Next to her on her left she found herself shaking hands with a good-looking man of about her own age. He stood up as he greeted her, and she saw he was no taller than herself, but his broad shoulders and stocky frame gave the impression of size. 'Andy Watson, from London.' He smiled, hazel eyes bright with humour beneath dark lashes and bushy brows. 'Unattached, available, charming, with an absolute passion for all things Egyptian, as I suspect have we all, because that's why we're here.'

Anna found herself laughing. A little shyly she introduced herself as a divorcée also from London, recklessly meeting his eyes for a moment before she turned to greet the tall, thin man with mousy hair, almost gaunt features and the palest blue eyes who sat on her right.

'There are five of us on the cruise.' Andy leaned across her, reclaiming her attention. 'That's Joe Booth next to you, he's something in the City, and beyond him is his wife Sally, and this'—he indicated the slim, red-headed young woman on his left—'is Charley, who is sharing a cabin with Serena, over there.' He nodded at a woman seated with her back to them at the next table. The sixth person at the table, the only one there apart from her who appeared to know no one on the cruise, introduced himself as Ben Forbes, a retired doctor. He and Andy were, it appeared, sharing a cabin. He was, she guessed, in his late sixties, a large, florid man with small, bright, observant eyes, a wild thatch of greying hair and a rumbustious laugh that proved to be infectious.

As they were waiting to be served, their tour guide, Omar, came to the table and introduced himself. 'Welcome. Tomorrow we start with our tour to the Valley of the Kings. Karnac and the Temple of Luxor itself we shall visit on the last day of the cruise. Tomorrow we get up very early. We cross the river on the ferry, and then we go on a bus. The schedule will be posted each day at the top of the stairs, outside the lounge.' A strikingly handsome young man, who, when he was not working as a tour guide, was studying history at Cairo University, he glanced round at them and smiled. 'Please, if you have any problems come to me at any time.' He bowed and moved on to the next table.

Watching him, Anna saw him introduce himself to each of them in turn, then she noticed the man next to whom he was now standing. It was the man who had sat next to her on the plane; he must have been on the bus after all. She suppressed a quick feeling of triumph that she was after all on the same cruise as he was!

'Seen someone you know?' Andy asked.

She shook her head. 'He sat next to me on the plane, that's all.'

'I see.' Andy stared over his shoulder, then he turned back to her. 'So. It's brave of you to travel out here on your own. What made you decide to come to Egypt after dumping hubby?'

She winced. 'It is as you said. I have a passion for things Egyptian, if that's not putting it too strongly. My great-great-grandmother was an artist called Louisa Shelley. She came out here in the late 1860s—'

'Louisa Shelley? The watercolourist?' She had his attention completely now. 'I sold one of her sketches not six months ago!'

'Sold?' Anna frowned.

'In my shop. I deal in fine art and antiques.' He smiled at her.

Beyond him Charley leaned forward and smacked him on the wrist. 'No shop, Andy, please. You promised.' She surveyed Anna warily. 'Don't encourage him!'

Anna noticed that Charley's hand was touching Andy's. So, he was not as unattached as all that. She would have to be careful. 'If you're interested in art and antiques, perhaps I should show you my Ancient Egyptian scent bottle!' She smiled.

Andy leaned back in his chair, his head cocked on one side. 'Genuine Ancient Egyptian?' He waited attentively.

She shrugged. 'Well, it came from Louisa and I think she thought it was. I have her diary with me. I'll see if she mentions where she found it. I just thought it would be fun to bring it with me. Back to the place of its origin, as it were.'

'Indeed.' Andy watched as a Nubian waiter approached with their soup. 'You must show it to me some time. And I would love to see Louisa Shelley's diary. Are there any sketches in it, by any chance?'

Anna nodded. 'A few, tiny thumbnail ones. She did most of her sketches in the special sketchbooks she had with her.'

She was aware suddenly that at the next table the man from the plane had realised she was there. He was staring at her with such attention that she suspected he had been listening to their conversation. She gave him a small smile in acknowledgment—and saw him nod in return.

'Your flight companion has spotted you, I see.' Andy was amused.

'So it seems.' Anna picked up her spoon. The soup was made of vegetables, thin and lightly seasoned, but tasty. 'He was fascinated by the diary. I was reading it on the flight and he couldn't keep his eyes off it.'

'Indeed.' Andy's eyes narrowed slightly. 'Anna, you will take care of it, won't you? I'm sure it must be extremely valuable.' His eyes on her face were concerned, sincere.

For the first time in ages, Anna felt a small rush of grateful happiness. He actually seemed genuinely interested in what she was saying. 'You are not suggesting that he would try to steal it?'

'No, of course not. I'm sure he was just curious. A manuscript diary is not the usual airport reading.' He leaned back in his chair and beamed at Anna, before picking up a bottle of wine and slopping a little into his glass. He raised it to his nose speculatively. 'This may be a mistake. One should really stick to beer in Egypt unless one wants to buy French wine. Not bad, I suppose. Want some?' He reached for her glass.

'I'm beginning to suspect that this is not your first trip to Egypt,' Anna said. 'I'll know who to ask for advice.'

'Indeed you will.' He winked. 'Now, finish that soup. I can see the hors d'oeuvres waiting to come in.'

When the meal was at last finished almost all the passengers made their way up to the lounge bar and some of them, thence, through the double doors out onto the deck. As Anna stepped out into the darkness, and threaded her way aft between the tables and chairs, she could hear Andy and Charley laughing together in the bar. She leaned on the aft rail. The river was broad at this point, though she could see little in the darkness. The only sound came from the occasional slap of water against the mud.

'So, it appears we are on the same cruise after all.' The voice at her elbow made her jump. 'Forgive me for doubting your good taste.'

Turning, she saw the lanky frame and sandy hair. He was leaning over the rail, not looking at her, lost in thought. He turned and held out his hand. 'My name is Toby. Toby Hayward.'

'I'm Anna Fox.' His handshake was firm but brief.

They both stared out into the darkness for several moments. 'You know, I am finding it hard to believe I am actually here,' Anna said softly. 'Somewhere out there in the darkness is Tutankhamun's tomb, and ancient Thebes, and beyond that the heart of Africa.'

There was a chuckle. 'A romantic. I hope you're not disappointed.'

'No. No, I won't be.' Suddenly she was on the defensive. 'It is going to be wonderful.' Turning away from him, she ducked into the lounge.

Andy spotted her at once. 'Anna! Come on, let me buy you a drink.'

She shook her head with a smile. 'Thank you, but I think I'll turn in. We've an early start tomorrow.'

She was conscious that the door behind her had opened and Toby had come in. Ignoring the other passengers he walked straight through the lounge and out towards the cabins.

She followed him slowly, not wanting to catch him up as he headed for the staircase, but there was no sign of him as she made her way to her door and let herself in.

It no longer looked bleak and impersonal inside. Nor was it cold. It was warm and inviting, the bedside light on and the bed turned down. Her own belongings made the place look welcoming and friendly. The little perfume bottle, in place of honour on the dressing table, was reflected in the mirror. Suddenly she was very happy.

The diary was waiting for her by her bed. Perhaps, before she fell asleep, she would read a little more and find out how Louisa had first experienced the Valley of the Kings, then tomorrow she would know what to expect.

Louisa was ready at dawn. Hassan was waiting on the bank with three mules. Food, water and her painting equipment had been loaded into the panniers on one and Hassan helped her onto one of the others, then, keeping a firm grip on the leading reins of both, climbed onto his own. Of the Forresters or Jane Treece there was no sign. Louisa hid a smile of relief. They were going to manage to escape.

The Forresters had not so far proved to be the hosts she had hoped for. They saw no reason to visit the antiquities and, more importantly, they seemed to feel that they were responsible for Louisa's moral welfare. Though a dragoman had been hired for her she was not to be alone with him. In near despair of ever visiting the Valley of the Kings, Louisa had had to resort to secrecy. She had found Hassan sitting in the shade of the deck awning, writing in his own small notebook, and whispered instructions in his ear. Well aware that Lady Forrester might at the last minute insist on Jane Treece accompanying her as a chaperone, Louisa had told her that she would not leave until mid-morning. To Hassan she explained privately that they must leave at dawn.

She had woken while it was still dark, climbing into her clothes as silently as she could. She had discovered her dragoman to be a quiet, refined man. His loyalties, he made clear immediately, were to Louisa alone. Wherever she wanted to go he would take her.

'Does he have a name?' Louisa patted her animal's neck as they set off.

Hassan shrugged. 'I don't know. I hired them for the journey.'

'He must have a name. I'll call him Caesar. How does that sound?'

Hassan smiled across at her as they rode away from the riverbank and turned out of sight of the *Ibis*. 'That is a good name. I shall call mine

Antony. And this our beast of burden shall be Cleopatra.'

Louisa laughed in delight. 'Then we shall be such an intelligent party.' He was a good-looking man, of middle height, slim, dressed in loose blue trousers and a striped robe. Looking across at him surreptitiously, she wondered how old he was. It was hard to tell. His hair was hidden completely by his red turban and, apart from laughter creases around his large dark eyes, his skin was smooth.

'How far must we ride to the valley, Hassan?'

He shrugged. 'We will know when we get there. We have all day.' His smile was warm and without guile.

Louisa laughed. In Egypt, she had discovered, things happened when they happened. That was the will of God. With a contented sigh she settled onto the felt saddle and concentrated instead on trying to accommodate herself to her mule's pace.

They stopped briefly for a breakfast of slices of watermelon and cheese and bread before the sun was too high, then they rode on. The road grew steeper as they made their way into the hills, and eventually they turned into the hidden valley where she could clearly make out the square doorways cut in the brilliant limestone cliffs. Drawing to a standstill, Hassan slid off his mule and helped her to dismount. As she stood staring round, listening to cries of the circling kites, he unloaded her sketchbooks and paints and a Persian rug, which he spread nearby on the sand. He also produced some poles over which he draped a length of green and blue striped cloth to make her a shelter.

'I expected to see people digging. Excavating. Why is it all so empty?' She was overwhelmed by the desolation of the valley.

He shrugged. 'Sometimes there are a lot. Sometimes none. The money stops. Then they have to go away to find more. Then they return. Then you will see the wadi full of people.' Again the shrug of the shoulders she was beginning to know so well.

Digging into his mule's pannier he produced two candles and a small flare. Flourishing them he bowed. 'You would like to see inside one of the tombs now?'

She nodded. The tombs would be cool after the endless sun.

'We will start here.' He waved at one of the entrances. 'It is the tomb of Rameses VI. This has been open since the days of the ancients.'

As they entered the passageway, Louisa stared into the darkness and was completely blinded after the brilliant light outside. Then, slowly, her eyes began to acclimatise. The flickering light of Hassan's candle barely lit the walls of the long passage in which they found themselves, but then he lit the flare and in the streaming flame and smoke she could see hieroglyphs and gods and kings covering the walls and ceiling in rich colours. Standing still on the steep, sandy floor of the passage, she stared round in amazement and delight. 'I had no idea,' she gasped. 'No idea at all that it could be so. . .' she fumbled for words '. . .so wonderful!'

'Nice?' Hassan was watching her.

'Very nice.' She took a few paces forward, her shoes slipping on the steeply sloping passage. 'More wonderful than I had ever dreamed.'

The intense silence of the place was overwhelming, but far from being cooler in the darkness the tomb was as hot and airless as an oven.

They began to descend a long flight of roughly excavated steps. The candlelight condensed on the multicoloured walls, then as they reached the pillared chamber at the bottom it spread and faded again, mixing and losing itself in the vast darkness. A further series of passages led deeper and deeper into the dark, until at last they reached the burial chamber. Louisa stopped with a gasp. Soaring overhead in the flickering shadows two huge figures spanned the ceiling above her head.

'Nut. Goddess of the sky.' Hassan was standing beside her, holding the flare high, and she found herself suddenly intensely aware of his closeness to her. She glanced sideways. He was gazing up at the figures, his face a silhouette in the soft light.

He turned and caught her staring at him. She blushed. 'May I have the flare?'

'Of course, Sitt Louisa.' For half a second their hands touched as her fingers closed round the wooden shaft. Then abruptly she stepped away from him. 'Tell me about the goddess of the sky.'

Anna woke with a start to find the light in her cabin still on, the diary lying open on her chest. Daylight poured in through the slatted shutters, sending bright narrow wedges of light onto the floor. Leaping out of bed she slid the shutters back. Outside, the river was a brilliant blue, and on the distant bank she could see the palm trees, a strip of brilliant green fields, and beyond them in the distance a line of low hazy mountains, pink and ochre in the early morning sunlight.

Dressing quickly in a blue shift, she made her way up onto the deserted deck. She walked to the rail and leaned on it, staring in delight at the palm trees on the far side of the river. It was several minutes before she could bring herself to turn her back on the view and head down for the dining room and breakfast. At the door she met Serena, Charley's cabinmate, who the night before had been sitting at the next-door table.

About forty-five, slim and attractive with short, dark hair and huge, green eyes, she gave Anna a cheerful smile. 'See you later,' she said by way of hello and goodbye. She held the door open for Anna, then disappeared in the direction of the cabins. In the dining room only Charley was sitting at the table they had all shared the night before.

'Good morning.' Anna sat down near her. 'How did you sleep?'

'Not a wink.' Charley scowled. She was nursing a cup of black coffee. She sighed. 'I hate flying and I hate boats.'

Anna hid an astonished smile. She resisted the temptation to ask why, in that case, Charley had come on such a holiday, asking instead, 'Have the others had breakfast?'

Charley nodded. 'All early birds.' She gave Anna a sideways glance. 'Andy and I are an item, we've been together for several months.'

Anna watched while the waiter poured her coffee, then she stood up ready to go to the buffet laid out on the serving table. 'I thought perhaps you were.' She smiled. Charley's comment was a clear warning shot across the bows. Yet hadn't Andy said he was unattached? Piling up fruit and cheese and a delicate crumbling croissant onto her plate, she turned back to the table. Charley had gone.

Returning to her cabin to collect her sunhat, glasses and guidebook, Anna stood for a moment staring round. She had left the diary on the bedside locker. Hesitating briefly, she swung her suitcase down from the top of the wardrobe where she had stowed it, and put the diary inside. Locking it, she lifted it back into place. As she was collecting some suncream from the dressing table to toss into her bag, her eye was caught by the scent bottle. Should she have locked that away as well? She hesitated, glancing at her watch. They had been told to meet in the boat's reception area at six forty-five. She did not want to miss the bus. The decision was simple. She would take it with her. Picking up the bottle, she wrapped it in one of her silk scarves and tucked the small scarlet bundle into her bag. Then, turning, she let herself out of the cabin.

To her surprise, as she sat alone in the coach and waited, staring eagerly out of the window, Andy came and sat beside her. 'So. How are you this morning? Excited?'

'I'm fine. Very excited. Yes.' She recognised all the faces now. Near her were Sally Booth and Ben Forbes. And Serena, sitting next to an elderly lady in a cerise trouser suit. Then two more couples whose names she didn't know. And at the back of the bus she saw Toby Hayward.

'Did you bring your diary?' Andy was looking at the bag on her knee.

She shook her head. 'It's locked in my suitcase.' She grinned at him. 'I'm sure it's all right, Andy.'

He was still staring at her bag, and she glanced down to see what interested him so much. Her scarf had worked free and the little scent bottle was lying in full view on top of her guidebook.

'Souvenirs already?' He smiled. 'Don't let the pedlars badger you into buying anything you don't really want. They're awfully persuasive.'

She shook her head, feeling defensive. He had clearly not recognised it as antique. Wrapping the bottle up again, she pushed it to the bottom of the bag. 'I won't. I'm good at saying "no".' She caught sight of his raised eyebrow out of the corner of her eye and chose to ignore it.

As the coach lurched onto the narrow dusty road, she stared out of the window at the squat, square mud-brick houses on either side. She shook her head. 'I still can't believe I'm here, to be honest.'

He laughed. 'You are here, believe me. So, did you read any more of the diary last night?'

Anna nodded. 'A bit. I found the section where she went to the Valley of the Kings. There was a wonderful description of the valley. It was empty. Deserted. There was no one there with her accept her dragoman, Hassan. They sat and picnicked on a Persian rug.'

Andy laughed. 'I'm afraid it won't be like that for us. It will be packed with tourists. I've heard a lot of people say there are so many crowds there that it spoils it. No atmosphere, or not much. And no dragomen!'

'It's such a lovely term. I should love my own dragoman!'

'Perhaps I can be of service?'

She smiled at him. 'I don't think Charley would approve,' she said gently. 'Where is she, by the way?'

'Up front somewhere. With Joe and Sally. She's been chatting up Omar.' The lurching of the bus threw him against her for a moment. 'Have you got your camera?'

She nodded. 'Photography is one of my passions. I'm not likely to forget that.'

'Good. You'll have to take a picture of me in front of some great pharaoh so I can brag about my trip at home.'

They climbed out of the coach to queue for the short ferry ride across the Nile and found another identical, though older, vehicle waiting for them on the other side. When Anna looked round for Andy as they climbed aboard, she saw that Charley was by his side.

For this part of the journey she found herself sitting next to Serena.

'My first visit to Egypt.' The dark-haired woman was wearing a cool cheesecloth skirt and blouse of brilliant contrasting blues and greens.

'Mine too.' Anna nodded. 'You're a friend of Charley's, I gather?'

Serena laughed. 'For my sins. She rents a room in my flat in London. It was my idea to come out to Egypt, and before I knew it Charley was coming too. I suppose I was so enthusiastic and excited about it I sold her the idea.' She shook her head ruefully. 'She and Andy had been going out together for several months, and when he heard about it he half jokingly said he'd come as well. Charley was over the moon, but he realised he might have committed himself a bit more than he intended so he asked the Booths, and there we were, a veritable wagon train!' She sighed. 'I'm sorry. Does that sound as though I'm complaining?'

Anna shook her head. 'I should think it's more fun coming with friends than on your own.'

'Perhaps.' Serena did not sound too certain. There was a moment of silence as the driver turned on the ignition and the bus settled down into a violent but steady rattle. 'You're on your own?'

'Newly divorced and stepping out for independence.' Anna had a feeling that her jaunty tone had a wistful ring to it. She hoped not.

'Good for you.' Serena nodded. 'My partner died four years ago. For a while it was like losing half of my own body. We had been so close there was a physical loss; part of me had died with him. But it gets better.' She gave a big smile. 'Sorry. That's a bit intense for a first conversation, but at least you know there's someone who understands if you need a chat.'

'Thank you.' Anna was astonished by the wave of warmth she felt for the other woman. It wasn't the same, of course. Felix wasn't dead. And her feelings for him—had they ever been so intense?

Conversation was impossible above the noise of the engine, and they turned their attention to the fertile fields through which they were passing. Apart from the cars and buses the landscape was, Anna realised, exactly as Louisa had described it 140 years before. She stared out of her window at the intense green of this narrow strip of fertile fields, watered by narrow canals, and at the shade of the eucalyptus trees and palms which formed darker patches on the dusty road.

They stopped briefly to get out of the bus and photograph the Colossi of Memnon, two massive figures carved out of pink quartzite, standing alone on the bare rubbled ground. Then they were back into the coach and heading once again towards the mountains.

The bus park in the valley dispelled all her visions of Louisa's lonely visit to the tombs. It was packed. Acres of coaches, hundreds of tourists and round them, like wasps round a jam pot, dozens of eager noisy men, dressed in *galabiyyas*, colourful robes, hawking souvenirs.

'Ignore them and follow me.' Omar clapped his hands. 'I will buy your tickets and photograph permits, then you can explore alone or stay with me and I will take you into some of the tombs.'

Anna looked around in dismay. It was nothing like the place she had imagined. For a moment she stood still, overwhelmed, then she was swept into a loosely gathered queue making its way alongside the cliffs. She took her ticket from Omar and set off into the narrow valley. The mountains all around them were huge, ochre-coloured, rugged and deeply fissured. The square entrances to the tombs were black, enticing shadows scattered over the cliff faces. Some were barred with gates. Many were open.

'You look bemused, Anna.' Ben Forbes was beside her suddenly. 'Want to venture in with me?' He had his guidebook already open. 'Rameses the Ninth. This is a particularly splendid tomb, I believe. It is as good a place as any to start.' He led the way down a sloping ramp where they joined the queue of people waiting to go in.

They were in front of a large square entrance, the heavily barred gate standing open but overseen by watchful guards. Slowly, shoulder to shoulder with people of every nationality, they shuffled down the long slope into the darkness, staring at the walls and at the ceiling. Every available surface area was covered from top to bottom with hieroglyphics and with pictures of pharaohs and gods—the overwhelming colours ochre and lemon yellow, green, lapis and aquamarine and black and white, stunningly preserved and covered now in Plexiglass. She couldn't take her eyes off them, amazed at their beauty and power, and the sheer scale of them.

The further they walked into the tomb, the hotter it got. On and on they moved, through three successive corridors, towards a huge pillared hall and then, at last, into the burial chamber itself.

Ben glanced down at Anna. 'Well, what do you think?'

She shook her head. 'I'm speechless.'

He laughed. 'Not an affliction that seems to affect many people down here.' Slowly, they turned and started making their way back towards the daylight. 'What about going to see Tutankhamun's tomb next? He's back in there, you know, minus his treasure, of course.' As they came out once more into the sunlight, he gestured towards one of the smaller entrances.

This tomb was very different from the last one they had seen. Besides being smaller, it was simpler; there was no decoration, but there was something else. Anna stopped, allowing the people around her to pass on, unnoticed. Suddenly she realised what it was that was so strange. This tomb was cold.

She shivered, conscious of the goose pimples on her bare arms. 'Ben?'

She couldn't see him. A crowd of visitors were making their way into the inner chamber. She turned round, half expecting to find someone standing behind her. There was no one there. 'Ben?'

Confused, she put her hand to her head. The tomb was no longer cold; it was as hot as the other they had visited and she could hardly breathe. Panic-stricken, she pushed her way forward. She wasn't usually claustrophobic, but the walls seemed to be closing in on her.

She stared round frantically and, diving for the next entrance, she abruptly found herself standing in the burial chamber itself, looking down at the open eyes of the young king Tutankhamun. He lay gazing up at the ceiling of his dark, hot tomb, divested of the riches which had bolstered his royalty, but still awe-inspiring.

'Anna?' Ben appeared beside her, his camera in his hand. 'Isn't he amazing?'

She nodded. The bag on her shoulder had grown very heavy. Why had she not taken out her own camera? She was pulling open the zip of her soft leather holdall when a strange wave of dizziness hit her. With a gasp, she straightened, leaving the bag to subside into the dust at her feet, spilling its contents over the ground.

'Are you OK?' Ben asked. He stooped, and hastily began pushing everything back into the bag for her. She saw a flash of scarlet as the silk-wrapped scent bottle was scooped out of sight, then Ben's arm was round her shoulders.

'I felt weird suddenly.' She pressed her hands to her face. 'Too much excitement, and too early a start, I expect.' She forced herself to smile.

'Perhaps that is a sign that it's time to go up for some fresh air.' He took her arm. 'These tombs are a bit overpowering.'

'There's something down here, isn't there?' Anna could feel the perspiration on her back icing over. She was shivering again. 'I thought all that business about the "curse of the mummy's tomb" was rubbish, but there is an atmosphere. I do want to leave. I'm sorry.'

'No problem. Come on.'

Grateful for the strength of his arm, she stumbled after him, back towards the entrance corridor and the blinding sunlight outside.

Once sitting in the shade of the visitors' resting area, she felt better. They both drank some bottled water, but she could see Ben was longing to move on. 'Go without me, please. I shall follow on in a few minutes.'

He gave her a searching look. 'Are you sure?'

'Of course.'

She desperately wanted to get away from the crowds, to find the place where Hassan had pitched the makeshift shelter, and to experience the silence as Louisa had done, so she began to make her way up an empty track that led away from the centre of the valley.

Almost immediately, the sound of the crowds diminished and disappeared. The heat and the silence were overwhelming. She stopped, staring around, scared for a moment that she might lose her bearings, but the path was clearly marked. Just empty. Somewhere near her she heard footsteps and the sound of scraping on the limestone. She frowned, shading her eyes as she scanned the cliff face. There was no one there.

Once more she began to feel uneasy. She had the strangest feeling that she was being watched, a weird sensation that there was someone near her. She stared up at the cliff face, narrowing her eyes against the glare, then took a few steps further up the path. The cliffs were arid, silent, but for the rock martins swooping into holes in the cliffs. The feeling that there was someone there at her shoulder was suddenly so intense that she swung round. Tiny eddies of dust swirled momentarily round her ankles in an undetectable breath of wind, then the air was still again.

Stubbornly she moved on. It was round here that Hassan and Louisa had sat together on the rug and Louisa had begun one of her paintings of the rugged hillside.

'Do I gather you too prefer to be away from crowds?'

The voice, a few feet from her, shocked her out of her reverie. She spun round. The lanky figure of Toby Hayward was standing above her. 'I'm sorry, I didn't mean to startle you. I didn't see you until I came round the corner.'

Astonished at how relieved she was to find out the presence she had felt was that of a real person, she managed a smile. 'I was dreaming.'

'The right place for it.' He stood for a moment in silence. 'I find it hard to catch the atmosphere with the crowds down there,' he said. 'So many of them, and they snap endless pictures, but don't look. Have you noticed? Their eyes are closed.'

'The camera remembers. They're afraid they won't,' Anna said quietly.

'I'm sure you look as well.'

The tone of his voice disturbed her, so she decided to change the subject. 'I was trying to picture this place before it was commercialised.'

'It's always been commercialised. They probably brought guided tours here before the corpses were cold.' Folding his arms, he stared up at the cliffs. 'Did I hear you right last night? You are a relation of Louisa Shelley?' No apology for eavesdropping, she noticed.

'I'm her great-great-granddaughter, yes.'

'She was one of the few Victorians who empathised with the Egyptian soul.' He had narrowed his eyes, still studying the rocks.

'How do you know that's how she felt?' Anna stared at him curiously.

'From her painting. There's a set of watercolours at the Travellers' Club.'

'I didn't know that.'

'On the staircase. I've often studied them. She uses a wonderful depth of colour. She sees the shadows, the textures.'

Anna looked at him with a new interest. 'You talk like an artist.'

He snorted. 'If you mean a painter, yes, I'm a painter.' He was still staring up at the cliff and she took the opportunity of looking at him for a moment, surreptitiously, taking in the rugged features, the thatch of unruly greying-blond hair beneath the faded blue sunhat.

'Louisa loved Egypt. I'm reading her diary, and it's apparent on every page.' She gave a wistful smile. 'I almost envy those Victorian women. They had so much to contend with and yet they still followed their dreams. They worked so hard for them—' She broke off, aware that he was watching her intently.

'It sounds to me as though you too wished you'd had to work hard for a dream,' he said quietly.

She shrugged. 'Perhaps. But I'm not the intrepid type. Breaking away from the group and coming up here was pretty intrepid for me.'

He laughed, and suddenly his face looked much younger. 'Then we must encourage your intrepidness. Which tombs did your great-great-grandmother visit? Not young King Tut, obviously.'

'No.' Anna's smile died.

Watching her, he raised an eyebrow. 'So, what have I said now?'

'Nothing.'

'Something about Tutankhamun's tomb?'

She shook her head. He was intuitive, she would grant him that. 'I was in there. A little while ago. Something strange happened. Claustrophobia, I suppose. It made me need to get away from everyone and come up here.'

'And I spoilt your solitude. I'm sorry.'

'No. No. I didn't mean that.' She shrugged helplessly. 'The trouble is, it didn't work. The feeling, whatever it was, followed me up here.'

Again he gave her that long, disconcertingly direct look, scanning her face for clues. 'I think this whole valley could have that effect on people,' he said at last. 'In spite of the numbers of tourists who come here, the atmosphere is extraordinary. Have you met Serena Canfield yet? She was sitting next to me at dinner last night. You should talk to her. She is into Ancient Egyptian magic and stuff which might appeal to you.'

Anna raised an eyebrow. Was he gently taking the mickey or was he making the suggestion in good faith? It was hard to tell.

'I have spoken to Serena,' she said. 'She sat next to me on the bus, but we didn't talk about magic. My interest stems from travel books, people like Lawrence Durrell, and my mother's books about archaeology.'

'And Louisa.'

'And Louisa.'

'Can I see her diary one day?' He held her gaze once more, with that disconcerting directness that seemed to be his trademark.

She looked away first. 'Of course you can.'

He swung his bag back onto his shoulder. 'OK, I think I'm heading back down to the valley to see another tomb or two before we leave. Will you be all right on your own?'

She wasn't sure whether the question was posed out of real concern, or was a subtle way of telling her that he did not expect her to walk back with him. Indeed, no sooner had he spoken than he turned and began to lope back down the path. In seconds he had disappeared.

The silence and the heat flowed back over her in a heavy curtain. She began to retrace her steps, hoping at every moment to catch sight of Toby ahead of her on the path. But the path was empty, and before she knew it she was running back down towards the valley as fast as she could.

Arriving at last in the valley bottom among the crowds and the shouting guides, she made her way to the shaded resting-place, where she sat down and closed her eyes, trying to steady the thudding of her heart under her ribs. There was no sign of Toby anywhere.

It was Andy who found her. Sitting down heavily on the bench next to her, he took off his hat and fanned his face. 'Hot enough for you?'

She nodded, struggling to steady her voice. 'I thought the tombs would be cool. In the darkness.'

'More like Tandoori ovens.' He grinned. 'Are you enjoying yourself? You look lonely sitting here. I thought Ben was taking care of you.'

'I don't need taking care of, thank you!' Her indignation was only half feigned. 'But he was with me, yes. He's a nice man.'

'And so am I.' Andy raised an eyebrow. 'Can I escort you into another hellhole? We gather for our picnic in about an hour.' He glanced at his watch. 'Then this afternoon it's off to the Ramasseum and Hatchepsut's temple. There's no slacking on this trip!'

A shadow fell across his face. Charley was standing there looking down at him. 'I am sure Anna doesn't need an escort. If she needs someone to hold her hand, Omar can do it. That's his job, after all.'

Anna stood up hastily. 'I don't actually need an escort of any sort. Please, don't worry.' She grabbed her bag and plunged back into the sunlight, towards the shadow of another tomb entrance.

It was only when she was standing in the queue, her guidebook in her hand, that she realised Andy had followed her.

'I'm sorry. That was embarrassing.'

'Not at all. Charley is right. I don't need an escort.' She glanced behind them. 'Where is she?'

'Still over there in the shade. Egyptology is not her thing. She feels she has seen enough for one day.'

'I see.' Anna glanced at him sideways, unsure whether she should feel triumphant or sorry for Charley. She liked Andy. His friendliness had done much to put her at her ease among so many strangers.

'Hello there.' It was Ben, who had just emerged from the entrance in front of them. As the sun hit him he smacked his floppy hat back onto his head and grinned. 'One of the best tombs, this. Magnificent!' His face sobered at little. 'Charley! Are you going in too?'

Charley was suddenly beside them, her eyes smouldering with anger. 'Yes, I'm going in too. Stupid thick Charley is actually interested.'

'Stay here!' Andy's hand on Anna's wrist was like an iron clamp as she turned to move away. Startled, she frowned. 'Andy, please—'

'No. I asked you to visit this tomb with me. If Charley wants to come too, that's fine. She has a ticket, the same as the rest of us.'

Charley's face was red with fury. 'That's right. And I'm coming in.'

'Please do.' Andy's smile was, at least on the surface, as affable as ever. When Anna glanced round for Ben, he had gone.

As they walked down into the darkness, Anna spotted Omar ahead of them with some half-dozen of the other passengers from their boat who had elected to stay with him for the tour. With relief she hurried to catch up with him, aware that Andy was still by her side. Over the next twenty minutes or so, as Omar talked to them about the burial chambers, she slowly managed to distance herself from Andy and Charley in the darkness. By the time they had reached the inner pillared hall she had lost sight of them entirely.

It was as she was walking back, her concentration on the ceiling paintings, that her arm was seized. 'What do you think you are playing at?' Charley's hiss in her ear was full of venom. 'Why are you doing it?'

Anna turned in astonishment. 'Doing what? Look, Charley, you've got the wrong end of the stick. I'm not trying to do anything, I promise.'

'You're encouraging him!'

'I'm not. Andy is a kind man. He has seen that I'm on my own and he is trying to make me feel welcome. So is Ben.' She paused for a fraction of a second. 'And Toby. And your friend, Serena. That is all it is. They are nice people and I appreciate their kindness.'

She glanced round hoping to see Andy nearby, but there was no sign of him in the long queue of people shuffling from the depths of the tomb back towards the light. Someone jostled her and she stepped back. 'We're in the way, Charley. We have to move on with the others.'

'I'll move on. As for you, you can get lost!' The viciousness of Charley's remark left her speechless. She wanted to run after her, to argue, to defend herself, but at the same time some defiant corner of her mind was telling her to take no notice, to talk to Andy, and, as long as she found him attractive, and she realised suddenly she did find him attractive, to give Charley a run for her money. It was only a small corner of her mind though. A far larger portion was all for keeping the peace.

Tired and dusty, they returned to the boat late in the evening to be greeted by fragrant hot towels, handed out at the door to the reception area by one of the crewmen. Anna made her way to her cabin and, once inside, she peeled off her dress, stepped into the shower in the bath-room and turned on the blissfully cool water.

The only empty chair at her table, when she arrived at dinner, was between Ben and Joe. As she slipped into it, Anna saw Charley link her arm through Andy's and give it a proprietorial squeeze.

'So, how did you enjoy day one?' Ben said quietly in her ear as he poured her a glass of wine.

'Wonderful.' She smiled at him and caught his wink. 'I could get used to all this very easily.'

There was a sudden roar of laughter from one of the other tables and Anna turned. Glancing up, Toby caught her eye. With a sardonic wink he raised his glass and mouthed a toast at her.

She raised her own glass back to him and saw Andy turn to see who it was she was smiling at. He frowned. 'So how did your visit today compare with Louisa Shelley's?' he asked. 'Has the valley changed a great deal?'

'Out of all recognition in some ways. In others not at all. There really is a timelessness, isn't there?'

'As there is all over Egypt,' Ben put in.

'Louisa had the valley all to herself, of course. It must still be wonder-ful when all the tourists go and it's empty. There are so few places left where one can get away from other people.'

'The cry of a true misanthrope.' Andy grinned at her.

She felt herself blushing. 'No, I like people, but I like to be able to get away from them too, especially when it's somewhere where atmosphere is part of the attraction. It's the same in great cathedrals. It should be possible to get away from parties of noisy tourists and uninterested school-children who are just ticking off their list of trophy visits.'

'Hear, hear! Well said.' Andy clapped solemnly. 'A great speech.'

'And a sensible one.' Ben smiled at her. 'Which I think we would all agree with deep down in our heart of hearts.'

There was a moment's silence and Anna looked down in confusion. It was a novelty, she suddenly realised, to be listened to!

Exhausted, she went back to her cabin early and got ready for bed. Then at last she reached up for her suitcase, to retrieve the diary from its hiding place. She was looking forward to reading another section before she fell asleep.

'Sitt Louisa?' Hassan's shadow fell across the page of her sketchbook. Louisa glanced up. Her easel, her parasol clipped to the canvas, had been set up in the bows of the dahabeeyah as it slowly sailed south. The others on the boat had all returned to their cabins, having succumbed to the heat of the afternoon. Only the steersman, at the opposite end of the boat, had kept her company up to now.

'Before we left Luxor I went to the bazaar,' he said. 'I have a gift for you.' He held out his hand. In it there was a small parcel. 'I know you wanted to visit the souk yourself to buy a memento.'

Sir John and Lady Forrester, on hearing of Louisa's plan to visit Luxor again, had decided almost wilfully that now was the time to sail south.

She bit her lip. 'You shouldn't have done that, Hassan—'

'I am pleased to do it. Please.'

She took the parcel from him.

'It is very old,' he said. 'More than three thousand years. From the time of a king who is hardly known, Tutankhamun.'

For a moment the angle of the boat changed and the shadow of the sail fell across them. She gave an involuntary shiver.

'Open it.' His voice was very quiet.

Slowly she untied the string that held the paper closed. Inside was a tiny, blue glass bottle. With it was a sheet of old paper, crumbling with age, covered in Arabic script. 'It is glass. From the eighteenth dynasty. Very special. There is a secret place inside where is sealed a drop of the elixir of life.' Hassan pointed to the piece of paper. 'It is all written there. It tells the story of a pharaoh who needed to live for ever and the priests of Amun who devised a special elixir to bring him back to life. In order to protect the secret recipe from evil djinn, one priest hid it in this bottle. When he died, the bottle was lost for thousands of years.'

'And this is it?' Louisa laughed with delight.

'This is it.' Hassan's eyes began to sparkle as he watched her pleasure.

'Then it is truly a treasure and I shall keep it always. Thank you.' She looked up at him, and for a moment their eyes met. The silence stretched between them, then abruptly Hassan bowed and turned away from her.

For a long time Louisa sat still, the little bottle lying in her lap, then at last she picked it up. It was little shorter than her forefinger, and made of thick, opaque blue glass decorated with a white, feathered design. The stopper was sealed in place with some kind of resiny wax. She held it up to the sunlight, but the glass was too thick to see through it. Slipping it into her watercolour box, she tucked it safely into the section where the brushes and waterpot lived.

Picking up her brush again, she turned back to her picture, but she

The boat gave a slight shudder and Anna felt the steady forward thrust of the paddle wheels. They were on their way at last. Pulling the cotton quilt more closely under her chin, she picked up the diary again. So, the bottle lying there in her bag had originally been a gift from Hassan. And what a gift! It wasn't a scent bottle at all. It was some kind of ancient vial, a holy artefact from the time of Tutankhamun.

She shuddered. For an instant she was back in that dark inner burial chamber looking down at the mummy case of the boy king, and she remembered how she had become totally aware of his body lying there before her, and how she had dropped her bag—and the bottle—virtually at his feet.

Soothed by the gentle rumble of the engine deep in the heart of the boat, Anna turned back to the diary and read on.

That night, dressed in her coolest muslin, Louisa lingered at the saloon table after Augusta had retired to her cabin.

'Can I ask you to translate something for me?' she asked Sir John. She reached into her pocket for the paper that had been wrapped round the little bottle.

Sir John rested the cheroot he was smoking on a small copper ashtray, and took the paper. 'Let me see. This is Arabic, but written a long time ago, judging by the paper.' He glanced at her. 'Where did you find this?'

She smiled. 'I didn't. One of the servants found it in the souk with a souvenir he bought for me.'

'I see.' Watching him, Louisa could feel her first casual interest tightening into nervous apprehension.

At last he looked up, frowning. 'I think this must be a practical joke. A piece of nonsense to frighten and amuse the credulous.'

'Frighten?' Louisa's eyes were riveted to the paper.

'It seems to be a warning. The item it accompanies'—he looked up at her, his blue eyes shrewd—'you have that item?'

'A little scent bottle, yes.'

'Well, it is cursed in some way. It belonged once to a high priest who served the pharaoh. An evil spirit tried to steal it. Both fight for it still, apparently.' His face relaxed into a smile. 'A wonderful story for the gullible visitor from abroad. You will be able to show it to people when you go back to London, and watch their faces pale over the dinner table as you recount your visit to Egypt.'

'You don't think it's serious then?'

'Serious?' He roared with laughter. 'My dear Louisa, I hardly think so! But if you see a high priest on the boat, or indeed any evil djinn, please tell me. I should very much like to meet them.' He held out the piece of paper to her. 'Keep this safe, my dear. Your grandchildren will no doubt enjoy the story.'

Anna stopped reading for a moment. Beneath her she could feel the steady movement of the boat as it forged its way south. In the diary, Louisa, too, was making her way over exactly the same stretch of river. With her scent bottle. A scent bottle with a curse, haunted by an evil djinn. In spite of the heat, Anna shivered.

What had happened to that piece of paper? she wondered.

Her eyes wandered over towards the little dressing table, where she had left her bag. It was dark there; she could just see the outline of the mirror, the glass faintly echoing the light the lamp threw onto the ceiling. She stared at it sleepily and then she frowned. Deep in the mirror had she seen something move? She caught her breath as a shaft of panic shot through her. Gripping the quilt tightly to her chest she closed her eyes, trying to steady her breathing. As she groped for the switch to the main cabin lights, the diary slid to the floor with a crash. In the harsh clarity the overhead lights threw on the scene, she could see clearly that there was nothing there. The key was still in the cabin door. No one could have come into the room. Her bag was lying untouched where she had left it—or was it? Still trembling with shock she walked over to the dressing table. Her bag lay open, the scent bottle in full view on top of her sunglasses. Cautiously she touched her scarf. It had been wrapped round the bottle in the bottom of the bag, she was sure of it. Now the scarf lay on the dressing table, and across the silk lay a scattering of some kind of brown papery stuff. Curious, she reached out to touch it and rubbed some of it between her fingers. Then she swept it to the floor.

She glanced round. There was nowhere for anyone to hide in the room; nowhere. She threw open the bathroom door and rattled back the shower curtain. She looked under the bed, but already she knew there was no one there. How could there be?

With another shiver she bent down to pick up the diary. It had fallen open when it hit the floor, cracking the spine lengthways. She ran her finger sadly over the leather. What a shame. It had lasted so long undamaged and now it had been broken. It was as she was preparing to climb back into bed that she noticed that an envelope lay on the floor where the diary had fallen. She bent to pick it up and saw that the strip of sticky brown paper that had sealed it to the back of the diary had torn away. Forgetting her fright, in her curiosity she opened it. Folded inside was a flimsy piece of paper. As she had already guessed, it was Louisa's Arabic message. The words from Louisa's entry echoed for a moment in her head. *A high priest who served the pharaoh . . . an evil spirit . . . both fight for it still. . .*

Anna found that her hands were shaking. Taking a deep breath, she put the paper back in the envelope and, opening the drawer in the bedside locker, she slotted it into her leather writing case.

Climbing back into bed, she drew the quilt up to her chin and lay there for a long time, her eyes straying every now and then to the dressing table. At last she could bear it no longer. Climbing out of bed again, she reached down her suitcase from the top of the wardrobe and tucked the little bottle, still wrapped in her silk scarf, into an elasticated side pocket where it would be safe. Then she closed the lid, turned the key and hefted the case back into place. Finally she snapped off the main cabin lights and climbed back into bed.

Louisa was not sure what had woken her. She lay looking at the ceiling in the darkness, feeling her heart thumping against her ribs. She held her breath. There was someone in her cabin. She could sense it.

'Who's there?' Her voice was barely more than a whisper, but it seemed to echo round the boat. 'Who is it?' Sitting up, she reached with a shaking hand for her matches and lit her candle. The cabin was empty. Staring into the flickering shadows she held her breath again, listening.

A sharp crack followed by a rattling sound made her catch her breath. The noise had come from the table in front of the window. It sounded as though something had fallen to the floor. Knowing she would not rest until she had looked more closely, she reluctantly climbed out of bed. One of her tubes of paint had fallen from the table. She picked it up and stared at it. The movement of the boat as it lay against its mooring must have dislodged it and it had rolled from the table.

Her eyes strayed then to Hassan's scent bottle. It was standing on the table with her painting things. She frowned. She had surely tucked it into her dressing case? She remembered distinctly doing so before dinner. Perhaps Jane Treece had moved it when she tidied away Louisa's gown. She reached out to pick it up, but at the last moment hesitated, almost afraid to touch it. What if it were true? Supposing it had been the property of a temple priest in the days of the ancient pharaohs?

Drawing in a quick, deep breath she picked it up, took it back to her bed and sat down. Leaning back against her pillows, the little bottle cradled between her palms, she lapsed into deep thought, her imagination taking her from the high priest who followed the scent bottle, to Hassan. Why should he have given her a present at all? She pictured his face, the strong bones, the large brown eyes, the evenly spaced white teeth, and she found herself remembering the warm dry touch of his hand against hers as he passed her the flaring torch in the tomb in the valley. In spite of herself, she shivered. What she had felt at that moment was something she had never thought to feel again, the intense pleasure she used to feel at the touch of her beloved George's hand when he glanced at her and they exchanged secret smiles in an unacknowledged recognition that later, when the children were asleep, they would keep an assignation in his room or hers. But to feel that with a comparative stranger, a man who was of a different race and one who was in her employ? She could feel herself blushing in the light of the candle. It was something too shocking, almost, to confide even to her diary.

Anna woke to find the sunlight flooding across her bed from the open window. The boat was still moving, and when she went to look out she found a breathtaking view of palms and plantations streaming steadily by. For a few moments she stood still, transfixed, then she turned and headed for the bathroom.

After a hasty breakfast, Anna joined the others on the quayside, where a line of four-wheeled open carriages, drawn by an array of painfully thin horses, was waiting to take them to the Temple of Edfu. The shouting was deafening, as around the calashes and between the horses' feet a dozen little boys shouted for baksheesh, and urged the tourists towards their own particular choice of vehicle.

It was with some relief that Anna found herself in the same calash as Serena, along with Joe and Sally Booth. Their driver, whose name he informed them was Abdullah, could have been any age between seventy and 150. His skin was especially dark, gauntly drawn into deep creases, and his missing teeth rendered his smile particularly piratical. They set off at a canter, heading into the centre of town where the horses challenged lorries and cars with no fear at all. Holding frantically to the side of the carriage, Anna wished she had a hand free to take out her camera. There was something deeply primitive in this mode of transport that appealed to her greatly.

The calash lurched into a pothole and Anna fell sideways against her companion. Serena laughed. 'Isn't it wonderful? I am so looking forward to seeing the Temple of Edfu. It was built in the Ptolemaic period, but it is famous for its inscriptions and carvings. They were still faithful to the old Egyptian gods even in Roman times, you know.'

Anna found herself wishing she had spent less time reading up about the scent bottle and more on Louisa's diary entry on her visit here. As the calash hurtled up the main street, she heard a shout from behind. She turned in time to see another vehicle draw level with them. Its driver cracked his whip in the air above the horse's head and gave a shout of triumph as Andy leaned forward to wave at them. 'Last one there pays for the beer!' His call rang in their ears as his calash drew ahead.

Serena laughed uncomfortably. 'He's like a child, isn't he?'

Anna raised an eyebrow. 'I suppose you see a lot of him if he and Charley are together?'

'Not that much. Not as much as Charley would like.'

They left the calashes in the shade at the back of the temple and walked towards the entrance. Anna stared up in awe. The temple was huge, a vast squat building, rectangular behind the enormous monumental gateway, 130 feet high, carved with pictures of Ptolemy defeating his enemies. They stopped in front of it, listening as Omar summarised 2,000 years of history and the temple's place in it.

A white-robed figure stood near the entrance, beside the statue of the god Horus depicted as a huge hawk, and Anna found herself watching him. A black line of shadow cut across his dazzling white *galabiyya* as he leaned silently against the wall with his arms folded. She had the sense that he was watching them and she felt a sudden tremor of nervousness.

'What is it? Is something wrong?' Serena was watching her face.

She shook her head. 'Nothing really. I keep getting this strange feeling that there's someone out there watching me . . .'

'Not someone very nice, judging by your reaction.'

'No.' Anna gave a small laugh. 'I think Egypt is making me a bit neurotic. Perhaps we could have a drink before dinner this evening and I could tell you about it?'

About what? A nightmare? A feeling that someone had unpacked her bag in the dark of her cabin and moved her little scent bottle? A scent bottle haunted by an evil spirit? She shook her head, aware that Serena was still watching her curiously.

They were late back to the boat, exhausted and dusty after their visit. Warm lemonade and scented flannels were followed by lunch, and then, as the boat cast off and headed once more upstream, the passengers retired either to their cabins or to the sunbeds on the upper deck.

Later that afternoon Anna met Serena in the bar and they settled into one of the sofas in the corner of the room. Outside it was dark. They had moored alongside a stretch of riverbank near the Temple of Kom Ombo. Around them the others were assembling a few at a time. She could see Andy perched on a stool at the bar. Charley stood near him and they were engaged in a noisy conversation with Joe and the barman.

'So, tell me about these strange feelings of yours.' Serena leaned back against the cushions, her glass in her hand.

'It sounds a bit silly talking about it in cold blood.' Anna shrugged. 'But Toby mentioned you were interested in sort of psychic stuff.'

Serena smiled. 'Sort of? I suppose so. I gather this is to do with the man we saw at Edfu this morning?'

'Not him especially. He was real. But for some reason he made me feel nervous. He was watching us, and I keep getting this feeling that I'm being watched by someone. It's nothing specific—' She broke off, not knowing quite how to go on.

'Start at the beginning. I find things are much clearer that way.'

Anna smiled. 'Well, I have a diary in my cabin that belonged to my great-great-grandmother, Louisa Shelley. In this diary there is a description of how Louisa was given a little glass bottle by her dragoman as a gift. I have inherited the bottle. With it was a piece of paper, which I also have, written in Arabic, saying that the bottle has a curse on it. The original owner, a high priest in Ancient Egypt, is following it and so is an evil spirit, because a secret potion is sealed into the glass. I know it sounds ridiculous, but it's worrying me . . .' Her voice trailed away in embarrassment.

'You have this bottle with you, on the boat?' Serena asked quietly.

She nodded, relieved that Serena had not laughed. 'I brought it with me. I suppose it seemed right to bring it back to Egypt. I've had it for years. I always assumed it was a fake. An inadequate friend of my husband told us that it was. And Andy thinks it's a fake.'

'Andy Watson?' Serena's voice was sharp. 'Have you shown it to him?'

'I showed it to him yesterday. On the coach to Luxor.'

'He could be right of course.' Serena paused for a moment. 'But you are afraid of this curse?'

It wasn't an accusation, merely a statement of fact.

Anna didn't reply for a moment, then slowly she shrugged. 'I've only known about it since last night.' She bit her lip with an embarrassed little laugh. 'But I suppose, if I'm honest, it is beginning to get to me. Even before I knew the story, I had the strangest feeling there was someone watching me. Then, once or twice I had the feeling that someone had been touching my things when the cabin door was locked and no one could have been there. I've tried to persuade myself I was imagining it, but . . .' Once again she tailed off into silence.

'Let's take things one at a time. Tell me what the note says as far as you understand it.' Serena's voice remained quiet, but firm. It had an attractive, deep quality that Anna found profoundly reassuring.

Serena thought for a while in silence after Anna had repeated it to her, staring down into the glass she held in front of her.

'If Louisa felt there was a spirit guarding the bottle, then we must assume the bottle to be genuine, obviously,' she said at last. 'And if it's the same bottle that you have brought with you, then the chances are that it does have some kind of resonance about it.'

Anna shrugged. 'It might just be my imagination. After all, nothing ever happened before I read about it. If it's true, why has nothing ever shown itself in London?'

Serena turned towards her. 'Isn't it obvious? You've brought it back to Egypt, my dear. It has come home.'

Anna and Serena lingered over supper with the others, but by an unspoken agreement they had turned away from the lounge where the coffee was being served so that Anna could show Serena the bottle.

It seemed crowded in Anna's cabin with two people in there. Serena sat down on the bed while Anna swung her suitcase down from the wardrobe. Setting it on the floor she squatted down, unlocked it and threw back the lid. 'It's here.' She reached into the pocket and pulled out the small silk-wrapped bundle and handed it to Serena.

Very carefully the older woman began to unwrap the bottle. 'It's smaller than I expected.'

Anna sat down beside her. 'It's tiny.' She gave a nervous giggle. 'So small, and it's causing so much hassle.'

'Hush.' Serena pulled away the scarlet silk and gazed down at the bottle lying in the palm of her hand. Closing her eyes she stroked it with her finger. 'It feels old. Full of memories. Full of time.' Her voice was very soft. Dreamy. 'There is magic in this. Power.' There was a long silence. 'I can see a figure with my mind's eye. He's tall. His eyes are piercing. They see through everything. He has so much power,' she went on slowly, 'but there is treachery there. He has enemies. He thinks himself invincible, but close to him there is hatred, greed. Someone, whom he thought a friend, is near him. Waiting. They serve different gods, but he has not realised it. Not yet . . .' Her voice trailed away into silence. Anna held her breath, watching mesmerised as Serena's finger stroked gently on. 'There is blood here, Anna.' Serena spoke again at last, her voice a whisper. 'So much blood—and so much hate.'

'You're making it up.' Anna stood up and backed away from her. 'You're frightening me!' Suddenly she was shivering uncontrollably.

Slowly Serena looked up. Her eyes found Anna's face but she wasn't seeing it. Her pupils were huge; unfocused. Then abruptly Serena rubbed her eyes. She smiled uncertainly. 'What did I say?'

'Don't you know?' Anna didn't move from her position near the door.

Serena looked down at the little bottle still lying in her hand. With a shiver she let it fall on the bed. 'It is old. Very old,' she repeated, flatly.

'You said.' Anna swallowed. Her eyes were riveted to the bottle, lying on the bed. 'But what was all that other stuff? About the blood?'

Serena's eyes opened wide. 'Blood?' There was a moment's silence then she looked away. 'Oh shit!' She put her hands to her face. 'I didn't mean that to happen. I'm sorry. I have a tendency to be melodramatic. Take no notice. The last thing I meant to do was scare you.'

'But you did.'

'Did I?' For a moment Serena stood gazing into her face as if trying to read her thoughts. Then she reached out to the bottle, picked it up and firmly rewrapped it in the silk square. She held it out to Anna.

Anna took it reluctantly. Then she walked over to the cabin window and stared down at the wavy reflections in the dark water below them. 'How did you do it?' she said.

Serena shrugged. 'They call it psychometry. It's a kind of clairvoyance, I suppose. Reading an object. I've always been able to do it, since I was a child. It's not something to be cultivated lightly, as you can imagine,' she said with a hint of bitterness, 'but it has its uses. Sometimes.'

'What did your husband think about it?'

'Ah.' Serena smiled ruefully. 'Another woman, of course, goes unerringly to the crux of the problem. He vacillated between thinking me delightfully scatty and certifiably insane.' Her quiet laugh made Anna glance back at her. 'I began to study Egyptian mysticism two years ago after my husband died, and I came out here to get a feel of the place in a group before coming back on my own.'

Anna looked down at the river. 'So, what do I do?'

'You could throw the bottle in the Nile. Then my guess is you'll be shot of the problem.'

Anna was silent. 'It was Hassan's gift to Louisa,' she said at last.

'And what happened to them?'

Anna shrugged. 'I haven't read much of the diary yet, but I know she came home safely to England.'

'It's up to you, of course.' Serena leaned forward with a sigh.

'You said you were studying Egyptian mysticism,' Anna said slowly. 'So, perhaps there is something you could do. Could you talk to him?' Part of her couldn't believe she was actually asking; another part was beginning to take Serena very seriously.

'Oh, no, that doesn't qualify me to deal with this.' Serena shook her head. 'Anna dear, this is heavyweight. A high priest would be way out of my league. Probably out of the league of anyone alive today.'

Anna bit her lip. 'I don't want to destroy the bottle.'

'OK.' Serena levered herself to her feet. 'I tell you what. You read some more of that diary. See what happened to Louisa. How did she deal with it? I'll spend the night thinking about this; tomorrow we go to the Temple of Kom Ombo. Who knows, perhaps we'll be able to appease the guardian of the bottle by making an offering to his gods.'

Serena went back to the cabin she shared with Charley on the floor below, and, after locking her cabin door, Anna wrapped the small silk parcel in a polythene bag, tucked it into her cosmetics bag and, zipping it up tightly, she put it on the floor of the bathroom. Then she closed the door on it. For several minutes she stood in the centre of her cabin, listening intently. Then, turning off the main cabin lights at last, she undressed, climbed into bed and, in the light of the small bedside lamp, she picked up the diary and started to read. She wanted to see if she could find any references to the bottle and its fate. Leafing through the pages she found herself looking at a tiny ink sketch, captioned 'Capital at Edfu'. It showed the ornate top of one of the columns in the courtyard she had seen only that morning.

The Forresters decided yet again that it was too hot to do anything other than stay in the boat, so Hassan procured donkeys so that he and I could ride towards the great Temple of Edfu . . .

Anna glanced up. The room was quiet. Warm. She felt safe. Settling herself a little more comfortably, she turned the page and read on.

The donkey boy who had brought them to the entrance to the temple retired to the sparse shade of a group of palm trees to wait for them, while Hassan led the way across the sand. They set up camp in the lee of one of the great walls.

'Come and sit by me while I draw.' She smiled at Hassan and patted the Persian rug on which she was sitting. 'I want to hear the history of this place before we explore it.'

He lowered himself onto the edge of the rug, sitting cross-legged, his back straight, his eyes narrowed against the sunlight.

'The temple has only recently been excavated by Monsieur Mariette,' Hassan began, as Louisa unscrewed her water jar. 'Before he came the sand was up to here.' Hassan pointed vaguely at a spot about halfway up the columns. 'He cleared so much away. There were houses built on the temple and close round it. They have all gone now. The temple was built in the time of the Ptolemies. It is dedicated to Horus, the falcon god. It is magnificent, one of the greatest temples in Egypt.' Hassan's low voice spun the history of the building into a legend of light and darkness.

Louisa paused in her work, watching his handsome face as the web of his narrative spun on. Dreamily, she listened, lost in the visions he was conjuring for her, and it was a moment before she realised he had stopped speaking and was looking at her, smiling. 'I have put you to sleep, Sitt Louisa,' he said.

She smiled back, shaking her head. 'You have entranced me with your story. I sit here in thrall, unable even to paint.'

'Then my purpose has failed. I sought to guide your inspiration.' The graceful shrug, the gentle self-deprecating gesture of that brown hand with its long expressive fingers, did nothing to release her. It was Hassan who broke the spell. 'Shall I lay out the food, Sitt Louisa? Then you can sleep, if you wish, before we explore the temple.'

340

He rose in a single, graceful movement and reached for the hamper, producing a white cloth, plates, glasses, silver cutlery. Then came the fruit, cheeses, bread and dried meats. The place settings, so neatly arranged, were very close to each other on the tablecloth.

Washing her brush carefully in the little pot of water, she dried it to a point and laid it down. 'I have such an appetite, in spite of the heat.'

She slipped off the canvas folding stool upon which she had been sitting and sank cross-legged onto the rug. When she glanced up, he was offering her a plate. There wasn't a trace of servitude in his manner as he smiled the slow, serious smile she was growing to like so much.

Taking the lump of bread he offered she said, 'You spoil me, Hassan.'

'Of course.' Again the smile.

They ate in companionable silence until another party of visitors appeared in the distance and stood staring up at the huge pylon. The woman was wearing a pale green dress in the latest fashion, and Louisa reached for her sketchpad, captivated by the splash of lightness in the intensity of the courtyard. 'We women look like exotic butterflies one minute, and like trussed fowl the next,' she commented when the figures disappeared. 'Out of place in this climate. So uncomfortable, and yet for a while, beautiful.'

'Very beautiful.' Hassan repeated the word quietly. Louisa looked up, startled, but he had already turned away, intent on the food. 'Some of the ladies in Luxor wear Egyptian dress in the summer,' he said after a moment. 'It is cool and allows them to be more comfortable.'

'I should like that so much,' Louisa said eagerly. Then her face fell. 'But I can't see Lady Forrester tolerating me as a guest on her boat if I did anything so outrageous.'

'Perhaps on our visits away from the boat we could arrange somewhere for you to change so that Lady Forrester need not be made unhappy.' This time there was a distinct twinkle in his eye. 'I can arrange for clothes for you, Sitt Louisa, if you wish it.'

'I don't think I can bear it a moment longer.' She shook her head. The tight wads of her hair, her hat, her tight corset, her sturdy boots, suddenly everything stifled her. 'Can we buy some things for me to wear here in the village, on the way back to the boat?'

He shook his head. 'We need to use discretion. I shall arrange it before we reach our next destination.'

Setting one of the donkey boys to guard their belongings, they strolled a little later into the hypostyle hall and stood gazing around them at the massive pillars. 'You feel the weight of the centuries on your head here, do you not?' His voice was almost a whisper.

'It is all so huge.' Louisa stared up, awed.

'To inspire both men and gods.' Hassan nodded. 'Shall we go on?' Ahead of them the second hypostyle hall was darker still. He was walking ahead of her, a tall stately figure wearing a simple white *galabiyya*. The shadows closed over him as he moved out of sight. For a moment she stood still, expecting him to reappear, waiting for her to follow him. But he didn't. The silence seemed to have intensified around her.

'Hassan?' She took a few steps forward. 'Hassan? Wait for me!'

Her boots echoed on the paving slabs as she moved towards the entrance where she had seen him disappear. 'Hassan?'

It was too quiet. 'Hassan?' She reached the entrance and peered into the darkness, suddenly frightened. 'Hassan, where are you?'

'Sitt Louisa? What is wrong?' His voice came from behind her. She spun round. He was standing some twenty feet away in a ray of light from an unseen doorway. 'I am sorry. I thought you were still beside me.'

'But I saw you go in there . . .' She spun round towards the entrance.

'No. I said we would go and look at the room of the Nile. It is the room from where the water was brought each day for the priests' libations.' He came towards her, his face suddenly concerned.

'But I saw you go in there.' She was pointing frantically.

'No, lady.' He stopped beside her. 'I would not frighten you.'

'If it wasn't you, it was someone as tall, as dark, dressed the same . . .' She leaned forward on the threshold of a small inner chamber and her arm brushed his. She felt the warmth, smelt the cinnamon scent of him.

'See, it is empty.' His voice was close in her ear. 'Without a candle there is nothing to see. I shall fetch one from the hamper—'

'No.' She put her hand on his arm. 'No, Hassan. I can see it's empty.' For a moment they stayed where they were. He was gazing down at her with a look of such love and anguish that for a moment she found herself completely breathless. Then the moment had gone. 'Hassan—'

'I am sorry.' He backed away from the door and bowed. 'I am sorry, Sitt Louisa. Forgive me. There is much to see yet, and we have need of light for the inner sanctuary. *Istanna shwaiyeh*. Please, wait a little. And I will fetch it.' He strode away from her, his face impassive once more, leaving her standing where she was in the doorway.

She glanced back into the darkness. Her heart was hammering under her ribs and she felt hot and strangely breathless. She took a deep breath. This was nonsense. First she was having visions, imagining she saw him when he wasn't there, then she was reacting to him as though . . . But her thoughts shied away even from the idea that she was attracted to him. This could not be.

Anna was woken by a knocking on her cabin door. She stared up at the ceiling blankly for a moment, then squinted at her watch. Eight thirty.

Leaping out of bed, she unlocked the door and pulled it open. Andy stood there, wearing an open-necked shirt and chinos. He grinned at her. 'I'm sorry. I thought I'd missed you at breakfast because you were an early riser.' His gaze took in her short nightshirt and the long, bare legs, and his grin widened. 'You were planning to come to Kom Ombo?'

'Yes!' Anna ran her fingers through her hair. 'Oh God, yes! I should have set my alarm. I've overslept! What time are they leaving?'

'Ten minutes.' He stepped away from the door. 'I'll fetch you some coffee from the dining room while you get dressed.'

She whirled into the shower, grabbed a dress, shoved her feet into sandals, and was just placing her camera into her bag when Andy reappeared in her doorway with coffee and a croissant wrapped in a napkin. 'Ali even spread it with strawberry jam for you!' He handed them to her. 'Omar said we could just follow them on down the track towards the temple. We can't miss it. You can see the ruins from the window.'

Taking the coffee she sat down on the bed and sipped it, gratefully. 'Please, sit down. I'll be two minutes.' The croissant was warm, oozing butter and jam. Not a thing to eat with dignity.

He watched her, his eyes alight with amusement. 'You could have another shower before we leave,' he said after a moment.

She laughed. 'Nothing so drastic. I'm sure a quick wipe round with a flannel will do!' She drained the coffee and turned to the bathroom. Her cosmetics bag was still on the floor. She glanced down at it, and froze. It had been fastened. She remembered. Only moments before she'd had her shower, she had opened the bag and rummaged for some lipsalve. Her fingers had closed over the polythene in the bottom of the bag and she had left it there, letting it nestle under cosmetics. And now the bag was open and shreds of polythene were hanging out. For a second she was too paralysed by fear to move. Then common sense kicked in. She had been in a hurry. Andy had been at the door. The polythene had caught in the zip. There was no more to it than that. The bottle was still there. With an effort, she calmed herself and reached for the flannel, wringing it out under the cold tap. Seconds later she was ready.

A cheerful crewman pointed the way along the river's edge to where, in the distance, their fellow passengers were clustered around Omar as he gesticulated wildly ahead.

'Do you want to catch up for the lecture?' Andy glanced at her.

'I don't think so. You go on if you want to.'

'I read up on Kom Ombo last night,' Andy said. 'I'll fill you in, if you like.'

By the time they reached the colourful stalls near the entrance to the temple, he had covered thousands of years of history, from the temple's prehistoric origins, to its rebuilding in the Ptolemaic period. 'It's much older than Edfu; a double temple. Split in two down the middle. Half is dedicated to Haroeris or Horus the Elder and half to Sobek, the crocodile god,' he said as they walked. 'It was a temple of healing. People came from all over to consult the healer priests.'

The place was crowded with tourists and once more they found themselves shuffling forward in a queue to present their tickets.

'I thought you must have decided to give this one a miss.' Toby was suddenly there beside her as Andy, distracted for a moment, had drifted out of earshot. 'Dallying with our antique dealer, I see.' He raised an eyebrow in Andy's direction. 'Serena is looking for you, by the way. Do I gather that you decided to speak to her as I suggested? Was she able to set your mind at rest?' He gave her a quick glance.

'Set your mind at rest?' Andy had veered back towards them. 'About what? Is something worrying you, Anna?'

She shook her head. 'Nothing serious.' Omar was just in front of them now, pointing out winged sun discs over the two doorways. She moved closer. Trying hard to concentrate on what he was saying, her eyes followed his pointing hand to look at the bas-relief carvings, but almost at once she found her attention straying. She was trying to imagine what this great temple had been like in the past, capture its atmosphere.

'Anna!' Serena was pushing towards her suddenly from the other side of the hypostyle hall. 'There you are! Are you all right?'

'Of course. Overslept, that's all.'

' Well, you and I have a task to perform,' she said.

'A task?' Anna stared at her for a moment, not understanding.

'You can't have forgotten last night. We are going to make a sacrifice to the gods, my dear. Remember? If there were any I would suggest flowers. Perhaps, as it is, a libation will do. I brought something with me which I thought might be suitable.' She patted the large suede bag on her shoulder. 'We'll find a quiet corner. It's worth doing, Anna.'

They were threading their way through a group of French tourists, still heading steadily towards the heart of the temple.

'Did you look up the diary to see what Louisa has to say about the bottle?' Serena asked her.

'I did. But I'm afraid I was distracted into reading about her and Hassan at Edfu. I will have another look this afternoon.'

'OK, let's find a quiet place, if that's possible.'

'And what good will this do?'

'If we please the gods, his gods, it can do no harm. And maybe, just maybe it will keep him away, whoever he is. Here.' She beckoned to Anna and ducked through a small doorway into a dark chamber. 'See here.' She groped in her pocket and produced a slim pencil torch. The thin beam focused on a group of figures on the far wall. 'Yes.' Her whisper was triumphant. 'Haroeris with Thoth and Isis. We are in the right place. I looked it up last night. This is where we make our petition.'

Serena reached into her bag and produced a small plastic bottle. 'Here. Pour some into your palm. Offer it to the gods, and then pour it onto the ground before them. It's red wine. I took it last night during dinner.' She unscrewed the cap.

Anna held out her hands. 'I'm sorry, but I feel like an idiot.'

'Don't.' Serena spoke sharply. 'Quickly, put your hands together. I can hear voices. Make the offering.'

Outside in the distance Anna heard a guffaw of laughter, followed by a sudden animated burst of conversation.

She did as she was told and felt the wine trickle into her palms.

'Hold it up! To the great gods of Egypt. Haroeris and Thoth and Isis, Lady of the Moon.'

Anna repeated the names, and then added for good measure, 'Please protect us and keep us safe.' She held out her hands for a moment, then slowly parting her two palms, allowed the wine to splatter on the stone at her feet. The atmosphere in the small room was suddenly electric. She glanced at Serena, saw that she was staring at the wall, transfixed. She followed her gaze and gasped. Was that the shadow of a man superimposed upon the carving? For a moment she didn't move, then Serena brought her arms up and crossed them over her chest. Her bow towards the wall was deep and reverent. Anna hesitated, then copied her.

They had barely finished when two figures appeared in the doorway. 'I thought I saw you duck in here. What are you up to?' Ben pulled off his hat and wiped his forehead with his arm. 'Have you seen anything interesting? Have you looked at the mummified crocs yet?'

Joe had followed him in. Both men had cameras in their hands. Anna surreptitiously rubbed the red wine from her palms with a tissue. Serena had screwed the cap back on her bottle. She slid it into her bag, and in seconds all four of them were back in the sunshine heading further in towards the heart of the temple.

Anna glanced at Serena. 'Did you see it?'

Serena nodded. She put her finger to her lips. 'We'll talk later, back on the boat. Keep your eyes open, though. The gods are definitely around.'

After lunch Anna made her way up the ladder onto the sundeck and chose a chair at the extreme front of the boat. Clutching her hat and the bag that contained both suncream and diary, she made her way towards it between some intrepid sun worshippers braving the afternoon's heat and, sitting down, she swung her long brown legs up on the leg rest in front of her. Most of the others were resting in their cabins.

Suddenly, she heard footsteps near her and, desiring a moment or two's peace, she feigned sleep behind her dark glasses. After a while she half opened one eye and saw that it was Toby who had come up on deck and was leaning on the rail. There was a sketchbook in his hand, she noticed, though he hadn't opened it. He didn't seem to have seen her, concentrating all his attention on the river, where a graceful felucca was winging its way past them.

She lay still, Louisa's diary unopened in her bag. The hot air was heavy and it was hard to stay awake. Her eyelids drooped. The boat would soon be leaving Kom Ombo to travel on south towards Aswan. Once they had started moving, there would be a slight breeze. Stretching like a cat, she closed her eyes.

She woke with a start as she heard the engines beginning to rumble in the depths of the boat and felt a slight tremor running through the deck.

'We're just leaving.' Toby was still at the rail. He didn't turn round, but she assumed he was addressing her as there was no one else within earshot. He had opened his sketchbook and was sketching swiftly and fluently. This time it was a man in a turban rowing a small boat heavily laden with green animal fodder. Anna sat up and levered herself to her feet. She went to stand beside him at the rail. 'Those are good.' She had glanced down at the page of small sketches. He had made several of the boat, so low in the water there was virtually no freeboard.

'Thank you.' He drew for a few more seconds. 'That is the island where the crocodiles used to bask.' He nodded at a low-lying sandy dune ahead. 'They disappeared from the river after they built the Aswan Dam.' He finished his sketch and flipped his book shut. Turning, he leaned on the rail, his back to the water. 'Are you enjoying the trip so far?'

She nodded. 'Very much.'

'When are you going to let me see the diary?' He wasn't looking at her. She followed his gaze and saw the old book, unmistakable in its worn leather cover, poking out of her bag beside her chair. She frowned, but already he was squatting beside her bag. Throwing his sketchbook down, he picked up the diary and, without further delay, opened it.

'There aren't many sketches.' It was almost an accusation.

'No.' She was irritated by all this interest in her property and indignant that he had picked it up without her permission.

'I'm sorry I can't lend it to you. I'm reading it myself.' She kept her voice steady with an effort.

'And you don't trust me.' He squinted up at her suddenly.

'I wouldn't trust anyone with it,' she said as calmly as she could. 'It is a personal document belonging to my family.'

'And pretty valuable, no doubt.' He was still leafing through the pages almost greedily. He paused when he reached one of the tiny cameo watercolours. 'She was good. And her sense of colour. Do you see? She never falters—never hesitates. One stroke and it is perfect. You shouldn't bring this out in the sun, you know. It's not some cheap paperback novel to cart around as the mood takes you. This is priceless!'

'It wasn't in the sun until you took it upon yourself to open it!' Anna retorted. She could feel her cheeks burning, and was furious with him. 'If you'd be kind enough to give it to me.' She held out her hand.

For a moment she thought he was going to refuse. He was holding it open, staring down at it as though he were trying fix it in his memory for ever. Reluctantly, he closed it and handed it to her.

'I'm sorry. I didn't mean to upset you,' he said quietly. 'Would you believe me if I told you that I'm not interested in its monetary value? It's the drawings themselves. She captures the atmosphere as I would never hope to do in a million years.' Just for a second she saw through his defensive mask and glimpsed something of the pent-up frustration and anguish that seemed to be hiding there. He opened his mouth as though he were going to say something else, then changed his mind. He picked up his sketchbook and walked away. Anna watched as he disappeared down towards the lower decks.

There was no time to consider his outburst. Seconds later Andy appeared. He saw her and raised his hand. Hastily she returned the diary to her bag, which she pushed out of sight under her seat.

'Was that Toby Hayward I saw up here with you?'

Anna raised an eyebrow. 'It was.'

'Did he ask you about the diary?' he asked casually.

'He did.' She groaned inwardly. She enjoyed Andy's company, but just at this moment she could do without anyone's. Stooping, she scooped up her bag. 'Actually, Andy, if you will forgive me, I think I'll go inside. It's a bit hot up here for me and I might have a bit of a sleep before dinner.' She didn't give him a chance to reply. Leaving him standing there, she made her way below and headed back towards her cabin.

Reaching into her bag for her key, she pushed open the door. She stepped inside and stopped, gagging. The air was thick with a dusty, spicy smell. Choking, she threw the bag on the bed and scanned the room. She spotted a thin scattering of brown resiny fragments on the floor, near the bathroom door. For some reason the smell coming from them turned her stomach and she shuddered.

The bathroom door was open and slowly she forced herself to move towards it. Her cosmetics bag was lying on its side under the washbasin, the contents scattered across the floor. Of the polythene-wrapped bottle there was no sign. With an exclamation of alarm she bent and scooped the things back into the bag and looked round. It was only a small area. There was nowhere for the bottle to have rolled. There was nothing for it to hide beneath.

Closing her eyes, she took a deep breath, then she stood up again and went to kneel by the door between the bathroom and the cabin. The fragments were sticky. She stared down at her fingers with a shudder of revulsion. She couldn't shake the stuff off. It clung to her skin, permeating her hands with the cloying scent of cedar and myrrh and cinnamon. Frantically she scrambled to her feet and throwing herself towards the washbasin she grappled with the taps, turning them on full and rubbing her hands again and again on the tablet of soap until they were raw. Drying them at last, she stepped over the rest of the mess and, snatching up her key, she let herself out into the corridor and ran towards the stairs.

There were six cabins on the deck below, three on each side of a long narrow corridor much like her own. Each was numbered and all the doors were shut. Had Serena told her the number of her cabin? She stood there frantically, racking her brains. She couldn't remember.

Then from the opposite side of the passage she heard the quiet murmur of female voices. Raising her hand she knocked. The voices fell silent and Charley opened the door.

'Well, well.' She looked Anna up and down as though she were some odd form of low life. 'To what do we owe this pleasure?'

'Is Serena there?'

Charley shrugged. She stepped away from the door and went to sit at the dressing table, leaving Anna in the doorway. 'It's for you,' she called.

The cabin was exactly like Anna's except that there were two beds and two cupboards crammed into a space barely larger than that of her own. The bathroom door opened and Serena appeared, wrapped in a towel, her short wet hair pushed back off her face.

'Sorry, I was in the shower.' She stated the obvious with a smile. 'What is it, Anna? Is something wrong?' Her smile faded.

'Something's happened,' Anna blurted. 'I need to talk to someone—'

'Give me five minutes. Wait in the lounge. Then we can talk.'

Numbly, Anna nodded. She turned away from the door and made her way slowly back to the stairs and began to climb.

The lounge bar was empty. She stared out of the double doors towards the shaded deck with its awning and tables. It looked pleasant out there—cool out of the direct sunlight. Toby was sitting at one of the tables near the door, working away at a drawing, his back towards her.

She watched him for a while, studying his profile as his slim brown fingers moved swiftly over the page. From the direction of his gaze she assumed he must be drawing the graceful minaret she could see above the waving fronds of the palm trees on the opposite bank.

'Why not come out here and join me?'

She realised that Toby had put down his pencil and was leaning back in his chair. He must have sensed that she was there. Reluctantly she stepped out through the doors. 'Thank you.'

She pulled out a chair and sat down at his table. His sketch showed the minaret, as she had guessed, together with the palms and a group of colourful mud-brick houses.

'You're lucky to be able to record the trip like this.' She indicated the sketchbook. 'I have to resort to the camera.'

'Are you not a good photographer then?' He was drawing again, cross-hatching a shadow on the page, and did not look up.

She felt a quick flash of resentment. 'Why assume that?'

'I didn't. Your own doubt in the merits of your photography implied it. But you'd have to be singularly inept not to be able to take a passable clutch of snaps home for your album.'

'My God, that sounds patronising!' She exploded.

'Does it?' For a moment he appeared to be considering the matter. 'If so, I'm sorry.' He didn't look it. He merely raised an eyebrow. 'I see you are no longer trundling all your possessions around with you.'

'My possessions?' She stared at him, puzzled for a moment. Then she understood. 'Oh, you mean the diary.'

He gave an almost imperceptible shrug. 'Women seem to need to carry huge sacks of stuff with them wherever they go.'

'Anna?' Serena's voice behind her made her look round in considerable relief. The woman was standing looking down at Toby's drawing. 'I don't want to intrude,' she said with a smile.

'No. No, you're not.' Anna stood up hastily. 'I'll leave you to your creative processes,' she said to Toby with some asperity, and led the way to the ladder to the sundeck.

Serena followed her to the rail. Companionably she leaned on it, watching the passing scene for a few minutes. At last she spoke. 'So, aren't you going to tell me what is wrong?'

'Serena, there is something in my cabin. It's weird. Horrible,' Anna said eventually. 'And the bottle has gone.'

'Gone?' Serena swung to face her. 'Are you sure?'

'Quite sure. I left it in my cosmetics bag, in the bathroom.'

'Then it has been stolen. One of the crew perhaps—'

'No. I think it was something . . . someone . . . else.'

Serena eyed her, then went to sit on one of the sun loungers. 'Anna, sometimes when we're overwrought,' she said gently, 'we start to imagine things. It's easy to do.'

'No, I'm not overwrought.' Anna's voice was bleak. 'Our libation to the gods didn't work did it?' she murmured sadly.

'It seems not. But tell me what you've seen.'

Anna shrugged. 'Dust . . . incense . . . in my cabin. I don't know what it is, or how it got in there—I can feel them close, Serena. Louisa's good priest and the evil djinn.' She shook her head. 'I'm so scared.'

With a sudden crescendo of noise another cruiser drew level with them and began to pass them. A line of garishly dressed figures on the top deck waved and yelled at them. Anna raised an arm reluctantly in acknowledgment of a race conceded without ever having been declared, and turned her back. She looked down at Serena. 'So what do I do now?'

Serena climbed to her feet. 'Right. To the practicalities. There is something weird and horrible in your cabin. Let's go and look at it right now.'

The strange substance had gone, and with it the smell.

Anna sat down on the bed and Serena sat on the little stool she had hooked out from beneath the dressing table.

'I suppose you think it was my imagination,' Anna said.

'No, Anna, I believe you.' Serena smiled.

'And someone has taken the bottle,' Anna said. 'You know, in some strange way I'm almost relieved.'

'Why should anyone steal it?'

'It's an antique.'

They looked at each other for a moment, then Serena shook her head. 'No. Not Andy. No way. He thinks it's a fake. Who else knows about it?'

Anna shrugged 'No one. The diary is valuable. That might be a temptation to someone, I suppose. Both Andy and Toby have warned me about it, but no one would take the bottle.'

They sat in silence for a moment, a silence that was intensified by the sound of the gong below. 'Supper.' Serena shrugged.

'Do we say anything? Ask if anyone has seen it?'

Serena shook her head with a grimace. 'I'd say not. You're not accusing anyone yet. No. If it was me, I'd keep quiet for now.'

She did. The meal was a cheerful one and it was easy to let the conversation flow around her. Once or twice she put in a comment, but it was hardly necessary. The visit to Kom Ombo, the afternoon's leisurely cruise, the throb of the engines as they headed towards Aswan, had worn them all out. After the meal, most of the passengers gradually made their way up to the lounge bar to sit sipping after-dinner drinks and coffee.

As they disappeared from the dining room, Anna remained where she was. Ben leaned down as he left the table. 'Coming with us, Anna?'

She shook her head. 'To tell you the truth, I'm a bit tired.'

'OK.' He gave her a quick smile and moved on after Andy and Charley. Charley glanced over her shoulder as she left the dining room. The look she threw at Anna was triumphant.

She was the last passenger there, sitting alone as the waiters, Ali and Ibrahim, cleared the tables. It was Ibrahim who eventually approached her, carrying a cup of coffee, which he placed in front of her. 'You are sad, *mademoiselle*? Would you like a coffee to cheer you up?' He had a gentle face, deeply lined, and his dark brown eyes were very kind.

'Thank you, Ibrahim,' she said.

'It is no trouble, *mademoiselle*.' He bowed, then left.

It was an odd feeling, sitting in the empty dining room. It was almost dark, save for the spotlight illuminating her table, and there was no sound except the steady throb of the engine and the beat of the paddles as the boat slowly made its way upriver.

She sipped the coffee thoughtfully. Part of her was looking forward to going back to her cabin to read some more of the diary and get an early night; another part was, she had to admit, a little nervous. She sat for a long time after her cup was empty, staring into space, half asleep.

'Aha! So this is where you are hiding!' The doors swung open and Andy hustled in, two glasses awkwardly held in one hand as he let the doors swing shut behind him. 'I hope you weren't hiding from me!'

She looked up and smiled wearily, unable to stop herself glancing quickly behind him to see if Charley was in hot pursuit. 'As if I would!'

He put the glasses down on the table and pushed one towards her. 'A nightcap.'

'Thank you.'

'May I ask why so thoughtful, all on your own in here? A trouble shared and all that? If it would help.'

It was strange how relaxed she felt in his company. She glanced at him. 'It's my little scent bottle. It's gone from my cabin. I know you said it was probably a fake, but it's very special to me.'

'You mean it's been stolen?' He looked shocked. 'Have you reported its loss to Omar?'

She shook her head. How could she tell him that he, Andy, had been her chief suspect. 'I thought I'd look again before I say anything to anyone. It would create such a nasty atmosphere if I started throwing accusations around. Perhaps it will turn up.'

'If you're looking for a suspect, I'd ask myself about that Hayward fellow. He's been showing an inordinate interest in your diary.'

'He's no more interested than you've been, Andy,' she retorted. 'No, he's a bit abrasive, I grant you, but I'm sure he's not a thief.' She glanced at her watch, and sighed. 'So much for my early night.'

He took a sip of his drink. 'I get the feeling that the cruise has been a bit stressful for you so far,' he said.

She paused, considering. 'Yes, I suppose it has. I brought too much baggage with me. Not just Louisa Shelley and her diary and her scent bottle, but my own divorce and my worries for the future.' She shook her head slowly just as the double doors burst open and Charley stormed in.

'So, this is where you're hiding!' She stepped inside, allowing the doors to swing shut behind her. 'Why is it I'm not surprised to find you here, I wonder, Andy?' She walked over to their table and stood over them, looking down. 'Just tell me something. Are we finished?'

Anna stood up hastily. 'Look, this is nothing to do with me—'

Charley glared at her. 'It's got everything to do with you,' she hissed.

'No, Charley. It hasn't.' Andy stood up too. He slammed his glass down on the table. 'Long before we came here I was sick of your clinging and whingeing, and since we've been on the boat your temper has been atrocious. I'm sorry, I don't want to hurt you, but you and I are going nowhere together. And leave Anna alone. She's right. This has nothing to do with her. We were having a peaceful drink. That's all. No more. No less.' He paused and took a deep breath. 'Listen, this is a small boat. This is the holiday of a lifetime for most of the people on it. Don't spoil it for them. No one else need know about this. I know Anna won't say anything, and neither will I. So let's keep it private, and stay friends, OK?' He held out his hands towards her.

'Friends!' Charley almost spat the word at him. 'I don't think so. Do you know what you are, Andy? You're a smug, self-centred bastard!' She turned to Anna. 'He only wants you because of your diary. Once he's got what he wants, he'll drop you. Well, you deserve each other.'

Charley then stormed out of the dining room, flinging back the doors so hard against the wall that the sound reverberated through the boat.

Anna looked at Andy in stunned silence. He sighed. 'I'm sorry. I wouldn't have had that happen for the world. Stupid woman. I guess we've been working up to this for quite a while.'

Anna shook her head. 'I'm beginning to think this holiday is cursed.'

'What, from going into Tutankhamun's tomb? I don't think so.' He laughed. 'Come on, cheer up. Can I get you a top-up—?'

He was just reaching for her glass when they heard a piercing scream beneath them. They stared at each other in shock for a split second, then Andy turned and made for the doors with Anna right behind him. They ran down the stairs in the direction of the sound, to find that a crowd of people were already gathered around Charley's open cabin door.

'What's happened?' Andy pushed to the front of the crowd.

Charley was standing in the middle of the cabin floor, tears pouring down her face. 'It was a snake! In there!' She pointed at the floor where one of the drawers from the dressing table lay, its contents spilt all around it. 'It was in there!' She had started to shake violently.

Omar pushed forward through the crowd. 'What is this? What has happened?' He stepped into the cabin. 'Please, Miss Charley, be quiet so we can hear ourselves talk.'

Charley pointed at the drawer. 'There was a snake curled up inside it.'

'Did it bite you?' Omar's face had become ashen.

She shook her head.

He took a deep breath, visibly relieved.

Behind them, Serena had appeared in the doorway. 'What is it? What's wrong?' She pushed her way into the cabin and put her arm round Charley, hugging her comfortingly. 'What is it?'

'There was a snake in the drawer.' Omar shook his head mournfully. 'This is so strange. I don't see how it could happen—'

'More to the point, where has it gone?' Ben had pushed forward into the room, but behind him the crowd was dispersing, as one by one the other passengers made their way nervously back to their own cabins, looking uncomfortably around them as they went.

'It must still be in here or we would have seen it.' Andy stared round. 'Serena, take Charley into the bar while Omar, Ben and I look for it?'

Omar shook his head. 'We would not find it. Snakes can hide. They can make themselves invisible. I shall fetch Ibrahim. He is a snake catcher. He can call them and they will come.'

'Call them?' Ben echoed. He raised an eyebrow.

Omar nodded. 'His father and his father's father did this before him. They have power over snakes. If there is a snake here, he will smell it and he will catch it. I will fetch him now.'

Serena led Charley away. She glanced at Anna as they passed her. 'We'll talk tomorrow.' She smiled. 'Are you all right?'

Anna nodded. Only she and Ben and Andy were left now. She stepped into the cabin. 'Careful, Anna,' Ben warned. 'It might be a cobra. They are still common in the fields along the Nile.'

But her eyes were on the drawer. It contained a muddle of filmy female underwear—Charley's rather than Serena's, at a guess—a few strings of beads and there, nestling in the middle . . . She stepped closer.

'My scent bottle!' She bent and lifted it out. 'That is my scent bottle—stolen from my cabin!' she cried indignantly.

Behind them Omar had appeared. At his heels was Ibrahim, carrying a covered basket. 'Please to come away, peoples.'

Omar stood back and ushered them all out of the cabin, leaving Ibrahim standing alone in the centre of the floor. They froze, watching.

He stood quite still for several seconds, his head slightly to one side, listening intently. They could see the slight flaring of his nostrils as he sniffed the air. Moving across to the window, he ran his hand for a second across it. It was closed. Then he turned and surveyed the room. He was looking increasingly puzzled.

At last he shook his head. 'There is no snake here. *Pas de serpents.*' He frowned. 'But there is something strange. If it was in this drawer it was very small. The cobra, he grows to six feet. More.' He turned round and stared straight at Anna, who was still there in the doorway with Ben and Andy. '*Mademoiselle*, there is something the king snake guards . . .' His voice dropped away. 'The snake is afraid you will give it away, to a man.'

Anna's hands tightened round the little scent bottle. 'I don't understand.' Little waves of panic rippled across her skin.

Ibrahim nodded slowly. 'He has gone now, but there is a shadow in the air.' His long thin fingers wove a pattern for a moment in front of them, and then curled into a fist. 'He is angry and that is not good.'

'We cannot have a snake on the boat, Ibrahim,' Omar put in. 'We shall have to call in someone at Aswan if you cannot find it.'

Ibrahim's face darkened imperceptibly. 'Do you not trust my words?'

'Of course I trust you.' Omar bowed. 'It is the travel company. Their representative comes aboard at Aswan to see all is well . . .' He shrugged.

'And all will be well, *Inshallah!*' Ibrahim nodded. 'Now go. All go to your cabins. The king snake is not on the boat any longer.'

On reaching the reception area outside the lounge, Anna pushed her way through the swing doors. She could see Serena and Charley on the sofa in the corner of the bar. Someone had brought them cups of tea.

'It's all right,' Anna said as she headed towards them. 'The cabin is safe. The snake's gone.'

Charley looked up. Her cheeks were pale, streaked with mascara. 'Did they kill it?'

Anna shook her head. 'No, it disappeared. Ibrahim knows about snakes. He is certain it's gone. There's nothing to be afraid of.'

She sat down opposite them, glancing at Serena, then back at Charley. 'So, how did my scent bottle get into your drawer, Charley?'

She saw the shock register in Serena's eyes. Charley looked down at her hands. 'It was a joke. I wasn't going to keep it.'

'No?' For a moment Anna stared at her, frowning. She reached into her pocket and drew the bottle out, laying it on the table in front of them. 'So how exactly did you get into my cabin?'

'The door was wide open, and it was just lying there on your bed, covered in earth or something, and I thought why not?'

'On my bed?' Anna frowned.

'Yes. I didn't rummage through your stuff if that's what you think.'

Anna shook her head, trying to make sense of Charley's words. The bottle had been wrapped in polythene, in her cosmetics bag. It had been hidden. 'But you must have gone to my cabin for a reason.'

'I did. To talk to you. To tell you to leave Andy alone.' Charley groped in her pocket for a tissue. Tears were streaming down her face again. 'Look, I'm sorry. I shouldn't have taken it. But there is no harm done.' She stood up. 'I'm going to bed. Are you coming, Serena?'

'In a minute.' Serena hadn't moved.

They watched as Charley made her way across the lounge and out of the swing doors. Anna turned to Serena.

'Apparently Ibrahim is some kind of snake charmer. He called it the king snake, even without seeing it, and he said it was guarding something that was mine, which it is afraid I will give to a man. He said it was angry.'

Serena leaned back against the cushions. She shook her head. 'I'm out of my depth. The cobra was a very powerful symbol in Ancient Egypt. The uraeus, the symbol of kingship and the serpent goddess Wadjet— who became one with Isis—they are shown as cobras.'

Anna shivered again. 'But was it real?'

Serena thought for a moment. 'Charley seemed to think so. Real or not, Anna, I think you should probably regard it as deadly.' She ran a hand across her eyes. 'Dear God, I'm confused. It's late now. I think we should get some sleep. Can I make a suggestion? Why not hide the bottle somewhere safe? Out on deck, perhaps. Just until you can put it in the safe. Don't take it back to your cabin.'

Anna didn't argue. They let themselves out of the door onto the rear deck. 'The pot plants,' Anna whispered. 'I'll stick it in one of the pots.'

They made their way to the ladder and climbed up onto the deserted sundeck. There, arranged around the bows, were a dozen tubs of brilliant flowers, scarlet geraniums and hibiscus and bougainvillea.

Anna scraped a small pocket in the soil of one of the tubs and slipped the bottle into it, then covered it again. 'That's all right as long as no one pinches the plants!'

'They won't. The crew take great care of them.'

Back in her cabin, Anna searched the room three times before she at last turned back to the door and, pushing it shut, locked it. There was no sign of either the snake, or of the earth on her bed that Charley had described. She pulled off her clothes and climbed into bed. With a shudder she reached for the diary. The urge to sleep had gone.

Leaving the Forresters to entertain the passengers of a neighbouring dahabeeyah, Louisa excused herself on the grounds of a headache induced by the intense heat. She persuaded them that nothing would be better for her than for Hassan to row her over to the low, blessedly green Island of Elephantine.

He brought the small boat ashore on a narrow, sandy beach and helped her out. She stared around in amazed delight at the trees and flowers—hibiscus, poinsettia, bougainvillea, mimosa and acacia.

By now it was with no embarrassment at all that she took the bag from Hassan containing her loose, soft, green gown and native slippers, and then vanished behind some bushes. They were both used to the routine. Safely sheltered, she would change into the featherlight gown, while Hassan set out her paints and sketchbook and the basket containing their food and drink.

She smiled at Hassan as she settled at her easel. His eyes met hers. 'You look happy here among the flowers.'

'I am happy. It is beautiful here, Hassan. A paradise.' A hoopoe was flitting back and forth in the trees above their heads flirting its crest, its pretty pink and brown plumage a gentle contrast to the lush green.

'The hoopoe is a bird of good fortune.' Hassan leaned against the trunk of an acacia tree. He was watching her closely, an indulgent smile on his face. 'Would you draw a picture of the bird for me?'

She looked at him, astonished. 'Would you really like one?'

He nodded.

'Then of course I will.' Her eyes met his again. This time he did not look away. She felt a flutter of excitement deep inside her, and for a moment she found she couldn't breathe.

She swallowed hard. She had to stop this now, while it was still possible. But she was still looking at him, drowning in his gaze, feeling the strangeness of new infinite possibilities. She couldn't look away.

It was Hassan who broke the spell. In one lithe movement he was heading down to the beach, where he stood for a moment staring out across the water, clenching his fists. When he turned back to her, he was in control of himself again. 'I shall serve the food, with your permission,' he said formally.

Unable for a moment to trust herself to speak, she nodded.

She ate very little, her eyes on the Nile, watching feluccas sailing back and forth in the breeze. Lost in her dreams, she did not even try to keep track of the time. Slowly, the sun was moving across the sky.

'Sitt Louisa?' She realised suddenly that Hassan was standing at the edge of the rug. 'Shall I pack away the food? The flies . . .'

She nodded without speaking, and he bowed. Silently he filled the basket with the almost untouched bread and goat's cheese and fruit. When he had finished, he disappeared for a moment into the trees. He returned with a spray of scarlet flowers in his hand. He presented them to her as if they were the most precious gift on earth.

She took them without a word. Examining them closely, she took in their beauty, the perfection of petals and stamens, then she glanced up. He was watching her. She smiled almost shyly, self-conscious as a young girl, then she raised the flowers to her lips and kissed them gently.

Neither of them spoke. It wasn't necessary. Both knew that from this moment their relationship had changed for ever.

'Do you want to go back to the boat now?' She could hear the regret in his voice.

She nodded. 'There is always tomorrow, Hassan.'

'If it is the will of Allah!' He bowed almost imperceptibly. 'I will take you to see the unfinished obelisk where it still lies in the quarry where they were cutting it from the stone thousands of years ago. We will have to go on camels!' He smiled mischievously.

'Then you can be sure the Forresters will not want to accompany us!' she said with some spirit. 'I should like that, Hassan.' She watched as he loaded the baskets into the boat.

When he had finished he turned to her. 'You should change your clothes now.'

For one moment she thought of refusing, of climbing back into the boat in her cool, loose-fitting gown, but then she realised the folly of the dream. The Forresters would be scandalised. They might even refuse to allow her to travel any further with them. Taking the bundle of clothes from him, she retreated to the bushes with a heavy heart.

'My dear, we've been waiting for you.' Sir John Forrester was on deck, reaching down to hand her up onto the dahabeeyah. 'I particularly wanted you to meet our guests before they depart.' He led the way to the saloon.

Behind her Hassan had brought the food basket up on deck, and would then put her paints and sketchbooks in her cabin for her.

She turned and followed Sir John inside and found Augusta sitting there with their guests. Two gentlemen rose and bowed as she appeared.

'Lord Carstairs, Mr and Mrs David Fielding, and Miss Venetia Fielding.' Sir John made the introductions and ushered her to a seat. 'My dear, we have a special favour to ask you.'

Louisa brushed a wisp of hair off her face, aware that she must look flushed and untidy after her day on the island. She could feel the critical eyes of Venetia Fielding on her. She was David Fielding's sister, rather than his daughter, she guessed. Mrs Fielding was, in spite of her heavily draped efforts to hide the fact, clearly in an interesting condition; she looked exhausted.

'Sir John was telling us, Mrs Shelley, about the scent bottle in your possession and the Arabic curse that accompanies it. I wondered if I might see it?' asked Lord Carstairs.

She had been watching him while he was speaking. He had deeply burnished copper hair and a narrow, suntanned face with a thin, somewhat large nose that made him look, she thought with sudden suppressed mirth, like Horus, the falcon god. The effect was not entirely displeasing. He was a good-looking, imposing man.

'I'll fetch it for you, with pleasure.' She rose, thankful for the excuse to leave them for a few minutes to freshen her face and hands.

When she returned, she found that tea had been served. The Fielding ladies were laughing prettily with Augusta, and the three men had drawn a little apart around the saloon table. Unsure where to sit, she hesitated for a moment in the doorway. It was the gentlemen who rose and made room for her among them.

Sitting down, she produced the scent bottle and laid it in the centre of the table. The paper which accompanied it she pushed towards Lord

Carstairs. 'Do you read Arabic, my lord?' She smiled at him and was surprised to see his face light up in response.

'Indeed I do, dear lady.' He began to read out loud. His translation was substantially the same as Sir John's, and when he had finished he let the paper fall to the table, his eyes fixed on the bottle.

There was a long pause before he looked at Louisa again. 'And have you seen the spirits who guard it?' There was no levity in the tone of the question. She was about to shake her head, then hesitated.

His eyes narrowed. 'Yes?' It was the merest whisper.

She shrugged, half embarrassed. 'I fear that I am somewhat imaginative, my lord. This country encourages one towards all kinds of fancies.'

'Just tell me.' His eyes were locked onto hers.

She moved uncomfortably in her chair. 'Once or twice I have had the feeling I was being watched. And in the Temple of Edfu I thought I saw someone. I assumed it was my dragoman, Hassan.'

'But it wasn't Hassan?'

'No, it wasn't Hassan.'

'What did it look like? The figure?'

She could sense his excitement, hidden beneath an impassive face.

'It looked like a tall man in a white *galabiyya*. But it was no more than an impression in the shadows of the temple.'

'Yes!' This time the word was a hiss of satisfaction. She watched, a small frown on her face, as he stretched out his hand towards the bottle. With his fingers only half an inch from it, he paused, and she saw him take a deep, steadying breath, before at last he picked it up. Slowly his lids dropped and he sat silently, eyes closed, totally withdrawn.

'Yes!' he said for the third time.

Louisa could stay silent no longer. 'You seem very interested in my bottle, Lord Carstairs.'

The sound of her voice seemed to drag him back to reality with a jolt. He laid the bottle down on the table with palpable regret.

'Where did you say you got it?' His eyes sought hers and held them.

'My dragoman found it for me in the bazaar in Luxor.'

'Indeed. May I ask what you gave for it?'

The question floored her. She could not admit that it had been a gift. 'I gave him money for several purchases. I am afraid I have no idea how much he beat them down to in the end. Why do you wish to know?'

'Because I wish to buy it from you. I will reimburse you and give you the full value again, so you may purchase something else.'

'I am sorry, Lord Carstairs, but it is not for sale. Sir John, in any case, feels that it is a fake.'

'It is no fake!' Carstairs flashed a look of pure disdain at his host. 'It is genuine. From the eighteenth dynasty. Even so, the monetary value is not high. These are common in Luxor. Stolen, of course, from the tombs. But it pleases me.' He turned back to Louisa. 'Mrs Shelley, you would be doing me the greatest service by allowing me to have it. You could probably find several like it on your return to Luxor.'

'Then why could you not find one like it yourself, my lord?' Louisa enquired softly. 'Why must you have mine?'

Carstairs met her eyes again. 'I have a personal reason for wanting this one.' As though becoming aware of the strange looks being directed at him by the two other men at the table, he smiled, and Louisa instantly felt the radiance of his charm. 'The legend; it pleases me. You would be doing me an inestimable favour, Mrs Shelley.'

For a moment she nearly wavered, then with a shock she realised she had almost been swayed to do what he wanted. Almost. She had to force herself to put out her hand and lift up the bottle and the paper. 'I am sorry, I really am. But I intend to keep this for myself. I am sure you will find one just as intriguing, my lord.' Standing up she gave little bow. 'My lord, gentlemen, please excuse me. I am very tired after my visit to Elephantine Island. I shall retire to my cabin for a little while.'

In her cabin she sat down on the bed with a sigh, looking at the bottle in her hands. Hassan's gift. Since those special moments on Elephantine Island it had become doubly important to her. Almost without thinking, she raised it to her lips and felt the glass cool against her skin.

It appeared that the Fieldings, Louisa discovered during dinner that evening, had hired their boat, the *Lotus*, in Luxor two months before. It did not take Louisa long to work out that the reason for the Fieldings' protracted stay was their meeting with Lord Carstairs, whose own boat, the *Scarab*, had been tied up north of Luxor at Denderah. He was wealthy, titled, and recently widowed. Any family with an unmarried lady in her late twenties or early thirties would agree that he could not be allowed to escape. When both boats turned south to cruise towards Aswan, they did so in convoy, and Carstairs did not appear to have discouraged the obviously predatory plans of Venetia Fielding and her sister-in-law, Katherine.

'I don't think I would have risked staying out here in your condition,' Augusta Forrester commented a little tartly to Katherine during a moment's lull in the conversation.

Katherine blushed scarlet. Her husband came to her aid. 'It was not our intention to stay out here so long, dear Lady Forrester, I assure you.

I had hoped we would have returned to London long before this.' He sent a baleful glare in his sister's direction.

'Lord Carstairs has two delightful children, Augusta,' Katherine put in amiably, in an obvious attempt to change the subject. 'Alas, now motherless, poor little dears.' She smiled archly at Venetia.

'There is nothing delightful about them,' Carstairs put in. 'They are a couple of small heathens. I have lost three nursemaids already and I'm thinking of sending them off to a cage in the Zoological Gardens!'

Louisa suppressed a smile. 'May I ask how old they are?'

'Six and eight, Mrs Shelley. Old enough to be totally unmanageable.'

Louisa laughed. 'My two boys are the same age exactly,' she exclaimed. She shook her head sadly. 'I miss them so much. Are your boys out in Egypt with you, Lord Carstairs?'

'Indeed they are not! I left them in Scotland.' He leaned back in his chair and smiled at her. He had been paying her particular attention since she had returned to the saloon but not once, to her relief, had he mentioned the scent bottle.

It was not until the guests were on the point of leaving that Lord Carstairs dropped his bombshell. 'Mrs Shelley, may I suggest that tomorrow you might care to accompany us to the quarries to see the unfinished obelisk? It is a fascinating excursion and I have promised to escort David and Venetia.'

Before she could reply, Sir John sealed her fate. 'Excellent plan,' he boomed. 'She was intending to go there anyway. I heard the dragoman giving instructions to the cook to put up a picnic. Now there will be no need for him to go and he can stay here and help me.'

Anna shook her head. How unfair. Poor Louisa. That was truly sod's law. Or was she going to fall for the suave Carstairs and forget her burgeoning love for the gentle dragoman? She glanced at her watch. It was two forty-five. Her head was aching with tiredness, but she could not resist flipping over a few pages to see what happened next.

And so, I have ridden a camel and seen the fallen obelisk and dear God! but I am so afraid. When I returned to my cabin yesterday evening the lock to my dressing case, where I had hidden my little scent bottle, had been forced and the bottle was gone. The Forresters were furious and Roger Carstairs distraught. The boat's crew have been cross-questioned—even Hassan. Then I saw him. The tall man with the white robe. He was here in my cabin, not six feet from me, and he held the bottle in his hand. And he had the strangest eyes, like quicksilver, without pupils. I screamed and screamed and the reis *came, and then Hassan and then Sir John, and they found the bottle lying under my bed. They think it was a river pirate and are giving thanks for my safety. He would have had a knife, they say, and they think he had returned for what poor jewellery I have brought with me. But if so, why did he not take it before? What I could not tell them was that I reached out to ward him off and my hand passed through him as though he were mist.*

Anna did not have the chance to talk to Serena again until they were on their way to see, in their turn, the unfinished obelisk that Louisa had dismissed in two short lines. They sat side by side at the back of the tour bus as it bucketed over the potholed streets of Aswan.

'Louisa saw him again. The man in white. In her cabin!' she said. 'And he tried to take the bottle. I read the passage last night. She had met someone called Lord Carstairs who wanted to buy it off her—'

'Roger Carstairs?' Serena glanced at her. 'But he's famous, or I should say infamous. He was an antiquarian, but dabbled in black magic and things.' Her eyes widened. 'Obviously Louisa didn't give it to him?'

'No, she was adamant.'

'But he saw something in it?'

'Oh yes. He saw something, although it might have been the Arabic inscription that intrigued him. I'll read some more this afternoon.'

'Did you give the scent bottle to Omar to lock away?'

Anna shook her head. 'There were only a few minutes after breakfast and I didn't have time. And there were too many people about. I reckon it will be safe where it is.' She was silent for a moment. It would have been nearer the truth to say that she hadn't wanted to touch it.

Leaving the bus, Anna and Serena trooped dutifully across the quarry and climbed the path to stand looking down at the great obelisk. Almost completed, it lay like a vast, fallen warrior, still half embedded in the living granite, almost free until a flaw had been found in it, which had caused it to be abandoned. Anna was strangely moved by the sight.

'It's beautiful, isn't it.' Toby was suddenly beside them. He had his small sketchbook in his hand and was busy transferring the image of the obelisk onto the page. He glanced at her. 'You can feel the utter frustration they must have felt when they realised they had to give up on it.'

Anna nodded. 'So nearly finished. So almost perfect.'

'Did Louisa come here?' He was concentrating on the paper. 'Did she paint the obelisk?'

Anna shook her head. 'She came here, but she didn't write much about it in her diary. She was distracted, I think. She came with friends, or rather acquaintances, whom she doesn't appear to have cared for much. One of them was a man called Lord Carstairs.'

He gave a low whistle. 'I remember my grandmother telling me something about him when I was a kid. Grandfather heard her and was furious; he said she mustn't talk about him. I didn't understand why, then. But then his grandfather was a vicar, so I suppose that explains it. How on earth did she get to know an evil bastard like that?'

Anna shrugged. 'I don't think she did. They moored near his boat here in Aswan and he came to visit.' She didn't mention the scent bottle.

Squinting into the sun, she saw that Andy was heading towards them. Behind him, Charley and Joe and Sally Booth were standing with a group of fellow passengers, all of whom were staring down at the obelisk.

Andy arrived with a rattle of stones on the path beside them. He glanced at Toby's sketch. 'Not bad.' The tone of his voice implied that he had reservations.

Toby ignored him. He flipped the page and began another drawing.

Anna glanced from Andy to Toby and back. The tension between them was palpable. She frowned. Whatever it was between these men she didn't want it spoiling her day. Turning, she began to make her way hastily back towards the other group.

It proved impossible to speak to Serena again that morning. Even on the bus she found herself next to Ben—loquacious, enthusiastic and very large in the narrow seat next to her. Their return to the boat was followed almost immediately by lunch, and the news that they were going to have the chance to sail that afternoon in a felucca to Kitchener's Island—the Island of Plants.

Andy, Charley and the Booths were aboard the first felucca. She waited with the second group until it was their turn to climb down into their boat, where she found herself sitting once more next to Toby. He grinned at her briefly, but seemed disinclined to talk. As they disembarked on the island to explore the botanical gardens, it was Toby who handed her ashore.

As she gazed around she couldn't restrain her cry of delight. 'It's so beautiful! I hadn't realised how much I had been missing gardens and greenery.' Everywhere there were flowers and birds. This must have been how Louisa felt when she had landed with Hassan on the nearby Elephantine Island. She reached automatically for her camera. 'How can they have scheduled such a short visit here?'

Toby shrugged. 'That applies to every site we visit.' He stared round thoughtfully. 'I am going to come back to Egypt on my own next time. Spend several months here.' He had brought a brand-new sketchbook, she noticed. She wondered how many he had used up already.

'Aren't you tempted to use your camera at all?' she asked suddenly. She had glimpsed one in his bag.

He grimaced. 'I use one when there isn't time to sketch. But I have had time today.' He allowed her to see his page for a moment and she saw that already it was covered in small drawings. 'If I have problems when we get back to England, I'll get you to show me your photos.'

The assumption that they might see each other again, once they returned to England, filled her with strangely mixed emotions. Half of her was indignant that he should presume, if only in jest, that they might remain friends; the other half was perhaps a little pleased.

'Are you a good photographer?' His question was tossed over his shoulder as he drew.

'I'm not sure. My husband always called it my little hobby.'

He raised an eyebrow. 'Just because your husband patronised your photography doesn't mean it was no good.'

She frowned. 'No. No, it is good.' Unconsciously she had braced her shoulders. 'I've exhibited some of my work. I've won prizes.'

Toby stopped, looking at her with renewed interest. 'Then you're good. And yet your ex-husband's view of you still matters to you?' He shook his head. 'You must have faith in yourself, Anna. It seems to me that you've been suppressed for too long!' He grinned suddenly. 'Stop hiding your camera. You keep putting it away. Flaunt it. You're a professional. Be proud of it.' He paused. 'Sorry. End of lecture. It's none of my business.'

Slowly they walked on, together now by some unspoken symbiosis, drifting along the path to where, in front of them, a vista of the River Nile opened out, framed by a dead tree on the shore at the edge of a narrow sandy beach.

She squinted through the viewfinder of her camera at the river. Out on the water two feluccas had been tied together midstream, their sails lowered, and the sound of Nubian drums drifted across the water.

'Earlier, you said you'd heard of Lord Carstairs,' she said as she dug for a new roll of film in her bag. 'What was so evil about him?'

He gave a tight smile. 'Having been forbidden to speak his name at home, I naturally looked him up as soon as I could when I got to a library. It must have been in the 1870s, after Louisa met him here, when he was chased out of England for what would nowadays be called Satanic practices.' He snapped the point of his pencil and cursed. 'He ran some kind of secret society in London—a bit like the Hell Fire Club.

I don't know where he ended his days.' He produced a penknife and began to whittle at the pencil point. 'Did Louisa only see him the once?'

Anna shrugged. 'I read a bit of the diary each evening. Just enough to keep up with where we are on the tour. Remembering,' she added with a smile, 'to keep it away from the sun and other sticky hazards!'

He gave her a quick, mischievous glance. 'That still rankles, does it?'

'A bit.' She folded her arms.

'And am I going to be allowed to see it? If I don't touch it? I'll stand well back and let you turn the pages.'

'With my own fair, clean, unsticky hands! Yes, I'm sure I could allow you to see it on those terms.'

For a moment their eyes met. She looked away first.

'You quite fancy that chap Andy, don't you?' A quick look at her under his sandy eyelashes and he was drawing again.

'I don't think that is any of your business.'

'He seems to have dumped Charley, and she is making it everyone's business. Her complaints on the bus about you were not kind.'

'The fact that he dumped her has nothing to do with me!' Anna tightened her lips crossly

'So, you don't like him?'

'I didn't say that. But I am here on holiday. I want to enjoy myself. To see Egypt. And I don't want any complications.' Stepping onto the path she left him abruptly, ducking back between the bushes.

To her surprise he followed her. 'I'm sorry. It was none of my business.' He shut his sketchbook and tucked it into his bag.

'I think it's time we found the others.' She didn't glance back at him. The mood was spoilt.

It was early evening before she had the chance to talk to Serena again. They had taken the last two sun loungers on the sundeck to relax after their exhilarating sail back. The plants had been watered, Anna noticed. The decking around each pot glistened in the evening sun.

'I'll rescue the bottle tonight.' Anna grimaced. 'I don't like the thought of it being soaked.'

'You could dig it up now. No one would notice,' Serena said.

'Probably.' Anna smiled. But she didn't move. A glance around the deck had revealed Andy asleep beneath his straw hat, a beer beside him on a small table. There was no sign of Charley. And no sign of Toby.

Anna shifted uncomfortably in her chair and glanced again at the scarlet, green and orange of the plants. A tall figure was standing beside them. For a moment she could not move. She stared, taking in every detail of the long, white-pleated robe, the dark, aquiline features, the glittering eyes. It must be one of the crew. Slowly she raised her hand to her dark glasses and pushed them up onto her forehead so she could see better. Immediately he disappeared.

'Serena.' Her voice sounded strangled, even to her own ears.

'What is it?' Serena sat up, catching the urgency in Anna's tone.

'Look at the plants! Can you see anything? Him?'

Serena swung round to look. She shook her head.

'I saw a tall man. In a long white robe. He's guarding it! I saw him clearly. In broad daylight!' She realised that she was trembling all over.

'It's all right, Anna.' Serena hauled herself up out of her chair and perched on the edge of Anna's to put her arm round her shoulders. 'You're safe. There's no one there now.'

Anna grimaced. 'What shall I do, Serena?'

'I've told you, give the bottle to Omar to lock up. We've got some exciting trips over the next few days. We won't be on the boat much. Relax. Just be a tourist.'

It was after supper, as she was sitting with Serena in the lounge, when Toby came over and perched on the edge of a sofa near them. 'I think I owe you an apology, Anna. Sorry if I trod on any toes this afternoon.'

She shrugged. 'You didn't. Not really.'

'No, you were right. It was none of my business.'

Serena stood up.

Anna frowned. 'Are you going?'

Serena nodded. 'Forgive me. I'm so tired. I don't think I have ever been so exhausted or slept so well on a holiday before. I'll say good night to you both. Don't forget we have another long day tomorrow.'

They watched her walk away. 'Nice woman.' Toby beckoned over a waiter. 'Can I get you a drink, Anna? As a peace offering.' He smiled.

Anna sat back on the sofa and nodded. 'Thanks. A beer would be nice.' She glanced at him sideways. How could one man irritate so much one minute and intrigue her so much the next?

They sat in silence for a while, watching the others. It was she who spoke first. 'What do you do with all your sketches?' she asked curiously, as Ali put down the glasses on the table. 'Do you work them up in your cabin or something, or will they all wait until you get home?'

'Most will wait.' He signed the chit and tossed it back onto the tray. 'I have been working on one or two. I need to do some of it quickly to keep the colour, the heat, the light, in my head. One thinks one won't forget; the images are so vivid, so intense, but half an hour back in

Blighty with its soft greens and cloudy skies, and that intensity will blur.'

Anna smiled. 'I envy you your creativity.'

'Why?' Again the acerbic tone, the sudden direct look, which she found so disconcerting. 'Anna, remember, you are a photographer. It is the same for you, your medium is different, that's all.'

'No. No, it's not the same at all. You have genuine passion. Commitment. And you do it professionally. I just play at it.'

'Art as a hobby can be just as passionate, as you put it, as when you do it as a profession. After all, how do you know you won't want to do it professionally one day? You are good and you have proved it, and you have that depth of understanding, that sense of rapport as you focus on your subjects, which could make you first class.'

He raised his eyes to hers. She could feel the colour coming to her cheeks under the intensity of his gaze.

Toby buried his face in his glass, and she had the feeling that he was as embarrassed by his revelations as she was. When he looked up he was calm again. 'Louisa felt it, of course. The all-embracing intensity of this country. You can tell from her work. It must show in her diary too.' He put his head on one side. 'Would this be a good time to be allowed to look at it?'

Anna laughed. 'You won't give up till I show it to you, will you?'

'Nope.' Toby shook his head.

'OK.' She stood up.

She hadn't intended him to follow her, but when she tried to stop him with deprecating gestures of hands and shoulders, he merely smiled and kept moving.

The diary was on the bedside table. He spotted it instantly, and sitting down on the bed, picked it up. Immediately he opened it, holding it gently on his opened palms with a reverence she found very touching.

'Toby?'

There was no reply. She doubted if he had heard her. She watched, fascinated, as he slowly turned the pages, devouring the book.

Neither of them heard the step in the corridor outside. Only as the door was pushed back against the wall did Anna see Andy standing there looking at them. 'I want a word, Anna!' He sounded inexplicably angry and she smelt beer on his breath. 'Now, if you don't mind.'

She frowned as the restrained violence in his voice finally got through to Toby, who glanced up, resting the diary on his knee.

'Perhaps you could excuse us, Toby.' Andy stepped into the cabin. 'I'll put this away, I think.' Before Toby had a chance to react Andy had taken the diary off his knees. He pulled open the drawer in the bedside table and put the diary inside, then he slammed the drawer shut.

'Andy! What are you doing?' Anna said angrily. 'How dare you barge in here like this!'

Toby stood up, his face dark. 'What the hell is this all about?'

'A private matter.' Andy reached out as though to take his arm.

Toby flinched. 'Don't touch me, Watson. What the hell is the matter with you?'

'Nothing at all.' Andy moved back a little. 'I'm sorry to interrupt, but it is important I talk to Anna. Alone. If you'll excuse us.'

'Anna?' Toby looked at her. 'Are you happy with this?'

Anna was furious. 'No, I'm not. Get out, Andy! I don't know what this is about, and I don't care!'

'I'll tell you what it's about as soon as we're alone.' Andy stepped back to the door and stood by it, obviously ready to usher Toby out.

Anna could feel Toby's rage and resentment. 'Perhaps you'd better go, Toby. We'll look at the diary another time,' she said. 'I'll deal with this.'

Toby hesitated and she saw him look at Andy through narrowed eyes. For a moment she thought they were going to hit each other. Then, abruptly, Toby stepped past them out of the cabin.

'Whatever this is, Andy, it had better be good after that performance.'

Andy sighed. 'You mustn't trust him, Anna.'

'Toby? This is about Toby?' She was bemused.

His eyes focused on the closed drawer. 'That is a very valuable item, Anna, and you are too trusting. How much do you really know about Toby Hayward?' There was a moment's silence, then he made for the door. 'I won't say any more now. Not without checking, but don't be alone with him. Ever. And don't let that diary out of your sight.'

After Andy had gone, Anna stood unmoving for several seconds before going to the door and locking it. Had Andy been drunk? She wasn't sure. He was certainly beginning to annoy her. On the other hand could he be right about Toby? She went over and took the diary out of the drawer and stood, holding it clutched against her chest, deep in thought.

Toby was an attractive man, challenging to be with. Her initial resentment had changed to one of intrigued tolerance, and then even to a feeling of genuine friendship. But his reticence and his abrupt manner meant that she knew very little about him or his background.

Sitting down, she set the diary on her knee and opened it. To Toby it was a gateway into Louisa's creative soul. He was interested in it for its content and its revelations about Louisa's relationship with Egypt. To Andy it was no more than a valuable artefact. Still flustered, she looked down at the page in front of her. To her it was the gateway to another world, a world that she was finding infinitely seductive, if a little frightening; certainly preferable to worrying about these two men and their increasingly unpredictable behaviour. Determinedly she put them both out of her head and set about getting ready for bed.

It was very early. A transparent wisp of mist hung over the Nile, unmoving in the dawn light, as Louisa, wrapped in a woollen shawl, climbed on deck and went to stand at the stern of the boat. She could see some of the crew swabbing down the deck in the bow, but they were concentrating on their work and seemed not to see her.

She was interrupted by a shrill voice behind her that made her jump. 'Louisa! What are you doing out here? Come in at once. The boy has brought us breakfast!' Augusta was standing at the saloon door.

She ushered Louisa towards the table. Helping herself to a large portion of bread and crumbly white cheese, Augusta said, 'I am glad you are not proposing to go anywhere today, my dear. Sir John has sent a message for the consul to come to the boat to hear our complaint about the thief last night. Hassan should be ashamed of himself for allowing anyone to reach your cabin.'

'But, Augusta!' Louisa was horrified. 'We have no clues as to who he was, no evidence—'

'We have the evidence of your eyes, my dear. That is sufficient!' Augusta glanced up and raised an imperious eyebrow as Hassan appeared in the doorway. 'What is it?'

'Lord Carstairs, Sitt Forrester. He wishes to speak with you.'

They could see the tall figure of their visitor behind Hassan.

Augusta raised her napkin to her lips, flustered. 'Oh dear! And here we are, not properly dressed to receive guests.' She glanced at Louisa's shawl and then down at her own simple skirt and pale blouse.

There was no time to demur. Lord Carstairs was already bowing to them, dismissing Hassan with a gesture of his hand.

'So, I trust you enjoyed our trip to the obelisk yesterday,' he said at last to Louisa, when Augusta finally drew breath after her lengthy description of Louisa's ordeal the night before. When told that the scent bottle had miraculously been returned, Louisa had seen him relax. He made no further mention of the matter, asking, 'Are you planning any more sightseeing, Mrs Shelley?'

Louisa was about to deny any plans, when Augusta jumped in.

'Indeed she is, Lord Carstairs. She is planning to go to Philae tomorrow.'

Louisa gritted her teeth against the retort she wanted to make; her hostess no doubt meant well. Instead she rose to her feet, and with what she hoped was a gracious smile she said, 'I should certainly like to go there if there is time. Maybe on our way back downriver, after we have been to Abu Simbel?' She nodded to them both. 'Please, Lord Carstairs, don't get up. Forgive me, but there are letters I have to write this morning if they are to catch the steamer before we set off.'

Leaving the saloon with perhaps more haste than decorum, she made her way to her own small cabin.

Hassan had brought the felucca against the side of the larger boat in the soft, pre-dawn darkness. Silently Louisa handed him her painting things and her bundle of clothes and shoes. Her feet, like his, were bare and silent on the wooden boards.

As she climbed over the side, she felt his strong brown hands grip her waist, and a shock of excitement knifed through her as he helped her down into the boat. When she was in her seat, he cast off the rope and silently steered the felucca out into the main channel.

Louisa found herself gazing apprehensively at the neighbouring boats, the *Scarab*, which housed Lord Carstairs, and beyond it the Fieldings' *Lotus*. They lay in total darkness.

As the dawn call of the muezzin began to echo softly across the water, the felucca nosed into the bank. A boy was waiting for them with horses, three saddled and one, a packhorse, carrying panniers.

'We will ride five miles up the side of the cataract.' Hassan spoke normally now, well out of sound and sight of the *Ibis*. 'Then we find someone to take us across to the island.'

He watched as Louisa slipped on her shoes.

'You are worried, Sitt Louisa?' Hassan helped her into her saddle and stood for a moment looking up at her.

She shook her head. 'I was afraid Lord Carstairs might see us and call me back to go with him. That was not what I wanted.'

'Then it shall not be. *Inshallah!*' He smiled and turned towards his own mount. 'The bottle, Sitt Louisa? It is well hidden?'

So he too suspected that, once it was established that she had gone, someone might be inclined to search for it.

She nodded. 'It is well hidden, Hassan. It is in my paintbox.'

Hassan swung into his saddle. 'And the djinn, Sitt Louisa? What of him?' She saw him make the sign against the evil eye.

She shrugged. 'We must pray that the djinn will not bother us,

Hassan, and that our prayers, yours and mine, will keep us safe.'

A dozen times during the course of their ride she wanted to stop, to sketch the cataract villages, the beauty of the river hurtling over the rocks; the carvings and drawings etched into the cliffs by pilgrims on their way to the Temple of Isis, but he would not let her. 'On our return, Sitt Louisa. We can stop then.' He glanced behind them nervously, but there was no sign of pursuit.

Once or twice they saw glimpses of the temple as they grew near, then at last they were at the top of the falls where the river widened and they could see the island of Philae in front of them. They made their way towards the landing stage, where they could hire a boat to take them out to the island, and Hassan began to unload the packhorse.

Louisa could not take her eyes off the island. The beauty of the temple, reflected in the still, deep blue water, was breathtaking.

Her transformation into the cooler, artistic lady painter had taken place this time in a secluded spot behind some rocks where the cliffs had come near the waters of the cataract. Now, as Hassan rowed her towards the landing place, her hand trailed in the limpid water, and she had totally forgotten Carstairs and her fear that he might follow them.

'This place is called the Holy Island.' Hassan rested on his oars for a moment. 'The heathen god Osiris was buried on the small island of Philae, and the priests would visit him from this great temple. People came from all over Egypt and Nubia to pay homage to him and to Isis.'

'I believe it is still holy.' Louisa lifted her hand, trailing water droplets, to shade her eyes from the glare. 'You can feel it still.'

They found a place to sit in the shade between two of the huge carved pillars that formed the great colonnade in front of the temple. She began to draw at once, while Hassan unpacked their belongings. He squatted on his haunches beside her when he had finished, content merely to watch, and she became at once acutely aware of his presence near her. When she raised her eyes she found his fixed on her face. For a moment they stared at each other, then Louisa looked away. Hassan reached out and very gently touched her hand. She glanced at him again. 'Hassan—' She found she couldn't speak.

He gave her his serious, gentle smile and put his finger to his lips. There was nothing to say.

They stayed where they were for a long while. Slowly she became lost once more in what she was doing, and it was several hours before she stopped working and they ate the bread and cheese and hummus he had brought for their lunch.

Then it was time to explore. Louisa extricated the scent bottle in its small box and tucked it into her skirt pocket with a small notebook and a pencil.

Slowly they wandered across the island, totally covered as it was by temple buildings and the ruins of a Coptic village that had been built there many hundreds of years before. Here and there she stopped to make a quick sketch as they made their way towards the delicately elegant kiosk of Trajan. Set against the stunning blue of the water and the stark barrenness of the rocks, it was astonishing in its grace and beauty after the heavy stateliness of the main temple. Louisa laughed in delight. 'I am going to have to paint this. As we saw it first. From the river. Or perhaps from down there, on the shore.'

Hassan smiled indulgently. He enjoyed seeing her so excited.

'Can you feel the magic of this place, Hassan? It is in the air all around us. More than in the other temples.'

She leaned against a piece of fallen masonry and pulled off her straw hat to fan her face. As she did so, her eyes fell on the dazzlingly bright sand of a small bay below them. A boat had been pulled up there and a man in European dress was standing beside it. Louisa let out a little cry of dismay. 'It's Carstairs!'

'No, Sitt Louisa, that is not possible.' Hassan stepped closer to her, his eyes narrowed against the glare.

'It is.' Louisa felt a rush of anger and something not unlike fear. 'I was afraid he would do this!'

'There is no need for us to see him, if that is your wish, Sitt Louisa. This is a small island, but there are places to hide.'

'But he will have asked the boy who waits with the horses. He will have asked the man from whom we hired the boat. "Yes, my lord," they will say. "They are here. Give us baksheesh and we shall take you to them!"' She was almost stamping her foot in her vexation.

Hassan was staring at the shore, seemingly unworried. 'We will prove them all wrong. We will disappear into the shadows. Come.' He held out his hand.

Without any hesitation she took it and they ran back towards the great temple. Hassan swept all their belongings together into a pile and threw the Persian rug over them. 'See. There is no sign that a lady artist has been here. Merely a visitor who has gone to explore the ruins. Here, boy!' He beckoned a ragged urchin over and showed him a coin. The boy's eyes grew huge. 'This is for you if you guard our belongings. If a gentleman asks, you do not know whose they are and you have seen no lady here at all. Hear me?' The child nodded emphatically, money changed hands, and moments later he was seated on top of the pile.

Hassan smiled. 'There are several groups of visitors going round the temple now, Sitt Louisa. This could belong to any of them. The *effendi* will not search long.' Once more he took her hand. 'It is best if we go inside. There are a thousand pillars to hide behind, a hundred small chapels and corners and robing rooms. There are stairs which lead to the top of the pylon. He will not find us.' His face was alight with laughter.

She couldn't help but laugh with him. Like two naughty children they ran into the shade of the colonnade and hid behind the pillars.

A group of visitors moved into the bright sunlight for a moment and stood staring up at the huge relief of Neos Dionysos. From behind her pillar Louisa saw Carstairs hurry to the middle of the courtyard and hesitate, scrutinising the women with care. After a few moments he moved on again, satisfied his quarry was not among them. Feeling the touch of Hassan's hand, she turned away to follow him into the darker shade close to the wall and tiptoed with him towards the entrance.

'Where is he now?' Louisa breathed, peering round a pillar.

Hassan shrugged. 'We must wait to see what he does next. We do not want to be trapped by going further into the temple.'

They waited, Louisa acutely aware that Hassan's arm was touching hers, that his fingers brushed her fingers. Her heart was hammering in her chest, half from fear, half from excitement.

She felt him move slightly when Carstairs appeared beneath the archway and stood staring round him again. She felt he could see them, or somehow sense them near him. She held her breath.

As if afraid he could feel her gaze upon him she closed her eyes. Slowly she turned towards the entrance to the inner vestibule at the far end of the court. Beyond it lay the sanctuary.

When she opened her eyes she saw a figure was standing there watching her. He was tall, dressed in white, his dark aquiline face a shadowy blur. As she watched, he began to move towards her, drifting over the rough paving slabs. His arms were crossed over his chest, but as he moved closer he unfolded them and reached out towards her.

She didn't realise she had screamed out loud until Hassan pulled her against him, his hand across her mouth. '*Allahu Akbar; Allahu Akbar, Allahu Akbar!*' He had seen it as well. 'God is great; God is most great; God protect us.' He guided her steadily backwards towards the wall. '*Yalla!* Go away! *Imshi! Allahu Akbar!* God save us from both the evil spirit and from the English *effendi!*'

She had closed her eyes again, trembling violently, aware of the steady beating of his heart beneath her ear, and the strength of his arm around her. The box in her pocket dragged against her hip as she walked. It seemed to her that it was growing hotter and heavier with every step. With an exclamation of horror she broke away from Hassan and fumbled in the soft gauzy cotton of the gown. She wasn't sure what she intended to do. Take it out. Throw it away. Hurl it towards the sanctuary perhaps. The tall figure was still there when she turned. It seemed to have come no closer, but it was, if anything, more solid. She could see the details of the face now, the gold embroidery on his gown with the girdle at his waist, and what looked like the tail of a leopard hanging to the ground.

'Dear God save us!' she whispered as they shrank into the shadows.

'In the name of the gods you serve and of Isis your Queen, begone!'

The voice immediately beside them made Louisa gasp. She cowered back into Hassan's arms.

Carstairs was only a few feet from them now. His eyes were fixed on the apparition, his hand outstretched, palm foremost.

For a moment no one moved. Louisa had closed her eyes again. When at last she looked up, the tall figure had vanished. In its place was Carstairs, his face contorted with anger.

'So. You see the danger now of playing with matters you do not understand!' he said. 'I assume that as its keeper has shown himself here, you have the ampulla with you? It would be sensible to let me have it, I think.' He held out his hand.

Neither Louisa nor Hassan moved. Carstairs's face darkened. 'Let go of your mistress, you dog!'

Hassan moved back without a word. His expression grew hard. Louisa's fright turned suddenly to blind fury. 'How dare you speak to Hassan like that! He was protecting me.'

'Then he has done his duty.' Carstairs took a deep breath, visibly calming himself. 'The bottle, please, Mrs Shelley. For your own safety.'

'I am perfectly safe with Hassan, thank you, Lord Carstairs.' Her eyes met his and held them. 'And the ampulla, as you call it, need not concern you. Nor need any superstitions and visions you may have thought you saw. Whatever it was did not harm us.' She hoped he could not see how her hands were shaking as she hid them in the folds of her skirt.

'How grateful for my intervention!' he sneered. 'Do you realise, Mrs Shelley, what would have happened had I not been here? Do you realise what would have happened had the priest Hatsek appeared?'

Louisa stared at him defiantly. 'The priest Hatsek?'

A tight smile illuminated his face for a moment, then disappeared. 'The second djinn. The hieroglyphs are drawn on your piece of paper, Mrs Shelley. Clearly you do not recognise them.'

'No, Lord Carstairs, I did not recognise them. I read neither Arabic nor hieroglyphics, as you are well aware,' she said coldly. 'Nor do I believe in curses and evil genies!'

'Then you should. Their names are written clearly on the paper you showed me. Anhotep, high priest and servant of Isis, and Hatsek, servant of Isis, priest of Sekhmet, the lion-headed goddess. The lion-headed goddess is the goddess of war, Mrs Shelley. Wherever she went there was terror and death. The wind from the desert is the hot breath of her rage. Do you not feel it, even now? And were you not so afraid of the figure you saw just now that you threw yourself into the arms of your Egyptian servant?'

She hesitated and she saw the triumphant gleam in his eye. 'Please, Mrs Shelley, don't lie to yourself, even if you insist on lying to me. Had I not arrived at that moment, you and your servant would be dead!'

Louisa stared at him. Behind her Hassan folded his arms into the sleeves of his white *galabiyya*. His meek silence was belied by the disdain in his eyes. 'The ampulla, Mrs Shelley. Surely now you will allow me to take it?'

'Why should it be safer with you than with me, Lord Carstairs?' Part of her wanted to give it to him. Indeed she wanted to scream at him to take it, keep it, throw it in the Nile, if he wanted to. Another part of her felt a healthy flash of rebellion. Somewhere in the back of her head she could hear her beloved George's voice: 'Don't let him bully you, Lou. Don't let him take it from you. How do you know he didn't conjure that fiend up just to intimidate you? What does he want it for, Lou?'

She felt herself smile at the thought of her husband and the oh-so-sensible advice he would have given her, and she saw the surprise on Carstairs's face. He had expected her to cower in fear.

'I appreciate your help,' she continued, 'but whatever it was we all imagined we had seen, it has gone now. So, I shall return to my painting, Lord Carstairs, and allow you to continue your own visit uninterrupted.' She turned and, beckoning to Hassan, began to walk away.

'You have made him very angry, Sitt Louisa.' Hassan's low voice at her elbow slowed her steps. 'He will make a bad enemy.'

She pursed her lips. 'I make a bad enemy too, Hassan. I will not have him browbeat me into submission. Nor will I have him insult you.'

Hassan grinned. 'I am not insulted, Sitt Louisa. But he has powers, this man. Powers to dismiss the djinn. But not in the name of Allah nor of your Christian God. I think he has studied the evil arts.'

Louisa stared at him, shocked. 'But he is an English gentleman!'

Hassan shrugged. 'I am not a learned man, Sitt Louisa, but in my heart I feel things, and in this I know I am not wrong. He wants the bottle because the power of the djinn is harnessed to it.'

She hesitated. 'Do you think he was right? Do you think this Hatsek, if that is his name, would have killed us?'

They walked out of the shadow of the colonnade once more and into the sunlight, and felt the heat like a hammer blow on their heads.

'I do not know. I did not feel the fear of death. Terror. Yes, I felt that. But it was of the unknown.'

If either had looked back to see whether Carstairs was following them they would have seen that for several seconds he stood watching them, then he turned sharply on his heel and headed towards the inner vestibule and beyond it into the darkness of the sanctuary itself.

When they reached their belongings once more, Hassan gave the boy another coin, spread out the rug and began to lay out Louisa's painting things for her once more. 'When he walks past as he surely will you must be painting very hard,' he commanded. 'Do not look at him. Concentrate on the picture you will be making.'

Louisa smiled. 'And that will be enough? He will walk away quietly?'

'I think he will, if you surround yourself with silence.'

She smiled. 'That sounds very wise.'

She set up her sketchbook on the easel and started drawing. She permitted herself a quick glance over her shoulder. There was no movement behind them in the great pillared hall. The only sound was the desultory cheeping of sparrows.

'Do not be fooled, Sitt Louisa,' Hassan said quietly. 'Lord Carstairs is still here.' He squatted down in the shade of the pillar she was drawing, and she found herself reliving the moment she had thrown herself into his arms. He had been strong, reassuring. He had smelt of a pleasing mix of sweet tobacco and spices and clean, freshly laundered cotton.

Her tongue protruding slightly from between her teeth, she rinsed the brush again. She had sketched a man, she realised, beside one of the ornate columns in her sketch. Not Hassan. This was a tall, solemn man, with a dark handsome face, who stared, arms folded, out across the Nile towards the distant mountains to the west.

Near her, Hassan sat unmoving. He appeared to be asleep, but his eyes were fixed on the archway that was the only way in to the inner temple. It was a long time later that he rose silently to his feet and headed back the way they had come. She glanced after him, but he gestured at her to stay and she turned back to the painting. The courtyard was airless, the bright sunlight shimmering off the stones. The heat folded round her like a soft blanket. Her eyes closed. She could feel the weight of the small package in her skirt pocket. It was inert. Unexceptional. Safe.

With a sigh she removed her shoes and slipped from her canvas stool onto the rug that Hassan had spread for her, and, pulling the bag which contained her formal, more fashionable dress towards her, she lay down.

She woke about an hour later. The shadows had moved and the burning sunlight on her bare feet was searing her skin. She drew them up sharply and sat up, staring round. Hassan was not there.

Aware that her feet were painfully burnt, she wondered where he was. Scrambling up, she moved further into the shade. 'Hassan?'

The silence was so intense she frowned. It was as though she were the only person in the world. 'Hassan, where are you?'

Nothing moved. The sky above was white with heat and she couldn't look at it. Her feet still bare, she made her way down the colonnade towards the entrance, gazing this way and that between the columns. 'Hassan!' she called, louder now. What if Lord Carstairs had found him and sent him away? What if he had gone without her?

At the end of the colonnade, the sand was blinding in the direct sunlight. She realised suddenly that she had left her shoes and hesitated. Then she heard a voice behind her. 'Sitt Louisa?'

She spun round. 'Hassan! Oh, Hassan, thank God!' She flung herself at him. 'I thought you had gone without me.'

His arms folded round her. For a moment he held her, then she felt a featherlight kiss on her hair. 'I would not go without you. I would guard you with my life.'

She raised her face to look at him. 'Hassan—'

'Hush, Sitt Louisa. You are safe with me.' For a moment he said nothing more, gazing at her face, then he smiled. 'We have fought this; I thought it forbidden. But now I believe that it is the will of Allah.' He raised a finger and touched her mouth. 'But only if you will it.'

She stared at him, aching to touch him. For a moment she could say nothing, then slowly she raised herself up on her toes and she kissed his lips. 'It is the will of Allah,' she whispered.

For Louisa time stood still. It was as though all she had ever dreamed, ever imagined in her wildest fantasies, had coalesced into the next moments of ecstasy in his arms. She never wanted the kiss to end. When at last it did, they remained close together, staring into each other's eyes.

It was a long time later that he noticed her bare feet. 'You must not go without your shoes, my love. There are scorpions in the sand. Come.' He scooped her up into his arms and carried her back to the rug. Before he allowed her to sit down he picked it up and shook it. Then he grinned. 'Now it is ready for my lady to sit.'

Sitting down, she drew up her knees and hugged them. 'Hassan, I am a widow. I am free. But you. You have a wife in your home village. This is not right.'

He knelt beside her and took her hand. 'A Christian may not have more than one wife. It is written in the Koran that a man can love more than one woman. I have not seen my wife, Sitt Louisa, for more than two years. I send her money. She is happy with that.'

'I could not love you as a wife, Hassan. When summer comes I have to go home to my own sons.'

He looked away, sadness in his face. 'Does that mean we should chase away the days of happiness which lie within our grasp?' He took her hands in his. 'If heartbreak must come, let it come later, when there is happiness to remember. Otherwise there is nothing but regret.'

She reached up and kissed him again, but he had suddenly grown tense. He pushed her away.

'Hassan, what is it?' She was hurt.

'*Ma feem tish*! I do not understand. Lord Carstairs. He is there!' He waved towards the distant colonnade. 'I searched everywhere. There is nowhere on this island he could have been hiding.' He shook his head in anger. 'Wait here, my beautiful Louisa. Do not move.'

In a second he had left her, slipping like a shadow along the colonnade. Louisa held her breath. The silence had returned.

Anna woke with a start. She lay still, staring up at the ceiling of her cabin. Her head ached and she pressed her fingers against her temples. Her exhaustion was total. She had been engrossed in Louisa's diary far into the night, and now felt too tired even to sit up. It was when she glanced at her wristwatch that the adrenaline kicked in. It was almost ten o'clock in the morning.

The boat was deserted. She stood in front of the notice board outside the dining room, which had long ago stopped serving breakfast. This morning there was an outing to Aswan and the bazaar, followed by a short visit at midday to the Old Cataract Hotel. Slowly turning away, she wandered up to the lounge. Ibrahim called out to her as she made for the shaded afterdeck. 'You have missed your breakfast, *mademoiselle*?'

She smiled, touched that he had noticed. 'I'm afraid I overslept again.'

'You like me to bring coffee and croissant?'

'I should love it. Thank you, Ibrahim.'

While he fetched her coffee, she made her way to a table at the far end of the shady deck, beneath the awning of white canvas. Groping in her shoulder bag, she brought out her guidebook, then dropped her bag on the deck. She wanted to learn more about the priest of Sekhmet and there was, she remembered, a brief summary of the Egyptian gods somewhere at the beginning of the book. She flipped open the pages and stared down. There she was, Sekhmet, with her huge lion's head. 'The lion goddess unleashes her anger—' the text commented. Over the figure's head was a sun disc and the picture of a cobra. She shivered.

'You are cold, *mademoiselle*?' Ibrahim put her coffee and croissant on the table, together with a glass of fruit juice.

She shook her head. 'I was thinking about something I'd read here, about the ancient gods. Sekhmet, the lion-headed goddess. They show her with a cobra.' She glanced up at him. 'How do you know so much about snakes, Ibrahim?'

He smiled at her, tucking his empty tray under his arm. 'I learned from my father, and he from his father before him.'

'When Charley found the snake in her cabin, you said it was guarding something of mine. How did you know that?'

She saw him lick his lips, suddenly nervous. He gave her a quick glance as though trying to decide what to say, and she thought she would help him out. 'Was it a real snake, Ibrahim? Or was it a magic snake? A phantom?'

He shuffled his feet uncomfortably. 'Sometimes they are the same.'

'Do you think it will return?'

'*Inshallah*. If it's the will of God.' Ibrahim shrugged and with a slight bow and that infuriating phrase he backed away.

It was an hour later that she finally rose to her feet and made for the steps onto the upper deck. The boat was still deserted. She had seen neither passengers nor crew since Ibrahim had left her alone, but the river was busy. Tourist cruisers juggled for position along the narrow moorings; launches, feluccas, ferries, small fishing boats and motor boats plied up and down, some within feet of the boat's rail.

The flowers in the pots had been watered early, but already the deck was dry. She walked slowly towards them and stood at the rail, looking out across the river towards the sand-coloured hills, half shrouded in heat haze. This was the perfect chance to retrieve the bottle.

She moved towards the plant container where she had buried the bottle and stooped over it. She raked through the tangle of stems and roots and touched something cold and hard. Closing her eyes she steadied herself sternly and began to work it free of the pot. At last it came loose. Straightening, she began to dust off the clinging streaks of wet earth. It was as she did so that the deck suddenly grew cold.

She held her breath. Please God, no. Not again. Slowly she forced herself to look up.

Hatsek, the high priest of Sekhmet, transparent, wispy as a breath of mist, was dressed in the skin of a desert lion. She could see it—the tawny pelt, the great paw hanging over his shoulder, the gold chain across his chest to hold the skin in place. She saw his long lean legs, his sandals, his sinewy arms, and for a fraction of a second, she saw his face, the burning fury of his eyes. He had seen her even as she had seen him. He had registered her presence, she was sure of it. He knew that she was the one who had brought the sacred bottle back to Egypt.

No! She doubted that she had spoken the word out loud. Her mouth was dry, her throat constricted with fear. The silence around her was, she realised, total. In one frantic movement she spun round and lifted her arm to throw the bottle into the Nile.

As she did so, a hand closed round her wrist and the bottle fell harmlessly onto one of the sun loungers. Suddenly she could hear again: the boats, the cars, the shouts, and with them a familiar voice.

'What on earth are you doing?' It was Andy. He stood staring at her, puzzled. Then he grinned at her and bent to pick up the bottle.

There was a moment's silence as she stared at him, then turned to look at the empty deck behind her. She was hallucinating. Her tiredness, her obsession with the story—even her conversation with Ibrahim—they had all conspired to make her imagine she had seen something.

Andy squinted carefully at the bottle in his hand. 'It's not genuine, you know. All the genuine stuff is in museums by now.' He was rubbing off the soil, seemingly incurious about why it should be covered in wet earth. 'Do you see this?' He held it out to her, pointing at the stopper. 'The glass here has been machined. It's not even a particularly old fake.'

She did not put out her hand for it. 'It has to be over a hundred years old if it belonged to Louisa Shelley.' She swallowed hard. To her surprise her voice sounded quite normal, even defensive. If he was right, there could be no ghost. How could there be a ghost?

'Then why were you going to throw it away?'

She grimaced. 'I had my reasons, believe me.'

'Perhaps I had better look after it for you? Even if it's Victorian and not Pharaonic it has a certain curiosity value, you know.'

She hesitated. It would be so easy to give it to him, to forget the whole business. To abrogate responsibility.

Watching her face, he frowned. 'What is it about this wretched little bottle? First Charley nicks it; now you want to get rid of it.'

'It's haunted, Andy. There is a curse attached to it. It has a guardian spirit—' She broke off abruptly as she caught sight of his face.

'Oh, come on! I don't think so. Serena's behind this, isn't she!' He roared with laughter. 'Oh, my poor Anna. Listen, lovie. You mustn't be led on by her. Serena is as mad as a hatter. She got into all that psychic tosh when her husband died. You mustn't let her scare you.'

'It's not like that, Andy.'

'No? Well, I'm glad to hear it. They almost certified her at one point. That's why Charley went to live with her. Charley's mum and Serena's sister are close friends. I think everyone reckoned it was better Serena didn't go on living alone.'

'I don't believe you! Serena is knowledgeable. Reliable. I like her.'

He shook his head forcefully. 'Please, don't get involved with her over this stuff. I suggest you put that away'—he glanced at the bottle—'and forget it. Concentrate on enjoying your holiday.'

She smiled faintly. What was the use of trying to explain her feelings?

He leaned towards her. 'Listen, why don't you sit down for a bit and I'll go down and get us both a drink. After lunch there is a coach coming to take us to see the dam. Your genie of the bottle won't be able to get you there.' His tone was conciliatory.

She frowned. 'You still don't believe me, do you?'

'Anna, my dear—'

Her irritation was mounting. 'No, Andy. I have things to do in my cabin. I'll see you at lunch.' Picking up her bag, she walked away.

'Anna! Don't be cross. I'm sorry, I really am.' His voice followed her across the deck. Then its tone changed. 'Anna, listen. There's something important I must tell you. I was thinking last night. About Toby—'

She stopped. Slowly she turned round.

'There is something in his past. I was right. It's something serious. I don't gossip, but I think you should know this. I'm fairly sure where I remember seeing his name now. It was in the papers.' He paused. 'I think he was indicted for killing his wife, Anna.'

Her eyes widened in shock. 'I don't believe you!'

'I hope I'm wrong. But I had to tell you. So that you're careful.'

'I will be.' She was stunned. And angry. Angry at Toby and angry at Andy. 'That is gossip, Andy. You don't know for sure, and whatever it was it is clearly in the past or he would not be here now!' She spun on her heel and made for the steps. She didn't wait to see if he followed.

Letting herself into her cabin she threw the bag on the bed. Her eyes filled with tears. It was all too much. The sleepless night, the bottle, the ghostly apparition on deck and now this. She was, she realised suddenly, desperately hoping that Andy was wrong. That Toby was not the man he thought. And she was also certain that she had had enough of them both and their desire to get their hands on her scent bottle or the diary.

She took the bottle out of her bag. Pulling open the drawer in her dressing table, she tossed the bottle in and slammed the drawer shut.

At almost the same second there was a knock on the door. She swung round, her heart hammering. 'Who is it?' She swallowed nervously.

'It's me, Andy. I want to apologise.'

'There's no need.' She made no move to open the door.

'Please, Anna, let me in.' The handle turned. She hadn't locked the door and it swung open. 'I'm sorry I upset you. I just thought you should know.'

'You didn't upset me, and I wish you wouldn't keep barging into my cabin uninvited! For your information, I couldn't care less about Toby and I don't care if you believe me or not about the bottle, either!'

He gave a rueful little grimace. 'You could try convincing me.'

She hesitated, glaring at him. Then she shrugged. 'All right. Let me show you what Louisa says about all this.' She stepped over to the bed-side table and pulled the diary out of the drawer. Then she sat on the bed and flipped it open.

Andy came over and sat down on the bed, his eyes fixed greedily on the book. 'Show me,' he said quietly.

She glanced up at him, then quickly looking away again she began to leaf through the pages. 'OK. Look. Here: *"I reached out to ward him off and my hand passed through him as though he were mist."* And here: *"The figure was watching me . . . he began to move towards me, drifting over the rough paving slabs."* And look at this . . . And this. And look how keen Lord Carstairs was to get his hands on the bottle. Why would he be interested if it were not genuine?'

Andy rubbed his chin. 'I really am not into spirits and things, Anna. I'm sorry. I always look for a more down-to-earth explanation when unusual things happen.' He paused, obviously aching to see what happened next. 'So, leaving aside these spirits for a minute, what happened when she got back to the boat? Did Carstairs pursue the bottle?'

She turned over the page. There were two sketches there, one of a felucca swooping across the Nile as the sun set behind a sand cliff, and the other of a woman in Nubian costume, a veil draped over part of her face. Beneath them the writing flew across the page.

It was nearly dark when we drew alongside the dahabeeyah and Hassan threw a rope up to the reis *who was waiting for us. As I climbed aboard the* reis *shook his head in some perturbation. "Sitt Louisa, there is big trouble! You must go at once to the saloon." This was followed by a tirade of Arabic directed at my poor Hassan.*

Anna looked up. 'Are you sure you want to hear all this?'

Andy nodded vehemently. 'I certainly do. What happened next?'

Louisa saw at once that Lord Carstairs was sitting at the table in the saloon. Near him were the two Fielding ladies and Augusta. Sir John was waiting for her by the door.

'Thank God you are safe, Louisa.' He grabbed her by the shoulders and planted a kiss on her cheek. 'Roger told us what happened to you. We were distraught, my dear. What a disaster! What a scandal!'

Louisa stared first at him, then at Carstairs. 'What disaster, what scandal? I don't understand.' She was suddenly suspicious. 'Please, Lord Carstairs, what scandal is this you feel you have to report to my friends?' A sudden wave of anger gave strength to her voice and he looked up at last to meet her eyes. The extraordinary depth of his gaze was without expression, and for a moment her mind went blank. Desperately she grabbed at her composure, and as she did so he smiled. It was a smile of extraordinary warmth and radiance.

'Mrs Shelley, forgive me. It was my desperate and sincere concern for your safety that made me speak to the Forresters in the way I have. I would never knowingly have spoken of anything which might in any way harm your good name.'

'Nor could you, my lord! I have done nothing which could possibly incur such an accusation. How dare you imply that I have!'

She was aware suddenly of the eyes of the others in the saloon all fixed on her face.

It was David Fielding who broke the silence. 'I think, my dears, it is time we returned to our vessel. It has been a tiring day and I am sure Mrs Shelley would like a little time to rest and compose herself without us all here, too. Katherine?' He held out his hand to his wife, whose face registered naked disappointment at being denied the spectacle of the first-class quarrel which seemed in the offing. Venetia, clearly also aggrieved, turned on her brother in fury. 'We cannot go without Roger! We were all to spend the evening together, surely?'

David pursed his lips. 'I am sure Roger will forgive us on this occasion. We can always meet once more tomorrow.'

His mild-mannered politeness belied the determined note that had entered his voice. In seconds the two women were trooping up on deck and making their farewells. With Sir John and Lord Carstairs gone after their guests to bid them farewell, she found herself alone with Augusta.

'What is this nonsense?' she asked briskly. 'What has he accused me of? That man is a perfect nuisance. He followed me uninvited, interrupted my visit, and generally spoilt the day for me entirely. And now I return to find he has been making some kind of accusations behind my back.'

Augusta settled herself into one of the chairs and clasped her hands in her lap. 'He told us about Hassan, my dear, and his totally inappropriate behaviour. I cannot tell you how sorry I am. He was so highly recommended.' She shook her head, and frowned. 'And there was something else.' She paused. 'Roger informed me, discreetly, of course, that you were not properly dressed! In fact you were wearing some kind of native attire!' Her face had begun to glow quite pink, and she reached into her sleeve for a lace handkerchief to dab her upper lip.

'The dress to which he refers I brought with me from England,' Louisa said furiously. 'It is most certainly not native attire, as he puts it. It is both cool and sensible wear for the climate and is totally decent, I assure you.' Her anger was almost choking her suddenly. 'As for Hassan, he has never ever been anything other than respectful to me. How dare Lord Carstairs imply anything else! He insults me, Augusta!'

Augusta stood up, agitated. 'No, my dear. He was right to speak to John and me. He admires you, Louisa. He meant it for the best, my dear.'

'In which case I have now set your mind at rest in all particulars.' Louisa could feel her face flaming. 'Forgive me, Augusta. I need to go and change before dinner.'

Augusta gave a small nod, but she did not look up.

It was not until after dinner, when Augusta had gone to bed and Sir John and Louisa were sitting together in the saloon over cups of tea, that Sir John dropped his bombshell. 'I have sent a message to the consul to ask him to recommend a dragoman for you for the rest of the trip.'

Louisa put down her cup. 'I have no need of another dragoman. Hassan suits me perfectly.'

'I have dismissed him, my dear. He was a nice enough fellow, but not of the standard one requires. Don't fret. We'll find someone new for you, my dear. It won't affect your little drawing trips at all.'

Anna looked up angrily. 'Poor Louisa. How could she put up with it? Sir John was so patronising! And what a complete bastard Carstairs was!'

Andy was sitting beside her, staring down at the book on her knee.

His arm was pressed against her arm, she noticed suddenly, his thigh against hers. Embarrassed, she closed the book. 'Andy, it's nearly time for lunch. I can hear the others. They must have come back from their shopping trip. Perhaps we can read some more another time.'

He nodded reluctantly. 'Sure. I enjoyed that.' Standing up, he made for the door. 'I can't wait to find out what happened next.' He turned and winked. 'I'll leave you to get ready. See you in a minute.'

When she reached the dining room, the others were already seated. A chair had been left for her beside Andy, she noticed. She slipped into it, and leaned forward and grinned across at Serena, who was sitting opposite. 'I'm sorry I missed this morning's trip. I would have liked to have seen the bazaar. Did you buy anything nice?'

Serena nodded. 'I'll show you later.'

'I trust you had a nice morning too.' Charley was sitting on Andy's left and peered round at her. 'You wouldn't have been lonely. Not with Andy to keep you company.'

Ali appeared with a pile of hot plates and began distributing them round the table. Relieved at the distraction, Anna turned away, but Charley was not to be deflected.

'I suppose the bazaar was too common for Anna. After all, she's the descendant of a famous painter. She's just going to lounge around and wait for everyone else to dance attendance on her. I'm surprised she didn't have her own private boat. But then she wouldn't have had the chance to meet any nice eligible men.' She sat back triumphantly. 'Ali? Where is my wine?' Her call made the young waiter hurry over to the central table to find the bottle which had her name on it. She poured herself a glass and drank it straight down.

'Charley, go easy.' Andy leaned towards her. 'There's no need for this.'

'No?' She helped herself again. 'This Egyptian wine is crap.'

'It's fine.' Andy took the bottle out of her hand and put it on the table out of reach. 'Come on. We can all be friends, surely.'

The dining room was very silent, Anna noticed suddenly. People were embarrassed, concentrating on their soup, which was thick and spicy and garnished with fresh mint.

Anna glanced round the table. Charley had poured herself another glass of wine. She sipped it in moody silence, her fingers linked around her glass. As though feeling Anna's glance she suddenly sat up.

'I'm not going to let you have him, you know,' she said, leaning towards Anna. 'You're mine, aren't you, sweetie.' Her hand came down on Andy's and she raked a nail up the skin of his wrist.

He jumped. 'Charley!'

She smiled sweetly. 'Yes, Charley. And if sweet little Anna comes between us, I shall do more than steal her silly little Egyptian bottle to teach her a lesson, believe me—' She broke off with a squeal as a hand came down on her shoulder.

'That's enough threats, young lady!'

Toby, who had been sitting on the other table, was standing behind her. 'Come on. You're not eating and you're causing a lot of grief. I suggest you go and sleep it off.' He pulled her up out of her chair. Her glass of wine flew out of her hand, depositing its contents over Andy's shirt.

With a scream of rage, Charley whirled round and hit Toby in the face.

'Take your hands off her!' Andy was frantically wiping himself down with his napkin.

'Please, Mr Toby, let me deal with it!' Omar had appeared and was trying to pull Toby off.

'Leave it. I can cope.' Toby had the screaming Charley by the shoulders. 'I'll dump her in her cabin.' In seconds he had dragged her out of the room and the doors had swung shut behind them.

Serena stood up. 'I'd better go and look after her.' Andy leapt to his feet. 'No, you stay here. I'll go.' He threw down his wine-stained napkin and ran after them. But not before he had turned to Anna. 'I told you he was violent,' he murmured, then he had gone.

Serena sat down with a shrug and turned back to the table. It seemed only seconds before Ibrahim and Ali had replaced the cloth and were serving the main course. As they did so, the conversation in the dining room resumed—at a slightly louder pitch than before.

It was ten minutes before Andy reappeared. He had changed his shirt and trousers. 'She's asleep.' He slid into his chair.

'And Toby?' Anna studied his face. 'I hope you didn't hit him.'

Andy laughed. 'No, I didn't hit him. I helped him carry Charley to her cabin and put her on the bed. We took off her shoes and left her to it.'

'So, where is Toby?'

'Who knows?' He sat down and poured himself a glass of wine.

The meal continued in silence for several minutes, then Serena looked up. 'So, when do we leave to visit the high dam?'

'Soon.' Omar had heard her question. He stood up. 'People, please be quick with your coffee. We leave very soon.' He smiled round the room. 'Very soon, English time, please, which is today. Not very soon Egyptian time, which is next week.'

Anna caught Serena's eye as they all laughed. Egyptian indifference to time was one of Omar's favourite jokes—one he no doubt repeated to each succeeding group of passengers. She decided to sit beside Serena on the bus on the way to the dam.

Her decision was thwarted immediately by Andy, who inserted himself into the seat next to her. 'You don't mind, do you?'

She hid her impatience. 'Of course not,' she said, but when he stayed close by her side as the coach stopped at the high dam, she became increasingly irritated. They walked out onto the top of the vast concrete edifice and stood staring over the far side at Lake Nasser, the inland sea created by the building of the dam.

'It's amazing, isn't it.' Serena had followed them. 'But sad to think that there are so many temples and things lost under all that water.'

'They moved the important ones,' Andy replied.

Serena nodded. 'But they lost many more. The dam has not been all good news.'

'No?' Andy was impatient. 'How do you work that out?'

'Well, for one thing, the lower reaches of the Nile are becoming poisoned with salt from the sea, because the current is no longer strong enough to hold it back, and the lake is filling up with all the silt the annual floods would have deposited on the fields to fertilise them.'

Andy scowled. 'Of course. And there are all the unhappy little birdies too, no doubt,' he scoffed. 'And miserable thwarted crocodiles and all the sensitive magical things that the nasty electric fields interfere with!'

Serena closed her eyes for a second and took a deep breath. 'Buzz off, Andy. Go and annoy someone else, there's a dear.'

Anna glanced from one to the other and changed the subject. 'There's a dog down there on the dam wall and she's got puppies. I want to photograph her.' She led Serena away from Andy, and fumbling in her bag she took out her camera and began to snap the animals playing.

'He's really taken you in tow!' Serena watched as Andy wandered away from them. 'I take it you don't mind?'

Anna gave a wry smile. 'The jury is still out. He is a bit overwhelming sometimes.' She glanced at Serena. The other woman was staring out across Lake Nasser. Anna could not see her expression behind her dark glasses. 'But he's fun. He's attractive—'

'Don't trust him, Anna. Not completely.' To Anna's surprise, Serena suddenly caught her arm. 'Be careful, my dear. Please. You've enough problems and he is just the kind of person who could exacerbate the energies that are whirling round you at the moment.' She paused. 'Ever since we arrived in Egypt he seems to have been getting more aggressive and predatory! So watch yourself, please.' She turned and walked away.

Anna stared after her. 'Serena?'

Serena shook her head without turning round. She was moving swiftly away from the rest of the party along the dam.

'Let her go.'

Anna jumped. She hadn't heard Andy come back. He put his hand on her arm. 'She'll come round. She always does.'

She glanced up at him. 'Did you hear what she said?'

He shook his head. 'If you've been telling her what I said about her, I expect she was very rude!'

She frowned. 'You don't give me any credit for tact then.'

'Sorry.' His arm moved casually round her shoulders. 'Come and stand over here. I want to take a photo of you.' He guided her towards the wall. 'If you stand here, I can get the length of the dam in the picture.' He paused and frowned. 'What is it, Anna? What's wrong?'

She hadn't heard him. She was staring into the middle distance, her mouth open, her body taut with shock.

Only thirty feet away from her the priest Anhotep was watching her, his hand upraised, his finger pointing at her heart.

Andy leapt forward to steady her. 'It's a mirage, Anna. A trick of the light,' he said when she'd stammered out what she had seen. 'Come on. Let's get out of the sun.' He began to guide her back towards the end of the dam where a few trees provided a patch of shade.

'Andy! Anna! Wait!' Serena, glancing back at last, had realised that something was wrong. 'What's happened?' She hurried towards them.

'It was Anhotep,' Anna said shakily. 'Serena, he was here, just for a second, on the dam. But I left the bottle on the boat. Surely he should stay close to it? Why would he follow me?'

Serena's eyes were on Anna's face. 'You are sure you saw him?'

'She didn't see anything.' Andy put his arm round Anna's shoulder again. 'The sun is so bright it's easy to imagine things.'

'I saw something!' Anna stepped away from him sharply. 'He was looking at me! Watching me!' She shuddered.

Feeding on me. The words came to mind unbidden. *He's using my anger. My fear.* She gave a violent shudder.

Omar, who had been talking to Ben and a group of others, regaling them with a lively account of the building of the dam by the Russians, turned, attracted by Anna's raised voice. He frowned. 'There is a problem, people?' He strode quickly towards them. 'Anna is not well?'

'I'm fine.' Anna forced herself to smile. She could hardly confide in Omar. Between him and Andy they would have her locked up.

'Too much sun, perhaps,' Andy said. 'I'll take care of her. Nothing a cool drink in the shade won't put right.'

He began guiding Anna back towards their bus, but she stopped for a second and looked across to where Serena was standing.

'We'll talk about this later,' she said wearily.

On the bus Anna found herself sitting next to Ben, who was bombarding Omar with questions. Serena, who sat across from Anna, said very little. She appeared to be deep in thought, and when they returned to the boat she disappeared at once towards her cabin. Anna stared after her thoughtfully, then made her way to her own cabin, where she picked up the phone. It was several seconds before Serena answered. 'I wanted to talk to you some more,' Anna said quickly. 'Can you come here, to my cabin? That way we won't be interrupted again.'

Serena gave a quiet laugh. 'By dear, oh so attentive Andy? All right, my dear. Give me twenty minutes and I'll be with you.'

Sitting down on the bed Anna pulled open the drawer of her bedside locker. She would read Louisa's diary until Serena appeared. She sat for a moment looking at the worn cover. Had Phyllis had any idea, she wondered suddenly, what a time bomb she had unleashed on her greatniece when she had passed over the diary, and years earlier, the little scent bottle, a romantic present for a small, acquisitive child?

Louisa spoke to the *reis* in private, begging him to give a message to Hassan, but he merely shrugged and shook his head with cold reproach. The friendly smile, the twinkling eye of their captain had gone. Louisa climbed onto the upper deck and leaned against the rail, her parasol shading her from the heat of the morning sun. Miserably, she crumpled the note she had written to Hassan in her hand, then she let it drop into the water. It floated for a while, then sank slowly out of sight.

Some time later the squeak of oars nearby made her glance up, and she saw with a sinking heart that Lord Carstairs was being rowed over from his dahabeeyah. She watched, unsmiling, as he raised his hand in salute. Feigning not to notice, she turned away and walked across to the other side to look instead towards the town. Augusta had gone ashore with the Fielding ladies earlier that morning to visit the bazaar. Louisa had declined to go with them. She had no heart for shopping.

It was only a short time later that she heard a step on the deck behind her. 'Mrs Shelley. I feel I owe you a deep and heartfelt apology.'

She did not turn round. 'You do, sir. And you owe a greater one to my dragoman who has been dismissed thanks to your interference.'

There was a moment's silence, and Carstairs moved over to the rail and leaned on it beside her. 'Will you allow me to try to make amends? I understand they will start to take us up the cataract this afternoon. Will you allow me to escort you on a picnic on the rocks so you can watch as the *Ibis* starts her journey upriver? It would make a wonderful subject for your painting.'

As they stared out across the water, side by side, Louisa could see the horsedrawn gharries on the Corniche, the donkeys with their assorted riders, several boats pulled up on the sand near the quay. He watched beside her in silence. Half of her wanted desperately to accept his invitation; the chance to draw the boat from the rocks was too tempting to ignore. On the other hand she was still furious with him, still intensely aware of the disloyalty it would show to Hassan.

She gave in, in the end, unable to throw away the chance of watching and recording the event. And going with him did not mean that she had forgiven him, or ever would.

Gathering up her painting equipment later that afternoon, Louisa followed Carstairs down into his dahabeeyah, intensely aware that Venetia Fielding was watching them from the deck of her brother's boat. Even from that distance she could feel the woman's anger and jealousy.

They landed on an outcrop of rock above one of the narrower gorges between the islands, and Carstairs leapt nimbly ashore. The boatman passed over the picnic, her painting things and an array of soft tapestry cushions. Carstairs slipped the man a handful of coins in return and then waved him away. 'This will give us a splendid view as they pull the boat up against the current.' He smiled at her. Holding out his hand he helped her towards the cushions with effortless courtesy.

The rush of water precluded much speech. Leaving her to unpack her paints, Carstairs went and stood on the edge of the rock, staring downriver. He stood for a long time, seemingly lost in thought, then at last he turned back towards her. Propping her parasol behind her, Louisa had opened a sketchbook and was pencilling in an outline of the canyon.

'I'm afraid you will be bored, my lord,' she said, not looking up.

He shook his head. 'Indeed not. You are quite wrong about my boredom levels. I have infinite patience.' To her surprise, he lowered himself onto a cushion next to her and crossed his legs. She shrugged. Dipping her brush into her waterpot she selected colours from her box, mixed them, and began to brush the resulting shade swiftly onto the paper.

When next she looked at Carstairs, the sun had moved slightly and the shadows just beyond her were deeper than before. He was sitting in exactly the same position as he had been when she had last looked up, his eyes focused on her sketch but, she was certain, not actually seeing it. She stopped painting and laid down the brush. He made no move.

'My lord?' She spoke quietly. 'My lord? Roger? Are you all right?' His eyes were open, his pupils tiny points of black in the strange clear irises. He was, as far as she could see, in some kind of reverie.

After watching him for a few more seconds Louisa turned away. She went to stand by the water's edge, staring at the rocks, wondering if she should try to wake him. At that precise moment she saw the first figures appearing at the mouth of the gorge, the ropes over their shoulders. Within a few seconds the river was a turmoil of shouting, laughing men, as, with a dozen or so on each of the four lines, she saw them dragging the heavy boat up against the torrents of water.

'It's a splendid sight, is it not?'

She jumped at the voice right beside her. Carstairs was standing close to her, his eyes on the activity before them. 'It is indeed,' she agreed.

'Do you wish to make a few quick sketches? I shall unpack our food and I must find some baksheesh for the boys. The moment they spot us they will want to dive for us.' Suddenly he was all efficiency, unpacking the picnic hamper, laying out the small cloth, pouring the wine.

With a roar of triumph, the men dragged the boat closer and Louisa could see Augusta and Sir John now, on the roof of the forecabin. As she looked up they began to wave.

'We'll rejoin them once they are through the first rapid.' Carstairs passed her a glass of wine. 'Then you'll be able to experience it from the other end of the tow rope, so to speak. Shall we drink a toast?' He held out his glass, and for a second their hands touched, then he raised his wine and put it to his lips. '*Salut!* beautiful lady.'

However hard she tried to resist she could not stop herself from glancing up to meet his eyes. She felt herself relaxing back onto the cushions, so tired. He had moved closer to her now, bending over her. 'Louisa, my dear, shall I take your glass? We do not want to spill it, do we.' His mouth was close to her face, his eyes, holding hers, so huge they were like great whirlpools, threatening to draw her in and drown her. 'Shall I move your parasol, my dear, to shade you better? There.'

Her eyes were closing. She couldn't help it. She could feel his mouth on hers. It was firm, commanding. A thrill of excitement coursed through her veins and then suddenly he was sitting up.

'*Yalla!*' he roared. '*Imshi!* Go away!'

A small boy was standing dripping on the rock beside them.

As she dragged herself drowsily upright she saw the boy turn. He leapt off the rock back into the boiling foaming waters. 'Oh my God, he'll drown.' She heard her own voice, shrill and frightened.

'Of course he won't. How do you think he got here? He's only after baksheesh!' Carstairs plunged his hand into his pocket and brought out a handful of coins. Throwing them high in the air he watched them splash into the water round the small bobbing head. In a second the cheeky smile had been replaced by a pair of small brown feet.

'Your wine, my dear.' He was handing her the glass once more.

It was as though it had never happened. She brushed her hand against her lips, confused. He was kneeling now, in front of the hamper, producing bread and hard-boiled eggs and fresh white cheese and fruit.

She glanced at the parasol. It had been moved, so that it was between the river and the spot where she had been lying. No one on the boat would have seen what had happened, if it had happened at all.

Had she dreamed it? If she accused him of taking advantage of her, would he call her a liar?

He was smiling again now, beside her, reaching for her hand.

'Louisa?' His voice was clear above the roar of water. 'Don't fight it. Look at me. You know you want to.'

She took a deep breath, staring hard at the dappling of sunlight on the water, trying to resist. 'Roger, please—'

'Look at me, Louisa. Why fight it? Look at me. Now.' His hand over hers was ice cold. She felt her face lifting towards his.

'That's right.' His eyes were intensely overwhelming. She could feel herself being drawn in by them once more, her thoughts wiped from her mind, her body that of a limp, obedient doll.

'That's right. It's so easy this way.' He trailed his fingers lightly up her arm and took her chin between them, raising her face a little more.

This time her lips parted obediently beneath his, even though her body did not respond. She was totally without defences.

'The scent bottle, Louisa. You are going to make me a gift of it, my darling.' His lips were by her ear now. The words echoed in her mind. The scent bottle. A gift. The scent bottle. A gift. Hassan's gift!

Her eyes flew open. 'No!' She pushed him away violently. 'No!'

Scrambling up, she ran a few steps on the slippery rock and felt her feet going from under her. She threw out her arm to save herself, somehow recovered her balance, and stood swaying on the edge of the water.

It was at that moment that she saw the tall figure.

It remained there for a moment between her and Carstairs, hands outstretched, the face a mask of fury, then it was gone.

Carstairs seemed frozen to the spot. He was as white as the foam on the water around them, trembling violently, his eyes alight, but whether from excitement or fear she could not tell.

'Ahoy, Louisa! Ready to come aboard?' A voice reached her suddenly over the roar of the rapids, and she turned to see the dahabeeyah within fifteen yards of her rock. Sir John raised both hands and waved. In a moment one of the crew was there on the rock with them, packing their belongings. In another ten seconds, she was pulling herself aboard the boat, Carstairs scrambling up behind her.

'So, did you sketch us? Let's see.' Sir John held out his hand for her book. She gave it to him mutely.

Behind her, Carstairs leaned forward and put his hand on her elbow. His fingers on her bare skin were like cold India rubber.

Anna looked up with a start. She frowned and glanced at her watch. Nearly an hour had gone by and there was no sign of Serena.

Closing the diary, she pushed it back into the drawer. She was making her way towards the door when there was a knock.

Serena was standing there. One glance told Anna she had been crying. 'What's the matter? Oh, Serena!' She caught her hand and pulled her into the room. 'Please tell me it's not Andy. Has he been having a go at you because of me?'

Serena shrugged, then reluctantly she gave a slight nod. 'It's not your fault, Anna. He's been on the point of saying all this ever since I met him.' She sniffed and groped in her skirt pocket for a tissue. 'It's just that he was so cruel.' She looked straight ahead, her face crumpled and bewildered. 'I'm no use to you like this, Anna.'

Anna stared at her, aghast. 'What did he say?'

'Basically I'm to keep my menopausal madness to myself and not come near you any more or he'll make my life hell. And he can do it, believe me. He's done it before. He comes round. He phones. He implies that I'm going round the bend. He threatens me with psychiatrists and exorcists and God knows what!' Sighing, she shook her head. 'Even if I wanted to I can't be there for you. He's drained every particle of confidence from me. In this state I'd be mincemeat for your priests. My only consolation, I suppose, is that I don't even have enough energy now to make it worth their while trying to possess me.'

Anna closed her eyes. The temperature in the cabin seemed to have dropped. She was thinking of Louisa and her fear. 'What makes you think they would try to possess you?'

'I'm an initiate. I probably have the kind of energy they want. If I was strong, centred, I'd be able to fight them on their own ground and then maybe I'd be of some use to you.' Serena shook her head. 'But according to Andy I only have my self-obsessed paranoia left now.'

'I can still throw the bottle away, Serena,' Anna interrupted.

'That won't do any good! They're not tied to the bottle, Anna. I don't know why they didn't show themselves before. Maybe they knew you would bring it back to Egypt one day. But now they have found the means to gain enough strength, they are not going to jump in the river after the bottle and disappear in a plop of steam!'

'Then you must help me, Serena. I need you. I keep thinking of Louisa; of how frightened she was.' She stood up again, suddenly resolute. 'I'm going to have this out with Andy right now, and get him to lay off you.'

'No, please!' Serena caught her hand.

'Don't try to stop me. I've had enough of his interference. We've both said he is a bully, and this is none of his business.'

'He's made *you* his business, Anna. He fancies you, and to be honest'—she hesitated—'I think he fancies that diary of yours even more. At heart, Andy is always the dealer first; friend or lover second.'

Anna stared at her in silence for a moment, then without another word she spun on her heel and stormed out of the cabin.

Andy wasn't hard to find. He was sitting on a stool at the bar, watching Ali with his cocktail shaker.

'I want a word. Now.' Anna stopped in front of him, her eyes blazing. 'Your interference has gone far enough! It has to stop.'

She was aware of various other people in the lounge glancing at her quickly then looking away. She took no notice of them.

'So, Serena went straight to you, did she?' He scribbled his name on a chit and took the glass from Ali. He raised it to her in mock salute. 'I just wanted to save you from getting dragged into her drama sessions.'

'What makes you think you've got the right to have any say whatsoever in what I do or who I have as friends? I like her and I trust her.'

'Ouch! Do I infer from that that you neither like nor trust me? I'm sorry. I'd somehow got completely the opposite impression.'

She looked him in the eye. 'I like you, Andy, and I trust you. But that does not mean you can pick and choose my friends for me.'

Andy held her gaze. 'Similarly,' he said softly, 'may I remind you that my relationship with Serena is none of your business.'

There was a moment's silence. She stepped back and gave a small nod. '*Touché!* As long as your relationship with her doesn't interfere with my relationship with her!' She turned sharply away from him to find Toby standing behind her, holding Charley's arm.

'Is this a private war?' Toby gave her a wry grin. 'Or can we join in—'

He broke off as Charley lunged past him, breaking free of his restraining grip. 'Andy, you bastard!' Her words were slurred, her eyes unfocused. As Anna moved away she lurched forward, putting her hands out towards the bar. 'Andy? I have to do this for the goddess Sekhmet. She needs me. She wants me.' In the shocked silence that followed her words she stared round. 'Andy, what's happening to me?'

Anna turned at a slight pressure on her shoulder. It was Toby. He beckoned her away and, with a hasty glance first at Charley then towards Andy, she followed him.

'Andy? What's wrong with me?' Anna could still hear the pathetic high-pitched voice as they got to the door.

'You're drunk.' Andy's harsh rejoinder could probably be heard by everyone in the room.

'No!' She burst into tears. 'No, I'm not. I haven't been drinking. . .'

'Leave Andy to deal with her.' Toby ushered Anna towards the door.

Sekhmet. Had Charley really mentioned Sekhmet? Anna shivered. As she followed Toby out onto the shaded afterdeck she was frowning. 'She didn't look drunk to me.'

'I don't know that she was necessarily drunk when she kicked up all that fuss at lunchtime.' Toby sounded thoughtful as they leaned against the rail, looking out across the river. 'There was no smell of booze. I'd say she was ill. I suppose it could be the heat.' He shrugged.

Anna was gazing into the water. 'She did say Sekhmet, didn't she?'

He looked blank for a moment. 'Who?'

'Charley. Charley was talking about the goddess, Sekhmet.'

'Was she? She was ranting and raving like a mad woman.'

Anna bit her lip. She was silent for a moment or two and Toby took the opportunity to study her face. 'Can I buy you a drink before dinner?'

She shook her head. 'Thank you, but I think I'm going to go and have a quick word with Serena.' She paused, scrutinising Toby's face, suddenly realising that this was the first time she'd been alone with him since Andy's revelation. She frowned, her eyes on his, then she shook her head. That was not the face of a murderer. If it was, she was the worst judge of character in the entire world.

Serena was nowhere to be found. Her cabin was occupied solely by a quietly snoring Charley. She wasn't in Anna's cabin, either, or on the upper deck. Puzzled, Anna went back to her own cabin.

With a weary sigh she sat down on the bed. There was half an hour till dinner. Perhaps she would have another look at the diary, to see what happened when Louisa got back onto the boat.

Having thanked Lord Carstairs for arranging the picnic, Louisa went to her cabin to change out of her spray-soaked dress. Exhausted and depressed, she stretched out on the bed thinking about Hassan.

A knock on the door made her sit up with a start. She must have fallen asleep. The cabin was in total darkness and she groped for the candlestick on her bedside locker. Another knock rang round the small space as the flame caught and she realised it must be Treece, coming to help her dress for dinner. She groped her way to the door and unlocked it.

Roger Carstairs stood there, his head bowed beneath the low ceiling. With one swift movement he pushed her back into the cabin and stepped in after her, bolting the door behind him.

'How dare you!'

He pushed her sharply, so that she collapsed backwards onto the bed. 'Where is it?' he hissed, scrutinising her belongings.

'Where is what?' She shuddered. 'How dare you come in here?' she repeated. 'Get out! I'll call for help! There will be trouble if you are found in here with me.'

'I don't think so.' He laughed. 'The Forresters wouldn't dare cross me, especially when I tell them how eagerly you received my attentions this afternoon.' He reached down and caught her chin between his fingers, forcing her to look at him. 'Where is it?' he repeated.

'I've hidden it ashore.'

His eyes blazed. 'Not today. It was not possible today. Yesterday, then. You left it at Philae? Where?' He pushed her head back against the cabin wall. 'Tell me,' he whispered through gritted teeth. His eyes were dark pits, close to hers. She couldn't look away. Desperately she shut her eyes. 'I'll never tell you,' she said.

'Oh, you'll tell me. Believe me, you'll tell me.' He caught her wrist.

With a little gasp of pain she felt the small delicate bones crushed between his fingers. 'Help me!' Her cry was no more than a whisper. 'Anhotep, if you exist, help me now!' The candle flared.

Carstairs laughed once more. 'So, our little widow invokes the high priest, but she doesn't know how.' He pushed her back so violently against the cabin wall that all the breath was knocked out of her body. 'Where is the bottle? I have to have it. It contains power. Power only I know how to use!' His eyes glittered feverishly as his hand tightened round her wrist.

'Anhotep!' Louisa struggled ferociously. 'Don't let him hurt me—'

As the candle flame flickered and streamed sideways in the tiny airless cabin, she opened her eyes to peer past him towards the window. A figure stood there—misty, indistinct.

'Anhotep! Help me!' Her voice was stronger this time. Her fear of the man half-sprawled across her was greater by far than her fear of a shadow from the distant past.

Carstairs moved back slightly, aware of the change in the atmosphere and the strange behaviour of the candle flame. He glanced towards the window and gasped. In a second he had pushed himself off the bed.

'Servant of Isis, greeting!' He bowed low, ignoring Louisa who cowered back on the bunk, making herself as small as possible.

The cabin had become airless; the candle flame, a moment before flaring wildly and streaming smoke, had died to a tiny glow. In a second it would be out altogether. The figure was fading.

Louisa launched herself off the bed towards the door, groping for the bolt. Frantically she scrabbled for it as the light died altogether. As the figure vanished totally, Carstairs turned back towards her. She felt his hands groping for her shoulders, just as her flailing fingers found the bolt and felt it slide back. But it was too late, he was dragging her away from the door and thrusting her back onto the bed. She drew breath to scream and felt his hand clamp over her mouth. Once again she heard him laugh. There was excitement in the sound now, and triumph.

At the very moment he began to rip open her blouse there was a loud knock at the cabin door.

The knock was repeated and Anna looked up, frowning. It was dark outside the open window and the only light came from the small bedside lamp. Confused, she put down the diary, her mind full of Louisa's terror, and pulled open the cabin door.

'*Mademoiselle?*' Ibrahim stood in the doorway. He had a tray with a glass of hibiscus juice and a plate of bread and cheese. 'You are not well, *mademoiselle*? I was concerned that you were not at supper. I have brought you something to eat.' He slid the tray onto the dressing table and gave her a grave smile. 'There is one other thing, *mademoiselle*.' He reached into his pocket and brought out something attached to a fine gold chain.

'I would like you to wear this, *mademoiselle*.' He held it out to her. 'Please give it back to me the day you go home to England.'

She stared down at his hand, then slowly she reached out her own. 'Ibrahim, what is it?'

He dropped a small gold charm into her palm. 'It is the Eye of Horus. *Allah yisallimak.* It will help to keep you safe.'

She found her mouth had gone dry. 'Safe from what?' She looked up and met his deep brown eyes. He held her gaze for several seconds before giving a small shrug, then looked down at the floor in silence.

'Ibrahim? Is this to do with the old gods? And with the cobra?'

'*Inshallah!*' There was no shrug this time. Instead, the ghost of a nod.

'Then, thank you. Thank you very much.' She smiled suddenly. 'I wish I knew the right thing to say in Arabic.'

'You say: *kattar kheirak.*' His eyes twinkled.

'*Kattar kheirak*, Ibrahim.'

He bowed. '*Ukheeirak, mademoiselle.*' He gave her a huge smile. 'Now I must go and work in the bar. *Bon appétit, mademoiselle . . .*'

After he had gone, she stared down at the charm in her hand. It was an eye surmounted by an arched brow with below it a tiny swirl of gold. The Eye of Horus was, she knew, a symbol of protection and healing used for thousands of years to ward off danger and illness and bad luck. For a moment she held it tightly in her hand, then felt for the clasp and hung it carefully round her neck. It touched her enormously that Ibrahim should have trusted her with something so precious. She smiled. It had made her feel safe and cared for, something, she realised, she hadn't felt for a very long time. Savouring the feeling, she stood for several minutes lost in thought, then she sat on the bed again and opened the diary.

The candle held high in her hand, Jane Treece surveyed the scene. It was clear what had been going on. Louisa Shelley had been behaving like the trollop she had always suspected she was. With one disdainful look she took in Louisa's flushed face and torn blouse and the handsome, angry man hastily climbing off the bed. He was still fully dressed, so she had arrived in time to thwart their lust. With a self-satisfied smile Jane Treece cleared her throat.

'Would you like me to help you get ready for dinner, Mrs Shelley, or shall I come back later?' Her voice was at its most repressive.

'Thank you, Jane. Please stay. I should like to change.' Louisa's voice was shaking. She turned to Lord Carstairs and pointed at the door. 'Go.'

For a moment he hesitated, then with a smile he ducked outside. 'A *bientôt*, sweetheart. We'll continue our delightful discourse very soon.'

Louisa closed her eyes. She was shaking as she watched Treece light her bedside candle and the others on the dressing table. In a very short time the cabin was full of gently flickering light.

Without a word Treece gathered Louisa's discarded clothes from earlier that afternoon and folded them. Then she picked up the ewer and withdrew to fetch hot water and towels. Louisa glanced at her dressing case. It was still locked, the tiny key safely hidden in her sewing box.

With shaking hands she picked up her hairbrush and began to brush her long chestnut hair with slow rhythmic strokes.

She looked up as Treece reappeared. 'Thank you, Jane.' She bit her lip, trying to steady her voice. 'Has Lord Carstairs left the boat?'

'I'm sure I don't know, Mrs Shelley.' Treece put down the heavy jug with a resentful bang. 'Did you wish me to run and fetch him back?'

Louisa stared at her. 'You know I don't! The man is a vicious brute.' She found herself fighting back the tears. 'I only wished to be sure he had safely gone.'

There was a long pause as the woman considered her words and Louisa saw a slight softening of the grim expression on her face. 'I had thought to hear them say he was staying for dinner,' she commented as she took Louisa's ruined blouse and stared at it distastefully. 'The Forresters are thrilled to have made such friends with another member of the aristocracy and one of so high a rank. They would be very put out if they thought one of their guests had upset him.'

'Would they indeed.' With pursed lips Louisa reached for the soap. 'Please pour out some water.' She shivered, though the cabin was still very hot. 'I'll wear my silk for dinner, thank you, if you could find it for me, then you can go and help Lady Forrester.' She straightened suddenly and looked the woman in the eye.

'Please do not speak about this to the Forresters. As you rightly said, it would upset them.'

She intended to speak to Sir John herself, and soon. But she had no wish for the sour-faced Jane Treece to spread the word first.

Sir John was in the saloon on his own when Louisa walked in. He stood up hastily. 'My dear, you look beautiful!' He eyed her midnight silk gown, and, as though unable to stop himself, took her hand and kissed her fingertips. 'Louisa, m'dear. I fear I have some disappointing news. Roger has had to leave us. He had a message that there was a problem with one of the crew on his own boat, and he has had to go back. He asked me to beg your forgiveness for leaving so abruptly.'

'I don't think it was leaving he was begging forgiveness for!' Louisa said tartly. She sat down on the seat near him. 'John, I'm afraid I must ask you not to allow Lord Carstairs to set foot on this boat again. I didn't want to mention it in front of Augusta. I know she likes him, but he came to my cabin this evening and behaved with shocking impropriety.'

Sir John stared at her, his pale blue eyes huge. 'Louisa, I find this hard to believe. He is a gentleman in every way.'

'No, not a gentleman.' Louisa clenched her fists. 'Had Jane Treece not interrupted, he would have ravished me! He has some strange power which rendered me incapable of fighting him off. And he is trying to persuade me, by underhand means and by threats, to part with my little scent bottle. This is outrageous behaviour, you must agree!'

Sir John was staring at her. 'You say he tried to ravish you?'

She nodded.

His eyes left her face and dropped to the neckline of her gown. He was breathing very heavily.

'I thought it was exceedingly foolish of you to go out with the man unchaperoned, Louisa.' Augusta had sailed into the saloon unnoticed and now seated herself at the table. 'Did you appear for him, as now, *en déshabille?*' she asked.

Louisa blushed angrily. 'I did not, I assure you. I have found Lord Carstairs's behaviour totally unspeakable. I hope very much you will forbid him to set foot on the *Ibis* again.'

Augusta leaned back in her seat. 'I don't think we can do that. The man is a peer of the realm. I have to admit that he has made me feel uneasy, too, but I had thought his ambitions fixed on Venetia Fielding, so I am surprised he should jump on you. David Fielding has a large fortune and he has let it be known Venetia's dowry will be considerable.' She glanced at her husband. 'Is there a reason for his interest in Louisa?'

Sir John had seated himself at the table with his hands in front of him. 'He wants her little perfume jar. God knows why.' He drummed his fingers on the table. 'I think it has to do with his study of Ancient Egypt. I wish you would give it to him, Louisa, and have done. The man will pay whatever you ask.'

Louisa glanced at him. 'It is not for sale. I have told him that. And for me it is also now a memento of Hassan who bought it for me and whom you so unjustly dismissed—' She was about to say more but bit her lip. 'He was my friend, and that makes it doubly precious to me. I assure you, I will never part with it. Not as long as I live.'

Augusta was alone in the saloon the next morning, when Louisa left her cabin, dressed in a cool blouse and skirt. Augusta led the way on deck, where they sat sipping lemonade in the shade of the draped sail. 'Sir

John and I have been talking, Louisa,' she began. 'We believe we may have been too hasty in dismissing Hassan. I think perhaps we were misled by Roger. Unintentionally, of course,' she added hastily. 'Sir John has gone ashore with the *reis* to try to locate him.'

Louisa held her breath. She closed her eyes, trying hard to keep her expression composed. Her heart was beating very fast.

'Would it please you, my dear, if he should return to us?'

'That would please me very much. But what of Lord Carstairs?'

'If Hassan is here there is no need for you to be alone with him, my dear. I believe Roger was probably a spoilt child and has continued to behave as one now he is an adult. If he wants something, he believes he should have it, and that nothing should be allowed to thwart his desires. We must show him that, though he is still welcome on the *Ibis*, in this case he is not going to get what he wants.'

Louisa spent the rest of the morning on the boat sketching the cliffs and rocks. It was midday before the men began to return, ready to drag the boat up the last part of the cataract. With them came Sir John and Lord Carstairs.

Louisa had withdrawn to the far rail so that she could watch the proceedings from the boat. The men were forming up on the rocks, getting ready to heft the great ropes like tug-of-war teams preparing themselves to do battle against the elements. Out of the corner of her eye, she saw Sir John and Carstairs go below into the saloon where Augusta was sheltering from the sun.

A short while later Augusta emerged. Her eyes were sparkling as she came and stood beside Louisa.

'Such wonderful news! You are not going to believe it!'

'Sir John has found Hassan?' Louisa felt her heart lift in excitement.

'Hassan?' Augusta looked vague for a moment. 'Oh . . . no. I believe John has left word for him to follow the *Ibis* if he wishes to have his job back. No, no, far better than that. My dear, Roger Carstairs has asked John if he might call on you. My dear, he wishes to ask for your hand!'

Louisa stared at her. For a moment she was too stunned to react. An icy clamp seemed to have fastened itself over her lungs so that she could not breathe. Her mouth had gone dry.

Augusta clapped her hands. 'Of course Sir John said yes. He knew you would be thrilled! Roger was so apologetic about frightening you yesterday. He said that his love for you completely overrode his sanity. He has brought you the most beautiful gift, Louisa—'

Louisa rose to her feet. 'How dare he inveigle his way onto the boat and ask Sir John? He is not my father!'

Augusta looked stunned. She raised her hands and let them fall to her sides in a gesture of total bewilderment. 'He asked John because he is your host. This is his boat. We are caring for you, my dear.' She sounded near to tears. 'We thought you would be so pleased. Think of it. His title—'

'I do not want his title, Augusta!' Louisa snapped. 'And I most certainly do not want him or his gift. I shall not receive him. Please tell him to go.' She leaned against the rail, staring down into the water.

'Louisa—'

'No.' She did not look round. 'Please. Get rid of him.'

'I can't do that, Louisa.' Augusta paused for a moment, then, with a sigh she turned away.

As the mooring ropes were loosened and the boat swung into the channel, Louisa found herself alone on deck.

It was perhaps an hour or so later that Louisa made her way somewhat cautiously back to her cabin. She glanced into the saloon as she passed the door. Augusta and Sir John were there alone. Of Carstairs there was no sign. With a sigh of relief she turned towards her door and pushed it open. He was sitting on the bed. On the counterpane beside him was her journal and her dressing case.

At her gasp of surprise and fear he smiled. 'Please don't scream, Louisa. It would be so embarrassing. Just give me the key to this silly little box and we'll have done.'

'You've been reading my diary!' She was overwhelmed with anger.

'Indeed I have. And what interesting reading. You don't appear to like my company, my dear. Your penchant is for natives, I see.' He sneered at her. 'Luckily I'm not particularly worried by your views, either way. The key, please, or I'll be forced to break the lock.'

'Get out of my cabin!' Louisa could feel her anger mounting. 'Get out now!' She moved towards him and snatched the diary out of his hand. 'Do you want me to summon the high priest once more to my aid? Who knows what he might do to protect me.'

Carstairs laughed. 'Summoning spirits, my dear, is what I do, not you. I have trained for years in the occult practices which will bring forth the guardians of your little bottle. Is that really what you want?' He stood up suddenly and she fell back, her courage draining away.

Carstairs looked down at her, not hiding his disdain, then he raised his face and took a deep breath.

'Anhotep, priest of Isis, I call you forth here. Now. Anhotep, priest of Isis, show yourself before me now.' He flung up his arms.

Louisa gave a whimper. She could see the figure already, transparent in front of the window, the thin, arrogant face, the square shoulders, the strange, pale eyes. The silence in the cabin was suddenly intense, the atmosphere electric. Louisa closed her eyes.

'Did you call, Mrs Shelley?' Jane Treece's voice, immediately behind her, made her gasp.

For a moment she couldn't move, then she turned and clutched at the woman's arm. 'Yes, please. Would you show Lord Carstairs out? He was just leaving.' She had begun to tremble violently.

She closed her eyes as Treece led Carstairs away. When she opened them again the figure in the window was still there.

'**O**h God!' Anna spoke out loud. She shut the diary, put it down on the bed, and took a deep breath. She glanced at the dressing table and was about to cross to it when a cough outside her door made her jump.

It was Toby. He took in her dishevelled appearance when she opened the door. 'I was worried when you didn't come to breakfast, having missed supper last night. Are you OK? You look awful.'

She gave a brittle laugh. 'Is that your usual chat-up line?'

'No. As chat-up lines go, I can do better.' He smiled again. 'What is it, Anna? Your hands are shaking.'

She wrapped her arms around herself self-consciously. 'I'm all right.'

'No. You're not all right. Is it the sight of me, or is it that damn diary again?' He had spotted it lying on the bed. 'Anna, forgive me for saying so, but if it upsets you so much that you are missing the excursions you have paid thousands of pounds to come and see, is it wise to go on doing it?' He held her gaze for a moment, his expression fierce. 'Put it away. Read it when you get home, sitting in the garden.'

'I can't. I need to know what happens. Someone was trying to steal the scent bottle from Louisa. She thought it was cursed in some way.'

'And you too think that the bottle might be cursed?'

She glanced up, expecting him to be laughing at her, but his face was perfectly serious. 'Will you show it to me, Anna?' he said. 'Watson thinks it's a fake. He's made no secret of the fact. I'm not an expert but I do have a feel for things.'

She hesitated, then swept over to the dressing table and pulled out the drawer. She handed him the bottle and he took it, bringing it up close to his face and running his fingers over the surface.

'It feels right to me.' He glanced up at her. 'Hand blown. Rough surface with a lot of imperfections, crude in some ways, but more than that.' He frowned, running his finger over it again. 'I can feel its age. I couldn't date it for you. A museum would have to do that.'

'But it is Egyptian?' She looked up at him.

'Does Louisa Shelley say it is?'

'Oh yes.' She bit her lip.

'Then it is Egyptian.' He gave her a reassuring smile. 'Anna, why not find a nice bit of diary to read?' he suggested suddenly. 'Something cheerful. There must be nice bits in it. Come on, I'll help you. Then put it away and come sailing.'

She hesitated, and when she didn't say anything he sat down on the bed, picked up the diary and began to leaf carefully through it.

Without a word, she stood watching him, wondering why she had invited him in. Why she felt more comfortable with him than she did, she now realised, with Andy, in spite of Andy's accusations.

He looked up. 'Here. Look. This seems to be a good bit. See, the writing is springy and even and the picture is cheerful. May I read it to you?'

Shrugging, she sat down on the stool.

Hassan had returned the day they moored at Philae. The *Scarab* had moored a stone's throw from them and the Fieldings' dahabeeyah a few yards beyond that.

With quiet dignity Hassan had accepted Sir John's explanation that it had all been a misunderstanding, and he had slipped quietly back into the life of the boat as though he had never been away, except that now, Louisa knew, the Forresters must have guessed that her relationship with him was more friendly than any of them chose publicly to admit.

It was dark when Louisa crept out on deck to find Hassan waiting to row her ashore. 'I have told the Forresters that I wish to paint the river in the moonlight,' she said quietly. 'They no longer try to stop me.'

A huge moon shone across the water, throwing black shadows across the sand. They walked slowly, taking in the intense beauty of the night. All around them the temple pillars, the distant hills, the dunes, the sand, had turned from gold to glittering silver.

'We will go up on the wall,' Hassan whispered. 'I'll show you.'

Carefully they climbed the worn steps, pitch-black inside the darkness of the stone, and emerged once more into the moonlight. It was cooler up there and Louisa pulled a shawl close round her shoulders. They could see the whole island beneath them with the *Ibis*, the *Scarab* and the *Lotus* like small toys in the distance. Immediately beneath them the huge temple lay silent and darkly mysterious.

'You wish to paint up here, Sitt Louisa?' Hassan's whisper was somehow shocking in the silence.

She nodded, and he unpacked.

Louisa began to sketch the scene. Every now and then she was so overwhelmed by the surrounding beauty that she sat spellbound, her pencil at a standstill. Hassan sat cross-legged a few feet from her. He had seemed reserved since he had returned. Quieter. More thoughtful.

'You think much, my friend?' she said at last.

'I watch the night. And I watch you.' He smiled.

'And I you. Look.' She held out the sketchbook. There was a picture of him; thoughtful, handsome, a wry smile playing round his eyes.

'You do me much honour, Sitt Louisa.'

'I show only the truth.'

He moved closer to her. 'When they sent me away I thought my heart would cease to beat for unhappiness,' he said at last. 'You have been my sun and my moon and the stars of my heaven, Sitt Louisa.'

Slowly he leaned across and touched her lips with his own. She closed her eyes. The rush of warmth and happiness that enfolded her drove everything out of her mind but the gentle, handsome man who had put his arms around her.

'Keep us safe, great Isis, and hidden from prying eyes, I beg you.' Her murmured prayer rose into the darkness and spun out towards the moon as, far below them on the river, Lord Carstairs emerged on the deck of the *Scarab* to stand staring at the temple.

There was a long silence. Toby closed the diary and laid it on the bedside locker. 'So, Louisa Shelley found love in Egypt,' he said at last. 'Does that please you? Can you put away the book and relax and enjoy yourself now? There was no mention of curses there. Or evil spirits.'

She smiled. 'You're right. Yes, I'll put it away.'

'And you'll come sailing?'

She glanced at her watch. 'If it's not too late.'

'It's not too late.' He stood up. 'You get dressed and I'll check there's a boat left for us and see if I can persuade Ali to give us some sandwiches.'

She met him on deck and found that there was one felucca left from the cluster of boats that had taken the rest of the passengers on morning excursions.

After helping her to make herself comfortable in the boat, Toby scrambled back onto the *White Egret* to ask Ali for a couple of extra cans of juice, then he climbed in beside her and allowed their boatman to sail slowly away. With a sigh of deepest pleasure, Anna rummaged in her bag for her camera.

'Happy?' Toby glanced at her in amusement as she leaned back to photograph the huge sail, a white wing against the blue of the sky.

'Very. Thank you for digging me out of my cabin.'

He was sitting with his arm outstretched along the side of the boat, his hand close to her shoulder. He had kicked off his shoes, she noticed, and his feet on the warm planking were as brown as those of their steersman. He smiled. 'You needed rescuing. Like Rapunzel.'

There was a gentle ripple of water under the bow as the boat turned and caught the wind. The sail flapped once and then filled. Anna reached for her camera again. The boatman, standing on the bow near the mast, was staring across the water towards the far bank, his hand shielding his eyes. She aimed the camera at him, but he had seen what she was doing and his face split into a huge grin and he struck a pose for her, balancing, one arm looped around the mast.

Anna put her camera away and closed her eyes, allowing the sun under the brim of her hat. The heat on her face was sudden and intense and she could see the violent scarlet of her eyelids. She drew back hastily and as she did so the steersman put his tiller across, his companion stepped away from the mast and sat down opposite her to adjust the sheet, the boat swung round and the shadow of the sail fell across her face. The new figure on the prow of the boat, balancing on the planking in his gilded sandals, was staring out across the water, his arms outstretched, his head raised as he looked up directly at the sun. She gasped, and the three men with her in the boat glanced at her.

'Anna?' Toby touched her arm. 'Are you OK?'

She swallowed. The figure had gone. Of course it had gone. It had never been there.

She shook her head. 'Sorry. I got the sun in my eyes.'

'Not good, missee.' The boatman shook his head. 'Very dangerous.'

She shrugged and nodded and looked repentant, pulling down the brim of her hat. She didn't see Toby's frown or notice the way he leaned forward to stare past her at the front of the boat.

When they returned, pre-lunch drinks were being served in the bar. It appeared that Andy had already bought her one. 'Specially for you!' He presented it to her with a flourish. 'To say sorry. I won't interfere any more and I won't be bossy.' The boyish charm was firmly in place.

Anna smiled. 'It's not a question of forgiveness, Andy. It's just that I want to be able to speak to Serena whenever I like without your intervention. Where is she now?'

He shrugged. 'I don't know. Perhaps the felucca she was on hasn't come back yet, but when it does I shall buy her a drink, kiss her feet, pat her hand, anything you like.'

Anna smiled. 'Just being nice would be enough.'

'Then I shall be nice.' He grinned hugely. 'I am nice.'

When Charley and Serena appeared in the doorway, Ali smiled hopefully and said, 'Cocktails for the two ladies? Ali make very good cocktails. Lots of things. Very expensive.'

Serena shook her head. 'No, thank you. Fruit juice would be lovely.'

'I'll have one, Ali.' Charley climbed onto a bar stool. Her eyes were feverishly bright and the sun had caught her skin, dusting it with a fine scattering of freckles.

Serena took her guava juice and retreated to a sofa. After a minute Anna followed. Toby was nowhere to be seen.

'So, where did you get to?' Serena looked gloomily into her glass.

'I went sailing with Toby.' Anna glanced at her, conscious that she was blushing slightly. 'I saw the priest Anhotep again today,' she went on. 'At least—' She hesitated. 'I think I did. On the felucca.'

Serena pulled a face. 'I hope that he hasn't attached himself to you.'

'Attached himself to me?' Anna forced herself to lower her voice again. 'You are joking, I hope. Dear God! You mean I'm possessed!'

'No!' Serena sat forward sharply. 'No, you mustn't get the wrong idea. In no way are you possessed, but he might have formed an energetic attachment to you. It's as if he's using you as a petrol tank. He's low on petrol because he doesn't have a body of his own, so he's put a sort of suction pipe into your energy field so he can use your energy to move around and show himself and that means he's staying near you.'

'I do hope you are wrong.' Anna took a sip from her glass and, in spite of herself, shivered violently. 'How can I get rid of him?'

'If you are strong-willed, your intention might be enough.'

'I am strong-willed.'

'Then next time you see him, tell him to go. Don't be afraid or angry, that will weaken you. Just be strong. Challenge him. Once you are in a dialogue with him you can ask him why he wants the bottle so badly, and how you can help him, and then you can ask him to leave.'

'By then we'll be on first-name terms and I'll be asking him to dinner!' Anna retorted. She paused. 'I can't believe I'm having this conversation!' She leaned forward and put her head in her hands. 'I want to get rid of the bottle, Serena. I can't cope with it. This was supposed to be a happy holiday. And instead it's turning into a nightmare.'

There was a pause, then Serena leaned forward and touched her arm. 'Do you want me to look after it for you? I can say some prayers over it. Perform an invocation and a dismissal. Burn some incense.'

'Not with Charley there, I take it!'

'No, not with Charley there. Let me do it, Anna. I do know what I'm talking about.' A note of urgency had crept into her voice. She stood up. 'Let's do it now. While Charley's here.' She cast a look over her shoulder at Charley, whose giggles were growing increasingly shrill.

Anna nodded. Climbing to her feet she followed Serena from the room, and towards her cabin. Fishing out her key she opened her cabin door. Then she paused. 'Someone has been in here.'

She moved cautiously into the small room and looked round. The bed had been made and clean towels left on the quilt, but that happened every morning. This was different. She looked round, feeling the hairs on her forearms stir, but the room was empty.

She stepped over to the dressing table and pulled open the drawer. The bottle lay where she had left it, wrapped in the scarf. She lifted it out and handed it to Serena, who had followed her in. 'All yours.'

Serena nodded. 'Come with me to my cabin.' She paused. 'What is it?'

Anna was staring at her bedside locker. The diary was gone.

'Everything all right, ladies?' Andy was peering into the room.

'No, it isn't.' Anna faced him, distraught. 'The diary has gone!'

'Anna, I did tell you to take care of it! You knew how valuable it was.' He stepped into the room. 'Are you quite sure it hasn't fallen behind the cupboard or under the bed or something?'

'I'm quite sure. It was on the top of my locker.' She stood stock still by her bed. 'Someone has taken it.'

'In which case I think we can all guess who that someone is.' Andy shrugged. 'I did warn you, Anna.'

'If you mean Toby, I was sailing with him all this morning.'

'Were you with him every second of the time?'

'Yes.' She hesitated. 'Well, I suppose not every second.'

He had left her sitting in the boat before they set sail. What had been his excuse? To fetch some cans of juice from the dining room. At the time she had thought nothing of it.

Seeing her frown, Andy smiled. 'Exactly. Shall I speak to him?'

'No!' Her response was instantaneous. 'No, don't say anything. If anyone does, it'll be me.'

She didn't believe it was Toby. How could it be?

'Thank God whoever took the diary didn't take the bottle. What an irony that would have been!' she said.

Andy, following her gaze, looked at the silk-wrapped bundle in Serena's hands. 'Is that it?' he asked sharply. 'Why has Serena got it?'

'Because I have given it to her to look after,' Anna replied firmly.

'I don't think so.' Andy stepped forward and with calm authority took it out of Serena's hand. 'I think I'll look after this, if you don't mind. It will be safer with me. Besides, I'm not having Serena getting involved in any more of her mumbo jumbo and unsettling Charley. This whole boat is heaving with superstition and hysteria already, as far as I can see.'

Tucking it into his pocket, he turned towards the door. 'Don't worry about it. I'll keep it safe.'

'Andy!' Anna found her voice at last. 'Bring it back this instant!'

But he had gone, striding down the corridor and out of sight.

'I don't believe he did that!' Anna turned back to Serena, who had slumped on the bed. 'Just because Toby turned out to be a thief.' She paused. 'Or at least . . .'

'Exactly.' Serena looked up at her. 'Don't jump to conclusions on Andy's say-so, Anna, please.' She hesitated. 'I suppose the police ought to be called, if the diary really is as valuable as all that.'

Anna sat down beside her. 'I'll go and talk to Toby and I'll ask him outright. If he's taken it, it's to read, that's all. He'd never steal it. Never.'

'And the bottle?' Serena's eyes were suspiciously bright.

'Oh, don't you worry about the bottle. I'll get that back.' Anna folded her arms. 'If Andy really thought that by buying me the odd drink he'd lull me into quiet acquiescence, he's got another think coming.'

'But he was right about one thing, though. Word is getting round the boat that something odd is going on and we do have to be careful not to let superstition and hysteria, as he calls it, cloud our judgment.'

With a rueful nod Anna headed for the door. 'Point taken. Listen, I'm going to go and see Toby now. Don't worry about the bottle.' She smiled. 'Let's see what Anhotep does about it. I'm more than happy not to have it for the time being.'

Serena levered herself off the bed. 'I'll see you later then. I do hope Toby's not a thief. To tell you the truth I rather like him.'

'So do I.' Anna pushed away the thought as she made her way to Toby's cabin. She clenched her fists. Who else could have taken the diary? Who else knew about it? Who else would have any interest at all?

Standing outside his door she took a deep breath and knocked quietly. There was no reply. She knocked more loudly. There was still no response so, glancing left and right along the deserted corridor, she gently tried the handle. The door opened; he hadn't locked it.

She peered inside and caught her breath. The cabin itself was identical to hers in layout, but there the resemblance ended. He had turned his into a studio. In the middle of the floor was a folding easel, on it a sketchbook, clipped back to reveal a sketch of the waterfront outside the window. On every wall he had stuck sketches and paintings. On the dressing table were paintboxes and charcoal and pencils. She stared round in astonishment and took a step inside. When had he done all these? He must have been painting every free second between their trips ashore.

She took another step inside and the door swung shut behind her.

The paintings were beautiful. Vibrant. She stood in front of the easel and stared at the busy waterfront scene with its array of cruisers, their own little paddle steamer moored alongside a vast gin palace.

It was several minutes before she remembered what she was looking for and turned her attention from his paintings to his personal belongings. The drawers under the dressing table were filled with a jumble of shirts, a couple of sweaters and some underwear. She pulled open the wardrobe. A couple of pairs of trousers and some jeans and a jacket. She pulled back the quilt and looked under his pillows, then she bent and ran her hand along beneath the mattress. Nothing. With a sigh she stood up again, pushing her hair back from her face, when a slight sound from the door made her swing round to face it. Toby was standing in the doorway, one arm propped against the doorjamb. His face was hard, his eyes cold.

'Have you quite finished your inspection?'

'Toby!' Any further words died in her throat as he took a step into the cabin and, closing the door behind him, drew the bolt.

'Why have you done that?' Her mouth had gone dry.

'Because I want the chance to speak to you without Andrew Watson poking his nose in. You have a reason, presumably, for being here?'

She hesitated. A wave of real panic had swept over her. 'Toby, I'm sorry. I came to find you. I knocked. The door opened. I saw the pictures and . . .' She paused with a shrug. 'I came in to see them.'

'And thought you'd have a quick pry while you were in here.'

'I wasn't prying!' She was stung. 'I was looking for my diary. It has disappeared from the drawer in my bedside locker. You were the only person who knew it was there.'

'In other words, you thought I'd stolen it!'

'No. No, I didn't think that.'

'Then who did?' he asked softly. 'Don't tell me. It was Watson.'

She shrugged.

'And you believed him.' He folded his arms.

'You might have borrowed it. You might have wanted to study it.'

'Without asking you?' She could hear the indignation in his voice. 'Why on earth didn't you lock your cabin door if you mistrust everyone so much?' he said.

'That's the point, isn't it?' she flashed back. 'I did trust everyone!'

'Everyone except me.' His voice dropped. 'So, tell me, why do you not trust me any more? Why does Andrew Watson not trust me? What have I done to deserve all this suspicion?'

She found herself colouring. 'I don't know,' she said.

'You don't know.' He took a deep breath. 'Or you don't intend to say. My guess is Watson has been poking his nose in where it's not wanted and poisoning the well.' He sat down heavily on the bed.

Anna bit her lip. Her fear had evaporated. 'All right, I'll tell you what happened! I didn't believe him, not for a single second! Until this happened. And then . . . I'm sorry.' She hung her head. 'I was so frantic about the diary that I wasn't thinking clearly.' She straightened up. 'If I'm honest, I was hoping you did have it. If you haven't, who has?'

He considered for a moment. 'Do you really want my opinion?'

She nodded.

'I'm prepared to bet fairly large odds on Watson himself.'

Anna shook her head. 'He wouldn't. Besides, he was there—'

'He was there. He sympathised and he pointed the finger at me. I can see the scenario clearly, Anna.' He sat forward suddenly. 'Why would I want the diary, tell me that? He's the wheeler-dealer. He's the man who has the contacts.' He looked up at her. 'Well? Why would I want it?'

She shrugged. 'It's a historical artefact. It has Louisa's sketches. It's worth a lot . . .' Her voice trailed away.

'I don't need money, Anna. And I don't want Louisa's diary. Is that clear?' He glanced at the cabin window. 'Now, you'd better go.'

'Toby, I'm sorry.'

'Go!' The implacable coldness was back in his eyes.

'I am sorry,' she repeated and turned towards the door. Outside in the passage she stopped and took a deep breath; to her chagrin she was near to tears and she fled down the corridor.

Toby's cabin door reopened and he stepped out. 'Anna!' he called.

Ignoring the shout, she ran upstairs to her cabin. Throwing open the door she ran in, hurling it back on its hinges so that it slammed against the wall, rebounded and closed behind her.

With a sudden frantic gasp, she stopped dead. The cabin wasn't empty. The air was heavy with the sickly smell of resin and myrrh, and standing in the middle of the floor was a shadowy figure, tall, insubstantial, but unmistakable in its bearing. Anhotep half turned towards her and began to raise a thin wispy hand slowly towards her.

Anna screamed. Desperately she tried to turn back to the door, to move, to tear her eyes away from his, but she couldn't. Something held her where she was. She could feel her legs beginning to buckle, strange red lights flickering behind her eyes.

As she started to fall, the door opened and Toby flung himself into the cabin. 'What is it? What's wrong?' He stared round frantically as he caught her hand and swung her towards him. 'Anna, what is it?'

Behind her the cabin was empty.

'Is it Watson?' He pushed her away, more gently now, and pushed open the bathroom door. There was no one there.

'No, it's not Andy. It's Anhotep the priest. You read about him in the diary. The one who haunts my little scent bottle. He was standing here!' She indicated a spot on the floor about two feet in front of her.

She was shaking so violently that her teeth were chattering. Slowly she collapsed onto the bed and sat looking up at him, wondering suddenly if he was going to laugh; to ridicule her every word.

He stared round the small room again. 'Have you seen this apparition before? Didn't you see something on the boat this morning? Is that what you saw? The priest?'

Relief flooded through her. He believed her! She nodded.

'You told me the bottle was cursed. But you never told me how or why. Why didn't you mention all this before?'

'And have you think I'm mad?' She put her head in her hands.

'Does anyone else know about it?'

She nodded. 'Serena.'

'And what does she think?'

'She believes it. She knows quite a bit about Ancient Egypt. She's studied its religion and rituals. She was going to take the bottle and bless it or something, but then Andy took it away, saying that he was going to keep it safely for me.'

Toby sat down beside her. 'I think it's more likely he plans to flog it,' he said cynically. He glanced at his watch. 'It's lunchtime. Can I suggest that a meal in a crowded dining room would be a good thing for both of us? Very grounding. And no ghost would show himself there. We can cool off and rethink the situation. My guess is Andy Watson has both the diary and the bottle and he'll take care of them as long as they are potential money earners.' He paused, waiting for her nod. 'And this afternoon I suggest we talk to Serena. We need to consult her about what steps can be taken to keep you safe from any paranormal repercussions. Perhaps at the same time we could have a council of war about recovering the diary and thereby'—he paused and gave her a wry grin—'clear my name, once and for all.'

Anna, Toby and Serena held their council of war at the Old Cataract Hotel, sitting on the terrace overlooking the Nile.

'Did you see Andy's face when the three of us went ashore together?' Serena was stirring her cup of tea. 'He looked distinctly worried.'

'As well he might.' Toby sat forward and studied Serena's face for a few moments, then he nodded. 'Anna tells me you know about Ancient Egyptian ritual. By that I take it you have studied modern spiritual techniques and magic based on Egyptian texts?'

Serena met his eye steadily. 'I've studied with Anna Maria Kelim, if you've heard of her.'

Toby shrugged. 'I took a bit of an interest in these things when I was younger. The name rings a bell. But the important thing is that you know what you are doing. I suspect Anna's ghost or ghosts are not going to be deflected by a bit of New Age chanting.'

Serena didn't say anything for a moment, clearly taken aback by his directness. But after a few seconds' thought she said, 'I have some experience of rescue work—you know what rescue work is, don't you?' She glanced up at Toby and saw him give a curt nod.

'He may, but I don't,' Anna put in quietly.

'It means someone who works with earthbound spirits and helps them move on. Most "ghosts", if you like to use that word, are lost. Trapped. Unhappy. Nobody came to collect them or look after them. I have worked with one or two cases like that and helped them move on.' Serena sounded more confident now she saw she had an audience who respected what she had to say. 'I have never worked with a spirit, however, who has chosen to remain earthbound because it has unresolved business here. They are the scary ones. Unable to let go. Anhotep and his colleague are like that. And they are not just ordinary ghosts. They were trained priests, with knowledge of one of the most powerful occult systems ever known. They probably chose not to die.'

There was a short silence.

'And what has happened to the colleague? The second priest?' Toby put in after a moment. 'You haven't mentioned him.'

Anna shuddered as she recalled her terror at the apparition of Hatsek, the priest of Sekhmet, the lion-headed goddess. 'I've seen him. And so did Louisa, at the temple. He seemed the more evil of the two.'

Toby grimaced.

'You still believe us?' Anna looked at him. 'You don't think we're mad?'

'No, I don't think you're mad. I've seen ghosts.' Toby did not smile. 'Our culture is very foolish to dismiss out of hand anything it can't prove with an algebraic formula or a test tube. Luckily most other cultures of the past and many today are far wiser than us in the West.'

Serena put down her cup with a small clatter and shook her head in disbelief. 'I can't tell you how it cheers me up to hear you say that!'

'And me.' Anna gave a small hopeful smile.

'Good. Well, having rallied the troops we'd better decide what we are going to do.' Toby sat forward, concentrating. 'We have only a few hours before we leave for our trip to Abu Simbel.' He looked at Serena. 'If you are prepared to do an exorcism, or whatever you choose to call it, what would you need?'

Serena thought for a moment. 'We really should have the scent bottle itself to act as a focus, but I can try to do it without. Other than that I have the things I need with me for my own spiritual practice. Incense. Candles. A bell.' She shook her head. 'I haven't been able to use them, of course, sharing with Charley. And Toby, don't be angry, but I don't think you should be there.' She looked at him apologetically. 'I may be wrong, but I have a feeling that we would be safer, just Anna and me. Women are *de facto* servants of Isis. Women are less likely to come to harm.'

Toby nodded. 'I won't argue. As long as you think you'll be safe.'

Serena shrugged. 'I hope we'll be safe.'

There was a moment's silence.

'So, the next step is a raid on Andy's cabin to rescue the book and the bottle.' Toby drained his cup. 'OK, let's go. We may as well start right now. If Andy has gone ashore we can search his cabin straightaway.'

The door was locked.

'Try your key.' Anna glanced nervously over her shoulder. Andy and Ben were, it had turned out, sailing.

Toby fished in his pockets and eventually retrieved it. It didn't fit.

'Yours?' He looked at her.

She already had it in her hand when Ali appeared at the end of the passage. He came towards them. 'Problem?'

'We need to get into this cabin,' Anna said.

'OK.' Ali dived into the pocket of his *galabiyya* and came out with several keys on a ring. 'This one opens all. Very useful.' He unlocked the cabin door and pushed it open, then turned and shuffled away.

'Phew!' Toby looked at Anna and grinned. 'He didn't want to know why we needed to go in!'

'Probably thought it was ours.' Anna stepped inside and looked round. The cabin was cheerfully untidy, littered with clothes and shoes.

'It will be hidden. Drawers. Suitcases. Down the back of something.' Methodically they went through all the obvious places, searched under the mattresses, in the wardrobe, in the bathroom, even behind the framed prints hanging on the walls.

'It's not here. Neither of them is in here.' Miserably she shook her head. 'We've searched every square inch.'

'Have you indeed!'

The voice in the doorway brought her up with a jerk. She and Toby spun round.

Andy was standing in the doorway, staring at them. 'May I ask what exactly you are searching for?'

'I hardly think you need to ask! Anna wants her diary back, and her scent bottle.'

'And you think I have them?' Andy was looking very flushed. They could smell beer on his breath.

'I know you have the bottle, Andy and I want it back. And I suspect you've got the diary as well.' Anna fought to keep her voice calm.

'I've put the bottle somewhere safe, which is what you should have done in the first place! But to dare to come here and accuse me of taking your diary! That is outrageous! Get out! Get out now!' He caught Anna by the arm and swung her towards the door. 'Go on. Get out!'

'Leave her alone, you bastard!' Behind him Toby stepped forward. He caught Andy by the shoulder.

'Toby!' Anna screamed. 'No!' She snatched at his arm. 'Don't! What's the matter with you all? Why is there so much anger on this boat?'

Toby's expression was furious. He shook Anna off, his fists clenched. For several seconds the three of them remained unmoving, as if frozen in a tableau on a stage, then slowly the fire went out of Toby's eyes and he dropped his fist. He pushed Andy away.

Andy sat down on the bed. His face was white.

Anna glanced at Toby. 'I think we'd better go.'

He nodded. With a final glance at Andy he walked out of the cabin.

'Will you be all right?' Anna followed Toby, but in the doorway she paused, looking back.

Andy nodded.

'It was your fault. You shouldn't have touched me. And you shouldn't have taken my things.'

Andy looked up. 'I'm sorry, Anna. I'm not sure what came over me. This isn't like me, it really isn't. But you do believe me now, don't you?

He's a killer! Be careful, Anna. Whatever you do, be careful.'

Anna turned and left the cabin. Toby had gone. Shakily she turned towards Serena's cabin and knocked on the door.

Serena pulled it open. 'Did you find it—' She stopped in mid-sentence. 'Anna, what is it? What's happened?'

'Andy caught us in the cabin. He and Toby nearly had a fight.'

Serena bit her lip. 'Well, I suppose I can't honestly say I'm surprised. Come in.' She pulled Anna inside and closed the door behind her. 'Is Andy all right?' she asked suddenly, almost as an afterthought.

'He'll live.'

'And Toby?'

Anna shrugged. 'He was terrifying, Serena. He almost lost control for a moment. I could see it in his eyes. If I hadn't been there, I think he might have hit Andy.' She bit her lip anxiously, shaking her head. She didn't believe Toby was a killer, of course she didn't! But she had seen a side of him now which had frightened her and she was full of doubt.

Serena studied her face. 'Did you find the bottle?' she asked quietly.

'No.'

'That's a pity.' She was thoughtful for a moment, then she shook her head. 'I have got a theory, Anna. I hope it is wrong.' She hesitated. 'The thing is, the other priest, Hatsek, the priest of Sekhmet. He is here. On the boat. I have had my suspicions for some time that when Charley stole the bottle she was in some way affected by him; that maybe he is using her energy and that is why she is growing weaker. There is no question that she is becoming slightly unhinged. She never used to drink the way she does now.'

Anna nodded. '*And* she talked of Sekhmet in the bar the other day.'

'Yes, and now there's something else,' Serena continued. 'Toby and Andy. I think he could be feeding on their anger too. There's this atmos-phere on the boat. I can feel it intensifying. It's affecting us all.'

Serena moved over to the window and stared out. 'And then there is you. Anhotep follows you around. He must be using your energies.' She sighed. 'I've decided to go to Abu Simbel tomorrow. I need to get off the boat for a bit, distance myself from all this. Then perhaps when we come back—we have one day to see Philae before the cruise back to Luxor—at Philae maybe we can try something. Philae is, after all, the temple of Isis.'

'You think Anhotep won't follow us to Abu Simbel then?'

There was a short silence. Serena was watching a felucca drifting with the current past them. 'No, I don't think he'll come to Abu Simbel,' she said at last. 'I wish we knew what had happened to Louisa Shelley. She came through it. She coped.'

Anna nodded sadly. 'I can't bear not knowing what happened. But as you say, she coped. She went home and got on with her life.'

But what happened to Hassan? The question increasingly echoed in her head. And what about the priests Anhotep and Hatsek? They haunted Louisa, as they haunted her great-great-granddaughter. How had she made them leave her alone? A new wave of frustration and fury shot through her as she thought about the diary. Anna made a decision. She wouldn't go on the coach to Abu Simbel tomorrow. That would give her two days to search with no one on the boat to interfere.

Just for a moment she forgot that the priests of Isis and Sekhmet would probably stay with her.

The telephone by Anna's bed rang at a few minutes after 3.30am. The wake-up call was followed by a knock at her door and a cup of tea. She dressed quickly in jeans and a tee-shirt, then set out to find Omar. He merely shrugged when she explained she didn't want to go with them. *Inshallah*! It was up to her. Tell Ibrahim she would require meals, and enjoy her rest.

Finding Serena wearily lifting her overnight bag onto her shoulder, she whispered her decision. Serena nodded. Was she, Anna wondered, even a little relieved? She couldn't see Toby or Andy, but already the passengers were streaming across the gangplank onto the shore. There, a small charabanc was waiting to take them to the assembly point, where a convoy of coaches and taxis gathered every morning to leave under escort for the drive south across a desert which was also a military zone.

When they had all gone, Anna stood still for a moment, listening to the silence, wondering a trifle wistfully if she had done the right thing. The tour to the temple of Rameses was one of the high points of the trip. But it was too late to change her mind. She decided to go back to bed.

When she woke she was lying on her bed, fully dressed. She frowned, disorientated for a moment by the lack of bustle on the boat.

Slowly she climbed out of bed. She wasn't sure where she was going to start her search for the diary, but Andy's cabin seemed the obvious place. Either she had missed it the first time, or perhaps, even if it hadn't been there before, the diary would be there now.

As she expected, the boat was completely deserted. She ran to the reception desk, ducked behind it and lifted Andy's key off the hook where Omar had placed them all before they left. Slipping it into her pocket she made her way, for the second time, towards Andy's cabin.

Bolting the door behind her to make sure that on this occasion she was not interrupted, she went through the place systematically, checking every square inch until at last she had to give up.

There was no sign of the diary or the bottle, and there was nothing for it but to let herself out of the cabin and return the key to its hook. Then she wandered up the stairs, deep in thought.

Ibrahim was behind the bar in the lounge, polishing glasses. He greeted her with a big smile. 'Good morning, *mademoiselle*.'

'Good morning, Ibrahim. It looks as though I'm all alone for a while.'

He shook his head. 'Omar says three people for meals, *mademoiselle*. I cook for you all myself because the real cook has gone to see his mother in Sehel. But Ibrahim is a wonderful cook too. *Inshallah*!' He roared with laughter. 'Would you like a drink now?'

She ordered a beer and wandered up to the sundeck, wondering which other passengers had stayed behind. She watched another huge cruiser manoeuvre its way in towards the bank for a while, but it was too hot to stay on the top deck, so she made her way back downstairs to sit beneath the awning.

'Anna!'

The voice behind her took her completely by surprise. She swung round. Toby was standing in the shade, his sketchbook under his arm.

They stared at each other awkwardly for a moment, then he said, 'I thought you would have gone to Abu Simbel with Serena?'

'I couldn't go without knowing what has happened to the diary.' Anna squinted up at him. 'So, why did you stay?'

He shrugged. 'I wanted to do some more sketching'. He pulled out the chair next to her. 'May I?'

She nodded. 'Ibrahim said we could help ourselves from the bar. Just write it on the pad. He's gone to cook lunch.'

Toby grinned. 'Great.' He headed towards the door into the lounge, then he stopped. 'I take it you have searched Andy's cabin again?'

She nodded. 'I have indeed.'

'No luck?'

She shook her head. 'No.'

'Well, he won't have taken it with him. That would be too risky. He'll have left it somewhere safe on the boat. We'll have to be systematic, tick off each place as we search it.'

She realised, as he headed through the doorway to the bar, that she liked the way he assumed he would be helping her.

When Toby returned, he glanced at her over his glass. 'Of course, the safe! Have you thought of the safe? It's the obvious place.'

They found Ibrahim laying three covers at one of the tables in the dining room. From the open door into the kitchen came a wonderful smell of garlic and onions.

'Is it possible to look in the safe?' Anna sat down at the table and looked up at him pleadingly. 'I lent my grandmother's diary to Andrew Watson and I think he may have put it there for safety, not realising I wasn't going with them all this morning. I need it urgently.'

He nodded. 'I have the key. I will come and look for you.'

They followed him down to the reception desk and waited while he fiddled with the lock. At last he swung the small safe door open. It was full of envelopes and packets.

He rummaged through the packages, glancing at the larger envelopes. 'Andrew Watson!' He pulled one out.

'That's it! That's the right size and shape,' Anna cried in delight.

Ibrahim passed it to her. 'You look.'

She ran her thumb under the sealed flap of the envelope and pulled out the diary.

'Good! Good!' Ibrahim beamed in delight. 'Now we go to eat lunch.'

'Wait.' Anna stretched out her hand. 'My scent bottle. He was looking after that as well. If it's here it can stay, but I'd like to check.'

'Bottle?' Ibrahim frowned.

She met his gaze. 'The little bottle that was guarded by the cobra.'

Ibrahim shook his head. 'That is not here,' he said, without even looking, and slammed the door of the safe shut.

She glanced at Toby, who raised an eyebrow and grinned. 'Proof enough for you? Am I totally exonerated for ever?'

She nodded, hugging the diary to her chest. 'Proof enough. If you wish I shall grovel to you for the rest of my days.'

His smile deepened. 'A day or two will be sufficient.'

The third passenger did not join them for lunch, and they ate companionably before looking at the diary again. Anna began to read out loud.

In the coolness of late afternoon they had sailed away from the *Ibis*, beaching the boat near a magical lake bordered by palms. Hassan had sent away the Nubian donkey boy who had guided them into the dunes of sand. He would come back just after sunrise so they could return to the *Ibis* before the sun had gained its full strength. Now, as the sun was setting they could feel the first cold breaths of the desert wind.

'You are sure he will find us again?' Louisa gazed around her. Hassan smiled. 'He will come. There is nothing to fear. We are within sight of the river. We have only come a few miles upstream from where the *Ibis* is moored. Come.' He held out his hand and began to pull her up the narrow valley between the dunes. 'We follow this wadi, then I will show you my surprise.'

They began to scramble up the rocky heights of a small hill.

'There! The top!' He triumphantly hauled her up the last couple of yards and he stood back so that she could see what they had come to visit.

On the summit of the plateau stood a small, exquisite temple, similar to the kiosk at Philae. Louisa stared in delight at the delicate leafy carvings on the capitals, and the heads of the goddess. The temple was badly ruined, but it was a beautiful red-gold in the light of the dying sun.

Louisa stared at it in delight. 'Where is this?' she asked at last.

'It is the Temple of Kertassi.' He gestured around with his hand. 'This temple too is sacred to Isis. It is very beautiful, is it not?' He smiled.

Louisa stared up at the pillars with their long black shadows running down to the water.

'Soon the sun will go down.' Hassan put his arm round her shoulders. 'Look, it slips into the world of the gods as we watch.'

Louisa watched. She found she was holding her breath as the inverted crescent of light grew smaller and smaller until there was barely a sliver left. Then it was gone.

There were tears in her eyes as they watched the afterglow disappear, then at last it was fully dark and the stars appeared. Louisa stared up in delight. 'I can see every star in the firmament! The sky is like a black velvet cloak, sewn with diamonds!'

Hassan didn't speak. He too was staring up, lost in thought. They stood there together for a long time, until her sudden shiver reminded them that the air was growing sharply colder.

Hassan had carried one of their bags up on his shoulders. Now he let her start unpacking it while he went down to the spot where the donkey boy had left them and brought up the other two.

'I am afraid that I will fall asleep and miss the sunrise.' Louisa had pulled a rug around her as she sat in the centre of the temple watching him unpack the food by the light of a small lamp.

Hassan smiled. He had erected the tent and came and sat beside her 'Do not be afraid, my Louisa. I will watch for you.'

'All night?'

'All night, my Louisa.' He drew her against him. 'You are cold?'

She nodded. Her heart was beating very fast.

'The desert is very cold when the sun has gone.' He was gently stroking her hair. Nestling against him she raised her face to his and felt the touch of his lips in the dark.

Dreamily she let him guide her inside the tent and down onto the pile of cushions. She felt him drawing a rug around them, then gently, every move a caress, he eased her dress back from her shoulders and pushed it away until she was lying naked in his arms. Closing her eyes she felt her body relax. His hands, his lips, moved delicately across her skin and she felt herself an instrument touched into wild music at his command.

Far away across the desert a jackal howled. She tensed, but his hands soothed her, and as his mouth came down over hers she abandoned herself to the ecstasy which was building in every part of her body.

Afterwards she slept, secure in the crook of his arm. Faithful to his promise, he lay awake, staring out at the night.

Some time before dawn he dozed, then he woke suddenly. The sand near them sighed and hissed under the soft touch of the wind. His eyes opened and he stared into the darkness. There was another sigh of movement in the sand and he tensed sharply. There was someone, or something, near their belongings.

Carefully he drew his arm out from beneath her shoulders. She stirred and her eyelids fluttered. 'Is it dawn?' Her voice was soft and husky, her naked body warm and relaxed beneath the rug.

'Nearly dawn, my love.' He spoke in a whisper. 'Be still. Do not stir.'

He slid out from the rug and stood up, staring round in the darkness as he pulled on his clothes. He glanced round for a weapon. Piles of stone lay all over the place among the ruins, and cautiously he bent and picked up a couple of pieces.

Louisa strained her eyes. It had grown marginally lighter, but she couldn't see Hassan any more. As she pulled her gown silently over her head, something moved near the food basket and she held her breath.

Hassan's sudden shout brought her to her feet as she saw movement near the far pillar, and heard a gasp and then the grunt of men fighting.

After only a second's hesitation, Louisa bent in her turn to pick up a piece of fallen sandstone as a weapon and ran towards the sound.

Hassan was wrestling with another man, a man dressed in European clothing. As she drew closer she gasped. It was Carstairs.

Almost at the same second that she recognised him there was a sharp cry from Hassan and he reeled to the ground and lay still. Louisa froze then she threw herself towards him. 'What have you done? Hassan, my love, are you all right?' Dropping to her knees she touched his head, her eyes fixed on Carstairs as he stood over them. The wound on Hassan's head was wet and sticky. Without looking she knew it was blood.

Carstairs was holding a knife. 'The sacred ampulla. Or I kill him.' His eyes glittered as he stepped towards her.

'You're mad!' She was trying to protect Hassan with her hands.

'My sanity need not concern you, Mrs Shelley. Give me the bottle and I'll leave you in peace, otherwise I'll be forced to kill him. Are you insane coming out into the desert alone with only a peasant to guard you? Have you not heard of the bandits who rob travellers out here?'

'There are no bandits here, but you!' she shouted at him desperately. 'And you will answer before the law.'

Carstairs smiled. 'Who would believe you, crazed as you would be with horror and thirst and the ravages of the bandits who had captured you and left you to the noonday sun?' He slowly tucked the knife into his belt. 'In a minute the sun will come up, and with it will come the heat.' He put his hands on his hips. 'The ampulla, Mrs Shelley.'

'I don't have it. Would I bring it into the desert?'

He smiled. 'I can see I am going to have to persuade you to take me seriously.' He took two steps away from her and turned to face the east, his arms upraised. 'Great Sekhmet, hear me! Sister of Isis and of Hathor, Eye of Ra, goddess of war, send me the uraeus, your flame-spitting servant, that it may protect your priests and the container of their magic! Send it to me now!' His voice was echoing among the pillars. Louisa stared at him unable to look away, Hassan's head cradled in her lap.

Behind them, on the far side of the river, the first thin, blood-coloured segment of the sun appeared, sending horizontal rays of red and gold shooting towards them across the sand.

'Dear God, please save us.' Louisa heard the whispered words from her own lips as though they came from someone else.

At Carstairs's feet she saw a shadow move. A shape was appearing on the sand, a long brownish body, gleaming scales, small beady eyes. It moved towards him with one or two sinuous movements, then it stopped. It seemed to be watching him and, as he gestured towards them it reared up and spread its hood, swaying gently from side to side.

Hassan groaned. 'Move back slowly, my Louisa. Leave me.'

Carstairs smiled. 'Mrs Shelley is not in danger, you dog. The servant of Isis would never harm a woman. But men are different.'

'If you kill Hassan, you will never see the bottle again,' Louisa said. 'He has hidden it somewhere in the fields along the Nile. No one else knows where it is, not even I! Don't let it touch him, my lord, or you will be very, very sorry.'

'Why should I believe you?'

'Because it is the truth.' She held his gaze for several seconds.

He looked away first.

'So be it. But what has been called forth cannot be sent away!' he said softly. 'Until I have the sacred tears of Isis in my possession, my servant will guard them. Do not think this dog will escape me. I shall be watching him.' He smiled grimly. 'For all eternity, if necessary.'

The book fell from Anna's hands and she stared blankly ahead of her.

'The cobra in Charley's cabin. Carstairs conjured it up, not the priest!'

Toby reached across and taking the diary from her lap he put it to one side. 'Possibly. On the other hand, there are still cobras in Egypt.'

'But in the cabin of a pleasure cruiser?'

He shook his head. 'It seems to be more than a coincidence.'

They sat in silence for a while, staring at the river. It was Anna who spoke at last. 'The tears of Isis. It sounds romantic, doesn't it? That's the first time I think there has been a specific clue as to what is actually in the bottle. I've held it up to the light, of course, but the glass is completely opaque. It's impossible to see if there is anything in it.'

'You could take it to the British Museum when you get back to London, tell them the whole story and ask them to unseal it. They could do it under sterile conditions and find out what, if anything, is in there.'

Anna was staring dreamily into the distance. 'Science versus romance. That seems somehow a very modern solution to the problem.'

Toby looked grim suddenly 'Anna, what are you going to do about the diary? When Andy comes back?'

She hesitated for a moment or two. 'I don't know. I don't want the police involved. I have a feeling it wouldn't be wise to make an issue of it. He would only deny it and say I had lent it to him or something, and it would be very difficult to prove that I hadn't. I'll keep it locked up or with me at all times, and probably leave it at that.'

He stared at her. 'Anna, he tried to steal something which could be worth thousands of pounds.'

'I've got it back,' she said firmly. 'And he's got to live with the fact that you and I and Serena know he's a thief. He'll be sweating.'

He exhaled loudly and shook his head. 'OK. If that's what you've decided. It's your diary.'

Later, they dined alone in state by candlelight on Ibrahim's speciality, something he called *mulukhiyya*, which turned out to be a herb soup poured over white rice, followed by fried perch and vegetables. For dessert they were given dates and soft cheese and then Egyptian coffee.

Only when they assured him they could eat no more did Ibrahim bid them good night and leave.

'And so.' Toby smiled. 'We have a boat to ourselves.'

She nodded. 'Don't forget the captain is still on board.'

'But we don't see him.' Toby said. 'Perhaps he doesn't exist. Or perhaps he is Ibrahim too, with another hat on!' He glanced at her and slowly his face became thoughtful. It was several minutes before he spoke at last. 'What did Andy tell you about me?'

She bit her lip. 'He seemed to think you had some kind of a scandal hanging over you. I didn't take much notice.'

He grimaced. 'Why haven't you asked me if it's true?'

She hesitated. 'Because I believed—hoped—it wasn't.'

There was another long silence, then he said, 'It is true. Anna, I don't want there to be any secrets between us.'

She waited, aware that there was a sudden knot of anxiety somewhere in her stomach. 'What happened?'

'I killed someone.'

There was a long silence. She bit her lip. 'Why?'

His jaw tightened. 'He raped my wife.'

Anna closed her eyes. 'Did you go to prison?' she asked at last.

'For manslaughter, yes.'

'And your wife?'

'My wife is dead.'

'Dead?' Anna stared at him.

'She killed herself while I was in prison. The state took it upon itself to punish me. It did nothing about the man who attacked her and tormented her. While I was in prison it left her alone to cope with her unhappiness and her shame. She was pregnant when she died, apparently by him. She had no one. No family. My father was dead. My mother was abroad. She couldn't get there in time.' He stood up abruptly and walked away from her. He climbed up onto the upper deck and she saw him disappear into the darkness. For a long time she stayed where she was, then at last she turned and followed him.

'Thank you for telling me.'

'If I hadn't, Watson would have done so in the end, no doubt. People always remember these things even though it happened years ago now.' He turned to her at last. 'Do you want a drink?' The emotion was raw on his face. It was masked instantly. 'If you want to drink with a murderer.'

'You weren't a murderer; not if they said it was manslaughter. And yes, please, I think I'd like one very much.' She wanted to touch him, to reassure him and comfort him, but she sensed that now wasn't the time.

Instead she forced herself to smile, and it was she who turned and led the way down to the bar.

Toby poured two slugs of whisky, signed a chit from the pad by the locked till, and pushed one of the glasses towards her. 'Cheers! Here's to you and me and the mysteries of Egypt. *Inshallah!*'

She clinked glasses with him. 'Toby . . .' She hesitated. How could she put into words the strange mixture of feelings she was experiencing? Rage at the injustice of life. Sympathy. Pain for him, for his wife. Anger at the man who had ruined so many lives. It was impossible and, looking up, she realised suddenly as he met her eye that he understood.

'Shall we read some more about Louisa?' he said quietly. It was a signal to change the subject.

She nodded. 'The diary is in my cabin. Shall I bring it here, or shall we go there to read it?'

He studied her face. 'Which would you like?' He sounded hesitant.

She hadn't intended her words to sound like an invitation, but she realised that that was what they were. She reached out her hand.

In the cabin she turned on the bedside light. 'The diary is locked up. A classic case of bolting the stable door.' She laughed. There was a sudden tight knot of excitement in her stomach as she felt him standing very close behind her. She reached into her shoulder bag for the key to her suitcase.

Toby stretched out his hand and caught her wrist. 'Anna?'

She stood stock still. Then she turned and looked up at him.

They remained wrapped in each other's arms for a long time before Anna gently disengaged herself. 'Are you sure this is what you want?'

She was amazed that it was she who was taking the lead, she who had initiated this move, overwhelmed as she was by a desire for him so great it almost paralysed her. She had never felt like this before, this incredible, undeniable longing that had swept over her.

Toby smiled. 'It's very much what I want.' He drew her close once again and she could feel him searching for the zip of her dress. It slipped to the floor and she felt his hands on her burning skin, cool and firm as he stroked her shoulders and ran a finger down her throat towards her breasts. She gasped, raising her mouth to his again as he unfastened the hooks on her bra and then pulled her towards the bed.

It was much later, asleep in the crook of his arm, that Anna was woken by a violent knocking on the door.

She lay still, holding her breath, feeling him stir beside her.

They looked at each other for a moment. 'It must be Ibrahim.' Anna pulled on her dressing gown then headed for the door. Unbolting it, she pulled the door open and Charley almost fell into the room.

'Anna! You've got to help me!' Tears were pouring down her face. 'Oh God!' She glanced behind her down the passage, then, stumbling into the cabin, she slammed the door and shot the bolt across. She didn't appear to have seen Toby, who had reached over the edge of the bed for his trousers and was pulling them on. Anna put her arm around Charley's shoulders and guided her to the stool in front of the dressing table. 'What's happened? I thought you had gone with the others?'

Charley shook her head. She had grabbed Anna's hands and was clinging to them as though her life depended on it. 'Don't let him in. Keep him away from me!'

Toby was pulling on his shirt. He frowned. 'Who? Who is it, Charley? What's happened?'

'I was asleep. In my cabin.' She shook her head. 'I thought I was dreaming. I *was* dreaming.' Her breath was coming in short gasps, her hand in Anna's shaking violently. 'Then I woke up. I'd locked the door. I know I locked the door. But he was there.' She broke into fresh sobs.

Toby came and knelt in front of her. He took one of her hands. 'Charley, listen to me. You are safe. We are not going to let anything happen to you. Now tell us what happened. Who was in your cabin?'

'It was a man. In a green *galabiyya*. He was reaching out towards me.'

'Describe him. Was he one of the waiters?'

'No. No. He was very tall. He was wearing an animal skin round his shoulders—'

'A lion skin?' Anna had gone to sit on the bed.

Charley glanced up and shrugged. 'It could have been.'

Toby glanced at Anna, who grimaced. He tried another tack. 'Why didn't you go with the others, Charley?'

'I was going to. I wanted to.' She shook her head. 'I remember waking up early and Serena and I were getting dressed. Ali brought us some tea. Then Serena was ready, but I didn't feel well. I said I'd follow her. I sat down on the bed for a minute. Serena came back, and I think she asked me how I was, and I suppose I said I wanted to go to sleep.'

Anna stood up. 'That explains the third person on the boat. Serena must have told Ibrahim you were staying. What happened next?'

'I don't remember anything till I woke up and saw him standing there just now.' Charley began to sob again.

'Then what?'

'Then I screamed. I sat up and screamed and he sort of stepped towards me. Then he began to shake.' She shook her head, confused. 'He was shaking quite violently, then he—' She stopped and shrugged. 'He sort of wasn't there any more.'

'You mean he left the cabin, or he disappeared?'

She shrugged again. 'I didn't wait to see. I ran outside and I couldn't see anyone. Have the others gone yet?'

'Charley, they left yesterday. Twenty-four hours ago.'

Charley's eyes focused on Anna's face. 'No.'

Toby looked up at her with concern. 'When did you last eat, Charley?' He had taken her hands again. He glanced at Anna. 'Do you see how thin she's got?' he said under his breath. 'I can't believe it. In a week.'

Anna nodded. She had been studying Charley's face while Toby was talking to her. 'Serena thought the incubus was taking her energy.'

Charley's eyes were round again and Anna noticed she had begun to tremble once more. 'Andy will be so angry. He was going to sit next to me. And now you're with him'—she nodded at Toby—'and not after my Andy at all.' She shot a defiant look at Anna. 'Did you know he had your stupid little bottle with him? So if you've lost it again, you know it wasn't me.'

'He's taken it with him?' Anna stared at her. 'Are you sure?'

Charley nodded.

Anna's face had frozen. She was staring at the suitcase in front of the cupboard. Locked inside was the diary where only hours before she and Toby had read about the snake. The king snake, programmed to kill any man who touched the sacred ampulla.

She glanced at Toby. 'The cobra,' she whispered. 'The guardian of the scent bottle. Only women have owned that bottle. Louisa. My great-great-grandmother. My great-aunt. Me.'

'Oh shit!' Toby rubbed his chin. 'What do we do?'

'What is it? What's wrong?' Charley grabbed at Toby's arm.

'The snake you found in your cabin,' Anna said sharply. 'It didn't hurt you because you're a woman.'

Charley stared at her. 'Why? What do you mean?'

'It guards the bottle. Look, don't ask, Charley. Just believe it! Find Ibrahim,' Anna said to Toby urgently. 'Perhaps we can phone Omar and get him to warn Andy.'

'No! Don't leave me!' Charley clung to Toby as he turned towards the door. 'What about the man in my cabin!'

'We won't leave you, Charley.' Toby pushed her towards Anna. 'Stay here, both of you. I'll see if I can find Ibrahim.'

As he disappeared, Anna closed her eyes. She took a deep breath. 'If we can't contact Omar, we're going to have to find a way of warning Andy. Take a bus or a taxi or something.'

She unlocked the suitcase, took out the diary and pushed it into her holdall along with her sunhat, glasses and guidebook.

By the time Toby returned Anna was ready. 'I spoke to the captain. He knows nothing. Not where they are or where Ibrahim might be, though he thinks he has gone to visit friends. But he has ordered us a taxi. It'll be by the gangplank in ten minutes.' He turned to Charley.

'If you don't want to stay on board here we can drop you off at a hotel before we go. You'd be safe there.'

Charley shook her head. 'I hate all this. I want to go home.'

'A hotel can arrange that for you, if that's what you really want.'

It was Anna who went into Charley's cabin while Charley clung to Toby in the corridor outside. It was empty. Grabbing Charley's already packed overnight bag she closed the door behind her with a fervent prayer that the priest of Sekhmet would stay wherever it was he lived and would not follow them.

A black car was waiting at the water's edge. The young man at the wheel greeted Toby with some deference as they climbed in. In seconds they were heading south towards the Old Cataract Hotel.

'Wait here,' Toby said to Anna when they arrived. He took Charley's arm and bundled her out. 'I'll be five minutes.'

It was fifteen minutes before he returned, and Anna had dozed off. He seemed pleased with himself as they set off. 'Charley'll be fine. She can either stay there till we cruise back to Luxor, or they'll get her a ticket to fly back home early. And I've sorted us out, too. South of Aswan it's a military zone, so I've organised passes to go through the desert.' He leaned back beside her. 'Now, go back to sleep. I'll wake you when we get there.'

'Toby?' With a shiver she pulled her sweater more tightly round her shoulders. 'What happens if the priest of Sekhmet has got hold of her? What if he comes back when she's on her own?'

'The hotel staff will keep an eye on her. If anything happens they'll call a doctor.'

'And what could a doctor do?'

He shrugged. 'We'll be back in Aswan very soon, Anna. Once we've found Andy and relieved him of the bottle the urgency is over.'

They woke some hours later when the taxi lurched to a standstill in the car park at Abu Simbel.

'Good speed, yes?' The driver beamed at them.

Toby nodded. He reached for his wallet. 'Good speed. Good bonus.' As he began counting notes into the man's hand, Anna climbed out of the car. The heat hit her like a hammer blow as she stared round at the ranks of cars and coaches. 'How will we find the others?'

Toby raised a hand to the driver and watched as the taxi backed away. 'Is he leaving?' Anna stared after it.

'Not if he knows what's good for him. I've only given him the fare here. If he wants the rest he'll wait for us.' Toby smiled. 'Now I think we should try the great temple first.'

Joining the queue to enter the gates, Anna and Toby began to scan the crowds around them for faces they knew. They bought their tickets and made their way in, following a path around the side of a low hill. Suddenly they found themselves in front of one of the most famous sights in the world, the four colossal statues of Rameses II, set into the cliff face. In front of the temple the sea of swirling humanity threatened to overwhelm the façade, for all the enormous height of the statues. 'We'll never find them!' Anna gasped.

'Of course we will.' Toby stared round. 'I hope Andy comes to realise how much effort we are going to, to protect his hide.'

They were threading their way through the groups of tourists to the entrance to the vast rock-cut hall with two lines of four lofty columns. They stood close together, staring into the dark, aware of the vast crowds of people milling around the pillars. Only close to the doorway was it possible to see much. Everywhere the walls were covered in relief carvings of Rameses's victories. Further in all was almost dark.

'We'll never see them!' Anna was near to tears.

Suddenly there was a touch on her shoulder. 'Anna?'

It was Serena. She gave Anna a hug. 'What on earth are you doing here? Why did you change your mind? How did you get here?'

Anna returned her embrace with relief. 'It's a long, long story. Where is Andy?' She was looking round frantically.

Serena shrugged. 'I've no idea. He's not my favourite person at the moment. Why all the panic about him?'

'He left the diary in the boat's safe, but he has brought the bottle here with him. And probably the cobra too. And it will kill him. Carstairs summoned it to kill Hassan and any man who touches the bottle! And I mean man, not woman. That's why Charley and I—and you—were safe.'

Serena grimaced. 'So, you want me to help find him and warn him?'

Toby nodded. He tapped his watch. 'We'll do better if we separate, then we can search a bigger area. Let's all meet in half an hour outside the main door and hope one of us has located him.'

'God knows how you'll persuade him even to admit he's got it with him, never mind that he's in danger of being poisoned by a magic snake if he doesn't give it back!' Serena murmured as she and Anna separated and turned to push their way towards the interior.

The crowds were less dense once they had passed into the smaller chambers at the back. Anna stepped into the first and squinted at the few people looking at the reliefs in there, but none had the breadth of shoulders of Andy.

The next small chamber she looked into was empty. For a moment she stood in the doorway peering in, struck by the sudden stillness. Rebuilt to save it from the rising waters after the building of the high dam, it had been mobbed by crowds ever since. And yet now, in this small side room, she found an intense silence. She turned towards the sanctuary, deep in the heart of the temple. It was here, twice a year, that the sun's ray pierced all the way through from the entrance into the depths of the rock to fall on the altar, illuminating three of the four statues that guarded it. The temple had been aligned exactly as it had been in its original setting so that this miracle could take place in such a way that the fourth statue, that of the god Ptah, the creator god, Lord of Darkness, remained for ever in the dark, untouched by the sun.

Ptah, of course, was the husband of Sekhmet . . .

Anna stopped. The words floating out of the darkness towards her had come, she realised, from a group of people standing by the statues.

She felt her stomach turn over with sudden fear. Would Hatsek come here? Would he recognise this temple, rebuilt and swarming with unbelievers from a different age though it was?

Almost as the thought crossed her mind she knew that he would. She stepped sideways into the corner of the sanctuary, staring round. There were two other people in the chamber, examining the seated statues. Near them the air shimmered for a moment and grew cold.

Anna tried to turn back, but her feet were rooted to the spot. The sanctuary was growing darker, and in the strange chill that surrounded her, she could hear voices somewhere in the distance, chanting.

Light flickered to one side of the statues. It came from a lamp, she realised, set in a niche in the wall. In the foreground, on what she had thought was an altar, she could see the dark shape of a model boat.

And then she saw him, a tall man, very dark of complexion, his face drawn into harsh lines. He was naked but for a short skirt round his hips and the tawny pelt of a desert lion hung round his shoulders. On his feet she could see gilded sandals and in his hand was a long staff, with the angry, snarling head of a lioness at its top.

He was staring past her, not seeming to see her as he turned towards the entrance to the sanctuary. The chanting was growing louder, and she could smell the sweet spicy smell of incense. He was standing in front of the statue of Ptah, bowing, placing something before it.

Frozen with fear, Anna could see shadows moving across the chamber, two people talking softly at the centre of the sanctuary. The two scenes, two eras, seemed for a moment to coexist within the same place. The couple seemed not to see the priest standing near them. It was they who seemed wraiths out of time. It was Hatsek, the priest of Sekhmet about his sacred ritual, who was real in this strange, reconstructed place.

'Are you all right?' The touch on her arm shocked Anna back to the present. She recognised one of the women from their boat, Celia Grayshot—her husband was a retired vicar. Anna staggered slightly, her hand to her head and the woman put a supportive arm round her shoulders. 'Shall I help you outside, my dear?' she said. 'This is such a powerful, weird place, isn't it?'

Anna did her best to smile. 'I think I would like to go outside. I am feeling a bit odd.'

Serena was sitting on a bench outside. She jumped up in consternation as Anna and her companion appeared. 'Anna, what's wrong?'

'Too much heat, I think. Celia was kind enough to look after me.' She flopped onto the bench. 'No sign of Andy?'

Serena shook her head. 'None.' They watched as Celia, with a pleasant word and a wave, disappeared into the crowds in search of her husband.

'I saw Hatsek!' Anna said as soon as her companion was out of earshot. 'I heard someone say that Ptah was Sekhmet's husband!'

Serena thought for a moment. 'Did you feel your energy depleted?'

Anna shrugged. 'I suppose so. I nearly fainted; that's why Celia helped me. But it was fear, Serena. Cold, hard, total fear.'

Serena nodded slowly. 'I've made a decision while I've been here, Anna. I want to try to call up the priests. But on my terms. I think I can do it. If you like we'll try it at Philae, this evening. And it'll be all right, I promise.' She gripped Anna's hands. 'Did you bring the diary with you?'

Anna nodded. 'I'm not letting it out of my sight again!'

'Then may I suggest we find somewhere shady and have a drink first and we can look at it to find out if Louisa found a way of dealing with Carstairs's curse. Then we'll have another shot at finding Andy. Come on.' Serena stood up and held out her hand. 'Let's get out of the sun.'

After the rescue party had brought Hassan back to the *Ibis* from the kiosk at Kartassi, Louisa, alone and shaking with anger, had demanded that one of their crew row her over to Carstairs's boat, but when she got there she found he had gone. His *reis* shrugged when she asked for him. 'He say he go for three, maybe four days. No say where.'

Louisa instructed the boatman to take her next to the *Lotus* on which she could see David Fielding and his two ladies with their parasols. Venetia greeted her with a scowl. 'Katherine is resting. I don't believe she has the strength for visitors,' she called down frostily.

Louisa inclined her head slightly. 'It was you or your brother I wanted to speak to. Do you know where Roger Carstairs has gone?'

Venetia's face reddened perceptibly. 'I have no idea. You are the one I had thought privy to all his movements.'

'As I think you know by now, he attacked my dragoman, Hassan.' Louisa stared up into the other woman's face. 'If you see him I want you to emphasise that he is no longer welcome for any reason aboard the *Ibis*. I never wish to see him again and Sir John has forbidden him to set foot on the boat.' She smiled coldly. 'I have no doubt you find such news pleasing as it leaves the field clear for you, Venetia. But do beware. The man is a fiend.'

As they rowed back towards the *Ibis*, Louisa could feel the other woman's eyes on her back. When she climbed back on board, Venetia was still standing at the rail looking after her.

'Sitt Louisa?' Hassan, bandaged and much restored, was waiting on deck. 'You should not have gone to see him.' He was angry.

Louisa shrugged. 'You expect me to leave it at that? He tried to kill you! He is a dangerous man . . .' She shook her head slowly. 'Anyway, he wasn't there.' She reached over and touched his arm. 'We do not need to think about him. We can be happy.' She smiled at him pleadingly. 'We are going to stay here for a few days so I can paint the Sun Temple.'

He nodded. 'Of course, my Louisa. We will do whatever you want.'

He was holding the bottle in his hand. 'What shall we do with it?'

Louisa shrugged. 'Is there nowhere safe?' She took it from him. 'While Carstairs is away I shall find a place to hide it.' She sighed. 'So precious a gift, my love, and so dangerous. I intend to treasure this for the rest of my life. He will not have it.'

'For the rest of your life?' Hassan repeated quietly. He glanced at her. 'You will take it back to England with you then?'

Louisa bit her lip. The future was something she did not want to contemplate, but she knew soon there would be no escaping from it.

Louisa turned away from him. She walked to the end of the deck, then she turned back. 'I have to go back to England, Hassan.' She hesitated. 'To my children. But how can I leave you? I don't know what to do!' Her voice trembled.

There was a movement behind her and she realised suddenly that Augusta had appeared at the door of the saloon. Desperately she tried to compose herself as Hassan moved a discreet pace or two away from her.

'My Louisa, you must not cry,' he murmured. 'You and I will be together in our hearts, if it is God's will.' He smiled sadly.

She was staring out across the river. '*Inshallah!*' she whispered.

'Louisa, my dear. You cannot stay out here without shade!' Augusta's voice boomed out as her hostess sailed towards her. Hassan bowed and moved away as Louisa hastily dabbed at the traces of her tears.

'I saw you coming back from the Fielding boat earlier. You didn't say you were visiting them. I would have come with you, had I known.'

Louisa managed a tired smile. 'I had a message to deliver to Lord Carstairs. I hadn't realised he had gone.'

'Gone?' Augusta frowned. 'Where has he gone?'

'I don't know the answer to that question. I had the boy row me over to the Fieldings' to see if they knew, but Venetia said not.'

Something in the set of her lips made Augusta raise an eyebrow. 'She is not too happy about Lord Carstairs's interest in you. I'm afraid she still hopes for him herself.'

'Does she indeed? Well, she is welcome to him.'

'You are still implacable, my dear?' Augusta asked Louisa. 'He would be such a catch. Title. Money. And such a handsome man.'

'And a loathsome one.'

Augusta sighed. She glanced towards the stern of the boat where Hassan had settled in conversation with the *reis*.

'Once you are back in England you will feel differently about things,' she said gently. 'And it will be time to return very soon. Sir John has decided not to go any further south. The heat is becoming unbearable.'

Louisa followed her into the saloon. 'But I have asked Hassan to take me ashore to sketch the great Temple of Rameses.'

Augusta sighed. 'My dear, you have seen so many temples already. Surely you can draw it from here? You do not have to go ashore.'

'But I do!' Louisa felt a wave of panic sweep over her. Her longing to be alone with Hassan was overwhelming her.

'What's this, what's this?' Sir John strode into the saloon and stared round. 'What is it you must do, Louisa my dear?'

'She wants to go and see that temple this afternoon,' Augusta answered for her. 'I told her she couldn't. We are turning for home.'

'No, no. We must see the temple before we go. This is one of the wonders of the world, Augusta, or if it isn't, it should be. I shall go ashore with Louisa. Why don't you come too, my dear?'

Augusta shuddered. 'I have not been to visit any of these heathen places and I do not intend to start now. I shall remain on the *Ibis*.'

'Well and good.' He smiled at Louisa. 'My dear, you are looking very serious. Does my plan not please you?'

'I am sorry, but I imagined I would have time to paint this afternoon. I had no idea you would want to come with us.'

He frowned. 'Can you not make quick sketches, my dear?'

'I know that John will want to come back to me very soon, Louisa,' Augusta commented. She raised an eyebrow. 'Should you wish to stay longer on the shore I am sure that would be possible. Even if the *Ibis* sets off downriver I feel certain you would have no trouble catching us up in one of those little feluccas. You may have your few extra hours with—' She hesitated. 'With your paintbrush and your muse.'

Louisa glanced at her gratefully, but Augusta was not looking at her; she was sitting near the open door fanning herself vigorously.

They spent an hour inside the temple looking at the carvings and peering over the piles of sand towards its as yet unexcavated corners, then Hassan rowed Sir John back to the *Ibis*, leaving Louisa sketching the four great heads of Rameses. When Hassan returned he was alone, carrying a bag over his shoulder. 'I have permission to escort you wherever you wish as long as we join the boat by dusk. They will be leaving soon, but the wind, all that there is, is against them. We shall catch them easily.' He smiled and reached for her hand. 'Come. Pack up your painting. I want to show you a secret place on the far side of the temple, where we can find shelter from the sun and be alone.'

They found the dark entrance in the sandstone cliff and stood peering in. Hassan grinned at her and held out his hand. 'Shall we explore?'

They stepped into the shadows and Hassan dropped their belongings. He rummaged in the bag for a candle. 'Do you want to see inside?'

She frowned uneasily and shook her head. 'Let's spread out the rug and sit down here. No one will see us unless they come right up to the rockface.'

He shrugged and did as she bid, laying out the rug and reaching for the bag containing fruit juice and water and leather travelling cups. Then he frowned. 'What is this, my Louisa?'

'The scent bottle. I didn't know where to hide it.'

Hassan shuddered. 'It is accursed three times over, my Louisa. You should not touch it any more.'

'I know.' She stared at the little bottle as it lay in the palm of his hand. 'So small a thing to have caused so much trouble.'

Behind them, in the darkness, something stirred. Neither noticed.

They were both looking down at the small bottle. 'It was your present to me,' Louisa said. 'Right at the beginning.'

He nodded. 'I loved you, my Louisa, the first moment I saw you. But you were an English lady and I a lowly guide.'

When she shook her head he shrugged. 'That is the way your people see mine, my Louisa.' He smiled. 'And perhaps, if we are honest, the way my people see yours. *Inshallah!*'

'Whatever our peoples feel, you were my friend and now you are my love.' She moved towards him and their lips touched. Slowly they sank down onto the rug. With eyes only for each other they did not see the sinuous movement on the rock-strewn sandy floor of the cave.

As he felt the sudden agonising pain of the venom-filled fangs, Hassan leapt to his feet and spun round. The scent bottle flew into the air and rolled to the edge of the rug. For a moment he stared down at the wound on his arm near his shoulder, then he let out a cry of anguish, his face contorted with pain and grief as he stared at Louisa.

'Hassan!' She had seen the snake for only a second. Already it had slithered away out of sight. 'Hassan, what shall I do? Tell me quickly!'

His face had gone grey. A sheen of clammy sweat broke out on his skin as he gasped for breath, clutching at his chest.

'Louisa! My Louisa!' The words were slurred as the muscles at the side of his mouth froze. He slumped to his knees and then he toppled onto the floor of the cave. Around his mouth the skin was turning blue.

'Hassan!' She stared down at him in disbelief. 'Hassan, speak to me!' She touched his shoulder lightly with one finger, hardly daring to breathe. 'Hassan, my love. Speak to me . . .' Her voice trailed away into silence, as she knelt beside him. A slow paralysis seemed to be creeping over him as he looked up at her through dimming eyes, then between one anguished breath and the next his heart stopped beating.

'Hassan!' Her whispered cry of agony was so quiet it barely stirred the hot shadows of the cave.

She didn't know how long she sat there with his body. The sun moved round so it no longer shone into the mouth of the cave. The heat remained intense. She cried a little, then she sat, staring into space. She had no fear the snake would return. The servant of the gods had done its work and vanished back to the kingdoms from whence it came.

At last she moved. She bent and kissed the poor, tortured features, then, climbing stiffly to her feet, she stood for a moment and whispered a quiet prayer, before she turned away and staggered out into the sunlight. She barely remembered the walk back through the hills to the front of the great temple, or her tearful plea to the other visitors she saw there, and to the tall blue-robed dragoman from another yacht, who took charge, sending men for Hassan's body, calling for a boat to take her to the *Ibis*. She would not be allowed to see Hassan again, to attend his funeral which would be before dark, to know even the place of his grave.

She was dimly aware of Augusta's arms around her, of lying in her darkened cabin. She heard the anchor being pulled up, the creak of the rigging, and the gentle slap of the river water, then, lulled by a drink heavily laced with Augusta's laudanum, she slept at last.

Anna stared at Serena. Both women had tears in their eyes. 'Poor Louisa. She loved him so much!' Anna was clutching the diary to her chest.

They sat for a moment, lost in thought, then Serena turned back to her. 'I think we'd better go on looking for Andy, don't you?'

Anna nodded. Then she shook her head violently. 'I want this all to be a legend!' she cried suddenly. 'A story! I don't want it to have been true.'

A shadow fell over them for a moment and they looked up. Toby and Omar were standing looking down at them. 'Are you all right?' Toby touched Anna's shoulder gently. He had seen the tears in her eyes.

'We were reading about Hassan's death,' Serena replied for her.

Toby sighed. 'So, the bastard killed him, did he? Poor Hassan. I've told Omar why we feel we have to find Andy urgently.' He glanced at the other man. 'He's prepared to give history the benefit of the doubt even though he doesn't believe it himself, isn't that right?'

Omar nodded. 'It is only necessary to believe one is cursed for the curse to begin to work its way in one's head,' he said. 'I have told Toby that I think Andy has gone round to see the back of the temple. One can walk in to see how the artificial hill was constructed. I show you?'

They followed him back towards a small entrance that led into the face of the cliff. Omar gestured towards it. 'If you go in here, I think you will find him. I will search elsewhere in case he changed his mind and went somewhere else.' He bowed and disappeared into the crowd.

They plunged into darkness and found themselves in the huge hollow area beneath the artificial hill which held the reassembled temple. As they climbed the stairs Anna said, 'We're not going to find him. It's too crowded.'

'We'll find him.' Serena was emphatic. 'I promise you we will.'

Toby shook his head. 'I don't think he's here. Omar says they're all due to meet anyway in about an hour to get back on the coach.'

'It'll happen here. In Abu Simbel. I know it will.' Anna was frantic suddenly. 'We've got to find him.' She turned and began to push her way back towards the entrance. 'We've got to find him. We've got to! Andy!' Her cry was lost in the huge spaces around them.

'Let her go!' Toby called to Serena. 'I don't think he's here, but we'd better be systematic.' But Serena had already turned to follow Anna. He stayed where he was, frowning. Then he turned to scan the faces of the crowds once again.

Anna was pushing her way out of the entrance, staring more and more anxiously around her. She headed blindly towards the one place she hadn't looked—the smaller temple that Rameses had built for his wife, Nefertari. It was far less crowded than the great Sun Temple itself.

A frieze guarded the door to the temple. A frieze of cobras. For a moment Anna hesitated, then she plunged into the darkness beyond.

'Andy?'

He jumped. 'Anna! What are you doing here? You weren't on the bus!'

She shook her head. 'I wasn't feeling well. I came on later with Toby in a taxi.' Suddenly she wasn't sure what to say. She realised that Serena had stepped up beside her and she glanced at her helplessly. 'I need the scent bottle, Andy,' she burst out at last. 'Give it back to me. Now.'

He inclined his head slightly. 'What scent bottle?'

'Oh please, Andy. Don't play games with me.' She held out her hand.

He shrugged. His face was cold. 'I put it somewhere safe. On the boat. You don't think I brought it with me, do you?'

She held his gaze resolutely. 'I found the diary.' She paused. 'It was in the boat's safe, in an envelope under your name, but the bottle wasn't there and I want it back.'

'OK. So I didn't leave it in the safe. It's in my cabin.'

'It's not in your cabin. I looked there too.'

His face darkened. 'You had no right to do that.'

'You had no right to steal my belongings.' She took a step forward and was surprised that he stepped back defensively. 'It was *stealing*, Andy. It is worth a great deal of money, as you yourself pointed out.'

'Hang on a minute!' he interrupted. 'I only took it to make sure it was safe.' A patch of red had appeared above each cheekbone.

'Then you should have told me what you had done with it and not accused Toby.' She could feel her own anger rising to match his.

'Ah, Toby!' He folded his arms. 'Well, I was right about him!'

'What Toby did is in the past. He paid for it,' Anna said.

'Oh, he paid for it, did he, Anna? Is that what he told you?' Andy glanced at Serena. 'Well, I sat next to a chap on the bus called Donald

Denton. He's a retired doctor who used to live near Toby and he remembered the whole story. Toby killed a man who he claimed in court had raped his wife, but in fact the wife and this chap were having an affair and she was about to run away with him! And Toby murdered his wife as well.' His face softened. 'I'm sorry, Anna.'

'It's not true! She committed suicide.'

'Is that what he told you?'

'He told me all about it, yes.'

He sighed. 'And you believed him. I can never understand women!' He grinned, confident now that the diary and bottle were forgotten.

'Why don't you speak to Toby yourself?' Anna said. 'I'd like to hear what he has to say about your accusations.'

'Oh no! You're not setting us up for a sparring match, sweetheart.' He looked at his watch suddenly. 'Anyway, the coach is leaving soon. It's time we were heading back.' He strode past her towards the entrance.

Anna looked towards Serena. 'I don't think he has got the bottle with him. After all that, he was safe!'

Serena nodded. 'So, Andy lives to fight another day,' she said. 'And in more ways than one.'

Anna shrugged. 'I don't believe him. Not about Toby.'

'Good. He's a complete, congenital liar.' Serena tucked her hand through Anna's arm. 'Come on. Come back with us on the bus.'

Anna hesitated. 'We came in a car. Toby told the driver to wait.'

Serena wrinkled her nose. 'How very rich this ex-con must be!'

'I don't think so.' It was Anna's turn to colour. 'He did it for me. He cares, Serena. You saw how much he cares.'

They emerged from the temple and looked round. Omar was standing some fifty yards away. He raised his hand to beckon them over. 'We must go soon, people. The bus is waiting.' He grinned at Anna. 'I saw Andy. He says you found him.'

Anna nodded. 'I did indeed.'

'And there was no cobra?'

She shook her head.

'Jolly good!' Omar smiled even more widely. 'Now, please, we go.'

Anna was looking round. 'Serena? Where did Toby go?'

'He stayed in the hill when we left to look in Nefertari's temple.'

Anna sighed. 'I don't know what to do. He'll expect me to go back with him. I'll have to find the car.'

'Well, presumably it will be in the car park, near the bus. We'll find it and you'll have to choose.'

Andy met them in the car park. He was smiling broadly, gloating even. 'Well, you'll never guess what's been happening here!'

Anna's heart sank without knowing why. 'What's happened?'

'Your friend, Toby. The police came. They've taken him away, and your car has gone. I'm afraid you'll have to make do with the hoi polloi on the bus.' He gave a small bow.

'Toby's been arrested!' Anna echoed. She stared at him. 'You're lying!'

'You wish! No, I'm not lying.' He stopped and his face sobered. 'He had you fooled, didn't he? He had us all fooled. The painting must have been a cover for something. To make him look respectable.'

'But what's he supposed to have done? I don't understand.'

Andy shrugged. 'No doubt we'll hear all about it soon enough!'

Serena touched Anna's arm. 'Let's get on the bus,' she said softly. 'There's nothing you can do here.'

Anna sat with Serena at the back, too shocked and miserable to speak as the coach swung out of the car park and back onto the dusty road.

'You OK?' Serena asked.

She nodded. 'I think I've had enough of Egypt. As a holiday meant to cheer me up and restore my sense of self-worth it has failed totally.'

'Toby means a great deal to you, doesn't he?'

'Yes.'

'I'm so sorry, Anna. Andy's a bastard. I bet he's got the whole thing wrong.'

Behind her sunglasses there were tears in Anna's eyes. 'I don't understand any of it. But there must be something we can do to help him.'

It was like coming home. The crew with their friendly smiles were all back after their two-day break, with scented towels to wipe away the heat and dust of the desert and warm, freshly made lemonade.

Standing in the crowded reception area, sipping her drink before making her way to her cabin, Anna was suddenly confronted by Andy.

'Anna, I am truly so very sorry. It was crass, the way I broke the news to you. And will you forgive me for taking the diary? It was thoughtless beyond belief. Meet me in the bar when you're freshened up and we'll have a drink. Please.' His eyes were sincere and very kind.

'Andy, I'm so tired. I just want to rest.'

'Please, Anna. I want us to stay friends.' He paused, and grinned enquiringly at Omar who had stopped beside them.

'Your bag, Andy. You left it on the bus.' Omar handed over the bag and slapped him on the back. 'Luckily the driver spotted it.'

Andy thanked him and swung the bag onto his shoulder. 'Say in half an hour? In the bar?' he said to Anna. 'Please?'

She was looking at the bag. As he had lifted it up the side pocket had gaped open and she had spotted the flash of scarlet silk.

'Strange, this scarf looks so much like mine,' she said, and reached out and pulled a small bundle out of the pocket. 'My scent bottle. You had it with you all the time?' She spat the words at him. 'Why did you lie, Andy?' She shook the bottle under his nose. 'Why do men always have to lie?'

She marched away to her room, and read from Louisa's diary in an effort to take her mind off Toby.

Sir John knocked on Louisa's cabin door and pushed it open. Outside it was dark, and the river was bright with moonlight.

'Louisa, Lord Carstairs is in the saloon. I understand he came up to Aswan on the steamer. Are you well enough to receive him?'

She sat up slowly, pushing her hair out of her eyes. 'He's here? On this boat? I thought you had forbidden him to set foot on it!'

Sir John shrugged uncomfortably. 'He heard what happened. He wants to see you.'

For a moment she sat still, as if gathering her strength, then she pulled herself to her feet. 'I'll see him in the saloon.'

'Very well, my dear.' He nodded. 'By the way, a party of Nubians came to the boat this afternoon, Louisa. They brought your paints; the things which were left in the cave.' He looked down at his feet suddenly. 'They are very honest, these people. I rewarded them well.' He glanced back at her. 'I thought you'd want your things.' He went to the door and fumbled outside for a moment, turning back with her woven bag, which he placed against the wall, under the small table.

Roger Carstairs was waiting for her in the saloon, sipping sherbet with Augusta, when Louisa burst in. They both turned to face her and she saw Carstairs's eyes widen. In her deep-blue robe with her hair wild, her face white and tear-stained, she must have looked strange indeed.

'Please leave us, Augusta!' Her request was so peremptory that Augusta rose to her feet without comment and disappeared out on deck.

Louisa stood in front of Carstairs, her eyes fixed on his face. 'So, my lord, are you content?'

He eyed her coldly. 'What happened is unfortunate. You had the means to prevent it.'

'So it was my fault?' Her voice was very quiet.

'Indeed it was. I do not permit people to cross me, madam. But if you wish to prevent further tragedy, I suggest you give me the sacred vial.'

'Never!' Her eyes blazed. 'You will never have it. All the gods of Egypt saw what you did, Roger Carstairs, and they revile you for it. The priest who guards that bottle, the priest of Isis despises you!'

Carstairs sneered. 'Isis is no goddess of love. She is goddess of magic and her servant is the cobra.' He smiled. 'Where is the bottle?'

'I no longer have it. It is lost in the cave where Hassan died and there it will stay, buried in the sand and guarded by your snake!' She laughed suddenly, a quiet, bitter sound. 'If you search for it, I hope it kills you with all the certainty of purpose with which it killed Hassan!'

He gave a quick bow. 'It had not occurred to me that you would leave it at Abu Simbel. I trust for your sake that it is safe!'

He made for the door, but she was standing in his way. 'Don't ever set foot on this boat again. Not ever. The Forresters support me in this; and don't show your face anywhere decent people go. I shall spread word of your evil. In Luxor. In Cairo. In Alexandria. In Paris. In London. I shall make sure that the name of Carstairs is reviled throughout the world!'

For a moment he frowned, taken aback by the force of her words, then he smiled. 'No one will believe you.'

'Oh, they will. I'll make sure of it.' She turned and moved away from him, and stood still, her back to him. For a moment he hesitated, then she heard him leave the saloon.

She walked slowly back towards her cabin. Picking up her hairbrush, she was brushing out her long tangled hair when her eye fell on the woven bag lying under the table where Sir John had left it. Frowning, she picked it up and tipped it up over the bed. There was her small paintbox, the waterpot and water bottle, a packet of charcoal strips for sketching, and, under it all, the scent bottle of the priests. She picked it up and held it in her hands, then quietly she began to cry.

'So, that's how it came back.' Serena shook her head. 'And Carstairs had already sailed. He *was* reviled, of course. His name is still known for his carryings-on. I don't think he ever went back to England.'

'And he never got the sacred bottle.' Anna was staring at it. 'I think I should throw it into the Nile.'

Serena grimaced. 'No! No, don't do that. I want to talk to the priests.' She went to stand at the window, staring out across the river. 'Until this is all resolved they can't rest. We have to find out what they want us to do. Please, let me try.'

'And the snake?'

'The snake will not harm us. Can we do it, Anna? After lunch, while people are having a siesta. Please. I want to talk to Anhotep. Anna nodded. 'But first we must find out about Charley. Shall we ask Omar to see what's happened to her?'

Omar called the hotel on his mobile phone. When at last he cut the connection, he said, 'She is coming back to the boat. They say she is rested and fine and they are putting her in a taxi. They said the bill has been paid by Toby Hayward, and he was there this morning.'

'He was at the Old Cataract Hotel?' Anna looked at him stunned. 'Then where is he now?'

Omar shrugged.

Two minutes later Anna and Serena were outside Toby's cabin. Anna knocked. There was no answer, so she reached for the handle. The door swung open and they peered in. The cabin looked totally normal, if tidier than when Anna had last seen it.

'Where would he have gone?' Anna bit her lip miserably. 'If Toby was at the hotel, then he can't have been under arrest.'

'Perhaps Charley will know where he is,' Serena suggested.

They turned towards the dining room. Lunch was a subdued affair and Ibrahim and Ali served it with the minimum of delay. Only some forty minutes later Anna and Serena made their way to Anna's cabin.

They closed the shutters and, pulling the bedside locker into the centre of the room, covered it with a silk scarf. On the makeshift altar, Serena put candles held in small coloured-glass candleholders, a brass incense burner and a tiny carved statue of Isis. Then she laid an ansate cross—the looped cross which is the Egyptian symbol of eternal life—next to the statue, and finally she produced an intricate red amulet on a leather thong, which she hung round her own neck.

'What is that?' said Anna, leaning forward and squinting at it.

'It's called the tyet. It represents the knot of Isis's girdle. Or her sacred blood, which is why it's carved in red jasper. It is a powerful symbol.'

Unconsciously, Anna groped for the amulet which hung round her own neck. Serena saw the action and gave a quick nod of approval, before reaching into her bag for a box of matches. She lit the candles, then she moved to switch off the light. She stood for a moment in silence, her eyes closed, then she reached into her bag for the last time and produced a small metal object about twelve inches high, shaped rather like the ansate cross, with four pieces of wire stretched across the looped head. On the wires were strung small finger cymbals. 'This is a sistrum, the sacred instrument of the gods,' she said as she laid it on the altar. 'It is shaken to invoke, both to purify and to protect.'

Then Anna reached for the scent bottle, unwrapped it, and laid it reverently next to Serena's sistrum.

'Ready?' she breathed. Her hands were shaking.

Serena nodded. She reached into her bag for a box of matches and lit first the small incense cone.

Behind her Anna retreated to the bed and, drawing her legs up under her, watched breathlessly.

'Whatever happens, don't try to interfere,' Serena said. 'Don't wake me if I go into a trance. It could be dangerous for me. Just keep yourself safe and watch.'

As the first low chanting began to fill the room, rising and falling to the accompaniment of the rattle of the sistrum, Anna felt the atmosphere tighten perceptibly. Her eyes were fixed on the little bottle. As the reflection of the flame played on the glass it looked as though whatever was inside the bottle moved.

Anna clenched her fists. Serena's voice was growing stronger, as she lost herself in the phrases of her invocation. When she stopped, the cabin seemed to echo for a moment with the words of power, then the candle flames began to stream sideways as though in a strong draught. Anna swallowed, clutching the amulet tightly between her fingers.

She could see him—the tall figure—so transparent he was barely more than a shimmer in the air near the window.

Serena flung back her head and rattled the sistrum in front of her. 'Come! Oh, Anhotep, servant of Isis, come! Show yourself before me and before this vial of sacred tears!'

He was easier to see now, his features more distinct, the outline of his shape clear in the shadows of the candlelight.

Serena, her hands on the altar, dropped to her knees. Her head back, her eyes closed, she gave the sistrum a final rattle and laid it down. Anhotep was suddenly towering over her, and slowly as she stood up their two outlined shapes seemed to coalesce and become one.

She convulsed forward, shaking, then slowly she straightened again and opened her eyes. 'Greetings.' Her voice was completely unlike anything Anna had heard before. 'I am Anhotep, servant of the servants of the gods. I come to take possession of that which is mine.'

Anna's mouth had gone dry. She felt terrified. It was as though Serena herself had stood aside and lent Anhotep the flesh, the muscles, the organs he needed to function once more on the earth.

She could see a shadowy hand stretching out in the candlelight. It hovered over the little bottle and Anna noticed, with a shudder, that as it passed between the bottle and the candle flame it cast no shadow, although it was Serena's hand.

Then the cabin door flew open and light flooded in from the corridor.

'Help me!' Charley's voice was unmistakable. 'Help me! It's happening again. I don't know what to do—' She staggered slightly, then slowly she fell forwards into the cabin.

With a hiss of rage the figure at the altar turned. 'Hatsek!'

Charley scrambled to her feet and stood where she was, shaking violently. Anna looked from one to the other, paralysed with fear.

Whatever happens don't try and interfere!

Serena's words seemed to hang in the air for a moment.

'Hatsek! I curse thee for thy vile betrayal!' As the words filled the cabin Anna became aware of a second figure in the doorway.

She dragged her eyes away from Charley and saw that it was Toby.

'Curse thee for the deceit and slaughter!'

Charley took a step back, then she seemed to rally. 'Thou wert ever a fool, Anhotep!' She moved forward and reached out towards the altar where the candle flames streamed sideways. As her hand moved towards the little bottle, Anhotep let out a great cry of rage and lunged at her.

As the two women collided, Charley let out a scream and flung herself back towards the door. Behind her Serena slumped to the floor.

The two priests were gone.

'Turn on the lights, Anna, for God's sake!' Toby had caught Charley by the wrists. She was struggling frantically as he pushed her back into the room and down onto the bed beside Anna.

Anna leapt to her feet and dragged open the shutters. 'Serena!' She dropped to her knees beside the lifeless form lying on the floor. 'Serena, are you all right?'

On the bed behind her, Charley was sobbing hysterically. Toby sat down beside her and put his arm round her.

'What's wrong with Serena?' Anna cried.

'Don't you know? You heard her. She's what they call a trance medium. A channeller. She allowed the priest to talk through her, but without allowing him to possess her. She obviously knows how to protect herself. She'll be all right.'

'And Charley? What is she?' Anna looked up.

'The same perhaps. Or maybe she is possessed. I shouldn't have brought her back.'

'No, you shouldn't!' Suddenly she was shaking with fright and anger. 'Where have you been? Why did you disappear like that? We needed you!'

He was gathering Charley into his arms, rocking her like a baby. 'I couldn't help it, Anna. I'll explain later. Let's sort this mess out first.'

There was a groan from Serena and Anna stroked her hand. 'Serena? Can you speak to me? Are you all right?'

'What happened?' Serena's voice was hoarse. She frowned and rubbed her eyes, moving her head from side to side. 'Did Anhotep come?'

'Yes. He came.'

'Did he say what he wanted done?'

'He didn't get the chance.'

Serena's skin was pale and damp, her eyes unfocused. 'Why not?'

'Hatsek came. He appeared to have taken over Charley's body. It was terrifying.'

At last Serena turned her head towards the bed. She registered the sight of Toby with Charley in his arms. 'You? You brought Charley back? I thought you were supposed to be in prison?'

Serena struggled to her feet. She stood for a moment, swaying slightly, then she sat down stiffly on the stool.

Toby grimaced. 'Not lately, I'm glad to say. No, I was with a friend. I'll tell you the whole story, but not now. OK? Let's get this mess sorted out. What do we do with Charley here?'

Charley raised a tear-stained face. 'I want to go home.'

'Then that's what you shall do.' Toby stood up. 'I've got a friend at the consulate in Cairo. I'll get him to arrange a flight for you. Poor Charley. You'll be fine. Do you want to go back to the hotel for the night?'

Charley nodded. 'I liked the hotel.'

Serena and Anna watched as he guided Charley out of the cabin and up the corridor. Anna closed the door behind him and leaned against it.

'Oh, Serena, are you sure this is safe? Supposing you can't get rid of him?' She sat down suddenly, overwhelmed with exhaustion.

'I wasn't possessed, Anna.' Serena was folding the sistrum into its piece of silk. 'I was allowing him to use me.'

'Isn't that possession?'

'No. Possession is like rape. It is uninvited. A violation. A theft.'

'That's what happened to Charley?'

Serena bit her lip. 'I think that's what has happened to Charley, yes. Hatsek has been using her energy, sucking it like a leech. And he found it easy, when he needed to invade her personality, to walk straight in.'

'And is she free of him now?'

'I don't know. I really don't know. Oh, Anna, I feel dreadful about all this. If I hadn't interfered . . .'

'If you hadn't interfered I would probably have been carried off kicking and screaming to a mental hospital by now.'

Serena stood up and started to pack things into her bag. 'So, what do you want to do now?'

They looked at each other glumly, then Anna shrugged. 'Have you the strength to try again? We don't know if Hatsek will follow Charley back to London. What if he follows you or me? What if the cobra comes too? Somehow my coming here has activated this whole, stupid charade.'

'I suppose we should try again tonight,' Serena said. 'On Philae, as I originally planned. In Isis's temple.'

Anna's mouth dropped open. 'So soon?'

'Yes.' Serena nodded. 'It would be perfect. We're going to the sound and light show, right? There will be hundreds of people there, but they'll all be watching the show. We'll slip away and hope that no one notices us.' She picked up her bag. 'I'm going to go and have a sleep. I'm completely exhausted. I'll meet you later, OK?'

Anna nodded. She stayed where she was for a long time after Serena had gone, then she lay down on the bed and closed her eyes.

Twenty minutes later she gave up trying to sleep. She reached for the diary. There were only a few more pages left to read.

Louisa had dozed off at last. When she woke she lay still, looking at the darkened ceiling of her cabin. The boat was silent, but she could smell cooking from the crew's quarters and from far away, somewhere on the shore in the distance, she could hear the wail of a musical instrument.

The knock on the door was hesitant. With a sigh she called out to come in. Augusta peered round it, a candle in her hand.

'Please join us for supper, Louisa. You will fall ill if you don't eat.'

Louisa sat up. Augusta was right. There was no point in starving herself to death. After all, she had to return to England, to her sons. She managed a watery smile and said that she would join them.

Miserably she allowed Treece to help her on with her dark green gown and then gather up her hair into a knot on her neck. It was as she was leaving the cabin that she heard the other woman sniff in exasperation, then mutter, 'Such a fuss! And all for a native!'

Louisa's anger carried her out through the saloon onto the deck, where the others were waiting for her, sipping their drinks. It was as she took the proffered seat from Sir John that she turned and looked out across the river. It was broad just here, and palm trees grew down to the water's edge on both sides. Against the far bank she could see the two boats moored side by side. The Fieldings' boat and that of Lord Carstairs were brightly lit with lamps, and the music, she realised suddenly, was coming from a group of musicians on the deck of the *Scarab*.

She pushed past Sir John and walked over to the rail, staring out across the water. 'Are they having a party? A *soirée*?'

'Nothing like that, I'm sure. They've just asked a band of musicians to play for them. They have every right, Louisa—'

'But I thought he had sailed back to Abu Simbel!'

Sir John shook his head gloomily. 'Apparently not.'

'But I told him to go!' Her voice was angry. 'And he took no notice.'

'Louisa, he knows he is not welcome on this boat. But I cannot prevent him from sailing near us!'

'No, but I can!' She swept round and ran forward towards the crew's quarters. 'Mohammed! Call the boy. I want to be taken across the river.'

'Louisa, no!' Sir John hurried after her.

'You cannot stop me!' She turned on him. 'Don't even try. I shall not require you to come with me. I just need the boy to row me over.'

Behind them the crew had all leapt to their feet from their seats around the brazier. Mohammed stepped forward. 'If the lady Louisa wishes to go on the river I shall row her myself.'

'Thank you, Mohammed. I should like that. I want to go now.'

Her face was as white as a sheet as she climbed in the little dinghy. Mohammed began to paddle expertly across the dark water.

It was David Fielding who helped her up on the *Scarab*'s deck. Behind him she could see Venetia and Katherine ensconced on huge silken cushions, sleepily watching the entertainment. Roger Carstairs had been sitting near them. As Louisa appeared, he rose to his feet. He was dressed in a white turban and black robe, bound at the waist by a multi-coloured fringed sash from which hung his long curved hunting knife.

Katherine smiled in sympathetic welcome, but Louisa did not see the gesture. Her eyes were on Carstairs's face.

'Good evening, Mrs Shelley!' Carstairs bowed. Behind him the musicians had fallen silent.

'Good evening, my lord.' She was conscious that Mohammed had climbed over the rail after her and was standing close behind her. When she stepped forward he did the same. His presence was comforting.

'Would you care to sit down with us and watch the entertainment?'

'I have not come to be entertained,' Louisa retorted. 'I have come to ask why you decided not to go back to the cave?'

He smiled. 'Because I was informed that the vial was no longer there. You tried to trick me, Mrs Shelley.'

'The thing you wanted so badly that you were prepared to kill a man to get?' Her voice was very even.

'Oh yes, Mrs Shelley. I was prepared to kill a man.' He smiled. 'Though in the event I didn't have to. The snake did it for me.'

She laughed. 'The snake did it for you!' she echoed. 'Have you told your friends here what you did to get hold of my scent bottle?'

'Oh, Louisa!' Katherine's groan was anguished. 'Please, my dear, don't.'

Louisa turned on Katherine and the force of her words made the pregnant woman shrink back on her cushions. 'This man is an evil fiend, a practitioner of the black arts. You are not safe on this boat. No one is!'

'Louisa, my dear.' David Fielding put his hand on her arm. 'We all know you are upset. With good cause. But this will not help. What happened out there in the desert was no one's fault. It was a tragic accident. People are being killed by snakes and scorpions all the time out here.'

'No!' Louisa shook her head. 'This was no accident. Hassan knew about snakes and scorpions. That was his job! To escort me and keep me safe.' Her eyes filled with tears. 'Don't you see? Lord Carstairs did it. As surely as if he had plunged that knife into Hassan a second time!'

Carstairs shook his head slowly. 'These are the imaginings of an over-heated brain.'

'Are they?' She dashed the tears out of her eyes. 'So, you don't want the bottle?'

He tensed suddenly. She saw his eyes grow watchful. 'You know I am very anxious to acquire your scent bottle, Mrs Shelley. I have offered to buy it from you. I told you that you could name your price.'

'All right. My price is Hassan! If your magic is so powerful, you can bring him back to life!' She was smiling at him wildly.

He narrowed his eyes. 'You know it is not. No one can bring someone back from the dead.'

'So, you cannot pay my price?'

'I have offered you money, Louisa. Any amount you would like to name.' His voice was growing impatient.

She shook her head. 'Money is of no use to me.'

'Then anything else that it is in my power to give. Jewels. Land.' He frowned. 'I have already offered you my title and my own hand!'

There was a small cry from Venetia. 'Roger! You promised *me*!'

He ignored her; his eyes were fixed directly on Louisa's face. 'Well, what is it you want?'

She shook her head. 'There is nothing you can give me that I want,

448

my lord.' Her voice dropped suddenly to a whisper. 'Except revenge.'

At Louisa's last words the boat fell suddenly silent. Louisa held his gaze. 'I have the bottle here,' she said quietly. She slipped her hand into the pocket of her dress and drew out the bottle, wrapped in a piece of white silk.

His eyes widened hungrily. 'And you are going to give it to me!' He smiled in triumph.

She looked down at her hand thoughtfully. 'No,' she said at last. 'I am going to give it to the gods you claim to serve. You will never set eyes on this again, Lord Carstairs. Never!'

With one quick movement she hurled the parcel as hard as she could out into the darkness. There was a pause as every person on the boat held their breath, then a small splash far out in the river.

'No!' Carstairs threw himself towards the rail. He hung over it, staring frantically at the water. 'Do you realise what you have done?' He turned suddenly and caught her by the shoulders and shook her hard.

'Hey! Wait! Take your hands off her!' David Fielding grabbed his arm as Mohammed stepped forward. He had his own knife in his hand.

'No!' Katherine let out a scream. 'No! Someone is going to get hurt!' She pulled herself to her feet. 'For pity's sake! This has all gone on long enough. Louisa, I think you should go. You've made your point!' She broke off suddenly and clutched at her stomach with a groan.

'Kate?' David Fielding's cry was anguished. 'My love, what is it?'

She straightened up, her face white, and staggered back to the cushions. 'I'm all right.' She was breathing heavily. 'Louisa, you should go.'

Louisa had stepped back, tearing herself away from Carstairs's hands. 'I'm going. Mohammed, will you help me into the boat—'

Her words were interrupted by a piercing scream. Katherine had doubled up once more. 'My baby! It's my baby!' She tried to stand, reaching frantically towards her husband.

Louisa stopped at the top of the ladder. Turning round she saw a red stain spreading on Katherine's skirt.

For a moment nobody moved. Then Venetia put her hand to her head and fainted back onto the silken cushions. No one took any notice of her. Louisa stared round the assembled men in horror. They were paralysed, staring at the agonised woman and at the pool of blood appearing on the deck of the boat below her skirts.

'Carry her below into a cabin!' She stepped forward, pushing Carstairs aside. 'Now! Quickly!'

'We'll go back to the *Lotus*!' David Fielding looked round wildly for his own servants. 'She should be there.'

'There's no time. Take her below, David. My lord.' She turned to Carstairs with a contemptuous stare. 'See that the other men leave the boat. Presumably they can go across to the *Lotus*. Mohammed, will you go and fetch Lady Forrester to help me? Do it!' She shouted at the stunned faces around her as Katherine let out another scream. The sound sent the men scurrying in all directions and eventually it was Carstairs himself who picked Katherine up and carried her to the saloon.

With soothing words Louisa tried to make Katherine more comfortable, but Katherine's fear was contagious. Louisa could feel herself fighting down waves of panic as gently she took Katherine's hands and held them firmly. 'You'll be all right, Katherine. You'll be fine.'

'And the baby? What about the baby? It's not due for two months!' Katherine burst into tears again. 'It's David's fault. He wouldn't listen. He would insist on coming to this God-forsaken country. I begged him not to, but he wanted to bring Venetia. He wanted to try to find a man for her.' She broke off with a catch in her breath, wailing with pain.

When the pain had subsided Louisa leaned forward to sponge her forehead but already another pain was coming. 'It's your fault!' Suddenly Katherine was screaming in her face. 'If you hadn't come over and picked a fight with Carstairs this wouldn't have happened!' She clutched Louisa's hands more tightly. 'You shouldn't have come! Why did you?' She was panting frantically, sweat pouring down her face.

Louisa heard a noise at the door. She glanced round to see Mohammed hovering on the threshold. He had turned his head away to avoid looking directly into the saloon. 'Lady Forrester will not come, Sitt Louisa. She says she knows nothing of childbirth. No matter! I have brought a woman from the village who is wise in these things.'

Behind him a heavily veiled woman peered anxiously into the cabin. She had huge dark eyes, which glanced shyly round above the veil and rested on Katherine with a frown of concern.

Mohammed whispered to the woman and she slipped quickly into the cabin past him and approached Louisa with a bow.

'Don't let her come near me!' Katherine screamed. 'Dear God, I'm going to die and you bring me a native! Where is David? Oh God!'

With the door closed behind her the woman removed her cloak and veil and set down her basket of herbs and ointments. She looked at Katherine and took stock of the situation at once. Moving forward she placed a cool hand on Katherine's belly.

Katherine shrank back but the woman nodded and smiled.

'Good. Good,' she said. 'Baby good. *Inshallah!*'

'Send her away!' Katherine pushed at the woman's hand, but already the pains were coming again.

'David!' Her final scream was so shrill that the village woman forgot her shyness. She placed her hand on Katherine's stomach and uttered a couple of incomprehensible instructions to Louisa, followed by more easily understood gestures as she tried to pull Katherine to her feet and indicated that she should squat, ready for the birth.

Some time later the men waiting on the *Lotus* heard clearly the feeble cry of a baby. David turned at the sound. 'Was that it? Was that my baby?' He was shaking.

By the time David was allowed into the cabin it had been tidied, the woman's basket with the ointments of fenugreek and honey, acacia, birth-wort and tamarisk had been repacked and Katherine was propped on pillows, smiling at the tiny baby lying between her breasts.

Louisa crept upstairs and made her way towards the stern of the boat where Mohammed was waiting for her. Beside him the mooring line from the boat bobbing behind the dahabeeyah was tied to the rail. He rose and bowed to her as she approached. 'Sitt Fielding is well?'

'She is well, Mohammed, thanks to you. And the baby boy, too. Will you take me across to the *Ibis*? It is nearly day, and I am very tired.'

He turned to pull in the dinghy, then suddenly let out a cry. Coiled on the boards near him was a large snake. As he moved, it hissed. It lifted its head, the hood extended sideways, and swayed its neck from side to side, its eyes on his face.

'No!' Louisa stared at it for a moment, then she turned to her right, where Carstairs stood watching the scene. 'Call it off! Are you so evil you would kill another innocent man?'

He was smiling. 'I did not summon it, Mrs Shelley, I assure you.'

'Your assurances are worth nothing.' She stepped towards the snake, her heart in her mouth. 'Mohammed, get in the boat.'

'No, lady. I cannot leave you.' His face was chalk-white.

'Do it! It will not hurt me.'

Mohammed moved cautiously backwards a step at a time as Louisa reached out for Venetia's discarded parasol, lying near her on a chair. The snake was watching her now. 'Call it off, my lord.'

He shook his head slowly. 'I did not call it!'

'Then your powers are growing feeble.' She was aware of Mohammed behind her, slowly climbing down the little ladder into the boat. 'Please, Sitt Louisa. Please. Now save yourself,' he whispered.

Louisa gave a small smile. 'So, Lord Carstairs. Will you send me into paradise with Hassan?'

451

Carstairs gave a hiss. As the snake wavered and turned towards him, Louisa scrambled onto the ladder. Within seconds she was in the boat and Mohammed was paddling frantically for the *Ibis*. Behind them they could hear Carstairs's bitter laughter ringing out in the darkness.

Halfway across, Mohammed rested on the oar. 'Sitt Louisa. I have something for you.' He fumbled in his robe and drew out something small and white. 'When I went for Lady Forrester I saw it floating in the water. The silk you wrapped it in had caught the air. It never sank.'

Louisa looked down at the small, damp package with a slow, bitter smile. So, the gods had not taken the scent bottle after all.

Several boats were waiting at the quayside to take the queues of spectators out to the son et lumière at the Temple of Philae on its island. As Anna and Serena sat down in one of the launches, Anna found herself next to Andy. She frowned as he put his arm round her shoulder and said, 'No hard feelings, eh, Anna? Have you brought a warm wrap? Apparently the wind off the desert can be very cold after dark.'

She shifted imperceptibly away from him. 'Thank you, Andy. I'm well prepared for the evening.' She looked round for Toby and spotted him further up the boat. He was talking to the man at the wheel, and it dawned on her for the first time that Toby was speaking Arabic. She still wasn't sure what had happened out there at Abu Simbel, but somehow it didn't worry her. Toby would have a good explanation for his absence and when the right moment came he would give it to her. That was all that mattered.

'So, am I forgiven?' Andy was speaking in her ear. 'I only had your interests at heart, you know.'

She didn't know whether he was talking about taking the diary and the scent bottle, or whether he was referring to Toby, but suddenly she didn't care. The boats began to nose out into the river.

The temple was floodlit, reflecting all its serene beauty into the waters around it. Beside it, the kiosk of Trajan, described so eloquently by Louisa in her diary, stood up to one side of it, the columns delicate, almost ethereal against the midnight blue of the sky. Anna caught her breath at the sheer magic of the sight.

As the boats queued to come in turn against the landing stage below the temple, the passengers rose to their feet and made their way forward. Anna and Serena hung back, watching Andy inching his way up the boat.

'Perhaps if he sees us with Toby he will back off,' Serena murmured. They were near the front now, and each in turn found themselves being helped up onto the wooden landing stage.

Serena, who had stepped out first, stood apart from the others and waited for Anna. To her annoyance she could see Andy had done the same.

'Come on, you two. We want to be near the front!' Andy called.

Anna glanced at Serena. 'You go on, Andy.' She folded her arms. 'I'm going to sit with Toby.'

She saw the anger on his face. 'You are joking?'

'No. No, I'm not joking.' She returned his look coldly. 'Please, go on. You follow the others.'

For a moment she thought he was going to refuse, but suddenly Toby was there, waiting at the side of the path. Andy glanced at him in obvious disgust and joined the slowly moving queue of people. Toby smiled. 'Do I gather I scared him off?'

'You did.' Anna smiled back. 'And that was important because we're going to slip away into the sanctuary to have another go at calling up the priests.'

Toby glanced over his shoulder. 'You haven't a hope. Look at the lights. And there are men there, ushering people to their seats. Surely it doesn't have to be in the sanctuary? Near the temple will do. Look, follow me down here.' He ducked off the path between some low bushes. 'See?' he called quietly. 'The shadows are incredibly black where the floodlights don't reach. It's the contrast. No one will ever spot you down here at the water's edge. It's the perfect place.'

They followed the narrow path he had found round the side of the island until they reached a strip of bushes and a line of beach below the kiosk of Trajan. Toby crouched down in the darkness.

'Unless a stray spotlight comes this way, no one will see you here. You've got about an hour, I gather. I'll meet you here, at the end.' He looked round. 'Good luck. Be careful.' He kissed Anna quickly and turned away. There was a rustle of dried fronds and he had gone.

Serena was already fumbling in her bag. Her hands were shaking as she spread out her statuette, her ansate cross, the incense, the candlestick. Anna reached into her own bag and brought out the scent bottle. Unwrapping it, she laid it at the feet of Isis. She paused, looking up. 'Listen, it's starting!'

The lights suddenly went off all over the island. Serena caught her breath. The darkness around them was tangible. The show had begun.

It was hard to ignore the noise behind them: the disembodied voices, the music echoing across the water and the play of lights, but the two women concentrated on the tiny square of silk before them. Serena struck a match and held the flame over the cone of incense until a thin wisp of smoke began to rise. She turned to the candle. Its flame skittered sideways, then it steadied and burnt clear.

'Isis, great goddess, I invoke thee!' Serena was speaking in a whisper. 'Hear me, great goddess, and come to our aid. Summon thy servants Anhotep and Hatsek; let them settle their disagreements and decide on the future of this sacred ampulla with its contents of thy tears.'

She reached forward, and picking up the bottle held it up towards the indigo velvet of the sky.

'Isis, send thy servants here! Protect us with thy magic and send them to speak here, tonight, on thy sacred ground!' Serena's voice had risen dramatically. A faint flurry of wind touched Anna's face and she saw the candle flicker. Her hand went to the amulet at her throat.

Serena's eyes had closed. She laid the bottle down on the ground and then raised her arms again towards the sky.

Somewhere out across the water a bird gave a sharp cry, and a faint light appeared on the shore a few yards from them. Anna caught her breath. The light near them grew larger. It elongated into the shape of a figure and gradually appeared to grow more solid. Serena had lowered her arms and crossed them over her breast. She was kneeling, head bowed, waiting.

She's waiting for me to speak. Anna's mouth was dry with fear. She had to speak, to demand of the priest what she wanted. She looked towards the figure on the shore. It had moved closer. It was standing over Serena. She saw the shadow pass over Serena's face.

Serena's eyes opened suddenly with an expression of acute anguish. 'Traitor!' she screamed. 'You foul traitor! The tears of Isis belong to the boy king. They will save his life!'

Anna gasped. An intense pain gripped her head. She could feel her body growing hot and suddenly she was standing up.

'The tears belong to the goddess and I shall see they serve no other!' The words were being wrenched from her own mouth.

She saw Serena look up. Another blast of wind came from the desert, and as the candle flame shrank, Serena scrambled to her feet.

'Anna!' Her voice was coming from a great distance. 'Anna, be strong! Oh, great Isis, protect Anna. Make her strong! Anna, can you hear me?'

But Anna was far away. Looking up, she could see the high golden cliffs, the temple where the goddess had her home on earth.

Slowly she moved closer to it, listening to the sands whispering across immense distances. In that hidden temple lay all the secrets of eternity, guarded by just two high priests sworn to the service of the gods for all eternity. In her hand she held a knife, its blade pure gold, brought from the deepest heart of Africa to reflect the flame of the sun god and turn it into fire.

'Anna!'

A voice from thousands of years away echoed in the silence.

'Anna! For pity's sake, can you hear me? Anna?'

Suddenly it was as though Anna's head snapped back on her shoulders. A shower of ice-cold water caught her in the face.

Serena was shaking her violently. She let her go to scoop up another handful of water and lobbed it at her, then she caught her and shook her again. 'You didn't protect yourself, you fool! Hatsek was inside you! I could see his face in yours. I could see his hatred. You would have killed me, Anna!' Serena pushed her away so hard that Anna staggered and fell. Behind them the makeshift altar was scattered, candle and incense overturned, the ansate cross lying on its side.

Anna rubbed her face. It was wet with Nile water. Serena grabbed her and pulled her down into the shadows. 'You were Hatsek, don't you understand! He possessed you, Anna. He took you over!'

'He used my voice? Like Anhotep used yours?'

The sand. The desert wind. The blazing sun. They still filled her head, though the sky above her now was black and sewn with a myriad stars. 'He used my eyes. But he wasn't seeing this.' She gestured around her, confused. 'I saw the temple. The temple where Anhotep tricked him. Anhotep wanted the sacred water of life for the pharaoh, to use it as a medicine. But that was sacrilege.' She shook her head slowly from side to side. 'The servant of the goddess was a servant of the one God. Of the Aten. It was Anhotep who was the traitor.' She stared up at Serena, confused. She didn't know what the words pouring from her own mouth meant any more.

'No.' Serena shook her head. 'No, Anna. That's not true. They fell out. There was treachery and deceit. There was murder which had to be hidden.' She stared down at the ground and then with an exclamation of dismay she dropped to her knees. 'The bottle! Where is it? It's gone!'

Anna shrugged. 'Let it go. The priests have taken it. It's better lost. Whatever was in that bottle, whether they were priests of Isis and Sekhmet or of the Aten, the liquid was not something we were supposed to have. Let it go back to the gods.'

She turned and looked at the temple. The sound had stopped. The floodlights had come back on. A ripple of applause ran through the

455

night air. 'It is finished. We have to go. Leave it. Leave it all, here on the island of the goddess.' She turned towards the palms as a figure appeared out of the darkness. It was Toby.

He looked from one to the other and said, 'Well? Did it work?'

Serena shrugged. 'We've lost the bottle. It's gone.' She stooped and began to gather the other things into her bag.

'Anna?' Toby touched her shoulder. 'Are you all right?'

Anna nodded silently, still gazing out into the dark.

He frowned, then he turned back to Serena. 'We have to go. Have you got everything?' He glanced around. Then he stopped and pointed. 'There's your bottle. See? It's rolled down there into that dip in the shingle.' He stooped and picked it up. 'Anna?'

As she didn't appear to have heard him, Serena took the bottle from him. 'I'll take care of it.' She tucked it into her bag, then she touched Anna's arm. 'Ready?'

Slowly Anna nodded, and when Toby held out his hand she took it.

Andy was waiting for them near the landing stage. 'Well, what did you think of it?' He smiled at Anna. 'Fabulous, wasn't it?'

Anna nodded. 'Fabulous indeed.' She rubbed her face wearily.

'Except you didn't see it.' Andy leaned close to her, and she could smell alcohol on his breath. 'Do you imagine I didn't notice you slip away to hide in the bushes with lover boy?'

'Andy!' Toby dropped Anna's arm and stepped towards him. 'I've had enough of this! Just what exactly are you trying to say?'

'That you are a murdering, lying bastard and you should keep away from decent women.' Andy produced a bottle from the rucksack on his shoulder and took a swig from it.

'Toby, no!' Anna came back to reality with a jolt. She caught at Toby's sleeve. 'Leave it. Don't hit him. That's what he wants—'

She stopped mid-sentence and shook her head. Raising her hands to her temples she stared at him blankly. Something was happening to her again. She could see people staring, and whispering to each other as they saw Andy waving the bottle in the air. She could see Omar standing between Andy and Toby, gesticulating, but at the same time she could see the great white sun, the dazzling red-gold desert superimposed over everything else.

Her feet were moving slowly towards the boats. She had lost sight of Serena now. And Toby. She stared round wildly. Her eyes wouldn't focus. Then Andy was there, beside her again. He was smiling, holding out his hand towards her.

'Please to hurry up, people. Ibrahim will kill me if you are late for supper!' Omar grinned and shepherded his flock of tourists closer together, anxious not to lose them in the dark.

Anna hung back. 'Where's Toby?'

Andy laughed. 'He's probably been whisked away by Interpol. Him and the loopy Serena, both.' He reached across and caught her hand.

She pulled her hand away. 'Andy, will you leave me alone! I really don't need you pawing me.' She was finding it difficult to focus again.

The crowd was milling round the temple forecourt now, slowly filtering down the steps onto the landing stage, where the first motor boat had come alongside.

'Anna!' Suddenly Serena was beside her again. 'Are you all right?'

'Of course she's all right.' Andy was still there. 'I'm looking after her.'

Serena pursed her lips. 'What possessed you to bring a bottle of vodka with you? Have you any idea how much you offend the Egyptians, being drunk like that? You idiot!'

The man supervising the loading of the boat held up his hand. The boat was full. It nosed out into the river as a second boat arrived.

Anna was suddenly aware that Toby was beside her. She glanced at him and smiled. 'I'm afraid Andy seems intent on disgracing us all.'

'You surprise me!' Toby's voice was grim. 'Well, if he wants to make a fool of himself I suggest he does it elsewhere and somewhere he is less likely to fall in the river!' He took hold of Andy's arm and propelled him away from the edge of the landing stage to where Ben was standing. 'Can you keep an eye on him, Ben? He's being a damn nuisance.' He left him and turned back to Anna. 'What happened back there on the beach? You don't look right yourself.'

She stared at him, frowning. 'It was strange.'

The boat nudged against the platform and they made their way between the rows of seats. Anna sat down in the corner with Serena on one side of her and Toby on the other. She shook her head. 'I think I must be tired, that's all. I feel very weird.' She glanced up. Andy was making his way towards them. He sat down on a seat opposite her.

Ben had followed and sat down beside him with a shrug. 'I think this fellow needs some food inside him,' he commented cheerfully. 'He'll be fine once he's had some supper. Well, what did you think of the show, ladies? Did you enjoy it?'

'It was good.' Anna nodded and smiled.

'Not good.' Andy leaned forward and touched her knees. 'She didn't see it, naughty girl. She was canoodling with our rakish ex-con here.'

Toby's face tensed and Anna clutched at his arm. 'Don't rise to it. Please, ignore him,' she pleaded.

Andy turned to Anna, raising his voice to make himself heard over the chatter. 'So, did you bring that lovely little scent bottle with you to see the show? You two seem to be inseparable.'

'Yes, I brought it.' She smiled. The boat began to chug away from the island. Behind them the floodlit temple came fully into view, seemingly floating on the water as they headed back towards the shore.

'And did it perform magic for you? Did your priestly attendants manifest on the island of Isis?' He was grinning broadly.

'They did. Yes.' Anna was tight-lipped, trying to discourage him.

'So, what happens next?' He sat forward and tapped her knee. 'Are they going to show themselves on the boat? Do a turn for us? Did you hear that, people?' He stood up and raised his voice. 'Anna's Ancient Egyptian ghosts are going to do a turn for us.' He raised his arms above his head and wiggled his hips suggestively.

'Sit down, Andy. You are being a prat!' Ben pulled at his arm.

'They're not going to appear again, Andy,' Anna put in quietly. 'For the simple reason that I left the bottle on the island. It's buried in the sand. Gone for ever. No one will ever see it again. Nor will they see whoever it was who guarded it, so let that be the end of it. Please.'

Andy laughed. 'I knew you'd end up losing it. It was a fake anyway.'

'It is not a fake, Andy.' Serena suddenly turned on him. 'You're the fake around here. An opinionated, stupid, boorish, loud-mouthed oaf! I cannot tell you how tired I am of hearing your voice, your opinions.' She reached down at her feet and fumbled in her bag. 'For your information, Anna didn't lose the bottle. I picked it up and I brought it back with me. And if anything can prove just how stupid you are, this can. You know nothing about antiques. This is over three thousand years old!' She pulled out the little bottle and waved it at him.

'Serena! I had given that back to the gods!' Anna was furious. 'Give it to me!'

'Why? You don't want it, you threw it away! I am going to make sure that it is preserved safely.'

'Three thousand years old? That?' Andy sat down heavily. He snatched his arm away from Ben with a petulant shrug.

'Yes, Andy. This.' Serena cradled it in her palm. 'This is so sacred.' She sat looking down at it, aware of at least a dozen pairs of eyes on her. Serena shivered. She looked up at Andy. 'If I give this to you, do you know what will happen?' She was shouting over the noise of the engine.

'What?' Andy grinned. He held out his hand. 'Show me.'

'If I give it to you, a cobra will appear, here in the boat. A deadly poisonous, evil snake.' She smiled. 'And it will kill you!'

'That's enough!' Anna leaned forward and snatched the bottle out of Serena's hand. 'This has gone on long enough.'

'Show me!' Andy stretched his hand out towards her. 'Go on. Show me the magic snake! I want to see it!' He stood up once again and balanced unsteadily in front of Anna, holding out his hand.

'Andy, you're a fool!' Anna had raised her voice to make herself heard.

'Give it back!' Serena grabbed Anna's wrist.

'No. No, Serena, I'm sorry.' Anna edged away from her. 'This belongs to another age and to other people. They want it for their gods. Louisa tried to give it to the Nile. Now it's my turn!'

Standing up she raised her arm, but as she made to hurl the bottle out into the boat's wake, Andy lunged at her.

He missed her arm and staggered off balance. As she fell back into her seat, winded, he clutched at the rail, swayed for a moment, overbalanced and plunged head first over the side.

'Andy!' Serena's scream was echoed by others on the boat and alerted the crew. The captain threw the gears, dragging the wheel round in a small circle.

'Can you see him?' Toby and Ben were staring at the dark water.

'Torches! Has anyone got torches?' Toby kicked off his shoes and dived in as Ben reached over the side and freed one of the old cork lifebelts hanging on the side of the boat.

'Here you are, Toby!' He threw it as Toby's head reappeared. Two other belts followed, hitting the water near him.

'Andy! Andy, where are you?' Serena was leaning out over the side as one of the Egyptian crewmen jumped into the water near Toby.

Suddenly other boats were appearing out of the darkness, circling round them, dozens of passengers craning over the side, staring out into the dark. There was still no sign of Andy as a fast launch appeared and a spotlight shone out over the scene. Two, then three other men were in the water now, all of them diving.

'The water's pitch-black!' Toby reappeared, shaking droplets out of his eyes. 'You can't see a thing.'

He was treading water, turning slowly round, scanning the reflections around him.

Anna turned away from the rail and sat down. She put her head in her hands. 'He's dead, isn't he. And it's my fault! The gods have taken him! I've killed him!'

She looked up at Serena's face with tears pouring down her cheeks.

Serena turned to stare out across the water. 'If it was anyone's fault, it was mine,' she whispered. 'I wound him up. I produced the bottle.'

459

Another launch had appeared. The men crowding around its bows were dressed in police uniform.

'They'll find him.' Ben sat down next to Anna and put his hand over hers. 'He's a strong swimmer. It'll take more than a dunking in the Nile to defeat Andy.'

'They won't find him.' Anna looked at Serena. The boat was strangely silent now. The other passengers were sitting quietly, staring around, numb with shock.

Serena shook her head. 'As you say, the gods have taken him away. He mocked them, Anna, and he paid the price.' She bit her lip.

A slight shock ran through the boat as a launch came alongside and two tourist police officers climbed on board. There was an exchange with the boat's captain, then they made their way aft to where Anna and Serena were sitting.

One of the officers sat down next to them. 'This gentleman had been drinking alcohol?' he asked in heavily accented English.

Both women nodded. Anna said, 'Yes. He had brought a bottle of vodka with him for some reason. He stood up and'—she paused, feeling the tears returning—'he went in head first.'

'The water is very cold.' The man shook his head. He stared gloomily over the side. 'Could he swim?'

'Yes.' Ben cut in. 'He can swim.'

'Then it is not good news. He should have come up and shouted.' The officer turned to his companion and, after a quick exchange in fast, eloquent undertones, the two men made their way back to the captain at the wheel of the boat.

One by one the swimmers were hauling themselves back onto their boats. Anna saw Toby climbing out of the water. A few minutes later he was making his way towards her, wrapped in a rug.

'He just disappeared. The water is like ink in the darkness. You can see the lights if you look up, but nothing below you.' He shook his head. 'I didn't stop to think. I should have waited. Seen where he came up.'

'He didn't come up, Toby,' Serena said. 'We were all watching.'

'It was very brave to go after him.' Anna leaned forward to touch his hand. It was like ice.

It was a long time later that the passengers rejoined their ship. While Toby was whisked away by Omar to be seen by a doctor after his long, cold immersion in the Nile, the others trooped into the dining room. No one had much appetite and so it wasn't long before in twos and threes they began to make their way to their own cabins. Serena followed Anna to hers and they sat side by side on the bed.

'It was a stupid accident, Anna.' Serena put her arms round her companion. 'He was drunk.'

'It was our fault. We both wound him up. If I hadn't thrown away the bottle it wouldn't have happened.'

'No. It could have happened at any second, anywhere. Andy was like that!' Serena shrugged. 'He was a fool. A great big, stupid, malicious, lying fool . . .' Suddenly she was sobbing violently.

Anna stood up. She rubbed her eyes. 'I'll get us something from the bar.' She hesitated, then she went out into the deserted corridor.

Ibrahim was behind the bar. There were several people talking in subdued voices in the lounge. He looked up as Anna came in and frowned. 'You wore the amulet?'

She nodded.

Ibrahim shrugged. 'Do not take it off. Not even for one second. The gods are still powerful, *mademoiselle*. I am sorry for Monsieur Andrew but these things happen. *Inshallah!*'

'I keep thinking we'll hear his voice; that he swam underwater and crawled up on the rocks somewhere. That they'll find him alive.'

Ibrahim inclined his head slightly. 'All things are possible.'

'What will happen? Will they cancel the cruise?'

Again he shrugged. 'The police will come tomorrow. Omar will meet them. I expect they will ask for you. This is a very small boat. Everybody knew Monsieur Andrew. Everybody is sad.'

She nodded slowly. 'I just want to curl up and go to sleep.'

'You want to take a drink to bed?'

'Yes, please. And one for Serena.'

He nodded. 'I bring them to your cabin. You go.'

Serena was lying on her bed with Louisa's diary in her hands.

'I hope you don't mind. You'd left your bag lying open on the side table and I thought it would help to take my mind off things.'

Anna sat down beside her. 'Good idea.' She sighed. 'Ibrahim is bringing us a drink to the cabin. I suspect he is going to mix a knock-out concoction.' She smiled wearily. 'So, what happened to Louisa?'

Serena sat up and swung her legs to the floor. 'I think you should read it yourself.' She cocked her head at the sound of a gentle knock, and opening the door she took a tray from Ibrahim.

'There you are. Your knock-out drink.' She put a glass on the table next to the bed for Anna and sniffed cautiously at her own. 'For a Muslim and a teetotaller he mixes a fairly hefty cocktail.' She paused with a wistful smile. 'Don't dwell on things, Anna. It is absolutely not your fault. It was Andy's for getting stupidly drunk.'

Anna nodded. She could feel the tears very close.

'I'll leave you to read,' Serena whispered. 'We'll talk in the morning.'

Anna sat without moving for several minutes after she had gone then she reached for the glass. Serena was right. There were only a few pages of the close-packed writing left, and it would serve to take her mind off the present through what would inevitably be a sleepless night.

The three boats remained at their moorings for several days after Katherine's lying-in. Then, when she was sufficiently strong to transfer back to the *Lotus*, the Fieldings and the Forresters set off once more in convoy on the long journey north, leaving the *Scarab* behind. There had been no sign of Lord Carstairs since the day of the birth.

It was at Luxor that Louisa made her decision.

'I shall take the steamer back to Cairo,' she told the Forresters after dinner on the night they took up their moorings. 'You have been so kind and so hospitable, but I want to see my little boys again.'

In her cabin she began to pack away her painting things. Treece would deal with her clothes, but these were special. They had been packed and unpacked by Hassan. She opened one of her sketchbooks and stared for a long time at his face, the dark loving eyes, the gentle mouth, the hands which were so strong and yet so sensitive.

Behind her there was a loud knock on the door, and Treece came in with a branch of candles. She banged it down on the table. The woman's face was sour. Angry. Within seconds, Louisa knew why.

'Sir John says the steamer is fully booked. There are no cabins available until next week so you'll have to stay with us that bit longer.' She sniffed her disapproval and turned to fetch a ewer of water.

Louisa stood staring after her in dismay. She wanted to close this chapter of her life where every breath of desert air made her think of the man whom she had loved and who had died because of her.

Her gaze fell on the table. For a second her heart missed a beat. She couldn't see the little scent bottle. Then she spotted it, small, scruffy in its wrappings, half hidden by a box of charcoal. As Treece had banged the candles down a shower of wax had fallen across the table. A small lump hung from the dirty silk like a miniature stalactite.

As she stared at it she knew what she had to do. The next day she would get Mohammed to take her back to the Valley of the Tombs. She would bury the bottle there in the sand beneath an image of the goddess; it was she who must decide on its fate.

Anna's eyelids drooped. She took another sip from the glass. The diary was suddenly heavy in her hands, and she let it fall onto the covers. Staring sleepily towards the window of her cabin, she could see the stars above the skyline. With a sigh she reached out and turned off the light. Just for a moment she would rest her eyes before she climbed into the shower to soak away the stiffness and pain of the night.

As she sank further into sleep the shadows grew closer and the whispers in the sand grew louder.

She was woken by the sun. Hot. Red. Fiery behind her eyelids. Anna could feel the abrasive heat on her face, the raw bite of every breath in her lungs, the rasp of sand in her sandals. Slowly she walked towards the entrance of the temple, shaking her head against the haze that seemed to surround her.

She was drifting, rootless, overwhelmed with anger, then cold with fear as the gods came near and shook their heads and turned away.

'Anna? Anna!'

Voices echoed in her head, then died away, carried on the desert wind.

'Anna? Can you hear me? Oh God, what's happened to her?'

She smiled as the sweet scents of flowers and fruit blew across the sand from the temple buildings.

'Anna!' It was Toby's voice, Toby's hands on her shoulders. 'Anna, what's wrong?' He was far away, his voice an echo across time. There were other voices, bright lights in her eyes, fingers on her pulse.

Then all was dark. She slept. When she woke she felt the cold, sweet waters of the Nile on her lips. Voices again, echoing over untold distances, the silence and darkness again. She grew weaker every second.

'Anna!' That was Serena. 'Anna, you're going home.'

'**A**nna, are you awake?' Frances Hayward put her tray down near the door and, crossing to the window, she pulled back the heavy curtains so that the watery winter sunshine poured in across the patchwork coverlet. She turned to view her charge. The dark-haired woman she saw lying propped up on the pillows was pale and very thin, her large green eyes deeply undershadowed with exhaustion and strain.

'So, how do you feel?' Frances put the tray of coffee on Anna's knees, then sat down beside her.

Anna shook her head. 'Confused. Woolly. My memory is so muddled.'

She glanced at Frances. Her hostess was a tall woman with wild, curly grey hair. She had strong bones and a handsome face. The resemblance to Toby was there, oblique but unmistakable.

She met Anna's gaze steadily and smiled. 'Shall I tell you again? I'm Toby's mother, Frances. You have been here three weeks now. You remember who Toby is?' She raised a quizzical eyebrow.

Anna was playing with a small piece of toast. When there was no response, Frances went on, 'You met him on a Nile cruise. You became ill during your last few days there. Toby and your friend Serena didn't know what to do, how to contact your family, so they brought you here.'

'And you've been looking after a complete stranger?'

'It's been a pleasure for me. But I'm worried, my dear. You must have friends and family who are wondering where you are.'

Anna picked up her coffee cup and blew gently at the hot steam. The smell cut deep into her brain and she frowned, trying to cudgel her memory. There was so much there, just out of reach. There were pictures of sand dunes and shimmering heat, of the brilliant blue of the river and the green of the palms, but no faces, no names, nothing to pin anything to. She sipped the coffee again and frowned.

'Toby was wondering whether it would jog your memory if we took you to your house. If you feel strong enough, that is.'

Anna looked up. Her expression was suddenly more animated than it had been so far. 'You know where I live?'

Frances smiled. 'Yes, we know that much! But we couldn't leave you there alone, could we?'

They took a taxi across London later that afternoon, Anna wearing a pair of borrowed trousers and an elegant sweater from Frances's wardrobe against the cold wind.

The taxi pulled up outside a small, pretty, terraced house in Notting Hill and they all climbed out. Anna stood surveying the warm, grey brick, the square, Queen Anne windows, the blue front door with a half-moon skylight and a tiny front garden.

'It looks nice,' she said with a wry smile. 'Are you sure I live here?'

'I'm not sure of anything.' Toby put his arm lightly round her shoulders. 'See if your keys work.'

She glanced at him sharply then she rummaged in her shoulder bag and pulled out a bunch of keys.

The house smelt cold and unlived in and there was a pile of letters behind the door. Stooping to pick them up, Anna walked into the living room and looked round. The room was furnished with antiques, the polished woods set off with colourful rugs, cushions and curtains.

Toby reached for the light switch. 'Nice house.' He grinned.

On a table by the small sofa a light on the answerphone blinked steadily, announcing three calls.

'Only three and I've been away weeks.' Anna stared down at it.

'I expect all your friends knew you were away,' Toby commented sensibly. 'Aren't you going to listen to them?' He was standing with his back to the fireplace, his arms folded. 'There might be a clue.'

Anna shrugged. She reached out and punched the PLAY button.

'Anna, dear, this is your Great-Aunt Phyl! Where on earth are you? You said you'd come and see me the moment you got back. I'm dying to hear how you got on. Ring me.'

'Anna? Your great-aunt seems to think you're avoiding her. Ring her or me, for God's sake!' This was a cross male voice. Her father. She recognised it without a moment's hesitation.

'Anna? It's Phyllis again. My dear, I'm worried about you. Do please get in touch.'

Toby was watching her face. 'You recognised the voices?'

Anna nodded. 'And this house. It's all familiar. But it doesn't feel like mine.' She shook her head and put her hand to her eyes.

'I'm going to ring your aunt back.' Toby reached for the phone and punched in 1-4-7-1. After a pause he pressed the '3' to return the call.

The phone rang for a long time before it was answered. 'Do you want to speak to her?' Toby held out the receiver. Anna took it from him.

'Phyl?'

'Anna? Anna, thank goodness, my darling! I was beginning to think you'd fallen in love with Egypt and decided never to come home!' The voice on the other end paused. 'Anna?'

Anna shook her head. Tears were pouring down her face. She couldn't speak.

Toby took the receiver from her. He gave Anna a reassuring smile. 'Is that Anna's great-aunt . . . ? My name is Toby Hayward. I was on the cruise with Anna. She has not been very well. Is there any chance you could come up to London, or could I drive her over to you?'

He listened for a few seconds, hastened to respond to the anxious questions, reassured and nodded. 'OK. I'll bring her to Suffolk tomorrow. I'm so glad we've made contact.'

He put down the phone. 'We'll leave first thing in the morning.' He glanced at his mother, who had been standing quietly by the door. 'Do you want to help Anna find some warm clothes while we're here?'

Anna started idly picking through the post. She reached for a postcard, studied the picture and then read the back. Then another. At least two of her friends, it appeared, had also been on holiday recently.

'It's only my memory of the holiday that's completely gone,' she said wearily. 'The rest seems to be here, intact.' She broke off. She was looking down at a letter in her hand. It had Egyptian stamps. Her face paled.

Toby glanced at Frances. He put his finger to his lips. They both watched Anna as slowly she tore open the envelope. 'It's from Omar,' she said slowly. 'He wants to know how I am?'

She looked up and her eyes widened. The floodgates had opened. A torrent of memory, of noise, of images, of shouting, suddenly poured into her head. She sat down abruptly and stared wildly up at them.

'Oh God! Andy! I remember now. Andy died!'

Toby sat down beside her and put his arm round her shoulders. 'Do you remember what else happened?' he asked gently.

She was staring down at the letter in her hands. 'The scent bottle. The scent bottle of the priest of Sekhmet!' Suddenly she began to sob, tears pouring down her face. She looked up at Toby. 'I remember Andy falling in the Nile. His body disappeared.'

Toby nodded. 'They found him the next day, Anna—'

'And Ibrahim gave me an amulet.' She put her hand to her throat. 'I'm still wearing it! But it's valuable, I should have returned it to him!'

'No, he wanted you to keep it. He told me to tell you to keep it for ever.' Toby took the letter out of her hands and put it down on the table.

'What happened to Charley? Is she all right now?'

Toby nodded. 'She's fine.'

Suddenly it was all crystal clear in her mind. 'He needed me. The priest needed me when Charley left Egypt, and I let him in. Serena summoned him at Philae, and while I watched he jumped inside my head! I just let it happen! Where is Serena? What has happened to her?'

'Serena has been to see you several times, Anna,' Toby said. 'She's been so worried. She tried to explain to the doctor that she thought you had been possessed, but he was not prepared to listen. Ma wanted to bring in a clergyman, but Serena said that would make the priest angry.'

Anna shuddered. 'I've been so much trouble to you.' She looked up miserably. 'And it's all my fault.'

'It wasn't your fault.' Frances came and knelt in front of her. 'None of it was. How could anyone have known that these terrible things would happen?' She shivered. 'Come on. Let me help you pack some warm clothes. Then we'll go home. Tomorrow Toby will take you to see your great-aunt in Suffolk and things will start to get back to normal for you.'

Anna shook her head. 'Nothing can ever be normal again.'

It occurred to her for the first time that evening to wonder where it was that Toby went after the three of them had eaten together each night at the small round table in Frances's kitchen.

Frances laughed. 'Didn't he tell you? He's staying with someone called Ben Forbes. I gather he met him on this infamous cruise of yours.' She hesitated. 'Toby lives in Scotland, Anna. You knew that, didn't you? After his wife died he didn't want to stay in London any more and he gave me this house. Usually he stays upstairs in the bedroom you're in when he's in town, but he didn't want to crowd you.'

'He's been very kind to me,' Anna said thoughtfully. 'I don't know what would have happened to me if he hadn't been there.'

Frances smiled. 'I was so pleased he brought you here.' She was busying herself making them both a nightcap. 'I gather he told you about that dreadful time ten years ago?' She glanced up, and when Anna nodded she went on. 'He became very defensive after Sarah died; he cut so many people out of his life.'

It was the moment to ask questions. To find out more about what had happened. Anna hesitated and the moment passed. She accepted a mug of hot chocolate from Frances and sipped it slowly. 'Did Toby tell you the whole story of the trip?'

Frances shook her head. 'I'm pretty sure not. To be honest it all sounded a bit far-fetched . . . No!' She reached out her hand towards Anna as the latter opened her mouth to protest. 'I'm not saying it didn't happen. Just that I found it hard to picture it all. Andy's death was sufficiently dreadful for me. Perhaps that's all I can cope with at this stage.'

Anna nodded slowly. 'I would like to go and see his grave,' she said. 'Take him some flowers. Tell him I'm sorry.'

Frances glanced at her. She hesitated, obviously trying to decide how to respond. 'Anna, my dear, you weren't in love with Andy, were you?'

'In love with him!' Anna was shocked. 'No, of course I wasn't! Didn't Toby tell you about Andy and me? How he was trying to get hold of my great-great-grandmother's diary?'

Frances nodded. 'He told me. He told me a lot of things, but he left some out as well. Such as how you two feel about each other.'

Anna could feel her cheeks colouring. 'I know how I feel about him.'

'You're in love with him?' Frances caught Anna's eye and smiled.

'I think I might be.' Anna shrugged. 'But we've had such a short time together and that time was difficult!'

Frances snorted. 'That seems like an understatement! I won't ask any more, my dear. Just know that I'm so pleased Toby met you.' She reached across the table and squeezed Anna's hand.

Anna went over that short conversation again and again in her head as she lay in bed in her bedroom.

The diary lay on the small table in front of the window. The last thing she remembered doing on the boat was putting down the diary on the bed in her cabin, overwhelmed with fear and a strange, alien rage.

She reached for the book thoughtfully. Had he really gone, the priest who had invaded her head, or was he merely biding his time? She shuddered and looked down at the book in her hands. In the last section she had read, Louisa was planning to go out to the Valley of the Tombs to bury the scent bottle at the feet of Isis.

It was dawn when Louisa and Mohammed mounted their donkeys and headed westwards into the bright heat of the desert.

'Where will you put the bottle, Sitt Louisa?' Mohammed looked over at her at last. 'Which tomb do you want to go to?'

Louisa shrugged. 'Somewhere quiet and hidden so the bottle can rest in peace. I need to find an image of Isis so it can lie near her.'

He nodded gravely. The path had narrowed as they reached the mouth of the valley, and they urged the donkeys towards one of the dark entrances in the cliffs. Mohammed slid from his saddle and helped Louisa to dismount, then he reached into his saddlebag for candles. He shivered. 'I do not like these places, Sitt Louisa. There are bad spirits here. And scorpions.'

And snakes. The word hovered unspoken between them. Louisa bit her lip and forced herself to move forward, leading the way. 'We won't be here long, Mohammed, I promise. You have the spade?'

He nodded. Swiftly he moved in front of her, and she saw he had his hand on the hilt of a knife tucked into his belt.

They climbed the steep path to the entrance. Mohammed peered in. 'Is this the right place?' She saw him make the sign against the evil eye.

She nodded, reaching into her shoulder bag for the silk-wrapped bottle. She stepped ahead of him into the darkness, as he lit the candle in its little lantern.

'Sitt Louisa!' His strangled cry echoed into the tomb.

She spun round.

He was still standing at the entrance, flattened against the wall, frozen with terror. In front of him she could see the swaying head of the cobra.

'*No!*' Her scream tore into the shadows as she hurled herself back towards the cave entrance. 'Leave him alone! No! No! *No.* . .'

As the snake struck she threw the bottle at it and then went for it herself, grabbing at it with her bare hands. It thrashed for a moment in her grip—warm, smooth, heavy, and then it had gone. She was staring down at her empty fingers.

Mohammed slid to his knees, sobbing. 'Sitt Louisa, you have saved my life!'

'It didn't bite you?' Suddenly she was shaking so violently she too could no longer stand, and she found herself on her knees beside him.

'No.' He closed his eyes and took a deep breath. 'No, it did not bite me. See!' He held out the width of the full trouser leg and she saw the mark of the fangs and the long trail of the poison which had run down the cotton below the hole.

The bottle had gone. There was no sign of it on the path or in the tomb entrance. It had vanished with the snake.

Mohammed reclaimed their donkeys and they arrived back at the *Ibis* to find the boat in turmoil. One of the travellers planning to return north to Cairo had fallen sick and a berth had been found for her on the next day's steamer. There was very little time if she wanted to take it up. She must pack her belongings, say her farewells and arrange for her luggage to be loaded on the larger boat without delay.

Later, she was glad it had all happened so quickly. There was no time for retrospection. Barely time for goodbyes. Mohammed and the *reis* wept as she left the boat for the last time, as did Katherine Fielding who had, to her delight, named her baby Louis after her. Venetia offered a cold cheek with barely a smile; David Fielding and Sir John both gave her huge bear hugs. Augusta took her hands and squeezed them. 'Time heals, my dear,' she said gently. 'You'll forget the worst times and remember the good ones.'

She reached London on April 24th. A week later she was reunited with her sons. It wasn't until July 29th, on a hot afternoon as she worked in the studio in her London house, that she opened the first of the boxes of Egyptian canvases and sketchbooks and began to pull them out one by one. Carefully she stacked them round the walls, studying them critically, allowing herself for the first time to remember the heat and the dust, the blue waters of the Nile, the dazzling glare of the sand and the temples and monuments.

She stooped to pick the last canvases out of the box and frowned. Her old bag was there. She must have used it to wedge the paintings in place. She pulled it out and stared at it ruefully; there were still some paints left inside. She rummaged inside to retrieve them.

The scent bottle was still wrapped in the stained silk. She stared down at it for a long, long time.

She had thrown the bottle at the snake. Surely she had.

Dropping the silk to the floor she stood looking at the bottle as it lay on her palm. Then she shivered. Could she never be rid of it? There were tears in her eyes as she turned to the desk where she sat to do her correspondence. Opening the lid, she slid out one of the drawers and reached inside to touch the lever that activated a secret compartment. She laid the bottle inside it and stood looking at it for a moment. The piece of paper telling its story was still tucked in her diary in her writing case. One last look, one last thought of Hassan, and she pushed the secret drawer back. It clicked into place and she quickly shut the lid of the desk.

She would never touch the drawer or her journal again.

'Did you know all this when you gave me the diary?' Anna was sitting next to Toby in Phyllis's sun-filled sitting room.

Phyllis shook her head. 'I always meant to try, but somehow with my bad eyes I never got round to reading it.'

'So you didn't know about the bottle when you gave it to me?'

Phyllis shook her head. 'I would hardly have given it to you, sweetheart, if I'd known its history!' She was indignant. 'As far as I knew, the bottle had lain in that drawer ever since Louisa put it there. The Davenport and the writing case came to me through my father, of course.'

The three of them sat in silence for several minutes. In the hearth the fire crackled cheerfully, filling the room with the scent of apple logs.

'What happened to Louisa, do you know?' Anna asked at last.

Phyllis nodded slowly. 'I know a bit. My grandfather, as you know, was her elder son, David.' She paused thoughtfully. 'Louisa never married again. And as far as I know she never went back to Egypt. She moved from London some time in the 1880s, to a house down in Hampshire, which she left to David when she died. She went on painting, of course, and became a very well-known artist, even in her lifetime.'

'I'd love to know what she must have felt like when she found she still had the scent bottle despite everything she had been through to try to get rid of it. And why did she hide it? Why didn't she destroy it as soon as she found it? Wasn't she afraid the priests would come back?'

Phyllis sat back in her chair and stared thoughtfully down at the fire. 'Anhotep and Hatsek.' Phyllis whispered the two names softly.

Anna wondered for a moment if she had heard correctly. Her eyes widened. 'Then you have read the diary?' she accused.

'No.' Phyllis shook her head slowly. 'There is a painting of them, here, in this house. Their names are written on the back.'

Anna stared at her. She had gone completely cold.

'Where is it?'

'I never liked the painting, but I knew it must be valuable. So I kept it, but I put it in the back storeroom.' She frowned as Anna made for the door. 'Darling, wait. Be careful! Toby, go with her.'

'Where? Where are we going?' Toby hurried down the long passage after Anna.

'She's got a picture of the priests! In the storeroom. I don't believe it!' Anna pushed open the door of the kitchen and led the way inside. For a moment she stood still, staring at the door between the dresser and the sink. 'It's in there.' She swallowed. Her hand went to the amulet at her throat. 'Toby, it's in there!'

'There's no need to look at it.'

'There is. Don't you see, I've got to see if they looked the same to Louisa!' Taking a deep breath, she walked over to the door. Opening it she reached for the light switch. The room was small and almost filled by a large chest freezer. She stared round the walls and for a moment she didn't see the picture. Then she spotted it. Two tall, dark-skinned men were standing in the desert against a sky the colour of sapphires. One was dressed in white linen robes, the other wore an animal skin draped over his shoulders. Both wore strange headdresses and carried tall staffs. They were staring out of the picture towards the viewer with an expression of intense concentration.

'That's them,' she whispered, 'just as I saw them.'

'OK. That's enough.' Toby pulled her away. 'Come on. Back to the fire.' He switched off the light and led her back to the sitting room.

Phyllis was sitting on a cushion on the hearth-rug in front of the fire, an open box beside her. She glanced up as they came in. 'Did you see it?'

'How long has it been hanging there?' Anna threw herself down beside her great-aunt. 'I've never noticed it before.'

'Oh, my dear, I don't know. Thirty years? I can't remember when we put it there. You've just never noticed it, that's all.'

Toby sat down beside her. 'Anna, an awful lot of people can see something every day of their lives and not look at it,' he said gently. 'After all, you had no reason to notice it, did you? It meant nothing to you until you actually went to Egypt.'

'Unless I noticed it, and stored it away in my memory like some hidden nightmare to bring back later. Maybe going to Egypt reminded me in some strange subliminal way. Perhaps I created the whole thing out of my imagination.' She stared at them both hopefully.

Phyllis shrugged. 'I dug out some of my grandfather's old letters before you came,' she put in quietly. She pointed to the old tuck box in her hands. 'See if there is anything interesting.'

With shaking hands Anna drew the first envelope out of the box. She read it quietly and passed it to Phyllis with a smile. 'They are very early. Your grandfather is still at school in this one.'

She opened another, then another, slowly relaxing as she became immersed in the gentle day-to-day activities of a Victorian family. It was ten minutes later that she let out a little cry of surprise. 'No! Oh God, listen! This letter is dated 1873. It's from John. That's Louisa's younger son. "Dear David, Mother is not well again. I called the doctor, but he has no clue what is wrong. On her orders I went to the studio to fetch her a sketchbook. Imagine my astonishment when I was confronted by a large snake! I slammed the door and called Norton."' She looked up. 'Who was Norton? "We went in very cautiously and found nothing. It must have escaped out into the street through the open window."' Putting down the letter Anna stared into the fire. 'The snake came to England,' she said bleakly. 'It followed the bottle.'

'Does he say anything else?' Toby was frowning.

She shook her head. '"We did not tell Mother in case it alarmed her."' She gave a short laugh. 'How wise!' She leafed through some more letters. 'No, nothing else. These are from Cambridge . . . then the army. No, wait.' She held up another letter in excitement. 'This is Louisa's writing.'

There was a long silence as she scanned its pages. When she looked up her face was pinched. 'Read it out loud.' She handed it to Toby.

'"I have painted a picture of my persecutors in the hope of getting them out of my head. They haunt my dreams even now, so many years after my visit to Egypt." Who is she writing this letter to?' He looked up.

'It is addressed to Augusta.' She shivered. Hugging her knees she stared into the fire. 'Go on.'

'"Last night I dreamed about Hassan. Not a day goes by without him appearing at some point in my memories. But I dread his two companions in my thoughts. Will they give me no rest? They beg me to take the vial back to Egypt. Perhaps one day one of my sons or grandsons will take it for me."' Toby broke off, staring at Anna. 'That's you. Her great-great-granddaughter. *You* took it back.'

She nodded. 'But something went wrong. I didn't do it right, and I sacrificed a man's life as a result.'

'No, Anna. Andy died because he was drunk.' Toby folded up the letter and put it back in its envelope. 'There were no priests and no snakes in that launch, remember?'

Phyllis frowned. 'We haven't talked about you, Toby.' She changed the subject adroitly. 'Come on. Let's have all the details. What do you do for a living?'

Toby smiled. 'I'm afraid I paint, too. Not as famous as Louisa, but I can earn my living at it. I am also lucky enough to have inherited a bit of money when my father died, so I've been very spoilt. I'm a widower.' He hesitated, glancing at Anna. Then he shook his head and went on. 'I have a mother, no brothers or sisters, alas. I do not work for the CIA or the Mafia. I am not wanted by the police, as our poor late friend Andy seemed to think. I have a house in the Scottish Borders and another in London, which is where my mother lives. My passion, at least until recently, has been travelling and painting. I've supplemented my income by writing two travel books, both quite well received.' He grinned. 'If I write about our last cruise it will, I fear, have to be fiction, or no one will believe it!' He shrugged. 'That's it, really, except to apologise for abandoning Anna at Abu Simbel. I never got the chance to explain why I wasn't there when she needed me.' He shook his head. 'I met a friend of my mother's who was on a different cruise. She was on her own, and just after I had spoken to her she was taken ill. That was why the tourist police were looking for me. It was at her request. By the time I'd sorted her out, Anna had got on the coach and gone.'

Anna smiled. 'Being kind to ladies in distress again. It's a good excuse. You're forgiven.'

'Good.' Phyllis climbed to her feet with a groan. 'Well, dears. I think it's time for a stiff drink. You take these letters away if you want them. And the picture.' She paused. 'No? All right. I'll keep your priests on ice, as before.' She laughed. At the door she paused and looked back. 'Did I tell you, Toby? You've passed muster. I think you'll do.'

They arrived back in London very late, but lights were still burning in the house as they let themselves in. Frances was sitting at the kitchen table, reading. She glanced up at them. 'Have you had a good day? I'm dying to hear all about it. But first—' She stopped for a moment and they both saw a frown hover between her eyes. Then she went on. 'I've been riveted by your diary, Anna. I've hardly moved all day.' She stretched wearily. 'And I've got something very odd to tell you. I don't know how you're going to take it.'

She closed the diary, and Anna felt a sudden worm of unease deep inside her. Frances's face, usually so tranquil, was etched with worry.

'The villain of the tale. Roger Carstairs. What happened to him?'

Anna shrugged. 'He's never mentioned again in the diary after the Fieldings' baby is born, but I gather he was quite famous in his day.'

Frances glanced at her son and nodded. 'He was famous. He left Egypt in 1869 and travelled to India and the Far East. He surfaced again five years later in Paris.'

Toby frowned. 'How on earth do you know that?'

'He married a French woman, Claudette de Bonville and had two daughters. One of them was my mother's grandmother.'

There was a stunned silence as Toby and Anna stared at her. 'You are descended from Roger Carstairs!' Anna said incredulously.

'I'm afraid so.' Frances shrugged. 'He had two other children by his first marriage, of course. The elder, James, inherited the earldom, but it died out as neither he nor his brother had any children.'

'And what happened to Roger?' Anna was staring at Toby. He seemed as stunned as she was.

'He disappeared.' Frances shrugged. 'Rather apt, really. It was thought he went back to Egypt. I was looking through the family papers and records this afternoon. He left France under a cloud, after five years with Claudette, and travelled to Alexandria, where he stayed a couple of years. Then he moved on. As far as I know he was never heard of again.' She turned to Toby. 'Before you ask why you didn't know all this, (a) you have never been interested in family history and (b) my parents would not allow his name to be mentioned in the house. I'd forgotten about him until he turned up in Louisa's diary.'

Anna was still staring at Toby.

'I'm glad you ditched the bottle, Anna.' He raised an eyebrow. 'Or you really would have suspected me of coveting it!'

'You haven't inherited his powers, I hope.' Anna forced a smile.

'No, I haven't.' He was looking at her closely. 'This has upset you, hasn't it? Anna, it was more than a hundred years ago!'

'I know. I know it's a weird coincidence. I know it's not logical. It's just that I've lived in Louisa's head for so long.' She closed her eyes, stunned by the sense of despair which had swept over her.

'A lot of people's ancestors did evil things, my dear,' Frances put in gently. 'There has to be a place for forgiveness in history. That is what Christ teaches us. And although Roger Carstairs might have been an evil man, my grandfather, who was also Toby's ancestor, don't forget, was a rector in a village in the Midlands, a much loved and respected man, who did an enormous amount of good in the world. So our blood is not wholly tainted.' She stood up and smiled wearily. 'Now, if you will excuse me, it's very late. I'm going to bed. Good night, my dears.'

Toby and Anna watched her go in silence. Then Toby stood up and fetched a bottle of whisky from a cupboard. 'I need something a little stronger than hot chocolate at this point, I think. Would you like one?' He reached two glasses down from the shelf over the sink. 'Ma's right, you know. It doesn't matter.' He poured out half an inch of whisky in each glass and passed her one. 'No, I didn't mean it doesn't matter. Of course it matters. But it doesn't affect us. It doesn't, does it?'

Anna shook her head. 'Of course it doesn't. It's just that his memory resonates very powerfully in my head at the moment. It's all tied up with the fear and anguish I felt since the holiday.' She stood up. 'I'm going to go to bed, Toby. It's been a tiring day, going up to Suffolk and everything.'

She walked to the door, then she turned. 'Toby, I want to go back home tomorrow. Your mother has been incredibly kind, but I'm well now and want to be under my own roof. You understand?'

'Of course.' He couldn't hide his crestfallen expression.

'It's not because of Carstairs. I need to pick up my life again.'

He nodded. 'Will I be a part of that life?'

She hesitated. 'I am pretty sure you will, if that's what you want. But I need time. Too much has happened.'

'Sure. You'll have all the time you need.' He got up to open the door for her. As she passed him he leaned over and kissed her. 'Meeting you has been the best thing that's happened to me in a long time, Anna.'

She smiled. 'I'm glad.'

It was only after she had gone that he realised she had not said she felt the same.

Ten minutes later she heard his car start up and then drive away.

When she woke she looked at her watch and found it was after ten. She dressed quickly and ran downstairs to find the house empty. In the kitchen there was a note on the table: *I thought I'd let you sleep in. I'll be back at lunchtime. F.*

Thoughtfully she made herself some coffee, then she went back upstairs to the ground-floor sitting room. There was no sign of Toby. No message. She reached for the phone book and found Serena's number.

'I hoped I'd catch you. I wanted to thank you for coming to see me.'

'How are you?' Serena sounded cheerful. Anna could hear Beethoven's Sixth Symphony in the background.

'Serena, I'm going home this afternoon. Will you come round to see me there? I'll give you the address.'

'Something is still wrong, isn't it?' Serena's voice was concerned.

'Yes.' Anna managed to swallow her tears. 'Something is still wrong.'

Toby and Frances returned together at lunchtime with pâté and cheese and bread and a bottle of Merlot. They were not surprised to find Anna's case ready packed in the hall. 'I'll drive you back after lunch.' Toby gave her a glass of wine. 'We're going to miss you.'

She smiled. 'I'm not going far. And I hope you're both going to come and see me often.' She hadn't realised how formal it sounded, hadn't meant it to sound quite so final, until she saw Frances glance at her son. His face was bleak.

He forced a smile. 'You won't be able to keep us away,' he said. The words did not sound as though he believed them himself.

None of them ate much, and less than an hour later he was driving her across London and parking outside her house.

Anna climbed out and walked slowly to her front door leaving Toby to follow with her case. She reached for her keys. 'This isn't goodbye, Toby.' She turned and faced him on the step. 'There are things I have to work out by myself.' She took his hands. 'Please, be there if I need you.'

'You know I will.'

She reached up and kissed him on the lips. Then she turned and, hefting the case in by herself, she closed the door behind her.

He stood for several seconds staring at it blindly, then he turned away.

On the other side of the door, Anna stopped too. She dropped the case and her bag and took a deep breath, fighting back her tears. It was there again. The sunlight behind her eyes, the heat of the desert sun on her face, and the rich drifting smell of the incense of the gods.

Biting her lip, she stooped to pick some letters off the mat. Among them was a small parcel. Throwing the letters on the side table she stared at the parcel. It had Egyptian stamps. She turned it over and over in her hands, then she carried it into the living room and tore it open. Inside was a typed letter and a small bubble-wrapped packet.

The letter was from the Luxor Police Department.

The enclosed artefact was found in the hand of the deceased, Mr Andrew Watson, when his body was recovered from the Nile. It was later established that the item belonged to you. I hereby return it. Please acknowledge your receipt of the same.

'No.' She shook her head. 'No. Please, no.'

She put the packet on the table and ran to the front door.

'Toby!'

She scrabbled frantically at the lock and pulled it open. 'Toby, wait! Come back, please!'

His car was pulling away from the kerb, but already the car had joined the stream of traffic. He had never looked back in her direction.

She stood staring after him. 'Toby, come back. Please. I need you!'

Slowly she turned and walked back towards the house, feeling more lost and frightened than she had ever felt in her life.

At the traffic lights in Notting Hill Gate, Toby frowned. He drummed his fingers on the wheel. His head was strangely full of odd sounds, sounds he had never heard before: the plaintive chanting of distant voices, echoed by a harp and what sounded like the low, haunting notes of an oboe, floating over vast distances. He shook his head, puzzled.

Toby! The call came from far away.

Toby, come back! Please! He frowned. That was Anna's voice.

Seconds later he was spinning the steering wheel full circle and speeding back towards her house.

'Anna! Anna?' He left the car in the middle of the road, the door open, the engine running. 'Anna! Open the door!' Running up the path he hammered on it with his fists. The door swung open. Anna had not closed it properly when she walked back into the house.

'Anna?' Toby stared inside. 'Where are you?'

He ran through the deserted hall and threw himself into the living room.

'Anna!' He skidded to a halt.

The room smelt of Egypt. Of heat and sand and of exotic incenses.

The shadow was all around her. 'Anna, fight it, sweetheart! I'm not going to let him have you. Anna, look at me! I love you!'

He grabbed her hands and spun her to face him. 'Anna!'

She blinked, frowning. 'Toby?'

'I'm here, sweetheart. It's all right.'

She was coming back to him. The shadow was fading.

Gathering her into his arms, he kissed the top of her head.

'It came back, Toby,' she stammered. 'The bottle. Louisa couldn't get rid of it and neither can I. I threw it in the Nile but Andy caught it. He brought it back!' Sobbing, she glanced at the table where the little bottle stood. 'I'll never be free.'

He stared at it thoughtfully. 'There are a lot of things we can do, Anna. We can give it to the British Museum. We can send it back to Egypt. We can throw it in the Thames. But whatever happens, we're going to face this together.'

She looked up at him. 'You mean it?'

'I mean it. You are not alone. You'll never be alone again. And you are going to be free of Anhotep and Hatsek. I guarantee it.'

As he kissed the top of her head, he glanced up. On the shining, mahogany surface he could see fragments of dried resin, smell its cloying scent. As he watched, more appeared on the carpet at their feet.

Anna looked up at him. 'Serena is on her way,' she murmured. 'She'll help us, I know she will.'

Toby tightened his arms around her. 'Of course she will. And don't forget, I have the blood of Roger Carstairs and of my reverend great-grandfather in my veins to give me a start in the spiritual stakes.'

As she looked up at him he smiled. 'Courage, my darling, their combined shades have given me an idea. If I stand over that little bottle with a large hammer, I think the priests of Ancient Egypt are going to start listening to what we have to say to them for a change, don't you?'

BARBARA ERSKINE

Best-selling author Barbara Erskine met her first ghost on the day she moved into her beautiful sixteenth-century manor house in Essex in 1991. 'I was very stressed and the house was filled with so many people helping me move that, when I met an unknown young woman on the landing wearing a long Victorian-looking dress and white apron, I didn't even think about it. She was as real as you or me, totally solid, not like a ghost at all. Our eyes met, she smiled at me, and when she disappeared I thought she had just gone into another room.' Barbara then discovered that her home, built next to a Norman church on a site that had been inhabited since pre-Roman times, was known as one of the most haunted houses in Britain. 'We have ghosts from different ages who turn up in different seasons. I usually see them when I relax after a day's writing,' adds Barbara, as we sit chatting in front of the Aga in the kitchen. 'There's one who stands just in the doorway, behind you. We call him the Boot Boy, as he seems to be waiting for the day's orders. The dogs sense him too: Freya, my golden retriever, will take him a shoe to play with. I do find that there is sometimes a slight stigma if you see a ghost. People think you're slightly dotty or they are frightened by the idea. But if I see something I am more excited than scared.'

In fact, that is how Barbara felt when she went to Egypt on holiday with her friend and literary agent, Carole Blake. 'In common with many people, I suspect, my expectations of Egypt were so enormous that I was, in a way, almost reluctant to go there. Suppose it was not as wonderful as I'd hoped? Suppose the visit was a disaster and all my dreams and fantasies were shattered? The boat in which we sailed from Luxor to Aswan was very like the *White Egret*, but, I'm pleased to say, nothing as sinister happened while I was on her—although I did see a ghost in the passengers' lounge, which gave me the idea that ghosts could go on cruises!' During the trip Barbara took reams of notes and when she returned home undertook extensive research before she began writing *Whispers in the Sand*. 'I was absolutely fascinated by the number of intrepid Victorian ladies who, unsuitably dressed in voluminous petticoats and boned corsets, travelled to the most inhospitable of places.'

Writing has always been a part of Barbara Erskine's life. 'I started writing short stories while studying history at the University of Edinburgh.' Her first job was working for a publishing company, but she didn't concentrate on her writing as a career until she and her husband moved to Wales with their first son in 1974. 'Being a mother at home with a young child gave me the chance to do what I'd always wanted to do. I started researching and writing what became my most successful book to date, *Lady of Hay*.'

When I asked Barbara whether she had any plans for returning to Egypt, she looked wistful and said, 'Not at present, but, like Anna Fox, in the novel, I made my own offering to Isis at Philae. Like a coin in the Trevi Fountain, I am certain that will ensure my return one day.'

Jane Eastgate

601-011-1